The Sister

Max China

First Published by skinnybirdproductions: November 2013
Revised cover edition incorporating minor edits June 2014

Copyright © 2012 Max China
All rights reserved.
ISBN: 978-0-9571312-6-2 Paperback
ISBN: 978-0-9571312-0-0 Kindle

For my children, Charlotte and Sam

This book is dedicated to those who are always searching. For love, for meaning. For themselves.

Acknowledgements

I'd like to thank my family and all those around me for their enduring patience...Anya, who gave up her time, listening to pitch after pitch, and endless scenarios in the creation of this, my debut novel...and most especially, Chloe McDonald (author of The Trilogy of Noor) for her much valued advice and continuing encouragement, for which I'm extremely grateful.

Author's Note:

'The Road Not Taken' is a poem by Robert Frost, the first of his poems to appear in the collection *Mountain Interval*, published in 1916. It is partially quoted and referred to by a character in this novel, and can be read it in its entirety on the last page.

Chapter 1 – Prologue

Midsummer 2007

He'd always stayed away from deep water – it scared him, but this time was different: he jumped in to save someone; his efforts have exhausted him. He can't swim.

Did you save her?

Stripped of every thought that used to matter, he struggles. Snatching a desperate breath before going under again, he presses his lips tight, clamping his last breath inside. He sinks lower. Pressure builds, charging his head with ear-splitting pain: the sound of his heart grows louder. Deeper down, the murky water blankets the light filtering through. He closes his eyes.

Oxygen drains from his blood and lungs; every signal from every nerve attacks his ability to remain calm. His chest bucks against the urge to gulp. With only seconds to spare, his feet touch the bottom.

The brute will to live kicks in, and survival mode takes over, diverting every ounce of strength into powerful thighs. Driving up, he surges through the water, a human missile shooting for the surface. The initial burst of acceleration stalls against the mass of water. Without technique, desperation propels him further, and he thrusts his nose and mouth clear of the lake, out into the air. He sucks in a quick shot, before sinking again.

A Japanese mantra starts in his head. *Mushin no shin*...empty mind. All thought *must* disappear.

The instant he feels the lake bed underfoot he drives up hard again, a bubble about to burst.

Although his mind is empty, he knows that if he doesn't make it this time, without rescue, he is finished. Flailing his arms and legs, his frantic actions get him higher, and he pushes his mouth up to clear the water. *Just another inch.*

The effort in vain, the chance missed, he slips down again.

His heart sinks. He'd always known when the end came it would come by water...the end of living on borrowed time.

Someone's words spring to mind: *In those last moments, you don't see your whole life flashing by, but if you're lucky...you get to make some sense of it all.*

Reflex takes over. He gags on the first influx of water. Watching the huge bubble of displaced air break for the surface, he sees a distorted world within it. *You should have learned to swim...*

Chapter 2

North Cornwall – Summer 1967

Halfway across a sloping section of the woods, in a well-hidden clearing, a boiler-suited man was about to light a fire. Next to it, a small stew pot filled with rabbit meat. Discarded body parts, skin and offal, lay a few feet away. A cloud of bluebottles buzzed around the unwanted waste; the noise irritated him. Scooping the refuse up with a shovel, he swung it over his shoulder, catapulting the pieces with ease across the space between him and the water. They plopped in through the chickweed, releasing an unpleasant, sulphurous odour. With the remains gone, the flies dissipated, and silence returned.

As the match he struck fizzed into life, he heard voices. He blew it out. Moving low and keeping under the cover of scrub, he peered through the bushes.

A young man came into view, crossing over a ridge in the path further down. He was dressed in khaki and wearing a leather bush hat. A rangy dark-haired girl walked next to him. Both carried rucksacks, sleeping bags and climbing gear.

They were heading his way.

As they came into earshot, he kept back out of sight.

'You told Lei you were coming here?' the girl asked. 'Are you sure she won't get lonely and come down to join you – us?'

'No, Christina. She won't come here. Like I said, we argued, and now we're not talking...besides, she's scared of this place, what with all those old stories—'

'What old stories?' Christina stopped and looked at him, hands on hips. 'You're scaring *me* now.' Suspicion darkened her expression. 'By the way, Thomas, you didn't tell me why you'd argued. You haven't told her about us, have you?'

'No – now come on, let's get this tent up!' He laughed and pulled her in for a kiss.

Thirty minutes later, the man unfolded the two sets of new boiler suits he'd fetched from his car and laid them out by the stream bed. He took the left hand sleeve and the left trouser leg of one set and twisted the ends, joining and knotting them together. Then he repeated the action on the opposite side. He'd now formed two handles, with the main body of the suit becoming the bag in the middle. When he was finished, he did the same with the other one and then, unzipping the top of each, prepared them to receive their cargo of ballast.

The trek to the car in the heat and his latest exertions left him sweating profusely. A mass of flies trailed him while he collected fist-sized rocks from the dried-out edges of the nearby stream.

He counted out twenty-seven stones for each boiler suit. The number was important, the product of three, multiplied by itself three times – the ultimate lucky number. With the stones packed in, he hauled them up to the pond, placing the modified suits on the ground near the water.

Straw-coloured hair, mixed with dirt and perspiration from his forehead, stuck to his face. He drew his fingers across it and down his cheeks, wiping the sweat away, giving him the appearance of wearing light camouflage.

Moments later, he crept up on the tent, moving closer, listening to the growing sounds of passion. His shadow cast itself across the nylon wall. The moans coming from inside ceased abruptly.

Damn! He'd seen it too late. Moving in the opposite direction, careful to keep the sun in front of him, he stood perfectly still, head tilted, an ear cocked close to the orange fabric. Against the sunlight shining through from the other side, he could see their silhouettes, frozen in position, the girl with her knees drawn up, the man between, on top.

'I saw someone,' Christina whispered urgently.

'What? *Jesus!*'

'Thomas – there's someone outside.'

The stalker held his breath, expecting the top shadow to extricate itself, and come out to look. They remained locked together.

'There's no one out there, relax.' Slowly, the dark profile of his buttocks resumed their thrusting.

Outside the lover's nest, the man moved silently towards the entrance.

High above, a bird of prey cried, its keening piercing the air.

Chapter 3

20 August 1967

The Milowski family walked much further than they had intended to find the ideal picnic spot, choosing a wide-open meadow where Bruce could play with little chance of hurting himself. From where they sat on a spread of blankets, the field of vision was uninterrupted for hundreds of yards.

His grandfather stared up at the rocky crags and pointed. 'Can you see that bird, Bruce?'

'You've got good eyes,' Mrs Milowski said. 'I wouldn't have noticed it. Did you bring binoculars?'

'No, telescope,' he said, 'in bag, next to you." Although he'd lived in England for twenty years, a trace of eastern European accent remained, along with a tendency to leave words out. 'Pass to me,' he said, holding out his hand. 'Please.'

He focused on the bird. *A buzzard.* 'There, at top of cliffs. Probably, he lives there.'

He handed the 'scope over to Bruce's father, who trained it first at the sky, and then at the craggy outcrop.

'You want to look, Ellen?'

'Maybe later,' she said, tending to the baby.

'You, Bruce, you look…' He pulled the boy in close, and passing the telescope over, showed him how to work the adjustment wheels. 'Remember, if you can't see, turn those buttons I showed you.'

Fascinated, he stared through the lens, sweeping the skies and the landscape. On the other side, lower down, he caught a flash of bright colour. He fiddled with the controls until he brought the object into focus. It was a young woman dressed in purple, undoing her hair.

He lowered the telescope, and compared the image with what he could see with his naked eye. The difference amazed him.

His mother's voice drew him away from the distant world he'd discovered. 'Bruce, put that down for a minute and come and eat.'

When they had finished their food, Bruce amused himself by lying on his front, staring at the intricacies of the grass below his face, constructing fantasy adventures which involved cutting his way through the jungle, battling giant ants and spiders. Suddenly, he rolled on to his back and stared at the sky. Something had unsettled him. He didn't want to lie there anymore. 'I'm bored – can I go and explore?' he asked no one in particular.

His father and grandfather were deep in conversation, his mother, although busy with his two-year-old baby sister, turned her attention to him.

'Do you want to go off and play?'

'Can I?' he said.

'Yes, you can, Bruce, but I want you to stay where I can keep an eye on you,' she said.

Over the course of the next few minutes, he edged further away.

Mrs Milowski called out, 'Don't go any farther, Bruce!'

'I won't!' he shouted.

Waving to reassure her, he inched his way towards a fence separating the meadow from another field, a hundred yards away. On the other side, the vegetation was quite different from the one he was in now.

He paused, looking back at his family. His mother, distracted by his sister's crying, had turned away to soothe her, and the men were still in deep conversation.

He dropped to his knees and slid under the barbed wire, careful not to catch his clothes.

When Mrs Milowski realised that Bruce had vanished, she cried out, 'Bruce, where are you? I told you not to wander off.' Then, panic rising, she shouted at the top of her voice, 'Bruce!'

The men stood, their faces registering concern as they scanned the meadow, looking in all directions. 'What are you talking about? Where was he when you last saw him?' her husband asked.

'He was over there,' she said, pointing to the edge of the field. The little girl sensed something was wrong and began to cry. Mrs Milowski hugged her tight.

'Find him,' she said, clasping the child's head to her shoulder. She bit her lip, keeping her face hidden from the little girl, and her eyes squeezed shut. A large tear rolled down her cheek.

The men sprinted to the fence where Bruce had been a few minutes earlier. His father vaulted the wire and crossed to the other side of the field calling his son's name. Bruce's grandfather bent to pass between the strands, and standing upright on the other side, eased his palms into the small of his back to help it straighten up again. He watched his son a hundred yards away, charging in and out of the trees, wasting his efforts. *The young ... they have so much energy.*

Eyes half-closed; he stared through the ferns. The narrowing of vision enabled a sharpening of focus, and he was able to dismiss the animal runs at low level and pick out the fronds most likely bent by the shoulders of a child.

'Wait, I have found his path!' The old man waded through the undergrowth with a speed that belied his seventy-five years of age.

He pointed through the trees, and said, 'Bruce went that way.' A startled look crossed his face. 'Mother of God, we must be quick. He is in danger.'

Bursting through the undergrowth, driven by fear, they followed a trail only his grandfather could see.

Chapter 4

The girl in the purple seersucker dress climbed all the way up; to come down the way she knew *he* would have taken. At its highest point, Lei stopped to admire the view. She rested on a boulder smoothed by wind and age and imagined three weeks ago Thomas might have stopped there, too, taking a drink after the long climb, rucksack at his feet while he surveyed the dale stretching out below.

The valley sat between two granite escarpments almost a quarter of a mile apart. The landscape changed from rock to shale, dropping away sharply before becoming a gentle slope with patches of yellowish grass and scrub that grew wherever the roots could take hold, getting greener further down the hill where it flattened out around the stream.

A student in geology, she took in the extent of the flood plain and the displacement of pebbles and sandy deposits; it told her how, during heavy rain, it became a full-fledged river. She imagined the roar of the water, white and foaming, fed by the fingers of channels funnelling off from the slopes. The waters would swell, spilling out over bends that could contain it no more, settling back when the rains ceased, becoming once again a thin ribbon of water to gurgle its way over smooth stones, around rocks and boulders, before disappearing into a wooded glade.

The woods concealed the site of a tragedy, a system of workings and shafts, where thirty-nine miners lost their lives during one black day in the summer of 1857. A combination of freak weather and poor engineering had caused the mine to flood and collapse. Soon after the deluge, downhill from the mine's entrance, a large swallow-hole had appeared in the ground and filled with water. Silt plugged its fissures and cracks, building up over time until the pond became permanent. Ferns, nettles and blackberry bushes grew up in the gaps between the variety of trees that had taken root around it over the years, encircling and completing its concealment.

Seen from high above, the body of water appeared malignant, vigilant. The texture of the vegetation surrounding it, forming warty upper and lower lids, totally shaded and utterly black, like the open eye of a giant, perfectly camouflaged prehistoric creature.

A buzzard circled lazily against the silent backdrop of a cloudless blue sky. The mid-August sun beat down without mercy. In the meadow below, the girl was only visible above the waist.

Lei stopped to unhitch her rucksack. Cool fresh air passed over her back. She untied her jet-black hair and shook her head, allowing the glossy mane to cascade almost to her waist. After flexing her shoulder blades, she resumed walking, carrying the sack by the straps. Its weight made her change hands frequently. Her fingers trailed through the dry tips of the long grass without a sound, but every stride whispered and rasped against the serrated leaves, scratching her legs, which stung as perspiration formed and found its way into tiny cuts. At first, thinking some sort of insect was biting her, she looked below her knees; the skin was red and blotchy. Already she'd hiked around seven miles, and sensing she was close to her destination, she took a map from her backpack to check.

The sudden disappearance of her boyfriend, and the guilt she felt because of it, had left her a little unstable and more likely to take risks. Earlier, she'd traversed a ledge she should never have tackled without equipment, but she no longer cared.

She was breaking all the rules that she'd spelled out to him. *Always tell someone where you're going, when you'll be back, and never go alone.*

Thomas was a caver and abandoned mine explorer. When he'd said he was going to scout the site of an old mine disaster, she'd refused to go with him. They'd argued about it. *If you don't come with me, I'm going alone!* She didn't believe for a minute he'd carry out his threat. Lei had been sure he'd find someone else to accompany him, but the next thing she knew, he'd disappeared. It turned out he had gone on his own, and she felt incredibly guilty. *If she'd only gone with him...*

Now, she was going there anyway. The derelict Victorian mine complex down in the valley. The last place he'd still been alive.

In her heart, she knew he was dead, but she was convinced that if his spirit lingered, it would linger there. Rescuers found his tent pitched near the mine's entrance. It was empty, his equipment missing. Unable to find any trace of him outside, the rescue team concluded that he must have decided to sleep in the mine. Perhaps, because of the recent heatwave, he'd found the constant temperature inside preferable. A few hundred yards into the mine, a fresh roof fall had rendered the whole section unstable, making it impossible to continue the search. In places like that, a single cough would be enough to trigger a further collapse. He wouldn't have stood a chance. The mine was now his grave.

It had taken Lei three weeks to summon the strength to travel there to pay her last respects, going on impulse when she realised the date, and what day it was. *Ghost Day.* Her Chinese origins meant she believed, that for one day only, the gates of Heaven and Hell would open, allowing the dead a reunion with the living. Thomas hadn't had a proper ritual send-off. The gods had granted her the opportunity to do it on this day. Suddenly it felt important.

With little time left to prepare, she phoned work and reported in sick. She told no one she was going.

The rucksack contained offerings to nourish and guide his spirit. A part-time florist, she had brought scissors and string and made a wild flower bouquet as she sauntered along. She'd build a rocky shrine and then place lit candles inside, with joss sticks, food and a poem she'd written for him. When today was over, she'd return to Hong Kong. There she would learn to live without him, but she'd remember him most especially on this day, every year into the future.

Three years together, gone...just like that. Her throat tightened at the thought.

Over to her right at the bottom of the hill, a scattering of trees marked the edge of a densely wooded area.

Eager to get into the woods and out of the sun's direct heat, she quickly crossed a field of swaying ferns.

At the margins of the wood beyond the canopy, dappled light dropped through the leaves, making a patchwork of sunshine and shade on the ground. It looked so cool and appealing that she wandered in deeper.

So peaceful and quiet, only the occasional buzz of a fly and the gentle gurgling of a brook broke the silence. She approached the water's edge. In the curve of a long looping bend, there was a place where the banks flattened, making an expanse of pebbles like a small beach.

Her new Doc Martens were the most comfortable trekking boots she'd ever worn, but they made her feet hot, so she removed them, along with her socks. She couldn't wait to dip her toes in the cold water and crunched unsteadily towards it, holding the footwear by its laces. With stones digging painfully into her bare soles, she skipped and jerkily tiptoed to get to the stream quicker.

Nearer the water, where larger, smooth grey boulders sat in the margins, Lei stepped in something slimy; the mud below oozed, blackening her foot as it sank into it, releasing a sulphurous odour. She found a rock with a flattish top, hitched her dress up, sat down and dangling her bare feet in the cool stream, rinsed the black sludge from between her toes. She put the boots back on, before crossing the shale again.

The sound of gravel crunching behind made her jump. Heart thumping wild and afraid, chest tight, she spun around sharply. *Nothing there!*

She sighed with relief. Turned, and froze.

A stranger stood before her, the rank odour of sweat and stale cigarette smoke assailing her nostrils.

His eyes made his intentions clear.

Chapter 5

He didn't give Lei a chance to scream. Clamping her mouth with a powerful hand, he fastened the other at the base of her skull, pressing against it hard. The force of his grip made her eyes bulge, filling them with fear.

Afterwards, he smoked a cigarette, thinking about the girl he'd just met.

If she'd come by tomorrow, she'd have missed him; it was his last Saturday; he'd finished the demolition contract he was working on, and he was pleased about that. *Never stay too long in one place.*

He couldn't explain it, but he had known there would be one more. Things happen in threes. Was he really to blame if the Devil sent them his way?

He'd already committed the girl to memory. Blessed with photographic recall, everything stayed in his head. He never took trophies from the women he killed, and although he left nothing behind, he had taken something from a man two weeks earlier. It didn't matter; he could have found it left behind on the beach, or at a jumble sale. *How would they find you, if you told no one, and left no trace? They'd have to catch you in the act.*

He took a long last draw on the butt of his cigarette and flicked it into the water.

At the edge, she waited for him.

Stooping, he picked the body up in one smooth, effortless movement. He heaved her over his shoulder and gathered her possessions with his other hand. He was ready to take her beyond and into the woods. Her lifeless arms trailed limply down his back.

A scraping of pebbles close behind stopped him dead.

What the...

The man dropped her roughly to the ground, turning and looking in the direction of the sound in one fluid movement.

A small boy had slipped over on the rocks. Stunned, he lay still for a moment before rolling over onto his feet and scurrying for cover.

Not quick enough, kid...I've seen you! You've given me no choice, but to get rid of you. This is going to be easy. With his last victim's body left unattended out in the open, the last thing he needed was a chase.

'Comin' to getcha,' the killer mumbled and started towards him.

Bruce hurried, scraping across the shale until he reached the cover of the low scrub that grew in patches along the bank. After fifty yards, the bushes ran into a huge boulder – a dead end. He had to make a choice, run, or gamble on staying put. He was of two minds, and one of them didn't seem like the mind of a seven-year-old. An inner voice told him to stay still. The urge to move gnawed at his legs, making them twitchy. His ragged breathing deprived him of oxygen, and left him close to panic. He wondered if his parents or grandfather would find him in time.

He squeezed his eyes shut and took a deep breath. *Stay put!*

Where are you, Dad? He remembered taking the car for repairs with his father one Saturday morning. The mechanic wore the same style of clothes the man looking for him now was wearing; a garage suit covered in grease, black where it should have been blue. The garage man kept a guard dog, which escaped while Bruce played in the storage area behind the workshop. Freed from its cage, the enraged animal attacked a group of people who'd called in to view cars. In the chaos and confusion that followed, it evaded capture, and then it saw Bruce. The dog advanced on him, emitting a low growl; it seemed wary of him. The boy closed his eyes and said a silent prayer. His hand closing over his seashell, he pulled it from his pocket and held it out for protection. *Where are you, Dad?*

Saliva flew as it snapped at him. He felt the heat of its breath on his face as vicious jaws snatched at empty air, driven back by a mighty kick. *It was his dad!* His father scooped him up in his arms; a group of men managed to keep the dog contained. *The shell, it's magic! It brought my dad to save me.*

The tramping of heavy boots sent loose stones skittering, clattering across the hard-packed surface between the rocks nearby and abruptly stopped. There wasn't a sound in the air, apart from his heart beating heavily in his ears, and his ragged breathing. Bruce fought to control it. In...out...in...out.

He heard the rasp of a match and three quick sucking sounds. A waft of cigarette smoke drifted into his nostrils, the urge to cough was hard to suppress – he did it inwardly, without opening his lips. His small body jerked with each attempt to keep the sound inside. The tiniest gasp escaped.

A spent matchstick dropped out of the air and on the ground next to him.

The boy shut his eyes tight, mouthing a silent prayer.

'Your God doesn't scare me, kid!'

At that, the boy produced a seashell from his pocket and held it out at arm's length, eyes closed, holding it blindly in front of him like a talisman to ward off evil.

'What's that, huh? You're gonna need more than that, kid!' The killer was about to snatch it out of his hand, when he heard shouts; men calling out, there were at least two or three of them, and they were getting closer.

'Bruce! Can you hear us? Bruce!'

'Mother of shit!' he cursed under his breath, eyes burning into the boy. 'Listen to me, kid, today's your lucky day, but if you tell anyone what you saw...I'll find you, and I'll kill you all...your mum, your dad...all of you. Have you got that, *Bruce?*'

He nodded, terrified.

The killer turned sharply, rushing back to where Lei lay, scooping her up again and checking to ensure no trace of her remained.

His arm clamped her body down on to his shoulder as he carried her out of sight.

Hidden by dense vegetation, the killer worked faster than he'd have liked, wrapping the arms and legs of the weighted suit around her. He knotted them together. The voices were getting too close for comfort. He gathered her up and heaved the human parcel into the pond, throwing the rucksack and flower bouquet in after her. The bag filled with water and sank. The poem she'd written in memory of her boyfriend, floated up to the surface and unfurled, the blue ink blurring as the paper soaked through: an epitaph for a missing person, penned by another, who would remain undiscovered for a long time.

On the bank, he found one of Lei's boots. Frantically he looked for the other one - he was sure he'd picked up both, he *knew* he had. He jammed a large stone into the boot he was holding and lobbed it into the dense water. His search for the missing one failed. *It has to be somewhere in this long grass!*

With time running out, the killer gritted his teeth and spat a curse at the kid and the men who'd rescued him. The boiler suit containing the stone ballast was only half tied to her body. He wasn't worried about that, it was secure enough, but the boot was a trace of her and if anyone came looking and if they *found* it...

He watched the younger man examine the kid's head where he'd banged it, pulling his hair back to look deep into the hairline. Apparently satisfied there was no serious injury, he'd playfully cuffed at his ear.

The old man remained squatting and spoke to the boy, who nodded. Slowly, he stood and moved away from the others, staring beyond the edge of the woods.

The killer knew the old man couldn't see him crouched in the shady darkness behind the bushes, but he seemed to stare exactly in his direction. *Had the kid told him?* He backed away silently, deeper into the shadows. The stench of sulphur was thick in his nostrils, and drifted on a slight wind that had picked up, spinning the dry leaves in small whirlwind circles. The breeze swept particles across the dusty surface and carried on up the slope, before subsiding at the feet of the men and boy, exhausted. Drops of rain began to fall.

Bruce's grandfather turned in the direction of the rattling leaves and stood with narrowed eyes focused on the darkness beyond the tree line, further down the hill.

Something was in the shadows.

His hackles rose, sharpening his senses. A cocktail he'd last tasted during the Second World War on his lips again. The flavour was familiar. It was the taste of fear.

His memories carried him back to the horror; you never forget how it feels.

He'd fought in three wars and survived them all; he was more attuned to minute changes in the atmosphere and unnatural silences than his compatriots, and possessed a burning desire to remain alive. He smelled the scents of fear and death as they lingered in the sulphurous air, and hanging alongside was the faint whiff of cigarette smoke.

With his focus concentrated on the tree line, Bruce's grandfather walked slowly backwards, afraid if he turned, something would hurtle out without warning and take them all. Only when he had joined the others, did he turn round again. Spreading his arms symbolically, they came under his protection, and he shepherded them away. 'Come on, we'd better go.'

Chapter 6

The killer calculated that from the direction of the family's retreat up the hill, wherever they'd come from, they wouldn't have hiked all the way in with a kid that age in tow, meaning they couldn't have parked anywhere near where he'd left his vehicle.

The rain picked up. Heavy droplets crashed through the leaves, spotting his back, dotting the ground around him. He fished his cigarettes from a pocket outside his overalls, took one and lit it and, not wanting the packet to get wet, replaced it deeper inside his clothes. When he'd finished smoking, he packed up his gear and headed off to retrieve his car from the rusted tin agricultural shed where he'd been sleeping for days. It cost nothing, and apart from that, the big advantage over staying in contractors' digs was he didn't have to talk to anyone. He didn't like people.

The disused barn was at the end of a potholed dirt track. No one had been there for years.

He heaved open the door. It thundered noisily on its runners. Four hundred yards away, a flock of crows flew up from their roost in the trees. *Was it me who disturbed them...? Or is someone else over there? No time to look now.*

He started the engine and turned the car up the track. It rode more like a camel as it bumped and rolled on its suspension. The wipers smeared across the screen before finally cutting through the accumulated grime. After ten minutes, he was relieved to turn on to the smooth tarmac of a country byway and soon after turned on to the main road. He didn't notice the white and green Lotus Cortina hurtling up behind him. It swung out at the last possible moment, overtaking him on a bend, horn blasting as it roared by. *That idiot is going to kill someone driving like that!* Outraged, something inside him flipped, and flooring the accelerator, he gave chase, flashing his headlights at the car in front.

The young man slowed.

The killer caught up; close enough to see eyes looking back at him in the rear-view mirror. With crew cut hair, shorn off at the sides, the shape of the man's head annoyed him. His palm smacked down hard on to his hooter, holding it down continuously, as if doing so would make it louder.

He aimed a two-finger gesture into the rear-view mirror, and to reinforce the message, stuck his right fist out the window and rotated it up and down before accelerating away into the distance.

Unmanned roadworks came into view, reducing traffic to a single file. The lights turned red, and cars started streaming through from the opposite direction, blocking the reduced lane.

The Cortina rolled to a stop. With no place to go, he adjusted the mirror nervously, watching as the battered car rattled to a halt behind him. In his head, an imaginary scene unfolded. *The driver behind gets out and approaches him. He jumps out of his car...What are you after, man? Do you want some of this, eh? Yeah? Well, hold on to that then! The man goes down from a single punch, and he kicks him around in the pouring rain...*As he'd imagined, the man got out. He watched in horror, the fantasy evaporating when he saw the size of the figure approaching in his mirror. His elbow pushed the door lock down. He'd lost his nerve.

The man stopped by his window. All he could see looking out from the driver's seat were the man's hips and mid torso. The distinctive brass buckle on the leather belt caught his attention. It depicted a skull and cross bones and its empty eye sockets had been picked out in blood red paint.

How can you take someone who wears a buckle like that seriously? It was all a show! Who does this guy think he is – a bloody Hells Angel?

'Angel' tried the door handle. An entirely different perspective dawned on the man in the car. *He's trying to get at me!*

'Angel's' face suddenly appeared, pressing hard against the window, contorted, one eyeball almost touching the glass. The crazed eye locked on to him. Tilted, as if pushed by a rhino, the car leaned over. Cortina man shrank into his seat, compelled by fear into looking straight ahead as the big man's lips parted, releasing a shout so loud, it hurt his ears even though the windows and doors were shut. 'OPEN IT!'

Turning in his seat, he looked at the white foamy spit as it mixed with rain on his window. Outraged at this blemish, he shook his head defiantly. Newfound defiance held his rising apprehension in check. His mouth felt dry. At least he was safe in his car.

Abruptly, Angel stood upright and leaned his hip against the door.

From out of sight above the roofline of the car, the voice had become calm, the contrast to the moment before welcomed. 'You really should be careful who you stick your fingers up at, you know,' he said. At this point, he was giving him a chance.

Cortina man tilted his face and pressed it against the window, to try to see him better. He should have put a hand up and mouthed *sorry* from the safety of the car, but he didn't; the sight of the spit on his window combined with his fear, made him erratic. He heard himself say, 'Oh yeah, why's that then?' For the second time in as many minutes, he *knew* what would happen next. He cursed his stupidity.

The response was swift and decisive without concern for personal injury. A single punch exploded through the glass of the window, driving rough cubes of it deep into his face as the fist connected.

Angel's reply was the last thing he heard as it trailed him into unconsciousness. 'Why? Because, my finger-happy friend, next time I'll kill you!'

Angel marched quickly back to his own car, climbing in as the lights turned green. Flooring the accelerator, spinning the wheels, he headed off down the wet road, narrowly missing the stationary vehicle.

Police found the driver of the Cortina slumped in his seat two hours later. In hospital, when he'd recovered sufficiently for police to interview him, he was unable to recall what had happened.

No one responded to an appeal for witnesses.

Chapter 7

Southern Ireland.

Miles away across the sea at Celtic Deep, a thirteen-year-old girl hovered between light and darkness. The fever that had burned her up for the past two days had broken at last. She opened her eyes. The light, though dim, stung them as she blinked to focus. Her mother smiled at her; relief clearly visible on her face. As she reached to turn the flannel on her forehead, she thought Vera's eyes looked greener than usual. *Such a pretty girl...*

'Praise, God, you've come back to us.'

Vera simply looked at her and said, 'It isn't safe outside.'

'What's not safe, Vera? You're here, safe with us. There's no need to worry about anything.'

'Yes there is, Ma, I *saw*. There's a man...' Vera turned her head on the pillow, cutting eye contact, staring with consternation at a point beyond the wall. Her mother's questions faded from her consciousness as she closed her eyes once more.

Vera became moody and withdrawn, sleeping for hours during the day, then wandering restlessly in the night.

The doctor advised Mrs Flynn to keep her off school for two weeks. Her convalescence took longer than that. A pale and sickly child, Vera had been the only one in the family to have ginger hair. Her mother thanked the Lord it was the colour of bright copper, and not orange, but even so, at times other children taunted her mercilessly. Vera refused to leave the house, even when she'd recovered, and she would not say why.

Finally, her mother lost patience with her reluctance to venture out, so one Sunday morning she dragged Vera out of bed and announced she was taking her to Mass. Despite her protests, Vera dressed, but when the time came to leave, she would not go. Her mother hauled her outside, screaming and kicking all the way to the church. Once inside, she lapsed into a strange silence. They sat at the back, in the only available pair of seats together. Vera shivered, her teeth chattering noisily. She made a grrrr-ing sound as she shook. Concerned, her mother looked across at her, half thinking she was faking something to get out of the service. Suddenly, Vera's leg spasmed, and her foot struck the pew in front with a dull thud.

'Vera – what are you *doing*?' Her mother hissed under her breath. Both legs stiffened, stretched out taut, her backside raised off the seat as her back arched. She collapsed between the pews, trembling.

A woman asked, 'What's the matter with her?'

'I don't know,' her mother said. 'She seems to have had some sort of fit.'

Two men carried her outside into the air and laid her down. A small crowd gathered around her prone body.

'Vera? Vera love – are you all right?'

Slowly, she turned her face towards them. It had blistered so badly that the group of people surrounding her, gasped as one.

'Holy Mary! Fetch Doctor Robert, someone, and be quick about it!'

Vera barely managed a whisper, 'I said it wasn't safe outside.'

They took her back inside the church.

The doctor arrived and following a brief examination, could offer no immediate diagnosis. 'I believe it's an allergic reaction. Her recent illness has weakened the body. I'll prescribe something for her skin. In the meanwhile, let's take her home. I'll give you a lift.'

Inside the house, he scribbled out a prescription and handed it to Mrs Flynn. 'She's to rest. Get her drinking plenty of fluids. Call me if you need me, but otherwise, I'll be back in a couple of days.'

Her newly healed skin was smooth and pink. It became clear she'd be unable go outside, whether the sun shone or not. The smallest amount of ultra-violet light triggered severe burns. The doctor, mystified, took blood and tissue samples and sent them away for testing. No medical evidence was found to support any known ailment. Dr Robert suspected she'd somehow triggered a psychosomatic illness so she could avoid going out. Forbidden to leave the house until someone came up with an effective solution, Vera made sense of things from her bed. She resigned herself to a past she couldn't alter, and she looked at ways she might bring about a change in the future.

It came to her suddenly. To do that, she would have to be outside, and in order to do *that*, she'd have to cover herself up completely during the day. Mostly she would go out at night while the rest of the house slept. It was on one of those nights that she wandered down to the beach. The sea was speckled, flecked with silver moonlight. It was then she saw it for the first time. Sitting amongst the millions of other stones on the foreshore, it glowed, its blackness exposing it just as surely as if it were white. Vera stooped to pick it up. At first, she thought it must be a black marble. She knew straight away it was unlikely to be glass because, although perfectly spherical, it had the heavy weight of some type of metal. Even at her tender age, she knew the chances of such an object occurring naturally would be almost non-existent.

She held it up in front of her, between her thumb and forefinger, amazed such a relatively small thing, when placed at a precise point in her line of sight, could eclipse the silvery orb. For a fleeting second, she had the feeling that the world was within her grasp. Celestial light seemed to lay a pathway across the water to where she stood. Vera remained spellbound, giddy and incredibly light on her feet, until a passing cloud broke the spell and allowed the return of her senses. In that moment of insight, she understood she could make herself bigger in the overall scheme of things by altering her perspective on life, by moving her standpoint.

She'd seen a way into the future, a way to make things safe, to put things right: she'd seen the difference she could make. All she needed to do was work out how. The stone in the palm of her hand, blacker than black, held the moon in miniature, and reflected it in the curves of its own dark skies. She felt like an astronaut looking down from outer space onto a distant world. The night never felt fresher or more alive than it did for her then.

There's something special about this stone... At only thirteen years of age, she had all the time in the world to find out what it was.

She closed her hand over it, slipped it into her pocket, turned, and started the long walk home.

The following Thursday, Mrs Flynn announced, 'We're going to Mass this Sunday, come hell or high water,' she said, and paused, expecting resistance. 'So, it's the confessional for you tonight.'

'What for, Ma? I've done nothing wrong.'

'I know that child. It's just that you've not been to confession since I don't know … a long time now. I'm wondering if it might help with things, you know…' She took Vera's hands in hers. 'And I want God's light to shine for you; you've spent so much time out of the light of day. I'm afraid the darkness might take you.'

Vera didn't respond.

'We'll go tonight. It's Father O'Malley. I always feel more cleansed when I confess to him, more so than the other one…' She snapped her fingers several times in quick succession, 'What's his name, I can't for the living bejesus think what it is … can you, Vera?'

At last, Vera answered. 'It's Father Hughes.'

The church sat in the middle of a graveyard surrounded by dry-stone walling, its windows half-aglow with dim light.

Mrs Flynn pulled the door, and it creaked open. There were already almost a dozen people lined up along the front pew awaiting their turn. For some of them, it was a chance to socialise while they waited, and they whispered among themselves in hushed tones.

Vera sat one place from the end of the seat, leaving a space for her mother.

On the bench, the other women had perfected the art of speaking so no one else could make out what they were saying; the odd word was recognisable, but with no context, the rest was meaningless.

Vera's mother would go in after her, and she was already running through the little things she'd done since she last confessed. *Is it a sin to eavesdrop? It didn't matter; she'd add it to the list anyway and the Father would tell her.*

This last thought raised concerns for Vera. At last, her turn came. She entered the booth and closed the door behind her.

'Bless me, Father, for I have sinned. It has been a while since my last confession because I haven't been very well. Since then I think I have been good, although sometimes I catch myself listening in on other people's lives, and their thoughts. Worse than that though, the other night I dreamed the doctor died, and then he did.'

'Doctor Robert? I saw him, not half an hour ago. I can safely assure you; he is not dead.'

'He *does* die, Father.'

The priest sighed. 'My child, we all have dreams, and sometimes they are strange. Purity of thought leads to purity of vision, but you cannot control what you dream about, so how can it be a sin? You spoke what was on your mind, and through me, God has listened to you. I can't see that you've sinned at all. However, since you're here, pray to God and our Lady that they continue to guide you.'

She made her way up to the front row before the altar to wait for her mother so they could pray together. When she returned, they both kneeled and crossed themselves. Vera whispered her prayers aloud; her mother kept silent, keeping the number of Hail Marys and Our Fathers a secret. Vera chose not to intrude on what she'd done, although judging from the length of time her penance took, it must have been something at least a little bit bad.

On the way home, with only the moon to keep the darkness at bay, she asked her mother, 'What is contraception?'

'Where did you hear that word?' her mother demanded.

She'd picked it up in the confessional, a trace of someone's guilty secret. Uneasy at the tone of her mother's voice and afraid she'd land herself in trouble, Vera lied, 'I can't remember...'

In her mind, she was at her next confession already.

A white lie isn't a sin. Is it, Father?

She had a feeling she wouldn't go to Mass with her mother that Sunday.

Chapter 8

Bruce remembered the first time he'd visited the seaside with his parents when he was four years of age. They'd gone to escape from where he lived in the 'Smoke', a name he'd often heard London referred to in those days.

Outside the railway station, he'd cried out in his excitement at seeing the white gulls wheeling low across the waves, screeching high and shrill, squabbling over scraps.

Later on the beach, everyone retreated from the incoming tide to the top of the embankment. The lapping water washed the rocks with a white foamy lather, and swept up to the high watermarks left on previous days with a 'shushhh' coming up, and a 'shishhh' as the sea rushed back again. Bruce watched this gigantic, breathing creature full of fishes and monsters, thankful it could climb no higher up the sloping wall.

The water…something about it terrified him, even then.

An old lady walking past with her dog stopped to talk, trying to tease him into conversation.

Bruce didn't answer.

She fished in her pockets and pulled out a large seashell.

'Here, I have something for you. Would you like it?' she said. 'It's a special shell, a magic shell.'

He took it in his hand, turning it over and around, feeling its smoothness. The way it fitted so neatly into his palm confirmed it for him. It was special. He was in awe of it already, and he didn't know why.

'How is it magic?' he asked the old lady.

She leaned down to whisper in his ear.

'It's captured the spirit of the sea, so that wherever you go with the shell, a part of the sea goes with you.' Her outstretched arm cut around in a wide arc, indicating the horizon before him. 'When you get home, and you miss the seaside, hold the shell to your ear like this.' She cupped a hand over her ear. 'And listen.'

Bruce moved the shell close to his ear.

'Not now!' She laughed. 'You're here anyway!'

His mum smiled at the lady and thanked her.

'Come on, boy, it's time to go,' she said.

The old lady walked away. He watched her go. She must have had a feeling he was watching her because she turned around and waved at him again before going on, her black Labrador following bandily, on elderly limbs.

He handed the shell to his mum to look after.

That night when she came to his room to tuck him in, just before turning out the light, she took the shell from her pocket and placed it on his bedside table.

She kissed him goodnight. 'Night my little angel boy, don't let the bedbugs bite!'

'I won't,' he promised.

After she'd gone, the two-inch gap she left between the door and frame threw a bar of light across the room. It bathed the shell, making it brilliant against the darkness surrounding it, highlighting the mysterious entrance to its cave. Bruce reached out and took it from the table, turning it to hold up to his ear as the lady with the dog had shown him.

First, he smelled the salty tang of the sea, and then he heard its whispered whooshing from deep inside. It scared him.

The spirit of the sea held inside the dark cavities deep within. A whole world captured in such a small thing, was magic indeed.

It sparked a fascination in him. Although it frightened him, he carried it with him everywhere.

During the night, he dreamed he was on an island surrounded by the sea and the tide was coming in. With no rocky walls to hold it back, he retreated until he stood on a higher piece of ground in the middle. The waves licked at his bare toes. He couldn't swim, but he was holding the shell in his hand. It occurred to him that if he could listen to it, and it *was* magic, then maybe it could listen to him.

So he held it up and spoke into its cave, pleading with the spirit of the sea to save him, and holding it to his ear, he thought he heard it say, 'I will carry you, but you must learn to hold your breath and swim.'

In the morning, he asked his mum if he could have swimming lessons. 'It's *important,*' he told her.

Mrs Milowski looked at him thoughtfully; she'd never learned. Scared of the water, she'd always believed it was far too dangerous to play around in. 'We'll see, Bruce, we'll see...'

For a few weeks, Bruce managed to blank out what he'd witnessed from his memory. Even at that tender age, he possessed an uncanny ability to dissociate himself, instilled in his genes perhaps as a mechanism evolved from the great capacity for survival of his ancestors.

Tonight, he was unable to keep it out, no matter what he tried. Back then, he hadn't understood it. His mind felt an invisible force constantly pulling and redirecting it. He tired fast and stopped resisting, observing his thoughts as they flowed freely.

He was back at the edge of the field. Mum kept calling, telling him not to go any further, and every time she did, he saw himself stop and wave to her. He managed to inch his way to the fence. A curious sensation took him above and behind himself, as he watched how he'd scrambled on his hands and knees below the barbed wire into the next field, instinctively keeping low to avoid catching his clothes.

I did it!

Across a silent sea of rippling ferns, there was a wood on the other side. The wind whispered as it blew, animating the mysterious feathery fronds. He walked among them, away from the sunshine, into the darkness of the woods beyond. Bruce watched himself enter the dark shadows the trees cast.

He followed the coolness in the air, which led him to a small stream, and he felt cold as 'other Bruce' skipped on and off rocks along the bank, challenging himself to leap greater and greater gaps between the rocks, oblivious to everything.

Even expecting it as he was, he still jumped at the sudden appearance of a man standing up, throwing the woman over his shoulder. 'Other Bruce' skidded as he landed, slipping partly into the brook. The resounding thud of his head against the rock made him hunch his shoulders as he recalled the pain. He scrambled hastily from the water, dazed and full of fear. Is this just a nightmare? Where are you, Dad?

The man was now just a few feet away.

He wanted to scream, but his voice wouldn't come. It was stuck in his throat. His legs felt disconnected from his body. The man was almost upon him, and he couldn't even run away.

Something wet and warm ran down Bruce's leg. Oh, now he'll be in trouble with his mum! He checked his pyjamas and felt considerable relief at knowing it had only happened to the 'other Bruce'. Wait a minute... It did happen to me! Suddenly, he was travelling...backwards and upwards, faster than falling, faster than he'd ever imagined he could move – then stopped – hovering like a bird of prey, looking down. His father and grandfather burst through waist-high ferns, leaving a trail of flattened fronds behind them.

Bruce cowered on the ground as the man bent over him.

Distracted by the voices calling out, the stranger stood, stared hard at the frightened boy and locked eyes with him. He put a finger to his lips and whispered, 'Shhh...or I'll kill them all.' Then he turned and sprinted away, back to where he'd left the woman, and swept her up over his shoulder with one arm. Her head came upright, balanced for a moment at the point of flopping back down. Eyes bulging; tongue stuck out of her beetroot face; she seemed to fix Bruce with an angry expression.

He tried to look away, but failed in this version as well, the look on the woman's face burned itself into his memory.

Then the man was gone.

He suddenly remembered the shell! It had saved him again. In the dream, he was telling them what had actually happened, and he was afraid the man would know and come to kill them all. His father checked the bump on his head while his grandfather walked further down the slope to see if there were any sign of what Bruce had just told them he'd seen. There was none.

They spoke together rapidly, too quickly for him to understand. What he could tell though, was that his father didn't believe him. 'It is the bump he has had on his head!'

His grandfather disagreed. 'No, I feel him...somebody bad.' Squatting next to him, looking deep into his pale blue eyes, he said, 'Bruce, remember when you hear this?' His arm extended and came around in a semi-circular sweep.

'I can't hear anything,' Bruce said, confused.

In his heavy Eastern European accent, his grandfather explained patiently, 'Yes, you hear nothing. Remember, when you hear no birds in the forest...the birds, they warn you it is a bad place. You understand?' Bruce nodded; his brain jarred, making his head throb.

His eyes snapped open. The room was dark. Bruce was back in his bedroom. Closing them again, his fears subsided; it was only a dream. Something made him open his eyes once more; part of his dream was still with him.

There was a presence in the room. He knew it sensed him. Not moving, hardly breathing, he didn't dare cross the room to turn on the light. He wasn't sure where this thing was. It was everywhere around him; it was in his head just like when the garage-suited man was after him. His voice paralysed; he remembered what his mother had told him about the living and the dead. *You don't have to worry about the dead – only the living can hurt us.* Whatever it was in his room with him, it wasn't alive. He reached for the seashell that had protected him since he was four years old and, holding it tight, crossed the room to switch the light on; the urge to check under the bed quickly countered by the fear of what he might see. At last, exhausted and feeling safe with the light on, he slept.

A black fly started up, buzzing around, knocking against the lampshade. The droning announcement of its presence made him fearful. *If the room were in darkness, would it settle? Can I find it and swat it the instant the light goes back on?* He extinguished it, turning the room inky-black. The fly cut its engines. *Silence.* Then something cold and wet settled on his lips. He spat furiously, fumbling for the light switch. He crossed the floor and opened the window, hoping the fly would go out. Its abominable noise stopped. Sleep crept into his worried mind and took over.

Something wormed its way into his subconscious. Teeming sounds, distant and surreal, like a tiny Middle Eastern bazaar, drew him from his sleep. He opened his eyes. The spotlight that the lamp shade threw up onto the ceiling, revealed a moving carpet of tiny insects, moths, midges and mosquitoes, and at the centre of it, unmoving...sat the orchestrator of it all. The bluebottle.

Suddenly, Bruce knew he was not alone; the presence that had previously intruded on his thoughts was back in his head, and he knew something else lurked in the shadows under the bed, waiting for him. In stark terror, he shook as his imagination took flight.

Too afraid to look, he tried emptying his mind the way his grandfather had taught him. Deeply breathing in and out, he calmed himself, thinking about his father and grandfather. They always knew what to do, no matter what.

He floated in the transition between sleep and wakefulness.

Clunk! The sound reverberated through the bed, jolting him upright. A few weeks before the same thing had happened, and his mum said it was only the springs settling in the mattress. Uneasy, he tried to relax again.

Clunk! This time, he looked under the bed.

He screamed.

The whole household came running to investigate. In a small voice, he told everyone he was okay; it was only a nightmare. He dared not tell them the real reason.

The following nights, Bruce would lay there like that, fighting sleep. He'd see what happened over and over again, from perspectives that couldn't have been his. Sometimes it felt as if someone else was in his head; he kept seeing the woman's beetroot face, and the killer, finger on lips – *'Shhh...'* he fought to keep the thoughts down until exhaustion forced him into sleep, and then he'd wake in the grip of a nightmare, stifling a scream, afraid of the darkness in his room.

Over the years, he gradually weaved an insular blanket to throw over the intrusive thoughts and fears that plagued him. He hadn't removed the root causes, but he'd never consciously allow them to trouble him again.

Chapter 9

Southern Ireland 1969

Brenda Flynn was Vera's aunt; once considered the life and soul of parties. She was always telling jokes and many a stranger ended up with sore ribs after she'd elbowed them hard on delivering the punch line. While they doubled up in pain, her raucous laughter infected everyone around to join in, none more so than her previous victims.

Life changed dramatically in 1969 with the death of Brenda's husband in a farmyard accident. One cold morning, he started the engine and left it to heat up, then reaching back in to pull something off the front seat, he snagged the gear lever; the tractor started forward with him half in and half out. She saw it as she ran out to take him the sandwiches he'd left behind on the kitchen table. He lost his footing trying to get back into the cab and fell under the back wheel. Widowed and childless, part of her died that day, too.

She became embittered and sour.

A few weeks later, her brother and his entire family burned to death when their home caught fire. All perished apart from Vera. Alerted by the flames, villagers found her wandering, aimless, outside the house. The fire brigade pinpointed the upstairs landing as the origin of the fire. They always left a candle burning there because of Vera's sleepwalking, in case she couldn't see and fell downstairs.

With no family to look after her, she faced the orphanage. Fortunately, her aunt would not allow that, as Ireland in those days was no place for a child to grow up in a Catholic institution.

Her niece was only thirteen, but Brenda never knew what she was getting herself into. Something played on the child's mind; whatever it was, it wouldn't let her rest. One night, despite what they say about never waking a sleepwalker, Brenda did just that, questioning Vera about the fire while she was in her somnambulant state.

'Is that how the fire started, when you were on your wanderings?'

Vera did not appear to wake fully. 'No, it was the dog, chasing a rat. It knocked the candle over at the top of the stairs. When I saw what happened, I was on the beach, too far away to get back to warn them.'

The older woman stared in disbelief, and wondered if the child before her was truly awake.

In her mind's eye, Vera saw it all again, the way the fire caught quickly, the draught funnelling through the stairwell fanning the flames, the melted wax turning it into an inferno. The next thing she knew she was outside in her nightie, warmed by the heat of the fire.

She didn't tell her aunt she'd warned her mother about the fire three nights before. She didn't tell her because she was a child who'd not yet made sense of it all, who was afraid she'd frighten her and because she'd *known* it would happen in advance and didn't do enough to prevent it from happening. There was something else, too, that she didn't tell. While she was on the beach that night, she'd projected herself into her parent's bedroom to warn them. Her ma sat astride pa, riding him. Her father had seen her, but believing her to be sleepwalking, whispered, so as not to wake her, 'I don't want disturbing taking what little pleasures there are to be had in this life. From now on, I'm locking that door.'

'Wait,' her mother said, raising herself off him. She'd seen Vera, too. 'There's something wrong. What is she doing here? Why is she pulling that face?'

'She's only sleepwalking again, don't worry love. Get back into bed and be quiet, and then she'll go away.' Vera looked sad. She knew she should have tried to wake the others first. It was already too late as her projection left the room.

One minute she'd been there, the next she was gone. They didn't question it until they heard the screaming. Her pa never noticed the heat of the door handle as he opened the door. A massive fireball engulfed them. It was only afterwards that she realised she couldn't directly interfere with what fate had planned.

Finally, Vera spoke. 'I tried to wake them.'

Her aunt berated her, 'You stupid, stupid child, you should have tried harder! What you did not do killed your parents.' She couldn't believe her own words as they tumbled out of her mouth. What she'd have given to call them back unheard; but it was too late.

It started a chain reaction. Vera retaliated by telling her she'd killed her own husband.

Stunned into silence, Brenda reacted with undisguised venom. 'What did you just say?'

Vera was afraid of her anger.

'What did you just *SAY?*' she shouted; the veins in her neck stood out, and her piggy eyes bulged almost out of their sockets.

Vera looked down; she spoke quietly. Brenda leaned in to hear her better.

'The last time you were in the tractor, you left your jacket on the front seat. Uncle Tommy started the engine to warm her and jumped down. Seeing it there, and not wanting you to feel the cold, he reached back in and pulled it across the seat. As it came, it snagged the gear lever; he wasn't really looking. He felt it catch, and he tugged it harder. It slipped into gear. You know the rest.'

Now she knew how it had happened as seen through the eyes of the child before her.

She'd been blissful in her ignorance. Now she knew that, in the simple act of leaving her jacket behind, she had contributed to his death.

She wept softly.

Vera woke and put her arms around her neck. 'I'm sorry, Aunty Flynn. I thought you might have wanted to know what happened.' She'd just discovered that the truth had the power to hurt.

After that, she always asked if someone wanted the truth first.
Brenda never woke Vera while she was sleepwalking again.

Chapter 10

Late May 1969

In the early summer of 1969, two memorable things happened to Dr Ryan, and they both occurred on the same day. One: a rainstorm, the likes of which he'd never encountered before. The other: meeting Vera Flynn for the first time.

Rain, driven on demonic winds, lashed horizontally – millions of thin, watery nails unleashed, wave upon wave, like sheets that seemed to undulate in all directions as they rode the currents. Dark skies subdued the light, making everything leaden and drab.

The soft red of the car stood out as it wound its way down the lane, the driver slowly easing in and out of the unavoidable water-filled potholes. Huge splats of machine-gun bullet rain drummed against the windows, producing a secondary mist that cut visibility, so that Ryan perched as far forward on his seat as the wheel allowed, his nose only inches from the inside of the screen. He wiped a swathe of condensation clear with his hand. *As soon as I have enough money,* he told himself, *I'm getting a car with a decent blower.* The wipers of the old Ford couldn't wipe quickly enough to keep up with the rain. The dampness raised a sweet, stale odour from the upholstery inside.

Beyond the misty veil, the farmhouse was barely visible. Set back from the road, he saw it only at the last moment. Pulling quickly into the gateless gap in the stone wall between the pillars, he parked as close to the front door as he could.

Ryan switched the engine off and braced himself, ready to jump out. One – two – three, he flung the door open and dashed out straight into a puddle, cursing as the freezing water swept into his shoe, and soaked his sock. This was the Somme, a war zone masquerading as a driveway with water filled, muddy craters everywhere.

He grabbed his bag from the back seat of the car and, head down against the rain, zigzagged between craters to the front door. A woman watched his approach through a porthole she'd wiped clear through the mist on the glass. As soon as he lifted the knocker, the door opened, and he stepped inside, stamping and scraping on the mat to rid the rain from his shoes.

'Mrs Flynn?' he enquired.

Possessing the heavy, blunt features and ruddy complexion of someone who had spent a lifetime working outdoors, she looked from his bag to his face and said, 'Where's Doctor Robert?'

'He's, um … indisposed, so they sent me instead. Sorry, I'm Dr Ryan.' He extended his hand. She ignored it.

'What's happened?' she said, eyes narrowing.

'I think he's had an accident, and that's all I know.'

She looked at him suspiciously and turned away, removing first her coat, then the scarf covering her head, to reveal a tangle of surprisingly snow-white hair, distinctly at odds with her age.

He took the opportunity to ask some questions. 'What seems to be the matter with her?'

'She was outside yesterday – you remember how dull it was – when she came back in, she looked as if she'd suffered the most terrible sunburn, blistered and all.'

Ryan frowned as he discounted sunlight from the list of possibilities. 'Has this ever happened before?'

'When she was thirteen, by all accounts, something similar happened one Sunday morning at Mass.'

'How old is she now?'

'She's fifteen.'

'Uh-huh, let's take a look at her then.'

She led him down three steps from the hallway. The flag-paved floors did little to make the house feel warm. Ryan shivered; the dampness had seeped into his bones.

They stopped outside the last door down on the left. She knocked and entered without waiting for a reply, ushering him in behind her.

'Vera, the doctor's here.' She did not turn away from the window. Ryan looked around the room; it was a dirty white and sparsely furnished. No two sticks of furniture matched. A small mirror hung over a pine chest of drawers, a rickety looking chair in front of it. Over by the wall furthest from the window, was a child's bed. The blanket covering it was green, and the sheet from underneath it folded down over the top to form a collar. A single pillow was propped upright against the wall; the sag in the mattress indicated how much use it had seen over the years.

The other side of the room, opposite where Vera sat, was a table with a collection of paintings on it. He moved closer to inspect them. The girl had talent and a vivid imagination. The top painting was an aerial landscape view. She must have recreated it from a photograph, or remembered looking down on it from an aeroplane. The centrepiece drew his eye deep into the painting. A black hole of nothingness stood out stark against the greenery of the tree canopy surrounding it; bottomless and empty like the well of a dark soul, it stared up at him. Pointing to the painting, Ryan remarked, 'Very imaginative.'

'Not imagination at all, people have died there,' Vera said without turning around. Unsure what to say, Ryan looked over to the easel next to the table. On it, a half painted canvas depicted stormy skies. Crows or ravens rode the thermals above misty mountain crags and, in the foreground at the foot of the cliffs, two black horses pulled a funeral carriage; one dragged a man behind. A procession of faceless people followed. Ryan switched his view from the painting to the window and beyond. The room was too cold for condensation to form on the glass. Dressed only in a thin nightgown, if she felt the cold, she showed no sign of it. Her eyes seemed fixed on the grey cliffs in the near distance. Taking a step back, away from the window, he'd almost staggered as he recognised the scene. *It was the backdrop to her painting.*

Her hair was the palest shade of ginger, and it spilled down over her shoulders. The way she sat hunched made her backbone stick out through the fabric of her nightdress; her skin was as fine and white as porcelain. He'd not expected to see such delicate beauty after seeing her mother.

'Vera?' Ryan spoke softly.

She turned to look at the young doctor, the expression on her face serious, her eyes green and feline, fixed on him.

'Doctor Robert won't be coming will he,' she said.

'No, Vera something happened, he—'

'Died in his sleep last night,' Vera looked from him to her aunt. 'And she's my aunt, *not* my mother.'

Mrs Flynn's piggy eyes were as wide and round as they could go. Her hand covered her mouth, stifling a gasp.

'How could you have known about Dr Robert, Vera?' Ryan said, also taken aback.

Without answering, she moved over to the painting. Her hands worked with incredible speed. Vera's aunt and the doctor watched transfixed as she mixed colours and painted the outlines of three additional characters. She left them unfinished, but clearly recognisable as a man and woman, carrying a pinkish baby.

The significance of the earlier work troubled him, and a feeling of apprehension passed through him as it became clearer. He wondered if he should ask about the addition of the new figures.

Vera raised her eyes from the painting and stared over the top of the canvas at him.

She smiled with all the self-assurance of a grown woman.

Embarrassed, Ryan attempted to usher Vera away from the window to the bed, where he could more easily examine her. She refused to move from her chair, and no amount of coercion could persuade her otherwise, so he conducted his examination right where she was, by the light of the window.

He checked her eyes, ears and throat, pausing between to make notes. 'Say aah...'

Mrs Flynn, having provided a running commentary of Vera's symptoms throughout, now demanded his diagnosis.

He held his hand up for her to wait while he finished note taking. Conversation and writing at the same time wasn't good for him. Some people could do it. He could not.

Even without talking, he made enough mistakes, so he always drafted in pencil. It made it easier to correct if the need arose. Scrawled out corrections looked so unprofessional; he'd sooner rub them out and start again. He clicked a further millimetre of lead into the nib and examined it before continuing.

'Dr Robert would've had the answer by now. What do *you* think it is, Dr Ryan?'

'Give me a minute, please.'

Although he was a doctor of medicine, he longed to qualify as a psychiatrist. He had a flair for it, an affinity with people and a clear understanding of how their minds worked. To put bread on the table, however, he'd had to take a job as soon as he'd qualified as a doctor. Often, while making his medical diagnosis, he'd include a psychological evaluation he'd keep to himself, but this time his analysis was for her aunt. Despite making an allowance for her anxiety, he marked her down as an impatient woman.

She was asking him questions again. 'I know you must have *some* idea of what's going on with her. What is it, in heaven's name?'

He knew she wouldn't drop it until he gave her something, so he effectively summarised what she'd already told him. 'Mm-m, she looks anaemic. From the diet you told me she has, it's unlikely that's what she's suffering from. Her complexion is naturally pale, a well-known characteristic of her hair type. You said she can't go out on sunny days without blistering and yet she blistered up with sunburn when the weather was dull like this yesterday – if I have that right?'

'That is what I told you.'

Where had all the blisters gone? Ryan frowned. 'She has no melanin in her skin – was she always like this?' The pigmentation of her eyes and hair were normal. If he didn't know better, he might have thought she was suffering from a type of albinism. It puzzled him. She was as pale as alabaster, even in the grey of the dull day; she was almost pure white.

Vera continued to gaze out of the window. Her eyes were almond shaped, her face elfin. She didn't look hot; she had no difficulty breathing; her pulse was normal. He decided to check it again and took her hand in his, turning it over, so the back of it lay against his palm. It was surprisingly soft, yielding and warm; his thoughts turned inexplicably to images of post-sexual spooning.

Ryan shook his head involuntarily to get the image out; with his other hand, he spread her fingers and inspected her palm. Opened fully, it was remarkably unlined, completely unblemished. His intention was to take her pulse, but he waylaid himself into examining the structure of her hand. They were not the hands of a girl that worked physically at all. Her fingers were long and slim; there was a slight callous near the tip of her middle finger, and he already knew it wasn't from writing. He guessed she must do a lot of painting.

Ryan felt for her pulse, frowning as he manoeuvred his finger around the inside of her wrist, he found no trace, feeling only the throb of his own heart in his fingertip.

He became aware of her turning away from the window; her eyes had changed appearance, no longer feline, they were now wide-open sea green and had settled on him. For the second time she smiled as a woman and then her pulse began strongly, it mingled and beat in accord with his. Ryan suddenly felt self-conscious under her gaze and looked away to break contact.

She spoke for the first time since she'd mentioned Dr Robert. 'Talk to me, B. Ryan, I don't bite.'

Ryan found himself taken aback for the second time that morning. How could she know his first name began with a B? Her eyes led him to the bag; the nameplate on it said 'B Ryan'. *So that was how she did it!* He smiled in recognition of the simple fact. She could be no more than fifteen, but she had the knowing smile of a woman. He looked away.

'Vera, are you allergic to anything you know of that you might have come into contact with in the last few days, yesterday perhaps?'

She didn't respond; instead, fiddled with something she held in her free hand.

He caught a glimpse of a shiny black object between her fingers. The quizzical look on his face, prompted her to tuck it away behind her back.

Although he was curious, he decided not to ask about it.

If he had, she'd have told him it was just a stone she'd found two days before on the beach.

'I'd like to get you in for a blood test. The hospital will contact you with an appointment.'

'She needs something doing – and now!' Mrs Flynn exclaimed, louder than she'd intended. She covered her mouth with her hand, her eyes round with embarrassment.

Ryan turned to look at her. 'What am I missing here?'

She didn't reply.

He looked from one to the other for a clue, and noticed she'd shot her niece a sharp look. Vera glanced almost imperceptibly at the bed. He eyed the hollow caused by sagging springs.

'Have you been sleeping well?'

Her aunt chimed in and answered for her, small round eyes rolling anticlockwise towards the ceiling. 'That one hardly sleeps at all for nights on end. I'm telling you. You can hear her walking about, creaking open doors like a noisy ghost all night long. She isn't asleep, and she isn't awake either. When she *does* sleep, you can't wake her up at all!'

Vera gazed steadily at Ryan; he pretended not to notice, but the heat under his collar gave him away. His discomfort made her smile.

'Vera, when did you last get a good night's sleep?'

She made brief eye contact, and then looked over to her aunt. 'Last night, the night before...'

'Since when?' Mrs Flynn scoffed.

'Since last night, and the night before!'

'Wilful child, how dare you take that tone with me!' She moved within striking distance, the back of her hand raised above her left shoulder.

Jumping between, arms outstretched, he kept them apart. 'Let's not be squabbling now,' he said, holding his hand up to Mrs Flynn as if stopping traffic. 'So, Vera, you would say you sleep all right?'

She hesitated for a moment. 'Well, *I* would say so.' She shot a defiant look at her aunt, knowing she'd say differently.

'That bed looks uncomfortable, you might try turning the –'

'Don't you think we've tried that!' she snapped. 'The springs are poking... Soon they'll poke through this side as well.'

The idea of having a new mattress delivered anonymously occurred to him, but he guessed they would know it was from him. *When pride was one of the only possessions people had left, you couldn't afford to hurt it.*

'How did you know about Dr Robert, Vera?'

She swivelled away from the window to face him square on, a faint comma of a smile appeared at the corner of her mouth, enigmatic, like the one in the painting of the Mona Lisa. A brief appreciation of Da Vinci's talent crossed his mind. *How do you capture something as transient as that in a painting?*

Mrs Flynn's face illuminated, and she glanced at Vera, a mixture of pride and awe. 'She has the sight. I wasn't sure before, but now I'm convinced of it. This morning before you even arrived, she taunted me about Dr Robert. I didn't see how it could be true, but that smile of hers just confirmed it.' She shook her head slowly. 'A blood test indeed!' she guffawed. Fixing him with a hard stare, she pushed her face to within inches from his. The smell of her breath stunned him as she rasped, 'Buy me a chocolate teapot!'

He chose not to respond, and instead cleared his throat into his clenched fist.

'I'm a doctor, but I'm hoping to become a psychiatrist. I'd love to understand a little bit better what you're going through. Could you help me with that?'

Vera's eyes softened; he saw a kind of fleeting sympathy there. A second later, it was gone. 'Doctor, I don't think I can do that, I believe it's beyond your powers of comprehension.'

His voice was soft, but determined. 'Try me.'

'Dr Robert was riding to my house on a mare the colour of midnight, its mane tied off in black ribbons and bows. A storm rose from hell. The animal was uncontrollable, too fiery for him, unbroken. He fell from its back and lay in the mud. It was the same horse that dragged poor David Robert behind, the same one that led the funeral procession.' Vera pointed to the painting. 'Oh, I knew he was dead, but he didn't die like that,' she explained. 'He woke up clutching his chest, his bulging eyes almost popping out of his head. Knowing it was the end, he grabbed for a note pad and scribbled and scrawled and didn't finish it all. He tore the page from it – now you tell me – why would he do that, if he hadn't finished?'

There hadn't been a note!

He felt the hair on the back of his neck rise. *What if it were true? What would that mean?*

She seemed to read his mind.

'You were there this morning, it's why you were late...there *was* a note. It slipped under the bed off the bedside table, the draught from the door blew it there when the housekeeper went in to wake him. She found it after you left. Do you want to know what it said?'

The cold truth of what she was saying started goose bumps rising; a chill ran over him, and the hair on his arms stood up as if in an electrostatic parade.

'Will you tell me?'

Vera beckoned him closer. 'Yes, but it's for your ears only.'

Mrs Flynn looked fearful. She shook her head and said emphatically, 'I'll not leave the room!'

He bent forward and inclined his head towards her. She leaned and whispered something in his ear.

What she said made him stand erect and incredulous. She gave him three predictions, and of those, one came true within the hour. The second would be confirmed in the not too distant future, while the third would remain a secret until the time was right to reveal it, many years hence. She played her tongue suggestively across her lips, her green eyes shiny with unmistakable desire.

Mrs Flynn was outraged. She grabbed his bag, shoved it into his arms and ushered him out. 'That's enough! What sort of doctor are you anyway!'

Ryan blustered, protesting.

Her finger pointed to the door. 'Out!' She started moving towards him. He had the distinct impression if he didn't leave right away, she might help him on his way.

The sun came out beyond the confines of the room. Not visible outside the window, it didn't shine in directly, but the increase in light drew his attention to the painting. At the top was a tiny church with an illuminated cross. *How did I not see that before?* For no particular reason, he noted that the window faced north.

The business with Dr Robert and Mr Ryan's subsequent visit made Brenda Flynn's mind up for her. Vera's little predictions were becoming all too frequent and always coming true.

Keep her on the side of God, away from the Devil. After what she'd seen of her flirting with Ryan, it was time to act.

She reported Vera to the church and told them all she knew of her devil's curse.

Chapter 11

Ryan had waited for three weeks for the results of Vera's blood test to arrive before he called the hospital. He'd hung on while the lady at the other end checked the records, papers rustled dryly as she leafed through them next to the receiver on her desk. In the background, two women chatted excitedly about their holiday plans. Finally, she picked the phone up again.

'Hello, Doctor Ryan, are you still there?'

'Yes,' he replied, rather wearily.

'Thanks for holding. Vera Flynn, you said? I'm sorry we don't have a record of an appointment in that name.'

'Thank you for your time.' While waiting, he absentmindedly doodled on his paper blotter and after he'd put the phone down, he examined the series of shapes, squares within squares, elaborate crosses and concentric circles he'd drawn. They had no apparent meaning: he wondered what a psychiatrist might have made of them.

Besides psychiatry, his number one interest was the paranormal. When he first met Vera he hoped studying her in more depth might confirm some universal truths he suspected were common to all beliefs, pagan, conventional religion, or otherwise.

Initially, he didn't believe in God or any other supreme being, but what he found repeatedly was that the more deprived and disconsolate the people, the greater the likelihood there was they'd be devoted to religion. He also discovered these people were more likely to have visions of a religious nature, to experience miracles, and benefit from miraculous cures.

There had to be a link, something binding it all together, something that made it more than just mere happenstance. There just *had* to be...

Vera had been born into grinding poverty. Her family, all Catholics, attended church every Sunday. If she truly knew what happened to Dr Robert *before* it happened. If she'd really seen it unfold from afar, as she said she had; the writing of the note, blown from its place... He scratched his head in frustration; he had more questions than answers.

Doctor Robert had died before he completed the note. The first of the three things she whispered in his ear proved to be true. She'd told him about the note before anyone else knew of its existence. The first part read: *I think the Flynn girl is...* She told him what the doctor *would* have written. *Working against God.* At that point, she'd inserted her tongue into his ear, so quick, warm and sensuous.

Sitting at his desk, he touched his ear and remembered how stunned he was when she'd licked him. If there truly were a God, why would he create someone like her: If only to oppose Him?

Over the years, he'd found a reversal of his atheism; it came slowly. He became a believer. He'd seen far too many things to remain a sceptic. Back then, he'd yet to learn.

Finally, he plucked up the courage to find out why Vera hadn't taken the blood test.

He lifted the telephone again and dialled, it took a long time to answer.

'Hello?'

'Mrs Flynn?'

A two-second pause ensued. 'Who *is* this?'

'Mrs Flynn, it is Doctor —'

She stopped him short. 'You can't speak with her!'

'Wait, I didn't ring to talk to her. I rang to find out if everything was all right.'

'Why wouldn't it be?' she growled.

'She didn't show up for her blood test, and I just wanted —'

'Mr Ryan, she doesn't need any medical test, and she doesn't need the likes of you. Anyway, she's gone now.'

He hesitated a second. 'What do you mean...gone?'

'She's joined the sisterhood,' she said.

'That's impossible, she's too young!'

'She's an *exceptional* case, Mr Ryan,' she said with pride. 'Accept it. Let it go and leave us be!'

The phone banged down.

Cut off, he scowled at the receiver. At the time of his last visit, he'd sensed animosity between them, and now he was unlikely to discover what it was.

He did as she asked and let it go.

Chapter 12

Sent initially to a convent for further study, it didn't take long for Vera's unique gifts to manifest themselves. The preliminary assessment reported: *The girl appears to have the ability to read the past lives of people, to see deep into the very soul and nature of those subject to her scrutiny, indeed, even going so far as to predict the future – without evidence of trickery or deception.*

When word of Vera's supernatural abilities reached bishop level and beyond, it was inevitable the Vatican would take an interest. They sent two emissaries for her.

Once in Rome, specialist doctors hooked Vera up to EEG sensors and took electro-encephalograms while she slept to measure her brainwaves. After conducting psychiatric tests, polygraphs and other neurological evaluations, the investigators found no evidence of fraud or deception, and reported that the abilities she displayed were inexplicable, and beyond scientific understanding. A great deal of secrecy surrounded their conclusions and, with special dispensation from the Holy See, the church accepted her as a novice nun. She became Sister Verity and spent the next few years in the Vatican, where she studied, and was herself studied by theologians in supernaturalism.

Prior to the burgeoning sex abuse scandals of the eighties and nineties, the Church was keen to keep its own house in order, to avoid scandal and negative publicity. In Sister Verity they'd found someone who was capable of sniffing out and identifying the rot, God's own bloodhound. Sister Verity became widely known as simply 'The Sister' within the inner circles of the church.

In this role, she'd attend confession in selected parishes, and it was there in the confessional that she was able to establish the veracity of the priests. Her exposures were kept in-house in most cases, but some were too big to contain.

The newspapers ran headlines over the next few weeks: *Priest accused of child molestation – More victims come forward – Accusations going back decades – Bishop knew of allegations – Priest commits suicide!*

At first, she'd been only too willing to assist, later becoming unhappy, not only at the way in which the Church handled things, but also at the regularity with which she uncovered these people. 'Let he who is without sin, cast the first stone', was stretching the point. Although she was not without sin herself, the extent of sin she found in those holy places alarmed her. Inevitably, she came up against priests she had reported to the Church authorities the first time around, only to find them transferred to another parish in the hope they would mend their wicked ways.

Her last case had been the final straw.

One of the things she needed to do while waiting in the confessional was de-tune herself from the box itself, or she'd be hearing how Mrs Dalton or some other poor soul, had confessed to stealing eggs and potatoes to feed her starving family, while shame kept her from telling the priest that she'd also been sleeping with the milkman and the coalman while her husband was in prison, and her conscience had guilted her into thinking half a confession was better than nothing.

Well-worn hollows, formed by many different elbows, dished the shelf by the screen. The atmosphere was heavy and oppressive. It wasn't right. Placing her hands onto the wood, she focused beyond the fabric of its construction. So much guilt, unhappiness, sorrow and pain, had been absorbed. The image of a choirboy came to Vera, sitting on the pew outside, deliberately timing his arrival so he'd be the last in the queue.

'Bless me, Father, for I have sinned, it's been too long since my last confession, and since then you have had me indulge in vile practices with you, Father, and it has to stop!'

The priest was calm. 'You want to turn your back on all the special privileges your position brings? You no longer want to be in the choir?'

The boy blurted out, 'I'll not be doing those things anymore; it's against God and nature!'

The priest hissed through the grille, 'It stops, when *I* say it stops!'

'No, Father, it ends now or I go to the police!'

'Then go to the police! Do you think they'll take the word of an illegitimate orphan against the word of a priest?'

He could have only been thirteen, his voice newly broken. Unsure, he rose suddenly and dismissed himself.

Father O'Donohue swept out of the confessional behind him.

The boy didn't make it out of the churchyard.

Strong as Vera was, she came close to her breaking point. After six years of service, she decided it was time to leave and she left without permission to do so, returning to her home one last time to retrieve the stone from its hiding place.

When they'd originally come for her years before, she'd dropped it into the water butt outside the front door of her house. She took it from its slimy drawstring purse, held it and closed her eyes. It was the first time she'd touched it since her friend, Mick, had been run over attempting to negotiate his way through a railway crossing whilst drunk. When that had happened, she'd wanted to throw it away. Now that she knew she possessed the ability to interpret what the polished black sphere merely amplified, it would become a supplementary tool, and as part of her calling and destiny, it was far too important to discard.

As for the paedophile priest, she'd find a way to ensure he paid for his sins.

Chapter 13

New Year 1975

Although it was just before sunrise, the streets of Brighton were already busy. Traders exchanged friendly banter as the day's business commenced. Roller shutters clattered as shop windows were exposed. Van doors opened and then boomed shut, twin amber flashes and beeping sounds signalled the setting of alarms.

Nobody noticed the diminutive hooded figure in the grey satin cape as she hurried by, late for an appointment. Despite the loose fit of the clothing, the form was unmistakably female. The sharpness of the air caught her breath, turning it into misty trails of cloud that evaporated in her wake. She glanced up at a clock as she passed. It confirmed she was five minutes late.

Vera disappeared into a labyrinth of alleyways, before finally locating the impatient looking Mrs Smith.

'Sorry, I'm late,' she said, struggling to catch her breath.

The older woman forced a thin smile, and turned to unlock the door. She made no attempt at friendliness.

Decorated Romany style, red with the fine detailing picked out in yellows and greens, the shop's double front showcased the cleverly staged scenery. Set well back from the windows, one side depicted daytime, with all its sunny greenery, painted full size on canvas backdrops. The other showed night, dimly lit by an array of tiny star lights set into the black ceiling. Here, men sat about a campfire, drinking, smoking, engaging with each other, their faces half-aglow against the firelight.

Vera imagined for a moment that she saw it flicker into life. The focal point behind the shop front was a traditional bow top caravan, complete with steam-bent, carved wooden profiles, lavishly decorated in shades of red, green and gold. It looked authentic, and for all the world, as if the builders, unwilling to move it, had constructed the shop around it instead. She'd never seen anything quite like it before.

Beyond the lobby, there were four steps going up from ground level into the vardo. A pair of heavy crimson velvet tasselled curtains hung either side of the narrow entranceway. A horseshoe, hung above the door, for luck.

She followed as Mrs Smith entered.

Once inside, she pulled her hood down, revealing long, fine hair the colour of pale flame. Her complexion was creamy, and her green eyes striking; they conveyed wisdom beyond her years. 'Why is it so gloomy in here?' she said.

'There's not enough electricity to fire the bulbs up to their full extent,' the older woman explained, 'besides, it's advantageous if they can't see you properly.'

Surprised at the lush décor, the younger woman's eyes settled on a painting that dominated one wall. A beautiful and mysterious looking fortune teller in traditional garb had been captured by the artist in part profile, one eye narrowed, she peered into a crystal ball held aloft in her left hand. She realised with a smile that she'd positioned herself in the middle of the scene used as the backdrop for the portrait.

Mrs Smith sat. Vera remained standing and looked at the cloth covering the table between them, the colour and texture of it reminded her of fine green grass.

'C'mon Sister, take a pew,' she pointed at the red velvet seat opposite.

A sudden whiff of the past caught Vera off guard and, for the tiniest moment, she wondered if the woman knew about her. She didn't; it was pure coincidence. A habit she had of calling fellow Irish women 'sister'.

Vera acknowledged with a smile. 'I guess we're *all* Sisters here.'

'What did you say your name was, dear?'

'I didn't. Call me Sister, that'll suit me fine,' she said.

'Have you done this kind of work before?'

'No,' she said, shaking her head.

'Y'know, I used to call meself Petulengro in the early days, before I came here. I had to change it, seeing as that isn't me real name. What's yours?'

'It's Vera.'

'Then it looks like *you'll* be having to change your name, too!' The older woman laughed, 'What will you call yourself?'

'I thought we agreed a minute ago, call me Sister,' she smiled enigmatically.

'*Sister Petulengro…* Now *that* does have a good ring about it.' Mrs Smith's eyes shone as she continued. 'It's not too hard; they do half the work for ya. Okay, so this is how it we'll do it. You'll watch me for a few days and, if you're smart, you'll be up and running in no time. Remember, tell 'em what they want to hear. It's what they pay you for.'

Vera nodded her head. She needed the money too much to spoil her chances of a job with an argument about morals and ethics.

Chapter 14

As word of the new 'teller spread, one after another they came, in through the shop and into the vardo. Her clients were almost exclusively women. Some girls came by just for fun, and she didn't object to engaging in what they wanted to hear. Vera saw no harm in holding their palms upwards in her gloved hands and telling them...*You'll meet the man of your dreams.* They hailed from a variety of backgrounds, rich, poor, widowed, and divorced. It made no difference to her. All had one thing in common. They craved answers.

The Sister needed no props, no crystal ball, no cards, no tealeaves or hot sands. She needed only impressions, nothing more than that.

Not allowed to intervene directly, she *could* point the way. At times, she strayed a little off the path, away from the one recommended by Mrs Smith.

She saw there were times when the truth would be more beneficial, although not without pain. It wasn't long before she was giving them a choice. *Do you want the truth? Before you give me your answer, search your heart. It may be that deep down you already know. The truth, when it comes from someone else, has the power to hurt as well as heal.*

In many cases, the answers were there, but unable to face them, they needed them spelled out. Others just needed a clue. A few thought they might use the information to their advantage. One such woman had been carrying on an affair; her husband threatened to kill himself. She wanted to know if he'd really do it.

Sister held her gaze. 'You want the truth?'

She nodded.

'I see a lot of blood, and you can't honestly blame him, can you? You, sleeping with another man in his bed ...'

'Blood? Whose blood?'

'Yours,' Sister said.

The woman's features stretched; her mouth gawped; her eyes widened as a mix of horror and disbelief took hold. She'd not told anyone of her situation...*so, how could she know?* Afraid to hear more, she grabbed her coat and left in a hurry.

Sister's thoughts turned to the last time she'd connected through the medium of skin. The experience had been too intense, even painful for her. The stone insulated her from that direct contact, yet still achieved almost the same results. Perfectly round and of a similar composition to Obsidian, from the instant she'd picked it up, it appeared to have a life of its own. Struck with an immediate discourse, a transfer of impressions, she'd wanted to absorb them, follow them all, just like a bloodhound trailing a scent. Her senses were overwhelmed to such a degree; she was afraid she might fall over. She would learn to ignore the distractions it threw up at her.

The night she'd found it; she put it in her pocket and then picked up other stones on her way home and held them for a moment. None of them behaved like the black one. She grasped the mysterious stone ball again, expecting a further transfer. Nothing happened, not a thing. Whatever was in it before had now gone.

She let herself in when she arrived at her house and, upstairs in her room, held it against the lamp. It was too dense to allow light to pass through.

The following day, Vera recalled putting it down on the kitchen table in front of Mick McMurphy. Although perfectly spherical, it rolled loopily across the top, almost coming to a stop before wobbling and changing direction, lolloping around in a small circle, almost to a halt, rotating at right angles to its former position, and then as if driven by something inside, it did it all over again, a miniature perpetual motion machine.

He picked it up and stroked an eyebrow, somewhat mystified. 'That's a meteorite thingy,' he said, holding it close to his eyeball, trying to fathom it. 'It melted when it came in through the atmosphere and turned into thousands of tiny balls when they fell into the sea.' He was deadly serious.

'Aww, c'mon Mick, you can't really know that!' she scolded, and crossed her arms in front of her chest.

His face was a picture of amused indignation as he protested, 'Yes I do, actually, or how else do you think it turned into that shape!'

She smiled at him. *He's such a joker.*

He plopped it into her outstretched palm. The moment it touched, a fragment of Mick's life had flashed in her mind's eye. Afraid, she grabbed at his hand; the jolt from it almost felled her. The impressions rushing into her were the same as the stone, but amplified many, many times. She looked at her friend. *Oh, please God, it cannot be.*

Bemused by her expression, he said, 'What?'

Vera spoke very slowly, quietly. 'I'm not sure. Promise me, Mick, that you'll be careful...'

She knew what she knew; something akin to a code of conduct meant she could do nothing about it. When he'd handled it, she drew off what the stone absorbed from him, and after that it was clean again. She took from the stone, and it took from her. Her skin, already pale, became more sensitive still, so that even dull daylight could burn her.

'She has no melanin in her at all.' She recalled what Ryan had told her aunt, and it meant she needed to cover herself from head to toe whenever she ventured outdoors. And because of it, she preferred to spend her days inside, introspecting alone at the window, making sense of her precious black stone, watching other kids play, listening to the peals of their laughter. She put the memories of childhood behind her.

Now, it was like that again. All day spent indoors, but at night, quiet and inconspicuous, she began pastoral work, visiting the homeless, the tramps and winos that congregated in the quiet, dark alleyways away from the main roads leading from the seafront; outside the boarded up pubs and guesthouses. Her association with the stone charged her with an energy she hadn't possessed before she found it and, by now, she had an understanding of its powers.

Without the sphere, Vera could already see what was to come. What it did, was allow her to reverse engineer from the future to the past, something akin to analysing the moves that resulted in checkmate once the chess was over. She'd seen the rope of life with its many fibres and strands, its loops and its coils, the coming together and the pulling apart. She understood at last, exactly what fate held for her, just as she had the night she found it, when the stone had eclipsed the moon.

She watched from the shadows as a group of rough sleepers gathered around a fire burning in a perforated oil drum. In hushed tones, one was talking; he had a blanket draped over his head and shoulders. The others, mostly, listened in awe.

'Midnight it was, I couldn't sleep because I hadn't had a drop for hours. I was shivering, sick and cold to the bone; I wanted to die. Not knowing what else to do, I closed my eyes and prayed. When I opened them, she stood above me, in that cape o' hers, all alight as if she'd a fire burning behind her. She leaned over me, her hand out straight – like that – and I swear it glowed. I was scared; I never seen anything like it, and she was smiling, and I felt warm. The next thing I knew it was morning. I've not had a drop since.'

A murmur rose amidst the men. Some believed him. A few wanted to believe. The others were too far gone to care.

'Well, how come you're still on the streets then?'

'God did not build Rome in a day. All in good time, Czech, all in good time.'

Czech, a good man who'd lost his way. She smiled. They didn't need her tonight.

It didn't take long for Vera to achieve a mythical status among the down-and-outs in Brighton. Some swore she could perform miracles, or they'd say she could be in two places at once. They christened her, 'Our Lady of Brighton'.

When the church heard the rumours of a miracle Lady, they sent emissaries to investigate. She knew they were coming and stayed away from the streets at night. It didn't occur to them to look for her in a fortune teller's kiosk in the Lanes of Brighton during the day. The following Easter Sunday, Vera resumed her services. Through her, tramps, winos and the lost, lonely and disconsolate, found a God they could believe in.

The little bell above the door tinkled, taking her out of her reverie. She looked out from the darkness where she sat, not seeing who it was, but knowing.

'I've been expecting you.'

Chapter 15

Brighton June 1975

Ryan was not looking for an affair as he strolled along the seafront past the pier that morning. A few seagulls squabbled on the ground over scraps on the promenade, their loud cries attracting new screeching arrivals from the sky above into the fray. As the size of the group grew, he wondered absently how many gulls it took to qualify as a flock.

He turned away from the front and headed towards the heart of the town. *A shepherd and his flock…a congregation of people.* The definitions took on a religious connotation and he found himself wondering what had happened to Vera Flynn.

Inevitably, he arrived at the point in his recollections where she'd made the second of her predictions. The first was, of course, uncanny, and left no doubt she was in possession of something extraordinary: the ability to foretell at least the near future. When she'd whispered the second prediction to him, it was far into an indeterminable future. The warmth of her breath was on his ear once more, and the tingle of pleasure her tongue had sent through him as she pushed it deep inside, sealing the memory there. As he thought through the coming about of, and later the consequence of her suggested future, he felt the stirring of an erection.

He still thought about her occasionally over the years. How he'd have loved the chance to study her.

He reflected on the order of things, on the million and one thought processes discarded every hour of every day and deliberated on the sensory impressions filtered out as unimportant to survival. He also considered the unlikelihood of successfully predicting what would happen in the next minute. Oh, you might have a clue in the here and now as to which way events might turn, based on chance, probability and the ability to guess well, but to predict something an hour before, or the *day* before? The odds were beyond calculation. What mechanism could be involved in singling out from all other perceived information, a moment in time that did not yet exist? He sought answers from beyond the bounds of established convention, visiting mediums and their like.

He'd yet to find a single one with any special ability, other than well-polished trickery.

At first, Ryan walked past the shop by a few paces. A distinct impression formed that he should go back. *There's something different about this place.* He stopped, retraced his footsteps and then, peering through the window; decided to go in. A tiny bell signalled his arrival.

A soft female voice came from the gloomy interior. 'I've been expecting you.'

What? This was a new ploy. He squinted into the darkness.

'Turn the sign around on the door, Dr Ryan, and lock it for me, will you?'

He did as she asked without question; a sense of unreality pervaded as he turned the sign to *Closed* and, crouching, turned the key in the lock. He stood and sensing someone right behind him, he spun around.

She was there. He'd *known* it would be her. She lifted her face to him, her eyes a myriad of changing shades of green. He saw himself in miniature reflected in their opalescence.

Vera's soft lips parted as they touched his; she orgasmed almost instantly, shuddering against him, electrifying him; he marvelled at the joys of her, knowing it had barely begun. What he'd known for a long time would happen was happening. The second prediction was coming true.

It was an experience he would later note, like being born again.

She'd broken her vow of chastity. Abandoned by her powers, he again lost the chance to study her. Perhaps it was fated he shouldn't know more and once he'd served his purpose, she never allowed him to sleep with her again.

Chapter 16

A few months passed and Vera closed the shop on medical advice. Ryan had invested in her practice, buying the unit to keep the pressure off her. A year later she was ready to open up again, he helped her with the cleaning and preparations. Despite her weakened state, she now considered it safe to handle the stone again. She took it from her pocket, removed one of her gloves and, making a fist around it, closed her eyes. A renewed vigour infused her, restoring her fully. He was incredulous as he watched the change.

Later, he added to his notes. *Vera seemed to relish losing her powers. I'm sworn to secrecy over the reasons for it, but she seemed to know it served a greater purpose. She enjoyed the freedom from responsibility more than anything, although the events of the past few months seem to have sapped her strength. I examined her in my capacity as a medical doctor and, as I signed the necessary paperwork, she decided to share something with me.* He outlined what he'd witnessed, and concluded. *She keeps a mysterious black sphere about her wherever she goes – she calls it 'The stone'. It seems to invigorate her. I suspect it is the source of her power.*

She remained close to him, even working with him as he sought to make scientific sense of her. She wouldn't elaborate about the stone, other than to say it was her talisman. Without gloves, she wouldn't allow him to handle it, telling him he'd taint it.

'Taint it with what?' he'd asked.

Because she couldn't lie, she chose her words carefully. 'Some things are beyond human comprehension.'

'I'd like to examine its composition further, I've never seen a material quite like it, it's almost obsidian, but how did it become so perfectly spherical?'

Vera replied, truthfully, 'I don't know.'

'If—'

'No more questions,' she said, closing the matter firmly. 'You asked if I could help you in the more extreme cases, to unravel what you cannot?'

'That's right, I did.'

'The answer is, I can, but only if it plays a part in the bigger plan.'

'What plan is that?' Ryan asked.

'I can't tell you, it's always changing.'

'But you will help me?'

A vague smile was on her lips as she handed him a sealed envelope.

'What's this?' he said as he took it.

'Inside the envelope is the third prediction I told you of when I was thirteen. You must not open it until the day comes.'

'And how will I know when that is?'

'You will know,' she said.

Two of her predictions in regards to him had already come true, and he'd witnessed countless other accurate forecasts of the near future. He had no doubt that, in the fullness of time, the third would come to pass as well.

Chapter 17

Tuesday 15 July 1975

A shrill unearthly wail cut through the air, curdling the blood, suspending time, silencing everything.

High in the hills, the expedition line stopped abruptly, and then began to move again, reversing its direction. A head count revealed four boys missing, the remaining eleven boys and three teachers snaked back along the path, descending fast.

Above, silent and unnoticed in the cloudless sky, a small cruciform fleck circled lazily against the sun. The buzzard observed the unfolding drama below with avian indifference.

Kirk found Bruce Milowski rocking backwards and forwards in a foetal, squatting position, close to the edge of the pond, rambling to himself incoherently about evil spirits and moving shadows. Wild-eyed, he told Kirk how the water had sucked each of his friends under, one by one.

'I tried, I really tried. I threw Brookes my shell, and he caught it. It should have saved him...' he gnawed on his knuckles until the skin broke.

'What are you talking about, boy,' Kirk said, 'you're not making sense.'

'Because I can't swim – don't you see?' Without warning, he repeated the blood-curdling scream that first drew them back down the hill. Up close, it was ear splitting.

Milowski's behaviour spooked the other boys, infecting them with wild fears and imaginings. A sense of panic rose among them, the atmosphere palpable; filled with blind dread and confusion. Kirk recalled similar scenes in the war. *These kids are shell-shocked.*

A noxious odour drifted out from the deep, water-filled hollow and registered with Kirk, triggering memories. He'd once lost three men while crossing a swamp in Borneo, a pocket of marsh gas and hydrogen sulphide had erupted from the mud in such concentrations that it killed them within seconds, before dissipating in the open air.

Behind him, his colleague stripped off, preparing to go into the water.

Kirk caught a movement out of the corner of his eye. The PE teacher in his underpants ran by, ready to dive in. He'd almost reached the edge.

'Stop,' Kirk's parade ground voice barked. The other man stopped dead. 'You can't go in there.' He pulled the inside of his collar up, covering his mouth. 'The gas, it's poisonous, keep back.'

Kirk delegated him to run for help instead.

Even away from the water's edge, the smell was overpowering. On the lower banks, the corpses of several different species of birds provided a testimony to its lethal potency.

Somebody put a red blanket over the surviving boy's shoulders. Two teachers tried to comfort him.

Milowski watched the scene descend further into chaos. In his detachment, he was as far removed and indifferent as the buzzard that continued circling the skies above.

He began rambling again. 'You could see the sky in the water, but then it turned black! The shadows, they live in the water, and they've got out. They're going to get us all!' he paused, suddenly quite lucid. 'I let him have my seashell, I threw it to Brookes, and he caught it. I thought it would save him…' Then he screamed again, a few of the boys started to cry. Kirk slapped him hard, the sound cracking like a rifle shot. Everyone turned to look at him. He immediately put his arm around the boy's shoulder.

'You're in shock, kid, calm down. You're safe now; it's going to be all right.'

The slap had snapped the hysteria out of him and he shivered once, the reversal of his state was unnatural in its immediacy. He sank to his haunches, squatting twenty-five feet from the edge of the water, quiet, almost catatonic and stared across it, contemplating the loss of his friends. Empty and bewildered at what had just happened, unable to accept its reality, he'd already begun to seal the memory. He'd put it away in a bubble and not remember it again for a long time. The last part of child in him had finally gone and, with it, more than that. The blind faith he'd held in the power of his magic seashell. And with that, his belief in God disappeared, too.

He refused to move, even after the emergency services arrived.

An unmistakable smell of sulphur rose from the stagnant pond, churned up by the activities of the dive teams, and swamped his senses. He got the inescapable feeling that if there really were a hell, that's where he was already. Struck with the conviction that something else was going to happen – he sat, watched and waited.

Only four-wheel drive vehicles were able to get close. They had little tents erected in a cluster near the entry point for the divers. One of the trucks, a pick-up, had an A-frame bolted onto the back. A heavy-duty hook connected to a steel cable winch hung from the top pulley. Milowski wondered why they needed a piece of equipment like that.

Two hours later they pulled the first body out, clothes heavy, skin pale against the black waters that left trails and traces of silt as it drained off. Even through all the dirt and filth, his bright copper-coloured hair marked him out in death as unmistakably as it did in life.

It was Brookes. The last one to drown had become the first one out.

Milowski sat staring at the scene playing out before him.

Kirk eyed the fifteen-year-old youth crouched beneath a red blanket draped over his head and shoulders, a corner of it extended to a point just below his haunches, almost touching the top of the trampled grass. *It hasn't hit him yet.*

Two teachers and a paramedic were trying to coax him away. He brushed their hands from his arms and shoulders without saying a word, becoming increasingly agitated; his demeanour suggested he might explode at any moment.

Unable to persuade him to leave, the teachers shrugged at each other, at a loss for what to do next.

Kirk marched over. 'What's his name?'

'It's Bruce Milowski,' the PE teacher said.

The ex-army officer nodded and tried to repeat the surname without success. Anti-communist sentiment, a throwback to his military days, would not allow him to get beyond the first three letters before his tongue felt tied and alien to him. It might have been appropriate under the circumstances to call him by his Christian name, but given his background, he struggled with that, too.

He lowered his voice, almost sounding gentle. 'Listen, boy, I'm going to stay with you, all right?'

The water seemed to hold a continuing fascination for him. He didn't answer.

'All right?' Kirk said again and laid a heavy hand on his shoulder.

Milowski nodded without looking round.

Kirk squatted down next to him. With his broken nose, beady eyes and square jaw, his face was at odds with this newly found gentleness, and he managed a lop-sided grin that showed off his chipped teeth. His eyes didn't miss a trick. A veteran of the Korean War, he'd seen this sort of thing before; the boy was suffering from shock. On the battlefield, he'd have put himself in danger just sitting there, but not here.

The paramedic leaned down and spoke quietly in Kirk's ear.

'We need to get him out of here.'

Kirk stood up; he and the medic were the same height, but the former soldier's bearing commanded respect, something the other man resented.

'The boy is already in shock – if we try to take him now – under duress, we may do more harm than good.'

'I'm sorry,' said the ambulance man, 'I don't agree. He needs medical attention…'

Kirk put a halting hand up, stopping him short. 'Yes, he is in shock, but I believe he should be allowed to see the recovery of the bodies. It's what he wants. Then we'll take him out of here.'

'He's a young boy, and we are not in the army now, *Mr* Kirk.'

The men eyed each other, the medic angry, Kirk indifferent.

The younger man broke contact first, 'Well, he's your responsibility.'

'I know that, son,' Kirk said quietly. 'And it's just Kirk, not mister...okay?'

A fresh belch of sulphur invaded their nostrils; the medic pulled a face, and burying his nose into the crook of his arm, marched across to the nearest policeman. The officer listened, looked over and then started making his way towards them.

'Can I speak with you, sir?' The constable addressed Kirk, but looked closely at Milowski, who hadn't taken his eyes off the waters, watching as the frogmen surfaced, dived and resurfaced repeatedly. 'Over there, if you don't mind.' He motioned with his head.

Kirk pressed his lips firmly together and shook his head. He indicated the boy with a flick of his eyes. 'Can't leave him. Talk to me here.'

'This isn't a rescue operation, sir, this is a recovery situation.'

'I know that, officer,' Kirk said, leaning in close to him, speaking in a low voice. 'You see, I myself was an officer in the British Army, served in Korea, 1951. I think I know a thing or two about the way young men react when they see their friends die right in front of them.'

'Sir, with respect, that isn't the point here. There's no hope of finding the other two alive. The operation may go on for hours – might even have to resume in the morning. You can't stay here all night. The paramedic told me you felt the boy might get some sort of closure from seeing the last two boys recovered.'

'He might resent allowing himself to be persuaded otherwise, another emotion to deal with after the guilt and grief. Believe you me; I've seen the after effects too many times,' Kirk continued, 'I take full responsibility.'

The policeman reflected on what he'd said and looked over at Milowski, then back to the former soldier. 'Just keep him out of the way.'

Kirk returned to the boy's side. 'You sure you want to stay?'

He nodded without taking his eyes from the waters, he wanted to see them all recovered.

Kirk lit a cigarette, pulled deeply, holding the smoke for a few seconds, before blowing it out of the corner of his mouth, away from the boy. He cupped it inside his hand, protecting it from the soft rain that had started to fall.

The next body, hauled out a few minutes later, looked as if it came from under the mud, coated all over as it was with a thick, tarry substance. Milowski got onto his feet, peering at the body apprehensively. He couldn't tell who it was.

The frogmen heaved the body onto a tarpaulin, ready to haul it up the bank.

One of them held up a short, slimy and blackened branch. Horror dawned in his expression; he dropped it down in front of him.

Someone screamed, 'Jesus!'

Kirk stared open mouthed in disbelief. Part putrefied, and part skeletonised; it was a forearm dislocated at the elbow, with the hand intact.

The diver fell to his knees, retching and muttering curses in between.

Still unable to pronounce Milowski's surname, he said simply, 'Look away, kid.'

The rain increased, falling with a vengeance, and then the heavens fully opened, forming a veil of obscurity in front of them, dampening the noise of the men calling out with a steady sissing sound.

He realised with horror that this tragic accident had become something else.

The police officer was striding their way, his face grimacing as the water ran off it, dripping from his eyebrows and nose.

Kirk guessed from his expression what he was going to say. 'Come on, kid,' he said, and stood before the policeman reached them. Tapping the unresponsive boy's shoulder, he shouted above the noise of the rain, 'We'd better go!'

Chapter 18

In the school the morning after, rumours circulated about a tragic accident. Everyone had gathered in the main hall. The air was heavy with expectation as the Headmaster approached the centre of the stage, he carried a sheaf of notes in his hand, which he placed on the lectern and, shuffling the papers, the sound rumbled, seeming to echo from the high walls. All eyes were on him as he switched off the sound system and stood immobile, looking down, collecting his thoughts. Then he straightened and looked out over the assembly.

His voice, loud and clear, projected without the aid of a microphone. 'You will by now have heard about the tragic events of yesterday afternoon.' He spoke highly of all the boys. 'Christopher Brookes, the champion swimmer who proudly represented his school at County level. David Jones hated cross-country running when he first joined the school, but he blossomed into a keen long distance runner. And finally, Kenneth Walker, stalwart of the debating society...had the career makings of a barrister or politician.' The Head put aside his notes and continued.

'Let us be quite clear. This is a tragedy, the likes of which have never before been experienced by this school. Three young lives snuffed out, taken from us all,' he snapped his fingers to make the point, 'like that.'

He watched the clock high on the wall opposite him. A few seconds before the red second hand reached the twelve o'clock position, the Headmaster said, 'Let us pause and reflect. We will observe a minute's silence.'

When the hand had completed its three hundred and sixty degree sweep, the Head waited for another moment before speaking again.

'Some of you may hear rumours concerning the unrelated, coincidental discovery of further bodies. This is the subject of an ongoing police investigation, and it is important we keep those events entirely separate in our minds. Apart from location, there's nothing to link them at all.' He turned the page over and placed it at the bottom of the sheaf. 'This tragedy came about because extremely hot temperatures led to a desire to swim in unsafe and unfamiliar waters wholly unsuitable for any sort of bathing. It serves as a warning to us all, of the dangers of swimming outdoors, in ponds, rivers or lakes...

'Finally, let us not forget the surviving boy. We must ensure he has the weight of our support behind him in the forthcoming weeks and months. He is currently undergoing therapy that will assist him in coping and coming to terms with this tragedy. I ask all of you, unequivocally, to help him in every way you can.'

Kirk stood at the back of the hall; head bowed. With assembly over, he followed the Headmaster into his office.

Chapter 19

Ryan's intercom buzzed. 'I have your next appointment, Dr Ryan, it's Bruce Milowski.'

'Thank you, Penny, and, by the way, it's pronounced "Miloffski" and not, "owski".'

'Shall I send them in?'

Penny was still holding the receiver, awaiting his answer, when the psychiatrist came out to greet them.

'Miss Milowski...Bruce. I hadn't expected to see either of you again.' Shaking their hands in turn, he placed a hand in the small of her back as he steered them into his office. Mrs Milowski coloured up red. *It's not Miss.* She concluded that correcting the doctor would only increase the potential for further embarrassment.

Penny seethed. He never came out to greet anyone. What was so special about those two? It wasn't the boy. *The way the bitch just blushed up as if she's in heat; she's trying to get something going on.*

She'd not tolerate it, not right under her nose.

He'd last seen Milowski eight years before while still a medical doctor. The boy had fallen and banged his head on a rock after becoming lost. It had been enough to trigger a mild post-traumatic stress reaction in the seven-year-old, and the boy had had trouble sleeping. After a brief examination, he'd assured Bruce's mother that he would recover with no long-term effects. The boy had been one of his last patients prior to his Irish sojourn. It seemed odd to be treating him again. He'd grown into a young man with a troubled look on his face. Rebellion, defiance and denial, all those things were there, not altogether hidden behind the mask he wore. Ryan disarmed him with a warm smile; he had the confident bearing of a teacher about to take a class, the expression on his face sympathetic and priest-like.

The young man before him could have passed for older than his fifteen years; already there were signs of stubble on his flat cheeks and jawline. The boyhood features had gone, his face more pronounced and square, but the eyes were the same, pale blue and defiant. He now possessed broad shoulders and muscular arms that strained against the fabric of his sleeves. The tightness of his clothes gave him the appearance of a hillbilly kid, whose parents had dressed him in hand-me-downs because they couldn't afford to buy new ones. Miserably self-conscious about such things, she noticed the doctor eyeing what her son was wearing. Their eyes met. Ryan responded with a vague smile.

Quickly, she turned away, embarrassed. 'We can't keep up with him, he's growing so fast. I'm sure he's grown an inch since the accid—'

Bruce shot her a glance, and she stopped herself mid flow. They never talked about the accident. He'd block any attempt, by flying into a rage, and she didn't want that in front of the doctor. She moved a step closer to her son, measuring her own height against his. 'I'm sure it's about an inch in the last two weeks.'

The awkwardness of the moment was not lost on Ryan. 'Mm-m, please sit down.'

She sat; her son remained standing.

'You, too, young man, if you don't mind.'

The boy was reluctant to do as he was asked, exhibiting the sort of oppositional defiance common in adolescents. He was about to repeat his request, when the boy suddenly shuffled his feet and sat. So far, he'd not made eye contact with Ryan at all.

Ryan explained briefly that he practiced certain pioneering aspects of psychiatry, which he felt appropriate for Bruce's particular problems. When he'd finished, he opened a file and took out the consent forms Penny had prepared earlier. 'I'd prefer it if we left any questions we may have until after our initial consultation. Time is a precious commodity, and I often find any queries – well, most of them anyway – are dealt with during the first session with me. Are we okay with that?' His eyebrows rose, corresponding with the question. Neither of them answered.

'Good, this will take around two hours. You can wait for him here, or you might like to take a walk. My secretary can tell you where all the best shops are; there's a High Street not half a mile away.' Ryan pushed the paperwork across the desk in her direction. 'If I can just ask you to check all the details are correct.'

She pulled a pair of tortoiseshell reading glasses from her handbag and put them on.

'Yes…' she sounded unsure. 'Except for the surname, it is spelt wrong, there's only one L in it.'

'I'll get that changed. Can I get you to sign the consent forms?' He passed them to her; she read them carefully, and placed them on the desk.

'You won't be prescribing any drugs for him, will you? I'm dead set against them.'

'For me, that's the last resort. As I said just now, we tend to concentrate on therapy.'

She made small circles above the paper, holding an invisible pen between her thumb and forefinger.

He handed her a pen.

'You'll be able to help him, won't you Dr Ryan?' she said anxiously, pen poised above the page as if it were a condition of her signing.

'We'll do our best.'

Reassured, she signed quickly with a flourish, her large signature stylish, yet utterly illegible.

'Mrs Milowski.' He waited at the door, holding it open for her. 'We'll see you in two hours.' As she passed him, he bowed slightly.

Sitting back down, he traced his cheekbone with the edge of his finger. 'It's hot isn't it?' He poured two glasses of water and held one out to his patient. 'Would you like a drink, Bruce?'

'There's nothing wrong with me,' Bruce said, eyes sullen.

Ryan raised an eyebrow at him, tapping his notepad. 'It says here you've become withdrawn and forgetful.' He traced his finger across the paper. 'And here – that you are now prone to losing your temper,' Ryan leaned back in his chair. 'It also says you've been having trouble sleeping, keep waking up with nightmares…' The boy's head drooped onto his chest. 'Would you like to tell me about that?' he said evenly.

Bruce shook his head.

'Mm-m, so let's talk about the accident,' Ryan's voice lowered, becoming gentler. With his right hand insistently clicking the lead out of his silver pencil, it sounded like a miniature metronome. Milowski squinted at it. The metal was polished, shiny from everyday use. It caught a flare of sunshine, which illuminated its whole length, radiating a beam so bright, everything else paled against it; the desk and then even Ryan, began to fade.

All he could see was the pencil and Ryan's face hovering above it. He found himself drawn ever closer into the miniature elongated reflection of the window.

Something changed in Bruce's perception; he felt he was looking out through the mirrored image, at himself.

In the distance, he heard Ryan's voice; he felt as if he were floating a few inches above where he sat, detached, but still aware. Bruce heard his own voice speaking, disembodied and distant, present at the accident scene once more. Milowski's recollections unfurled, rolled out like a tapestry.

'We let the others go snaking up the hill, the line of them thinned as it stretched out. When we realised we were going to get away with it, we moved further down the hill. Jones was on the other side of a mass of ferns that swayed like the sea. I think he was tempted by the dark shade of the trees beyond. "Look down there! Let's go and see," he shouted. His pale blue eyes brimmed full of excitement. "That little stream we saw earlier, does anyone else remember it? I wouldn't mind betting that it opens out in those woods. That's why it's so green down there. I don't know about anyone else, but I'm so hot I wouldn't mind a swim if I can get one, or even just a paddle. Come on!"' Bruce hesitated, clearly immersed in his recollections.

'You followed him?' Ryan prompted.

The question took a moment to filter through. 'Yes, he charged off downhill. We shrugged at each other, and then raced after him. The others ducked beneath the top strand of the barbed wire fence. There was an old white tin sign with faded red letters swinging from the top wire, bent out of shape by a blast of shotgun pellets. None of us bothered to try and work out what it said. I was always the hesitant one. I parted the strands, and dipped under behind the others, careful not to catch my clothes. The quiet was overwhelming; hardly any light under the thick canopy of the trees. When I first saw it, the water didn't seem real. Chickweed grew all over the top, covering most of the surface in a green and black mosaic. The sky, reflected in the patches of exposed black water, looked like an oil painting.' Bruce tilted his head to one side and dipped it as if looking down, staring intently. He had become inanimate.

'Bruce...Bruce?' Ryan tapped his pencil gently on the desk until the boy had half turned towards the sound. 'What happened next?'

Concentrating harder, Bruce said, 'I had this weird sense of *recognition,* and it slowed me down. I tried to focus on what it was...where it came from. I can't quite put my finger on it...' he hesitated, biting his lip and then he exclaimed, 'I knew I'd been there before! I didn't recognise it, not from where I was then.

'I was back in a place I last saw when I was a seven-year-old boy standing a couple of hundred yards up the hill and I saw me gazing down to where I was standing then...my head's spinning...I can't remember what it was my grandfather had warned me about the place...I sprinted to catch up. Jones was hopping about, frantically removing his trousers and shirt, getting ready to dive in. The other boys shook their heads, plainly thinking that even *he* couldn't be that crazy...and then he charged towards the pond in his underpants. *He's actually going to do it!*

'Just at the very last possible point he could stop – he *did* stop; he was in the process of turning round to face us all with a gleeful smile, arms outstretched as if to say 'I fooled you', but he never finished what he started to say. He looked in disbelief at his foot as the ankle twisted and gave way, tipping him off balance. Panicking, he flailed his arms, wildly grasping at anything, reaching for a handhold, *anywhere...*grabbing at the air. He teetered on the edge, too far gone to come back, and plunged backwards into the water.

'Clouds passed over; shadows formed in the corners of my eyes. *I knew this feeling.* Something was wrong. I should have realised. I was too slow making the connection. Then I remembered what my grandfather said...that it was a bad place. By then, it was too late.'

Ryan observed the boy's eye movements, adding to his notes. *It's as if he is watching a film.* 'What do you see, Bruce?' he prompted gently.

Confusion furrowed Bruce's brow as he continued, 'It was as if I was standing outside myself. I watched my mouth as it shaped the word...*Nooo!* But nothing came out. I *might* have shouted it afterwards, I can't be sure. None of us could quite believe it. I stared down at where he'd lost his footing. Sticking out from the long grass, were the remains of an old boot lying on its side, the leather upper had cracked and blackened with age. The sole, wet and shiny, could have been new.

'In those few moments, the part of me that was observing latched on to every detail, as if my life depended on it. The deep, double splosh Jones made falling in, showed how deep the water was, and the stench that came up was worse than rotten eggs. The others were laughing and shouting. "That will teach you, you crazy son of a bitch!" "You can keep away from *me* when you get out of there, Jones!" Brookes cried, clapping his hands together with glee at the thought of this particular campfire tale. It all seemed to occur in slow motion, Brookes saw it first; the smile disappeared from his face, the same with Watson. Jones' chickweed covered face was a mask of horror; the light in his eyes disappeared—' Milowski snapped his fingers. 'Switched off just like that.

'He stopped moving – just stopped, and then he slid below the black water. Watson jumped in first, and a second later Brookes plunged in, too. The strongest swimmer in the whole school, he turned to me and he never said a word, but the look...the burning eyes...the jerky left-right-left movements of his head...each carried a warning. He seemed to say. *"Whatever you do...don't jump in!"*

'Something was very, very badly wrong down there. I became even more detached than before, and I saw myself struggling with the urge to jump in after them, moving this way and that, two or three paces left, two, three paces right. In my head, I knew I couldn't swim. That day, my fear of water saved my life. The scene was now a deadly play, and I – not knowing what else to do – stood there watching as the fight for life took centre stage. I watched myself, as in desperation, throw my magic seashell to Brookes, and he caught it!

'For a split second, our eyes locked onto each other, united by the power of the shell. I saw myself as I punched the air and exclaimed. *Yes!* One millisecond...and then he slipped under silently, a look of disappointment on his face. He looked as if he wanted to ask me something. The black water swallowed him and three large bubbles of air broke the surface before the carpet of weed covered it over again. Apart from the smell, there was no sign anyone had been in the water at all. I watched myself as I sank to my knees; a shrill, unearthly wail cut through the silence. I wondered who was screaming and then I realised. *It was me.'*

When Mrs Milowski returned just under two hours later, she walked into the reception and sorted through the magazines on the side table, selecting the most recent, a five-year-old National Geographic. She was much more comfortable leafing through it there than she would have been at the doctor's or even the dentist's. She was paranoid about germs and infections; she thought it less likely she'd pick up anything in a psychiatrist's waiting room.

There was an article about the plight of Native American Indians, and the reported high incidence of alcoholism among them. She began reading it, quickly becoming engrossed. Over the page, someone had written in light pencil, 'low self-esteem'. A short electronic buzz snapped her attention back into the room. She saw the red indicator light outside the door change to green. The receptionist was just returning with a small plastic watering can. She started watering all the plants that decorated the waiting area.

'Excuse me.' Mrs Milowski pointed at the green light. 'Does that mean he's finished?'

The receptionist, half-surprised at the interruption of her duties, said, 'He'll be out in a minute.' Her smile was thin. 'You can't beat some nice foliage to brighten a place up can you?' she added as an afterthought.

'No, you can't,' she said, putting the magazine back onto the table. She pointed at the lights outside Ryan's door. 'They're like traffic lights, I suppose.' She observed from the name displayed on the counter top that the receptionist's name was Penny.

'Sorry?' Penny said. 'Oh no, not quite; there's no amber, you see? Just stop or go. I'll let you in on a little secret,' Penny whispered, beckoning her closer. 'He had that put in after I walked in once while he was treating a lady.' She winked theatrically. 'When he's with a patient, he doesn't like to be disturbed, if you know what I mean.'

The casual way Penny breached Ryan's confidentiality bothered Mrs Milowski. The two women eyed each other briefly; Penny was about to speak when the door opened and Ryan brought Bruce out. They shook hands. The firmness of the boy's grip surprised the psychiatrist, crushing his arthritic finger. He winced.

On the way back to the station, Bruce's mother tentatively started a conversation without expecting much in return. She'd grown accustomed to his silences. 'So, how did it go?'

'He's a really nice bloke, Mum. It wasn't what I thought it would be, although he did try to hypnotise me, and I wasn't having any of that.'

Mrs Milowski couldn't hide her surprise. 'He tried to hypnotise you? He never said he was going to do that.'

'It doesn't matter. He tried, but he didn't.'

She gauged her voice so that it sounded normal; a little scared of what his reaction might be. 'What did you talk about?'

He frowned; suddenly he couldn't remember much about the session at all. 'Not a lot, just...Mum can we leave it for now?'

'Not a lot...Bruce, you were in there for over two hours! You must have talked about lots of things.'

'Mum!' he said firmly. 'I've just had hours of soul-baring or whatever; I can't remember. Right now I feel drained.' The crease in his forehead deepened. 'Although I do remember something...he wanted to know why I threw my seashell to Chris.'

Chris Brookes, one of the dead boys – this was a new development. When she'd realised his shell was missing – he'd treasured it since he was a small boy as if his life depended on it – she'd asked him where it was. He'd flown into a rage. Choosing her words carefully now, she asked, '*Why* did you throw it at him? Did you tell the doctor?'

He gawped at her blankly. 'I...can't remember.'

She decided not to press him further.

Once on the train, she checked the consent paperwork she'd signed, and though she couldn't remember specifically seeing it, there it was. *Some treatments may involve the use of hypnotherapy.*

If she'd seen that before, she wouldn't have signed. Hypnotherapy was a form of treatment she frowned on. She didn't agree with messing with people's minds. Sitting back in her seat, she smiled. It was the longest talk she'd had with him since the accident.

Chapter 20

By the time they returned to Doctor Ryan's the following week, Mrs Milowski had realised that despite the initial improvement, the effects of the last visit were just temporary, diminishing progressively with her son returning completely to his post-traumatic sullen self after only four days.

They sat quietly in the waiting room. The green light was on when they'd first arrived. It had just started to irritate her that they'd gone five minutes past their appointment time, when the door opened and the psychiatrist bounded out cheerfully. 'Mrs Milowski, Bruce. How are we today?' He made no apology for his lateness.

'Doctor, please call me Ellen, it's a lot easier.'

This informal suggestion triggered a scowl from Penny and, seeing it, Ellen suddenly realised the receptionist thought she was flirting, and went red with embarrassment. The more she thought about it, the redder she went. 'I'm so sorry,' she said self-consciously. Men often assumed the reason she blushed so hard because she was attracted to them. Most of the time it wasn't true, and certainly not in Ryan's case.

He reassured her with a sympathetic smile. 'You know, Ellen, there are treatments available for that.'

The heat generated by her blushing formed a slight sheen of perspiration that glossed her skin. 'We'll get my son sorted out first, then perhaps...' She fanned air towards her face with magazine in a futile effort to cool it. Bruce glanced at her with irritation. He knew she'd never sort it out, opting out with a comment like, 'I find it too embarrassing', as she always did.

He gestured for the boy to follow him. 'Shall we begin?'

They disappeared through the door, and it closed behind them. A few seconds later, the red indicator bulb illuminated.

Mrs Milowski felt Penny's eyes boring into the back of her head as she walked out of the room.

The doctor walked to the window and opened the Venetian blinds; the light coming through the horizontal slats projected across the room onto the opposite wall, recreating the image, distilled into alternate grey and white bars. When he returned to his seat, Bruce had switched places, sitting in the chair his mother had occupied last week. From there, he could see the books on the shelves better. He narrowed his eyes to focus, but could make out only the larger titles printed down the spines: *Strategies of Representation in Young Children, Children's Drawings, Foetus Into Man.* Below, piles of old *Nature* magazines stacked on top of a range of sliding glass-fronted cabinets that were filled with similar reading.

'Have you really read all those?' he said, indicating the bookshelves.

Ryan revolved around on his chair to look at them and then spun back to face his patient. 'No,' he chuckled. 'But they look pretty impressive don't they?' His glasses had slipped to the end of his nose, and he pushed them back up. Almost immediately, they slid down again.

The silver pencil that shone so brightly last week was resting on top of a pile of loose notes. He tried to get a closer look without being noticed.

'Are you looking at my pencil?' he asked him. 'Would you like to have a closer look?'

Picking it up, Ryan handed it to him. It was far heavier than Bruce expected. It appeared to be very old, the engravings on the barrel worn away to a shiny, polished surface where his fingers rubbed. He saw his face in miniature, as if he were looking into a fairground novelty mirror, all big nose, receding jaw and bulbous top of the head. Faintly amused, he moved it back and forth, and then clicked out the lead, two, three clicks. Ryan watched his patient warily, as if afraid he'd run off with it at any minute.

'It's beautiful,' Bruce said, returning it.

'Yes, it was my grandfather's. It's been in the family for years, and it's been with me almost since the beginning of my career. Made by Sampson Mordan...'

He snapped out of his memories quite suddenly, 'Right, we digress.' Clicking out the lead to the correct length, he tested it against his thumbnail. *Perfect.*

'Last week, you were telling me about the feeling you had, just before your first friend fell into the water.' He scrutinised Bruce over the top of his half-moon glasses. One of his eyes appeared faded, and watery; the other strong and deep blue. He seemed able to see right into Bruce, who shifted uncomfortably.

'Now I understand he was messing about when that happened, he stopped dead on top of an old shoe that caused him to lose his balance and fall.'

'I don't remember telling you that, but yes – it's true.' There was a note of concern in his voice. The psychiatrist continued, ignoring his comment. 'Then one by one, the others launched themselves to the rescue, and they all perished...' He allowed his words to trail.

Bruce nodded without speaking, he appeared to be deep in contemplation, staring at the light and shadows the blinds made on the wall.

'You were a non-swimmer and made no attempt to join them in the water.'

The whiff of sulphur, released in his memory, smelled real enough to make him shudder. He was unable to go back beyond that point. He simply had no conscious recollection of it.

Ryan pressed on to where the obstacle of guilt needed removing, or climbing over. 'The difference between you and them, the reason you are alive and they are not, is not one of cowardice. Neither is it because you failed to prevent the accident from occurring. The explanation is simple; on the day that events conspired to claim your friends, you were *lucky.*'

He studied the carpet, losing himself in its swirling patterns. Ryan coughed once to clear his throat. 'Bruce, look at me. You are not to blame.'

He glanced at Ryan. 'I let them down, there's no getting away from that. I had the ability to prevent what happened, and I did nothing about it. Instead of reaching in with a long branch, what did I do? I threw a fuckin' seashell to Brookes, because I thought it had magic powers,' he said bitterly, staring at the carpet again. 'Yeah, I know it wasn't my fault, but that doesn't make me feel better; I know I was lucky, and you know something? That just makes me feel worse...and I still can't sleep with the shadows that bother me...'

'What shadows?'

'I can't tell you, you'd think I was crazy.'

'Bruce, if you don't help me, I won't be able to help you.' He could tell he wouldn't give it up easily. The boy had slipped into the same defiant mood he was in the week before. Putting a new lead into the pencil, he clicked it out, and then pushed it back in flush. Not satisfied, he clicked it twice more, until he'd got it just right. Then he turned it and a slanted beam of light appeared on his forehead; it caught Bruce's eye.

'Help me to help you. Tell me about the shadows that disturb you at night.'

Later that night, Bruce dreamed he saw his grandfather again. His mind tricked him into believing he was still alive and trying to tell him something, but he couldn't hold on to what he was saying, only the words *Remember Bruce*, before he was snatched off somewhere else without the chance to say goodbye. This disturbed him. And then he was with the boys again reliving the moments before the accident, watching it unwind, seeing it from another point of view. For a second, he had the notion he might have been the buzzard looking down, and then dismissed the thought. *Buzzards don't think, do they?* Taken through time, he saw the killer's face again, for by now he knows he was a killer, and the girl... *It was the same girl, the one in the purple dress.*

Frightened, he blanked them all from his mind, but she still whispers in the quiet moments and follows him, staying in the shadows.

Ryan reviewed his notes on young Milowski. *Making progress, but painfully slow.*

Despite successfully regressing him to the incredibly early age of ten months, a fact he'd had to verify with Bruce's mother, there were still several black holes he couldn't penetrate, areas he could not get the boy back to. He decided to take him to see Vera Flynn; she'd help Ryan understand the inner workings of his mind. All he needed to do at the next session was to get Mrs Milowski's agreement. Then he'd take him on a therapeutic day trip to the seaside. Vera wouldn't object; she loved helping people.

Reception buzzed him. 'There's something wrong with a lady in the waiting room; I don't know what to do.'

'What's up with her?'

'She's talking gibberish, and she doesn't look at all well.'

'I'll be with you in a moment.'

While he was gone, Penny entered his office, carrying his mid-morning cup of tea. He'd carelessly left his private drawer open and Milowski's file was out on the desk.

If it wasn't for that boy! She put the tea down and read the first page, turning it onto the next, keeping one hand close to the saucer. If he came back suddenly, she'd say, 'I just put your tea down for you.' Blood pressure pulsed at her temples, each stolen moment increasing her chances of getting caught. What she read was enough to start her scheming; she glanced over at the open drawer. *She'd never seen it left open before!* The temptation was almost too much. If she was caught going through it, she would have no excuse. She'd find a way another time.

Later that afternoon, when the doctor was with one of his patients, she made a telephone call.

'Mrs Milowski?'

'Speaking.'

'It's Penny, Dr Ryan's secretary.'

'Oh, is everything all right? We are still seeing the doctor tomorrow, aren't we?'

'Well, actually I was just ringing to make sure you're still coming; only I noticed you hadn't signed the consent form for the new stage of treatment the doctor is proposing.'

'I'm sorry, you've lost me there.'

'Well, Mrs Milowski, it appears the hypnotherapy isn't working as well as he'd hoped; he wants to try a new treatment.'

She'd tolerated the hypnotherapy, only because it appeared to be getting results.

'What new treatment?'

'I'm not sure it's my place to say.'

'What new treatment?' she repeated.

'He is to take him to see a clairvoyant.'

'Oh, is he now? We'll see about that.'

Bruce never returned to Dr Ryan's practice. Penny congratulated herself on the way she'd removed her rival for his affections. *One day he'll realise he's in love with me.*

Next, she would deal with the medium.

The following afternoon, Ryan quizzed her about the cancellation; she told him that Mrs Milowski had cancelled citing personal reasons. 'She was adamant – saying she knew what you were planning to do, and if she heard anything further – she'd go to the press with the story.'

'Really?' He viewed her suspiciously. 'It all seems a bit melodramatic to me, and I have to say, confusing.'

'Would you like me to get her on the phone for you?' she said sweetly.

'No, what would be the point?'

She found it hard to suppress her happiness at that moment, and turned away. When she looked back at Ryan, he had her fixed in the sight of his narrowed eye.

'I have a job for you. I want you to prepare all the old files for archiving.'

She couldn't conceal her indignation. 'I'm on the verge of retirement, and you are asking me to do a junior's job?'

'That's right, Penny.'

'After all I've done for you,' she fumed. 'Okay, I'll start with that one!' She snatched at Milowski's file.

The doctor closed his hand firmly over the edge of the binder and moved it out of reach. 'Actually, you won't. I'm keeping this file.'

She seethed with barely restrained anger.

Hell-bent on causing trouble, Penny dosed his tea with laxative, hoping when the urge to go came over him, he wouldn't have time to lock his cabinet. He only ever left the cabinet unlocked when he was in his office, and he never left the key lying around. It was obvious that whatever the cabinet contained, it was important and highly confidential. A few minutes later, Ryan dashed by, heading for the toilet.

She rose quickly from her desk and let herself into his office. The keys were in the cabinet; she couldn't believe her luck. With a window of opportunity at the most a few minutes, she opened the drawer. It had names in it she'd never heard before. Milowski was there, as was Solomons, but the others... All the folders were ribbon-tied and housed within individual sleeves. She lifted Milowski's file out, and tugging at the knot that secured the ribbon, dropped the entire folder on the floor. *Shit!* Gathering everything up, she hurriedly assembled and retied it. Now, she'd be lucky to look at just one before he returned. Her nerves on edge, she found what she was looking for right at the back. *How long had he been gone?*

With her heart pounding in her ears, she withdrew the file and untied it. Starting at the end and working backwards, she found his inconclusive notes, which she read with great speed until her nerve broke. Rapidly retying the ribbon, she placed everything back as it was, returning to her desk. Ryan didn't emerge for another five minutes, when he did, he was wearing a troubled look.

Penny took her diary and made an entry of all the points she remembered. The last was a reference to an unearthly black stone. *She keeps the stone about her wherever she goes. It seems to invigorate her. I suspect it is the source of her power.*

Penny smiled inwardly. Although she didn't believe such things were true, she knew enough to know that if she were able to get that stone away from Vera, she'd be likely to implode. After all, she must be fragile to be in the care of a psychiatrist.

Chapter 21

The funeral was the worst day of his life. A young girl in bright summer clothes approached him. A black hat and veil her only concession to the sobriety of the event.

Bruce couldn't make out her face clearly, but he knew whom it was. His stomach knotted. Exerting every inch of self-control, he tried not to fall apart in front of her. The control didn't extend to his voice. It clunked in his throat like a glottal stop. Instead of trying to talk further, he nodded at her.

'Why didn't you save him?' Brookes' little sister asked him tearfully.

He couldn't even say he'd tried.

'He was your best friend, Bruce. What did you do to try to save him?'

I threw him a seashell. The answer seemed so ridiculous now, but at the time, the sheer belief in its power to effect some miraculous turn-around in events had never been stronger. He saw the look on Brookes' face when he caught it. *He* almost believed in it, too. If only...

He cleared his throat and it hurt, the lump growing more painful as the tears started in his eyes. He looked at her sincerely. 'I couldn't swim, Leanne. I never could. I'm sorry.'

She looked at him contemptuously. 'You didn't even *try* – I hate you!' she said.

Not as much as I hate myself, Leanne.

She turned sharply on her heel and walked away.

Whether it was by design or accident, Bruce never knew for sure, but when the summer holidays were over and he returned to school, Kirk was his new form master. Kirk renamed him Miller because he either would not, or could not pronounce his surname, and in doing so, he threw a lifeline to a struggling boy, who would use the nickname as a rope to clamber out of his despair. A few of the other boys told him he shouldn't put up with it, and each gave a reason why. The most bizarre and likeliest – given the teacher's background – was that he was anti-communist. Bruce defended himself against the implied suggestion. 'Well, I'm no communist and neither is anyone in my family.' If he'd told his father, there would have been hell to pay.

When the first day was over, Kirk asked him to stay behind after school.

'You know something, Miller, when I wasn't so much older than you, I joined the army. I won't bore you with all the details. I'd always wanted to serve my country, so I signed up with the Gloucestershire Regiment. A few months later, the Korean War started.

'In late April 1951, for three days from 22nd through to the 25th, a battalion of us managed to hold off not just dozens of Chinese soldiers, but thousands of them.' He fiddled with a piece of chalk he was holding, looking at it intently as he continued to speak. 'During that time, I never once doubted I'd come through. You know why?'

Miller shook his head.

'I had God on my side, and you know what? I *did* come through.' Scratching the back of his neck, he weighed how much to tell the boy. 'I escaped. Not many did...but I did and I met up with friendly forces a few days later.'

Miller listened with an expression that bordered on interest.

'It was hell. It changed me. It changed all of us. I was no longer the person I once was, but that was all right because he was still somewhere inside me. Still there, but shell-shocked and a little bit left behind.' His voice softened. 'You know, I felt guilty,' he snapped the chalk in his hands. 'That I pulled through unscathed, when so many were captured or killed. I felt *guilty*,' he said, as he searched Milowski's face. 'There was a reason for it. I was lucky, chosen, or whatever it was, I'm still waiting to find out. I might never know, but I'm not going to drive myself crazy dwelling on it.'

Miller contemplated the two pieces of chalk Kirk had laid back on the desk, arranged in the groove. He pushed them back together next to a pencil. Only the faintest crack was visible where they joined.

'Look at me, boy. In a way, what happened to you is the same. You just have to put yourself back together the best you can.' He studied him. 'Do you understand me?'

'I think so, sir.'

'Good – before you go, let me show you this poem by Robert Frost, an American. It helped me through some tough times, when I wasn't able to make sense of it all.'

He handed him the book, open on the page. 'Read it aloud for me.'

The words seemed to come naturally to Miller as he read them.

'Two roads diverged in a yellow wood,
And sorry I could not travel both
And be one traveller, long I stood
And looked down one as far as I could
To where it bent in the undergrowth...'

He'd almost read the whole thing when, just at the last line, Kirk joined in, saying, 'I then took the other one.'

Miller frowned. The line didn't match that in the book.

'*My* road, Miller, the line I chose...my life.' There was a distant look in his eyes. He settled them on the boy in front of him. 'When I joined the army, I made my choice. I *chose* my road, but you, you had no choice. You're stuck on the road you're travelling now. Follow it – make the best of it. You have your cards; play them as well as you can. Not one of us can undo time. There's no going back – is that clear to you?'

The tightness in his throat strangled his voice and he couldn't speak, so he just nodded.

'Once the inquest is over, you are to put it all behind you. You can do that, can't you?' He crossed the classroom to the door and held it open.

Miller stepped past him and, once outside, turned back and said, 'I'll try, sir.'

Watching him go, Kirk whispered under his breath. 'That's the spirit, boy.'

Chapter 22

North Korea – 27 April 1951

Kirk opened his eyes. Out from the darkness of a sleep devoid of dreams, he looked up into a dense canopy of green. *Dawn.* The dew from the covering mist collected on the broad leaves, accumulating until it bent them, running off the edges as they tipped under its weight, peppering the ground around him. For a moment he wasn't sure where he was. A large splat dropped down on him, wetting his face, waking him into reality. His bones ached from the damp and cold.

He struggled to recall. *How long is it since I lost the others – one night or two?* Exhaustion loosened his grip on the passage of time.

Once he made it to safety, he promised himself he'd sleep for a week, but in the meantime he must go on. He raised himself to his feet through sheer force of will. The sound of sporadic gunfire cut through the air, along with enemy shouts and voices he couldn't understand. Maybe they were talking about him. *Do they even know about me?* Maybe they were looking for other escapees.

Out of the babble of voices – quite clearly and unexpectedly – a Chinese rendition of a cut glass English accent said, 'We are going to find you, English.' A bullet smashed through the foliage next to him as if punctuating the statement, followed by the unmistakable single crack of a sniper rifle and raucous laughter. The vaporised sap from the shredded leaves reminded him oddly of fresh-mown grass and Sunday mornings. He shivered and then taking his pistol out; he checked it – four rounds left.

Folding a leaf into a chute, careful to leave it on the stem, he directed a few drops of dewy water into his mouth before moving slowly through the undergrowth.

In those two nights and three days, Kirk lived his whole life with a burning intensity and brightness of being he'd never again experience. Apart from his pistol, he possessed only a machete, a length of piano wire and the clothes on his back. Unsure which way to go, and guided by little more than intuition and the growth of moss on tree trunks, he took the road less travelled by.

He went south away from the river. His heavy heart told him if he kept trying; he would eventually get away.

Kirk opened his eyes, drenched in sweat, and in his own bed.

By day, he was a teacher. At night, sometimes, he was a lost soldier again. Over the years, the frequency of his wandering nightmares had diminished, but he avoided talking about his experiences. He knew if he did, it would trigger a series of unpleasant dreams that could go on for days. In Miller's case, he rationalised it was worth it.

A murder of crows entertained him from the trees. Cawing and calling, squabbling and scrapping, reluctantly roused from their roosting places, circling out and away finally, on black wings opened against the brightening grey light of dawn.

Kirk watched the birds in the morning, and he watched them at dusk when they arrived back at the tree; carrying out the procedures of dawn in reverse, governed by instinct, trapped in the loop of the cycle of life.

Gritting his chipped teeth, he wondered where in the nightmares his dreams would dump him tonight. He thought about Japan.

You just can't get away from some things.

Chapter 23

Mid-September 1975

Two months after the tragedy, the newly renamed Miller attended the inquest in a daze.

The following day, the local newspaper billboards carried the headline: *Drownings at Devils Pond: Coroner Records Accidental Death Verdict.*

Kirk sat with a newspaper arranged in his lap, a cup of coffee in one hand, turning the pages with the other. He was searching for the article with the vested interest of someone who had been involved and wanted to read the reporter's perspective. Steamy tendrils rose on the thermals from the surface blackness of the hot liquid and drew his eye. He stared through the steam absently, reflecting on the proceedings of the day before.

A crowd of news reporters had crammed into the courtroom, easily dwarfing the group of relatives and friends. However, if the journalists expected new developments, they were disappointed.

Kirk recalled how Miller had taken the stand to give evidence. At the start, he'd appeared oddly detached, distracted even, leaving sentences to trail as his thoughts wandered. Several times, the coroner had to prompt him to continue. By the end, he'd broken down. As he made his way unsteadily to his seat, his father rushed to help him.

Next, an expert witness delivered a lengthy report on his findings. 'High levels of exposure to hydrogen sulphide gas would have resulted in a rapid loss of consciousness. Actual deaths from breathing large amounts of this are quite well documented, but most of these have occurred in work settings.' Several people exchanged looks as the expert hit his stride, needlessly going into finite detail. 'In places like sewers, animal processing plants, waste dumps, sludge plants, oil, and gas well drilling sites, as well as tanks, and cesspools—'

The coroner interrupted, 'I think we get the gist.'

Clearing his throat, the expert continued. 'There's evidence the site was used earlier for mining operations. We picked up the highest readings I have ever encountered.'

When he'd finished, the coroner remarked, 'It seems to me that this place known as 'Devils Pond' should be made inaccessible, or better still, filled in entirely.'

The coroner read the post-mortem results, concluding that whilst high levels of hydrogen sulphide gas undoubtedly rendered all three boys unconscious, the actual cause of death was drowning.

In describing the case as a tragedy, the coroner also said it highlighted the dangers of swimming in unknown waters during hot weather.

Back from his thoughts, Kirk continuing reading and found that, with no fresh information to report, the rest of the article concentrated on the number of bodies recovered from the water, regurgitating earlier reports, re-quoting what various sources at the scene had said at the time. He scanned for anything he hadn't read before.

The first boy's body took two hours to recover. *He knew that, he'd been there.* He jumped two-thirds of the article and continued further down the page. *The operation recovered thirty skeletons in all. Twenty-three were thought to be much older than the rest, possibly dating from the mine disaster one hundred and fifty years ago.*

Murder squad detectives are concentrating their efforts on the bodies found wrapped identically in boiler suits and weighted with stones.

Forensic pathology identified five sets of female remains, and those of two men, one of whom was middle aged with a malformation of the upper jaw. Identified as in their late teens or early twenties, apart from the skeleton with the deformity, all had died up to thirty years earlier, assumed to have fallen prey to the same killer.

At the time of the report, the identities of six murder victims remain unknown. The seventh's name is being withheld until relatives are notified and is thought to be a young Chinese woman who has not been seen since 1967.

The investigation continues.

Kirk knew all of that from other articles he'd read, but the footnote at the end of this particular article contained something new.

Last week, local farmer, Robert Scraggs, announced his intention to fill the pond saying, 'I was fed up with the rumours of evil spirits and the Devil, and that. The pond's on my land. It's down to me. I'll fence it off and leave it to grow wild. It'll cost me a lot of money, but it's worth it for the peace of mind.'

When asked about the many rags tied up in the trees, Scraggs replied, 'Those clooties? They've been there as long as anyone can remember. A new one appeared last week, never seen any like it before; bright yellow silk, no one knows who puts them up. It's another of the many mysteries that surround these parts. They say the Devils Crake...'

Already aware of the local superstitions, he skipped the rest, but wondered who had written the article. The reporter's name was Henry Black.

Chapter 24

Amateur boxing coach, Mickey Taylor, first met Thomas Carney when his mother found a cleaning job at the gym and took him there one night after school.

When the boy was twelve, his father was shot by a hit man in a case of mistaken identity and had died three months later. Although devastated by the tragic turn of events, Thomas reacted by lashing out at the world and getting into trouble at school. By the time he was fifteen years old, his mother had sold up and moved south to get away. Already getting himself into fights all the time, the last thing she needed was to have him running with the gangs as he grew older.

Mrs Carney had asked Taylor if he could teach him to box, she knew his dad would have wanted that and she hoped it might keep him out of trouble.

'How old is he?' Taylor said.

'Sixteen.'

'Get him some kit; bring him back when you have and we'll see what we can do.'

Taylor admired her courage. It took balls, not only for an attractive woman to walk into a place like that, but to keep coming back. It was only natural to expect the men and boys to eye her lustily and speak in undertones about what they'd like to do to her, given the chance, but one of the men, speaking louder than usual, made a comment within earshot.

'I heard that! her high Manchurian accent cut through the gym and, marching straight up to him, face blazing with anger, she said, 'I'm not having that, you keep your filthy thoughts to yourself. You apologise and right now!'

The offender's name was Gerard, and he made the mistake of trying to laugh it off. A group of his cronies joined in. Thomas stepped in quietly, saying, 'She said apologise.' There was a firmness and quiet certainty in his voice. Terry, the club's assistant coach, intervened. Taylor stopped him. He wanted to see what panned out. Gerard looked at Thomas and laughed. 'And if I don't?'

The whole gym had ceased activity; all eyes were on the growing confrontation. The boy was outwardly calm, but insistent. When he spoke, his voice seemed loud against the silence. 'Apologise,' he demanded. The word hung in the air. Gerard moved within striking distance; Thomas balled his fists. Taylor planted himself between them. 'Sort it in the ring, guys.'

Terry prepared the gloves and, once they were ready, they entered the ring, where Taylor waited to referee. Nobody expected it to last more than a few seconds; after all, it was a contest between a fully-grown man, and a sixteen-year-old boy.

'Sort it out like men,' Taylor told them as he stood between the opponents, 'now shake hands.' Carney refused.

'Box,' Taylor said, stepping out of the way.

Thomas came forward, unafraid. His opponent poked his tongue out, mocking him. The boy stung him with a jab to the mouth, bloodying his lips.

Gerard wiped blood from his mouth onto the back of his forearm and staring at it in disbelief, his face became a mask of rage.

Is this where the expression seeing red comes from? Taylor thought.

The man exploded, striking out in anger, catching the boy high on the shoulder, hard enough to spin him half way round. Another shot deflected by his glove; a further one glanced off the top of Thomas's head, catching him as he bobbed under it. Thomas cut loose with a rapid, left, right, left combination. It lacked the power to trouble his opponent.

Gerard began to relish the prospect of teaching the kid a lesson. He threw a few more energy sapping punches, but couldn't nail him with a clean shot. Then he did something dirty. In the instant that Taylor looked at the clock on the wall, he butted the boy full on the nose. Thomas dropped to one knee, holding his face.

Terry yelled, 'Mickey – he's just fuckin' nutted him!'

It took two men to restrain Mrs Carney from getting into the ring. Gerard knew he'd gone too far, and he held his arms out away from his sides, exposing the palms of his gloves as he muttered a half-apology.

A few of the men watching started turning hostile, muttering threats. One mounted the apron and tried to get into the ring to get at Gerard.

Terry pulled him back, calming him. 'Leave it, Roy, we'll not be having a free-for-all. See that look on Mickey's face? He's not going to let that lie.'

Gerard's cronies, sensing perhaps that they could become targets for the other men's anger, began backing away towards the exit.

With the situation on the verge of getting out of hand, Thomas made it to his feet and advanced unsteadily in Gerard's direction. Taylor stood blocking him. 'You've had enough, son.'

Carney wobbled; his eyes rolled, one arm hung by his side. Slowly, his legs buckled, and he dipped into a collapsing pirouette. As Taylor reached to catch him, he sprang back to life. Ducking under Taylor's arm, he kicked his assailant in the balls and as Gerard doubled forward, the kid brought his head down sharply with both hands, to meet the force of his upcoming knee. Gerard, stunned for a second, stood bolt upright on his feet. Carney administered the coup de grâce: a footballer's head butt delivered – because he was so much shorter – from below, straight into his teeth, felling him. His mother led the cheers from the group of men around the ring.

At the hospital afterwards, when Thomas received stitches to the jagged wound in his forehead, a broken tooth fell from his torn flesh onto the floor. The two-inch scar didn't bother him. He wore it with pride.

Miller's school days passed by in a blur and he left without a clear idea of what to do with his life. He followed Kirk's advice almost to the letter, and it helped lead him out of the trough of guilt and self-loathing he'd slipped into. Still shy, but more outgoing than his other persona, he set about toughening himself up, taking long, cross-country runs. The solitude and peace were good for him. Out there in the wilds, he tuned in to nature. He learned to anticipate the birds that flew up, disturbed by his approach. He taught himself to listen, as well as to see. Slewing along undercover unseen, a grass snake announced itself with a pungent discharge, reminding him of the importance of smells.

As he ran, he shadowboxed, snatching at flies in the air. *The day I catch one, I'm joining the boxing club.*

A couple of days later, he found himself opening the street door into the gym one of his friends had recommended. Oddly enough, the smell hit him first; the stale odour of toil, sweat and boot leather, which he'd later discover was partly the tang of well-used gloves. *No wonder they call it a stable of boxers*, he thought.

Halfway up the stairs, someone opened the upper door and the sounds of the gym came alive. He could hear trainers coaxing more effort out of their fighters and the sound of skipping ropes, swishing through the air faster than the eye could see and the squeak of boots scuffing against wooden floors, grunts of effort, the pounding of heavy bags and the staccato drumming of a half dozen speedballs. The atmosphere buzzed with vitality.

Once inside, he approached the nearest instructor, a pug-faced man with a flattened nose-bone. 'Is Mickey here?' he asked.

Turning his head towards him, the man looked him over and then pointed to the ring in the far corner. 'That's him, over there.' Waving an arm in the air to attract the other man's attention, he called out, 'Hey, Mickey, newbie to see you!'

Mickey glanced up and beckoned him over. With his hands on his hips and a grubby white towel draped around his neck, he looked like a cornerman from another era.

'What's your name, son?'

'It's Miller.'

'What's your first name?' he said, looking at him intently.

'It's just Miller,' he said, his face deadpan.

A glint of amusement flashed in the trainer's flinty eyes, and he wiped his hand on the leg of his grey tracksuit and offering it, introduced himself. 'Mickey Taylor.'

They shook hands.

'We're going to need your first name for the application,' he said, taking a form from the clipboard on the chair next to him. 'Fill that in, then we'll get started.'

There was a time when he only allowed proper fighters to train in his gym, but he'd relaxed the rules in recent years because he couldn't afford to turn money away. Among the usual array were various non-combatants: nightclub doormen, friends of fighters, wayward kids and the occasional policeman.

The boy in the ring was a middleweight prospect. Even though he was only sixteen years old, Taylor was sure he could take an ABA title and turn pro in a few years. There were always two, or three, sparring partners lined up ready for him.

Miller watched from ringside with interest until Taylor said, 'Don't stand there gawping, go and see Terry and he'll get you started.'

The warm up routine was a basic lesson in stance, and a demonstration of bag work, followed by skipping. Twenty minutes later, he'd built up a sweat and Terry started him on the pads. Miller bobbed around in front of him, picking off the moving targets with ease. Terry moved faster, becoming more and more nimble on his feet, boots squeaking as he shuffled and turned, switching direction, making the pads harder to hit. Miller stuck to him closer than a shadow, catching the padded targets at will, with either hand.

Taylor, delivering coaching points to his boy in the ring, found his attention drawn by the blur of movement and the thwack of leather against leather, as the newcomer's gloves repeatedly struck home. 'Terry, send him over,' he called out.

'You said on the form you hadn't boxed before, son,' Taylor said.

'I haven't,' he said.

Taylor gave him a sceptical look. 'Are you sure? What do you reckon, Terry?'

'If he hasn't, then I'm a Chinaman.'

Taylor scratched the back of his head. He couldn't think why the boy would deny it, but then he didn't seem to want them to know his Christian name either. Taylor was puzzled. *Let's see how you handle yourself in the ring, eh?*

'Are you up for sparring, boy?'

'I'm ready,' Miller said.

'Let's get you gloved-up. Do you have a gum shield with you?'

'No, we're only sparring. I won't need it.'

Terry raised his eyebrows.

Taylor leaned forward and whispered to his protégé, 'Don't take it easy on him.'

Thomas, who stood watching with each of his gloved hands resting on the top rope, stuck out his gum shield, a bored expression on his face.

As Miller slipped through the ropes onto the canvas, Taylor said, 'No shame in it, boy. Just nod to me if he hurts you and I'll stop it, all right?' Moving back, he clapped his hands and said, 'Box.'

Carney came straight at him, arms pumping out a variety of punches. Working behind a ramrod, stiff left jab, he hooked, crossed and attacked.

Switched off from all conscious thought as his grandfather had taught him, Miller bobbed and slipped everything Carney threw at him. Only movement mattered; he closely defended and countered. Pure instinct took over. The countdown buzzer kicked in; Carney finished strong, it was all he could do to stay out of trouble; he flicked his eyes up at the clock – two seconds to go. Carney connected with a body shot which staggered him. Although he made it to the corner, the punch caused a delayed reaction. A full half minute later, he stumbled as it folded him at the waist.

Taylor called out, 'Next!' With a note of self-satisfaction in his voice, he said, 'He's been perfecting that shot for weeks, killer isn't it?' Miller nodded with a pained smile.

He only had himself to blame for allowing his concentration to waver.

In the showers afterwards, Carney approached with Taylor, who asked Miller for his real name.

A puzzled look crossed his face. 'It's exactly as I wrote on the form.'

'Why did you tell me you'd never boxed before? Thomas could barely lay a glove on you. You're not a ringer are you, son?' Taylor was priest-like, inviting confession.

'I used to spar with my grandfather when I was a kid about ten years ago. That doesn't count as boxing, does it?'

Taylor rubbed his eye. 'He must have been some kind of trainer, your granddad. Why won't you say what your first name is, son?' He held the application form out in front of him. Pointing to the entry by the first name, he said, 'You don't expect me to believe your name is just Miller, do you?'

'I told you when I first walked in that my name's Miller. I don't want to be called Mickey, or Tommy, or anything else. I just want to be called Miller, end of story.'

Chapter 25

Two and a half years later, a few days after his nineteenth birthday, Miller was walking home in a vicious rainstorm in the early hours. In the future, he'd remember this night many times. The memory, when it started, was monochrome.

The drab greyness of the rain and its incessant hiss deflated him, and he pinched his face against it, eyes reduced to slits and though the insides of his pockets were damp, he dug his hands further in, looking to warm them.

A car drew up alongside. The passenger door swung open. Leaning across with his face peering up at him was his old form master, Kirk. 'Get in, I'll drop you off.'

He was so close to home that a lift now made no difference to him; already soaked from walking in it for so long, he simply didn't feel the rain anymore. 'I'm all wet, sir.'

'Get in,' Kirk insisted. 'We have quite a bit of catching up to do.'

The drive took only a matter of minutes and when they arrived outside his house, their polite exchanges extended into deeper conversation. Kirk asked him about his life and how he was getting on, adding, with a grin. 'Are you still making your way through enemy lines?'

He listened as Miller explained how he suffered from feelings of unworthiness, how they'd undermined him and sapped his will to do anything, so in the end he'd dropped out of his psychology course halfway through.

'Have you seen anyone about these feelings?'

'No, not now, originally I did, but stopped before I came into your class at school. I thought you knew all about my background?'

'I probably did at the time. I'm only human, though, sometimes I forget things other teachers wouldn't,' Kirk said, turning off the wipers. 'So how close were you to completing your course?'

'This would have been the last year,' he said.

Kirk shook his head in dismay. 'You need a purpose in life, something you can do to snap you out of it. Psychology is a fascinating subject. You were sufficiently interested to start, weren't you?'

Miller nodded. 'Do you know much about it, sir?' Although he was tired and wanted his warm bed, he sensed the older man needed to talk.

'So what happened?' Kirk asked, turning the engine off. 'What went wrong for you to lose interest now?'

Miller took a deep breath, and held it a full ten seconds, saying as he exhaled, 'Everything.'

Kirk listened intently as his former pupil started and then faltered; as he tried explaining how he'd lost the only girl he'd ever loved. 'Her name was Josie and she put the colour back into my life...' He fell silent.

'Tell me about her,' he said, and rested a hand on Miller's shoulder.

'I can't,' he looked down at Kirk's hand. 'Your hand is cold.'

'That's right, and your clothes are saturated. In Tibet, the novice monks go outside, ordered by their master, onto the mountain slopes in the freezing cold, wrapped only in wet sheets. They have two choices. Freeze, or learn to generate Tumo, an intense body heat. Those that do, succeed in drying several of them throughout the night. Quite an achievement, wouldn't you say?'

'How do they do it?' he said, thinking about it.

'Our minds are gifted with powers we don't understand. All we need to know is how to tap into them, and that's not something I can tell you. How did you meet your girlfriend, by the way?'

Strangely, he no longer felt cold. 'I came across her one night, surrounded by a mob; two girls kicked, punched and pulled her down to her knees just because she was pretty, I guess. She'd fought back, but it was futile, her face had contorted with the pain of each new blow or wrench of her hair. I watched for only a split second before I intervened. I knew I ran the risk of coming under attack myself. I grabbed her hand and pulled her away. A dozen hard-faced youths encircled us; I kept my left arm around her and marched to the edge of the circle as if I couldn't give a shit. The pack closed in on us...' he said, his words trailing off.

'And then what?' Kirk asked.

'Someone yelled, "Leave him!" It had come from behind the mob; they dropped their aggressive stances and parted to let us through. I looked closely at them, trying to match the voice to one of the faces, and then I saw Thomas from the boxing club. I nodded in recognition and as I walked past with my arm around the girl, Thomas grunted, "All right." That was how I met her. We were very happy, right up until the beginning of last month.'

'Okay-y-y, so what happened last month?'

Kirk felt the muscles tense beneath his hand, but he kept his grip firm and reassuring on the young man's shoulder. For a second, he thought Miller would clam up again. 'Take your time,' he said.

'She died. She was out with a hen party on their way back from France and fell overboard on the night ferry; although they looked, they never found her body.' He slumped forwards. 'That's it for me now. Everyone I ever get close to, dies. I couldn't stand the pain, or the thought of going through it again.' Miller said, darkly.

Kirk lifted his hand from him, perhaps afraid at that moment Miller's jinx might get him, too. 'It will take time, boy, believe me. You'll learn to love again, but first you must rid yourself of that defeatist mentality.'

He sat up straight, angrily demanding, 'And how do I do *that* then, Mister Kirk?'

'It's just, Kirk, as you well know,' his former teacher reminded him. 'How do they dry the sheets on a cold mountain, Miller? Well, I did say I couldn't tell you, but I'd suggest it is sheer force of will,' he looked at him, knowingly. 'You will find a way.'

He opened the window a crack, the sound of the rain came in. Lighting a cigarette, Kirk peered closely at it as if it held a deep secret. 'I don't think I'd have smoked if it wasn't for the war. And if it wasn't for cigarettes, I don't think I'd have made it through.' He drew hard on the filter; the tip glowed and bathed his blunt face with an orange glow. 'I'm sure I mentioned some of this before.'

When he spoke of the war, it was *his* war, the Korean War, but knowing time was short, he condensed the part he'd played into a mere summary. '...and when it was over, I met up with a couple of dozen men from my unit, most of whom had been held prisoner by the Chinese. They told me about the mistreatment they were subjected to – degradation, abuse, and brainwashing. Some had changed beyond the point that you might have expected the experience alone to change them. Today is the 25th April, and the thirty-second anniversary of my escape through enemy lines.' For a moment, he drifted. 'You know, boy, I escaped, but I never got away. I'm *still* getting away. Most of the others that made it, made it out within hours. I got left behind and it took me two, even three days... Anyhow, look it up, do your own research, we don't have time to get into it now.'

'I will,' Miller promised. 'And what about you, sir, are you still teaching?'

Kirk looked across the seat at him, the cigarette end glowing as he drew on it. He sucked the smoke deep into his lungs and blew it at the gap in the window, where it siphoned into the outside air. 'No, I felt it was time for a change, aim at new targets.'

'So what is it you do now?'

'I'm still in education, a freelance trouble shooter. I weed out kids with problems. It's a challenge, but I enjoy the freedom it gives me.' Changing the subject back to Miller, he said, 'So you wanted to be a psychiatrist?'

'Yes, I did. To be truthful, I don't find it that appealing anymore, not in isolation and coupled with something else, maybe. I'd love to be a private investigator. It's been an ambition of mine, ever since I first persuaded my mum and dad to allow me to read True Crime magazine. '

'Really?' said Kirk. 'That's interesting.'

Miller watched the rain rolling down the windscreen. After a lengthy pause, he said, 'Do you remember the scene of that accident?'

'Of course I do. What's on your mind?'

'Well, nothing particularly, it's just that I've since found out you originally came from that neck of the woods, and I wondered if you ever heard—'

'Any rumours about the place? Of course I did, all us kids from around there heard them. I knew the place as Devils Pond, or Witches Pond as they called it sometimes. Apparently, there was an accident in the mines nearby, in the 1850's, and they lost a number of miners in a flash flood or something. They didn't recover all the bodies, about twenty or so were washed away underground.' The older man was quiet for a moment as he allowed his memories to come back to him. 'As far as I know, that's where the extra bodies came from that they found in the pond while looking for your friends.'

'Yes, I heard that. I'm not sure they ever conclusively proved who they were. What about the other four bodies, did you hear any more about them?'

'Not really, the press had a field day, though, I do remember that. The bodies had been wrapped in boiler suits and weighted down with stones, hadn't they?

What was it they called them…' He snapped his fingers as he tried to recall. 'The Boiler Man Killings.'

'I wonder who it was. I don't think they ever found him.'

'The police are useless,' Kirk said absently as he yawned. 'Might be a good first case for you to investigate.'

Miller caught the yawn from him. 'Maybe one day, but for now I still have too many bad memories.'

'Try to discover to whom the unidentified remains belonged; they never did find out who they all were.'

'I think I'd like to look for *living* missing people, though, not dead ones. I don't think I could do that. I don't feel anything if someone is dead. That's why I never looked for Josie when she went missing. I *knew* she wasn't with us anymore.' He sighed. 'If I'm going to look for missing people, they'll have to be still alive.'

'Well, I wish you luck with whatever you choose to do. Two roads diverged in a wood, and I...I took the one less travelled by, do you remember that poem?'

'I do,' he said solemnly. An irresistible tiredness washed over him and he yawned again.

Kirk reached over and took Miller's hand quite unexpectedly and, shaking it, said, 'Good night, Milowski, I hope you get on okay. Keep out of trouble,' he pronounced the name perfectly.

'You can say my name?' he said in amazement. 'I always thought you suffered from word blindness when it came to saying my name.'

'That's right,' he said, with a glint of humour in his eyes. 'I always *could* say it.'

Sometimes, you see a painter on the beach, or in the fields, dabbing his brush at the canvas then standing back, coming forward again, executing the finishing touches, before finally standing back once more with a smile, satisfied at last with his work.

Kirk was a teacher, but as Miller left the car and glanced back in at him, he had a satisfied smile and look of a painter about his face.

'Goodnight, sir.'

Miller ran up to his front door through the sheets of rain and when he turned back to wave, the car was almost invisible. Kirk had let the brakes off and the car began rolling forwards, down the hill silently. It disappeared into the mists, sputtering to life as he jump-started the engine. The red taillights illuminated briefly, and then they vanished, too.

Miller wondered as he closed the door, shutting out the driving rain: *Does it rain on Armageddon?*

Chapter 26

The following night, in his dreams, Kirk instructed him in unarmed combat, Korean style. 'Taekkyon,' he explained. 'Is actually a forerunner of Tae kwon do, I learned it during my national service in Malaysia.' Moving like a shadow, he said, 'Copy me.' And Miller did.

Unable to wake fully, he surfaced briefly, blinked his eyes and then drifted back into the depths, into Kirk's jungle. Behind him, the relentless sounds of pursuit as faceless enemies crashed through the undergrowth, preceded by their urgent voices, bugle calls and the barking of dogs. They were on his trail. There was no going in any other direction than forwards. He ran.

The pale light of dawn breaking through the trees marked the edge of the forest.

Tired of running, weak-kneed, every breathed ragged and hot, driven by an indomitable spirit, Miller pushed on across the exposed open ground. Low vegetation snagged at his heels, almost tripping him as he made his way up the slope, where the line of darkness at the top met the brightening sky. *The light at the edge of the world.*

Moments later, a mass of shadowy figures swarmed out of the tree line, their shouts took on a new urgency. They had seen him. The dogs, unleashed, raced forwards, closing the gap on him. Shots rang out. A bullet snatched at his shorts as it tore through. Another ricocheted off the rocks next to him; he stumbled over the crest and teetered on the edge of a sheer rock cliff, hundreds of feet above the water, the sea. If he didn't jump, he knew he'd die and if he did, it was unlikely he'd survive the fall. And if that didn't kill him, he'd drown in the sea. Already leaping as these things crossed his mind, he dropped through the air that tugged at his clothes, making him cold. The dark waters below approaching faster still, he saw the white foam tips of the waves crashing, heard their hollow roar. Praying he wouldn't hit the rocks; he braced himself for impact.

His bed seemed to bounce in the instant before he awoke.

Miller didn't stir for a few moments, replaying what he remembered of the dream. The beginning was lost in a haze, but he had an overwhelming feeling he'd gained another chance, a new path to follow. Throwing back the bedclothes, he got out of bed.

In the library half an hour later, Miller sat down with a book and read about the Korean War, the role of the Gloucesters and how rumours had spread among the men during captivity that the Chinese had singled out their Colonel for special treatment: brainwashing.

Returning the book to the shelves, he sought out books on brainwashing and mind control. Finding them, he flicked through the pages at speed. *Thought to be among techniques used by religious cults...* He stopped dead and leafed back through perhaps twenty pages before he found the words again and then studied the relevant text with a deep frown of concentration on his brow. *Cults?*

When he'd finished in the library, he made his way to a cafe; he'd not yet eaten that morning. Taking a newspaper from the courtesy read rack, he experienced a strange lingering sense, a calling almost, a definite sense of something, like rain in the air before a storm. He couldn't quite finger it, but he knew it was coming. A half-enlightened moment followed, and as he unfolded the paper he realised he'd known what he would see all along.

Heiress Disappears in Mysterious Circumstances.

The article was a lengthy one and he read it twice. Unable to explain the feeling, he knew somehow that she was still alive.

On his way home, Miller purchased every single daily newspaper he could find and spread them out all over his lounge floor. His thoughts nagged at him. He was no longer reading about the heiress; he was looking for something else, but what?

Rolling over on the carpet and propping himself up with his elbows on top of the Times, his fingers absently turned the pages and then, frowning, he stopped. Two-thirds of the way down the page was a short piece on the emergence of a particular cult operating in every major city in Europe, but particularly the popular tourist spots.

The following day, he had a hunch and he travelled to Piccadilly Circus, hoping to witness the cult recruiting first hand. In the shadow of the winged statue of Eros, he found them.

The rain before the storm still threatened, the feeling it was coming persisted. Thinking about the two roads Kirk had spoken of, he knew this was the right one.

The heiress's name was Olga Kale and he began to investigate the case in an unofficial capacity. Earlier reports suggested Olga had left London to visit Amsterdam, passing through Belgium, France, Spain and Italy. She had then inexplicably returned to Holland's capital. He was thinking. *She'd have gone east. Why would she go back to Amsterdam?*

That night he decamped into his bedroom and followed the half-remembered advice his grandfather had given him about solving problems overnight, whilst asleep. *Take the problem to bed with you, think about it, write it down, take books, photographs everything to help you focus, and then sleep.*

Miller slept in his bed using the newspapers as sheets. Every time he moved, they rustled dryly. Imagining pages turning over, images sharpened in his mind.

When he woke up in the morning, he'd worked it out. She'd been in Rome, where a convention attended by two thousand people had taken place. She had to have met someone who'd convinced her to go back with them to Holland, where the cult's headquarters were. It couldn't be a coincidence.

Miller drew out the last of the inheritance his grandfather had left him and flew to Amsterdam the following day.

Chapter 27

Three weeks later, Miller found himself sitting opposite a man he'd met for the first time only a few minutes earlier. The office was clearly that of a very wealthy man.

'I thought it was important to meet you,' Donovan Kale said, 'and to hear your account of things, first hand.' He ran his hand through his thick dark hair, revealing a few strands of grey. Thin faced with a single deep vertical crease on each cheek, his deep brown eyes narrowed as he focused them on the young man before him.

Miller was still jittery, the nervous energy draining rapidly from him as exhaustion took over.

The older man steepled his hands. 'Go on, in your own time.'

Never particularly good at explaining things, he took a deep breath and just started talking. 'It wasn't long after Josie disappeared, and I didn't care about what happened to me anymore, but then I met an old teacher of mine.' He caught the look of confusion on the other man's face and paused. 'Am I making sense? I don't make sense at the best of times. I'm tired.'

Kale nodded, and said, 'Go on, it's okay.'

Suddenly keen to get the whole thing off his chest, he continued, 'And the other thing was I think I wanted her out of there; because I knew what it was like to have someone go missing. It became an obsession to find Olga, I don't know if you can understand that. I just had to do it.' He looked for a reaction from Kale, who rolled his hand over, gesturing for him to continue.

'I got myself recruited. I couldn't believe how many people they'd squeezed onto that bus. For a moment as we were driving, I thought, what if they have more than one commune that they can take them to? I needn't have worried.

'They'd taken over a former school and its entire grounds. The place was enormous, and once inside there must have been six hundred lost souls in various states of delusion. They made us all feel extraordinarily welcome, bombarded us with love and affection, lots of touchy-feely contact. If it wasn't for the fact that I could switch off – dissociate myself – they'd have had me. They nearly did anyway.

'They kept the new ones separated at first, singled out for special treatment. It was three days before I saw her; she had this beatific smile on her face, and she was *gone* – brainwashed already, but I saw where they kept her at night. The place had four separate accommodation wings, which they locked down at lights out. They allowed a limited amount of association, supervised by trusties, or *premies*; I think that's what they called themselves.

'To get over to her wing, I had to cross a central hub, which was the main surveillance area. Security patrolled outside, so going that way was out of the question. The chances of getting to her undetected were virtually zero. I was lying in my bunk when it came to me. I'd cross over using the underground heating ducts. When we'd first arrived, I noticed that the distance between the ventilation bricks and the underside of the windowsills probably meant there was an under floor void at least four feet high. I waited until everyone else was asleep and then lifted a panel in the corridor floor.

'Once below, I carefully replaced it and started towards the centre, holding the pipes as navigation. I've never been in such a dark place in all my life. It took me forever to reach it. I could hear the guards pacing the floor above. I lost count of the number of times I banged my head where lines of different pipes crossed over.

'My back hurt from bending forwards at the waist, the actual depth of the walkway must have been about four and a half feet, decreasing as I neared the central hub, so I had to half crawl. To my advantage, the pipes were noisy. Security wasn't expecting anyone to do what I was doing, so any noise I made went unnoticed. When I finally got to the middle, the darkness and confined space had left me so disorientated, I lost all sense of direction.

'I handed myself over to blind chance, and miraculously ended up over on her wing. The access points into, and out of the ducts, were around every fifty yards or so and detectable by the short cat-ladders that stuck out beyond the pipelines. I listened for a long time to make sure it was safe to come out. Although the lights were out, after having been in total darkness, I could see easily. I was just figuring out how to find her, when she came out half-asleep to visit the toilet. I couldn't believe my luck; I knew then I had God on my side.'

When he'd finished telling his story, the man opposite who had listened without interruption, finally spoke again.

'You acted with no authority, completely off your own back, putting yourself at considerable risk – on the strength of what you read in the newspapers.'

Miller felt the spotlight heat of the man's eyes as they searched him.

'I assume you thought you'd be well rewarded if you had pulled it off?'

He shook his head. 'I never gave it a thought.'

Kale said nothing, but the expression on his face and the tilt of his head made it clear he expected an explanation.

'I did it because I wanted to feel worthy again. When Josie disappeared I knew how that felt. When I saw the papers, I just had to do something. You see, I had some bad luck when I was a kid.'

'What sort of bad luck?'

Miller told him. He listened intently.

'Listen, boy, call me Donovan, by the way. I'd like to give you a reward.'

'I didn't do it for the money,' he said.

'Well at least let me cover your time and expenses. It's the least I can do. How much do you want?'

Too tired to argue, he hesitated and then said, 'Two hundred and fifty pounds, that's all, just for fares and that.'

Donovan took out his chequebook. 'Who do I make this out to?'

'My bank account is in the name of Bruce Milowski.' Seeing the confusion on Kale's face, he added. 'It's my real name, but that's another story.' He started to explain and then thought better of it.

The older man smiled for the first time. Something about this kid appealed to him, apart from the fact he'd just rescued his daughter. He scribbled the cheque out and put it in an envelope, sealing it closed. Then handing it over, he said, 'If there's anything I can do for you son, you know where I am.'

They shook hands and Kale summoned his driver to drop him home.

The following morning at the bank, he completed the paying-in slip and passed it under the glass screen to the teller. She looked up at him, a mix of joyful confusion on her face. 'I think you might have made a mistake,' she held the cheque up to the glass for him to see. 'Because this slip should have another three zeros on it.' Miller was stunned into silence

The cheque was for a quarter of a million pounds, enough to set him up for a long time. He never forgot his good fortune and, afterwards, he divided his time equally between those who could afford to pay and for those that couldn't, he worked without pay. The rich subsidised the poor, a private investigator version of Robin Hood for modern times.

Kale used his wealth to have the cult shut down, by fair means or foul, routing its leaders. They simply disappeared, presumably afraid to face legal proceedings. And he was responsible for repatriating and reuniting nearly one hundred young people with their families. When his accountants untangled the web of financial dealings, the huge amount of revenue generated by the organisation astounded him, and naturally he took steps to relieve them of that wealth.

Without money, they would find it difficult to start again.

Chapter 28

June 1980

The mute scrawled a question onto the paper pad and passed it to the man standing opposite him. Without turning away from the window, Carlos took the pad and looked at it.

'What will we do?' The note read.

Carlos raised his amber eyes and gazed across the Istanbul skyline, the sunlight turning them the colour of molten gold.

'We take over what's left and start again.' He turned to look at his friend. 'Hasan, we will rise from the ashes, bigger than before.'

Hasan scribbled quickly and pushed the new note at Carlos.

'What about Kale? Do you want me to kill him?'

Carlos smiled. *Hasan is so loyal.*

'No, my friend, he took nothing from us. Instead, he has provided us with an opportunity.'

Hasan's broad face looked fierce; lips pressed tight together; an eyebrow rose in unspoken query.

'We will destroy the opposition. There is no better time to do it. The religious world is in disarray.' Carlos took a small box from his hip pocket and opened it. 'We are about to build a new church, Hasan. I have seen it.' Tilting his face upwards, he put a coloured contact into each eye, turning them dark brown. 'I will call our movement, The Church of The Resurrectionists of Monte Cristo. This will be the new church and nothing will stand in our way. First we will rid the world of the major cults, and then the old church will fall to us.'

Hasan nodded appreciatively. There was no doubting the ability of Carlos to do so.

Chapter 29

23 July 1983

The Hammersmith pubs had steadily filled with people since six o' clock. With Dire Straits playing the Odeon that night, drinkers in this particular watering hole wasted no time loading up on drink. It was a huge pub with a rough reputation; real spit and sawdust, hot and sweaty, a feeling of edginess and danger permeated the air. On concert nights, the extra crowds created a heady atmospheric cocktail of excitement, which attracted all kinds of men and women, from office staff to hippies, hospital workers to labourers. Most of them would go on to the show.

In this pub, lone outsiders could find themselves vulnerable and unwelcome. Those in groups were relatively safe, but it wasn't uncommon for people to have one drink and then leave.

Two Americans were talking loudly at the bar, their voices raised above the din of the crowd. 'Have you ever felt in real danger?'

'Sure I have, and you know something? I'm not feeling real comfortable right now,' he said, anxiously eyeing the mean-looking giant of a man who'd appeared at his friend's shoulder, belligerently looking him up and down, measuring him.

The big man poked him in the back.

Carefully putting his beer down, he caught the cautionary expression in his friend's eyes, the unease registering with him, he turned around slowly and then froze. Staggered by the man's size, his knees, perhaps eager to run, bucked involuntarily, and he stumbled, fighting to control limbs that had turned jelly-like.

'Is it because I'm Irish you think you're in danger? You think I'm wit the fuckin' IRA or something, eh – is that it?'

The American garbled his words. 'I – I wasn't talking about you.'

'So, I fuckin' *imagined* it all, did I?' The Irishman didn't care there were two of them. He was spoiling for a fight.

A moment of dread silence hung between the Americans.

A voice called out, 'Jack? Jack Doherty?'

The big man turned round. 'Mickey fuckin' Flynn!' he said and the two of them shook hands vigorously.

'Can't you see I'm busy, Mickey?'

Flynn took in the scene instantly. 'Uh-huh, leave the poor fellas be. C'mon let's be getting some drinks in!'

Doherty glared at the two men, who abandoning their unfinished drinks and left in a hurry.

Flynn and Doherty drank together for another couple of hours, after that, Flynn made his excuses. 'I gotta go, Jack. The missus, well you know, we only married last month.'

Doherty put his thumb onto his friend's forehead, stuck out his tongue and said, 'I thought you was a *real* man, Mickey!'

Flynn walked out backwards, still bantering; he bumped into a stranger at the bar. He apologised instantly. The stranger eyed him coldly.

Doherty watched from further up the bar; he didn't like the way the stranger looked at Flynn. With Mickey gone, he could have a bit of fun. Easing away from the edge of the group of Irish he stood with, he headed in the other man's direction.

He brushed past the stranger making body contact with the whole of his top half, and although the force and friction was enough to make the stranger adjust the plant of his feet; he did not stagger as most men would have. He felt solid, heavier than he looked, but Doherty wasn't worried. At a full head taller, he'd easily knock him out if it came to it, no trouble at all.

'Watch where you're going, all right?' the Irishman warned him.

The man turned to face him. Up close, he had the look of a fighting dog, scarred face and mashed lips. There was no fear in his eyes. They were dark like black stones, empty, but alert. He shrugged nonchalantly. The way he stuck his chin out, an invitation; he wasn't scared. He *wanted* it. Warning bells echoed at the back of Doherty's mind, and he thought better of it. He looked around quickly; no one was watching. 'Don't let it happen again,' he mumbled, before joining the rest of his group at the bar.

'What happened there, Jack? I thought it was going off?' Davey O'Connor said.

Someone *had* seen.

'Just a little skirmish that's all. I gave him a chance to drink up and go.'

'What Jack Doherty giving out second chances?' Davey looked at the others, in mock amazement. 'I must be fuckin' dreaming – somebody pinch me.'

'I'll do more than pinch you, O'Connor – I'll put you in the land of dreams for a week!'

A few minutes later, watching as the man bought another drink, the group of men looked around at each other. A series of nods, winks, and half-shrugs, decided their course of action. They goaded a reaction from Doherty.

'Holy Mother!' Davey rolled his eyes heavenward. 'He's only gone and got himself another pint, Jack.'

'I see your man is still there,' O'Connor's brother said. 'I don't think he's going, big man.'

Doherty put his pint down and wiped his lips. Most people wouldn't hang about when they'd had a friendly warning like that from him. The way the stranger stood there looking like he'd not a care in the world, infuriated him. He made a beeline for him, approaching from behind. *I'll fucking teach him.*

This time as he squeezed past, he cranked his hips and wound the upper left side of his body back as if cocking a spring and then released it with perfect timing, his shoulder slamming into the smaller man, who, about to take a sip, almost knocked his teeth out on the glass.

'Sorry about that!' Doherty said sarcastically, with a wink to his friends and a grin to a big-breasted girl wearing a nurse's uniform. Her dark eyes flashed back at him, registering interest. Distracted, the big Irishman veered towards her to try his luck.

Her eyes widened as the stranger came into view from behind, with bad intent written all over his face. He never said a word, instead exploding a mighty punch that bounced off the back of Doherty's head; it made a sound like dropping an overripe watermelon onto the floor. Although he'd anticipated some sort of retaliation, he hadn't expected *that*. The power buckled his knees; he stopped himself short of colliding with the nurse, putting his hands on the wall either side of her.

Silence descended over the pub.

Shocked by her unexpected and precarious position, the nurse stood open-mouthed. This close the Irishman's eyes, so full of life just a few moments ago, were now dull and empty. He didn't look at her; he was in survival mode.

Unable to finish the onslaught without risking injury to the girl, the stranger pulled his opponent round by the shoulder. She edged along the wall to safety.

Those few split seconds allowed Doherty a degree of recovery and the chance to launch a last ditch attack on the stranger. For a man of his stature, he struck with surprising speed. Three powerful, short and choppy head shots, left – right – left, the crowd gasped; the stranger rode the punches, taking the brunt of the power out on his forearms, but the last one hooked around his block and glanced off, catching him square on the temple. The stranger shook his head to clear it, his eyes briefly out of focus. He sensed victory and moved in for the kill – one more shot would finish him – he lined him up carefully, getting into range, ready to deliver the final blow.

The stranger exploded into action – ducking under, coming forward as the bigger man's punch scythed through empty air, he drove his left elbow into the Irishman's lower ribs, snapping them, stopping him in his tracks. A look of anguished surprise appeared on his face as his faculties struggled to keep pace with his instincts. He folded, leaning in to favour his broken side. In a split second of clarity, he saw his opponent's hips swivel, a desperate message relayed from his brain – too late for his deadened body to react. A solid right smashed the front of Doherty's face in, crushing his nose and mouth. The force of it disconnected him from his senses; his eyes were lifeless. A left hook clubbed in, a meat tenderiser masquerading as a fist. Very few – if any – in the crowd, would have ever witnessed an attack of such murderous savagery in their lives. There was a stunned silence as the big man toppled like a demolished skyscraper, knees buckling under him. His right eyeball – dislodged from its socket – hung down below his cheekbone as he fell to the ground.

Someone screamed and then the manager shouted, 'I've called the police!'

Two bouncers flanked him; he flashed a menacing glance at each of them. 'Don't worry boys, I'm going.' The doormen had an unspoken understanding; when it was time to fight – they'd fight, but only if they had to. They had seen what he'd just done and were in awe of his power. Both stood aside, knowing if they tried to stop him they'd have their hands full; they might not be able to contain the man, so they let him pass.

Over by the bar, Davey O'Connor picked up a stool and moved close, a dangerous look on his face. Tucked in behind him, his younger brother advanced with a knife held low.

'Come near me with that, sonny – and I'll kill you wit' it,' the fighter remarked without emotion.

A doorman stepped between, addressing the Irishmen. 'Let it go, boys. Jack picked on the wrong man tonight.' A tense moment followed. The O'Connors reluctantly stood down.

The stranger backed out cautiously through the door and into the street. No one tried to stop him.

By the time police arrived, he'd vanished.

Chapter 30

After the show, the 'Sultans of Swing' still ringing in her ears, the nurse rolled out unsteady on her feet, dark hair sweaty and dishevelled from dancing. Someone had given her a joint in there and it hadn't done her any favours. Separated from her friends by the tide of people flooding out of the venue, she gave up looking for them. She stumbled along the back streets, not noticing everyone else had disappeared, unaware of the man following behind.

She tripped, falling against a wall and, muttering curses about her shoes, removed them. Glancing up, she recognised the man who now stood before her.

'Oh! You're that *really* tough guy from earlier. Are you following me?' Her face bore no real expression and the vaguely quizzical look that did form there, reverted to drunken blankness almost immediately. They had stopped outside a house with black railings set in the top of a low garden wall. A locked gate led up the steps to a three-storey house. The windows, surrounded by white painted decorative stonework, stood out in contrast to the dirty buff coloured brick walls.

At first floor level, there was a security camera pointing down over the front door towards the gate. He spotted it. 'Come on, the car's round the corner,' he said.

She started to move off slowly.

The amount he'd seen her drink, she should be all over the place. *She must have the capacity of an elephant.*

As she struggled to compose herself, she held a single finger up and focused on it, using it for controlling her body and conducting her words. She waggled it in front of her, keeping approximate time as she spoke. 'Oh, I get it. You just want to make sure I get home safe and sound!' she taunted him. 'I'm a lover, not a fighter!' She didn't know who sang it, or even when. 'Michael!' she exclaimed in a loud voice. 'I keep forgetting his name. "That girl is *mine*..."' She giggled and started singing a crucified version of Dire Straits' 'Romeo and Juliet'.

'Are you coming?' he said, pulling on her arm.

She looked confused. It was hard to tell from her body movements whether she was resisting or just trying to control her feet.

As they turned into another smart street of terraced houses, the unlikely couple came into the sights of two young police officers. One of whom had just finished speaking into his radio. 'John – there's a disturbance at a party down the road – let's go!'

'You go on ahead, I'll catch you up. I want to check those two out,' he said, pointing across the street as he crossed over. His colleague strode off, quickening his pace as he got further down the road.

'Are you all right, Miss?' he enquired.

She didn't answer straight away; she tried without success to think of something witty to say so he wouldn't realise she was drunk.

'Yes, I'm really tired.'

'I can see that,' he said, his voice edged with polite sarcasm.

'Do you know this man?'

'Course I do! He's the one who had the fight earlier,' she said, referring to it casually as if the policeman already knew about it. The stranger cringed.

The officer looked away from her to the man, noticing the swollen right eye, the damage to his mouth. 'How did that happen?' he said, fixing his gaze on the wounds as he took his notebook out.

'I had a bit of an altercation over a spilt drink. No harm done. Looks worse than it is; we shook hands and had a drink together after.' He jerked a thumb in her direction. 'She's a nurse. I know her from the Hospital. I'm a porter there.'

The officer looked at her uniform and asked her again. 'Are you sure you're all right, Miss?'

She started humming '*The Girl is mine*', her eyes lighting up as she suddenly exclaimed, 'Michael!' She covered her mouth, surprised at the loudness of her voice. 'Michael, that's his name. I keep forgetting. 'Course I'm all right! *He's* taking me home.'

'That's right. That's what I'm doing,' the man said.

'What's your full name and address, Michael?' The officer asked.

Before he could answer, violent shouts from the disturbance further down the street drew the officer's attention, distracting him. The constable broke into a jog, turning to call back.

'Michael, make sure you get her home safely, okay?'

'Oh, I will,' said the stranger softly behind the officer's back. 'I definitely will.'

Her left leg buckled, pitching her down and away from him. Catching her before she hit the pavement, 'Michael' manoeuvred her into the front passenger side of the car with difficulty, brushing his hand across her breasts as he strapped her seat belt on. Although her eyes were closed, she wasn't actually asleep. She mumbled something unintelligible and then sighed, exhaling slowly. Within moments, she began to snore.

Michael started the engine.

Ten minutes later, her head lolled and bucked with every pothole the car went over as it lurched its way down the dark lane, headlights bouncing up and down, illuminating the shadowy trees before coming to a halt. He turned the lights off and the moon, almost full, bathed the car in its silvery light.

For a moment he watched her shallow breathing, and then he leaned over, inhaling her exhaled breath, running his hand up the inside of her thigh. She stirred. He hesitated and then hooked a finger into her panties, pulling them to one side.

'Huh?' she said groggily. 'I hope you didn't do that on purpose.'

Chapter 31

Kathy Bird never made it back home that night. The weeks and months rolled by, turning into a long nightmare from which there was no awakening. The appeals and campaigns were in vain; they didn't turn up anything. The case even featured the following year on the pilot Crimewatch programme. Nobody came forward with any new or significant leads.

After a year of endless campaigning, on the first anniversary of her disappearance, her mother broke down.

'I can't take this anymore; she's gone, hasn't she?' Her small shoulders looked frail, slumped in defeat. She shuddered as she took another breath. A deep sob racked her chest. 'We're never going to see her again,' she said it as a matter of fact, a strange light in her eyes.

'Don't ever say that again.' Kathy's father took her in his arms and held her. 'She isn't dead. If she was, I'd know. I would feel it.'

'You believe that?'

'I believe it with all my heart.'

Her lips found their way onto his. The surprise both of them felt, melted into a kind of urgency, a clinging to life and each other that they hadn't experienced since she'd disappeared. She began to act strangely as if in possession of a new vigour. He was unsure exactly what she was going through, but suspected from their frenzied and frequent couplings that she was hoping for a baby. Finally, he'd asked her as they lay in post sexual silence.

'Yes, I want another little girl or I'm going to go crazy.'

'What if you do get pregnant and it turns out to be a boy?'

She rolled over onto her side and looked at him with absolute conviction. 'It *will* be a girl.'

Her parents named her Stella because the name reminded them of the stars. Mrs Bird brought her up as far as she could tell exactly the same way as she did Kathy.

Not long after learning to walk, Stella realised there was a room that was always kept shut. When she was tall enough to operate the door handle, her mother took her inside to satisfy her curiosity. 'You have a sister; you look just like her, apart from your hair. She had dark hair.' She told the little girl all about Kathy, every little thing she could think of.

Stella stared at her mother and asked innocently, 'If she is my sister, where is she?'

Her mother gazed into the distance beyond the window. 'She's out there somewhere, lost. We will find her one day, your father and I.' Her eyes misted with tears as she continued, 'For now, all we have is that photograph, and you of course.' She forced a smile. 'She'll come home one day.'

Stella did not recognise the look in her mother's eyes – not in those days – as she stared out of the window into a distant place. It would be years before she realised her mother was lost, too, and that while Stella was young enough to depend on her, she was just distracted enough to continue to cope.

As Stella got older, a fear grew up inside her mother. Terrified at losing her, too; she lost faith in Kathy ever returning. It all proved too much. When she reached eighteen years of age, her parents killed themselves in a suicide pact.

Chapter 32

North Cornwall, July 1991

The driver possessed photographic recall, or more accurately, an eidetic memory. His mind was like an on-board video camera. When he wanted to remember something vividly, something turned on in him and recorded it forever. It meant he could switch his voice to match any of a repertoire of famous actors, or any voice he chose from his considerable memory banks. It was why he never needed to take trophies. All the details – sight and sound; touch, taste, and smell, were only a moment of concentration away.

Summer of 1967. The last time he came here. Apart from its freshly painted appearance, the signpost looked the same, but he noticed the directional pointer to the old mine had been removed. Few used to go in that direction anyway, now it would be less. Back then most preferred the walk across the top from the other side of the hill.

Ahead, the road shimmered with rising heat, silver phantom images of water pooled like distant oases, never getting any closer, eventually disappearing as the road changed direction.

Soaring temperature levels charged the air with static. Sweat ran down his face in rivulets. The heat was making him cranky.

A ferocious electrical storm had disturbed him as he slept in the car the night before. Alerted by a flickering flash of pale blue light, he'd sat up, half-dazed, listening to the thunder rumbling away in the distance and, lighting a cigarette, he waited for the rain. None came.

A trader in just about anything, he was a travelling man, always doing a bit of this and that. An asbestos removal contractor by trade, he looked far too bulky for a job usually carried out by smaller men. He felt like Gulliver on a few of the sites he'd worked on, the other guys were so small. Self-employed, it gave him an excuse to be places, and the dirty work a reason for keeping a few spare sets of work clothes in the boot. He criss-crossed the whole country and soon became familiar with places he'd never have found otherwise.

Sweet Mary, it's hot! The cloying heat enveloped him like a cloak of steam. Even with all the car windows open, the inside was like an oven, the fan just pushing warm air around. He'd have loved to floor the accelerator and get the air moving faster, but on this stretch of road the police often lurked in the bushes, stepping out with the speed gun and zapping any car doing more than 40 miles an hour. Although he *was* tempted, the thought of the police pulling him in kept him on the limit.

He reached over and pulled a cigarette out of the pack on the dashboard, and lit it with one eye on the road, the other on the cigarette. It made his eyes cross, and one stuck there, an ongoing residual effect of the lazy eye he'd suffered from as a kid. Afterwards, it ached as it always did, and he shook his head to clear the pain.

He leaned forward to drop the lighter back in the tray; his shirt, damp with sweat, felt cold and uncomfortable when he sat back again. To and fro he rocked, easing back against the seat several times despite the discomfort, just to feel the coolness on his back.

The first few deep drags burned the back of his throat as he inhaled, and though he knew it was a crazy thought, it helped to cool him down.

He mused about the benefits of smoking. *Cigarettes make so many things so much more tolerable. If you were down, a cigarette would lift you. In a temper, a cigarette would calm you down. After sex and drink, a cigarette was the best thing in the world, and if you combined all three...* He grinned at the thought, then toyed with the order. *Sex first, then a cigarette...*

The doctor recently told him the amount of cigarettes he smoked would kill him for sure. *That may be so, Doc, but I know someone who smoked all his life. He was told by a doctor to stop and a few weeks later he died of a heart attack. Giving up cigarettes killed him.*

'That won't be me,' he said, surprised he'd said it aloud.

Around a snaking bend in the road, halfway up the hill, a car park sat among the trees, three sides of it contained by man-made mud banks. A wooden sign pointed in the direction of several footpaths.

He guessed if anyone were walking today, it would be at the top, to catch the cooling breeze that always seemed to blow up there.

Tired of driving, he found some shade, parked and closed his eyes.

Too hot to settle, he gave up on trying to nap. A coffee might perk him up; he poured one from the thermos. It was so warm outside there was no steam. Fooled into thinking it wasn't that hot, the liquid scalded his lips. *Mother of Shit!* He spat through gritted teeth and bunching his left fist, threatened the windscreen with it.

'Jeez!' It took a lot of self-control to stop from punching the screen out. Now he needed a cigarette.

The coffee made him want to piss. Although there were a couple of other cars parked and he hadn't seen anyone around, he decided to go into the bushes to urinate. He wouldn't want some old woman to say he flashed his cock at her. A smirk crossed his face at the thought. *Would you be able to tell us what he looked like?* 'Well, Officer, I didn't actually *see* his face.' Shaking himself off, he zipped up his fly.

Destiny pulled him along the valley path. He wondered if the stream still ran on the same course, if the woods had changed. The demons of dark desire came alive at the memory of the naked girl and the others he'd met there. He suddenly remembered the boy. *Did I give you bad dreams, kid?* He decided the kid was too young to understand what he'd seen, but the old man...he'd given him the creeps. He'd looked straight at where he hid in the undergrowth. *How did he know?* Although he shook his head, he acknowledged if it hadn't been for that, he might have been tempted to stay, and if he had... Y*eah, did me a favour.* He was back today; if anyone should ask, he was watching for birds – his favourite pastime.

You never know who you're going to bump into. The element of surprise was what he loved best.

Half an hour later, he reached the broad shale beach, where the stream flattened out on a bend, before dropping away. The water gurgled, as it darted shiny and silver, through the rocks. The dense woods looked unchanged, except that someone had put up more clooties. This puzzled him; there were dozens of them tied in the branches of a whitethorn tree hanging over the bend in the stream. There wasn't a spring there. What did these damn ignorant, new age, seekers-after-something, think they were doing? Fighting back the urge to tear them down, he lit a cigarette. The smell of the woods set his heart thumping as a parade of memories started in his head, he felt himself becoming aroused. About to embark on a few minutes of fantasy, he unzipped himself, and then almost panicked when he heard female voices carried on the breeze. Tilting his head, he stood still, listening intently, tuning into the direction of the sound.

He moved away from the undergrowth, and stopped in his tracks, retreating into the cover of the shade once more. Three girls were moving away from him. He looked at the stub of the cigarette, took one last drag, right down to the butt and flicking it away, started up the slope just inside the tree line, stalking them.

Higher up, the path moved away from the trees leading to an open meadow of tall grass. From there, it climbed steeply up to the ridge. The stalker closed the gap with surprising speed, halving the distance between them. One girl lagged behind. The other two, clearly engrossed in conversation, marched on ahead, oblivious to the lengthening gap.

He measured the distance to the top and gauged the pace with which they were walking.

It was too risky. If he'd given in to reckless temptation every time the desire was on him, he'd have been behind bars long before now for sure.

Outlined by the sun shining through their thin summer dresses, the silhouettes of their bodies bound him in a spell. The leader girls were skinny; he'd no time for skinny girls. The other had fallen behind, now over a hundred yards from her friends. Fully developed, the shape of her excited him; the roundness, the curves, the gap at the top of her legs where the sun glared through the thin cotton dress. His brief masturbation stirred up feelings, which now overpowered him. The two girls disappeared over the lip at the top, out of sight. He knew it was too risky, but if he moved quickly…

The long grass allowed him to creep close to her, just outside her peripheral vision. He avoided looking at her directly, just in case she got the feeling that someone was watching her.

Despite his precaution, she turned quite suddenly and looked in his direction.

He dropped out of sight instantly. A few seconds later, he peered out from his hiding place, heart hammering, and mouth, watering. *Too late to turn away from it now.*

He broke cover on her blind side, crossing the space between them like a lion closing in on its prey and then he was on her, drawing the cold steel tip of his knife across the skin of her face, she shivered at its touch. Sweet, plump, beautiful, within seconds he was inside her. The realisation she was a virgin drove him crazy; when the revulsion on her face registered with him, she only hastened the end.

He started to choke the life out of her. What happened next took him aback, for a second she looked different, as if someone had swapped places with her. Those few decisive seconds saved her life. As he tightened his grip around her throat once more, a clear commanding voice shouted at him. *'GET – OFF – HER!'* The voice held no fear. It stopped him dead. He looked up sharply; he could have killed all three if he chose. That was what set him apart. He was clever. Sparking a manhunt didn't feature in his plans. Quickly turning away, he took off and ran, crashing and stumbling back to the car, his only thought was to get away. This time he'd fucked up, gone too close to the wire.

It had been too risky; he shouldn't have gone for it; he knew that, but he'd gone for it anyway. *Jeez!* Out of control, head spinning – he couldn't focus. What just happened had never happened before. These were credible witnesses to his crime, not like the kid.

Change unsettled him. Now it was inevitable. A fury rose within him, and it was hard to control. If he didn't get a grip, he'd end up doing something stupid and all the years of meticulous care, undone by a few crazed moments. He had to get home; he would shave his face clean, cut his hair and dye it.

He roared out of the car park, out into the country lane. In a daze, driving faster than the road allowed, he pulled a cigarette from its pack, lit it and almost careered off the road.

Deep inhalation, slow exhalation, deep, slow, calming, he wound his window down to get air into the car, to cool down and clear his head.

He arrived at a T-junction and turned left. He was now on a B road headed towards home.

'Be careful now!' he hissed to himself. 'Slow *down*. It's the last thing you want, bombing along drawing attention to yourself!'

The police would be out looking soon, and he wanted to get as far away as possible from where he'd just been. He started getting angry, berating himself with a woman's voice. It startled him. *His mother's voice? Sweet Jesus, am I going crazy? If she'd kept up with her friends, it would never have happened.*

The more he tried, the harder it was to concentrate. He ran through the things he'd have to do now. The job he had lined up. *Can't take that now; she's fucked that up for you. No, wait. If you don't, will somebody think... No – just get away. You can think it through later.*

That night as he lay in bed, he counted the way he always did, to bring his thoughts into order. He drifted afterwards until he thought about all the girls he'd ever known, albeit, most of them he'd known only briefly, playing through the different outcomes that might have been. *It beats counting sheep.* A few minutes of that and he'd be asleep, but not tonight. Tonight he was thinking about the one that got away.

In his entire career, it was only the second time there'd been witnesses, but it bothered him. The first time was sheer bad luck, and he never gave it a second thought. How could he have known that a kid would get lost and have half his family looking for him? No, this was different. He'd lost control, gone too far, and that disturbed him.

They were probably all over her body right now, looking for hair, clothing fibres, bits of skin and worst of all – he'd shot his semen inside her. If he hadn't been disturbed, he'd have carted her off, and they'd have had nothing. Still, they had to catch him first. He would make sure he was never careless like it again.

He cursed himself. After the kid saw him, he should have just stayed away. It was the old man – who'd been with him – he'd jinxed the place. As he dyed his hair dark brown and cut off his beard, he made his mind up; he wouldn't be going back there again.

Soon, he was back to thinking about the girl. He cursed her under his breath. She'd seriously fucked things up for him. The atmosphere. The associations. The lure had been just too much. Trailing behind her friends like that, letting him know she was lost and lonely. He'd just had to have her. He should have taken her straight down to the stream, fucked her there and then got rid of her. He'd allowed his cock to rule his head. His old man used to say. *You can't let your cock rule your head; it has no fucking brain!* Sound advice and he might have listened if the old man had practised what he preached. He gritted his teeth at the memory of the old man; he hated him and all he wanted to do was forget; that's the trouble with a photographic memory. You don't forget. You bury, but you do not ever forget. He balled his fist and crashed it into the wallboard, leaving a crater there.

He stared at his knuckles – unnaturally white for a second; the torn skin peeled back, turning red as the blood bubbled up and dripped onto the floor.

'FUCK!' The scream silenced the whole camp. The residents outside looked warily at each other. Not one of them cared to knock to ask if he was okay. When he was like that, they knew better than to disturb him.

In the bathroom, he stared at the face looking back at him. Older, but still powerful, a gleam of madness shone in his wild, blood-shot eyes. *I would not want to meet you on a dark night.* A half grin pulled painfully at his scarred top lip, preventing a full smile. He'd not smiled fully since he'd split the scar when he was a kid.

Lying on his bed, he tried to put her out of his mind, but she clung there. Photographic memories, you can't get rid of them; a flashbulb moment of concentration had burned them into his consciousness. He wasn't sure how it all worked, but if it wasn't important to him, he'd forget it. His old man said, '*You can't even remember what you had for breakfast, yet that little girl with the red hot pants next door, from ten years ago – you remember her like she was here yesterday!*' Now he was older and understood things better, he thought it might be to do with capacity. He'd read the mind works like that, keeping all the important things at the front and letting the mediocre drift to the back, forgotten. The more you thought about things, the fresher they kept. An article in a magazine about Ted Serios stated he could create an image in his mind and transmit it onto film, often using iconic buildings and structures. Serios produced images, which, although recognisable, were clearly not photographs, merely impressions from his memory. *Just imagine if I could do that. Somebody walks past with a camera while I'm reminiscing. They go into the chemists to get it developed. The technicians see it all on film. Next thing, he's arrested. No other evidence, no body, nothing. The Judge: 'How do you find the defendant, guilty or not guilty?' The foreman: 'Guilty.'* Oh, boy, the fun he could have with people that he didn't like, just as long *as they carried a camera.* A painful grin stretched his lips; he looked as if he were sneering. *She* was in his head again.

'Don't hurt me!' The flimsy moment of resistance inside her confirmed she was a virgin as he pushed through. The memory made him hard again.

It was a sign, and he should heed it. He'd give it a rest for a while, he'd done it before. It was nothing new. Change – he hated it, but he'd find something else. Necessity, the mother of invention, and the Devil makes work for idle hands. He was getting bored.

He'd always lived among travellers; his bare-knuckle prowess guaranteed him a reluctant welcome wherever he turned up within the community. It hadn't always been like that.

Widely regarded as a nutter, he had no friends, and although he kept himself to himself, he was often heard arguing with someone, or calling out in the quiet of the night. It was for this reason they pitched him well away from everyone else in the camp.

In his secret life, however, his disadvantages made him determined to compensate, and he'd disappear into remote places, taking with him books and plays. He would read aloud, playing different roles, experimenting with speech and elocution, speaking in a high, trill voice, alternating with low ones. He listened to tapes of famous speeches; he learned to speak just like Churchill, his voice indistinguishable; he could imitate Burton, *anybody* he set his mind to.

The seeds of his plans had germinated back then before he became a fighter.

While her speech impediment didn't impede the respect and admiration she received from the community, the father was widely regarded as no good. Both parents had harelips, a trait, which inevitably, passed on to him. The money he earned from fighting, he wasted mostly on gambling, but he did have the sense to invest in a number of strategically placed properties around the country. No one knew exactly where the properties were.

A licenced asbestos removal contractor, he'd occasionally engage in honest work, always keeping a pack of disposable boiler suits in the car, just in case a job came up, along with sets of paper over-shoes, gloves and a suitable mask to exclude the deadly fibres.

One morning, preparing to remove asbestos from a police station, he had a brainwave. If the kit were capable of keeping asbestos out, it would keep fibres in. Once dressed, he used heavy-duty tape to seal the joins between sleeves and gloves, trousers and shoes to prevent contaminating himself. It was a discipline he would follow, that also ensured he'd leave no clues behind.

The police had only ever stopped him once, and that was because an indicator light wasn't working. The lone policeman noticed his muddy tyres.

'Been off the beaten track have we, sir?'

He took a deep breath and explained that he'd been working on a building site.

The copper decided to check over the rest of the vehicle and asked to look in the boot. Shining his torch over all the boxes, he saw the disposable overalls and paper over-shoes, the duct tape and selection of facemasks. He eyed him suspiciously. 'What's all this for?'

'Can I get my papers?' he said.

Hand on his truncheon, ready, the policeman nodded.

While rummaging in the boot, he explained that he had to supply his own gear; otherwise, the tax office would take away his self-employed tax status.

The officer picked up an old mask. 'I didn't think people used these anymore?'

'You can't beat the old ones you know, if it's just a quick job, I throw that one on and well, it's job done.'

He handed his business card to the policeman, who examined it carefully. It read in large letters Freelance Asbestos Surveys and Testing Services – 24-hour service. Below that in smaller letters was a contact name and telephone number.

'Just one fibre, that's all it takes. Twenty, twenty-five years later, the insides of your lungs thicken, and you get...'

The young officer had heard enough. Suddenly he was keen to get away. He handed the card back quickly, fearing it might be contaminated, unaware that he'd just allowed one of the most prolific criminals the country had known in a long time to continue on his journey.

His rules for survival were simple.

Never stay still. If you do, the past has a way of catching up with you. Always keep moving; always keep changing. If you stay the same, someone will get to know who you are.

Unpredictable and unstable, it made him hard to pin down. Not for him the niceties of polite conversation, he couldn't do it anyway, could never be himself, the abrasiveness in him sprang from an inferiority complex over his condition, but it kept people away from him, and that was how he liked it.

Chapter 33

The Sister had packed, ready for her journey. Seventeen years in Brighton almost over. They would come for her before noon, by then she'd be gone. Rosetta was already waiting with their bags at the rear of the shop. *Rosetta.* When that girl was conceived, she thought her powers had deserted her forever. For a while, she enjoyed normality. She was almost disappointed when they returned.

It seemed to her a good time to be starting a new life far away, to resurface in a distant corner of the country where she'd keep a low profile. However, first she had an appointment to keep, one last favour to grant her benefactor.

The tiny bell over the doorway tinkled, and a heavily pregnant young girl came in. Sister took one look at her, the girl was in need, tortured inside because of her faith. When she'd asked her if she wanted the truth, she didn't hesitate, answering straight away. 'I want the truth.' Her strong chin lifted defiantly.

Used to knocks, this one.

Sister's green eyes settled on the dark haired girl before her.

'Well, Jackie, I'd like you to hold this a moment for me.'

The girl took the stone and clenched it tightly in her right fist. Eyes narrowed with suspicion; she looked directly at the fortune-teller. 'I don't recall telling you my name.'

Sister smiled serenely, their eyes met. 'That's right … you didn't. You can call me, Sister.' She reached over to retrieve the stone, thinking she should have used it more. It would be years before she understood it fully.

Before she'd even touched it, she had an idea of what would happen. Emotions hung in the air, like sheets on a washing line disturbed by a rising wind, rippling wildly and softly flapping. Sister's head tilted backwards; her body arched away from the seat; her knees jerked up suddenly, hitting the underside of the table.

This was something new, and nothing could have prepared her for it.

Jackie stared at her mortified. Frozen in a contorted position, Sister's eyes moved rapidly as if she were watching a dream. Her breathing became strangely erratic as she exerted herself. Concerned, unsure if she were in the grip of an asthma attack, Jackie leaned forward, and as she did so, thought she heard whispers carried on her breath. She listened closely, trying to make out what the medium was saying.

'Why they can never wait those two, they know I'm not as fit as them.' The words, she recognised them. They were her own. Memories from that day had burned so deeply into her subconscious; she'd never forget it as long as she lived.

This woman was reading her memories and projecting them back to her. Somehow, the two of them had joined each other in this particular part of her past.

Jackie struggled to keep up with her two friends; on legs like lead weights, her whole body felt heavier than normal in the searing heat. She cursed her plumpness.

'Oh, Jackie, it's because you've developed better than they have,' her mother's voice whispered to her through the mediums lips. The old insecurities stirred; she felt strangely depressed. She knew what would come next. She saw herself looking up the steep path; they were already at the top. They didn't even look round.

'They don't even care if I'm all right down here,' she muttered. Their voices, like a distant radio play; blew towards her on the breeze. 'Harry Solomons.' Those words, she made out distinctly. The voices cut out suddenly, as the ridge above interfered with the wind's transmission. Jackie picked up the pace, as she tried to catch up, straining to hear what else they were saying, '...with him behind the bike sheds.' What was that about the bike sheds? Their heads and shoulders disappeared from view as if they were going down invisible stairs on the other side. Shrieks of laughter pierced the air.

She never did find out exactly what they'd been saying, but she remembered the sadness she'd felt at that moment, left out and alone.

Karen and Gilda were so similar that inevitably, they always kept her on the outside. The other two girls homed in on her insecurities and never let up, driving tiny wedges of doubt into every crack they could find in her fragile make-up. 'Two's company, three's a crowd,' her mother whispered. Jackie's heart grew heavy at the thought they weren't truly friends.

Through Sister, her mother chided her. 'Why don't you ever stick up for yourself? You only have yourself to blame if you let people treat you like that! If you don't ever fight back, they'll know they can get away with it, and they'll end up walking all over you!'

She started a conversation in her head that she had never had in reality. 'Yes, Mum, I should start with you. You never have a good word to say about me. You criticise me, when all I am, is what you made me.' The recollection of her frustrations stung her to tears.

She realised her mum had made her a scapegoat for her own failings, made her feel that she was somehow responsible for them. She in turn one day would pass her own low self-esteem to her daughter.

Jackie's legs gave up on her, and she let the others go on. In a minute, they'd stop to let her catch up, she'd find something funny to pipe up with – get the other two laughing, and for a while they'd all be close again. Those happy moments were what she lived for. Life for her was a cycle of reward and failure, always struggling to please someone. Her mother's distant personality had created that in her, now Jackie recreated it in her relationships. All her friends ended up treating her the same as her mum did.

'Is this how your life will always be? Always the victim, always victimised? No, that's not going to be me,' she said to herself, and with new determination, quickened her step, trying to catch up with the others. Their faint voices carried on

the wind towards her. Sister's breathing whispers became ragged, and she couldn't make out what she was saying, her eyes no longer green, slowly turned brown. Jackie knew exactly what was coming next.

She reached a flattened off area, a narrow wild flower meadow below the top. She'd decided to shortcut the distance between them, by moving along parallel to them from below, the grass each side of the path was up to her waist. The field was sunny, dried out greens and yellows, seeds from faded heads stuck to her clothes as she brushed past. Time slowed down, spent blooms bobbed, she thought herself in tune with nature. She remembered how so much more alive she'd felt, more than ever before, how she wanted to cry out with happiness, or sing. Her arms thrown out, hands outstretched level with her shoulders, she'd spun like a whirling dervish, letting go of her emotions, her long black hair flew out around her. The widest of smiles hurt her face. It didn't hurt for long.

A powerful hand clamped across her mouth from behind. The hand reeked of sweat and tobacco. It all happened so fast. He was holding a knife, and he'd forced her to the ground. 'Don't hurt me,' she whispered. Her vulnerability sent him into a frenzy, pulling hard at her clothes, ripping them from her.

'Don't look at my face!' he commanded.

Shaking with fear, whimpering, she squeezed her eyes shut.

He was on her panting and sweating; he smelled like an animal. Something popped inside as he drove himself roughly into her; she gasped. She'd always imagined there would be more pain. Then came the awful realisation; she'd become involuntarily wet as she continued receiving him, she felt that she'd betrayed herself. She kept her face turned away; his sweat dripped onto her; its foul saltiness found its way into her mouth; she gagged dryly as if invisible fingers had forced their way down her throat. Jackie became aware she had a witness sharing her ordeal, she watched transfixed as the medium retched at the precise moment she did, eyes bulging as his foul sweat poisoned her, too.

'So I make you feel sick do I?' He didn't wait for an answer. His hands tightened around her throat, squeezing the life out of her. Sister grasped at her own neck, helplessly reliving Jackie's ordeal alongside her.

The rapist picked up a beat, thrusting up and down rapidly like an engine piston, gathering momentum. He shuddered as he spent himself inside her, lay atop her motionless a moment before pushing down with all his might; he began to crush her throat.

Jackie looked up at the sky in a daze, exactly as she did that day as if looking through an invisible ceiling. She thought she saw herself, a reflection, a trick of the light. She'd taken on a ghostly appearance. Hair no longer dark, eyes no longer brown, a voice rasped, 'Leave her alone!' It didn't seem real.

Startled, he turned around to look; the voice had given her vital seconds. She was choking; he was spooked. She heard Gilda's familiar bossy voice nearby.

'Leave – our – friend – alone!'

The rapist hid his face, rolled away and launched off down the hill, making his escape. She heard him thrashing through the long grass.

Her two friends ran to her. She was rubbing at her bare flesh with clumps of grass held tight in her hands, trying to clean herself, trying to get his smell off her.

'Why didn't I fight back?' she whispered. 'I should have fought back!' She began to sob.

What happened that day started a life-long friendship between the girls.

Two blamed themselves for what happened to the third. Jackie developed an obsession with cleanliness and a pathological hatred for cigarette smokers; she would never be the same.

Sister sat with her head forward over the table, breathing in great gulps of air. When she'd recovered sufficiently, she levelled a look at Jackie.

'Sweet mother of Jesus, so that's what happened to you!' Jackie didn't answer; there was no need to speak. There was pain for her in The Sister's eyes. Jackie wept; relieved at last, she'd been able to share the experience with someone who understood.

'And the child, it's his, isn't it?'

Jackie nodded.

'And you asked me for the truth, didn't you?'

Jackie nodded again.

'You already know the truth!'

Jackie looked at her; wetness smudged the mascara round her eyes, making them look large and afraid.

'That child deserves better than you would give if you kept it.'

Jackie paused between each word as she repeated, 'If – I – kept – it…?'

'That's right, if you kept it. You won't have an abortion because you're a good catholic girl, but 'Good Catholic Girl', you've been tainted. No, it's not your fault, not at all. You'd come to resent it, the child. You don't think so now. You don't believe it, but if you kept her that is what would happen.'

'Her? You know it's a girl?'

The Sister continued, 'She can't help how she came to be, but you'll punish her for it.' She rested a gloved hand on Jackie's forearm. 'It would be the kindest thing, to give her a chance to be loved by someone else in the way that you cannot. It's for the best, Jackie, in your heart y'know it's the truth.'

The tiny bell over the shop door tinkled as another customer arrived.

She helped Jackie out and down the steps.

'Keep well, Jackie. Oh, and there's something else. I'll be looking out for you from now on.' She touched her forefinger to her lips as if it were a secret.

Jackie thought she recognised the man in the lobby. She pointed at him and then at Sister. With the question on her face, she did not have to speak.

'Hello, Jackie,' the man said with a half-smile, he looked different without his glasses. 'Even psychiatrists need a bit of help with the future, from time to time.'

She supposed that was how he came to recommend she came here. She made her way out of the gloomy shop, back into daylight. Freed of making the decision by herself, she felt incredibly light on her feet despite the additional weight she was carrying. She held her belly in both hands. The cold light of the day only strengthened her resolve.

She wondered what help Dr Ryan needed with the future.

Chapter 34

On Sunday morning, two days after her consultancy with the Sister, Jackie doubled up in pain. The baby was coming early. That evening just as darkness fell, she gave birth. It was a girl.

In a strange way, having the child gave Jackie something she could focus on. Abortion had been out of the question; it wasn't the child's fault, but she *knew* she couldn't keep it. In time, she'd grow to resent it, questioning every foible and fault, believing it came from him. It was far better she allowed the child a chance at life, free and unhindered from what her father was.

So when the time came, it was not without sorrow that she gave her up. She knew she must.

Tears came; she wept for the part of her that was gone and pined for what might have been. *It's for the best...* Cursing the Sister's words and the hand that fate had dealt her, she wiped her face dry.

Nature can be cruel and seemingly illogical at first glance. In the wild, a TV cameraman films a trio of prideless, nomadic male lions as they come across two isolated females. They attack their cubs. The lionesses fight desperately to protect their young. Once the males succeed in killing the cubs, a strange thing happens. Nature and instinct take over in an unexpected development. The females begin flirting outrageously with the males, parading with sexual swagger, back and forth, getting close, head rubbing, tails flicking across the male's flanks. The heat of a new breeding cycle begins, triggered by the savage loss of their cubs. They mate with the killers of their offspring. No bereft human female would behave in such a way with the executioner of her children.

Instead of shying away from men, Jackie became promiscuous. It was like a tidal wave. Her pent up sexuality, driven by the need to stay in control – ran wild. No man would ever hurt her again, and as if to prove it, the risks she took were outlandish, having sex with one-night stands in toilets, cars and alleyways – Until the night she saw Harry again.

Harry wasn't sure that it was her at first. It had to have been two years since they'd last met. Jackie was sitting on a soldier's lap, drunk, teasing him. Harry grabbed her by the hand and pulled. 'C'mon, you shouldn't even be in here.'

Her eyes widened with surprise. 'Harry!' she cried out – louder than she'd intended. The soldier, who up to that point had been laughing uproariously, suddenly went quiet. It seemed the soldier, a veteran of Northern Ireland tours of duty in the late eighties and lately a parade ground sergeant, had something of a reputation among the locals, because the whole bar grew silent. A few thin giggles and awkward throat clearings were the only sounds to penetrate the tense atmosphere. Pushing up out of his chair so quickly it fell back onto the floor, the soldier stood and pulled her round to one side of him. He'd invested a few drinks in her and wasn't about to give her up without a fight. A space cleared around them, tables and chairs scraping as the crowd sensing trouble, moved out of range.

Standing right in front of Harry, he jabbed a stiff finger in his face, stopping short of his left eye. His face was contorted; the rage of a hundred conflicts fought with his hands tied, was about to be unleashed. Veins stood out at the side of his crew cut head. He growled menacingly. A parched parade ground voice tempered by instilling the fear of God into thousands of new recruits, barked out. 'You! Get away from my girl!'

'Your girl?' Harry said, with quiet dignity. 'Is that right, Jackie?'

A short sledgehammer blow collided with his jaw and rocked his head. His legs disconnected from his senses, and as they buckled, and he dropped; he thought, somewhat crazily. *So you really do see stars!*

Knocked too far from consciousness to get up easily, he felt each thud of the soldier's boots, although he was mercifully detached from the pain. Distant voices reached through the swirling fog in his head; he latched onto them with the last of his awareness, pulling at the anchor they provided, helping him to recover. He heard the rain outside; he knew he was coming back. The warm rain cleared his head enough for him to hear voices protesting, outrage overcoming their fear.

'Hey – no – soldier, don't do that!'

'Stop him someone, that's disgusting!'

'Is that what they teach you in the army? You should be ashamed of yourself!'

The soldier ignored their disapproval, a hideous grin on his face as he continued urinating on the semiconscious man on the ground.

'You wanted to take the piss out of me? There you go; there's the piss out of me! Nobody – NOBODY – takes the piss out of me and gets away with it!' The soldier roared, shaking his shaven head from side to side, eyes daring intervention from anyone in the crowd around him. He stamped one more time on Harry, who doubled up on reflex, with a grunt.

He stood triumphant, one foot on the chest of his trophy. Jackie walked up to him.

'Here's my girl!' he announced loudly, putting his arm out theatrically, like a protective wing for her to come under. 'Come here to me, doll.'

Without warning, she unleashed a kick with startling accuracy, her toe point striking with an impact of around two thousand pounds per square inch – Harry worked it out afterwards – a kick so hard she ripped his trousers through the crutch, front to back, the soldier grunted, doubling up with the pain.

Hurriedly, she picked Harry off the floor and together they stumbled out into the night, leaving the soldier nursing his injured pride, amid fevered speculation.

'Did you see that kick? She must have been *trained* to kick like that!'

'No, it was just a lucky shot.'

'Lucky? My arse!'

They did not hear the rest. The voices faded as the neon glow of the bars dimmed. They made their way out of town, back to his house.

Jackie swallowed him alive with the shameless things she did. Harry was smitten from that very first night.

Afterwards, snuggled up close, safe and warm, they slept.

The morning stole into the room through a gap in the curtains. A thin slant of light slashed through the gloom, across the foot of the bed and projected onto the wall opposite, like a sword blade. Harry had his eyes half closed; a cupped hand shielded them from its brightness; he felt her stir.

'It's far too *early* to be the morning already,' she mumbled, turning away from the light.

'Where *did* you learn to kick like that?' he said, with an air of nonchalance.

'Is it bothering you?' she said.

'No. Yes, actually it is. I keep thinking about that soldier. I just wish I was the one that kicked him like that. You'll have to teach me,' he said, smiling. 'That's assuming, it wasn't just a lucky kick.'

'No, you're right. It wasn't,' she said, staring at the ceiling. 'When I was fifteen, my mum sent me to self-defence classes.'

'Did she?'

'Yes, she did.' Jackie slipped deep into thought. It had been like locking the door after the horse had bolted. She couldn't see the point of it, yet after just a few sessions, she threw herself into it with an anger and gusto that surprised her instructor. *'Imagine I'm going to attack you.'* He was unprepared for the anger she put into her counter attack; he subdued her, but it was a close run thing. It wasn't about the horse at all. It was about the stable door; it was about confidence, feeling safe and secure. Her mother, in all her wisdom, knew exactly what she needed to get her life back on track again.

His hand sought hers under the sheets; he squeezed it.

Looking at him then, she knew she couldn't tell him about *that* part of her life yet. He wouldn't have been able to handle it. *Honesty? What would be the point?* In that bar, she'd identified with Harry's defilement. In that moment, he'd become a victim of vile abuse, too. Just like her. Her arms and legs wrapped around him. 'I'm never going to let you go,' she said.

He squeezed her tight. 'I'm glad.'

They fell in love and never spent another night apart.

In the future, they'd talk often about that night. Sometimes, over dinner with friends, when the drink had flowed, and they'd run out of things to talk about, one of them inevitably would say, 'Come on, Jackie. Tell us about the night you met Harry again.'

She'd always protest at the start, but then she'd look at Harry to see if he minded. He never did. More proud of what she had done that night than embarrassed at the indignity he had suffered at the hands of the soldier. It had been her moment, so she retold it.

The more she told the story, the better at the telling she became. After losing touch for over a year, she'd invited Karen and Gilda for dinner, and once they'd heard the story, they gave her a round of applause. Standing, she'd given them a little curtsy. The pride in their eyes something she'd never forget. Finally, she had stood up for herself.

Ripped from arsehole to breakfast time. She never found out what it actually meant; she repeated it only because it'd been her trainer's favourite saying.

She smiled to herself. He'd have loved that kick.

Chapter 35

Miller sat in the garden of the five hundred-year-old farmhouse he'd rented. Bathed in the warm glow of pale sunshine, he looked out over the green barley fields; the pastoral scene suddenly enlivened by the unexpected arrival of the first swift, followed by the appearance of many more. He was never quite sure at which point exactly the first arrivals came in any year. *Was it April, or was it May?* They just seemed to appear.

When he was a child, he'd wanted to be a fighter pilot; his mind examined those childish dreams once more. The memories felt as though they belonged to someone else.

He watched as a swift skimmed the tips of the young barley, banking fast from left to right, flashing its soft white under-belly at the sun as it rotated on its axis – all the way round with incredible speed and agility, hurtling along, criss-crossing the field picking off insects invisible to the human eye. Miller allowed the periphery of his vision to widen. All over the field, scores of these birds performed similar manoeuvres. *How did they not collide with each other?*

A smile crept over his face. All those men who aspired to fly like birds, from Icarus onwards – shackled by the human condition and later by cumbersome aircraft. Even now, with all the technology we can muster, we'll never be able to do it like *that,* he mused.

The swift continued its breath-taking display of aerial skills; he grinned broadly as he acknowledged the bird's superior ability. Now *that* is an aviator.

Lost in the dappled light and darkness, in the lanes of his memory, he realised he'd been having flashes all his life. His grandfather knew – he'd tried to explain – he had *been* explaining. At that time, he was too young to understand, but the old man had sown the seeds – planted the koans that would enlighten him when he was ready, and just like the swifts arriving unnoticed – suddenly just there – all five of his senses acknowledged the arrival of another, that crept up without him noticing. A sixth sense.

Everything started falling into place, triggering memories of the chance games he'd played with his grandfather. The guessing, at first at the turn of a card which suit it would be, and as he progressed the game becoming harder, so that finally, he'd identify the card before it was turned over. Miller recalled the radio receiver lessons. The tuning in and out of transmissions, and later the overseas viewings, the old man speaking with his eyes closed. *'If I close my eyes and think of my home in Poland, I can see it – the new people who live there, their children. They work hard, and if I listen, inside my head I hear them speak – not what they say; only sound, but I can tell from the sound if they are happy.'*

He reached deeper into his memory, searching for more. Each recollection triggered a new one. *Do we ever forget?*

The gravelly voice was fresh in his mind. *'One day in the future you will wonder, just as I did...what is it for – this thing we have?'* Bruce remembered listening, putting on a suitably serious expression, matching that on the old man's face as he continued talking. *'I used to ask God, why choose me to live, when other men close to me die in war? And the Almighty does not say. I think it's because he knows I would give my life freely, for my friend, for my brother. I don't cry out, Oh, God, let me live! I have faith, and he has too much left for me to do. That is how I survive, and I learn some tricks, too, and I tell them to you.'*

His eyes misted and he swallowed hard at the realisation. The old man had known he wouldn't be around as Miller was growing up.

He'd been preparing him, but for what?

Chapter 36

June 2006

Miller watched the thin clouds stretching across the pale blue sky, vaporising in the growing heat of the morning sun. It was time to move on. He swung his legs down from the bed and sitting upright, collected his thoughts before moving off to shower.

Gathering his clothes, he felt the phone vibrate through the layers he held in his hands. He put them down and sorted through, locating his mobile. *Private number.*

'Who is this?' Miller said.

'Long time, no speak. You don't recognise me do you? It's Donovan.'

'Donovan?' he said, taken aback. 'You're right; it has been a long time. Is everything okay?'

'Can we meet?'

There had to be something wrong. Miller sensed it. 'Okay, I'm guessing you want to make it soon?'

'This afternoon,' he chuckled.

Miller checked his watch, 9:30. 'Where?'

'Amsterdam.'

The plane taxied in at Schipol airport just after 5 'o clock. With no luggage to collect, Miller cleared the terminal within thirty minutes. Kale had a car waiting to drive him to his house in Oud Zuid.

'You know, since you rescued Olga, I have been slowly, but surely infiltrating various cults on the fringes, taking them over, stripping them of their assets, shutting them down. Doing society a favour, and making money in return. Can't be bad, eh?'

Miller surveyed the priceless treasures in the sumptuous room. Many were religious icons.

'Well, good on you, Donovan, it seems like a worthy cause, but what does it have to do with me?'

'I have a little proposition for you,' he said, dismissing his bodyguard with a jerk of his head, pausing while the man had left the room. 'I'm going to need your help to take out the last few remaining organisations. The big three. The leaders are untouchable by any conventional means.'

'Donovan, it doesn't sound like something I can help you with. The last time I had anything to do with you after bringing Olga home, somebody tried to kill me – remember?'

'Of course I do. You will come under my protection. Nothing will happen to you; I guarantee it, and you will also be well rewarded.' Kale smiled. 'Remember how generous I can be?'

'Donovan, what do you mean by conventional means?'

'The leaders that control the big three are the same people, although the figureheads are different. The people behind the facade employ a former assassin named Carlos, to protect them, along with a powerful psychic who forewarns them of danger ahead. '

'What is it exactly that you want me to do?'

'The psychic, he works for me too. He told me about you.'

'Donovan, you've lost me.'

'No, Miller, I have found you. Working as a team, we can finish what started twenty-six years ago. Oh, and the men who tried to kill you recently – they work for the top man.'

He thought about how the men had stalked him on the lecture circuit before ambushing him. There was no doubt they intended to kill him, and they were still at large. 'The psychic told you about that?'

Kale tapped his forefinger on the side of his nose. 'Do we have a deal?' he said, leaning across the inlaid desk, offering a handshake.

Miller took it.

Chapter 37

Rose Kennedy had given up hope of having a child long ago. The cause of her infertility was a mystery; there was no medical reason for it. She'd tried everything and failed. And yet she still entertained the notion that she'd have a baby one day.

She reached her mid-forties and resurrected a love affair with her husband, a last ditch all-out effort before her body changed. *John, let's just try again. What harm can it do?* He was shell-shocked at first; they were engaging more than they had in their twenties. He knew most likely she'd only suffer more disappointment, but he was happy to go along with her.

On a February morning so full of bright sunshine, the light hurt her eyes; Rose felt sick. Although she'd never had a migraine before, she knew the symptoms. She assumed she'd been stricken with an attack for the first time in her life.

It wasn't a migraine; it was something else she hadn't experienced before.

She was pregnant.

Their son was born on Friday 22nd November 1963. Despite her age, there were no complications. Rose considered it a miracle. It was also the night of President Kennedy's assassination. The whole world was in a state of shock.

The family name was Kennedy. They would call him John, after his father. Because of the timing of his birth, and because it coincided with the president's sudden death, Rose insisted they paid tribute by giving their son the middle name, Fitzgerald.

It transpired JFK died at around 7:00 p.m. Rose always believed that her son was born at the same moment. She took it as a sign.

'One out, one in,' she'd tell anyone who'd listen, that her boy was destined for great things.

As he grew older, unsurprisingly, he became interested and well versed in the life story of the president, and the events leading up to and beyond his eventual demise and that in turn, led to a fascination with the FBI.

His father was a detective. From an early age, young John would study case histories of unsolved crimes. He would theorise, running them endlessly past John senior, who'd worked through everything with his son, with quiet, methodical patience, picking holes in the theories and hypotheses his son had put forward.

In time, the boy would redevelop and test the tightness of his angles *before* submitting them to his father, who by now realised that his boy, John junior, or Johnny as he affectionately called him, had a natural aptitude for the work.

Privately, he hoped that junior would follow in his footsteps, but chose not to reveal his wishes, preferring the boy to make his own decision when the time was right.

In his early teenage fantasies, Junior JFK, as he now imagined himself, had become an FBI Agent. Often, he'd wonder what the FBI Agents over there would have made of him.

He would smile as he imagined the headlines: *New Agent 'Junior' JFK, solves 25-year-old mystery.*

When the time came, it was inevitable that he'd enrol in the police force.

He quickly established a reputation as a tough, no nonsense workaholic, with no time for women, making his way with ease through the ranks to detective, solving many difficult cases, making enemies inside and outside the force. A few of these believed his father helped to smooth his passage through the ranks; others suggested he could be gay. Thickset and heavily built, no one repeated the suggestion to his face.

Although his police record was exemplary, something haunted him. One night, not long after he started as an officer on the beat, something had slipped by him. If he'd been more experienced, he might have realised something was wrong, if only he'd been more assertive, and if that fateful call hadn't come through... Thirty seconds, that's all it would have taken to run a check on him, but he didn't and besides, she did seem to know him. The timing of the radio call, it all came down to that really, and the judgement on which was more important at the time. The girl disappeared without a trace.

For twenty-three years, it was the only blot on an otherwise spotless career record, until the arrival of a group of cases, all within a short space of time, which seemed unsolvable by conventional means.

The Midnight Man, the Stalker, the Gasman. Serial criminals. After two or three repeat crimes, the press would coin them a nickname.

He picked apart their operational methods, dissecting every known fact. There was never any forensic evidence. No witnesses, except in the case of the Stalker, he'd been seen looking in the windows of lone women in the dead of night. He dressed all in black, wearing a matching ski mask. Aside from his build, they did not have anything else to go on. No one had seen his face.

A burglar called the Midnight Man, and a rapist christened The Gasman. He admonished himself for thinking of them by their Press nicknames; he hated the way the press did that. It sensationalised their low lives, giving them a kind of infamy and glory in which to bask.

In trying to live up to their images, these people sometimes actually increased their activities and whilst inevitably most would get careless and then caught, there was something different about these particular characters and the way they continued to evade the law. There was a link between the Stalker and the other two. He just knew it. Ordinarily he wouldn't have been interested in a stalker at all, but he felt that if he could catch him, he'd get a lead on the others.

In the end, he concluded that the only way to do it was to catch them red-handed.

For now, they seemed just too clever for that.

Chapter 38

Friday 24 November 2006

Kennedy thought about the woman he'd spent Wednesday night with, and smiled. He'd have preferred to spend another night with her. Instead, at Tanner's insistence, he was out belatedly celebrating his birthday with a dozen work colleagues.

He'd tried to call it off earlier in the week. Tanner wouldn't hear of it. 'Come on, sir. It'll do you good.'

'You're only so keen, Tanner, because you think you can inveigle Theresa along.'

'Sir, I have no interest in her whatsoever, I swear.'

The night turned into a pub-crawl. Of the original group, only he and Tanner remained, lurching through the half-lit back streets of Covent Garden.

Even when drunk, he always kept well clear of darkened doorways.

'Y'know, Tanner, one of the first things learnt, learned?' he hesitated. 'Whichever, by me in the force...on the beat. On patrol, Tanner was to be wary in the streets and who could be hiding in the doorways. Walk in the middle, that's the best thing,' he said, almost walking into a cast iron bollard. 'The fuck, did that?'

Tanner grinned as he manoeuvred around it on legs that no longer obeyed him. Although he knew he should get him home, he was enjoying the spectacle Kennedy was making of himself.

They stopped. Kennedy perched his buttocks uncomfortably on top of the bollard and mumbled something about calling a taxi.

Tanner cocked his head, theatrically making a point of listening to the steady, muffled hum of a hundred people talking all at once. It was a human beehive.

Kennedy extricated himself from his temporary seat, steadied himself and shuffled to the doorway closely marked by Tanner. Drawn like moths to a flame, they hovered outside the pub.

'Sounds busy in there tonight,' Kennedy remarked. 'Let's have one *last,* one more for the road, eh?' He opened the door; it released a blast of sound that made both of them wince. They walked inside.

Kennedy shouted above the noise, 'I always said I'd retire when I reached fifty.' Despite having nearly seven years to go, Kennedy said it as if he were fifty already, as if he were leaving the next day. 'Before I go, I want to make a big effort to solve all the unsolved crime that happened during my watch. No, not all of it, one in particular and I'm not going to leave it until the last minute either.'

Tanner opened his mouth to speak, but the effect of a few drinks delayed the activation of his vocal chords.

Kennedy was in the same boat, only a little quicker. 'After tonight... no, no don't interrupt, I'm serious here. After tonight, I'm going to have those files on my desk, tomorrow, no, Monday morning. I'm going to start putting them to bed, starting with them.' He snapped his fingers several times, prompting his memory. 'The old one... Yes, that one!?' The words petered out as he struggled to remember what it was he was talking about; he froze in position at the bar, exhausted of the last of his energy. Deep in a haze, he lost himself in the fug of smoke that hung in the garish yellow light. The sounds of the bar no longer clear, his head felt as if it were underwater.

Tanner had never seen the DCI so drunk before. Frowning concern and measuring his words carefully, he said, 'Do you want me to get us a cab, sir?'

Kennedy's bluff face was expressionless as his eyes struggled to focus on the last drop of amber fluid in his glass, debating whether to finish it.

'Ah, the hell with it!' He tipped his head right back as he drained the glass, banging it down harder than he intended; he slapped his colleague's back heavily, jarring Tanner's head forward. 'Let's go, Tanner!'

The following morning Kennedy couldn't remember much, other than talking about solving old crimes. Something concerned him about what he might have told Tanner. He couldn't hold the drink the way he used to, he hoped it hadn't loosened his tongue too much. A few times earlier in the evening, he had been tempted to talk. The temptation to regale your friends with tales of derring-do and close encounters of every kind never leaves a man, especially when he is in drink, and in the company of people he thinks he can trust. Even the greatest indiscretions can seem trivial in an alcoholic haze, when the need to bare your soul comes creeping up unexpectedly.

He pinched the bridge of his nose, unable to remember, but Tanner, he wasn't sure about him anymore. A couple of times while he was still sober, he caught a look on that thin face of his, he'd made a few remarks that seemed he might be resentful of his promotion.

Kennedy rose from his chair, grabbed his jacket off the back and called it a day.

When Monday came around, Kennedy did what he said he would; he picked up the phone and spoke to a television reporter contact he had, explaining he wanted to broadcast a cold case appeal on Crimewatch for information on a girl who had disappeared in 1983.

Later in the afternoon, Kennedy received a call about the programme.

He outlined the case in detail, sprinkling in for good measure the suspicion that the perpetrator had probably been responsible for other crimes – they usually can't just do it once and stop – and that by getting further leads, in conjunction with modern technology, there was an even better chance that any leads received, could result in solving this crime. Then he played his trump card. 'And you know what else? It would be especially good because your program first aired the case during its launch year.' Kennedy moved the telephone from one shoulder to the other. 'You didn't know that? Well, now you do,' he said, shifting the handset as the conversation concluded. 'Okay, let me know what they say.'

Five minutes later, his phone rang. The show would run the appeal.

Chapter 39

19 December 2006. Crimewatch.

Kennedy felt that if he could get the missing girl's sister to appear, there would be a better chance of a positive result. She agreed to do it only if they filmed her blacked out; she didn't want people pointing at her in the street, or coming up to her. Her mother had told her to be careful about media exposure. *When you put yourself on a platform, you open all kinds of doors for people. Most have genuine intentions, but you have to be careful.* Her mother had had a couple of unpleasant experiences, unwelcome attention and things like that.

His appearance was just before hers. He'd passed her in the corridor earlier, and she'd smiled and thanked him for all his hard work.

I wonder if you'd have said that to me if you knew I could have saved your sister, and if I'd done that, maybe your parents wouldn't have killed themselves.

He couldn't bring himself to tell her. Besides, when it was his turn to face the cameras, she'd find out anyway. At that point, he realised he hadn't thought it through properly; he should have asked Tanner to lead the appeal. The burgeoning rivalry between them had clouded his judgement. Tanner thought he'd been favoured with the DCI's job over him because of his father's influence, and he knew he'd have to field some awkward questions from him once he realised.

Kennedy knew he should have told him about the case years ago, after all; he'd told him about all his successes. But then, you don't crow about failure.

The presenter finished summarising the last case and then introduced the next one.

'This next case is about the disappearance of a young girl just over twenty-three years ago. She was last seen walking home after a Dire Straits concert. Described as 5'6' tall, Kathy had shoulder length black hair and blue eyes. She'd gone out straight from work and was last seen wearing her nurse's uniform. She was also wearing large silver hoop earrings, a small silver cross on a chain and a St. Christopher medal.'

The reconstruction began by showing posters of the Dire Straits concert that night, the cameras panned across hundreds of people queuing outside, showing the local pubs packed with concertgoers. A young, dark-haired girl sipped at her drink, dressed in a crisp new nurse's uniform similar to the one Kathy had worn that fateful night. The narrator was speaking. '*Kathy had a change of clothes with her when she left for work that morning. It is thought she lost or mislaid them. Her mother said at the time, 'There was no way she'd go out socialising in her uniform.'*

The show portrayed her as a young girl enjoying a night out, meeting up with friends at the show, drinking, laughing and becoming louder as the evening progressed. Then they showed her looking confused after losing her friends. They used actors to portray her friends talking about Kathy, how although she'd had a lot to drink, she was all right until someone gave her something.

'I saw this guy give her a joint, and she lit it. They argued about something; he tried to make her stop with the smoking; I think he was scared they'd be thrown out. She wouldn't listen. One minute she was there and the next she's gone. It was just before the end of the show; the band was doing their encore.'

The re-enactment then showed two police officers walking down a typical affluent North London street. They noticed a man and a woman, at first it appeared they were arguing, she was clearly worse for wear, and as the officers approached to check up on her, a call to a domestic disturbance came in. It was two hundred yards away. The older one tapped his colleague and said, 'Let's go!'

The other officer said, 'You go on ahead; I'll catch up with you.' The woman almost stumbled over; the man caught her by the arm and pulled her upright. She was giggly and seemed happy enough, but something about their body language had bothered him. He started walking over to them calling back to his colleague. 'I'll be right with you; I just want to make sure she's all right!'

The older one hesitated, weighing up the situation. 'Okay, but be quick,' he said, as he took off down the street.

The actor playing the young officer approached the couple.

The narrator cut in. 'We have in the studio with us tonight, the officer who approached the couple that night, he is still with the force, now a DCI.' He swung round to face the detective who'd had his features fuzzed out with a blurry disc.

'DCI Kennedy, I understand you were the young officer who spoke to Kathy that night. Can you tell us in your own words, what you recall?'

The more astute viewer might have thought it odd that they named him, but concealed his face. Kennedy himself had insisted on that, citing a delicate case he was currently working on.

'As I approached, I thought the man who was with her looked a little out of place, too old for her. I thought he'd probably just stopped to try to help her. When I got closer, I realised she appeared to know him; she kept calling out his name, 'Michael!' Like that, repeating his name two, maybe three times. She didn't sound distressed, quite the opposite really. A happy drunk.' He'd spoken at length after that, but when the show went out, they'd cut to the actor playing him that night. The officer had said, 'Are you all right, miss, do you know this man?'

'Ish Michael,' the girl playing Kathy said.

The officer looked hard at the other man's face; there was bruising around the eye and dried blood in the corner of his mouth.

Kennedy's original narration picked it up from there. 'I noticed he'd clearly been in a fight. I asked him how he knew the young woman in question, at this point I could hear raised voices coming from the other end of the street where my colleague was. Michael said he was a porter. *"I'm at the same hospital she works for."*

The reconstruction cut in for the last time with loud and aggressive shouting coming from the disturbance his colleague was attending and showed the young policeman telling Michael to look after her as he turned and ran down to help his colleague.

Subsequent investigations revealed no one matching that name or description was employed at the hospital where she worked.'

Kathy's sister was speaking, filmed in silhouette.

'I never met my sister. I was born after she disappeared, but thanks to my parents, I have a strong sense of having known her and what she was like.'

She talked about the disappearance being so out of character; she'd just started a new job, which she loved. 'That was all she wanted to be from when she was a little girl,' she said. 'Sadly, our parents are no longer with us or they would have made this appeal. They worked tirelessly towards finding out what happened to Kathy that night, they never…' her voice betrayed her emotions and trailed as her thoughts drifted. She quickly regained control. 'If there's anyone out there that knows what happened to her or knows anything at all, please call.'

The presenter summarised. 'Were you at that Dire Straits concert that night? Perhaps you saw Kathy. Does anyone recognise the man who gave Kathy the marijuana cigarette? Can you remember seeing her outside? Did you see Kathy with this man getting into a car after the officer was called away?'

Photo-fits of the man as he looked then appeared on the screen, followed by a digitally aged photograph showing how he might look today.

'Do you know this man? Does anybody recall the fight in the pub that night? Has anybody seen or heard of Kathy since that night? If you know of her whereabouts or what happened to her, we want to hear from you. Please call the incident room number on your screen. DCI Kendricks and his team are waiting for your calls.'

The show also covered an armed robbery on a jeweller's shop, an aggravated burglary, an appeal for information about a fifteen-year-old runaway girl thought to be living rough in the London or Essex area. DCI Kendricks also put in an appearance, appealing for help in solving a rape and attempted murder case.

The filming completed without a hitch, but when they broadcast the programme later, there was a problem with the editing. They'd mixed up the cases and the detectives who were dealing with them. Kennedy's name and contact telephone number were allocated to the rape case, and Kendricks' details to the Kathy Bird disappearance.

Apart from the mix up with the cases and the phone numbers, the show had gone remarkably well. They corrected the numbers in a bulletin at the end of the show.

When Kennedy watched a re-run of the programme – at the point immediately after they gave his contact details, he heard something in the background. Rewinding, he played it again. With the volume right up, someone could be heard speaking faintly in the background, something unintelligible and then quite suddenly and barely audible, *These people are vile*. Said off camera, it had cut in right after the piece by Kennedy. It *sounded* like him, but he knew the voice wasn't his; it only took a moment to figure out.

Kendricks said it!

Nobody else seemed to notice.

It wasn't right. He debated whether to complain about it. The comment was irrelevant, but Kendricks shouldn't have said it. He'd have words with him in the morning. He imagined himself talking to John senior about it. *Anyone can make a mistake, John, but if you feel that strongly about it...*

He thought about his father, and it took him back twenty-three years, to just after the news that he'd been the last person to see Kathy alive. John senior had picked it apart for him.

'She said she knew him; you had no reason to 'call it in'. They called you out to attend a disturbance; you did what you had to do. It was a million to one chance, something like that happening; you can't feel guilty about it. Everything you did was right. It isn't as if you knew he'd kidnap her, is it?'

'I should have known. I should have had a gut instinct.'

John senior had laid a reassuring hand on him. *'Those gut instincts take time and experience to recognise. You did nothing wrong.'*

Maybe, Dad, but it still haunts me.

Compared to the mistakes he'd made twenty-three years ago, the production errors paled into insignificance. By taking it no further, he set in motion a chain of events he couldn't possibly have foreseen. When he looked back later at the pivotal events around which everything turned, he'd realise the editors and their cutting room mistake, had started a lunatic off on his trail.

Chapter 40

Tina Solomons heard the front door open. She turned the television volume down and listened intently.

'Mum, is that you?'

There was no reply.

Tina swung both legs out from underneath her on the sofa. She was half way across the lounge before she heard the rustling of shopping bags. It was her mum.

She sighed with relief.

At the other end of the hall, Jackie Solomons heaved the last of the shopping bags in, and turning, back-heeled the front door closed. She leaned against it for a moment with her eyes closed. She could have slept there and then she was so tired. As Tina watched her, she suddenly sprang back to life. The few seconds rest had allowed her to snap out of it. *Come on girl!* She started putting the bags away.

'Don't look, Tina!' she called out. 'Most of these are for you.' It was almost Christmas. Tina smiled. The only time of the year, her mum was truly happy.

Half an hour later, after Jackie had showered, she entered the room dressed in a black silk kimono, her long dark hair tied back. From behind, she could almost have passed for a Japanese lady. She was carrying a plate with a couple of sandwiches on it. 'Want one?' she said, offering them to Tina.

'No, I'm all right, Mum – I had something earlier.'

'What's that you're watching?' Tina quickly switched the channel over.

'No, wait – go back a sec.'

After what happened to her, she never watched programmes like Crimewatch. She always felt that whilst the programme did a lot of good in respect of helping to solve crime and catch criminals, a lot of the viewers came from the same mould as people that craned their necks round to have a good look when they passed a road crash, human vultures flicking through the channels, looking for someone else's misery to feed on. It was part of the reason she didn't like Tina watching it.

The photograph had her hooked; caught on screen in the moment it took Tina to change the channel. 'Go back!' Jackie said.

The girl had reminded her of someone.

'Mum, it's *Crimewatch!*' Tina said.

'Put it back on. I want to see.'

When Tina switched it back over, the girl had gone, but Jackie had seen enough of her to register. *She looked like me.*

Jackie should have just walked away, but her curiosity was aroused.

'Who was that girl, Tina?'

'She's someone who's gone missing from near here.'

'Oh, Jesus – no!' Jackie's hands flew to her cheeks, partly shielding her eyes.

'It's okay, Mum, you don't have to worry. It's a cold case. It happened over twenty years ago.'

After that, Jackie knew for sure she should have gone to watch TV in the other room, but the preview, the glimpse of a girl who looked like her, kept her watching the whole programme and in doing so, started her remembering things she'd spent years trying to forget. It seemed she was destined to watch it tonight.

Such a long time ago. What was it, sixteen years? Since then she'd lost two children; married, had another child, lost a husband and built a thriving business.

The programme made compulsive viewing.

She found herself experiencing a rising level of discomfort after each case. She kept telling herself to turn the channel over, but she didn't want to miss the reconstruction of what happened to the girl in the photograph. She kept watching. The next case was a reconstruction so similar to what had happened to her; it triggered a whole series of recollections she'd not thought of for years. She couldn't take her eyes off the screen.

Although they showed the part using an actress, the interviewer spoke to the victim herself. She had waived her right to anonymity. She admired the bravery of the woman. It wasn't something she could ever do herself.

Her situation was different, best left in the past. Once the programme was over, she would re-submerge the memories. She knew she'd have a spate of nightmares for weeks. The same thing happened the last time she thought about her ordeal. After a while, they would occur only occasionally. It was partly why she kept a prescription of sleeping tablets in the bathroom cabinet; they helped to suppress her nightmares. *Don't have nightmares; do sleep well.*

Jackie knew she'd be taking an extra one tonight.

The programme had ended; she'd gone right through the missing girl case, without taking any of it in.

What she'd wanted to see, she'd missed. What she'd avoided for years was in her thoughts again.

Fate has a way of catching up to you. She didn't know who said it, but she was beginning to believe they were right. No matter how high the walls she built to hide behind, she was still afraid in the quiet of the night, still afraid of walking alone in wide-open fields and still wary of strangers.

What that woman did, brought her to the brink of confronting her own demons. She wondered if one day she might find the courage to pick up the phone, dial the number and say, '*I've just seen your programme, and I'd like to go on air to talk about what happened to me, because there's a chance it might help someone else who is going through the same thing, and also because I'd like the chance to purge myself of guilt by standing in the studio on television, in front of millions of viewers to say, 'Look it's me, Jackie Solomons; what happened to me wasn't my fault, and I shouldn't be ashamed!''*

She felt strangely empowered just by playing the role in her head.

Her attacker was probably in his fifties back then, which meant he'd be at least in his seventies now. The realisation made her feel physically safer than she had for a long time.

It put a different perspective on it all. She didn't feel afraid anymore, but it also reminded her *why* she could never do what that woman did; she was hampered by a secret. Something she'd judged best kept from her daughter. Oh, she knew about the little stillborn brother that came and went before her, but Jackie had never told her about the rape or the older sister she would have had if she hadn't given her up for adoption because the rapist made her pregnant.

She wondered what had become of her.

She never told Tina, because she was too young. It was just too big, too ugly a truth to tell. Now she was older; she still couldn't tell her.

As her thoughts shifted away from herself, parts of the reconstruction she'd just seen came back to her. *Missing for twenty-three years? She's dead.* Jackie was back to thinking about herself again. She might have gone missing too, if it hadn't been for her friends.

'What's up, Mum, you look upset – is it the programme? I'll turn it off.'

Jackie turned away from the screen to face her daughter, managing a thin, tired smile. 'It's nothing, love; I was just miles away thinking about that poor kid's parents, that's all.'

She picked up her plate; most of the sandwich remained.

'I'm off to bed, night, love.' At the door, she turned and blew her a kiss with her free hand.

'Night, Mum.' Tina watched her go.

Wide-eyed with weariness, even without make-up, she looked like Cleopatra. With her long dark hair tied back, she looked a little plump in her silk pyjamas, but still a very attractive woman. She couldn't help thinking how lucky she was that her mum was so pretty. It meant there was a fair chance that she would be when she reached her age. She smiled at the adage: *If you want to know what your girlfriend will look like in twenty years' time, look at their mum!*

Tina knew her mum was keeping something from her; she also knew she'd tell her one day when she was ready.

Lying in bed, waiting for sleep to come, Jackie thought about how she lost her father in 1979, killed in a car smash when she was four years old. He set off for work, and he never came home. It triggered a separation anxiety in her; that she'd struggle to cope with all her life.

Jackie drifted into thinking about the letters her mum and dad had written to each other. She'd found them in the loft, taped up in the same box where they'd been placed when the house was cleared after her father died. They'd lain together, in unsorted neat little stacks of pink and pale blue envelopes tied with thin and faded ribbons. She'd untied a pink one. A trace of perfume so faint it couldn't have been more than a few molecules, triggered an image of her mother in her favourite summer dress, standing against the light shining in from outside, her outline unmistakable, her face partly obscured, dark hair tied up the way she liked to wear it in summer, clear of her face, with the exception of a few loose tendrils deliberately left hanging down in front of each ear.

She'd unfolded them one by one, never imagining her father to be sentimental in any way at all. Reading the letters exchanged between them, she had realised she was wrong. Her father had been a sensitive soul. Sometime later, she'd sorted them into date order from start to finish. Different hands, different inks. Thoughts, dreams, love shared, lying side by side, folded up together like paper ghosts, echoes of lives gone by.

Sealing them back together, her eyes had filled with tears at the things she couldn't change.

Chapter 41

In the Midlands, a stranger watched the programme in his hotel room. He remembered the events of that night better than anybody else.

Whenever he could, wherever he was, he always tried to catch Crimewatch. He loved to see the clues the stupid criminals left behind. They were as good as caught.

The case Kennedy outlined reminded him of the 'Cornish Girl' as he'd come to call her; she was very much a part of a fantasy he'd played out over the years. What he would do, if he ever came across *her* again. The thought started in his head and spread to his loins.

He could see only the outline of the sister speaking from the shadows, captured in the contrast between light and darkness, she turned slightly; the shape of her face astounded him. Unmistakably female in profile, her dark bee-stung lips curved out and away as if she pouted especially for him. He whistled softly in appreciation, in anticipation of what she'd be like in the flesh. He decided he would find her. It wouldn't be difficult; he already had so much information to work with. As his dark fantasies unfolded, he caught a comment made in the background; his condition meant his ears were extra sensitive, more able to analyse speech patterns to perfection. His memory was second to none, with total recall, although he struggled with his own voice; he could replicate those of others with ease. He was born with a stutter and much like those who can sing beautifully with no trace of their impediment, he could do the same, imitating voices, using them instead of his own. His favourite was Clint Eastwood. Rewinding the sound in his head, he deciphered what someone off camera had said: *These people are vile.*

He growled as he slammed his fist into the wall with a dull thud that shook the partition so hard; it stopped the couple next-door mid-stroke in their lovemaking. He stared at the three bloody flaps of folded back skin on his knuckles.

Who the hell does he think he is, to judge me? You're going to pay for that Kennedy. You've made it personal now.

He sucked the blood from them and cursed him as he lay back on the bed, recalling the nurse as she was then, how he'd looked over at her as he left the stupid Irishman on the floor, how she smiled nervously at him, her dark eyes shining, so pretty in her uniform, dark hair tumbling down; she was so full of life back then.

He remembered how he'd hung around outside in a doorway, following her when she came out, trailing her all the way to the Dire Straits concert. As he tailed her in, he'd grabbed a ticket off a tout and scowling aggressively, had given him a five-pound note. The tout opened his mouth to protest, but then thought better of it, and pocketed the money.

He spent the rest of the evening, keeping her under close observation from the fringes.

At first, dancing at times with her arms up above her head, she reminded him of a Spanish gipsy girl with castanets. Later, losing herself to the sound, she'd let herself go, swaying and pumping along to the music. She hadn't known he was there, watching. After the ride home, they'd become *acquainted* with each other.

He touched himself and found he was hard.

The benefits of a good memory.

When he'd finished, he had the bones of an idea in his head. These people are vile. He'd make Kennedy eat those words. First, he would find the runaway; then he'd get the sister, and after that, he'd put the bite on Kennedy.

Chapter 42

After the Crimewatch interview, Stella felt oddly detached. She'd worried beforehand that she might not get through it without crumbling. She needn't have concerned herself; she dealt with it as she did everything else, from behind a shield that protected her, hiding her true thoughts and feelings. *Nothing can touch me here.*

She watched the show that night in the privacy of her own home. With no need for shields, she felt the old pain rising up in her, seeping out through the gaps in the wounds the last few days had re-opened. She tried in vain to seal them back up, but the floodgates had opened too far, she gave up resisting and began to cry so hard she thought she'd never be able to stop.

The release lasted a few minutes; a sense of balance returned to her and with it a vague feeling of disappointment at her lack of control. There was no point to it. Nothing would change. The well of grief would be emptied, but she knew it would just fill up again. Better to keep it in for when she was strong enough, for when she'd be able to grieve properly without having the fear she would never be able to stop.

She sat in the light of the small oriel window on its wide, triangular windowsill, the unread letter in her hand. There was no need to read it, she knew what it would say, and she understood it, in a way. She didn't need more words to twist into wounds that would never heal.

The belief her parents had clung to, was one day soon their beautiful long-lost daughter would just walk in the door as if nothing had happened, with an explanation that would make everything all right. *I got drunk* – this much they knew, she was seen by a policeman in the company of a man who'd never come forward. *I fell over and banged my head. I couldn't remember who I was. I met this guy; fell for him, head over heels. We left for Australia the next morning. I was always thinking – I'll remember who I am tomorrow and then tomorrow turned into next week, next month or next year, and this is your new baby grandson, by the way.*

When that didn't happen, there was always another plausible excuse. She'd heard them all. As time passed, her parents had stumbled and faltered. They lost the blind faith that had previously hauled them through.

Stella grew up in the shadow of someone she was too young to remember, someone she knew only from photographs. Sometimes, she'd examine the face in the portrait they'd had blown up to hang over the mantelpiece in the middle of the lounge. It was their favourite picture of her, smiling for the camera outside in the sunshine, in her crisp new uniform, in front of the holly bush in the back garden.

Twenty-three years ago had passed, and the colours had faded. It was getting harder to make out her features. She'd been absent from their lives, longer than she'd been in them.

Could you learn to miss someone you had never known?

She missed her for her parent's sake, but not the way they did. How could she?

She knew, or at least she thought she knew, what it must have been like for them, but to have waited that long and then given up… It made no sense.

She pursed her lips, deep in contemplation.

They might just have hung on for her to be old enough to fend for herself, but that made no sense either. If they'd loved her enough to do that – then surely they'd loved her enough to carry on. Maybe they just didn't love her as much as they missed her sister.

Stella found herself wondering what would have happened if Kathy had walked through the door the next day, the way they'd always believed she would. *What would happen then? What would I tell her?*

None of it made any sense.

She almost didn't go through with it, but she was thinking of herself, *she* wanted closure.

And what if she did come walking through that door, as a direct result of the appeal? She was as surprised as anyone was when she'd been told her parents died in an apparent suicide pact.

Her mother was a vet; they'd injected themselves with enough horse tranquillisers to stop an elephant.

She wasn't convinced her dad would have gone along with it entirely of his own free will.

The letter had arrived two days after they died. She didn't open it. There could be no explanation or justification.

She informed the police.

'You haven't opened it?' The policewoman said.

'No. There's nothing inside for me,' she said without emotion. The officer dipped down to look up into her downcast eyes. 'Would you like me to call someone?'

'No, I'm okay. I'll be fine. Go ahead and open it, or take it for evidence, or whatever.'

The officer opened it; the contents confirmed what they already knew; it was suicide, but there was an explanation.

The policewoman offered the letter to her. She declined.

'Leave it there.' Stella pointed to the mantelpiece.

'Would you like me to read it to you?' The policewoman asked gently.

'No, I know what they did,' her voice had risen, filled with bitterness. 'I know you're trying to help, but no. Thank you. Leave it there.'

They left me behind. That's what they did.

She stared at the pills in her hand, at the glass of vodka in the other.

'Probably shouldn't do this,' she said to herself, then cupped her hand to her mouth and swallowed. She took a swig out of the glass and shuddered, the neat alcohol contorting her face.

If those paracetamol don't shift this headache, it'll be because you mixed them with vodka. Hell, yeah!

Stella poured herself another, took a deep breath and slid her fingers into the envelope to pull out the letter. Drawing it almost all the way out, she stopped and crumpled the whole thing into a ball. She walked to the pedal bin and threw it away.

Chapter 43

Tanner rubbed his eyes wearily. It wasn't that late, but the accumulation of working long hours had started to get to him. He hadn't seen the programme, but still volunteered to take any interesting calls that might come in because of it.

Although the appeal generated a handful of telephone calls straight after the programme, only one of them had any promise.

A taxi driver recalled passing a couple who could be a match. She was very drunk, dressed in a nurse uniform – he assumed she'd come from a fancy dress party that he'd already picked up two lots of people from. A man was trying to get her into a silver Ford Cortina. He remembered it well because after he'd driven past, a fight broke out at the party, and his windscreen got broken by a flying champagne bottle.

'Can you tell me anything else about what you saw, could you describe the man?' Tanner knew it was a long shot. After all these years, it seemed stupid to ask.

'No mate, not after all this time. I'm sure it was her though, dressed in her uniform. It's got to be, right?'

A silver Ford Cortina – It couldn't have been a rare kit car they could have easily traced, could it.

The lines had gone quiet; nothing had come in for over an hour. Checking his watch, he decided give it another thirty minutes before going home.

With just a few more minutes of his self-imposed deadline to go, his telephone rang again.

'Tanner,' he said wearily.

'*Switchboard* – I have a caller from Dublin regarding the Crimewatch case; he thinks he might be able to help.'

'*Dublin?* Okay, put him through.'

'Detective Inspector Tanner speaking, can I have your name?'

The Dubliner answered with a deep, soft-spoken voice. 'It's Jack Doherty, some people call me 'One Eyed Jack', but only once to me face,' he said with a chuckle, and then pulled himself up short, remembering the gravity of the case.

'I don't suppose this means anything now. I never knew the girl was missing, but I remember her from that night. I'd seen her earlier at the pub, so pretty that young thing, in her nurse's uniform. When the photograph came up, I said to myself, that's her! Anyway, there was this bloke – see, we got into a fight. He half killed me; I lost an eye, so I did, was in the hospital for six weeks and when I came out, I slouched back to Ireland. Couldn't work, see? Anyway, the thing is, when he knocked me down to me knees that last time; I saw he's wearing this belt with a skull and crossbones buckle. I'll never forget it. See, I thought he was a bit old to be wearing something like that. He was in his fifties I reckon, but here's the other thing, he was a fighter, not much doubt about that, you don't get to be that fit if you don't fight regular. I mean he was thirty years older, but sharper than I was! I reckon somebody would have known a bloke like that on the circuits; you know – the bare-knuckle ones, travellers' fairs, and that—'

Tanner interrupted. 'What makes you think it's the same man?'

'The photo fit is an excellent likeness, but also the constable said he'd been in a fight, had some damage round the eye and mouth. The mouth was already like it when I saw him, something about that mouth... I know it in my water – it's him!' Then he added darkly, 'He's probably dead by now anyway, but if it was him that did for that girl – and for what he done to my eye – I hope he rots in hell!'

'If you saw him again, do you think you could identify him?'

'No doubt about it, none at all. He was...how can I put it? Unusual looking, like the man was crossed with a pit bull terrier.' Tanner looked at the E-Fit, trying to make sense of what Doherty had just said.

'Are you being serious? You said the photo was an excellent likeness.'

'Well so it is, but they don't have the lips right, there's something about the mouth.' By now, Tanner had the idea that the man's mouth could be a distinguishing feature – if they could get that right.

'Would you be prepared to help us adjust the photo?'

'Well, I'll try, but I don't know where you'd find another mouth that looks like his.' Tanner didn't bother to tell him about the advances in technology that would make the creation of a better likeness possible, but took his contact details, name, address and telephone number. 'Listen, Jack, thank you for your call, we're going to need to talk to you again.'

He immediately started through the files, the evidence the constable provided at the time. His description covered almost everything, right down to the skull belt buckle. He felt it was so unusual he'd even drawn a sketch of it. It was a screaming skull variant inside a wreath of laurels on top of the crossed bones. Something in Tanner's waters told him it had to be the same guy.

Impressed with the impeccability of the young PC's report, he looked for his name.

He couldn't quite believe he'd missed it the first time round. It was almost as interesting as the report itself.

The son of a gun! Why didn't he tell me about it?

The constable's name was John Kennedy.

Chapter 44

The following morning, Tanner walked right into Kennedy's office without knocking and sat down.

'Oh, *do* come in,' he said irritably. 'What's on your mind?'

'You never told me *you* were the copper on the beat that night.'

'It's always been on file, I thought you knew.' He reinforced the lie by shaking his head in disbelief.

'You led me to believe it just *happened* on your watch, you even said that the other night.' His deputy was gearing up for an attack. He'd seen it before. His father had warned him to avoid close friendships at work, and this was one of the reasons. It made it too easy for lines to get crossed.

Kennedy glared at him. 'It did happen on my watch.'

'Listen, you said—'

'Look, let me explain. I was little more than a kid and I wasn't feeling too clever about coming that close to our number one suspect and then letting him go. It *did* happen on my watch.' He'd taken some of the wind from Tanner's sails.

'It didn't stand in the way of any promotions though, did it?' Although his eyes burned with suppressed anger, he immediately regretted the comment. He sighed deeply and then said, 'I just think you could have told me before.'

Kennedy was surprisingly calm. 'So that's what this is all about, is it? You think I got this promotion because my father was in charge ten years ago? We're friends, but at work, don't you *dare* cross the line with me,' he said in clipped tones, barely in control of his temper. 'Is that clear?' His fist slammed down hard onto the desktop. The emphasis stopped Tanner's words at his lips. He stuttered, and then stalled.

The DCI stood and walked to the door, holding it open. 'Let me know if anything *relevant* turns up.'

Tanner spun on his heel and left.

Kennedy closed the venetian blinds, returned to his chair and, leaning back, stared at the ceiling. *I never agreed with you on a lot of things, Dad, but you were right about friends and business. Keep 'em apart.*

Chapter 45

Kennedy drifted back; he recalled the effect Kathy's disappearance had had on him. He seemed to have spent every single hour of his off-duty time canvassing passers-by. His persistence seemed to have paid off when he stopped a man in his twenties, who recognised her from the photograph he showed him. He'd been at the Dire Straits concert that night, and he remembered seeing her.

'Yeah, I saw her; in the foyer, she was wasted. I thought it was, well, I thought she was just drunk until I saw this guy pass her a doobie.' He made a furtive gesture towards Kennedy with his hand cupped. Kennedy almost held his hand out to receive the imagined offering. 'He palmed her twice, the second time it was a pill. I know that 'cos she dropped it on the floor, and he shot down really quick to pick it up before someone else swooped on it. He gave it back to her, and she popped it straight away, I remember thinking, *boy, she's keen*. She put the joint in her mouth, but never lit it as far as I could see. The guy leaves her. He didn't take any money from her; you know. I think he was hoping to score off *her* later, or maybe he knew her, I don't know, then he goes over and does a deal with someone else. I only took my eyes off her for a minute, but when I looked back, she was gone.'

'Would you recognise him, if you saw him again?'

'I can do better than that; I used to see him at the youth centre. I'm sure the guy's name was Hutchins. Gary Hutchins.'

He followed the lead, getting no further with the dealer until he threatened to have him busted right there and then. Nervously pushing his long blonde hair back from his face, Hutchins' complexion had paled. Kennedy gambled he was probably carrying, and he was right.

'What do you want from me?' he said, licking his lips nervously.

'You were seen handing Kathy a pill, what was it?'

'It was an aspirin… No wait what are you doing?'

Radio in hand, he said, 'I'm calling the Drugs squad.'

'No, no, wait. It *was* an aspirin, but dipped in acid.'

'You gave her an aspirin dipped in LSD?'

'It was two, actually; she asked if I had anything for a headache.'

Kennedy made no effort to conceal his disgust. 'Did she know what it was?'

'I don't know,' he said, half shrugging, 'but she knows what I'm like.'

Later that night, Kennedy arranged for a raid on Hutchins.

He tried everything, and although he couldn't consciously remember the registration of the car he and the taxi driver had seen; he'd heard it was possible under hypnosis to recall such details. A specialist tried to regress him, but without any success.

He concluded she was dead, or she didn't want to be found. He considered the impact two doses of LSD could have had on her. It was clear from a subsequent interview that Hutchins made no real effort to control the amount of LSD put on each tablet, he'd simply used an old ear dropper. Kennedy consulted experts, but their opinions were divided. There were just too many unknown variables.

Further investigations revealed Hutchins was responsible for any number of bad trips with the users ending up in hospital. He eventually spent four years in jail for drugs offences.

He remembered Kathy's parents, how they'd been in denial. *'She never took drugs!'* her mother said hotly, and her father agreed, nodding vehemently.

They continued to campaign tirelessly, putting up posters in shop windows, stopping to ask people questions in the street, for years. Eventually, shops refused to allow them to keep their posters up anymore, explaining; *it isn't good for business.*

At Kennedy's intervention, they'd managed to keep the official 'Missing' poster at the station for longer than usual, and beyond that, they kept one on display in the vets where her mother worked and another facing out onto the street from the window of their home.

In the end, it proved too much for them.

It was as if she'd disappeared off the face of the earth.

DCI Kennedy parted a couple of slats in the blind with his fingers and looked out over the office from the observation panel. *The one blot in my career copybook.* That he was unable to rectify it irked him. He suddenly thought about the guilty pleasures he enjoyed with Marilyn. *If that were ever to get out...* He nailed the thought. After all, he wasn't hurting anyone and as long as he kept it to himself, that was how it would stay.

Chapter 46

4 January 2007

Tanner rang the number the Irishman had given him, someone else answered; he gave him another number to try. He left a host of messages for Doherty to call him. He proved to be a hard man to pin down, it transpired he was in London visiting relatives over Christmas, and he'd left his mobile phone in Dublin. In the New Year, he finally received the message. He was still in the capital. Tanner arranged for him to attend the station for an interview.

When Kennedy met Jack Doherty at reception, he cut an imposing figure. At least two metres tall and very heavily built; his head was larger in proportion to his size than might have been expected. Kennedy couldn't help wondering if the smaller man had felled him with a headshot. The other man's hand engulfed the DCI's as they shook. He led him down to the interview room, where Tanner joined them.

Doherty was clearly not overly concerned with cosmetic appearances; he wore a large black patch over his missing eye. It reminded him of the cup from one of Marilyn's bras.

When all three had sat down, the big man insisted on giving them some background on himself, the sort of man he was, how he'd been looking for a bit of 'sport' as he called it that night. Jack described his opponent and the fight at length, and how he remembered the girl he'd since learned was Kathy in the pub. He never showed any emotion; his voice was low and flat, difficult to understand at times and there was a kind of sadness in his broad potato face. From what he'd said about himself at first, it was clear the experience had changed him, perhaps he was thinking about the girl, perhaps mourning the loss of his eye, or a combination of both.

'What makes you think you'll be able to give sufficient details to the technician after so many years, Jack?'

'Do you not think I'd remember the man that did this to me?' he said, fixing Kennedy with a look, and then he reached under the eye-patch and lifted it, exposing the stitched shut and sunken eyelid. 'And there's something else, let me tell you. When you fight a man, you don't watch his hands, you watch his face.'

Kennedy acknowledged what he said. It was a perfect example of 'Flashbulb' memory, where the effects of a traumatic event burned themselves into the brain in fine, recollectable detail.

Later, when he saw the results of Doherty's work with the E-Fit operator, he was certain that the man did indeed possess such powers of recall.

It triggered instant recognition for Kennedy. It was 'Michael,' no doubt about that in his mind. With Doherty's positive ID of Kathy's photograph: *'I'll never forget her face; it was all I could do to stop myself crashing into her.'* It meant they were in the same pub. It was all too much to be just coincidence. The interview had thrown up something else as well; Doherty had sketched the unusual belt buckle too. It was similar to the sketch he'd produced himself years back.

'Who *are* you?' he said to the E-Fit. Then he called Tanner in and briefed him.

'I agree with you, sir, it's got to be him. I'm not sure how we find him with what we have though. He doesn't match any of the 'knowns' on the database.'

'Have you followed up the bare-knuckle lead from Doherty?'

'I don't think we'll get anywhere with that one, the travelling community doesn't talk to the police.'

'So you haven't tried then?' His eyes bored into his assistant.

'I needed to wait until we interviewed the Irishman, sir.'

Kennedy gave him a withering look.

'I'll get right onto it, sir, but it's a bit difficult to know where to begin.' *You can be so impatient and unreasonable at times, sir,* he thought.

Where to start? Tanner sat in his own office thinking it all through. *Even if this character, was still fighting in his mid-forties, who'd remember him twenty-three years later?* Doherty gave the impression he was an accomplished fighter. *What if he was that good, a legend and hero among his own people?* He thought that he could pose as a writer who was doing a piece on the best bare-knuckle fighters of the last twenty-five years. If he could meet with community leaders, he could ask for any old photographs they had to support his story. He smiled to himself. *Now that's not a bad idea, Tanner.*

He ran it past Kennedy.

'It's a good idea, but it's a shot in the dark. I can't justify sending you in undercover based on a hunch.'

'I understand that, sir, but I have a friend who's a reporter – well used to this sort of thing – and in exchange for the exclusive when it comes out—'

'I can't *sanction* that, either, and you know it. I don't want the press getting hold of anything they don't already know.'

I can't sanction that, either. He frowned. Kennedy had said it with an emphasis on *sanction*. The expression on his face lent him to believe he wasn't expressly forbidding it, so he decided to get his contact to dig at it from another angle, but without revealing the real reason. Tanner made a call later that night.

The result was disappointing; the journalist was too busy to help, but if it could wait... It had waited twenty-three years; a few more weeks were hardly likely to make a difference.

Chapter 47

The stranger found a newspaper picture of Kennedy on the internet. Although the photograph was grainy and at least ten years old, he had no trouble recognising him when he came out of the station.

He pretended to be working on a motorbike in a bay in the car park just over the road. At almost 6:00 p.m., the DCI drove out in his car. He sparked up the bike and tailed him home.

He watched him at varying intervals for days. Sometimes, he left with a plain-clothes man about the same age as he looked in the internet photograph. At this stage, the other man was of no interest to him.

There was a pub about a mile or so away; they would drive and park nearby. They never stayed in the pub for more than a couple of hours. When he slipped in the first time to eavesdrop on them, they spoke in confidential tones. They couldn't keep their conversation from him as long as he could see them because he was lip-reading. From where he sat, he could only interpret one side of the dialogue. Reading Kennedy's face as well as his lips, he registered his concern in talking about his mother, '… she's sick, but fiercely independent…' '… Dad drinks too much.' It was clear she was totally dependent on his father's ability to carry on.

You're only as strong as the weakest link in the chain, you should know that, Kennedy.

His continuing surveillance revealed where Kennedy's parents lived, also leading him to his secretary's address. She'd left the station one evening with her boss in his car; he imagined briefly that he might get some footage of them together in a compromising position, but he'd dropped her off at a garage, where she transferred into another car and continued her journey. He followed her.

She lived alone with her teenage daughter. In the dead of night, rifling through the refuse in the bin outside her house, he quickly established there was no man living there. No beer cans, no letters addressed to Mr Dick Head. No man-things at all.

You could learn a lot from people's rubbish by examining discarded envelopes and empty boxes. If they had a cat or dog and how well fed it was. Near the top of the bin was a tampon wrapper. Someone was having, or just finished their period. From the mini size, he concluded it had to be the daughter. One of the best things about recycling, he mused, was that there was no more sorting through smelly food waste to build a profile of the inhabitants of the house. Picking up an old prescription box, the label revealed it belonged to Miss Terri Hunter. It was for Seroxat. He made no sound other than the dry, plastic whispering of the bags as he put them back where he'd found them. *No dog, no man, no surprises.*

Around midnight he fished through the letterbox with a specially shaped piece of metal. Sometimes his victims doubled locked the doors and then he'd have to find another way, but not tonight. Tonight was easy. He looked forward to warming up; the cold had chilled his bones, God, how he'd love to warm up with her. Silently opening the bedroom door, he listened to the soft sound of her breathing. His eyes adjusted to the light; he could make out her features, moving closer he leaned in over her and breathed in her exhaled breath. *Now you're mine.*

Theresa stirred and turned onto her side. Biting his lip, he lifted the cover exposing her voluptuous form. Reaching to touch her, he bit down harder and controlling himself; he withdrew from the room. He had things for her to do first and then after that; she'd be eating from his hand. His lips tightened at the thought, into a semblance of a smile.

He did not get home until the early hours of the morning, but he wasn't tired, instead strangely elated. Typing *Seroxat,* he googled it and found it was prescribed primarily for the treatment of anxiety, depression and obsessive-compulsive disorder. He wondered if she might be suffering from all three.

His observations also revealed the DCI had a taste for prostitutes. It quickly became apparent he was using one in particular, on a regular basis. He staked out her home, originally with the intention of finding a way to film him in the act. In order to do that, he'd have to break in and set up remote cameras he could monitor from outside. He already knew Kennedy had visited on three consecutive occasions, two Saturdays and a Friday. Patience would reward him with the opportunity to blackmail him and discredit him so thoroughly. He half smiled as he arrived outside the flat around midnight. Up on the fire escape, blended almost perfectly against the black metal landing, was someone dressed in dark clothes. He stood in the shadows watching, as the figure furtively peered through the gap in the blinds covering the back door.

A Peeping Tom!

Settling down into his haunches, shielded from the peeper's view by a row of low bushes, he checked the direction of the breeze. Satisfied it would not alert the man, he lit a cigarette behind his cupped hand and watched him. The cigarette inspired a shift in his thinking.

An hour later, he trailed the peeper home.

Chapter 48

In late January 2007, police authorities launched a joint coordinated action across several counties, code-named 'Operation Moonlight', in an effort to flush out the perpetrator of a one-man crime wave who was dubbed the Midnight man by the press. The campaign included the surveillance and monitoring of known criminals on a scale not seen for years.

At the same time, a series of prominent adverts announced in the local press. *We Buy Your Unwanted Jewellery – Platinum, Gold, Silver – Top Prices Paid!* Undercover officers took over vacant retail outlets and ran them as second-hand dealerships. *We Buy Anything!* By installing covert CCTV camera and recording equipment in the shops, detectives hoped some of the jewellery stolen in Midnight's raids would surface, providing a lead back to him. The operation caught droves of junkies, muggers and casual criminals, but none of the items recovered matched any of the Midnight cases.

Kennedy had set up just such a unit under his jurisdiction and he monitored the arrests with interest. The Crimewatch programme had failed to achieve the results he'd hoped for, and he began to harbour a secret wish that 'Midnight' would surface in his Manor. If he did and Kennedy caught him, it would be a real feather in his cap.

The activities of the Midnight man were traceable as far back as early 2001, when a series of 'creeper' burglaries began to take place all over the country. He never struck more than two or three times in the same town. The next victims would not be anywhere close, not in an adjacent town, or even county; they would be many miles away. He could strike in Scotland one day, Cornwall a week later, Essex after that. There was no discernible pattern. It was just as likely he'd strike on a council estate, as in middle class suburbia. Because he wasn't a ransacker, most victims wouldn't discover the robbery until the next morning, or even later. This type of robbery was a creeper burglary because the offender usually gained access to the properties while the occupants were asleep. It took a disturbing change in his modus operandi for his activities to attract the coordinated attentions of the police.

In early January 2005, a woman woke to find him leaning over her, masturbating furiously; he ran off. She said in her statement that he wore household gloves and a lycra outfit, similar to what cyclists or joggers wear; it could have even been a black ski suit. In the dark, she couldn't tell. She couldn't see his face either; he was wearing a three-holed, black ski mask. It would be only a matter of time before the Midnight Man raped someone.

The police did not publicise specific details for obvious reasons. The sheer number of victims involved in the robberies made it difficult to contain. Inevitably, someone leaked information about his habit of striking around midnight, leading to his soubriquet in the press.

The methods of entry varied from fishing for keys through letterboxes, to using specially shaped pieces of metal to reach in with and undo night latches. Sometimes, he'd simply pop a tiny piece of leadlight glass in a window and get in that way.

Usually, he only targeted the homes of single women, widows and divorcees. Mostly he took things that fitted easily into pockets, typically cash, jewellery and watches. Sometimes, and for reasons known only to him, he'd choose certain items that the owners wouldn't miss straight away, leaving Detectives baffled at his motives.

One thing was common to all the later cases; he telephoned the victims afterwards, to tease or torment them about their missing property, offering to return it in exchange for sexual favours. Sometimes he would taunt the victims with information he'd gleaned from their private paperwork, or intimate photographs he found inside their homes. He had a talent for locating hidden objects in wardrobes or drawers. He reserved a special brand of abuse for those who had sex toys, pornography, or fetish wear stashed somewhere in their homes. On occasion, he was also known to provide matchmaking services, tricking victims into contacting each other because he'd planted A's possessions at B's house.

Oh A, you're just going to love B, you have such similar interests, all you have to do is talk to each other, he would croon and then supply each with the other's contact details. Attempts at blackmail and extortion were also reported in a few instances, but the true number was suspected to be much higher because the victims were too scared, or embarrassed to report them.

He secretly recorded himself having sex with one of the victims in a guest room at a cheap seaside hotel, after agreeing to return a few sentimental items. As the victim later attested: *In return for a fuck, and if you are a smart girl and keep your mouth shut, no one else need know about this.* He'd worn a ski mask throughout her ordeal and rewarded her, by delivering a copy of the film to a national newspaper anyway. If he hadn't done that, the victim would have probably never come forward.

Detectives scrutinised the short film; he wore a blue lumberjack shirt and jeans. No identifying marks or tattoos were visible in any of the shots. He never spoke the entire time, just a series of guttural grunts. The victim was scared, but more than cooperative. She kept looking in the direction of the camera as if aware of the filming. At the end of the film, once he'd finished, she could be heard asking, 'Will you give my things back now?'

He responded with one word. 'Huh?'

Dozens of occupants had used the room since the shoot, contaminating any evidence that might have existed. Detectives concluded that he'd put the camera on the dressing table below the fixed mirror on the wall, probably concealed in a case or bag, with the lens facing the bed. A closer inspection would have revealed a disc shaped blemish in the lowest part of the mirror, patched up from behind with mirror film. If they *had* seen that, they might then have discovered the frame surrounding it unclipped at one end, allowing the mirror to slide, exposing the cavity, which housed the hidden camera and proof of the room's use for secret filming on many occasions.

No forensic evidence was uncovered, or at any other investigation scene either.

Kennedy finished reading his copy of the file on the Midnight Man.

He closed it. *The suspect remains at large.*

He summoned Tanner to his office.

'You wanted to see me, sir?'

'What's the latest with the shop?'

Tanner could tell he wasn't in the best of moods. 'The good news, which I think you might already know, is that we caught a few scumbags, house breakers and muggers. We've nailed a few for receiving, busted a handful of druggies. The bad news is we're no closer to catching this guy.'

'Guy?' Kennedy regarded him with disdain. 'That cuddly son of a bitch we throw onto a bonfire?' Kennedy held him in his sights. 'You never have any good news, do you?'

'Well actually, sir, you might like to know that the second hand shop we ran in the High Street? We made a profit when we liquidated the stock.'

Kennedy shot him with a look that wiped the smile from his face, adding, 'For someone so allegedly smart, the remarks you come out with are stupid at times.'

Tanner followed up quickly with a theory. 'You know I was thinking, sir, none of the stuff he's stolen has come to light anywhere. It could be he's got his own smelter at home, or maybe he doesn't do it for the money.'

Tanner's last remark had Kennedy thinking.

'But why else would he do it? From what we know, he gets some gratification from the act itself, but he gets his real kicks playing with the victims afterwards, like he...' Kennedy trailed off, biting his lower lip in deep concentration. A small piece of the jigsaw looked like a fit; he tested it from a number of different angles.

'You were saying, sir?' Tanner prompted.

Kennedy held his hand up, indicating he didn't want his thoughts disturbed. Although they had known each other for a long time, Kennedy insisted that he called him 'sir' in the office. Outside of work, it was John, but Tanner called him 'sir' all the time, rather than risk forgetting. In the office, Kennedy allowed only Theresa and his superiors to do that.

Kennedy stared at Tanner, who shifted in his seat. 'Sir, you were saying?' Tanner repeated.

Returning to focus, Kennedy said, 'It doesn't matter. Have we checked out links with organised crime, what about Danny Lynch? He uses pubs and clubs as a front for all kinds of illicit activities – nothing there?'

'Nothing so far, Lynch has been squeaky clean for months, sir.'

Kennedy scratched his chin. 'That means he's up to something...' Looking at his watch, it was almost six o' clock. *Where does the time go?* 'I don't know about you, but I could do with a beer, what do you say?'

Tanner shrugged his shoulders. 'Sure, why not?'

'I'll meet you downstairs in five minutes. How are we getting on with the leads from Crimewatch, by the way?'

Chapter 49

When Melissa lost her job as a tenant liaison officer at the local civic centre, she wasn't unemployed for long. She remembered a promoter handing her a card at a carnival event, where Fred Astaire and Ginger Rogers were twirling around on a float as it passed by. Also on board were Humphrey Bogart, Frank Sinatra, Jackie and President Kennedy, they had one thing in common; they were all look-a-like impersonators.

She met the agent, Max, in a bookstore near the town centre, and he took her through the back, into the dingy office where he worked. The desk was a mess of paperwork. 'Don't touch nothin',' he said, 'I know *exactly* where everything is.'

'You know when I first saw you; I came back here, and I said to Manny, you should see this girl. She looks just like Marilyn, and she isn't even trying.'

'Who's Manny?' Melissa asked.

'He's my dad, came over from New York after the war and started this bookstore with my mom.'

'Are you an American?'

He leaned in as if divulging a secret. 'Half-American when my dad's around and when I'm round my mum, half-English.' He winked at her, pointed and made a gun cocking noise with his mouth. She noticed he switched accents halfway through the sentence.

'Can you get me any work?' She smiled, hoping he'd say yes.

He looked her up and down, and stroked his chin. 'Hmmm, now that depends a lot on you.'

She felt her cheeks redden. 'Are you propositioning me?'

Taken aback, he blustered. 'No, no, that's not what I meant at all,' he said into his fist. 'I was just saying if you were to pad your top out or even better, have a boob job – I could get you *lots* of work.'

Max delivered assignments exactly as he'd promised and just as he'd said; her career really took off after she had the enhancements. By this time, she'd created her own website and taken to calling herself Marilyn Mooner.

It wasn't long before she found more lucrative work for Monroe impersonators, but for that she had to make herself available for private hire. Booked to appear at a party arranged by CID officers to make the fortieth birthday of one of their colleagues 'special', she was to sing one song, then mingle with guests afterwards. As she sang 'Happy Birthday to you', she sashayed towards the birthday boy, pausing twice on her way over to him, spreading her arms wide, making little up gestures with her hands, to rouse the guests into cheering louder. Literally making a song and dance of it, she pushed him down onto a chair and sat on his lap stroking his hair as she drew out the final 'Mr President'. The party went wild.

It marked the beginning of a torrid affair with the birthday boy, whose name was by a strange quirk of fate, John Kennedy.

Melissa also did appearances with 'Frank Sinatra', 'President Kennedy' and other impersonators. Hamming it up for other people's entertainment, she loved it.

Soon she was mixing with people on the fringes of the performance world, getting invites to parties attended by B-list celebrities. She loved the champagne and cocaine, the lifestyle and the glamour, and she discovered a love of money she'd never had before. It seduced her into surrendering her values, chipping away at them bit by bit.

She'd had a cheeky portfolio photograph of herself taken over a vent grille, trying to hold down her billowing dress. It was similar to the famous shot, except hers was more revealing, the billow allowed to float higher; the photographer captured that she wore no knickers in graphic detail. She carried the photo around with her to show prospective clients. Next to the breast implants, it was the best thing she'd ever had done. It catapulted her into the world of high-class escort girls.

As Marilyn, she acquired a number of very rich and powerful customers – she called them boyfriends – who lavished her with cash and gifts in exchange for favours.

Most of her boyfriends loved fantasy role-playing in varying degrees. Some took it further. There was one guy who liked to dress as Tony Curtis, another who used to croon Sinatra to her and of course, Jack Kennedy himself, who loved nothing better than to hear her breathily singing: *Happy Birthday...Mr President,* as he lay waiting, expectant and naked on the bed while she strip-teased seductively. She'd slowly make her way to him, pausing only to pose provocatively, timing the words of the song to end just as she went down on him, whispering to his cock. 'Oh, Jack, what will Jackie say?'

In a case of life imitating life, she also had an affair with a well-known gangster – Danny Lynch – who was under observation by the Serious Crime Squad.

It was in this way that Melissa first came onto the police radar. She came from a good background and the DCI thought she was just a casual girlfriend of Lynch's.

She kept a secret file on her clients, a diary or dossier, in which she recorded names, dates, times, secret photographs, films and physical details that only close intimacy would reveal. It was her insurance policy.

Once she had enough money behind her, she intended to write her memoirs, she'd change the names of those concerned and would sell it to the papers. It was her pension. The way she spent money, she was going to need it.

Melissa always kept Thursdays free. She'd spent the day doing absolutely nothing but pampering herself. She watched daytime TV, read magazines and dozed on her bed. She wouldn't have planned her life this way, but she wasn't unhappy.

It was early evening before she finally rose. She cleaned the make-up from her face, then showered, afterwards walking naked into the kitchen where she poured herself a generous shot of gin and popped a couple of Mogadon. After all the dozing and sleeping during the day, she knew she'd be awake half the night, and tomorrow was Friday, her busy day. She wouldn't want to spend it looking a wreck. She decided to pop another one; just to be sure, she caught the sleep train first time around. The bitter aftertaste made her grimace. She padded barefoot back to the bathroom to clean her teeth.

In the morning, she wouldn't even remember getting into bed.

Chapter 50

1 March 2007

Eilise Staples was groggy from the night before. It was still dark as the clock turned 6:30 a.m. Most of the camp was still sleeping; a few early birds had their lights on. They bumped along, in and out of potholes, down the track, away from the camp. In the darkness, the headlamps played off rippling puddles, reflecting the light, sending it down the lane at crazy angles in all directions. Her head still felt spaced out and woolly from smoking weed and heroin.

Wild bursts of wind drove staccato rain that spattered heavily against the tin walls of the white transit van. Watery machine gun bullets drummed in waves of sound that overwhelmed the creaking and banging of the metal body, masking the steady drone of the engine. The bodywork sounded as though it might twist off its chassis at any moment. One badly out of line headlight cut through the morning darkness, blinding the oncoming traffic. It attracted the occasional retaliatory flash from an angry driver.

On her last night in the camp, they were talking about the future. *No such thing as forever, nothing is forever, we won't be here forever so you might as well enjoy it while you can.* They were always telling her that, and in the end, it was what made up her mind to move on.

Eilise packed up her life into two heavy-duty black bin bags. They sat next to her in the van, on the seat and the floor between her feet.

Strawberry had left the camp a couple of days before. The driver was a friend of his and he, too, was a traveller. He had an interesting take on life; he seemed to know where he was going, he had it all mapped out in his head. When he spoke, he addressed her from the corner of his mouth without taking his eyes off the road. 'I'm doing the markets up to next Christmas, going to save the money I make; get myself some better wheels, maybe a camper. Then I'm going to take a long slow drive. France, Spain, Morocco. Wherever I want to go, anywhere in between, end up in Goa, always wanted to go there. Do a bit of work on the way. What about you, Eilise, you going home?'

Eilise wondered whether Strawberry had told him anything about her. She decided he wouldn't have. 'I'm going to meet my mother.'

'That's good. Do you get on with her and all?'

'I don't know...' she said, trailing off, uncertainty giving way to nagging doubt. She'd deal with that when it came to it.

'You don't know! What kind of an answer is *that* to a question about your mother?' She wasn't sure if his apparent dismay was serious.

'I haven't seen her for a while, that's all.'

'How old are you, Eilise?'

'Eighteen,' she lied. At only fifteen, it made her feel safer to say she was older.

'Well, best you get on back to your ma, then, it's about time. I'd take you all the way, but I'm doing the market this morning. Why don't you come with me? I'll drop you off after.'

'That's sweet of you, but no. If you drop me by the station, I'll be there by ten o'clock I reckon.'

The brakes squealed in the dampness as the van pulled to a halt.

She opened her door; he came round from the other side and reaching in, grabbed her bags; they were surprisingly heavy, but soft and full of clothes.

Through the taut polythene sack, he saw the shape of a teddy bear straining against it. If it wasn't for that, she could have been going to the launderette.

She pulled the fur-lined hood up over her head, over black hair already wet with rain. Light from the street lamps pooled on the pavement and under-lit her features, revealing a strong chin and soft brown eyes that peered down the slope of her nose. She had her lips pressed tight against the cold. Her face was wet with rain.

He couldn't tell if she was crying. He wanted to squeeze her in his arms, but he didn't. Instead, he stood awkwardly silent as he realised how small and young she looked. She didn't look at him.

After a few moments, he finally made a move, gently touching the underside of her forearm. 'You take good care, Eilise,' he said.

She nodded, unable to speak or look at him. She heard the van door boom shut, and then he was gone.

Lifting her bags clear of the wet pavement, she put them on the bench and sat next to them.

With no one else was waiting at the stop, she'd obviously just missed the bus. She knew that with her luck the next one wouldn't be due for a while.

Looking around, she noticed the steamed up windows of a café across the road. Picking up her bags, she crossed over.

A man watched her at the counter of the Station Cafe. What first drew his attention to her was the way she rooted through the pockets of her army jacket to find enough coins. A moment later, he recognised her. He couldn't believe his luck. He'd seen the runaway girl on Crimewatch. She was alone and desperately short of cash. Holding her coffee with one hand and bending at the knee, she gathered her two bags with the other. She reached the door and hoped someone would open it. Just as she was putting the coffee down to do it herself, a young builder scooted away from his table to do it. 'There you go, love.'

'Thanks,' she smiled and walked out.

The man observing her wiped the steamed up plate glass window and watched her struggle. She pulled her hood up over her head with the hand that held the polystyrene cup and waited to cross over to the bus stop.

She hadn't looked around in the cafe at all. The man was sure she'd not seen him.

He returned to his car and sat watching her, revving the engine to keep warm.

A small queue formed waiting for the bus.

Someone had smashed the glass panel at the end of the shelter, so it now caught the brunt of the wind funnelling down the slope, around and under the bridge. Hunching her shoulders, she turned her back towards the bitter blast and cupped her drink with both hands. She was sorry when it had all gone.

The dirty white baseball shoes did not have any heels, not like her old shoes; the hems of her jeans were wet and frayed from dragging on the ground. She'd stopped turning them up a long time ago.

The tea had cost part of the bus fare, as soon as it stopped raining; she would walk a few stops up the road. She thought about asking one of the people in the queue if they had any change, but not one had a sympathetic face. Not one of them even looked at her; all of them too wrapped up in their own little worlds, to care about a homeless kid. The bus pulled up; the rest of the queue disappeared onto it. The driver called out to her. 'Are you getting on?'

Eilise shook her head and took a step back. The bus pulled away, allowing the wind to blast at full force once more; it was getting stronger.

She couldn't have felt more alone.

A car pulled alongside her. The driver wound the window down; the wind dragged a cloud of cigarette smoke out, it hovered by the car for a millisecond, before it was snatched away as completely as if it were never there.

Leaning over, the driver asked if she wanted a lift. Eilise thought he looked about sixty years old; if he was younger, she might have thought twice. Still a bit fuzzy from the night before, she squinted, looking him over. He seemed okay, but something niggled at her.

I can't believe I'm thinking about getting into this rubbish bin! The biting wind and lashing rain narrowed her choices.

'What shall I do with these?' She held her bags up to show him.

'Shove them on the back seat.'

She ducked into the back of the car with her bags.

Chapter 51

Even before she'd shut the door properly, he started moving off. From behind, his hair looked like a haystack, thick, pale yellow. Eilise studied it. *It can't be his natural colour; the hair was too coarse to be blonde. It's an age thing. Men... These days, they can't face up to the fact they're getting old.* The combined smell of stale cigarette smoke and damp was overpowering.

'You going far?' His hips were off the seat, and his hand was deep in his pocket, looking for something. His voice sounded flat and bored. Finally, he pulled out a packet of chewing gum. 'Want some?'

'I don't thanks.'

The state of the back of the car was like nothing she'd seen before. It was worse than Strawberry's caravan at the farm.

She decided to come forward from the back seat, slipping between the seats quickly.

'Need some help, yeah?' He put his hand under her backside as she squeezed through; although he didn't touch her, she pushed it away.

'Thanks.' She frowned. In the front, black cigarette boxes were crammed into every available nook and cranny, in the parcel shelves, door storage compartments, everywhere; not one of them crushed, they looked like new, and there were dozens of them. There was a layer of dust on the dashboard so old in places; it had thickened into a semi solid state, disturbed only by the tracks left by fingers pulling cigarettes from the box on the dashboard, which was currently open, revealing three cigarettes.

She remarked dryly, 'Worried about running out?'

His thoughts – evidently on something else – jumped back into the present with a jolt. 'Huh?'

'I said are you worried about running out?'

'Got three left,' he said, fingering the box as he reached for another one.

'I was talking about all *those*,' she pointed them out with a broad sweep of her hand.

'No, they're all empty!' he said without humour. Lighting it, he drew on the smoke as if his life depended on it.

She sat quietly, looking out of the window, listening to the hiss of wet tyres and swishing wiper blades above the drone of the engine. The set of his face was grim; he seemed to be deep in thought. Finding the lengthy silence uncomfortable, she volunteered, 'I'm from Nottingham.'

'You could have fooled me; you talk like a Londoner,' he said, and then not wanting to give away that he knew her identity, he asked, 'What did you say your name was?'

'I didn't,' she decided to choose another name. 'My name's Ellen.'

'Eliza, I like that name.'

Is he for real? 'It's not Eliza, it's Ellen!'

'Is that right?'

After that, he continued calling her Eliza. Even after she corrected him, he carried on doing it and because he had one of those deadpan faces, she couldn't tell if he was having a joke at her expense.

'What did you say *your* name was?'

When he didn't answer, it prompted her to guess. She was renowned among friends for the accuracy of her guessing.

'William,' she whispered to herself.

Although her whisper was barely audible, he heard her. And even though it was a name he never used, the mention of it sparked paranoia in him. His fists tightened on the steering wheel, causing the knuckles to whiten. They reminded her of the fists of an old fairground boxer, back at the camp, who must have been in his seventies; his hands were gnarled and misshapen. One day when he caught her looking, he examined the front and back of them in a kind of awe at his own limbs. 'I used to pickle 'em in vinegar, I could still knock a nail in with 'em!' After that, whenever he saw her, he'd grin toothlessly at her.

The driver pulled the car over abruptly. He looked angry. She was scared of him. For the first time, she had an inkling she could be in danger. She was fascinated at the way his moustache grew down over his lips. There was a boy at school with a cleft palate, who spoke with a dull *clunk* in the enunciation of his words; she saw him just a few months back and he had the same type of moustache. This guy has a harelip. She just knew it.

'How did you know my name, Eliza?'

'Whoa, just a lucky guess, that's all,' she assured him.

'Is that right? *Oooh, just a lucky guess?*' His mimicry was faultless, but cruel.

A familiar hurt rose inside her; she moved to get out, but the onslaught of the continuing rain made her hesitate.

The man examined her expression and not wanting her to leave; he softened the tone of his voice. She did a double take, to see if it was the same man talking.

'Out of all the names you could have guessed, you get it right, unbelievable.'

Before she had the chance to reconsider her decision, he pulled out quickly without looking properly, into the path of another car. The other driver blasted his horn. William put two fingers up to the rear view mirror and spat curses at him.

The coffee cleared her head a little and it occurred to her he never asked where she was going. Maybe he thought she'd no place to go. A fragment of a song Strawberry was always playing drifted into her mind.

Like a memory in motion,
You were only passing through...
That's all you've ever known of life,
That's all you'll ever do.

The first time she heard the song, she asked Strawberry the name of the band.

'It's Concrete Blonde,' he said.

It could have been composed especially for her, so strongly did she identify with it, but this time she *was* headed somewhere. *Should she tell him where she was going?* She decided she wouldn't.

Cold right through; she stared out at the grey streets passing by; glad to be out of the wind and water.

'Where you going, Eliza?' This time he sounded genuinely interested.

'I've got friends in Romford, they're expecting me.' It was a lie, but she wanted him to believe someone, somewhere expected her. It made her feel safer.

'Hey, it's nine-thirty in the morning, and my day off. I'm not doing anything else. Why don't you let me take you there, yeah? First I have to go home, you know, freshen up a bit.' He winked at her. The way he changed from a few moments ago, into someone who now almost seemed friendly, sounded alarm bells. It was a bit too Jekyll and Hyde for her liking. She dismissed the thought, wondering if she might be able to cadge some money from him.

'Well, what do you say?'

She nodded; she was glad just to be out of the rain. If the atmosphere was strange, it was because she was coming down from last night. She robbed Peter, now she was paying Paul. She'd see what she could steal, do it at the first opportunity and then be gone.

Turning the radio on, he tuned in to a station he thought she might like. It was trance or techno, either way it was too loud. She couldn't be bothered to say anything.

She shivered. 'Can I turn the heater up?'

'I'll do that for you, love,' he said.

He cranked down the window a crack, and lit the third smoke he'd had since she'd entered the car. Tiny white flecks floated around, and she realised that the dust everywhere in the car was probably composed almost entirely of ash.

His window was open, but only enough to push out the cigarette end to flick the ash off, which he did frequently; he didn't seem to notice that most of it came back in.

Apart from the incessant smoking, something else struck her as odd about him. He was wearing sunglasses in the rain.

Chapter 52

Sunglasses in the rain? Eilise didn't attach too much importance to it. Maybe the light hurt his eyes, or he didn't want to be recognised. More likely, he just thought he looked cool.

'Undo those for me,' he said, handing her a pack of cigarettes.

'Do you mind if I change the music?' she asked.

'No, go for it!'

She found a station playing alternative country music, turned the volume down a notch and closing her eyes, she drifted off. Occasionally, she was aware her head was lolling from side to side, but she was too tired to do much about it, other than rest it up against the window, where it drummed and jarred her into a semi-relaxed state of dreamless sleep, until, on the verge of slipping deeper, a warning whispered in her mind. *Something's wrong.*

They had stopped. She sat up, instantly on guard.

He'd parked outside a tower block, behind a row of lock-up garages. 'Relax,' he told her. 'I have to put it away, or we'll have no wheels when we come back. Kids round here got no respect, no matter who you are,' he growled.

He left her in the car while he unlocked the garage door.

It had stopped raining.

She opened the passenger door, pushing it wide as she prepared to get out. Her eyes felt bleary; she rubbed them. She leaned in and grabbed her bags.

'Leave those there, no one will take them.'

'I'm bringing them anyway.' *All I have is in those bags.*

'Suit yourself,' he said, shrugging his shoulders.

They came round the front, up a wide flight of steps to the entrance. There was graffiti on the brickwork, as far as the artist could reach, above and either side of the doors. Inside, there was a draught blowing right through from somewhere, bringing with it the twin scents of lost hope and despair.

They took the lift up to the seventh floor. Inside the lift was filthy, the smell of stale urine overpowering.

He fiddled with his keys. The door to his flat was deadlocked top and bottom, as well as the night latch in the middle. Turning to face her, he said, 'You can't be too careful. These kids round here would be in like a shot, if they had the chance.'

She noticed someone had taken the number off, leaving a faint imprint in the paint behind it. *Seventy-one.*

Once inside, he shut the door and said, 'Get out of your clothes.'

'I'm sorry?' she said, surprised and indignant at the suggestion.

'We'll soon get them dry, yeah?'

Something to do with the way he asked a question, and then answered it for her, made her uneasy, made her think he might have a tendency to be controlling, just like her foster father. She didn't like the mixed messages coming through her head about him. One thing she knew for sure; she wasn't going to remove her clothes.

'They're already near enough dry, but thanks.'

After the state of his car, she was shocked to see that his house was quite tidy.

Now she was there with him; she wondered why she allowed herself to get into such a vulnerable situation. William was trying just a little bit too hard, and she sensed it.

What made her think he'd be such a pushover? She couldn't be sure, but maybe she shouldn't have accepted a lift in the first place. Anyway, she reasoned, what's the worst thing that could happen?

Her skin was beginning to crawl, the sensation of thousands of tiny insects roaming all over her, started her scratching. She sniffed and wiped a dewdrop from her nose.

He watched her with renewed interest; he'd seen these symptoms before. Her vulnerability turned him on. The look in his eye changed.

A distant voice was telling her to get the hell out of there, but she needed money for her addiction, and it defeated the voice of reason. The itching had spread under her skin; no amount of external scratching would rid her of it. There was only one thing that would relieve it. She needed another hit. The mind that controlled her addiction had won.

'I'm just going to have a shower, get changed. You'll be okay out here, *all on your own.*'

There was a slant to the way he said it that made her think, *surely, he doesn't think I want to join him in there!*

He filled the kettle and put it on. 'I'll only be a minute; we'll have some tea then get going, yeah?'

'Yeah, you take your time; I'll get the tea going. Where are the makings?'

He showed her. 'Won't be a minute,' he said as he left the kitchen.

She heard the shower turn on, the rattle of the curtain rings along the rail as he swished it across.

He started to croon wordlessly. 'Bah – bah – bah – bah – bob...'

At the sound of his singing, she was up, quietly and systematically rummaging through the drawers in the sideboard. She opened a Cuban cigar box. She probably would have used it as a hiding place herself, but still couldn't believe her luck. There was a polythene self-sealing sandwich bag, with two smaller bags inside it. One was half-full of fine brown powder; the other contained a dozen or so wraps.

She fished one out, held it to her nose and smelled it. It made her mouth water. It was heroin. *The guy is a dealer!*

If she'd had the time, she would probably have found his cash as well, but she decided she'd go with what she already had. She stowed the dope bags in her pocket and grabbed her bags from the floor, twisting the necks so she could hold them in one hand.

Down the stairs and into the hall, the front door seemed miles away. Taking long, exaggerated silent steps towards it, her heart pounded in her ears. Mouth dry, and suddenly aware she hadn't breathed for a while; she sucked air deep into her lungs and held it, before continuing past the cupboard halfway along the passageway until she reached the door. With trembling hands, she unlatched it top and bottom.

She didn't hear the cupboard door as it swung noiselessly open behind her.

Chapter 53

Eilise was halfway out of the door when a heavy hand wrapped around her upper arm, pulling her back in. Naked, and still dripping from the shower, he turned her almost effortlessly, putting himself between her and the door. He used his heel to push the front door shut.

She almost wet herself with fear.

'Where do you think you're going?' he rasped, his foul breath drew a gasp from her. 'Did you honestly think I was that stupid? I had you booked for a junkie as soon as I saw you! Yeah, that's right; it takes one to know one. You can't kid a kidder. I know exactly who *you* are – runaway girl.'

She tried to snatch her arm away; he tightened his grip, his fingertips squeezing in through her bicep, right down onto the bone.

'Ouch, you're hurting me!'

She stopped struggling. He relaxed the grip.

'You thought you could rob me, eh?' He wiped the spittle from his lips with the back of his free hand. 'Hand it all over!'

She reached in her jacket pocket and retrieved the drugs.

He snatched them from her.

She struggled to understand how he'd reached her so quickly. 'But how did you?' she said.

He didn't answer, instead spinning her round, so her neck was in the crook of his elbow, his other hand pushing her wrist up between her shoulder blades, forcing her back past the cupboard door. Inside she caught sight of a crash mat on the floor at the base of a gleaming fireman's pole. A long, dark red velvet curtain came down to within six inches of the floor and behind it; she couldn't be certain if her eyes had deceived her in that briefest glimpse, but she thought she saw the bars of a cage and a pair of bare feet. The fog in her head had fully cleared. Propelled forwards, she thought fast. *Could that really have been a cage with someone sitting quietly barefoot in there? Well, you wouldn't think so, but then, what sort of man has a fireman's pole installed in his house?* For one insane moment, she thought of Batman and laughed nervously. He squeezed on her windpipe, choking it off.

'Are you laughing at me?'

He had her so tight; she couldn't deny it. A tear rolled down her face. She knew she was about to die.

'I said, are you laughing at me!' he shouted so loudly, her ear exploded with pain.

Her feet were almost off the floor; only her toes remained in contact. Suddenly, a woman spoke calmly. 'Martin – no, it's enough. Let her go.' The voice came from inside the cupboard.

Still he crushed her.

'Martin!' The woman's voice sounded close to panic.

He released her. She fell to the floor, sucking in air. She knew if she were to survive, she'd have to be clever.

'Q-quiet. I've let her go.'

Eilise's bruised larynx kept her voice barely above a whisper as she spoke. 'Who's that you have in the cage, *William*? And why is she calling you Martin?'

He shut the cupboard door. The woman's muffled voice now barely audible, said something about a middle name.

Eilise asked him softly, 'What do you want me to call you?'

Turning and squatting down on his haunches, he was holding a knife. He pressed its edge against her mouth.

'Sssshhh,' The coldness of the blade against her lips terrified her, sparking an uncontrollable trembling; the control she held onto precariously at the door when he first caught her was lost. She spasmed and a warm trickle of urine ran down her legs. Struggling to regain composure, she forced herself to make eye contact with him, knowing she might have a better chance of getting out alive if she could connect with him.

He stared back at her with eyes as cold and black as stone. He let her go, wiped his wet lips dry on the back of the knife hand; he seemed to be looking at his reflection in the blade. When he spoke this time, there was a soft hint of Irish in his voice.

'She's been with me a long time, that one, she knows how to toe the line,' he lowered his tone so the caged woman wouldn't hear. 'And if you turn out to be as good as she is I might even decide to keep you. You know, look *after* you like I do her.'

She shivered at the thought. 'And if I don't?'

'Then you'll be dead.'

'Look, why don't you just let me go? I won't tell anyone, I promise.'

He held the knife out.

She should have stopped talking then, but her voice was like a disembodied thing. She heard herself telling him she was a junkie and she couldn't help it. Surely, he knew what it was like, surely he understood. 'I would lie, I'd cheat, steal or *anything* for my next fix.'

'Really, Eliza?' he took a wrap from the bag and held it up in front of her. 'Show me.'

Leading her upstairs, Martin produced a syringe and a spoon.

'I've never taken it like that before,' she said, too needy to be afraid.

'Welcome to my world.'

He prepared the makings, a half teaspoon of water, a measure of smack, a single drop of lemon juice. He heated the mix in the spoon until the powder dissolved, then dropped in a piece of cigarette filter. Eilise had only ever smoked the stuff before; she had the feeling she'd no choice in the matter. If she wanted it, he'd jack her up.

His lips hung open, slightly apart and wet as he drew the solution into the syringe. He wrapped one hand around her bicep and squeezed, she felt no pain, just a weird numbness as the veins struggled to maintain the flow of blood, becoming visible and raised. The other hand pushed air from the clear plastic cylinder. A dribble of liquid appeared at the tip of the needle.

She licked her lips in anticipation; he found a vein; he drew on it, a tiny cloud of her own blood swirled in the mix, she swore she felt it leave her body and then *whoosh!* He injected the contents into her. A feeling so high and so low took her above and beyond the limits of just smoking it. She relaxed on the sofa vaguely worried about what would happen next, she noticed his cock had become erect; she struggled to focus. *Holy shit he's going to...*

She struggled to recover her senses, but could not. He pulled her clothes off roughly; she was as limp as a rag doll, detached, powerless as though she were watching it happen to someone else. He moved on top of her, parting her knees, preparing to penetrate her.

'Martin, what do you think you're doing?' It was the voice of the woman from the cage.

He rounded on her. 'H-how did you get out?'

'Never mind that, leave her alone. She's no more than a child!' Eilise floated down from her sweet detachment and opened her eyes. The woman had long dark hair, it was bedraggled; her face was without make-up. Her eyes were pretty, but vacant looking, lost and haunted. She had a scar on her upper lip that disfigured her and made it hard for her to speak properly. Eilise began to lose consciousness again.

'You, child – how old are you?'

Eilise had to think about it; she'd lied about her age so many times. 'Fifteen.'

'I want her out of here, Martin,' the woman was angry. 'You can't keep her here.'

'After what she's done? No way!'

'And what did she do, Martin?'

'She stole from me and she told me she was eighteen as well. She stays as long as I want her to stay!'

He pulled her up without answering the woman, steering her into another room. He breathed menacingly into her ear. 'I'm going to get rid of her soon, and when I do...' He brushed himself against her. 'This room is yours...for now,' he said, before shutting the door.

She heard him lock it behind her. Eilise looked around, unsteady on her legs.

The interior of the room was spacious enough, but gloomy and windowless, a red bulb hung from the ceiling, the light it produced barely sufficient to see an unmade bed along one wall, a sink, a bucket and little else. She flopped down on the bed. Cold and naked, she found a way into its folds. She passed in and out of dreams she couldn't remember. Occasionally she thought she heard them arguing violently, sounds like someone thrown onto the floor so hard that the whole upstairs shook and finally, the cries of rough passion that kept her awake for hours. Eilise was terrified he'd kill the woman and then come for her.

She stayed in bed until the last residues of the drug had gone. There was no natural light and he'd taken her watch; she had no way of knowing how long she'd been unconscious. It felt like morning.

Pacing around in the confines of her cell, she wondered how long she'd be able to keep him off her. There was no way she'd spend her life locked up by a pervert. She had to get away.

Suddenly the door unlocked; he flicked the light on and came in carrying a tray with milk, biscuits and a preloaded syringe on one side.

'Supplies,' he said.

After that night, he kept her and the other woman apart, locked in two separate rooms. Eilise tried to speak up as close to the dividing wall as she could, trying to get the woman to talk, but she only succeeded in waking him and getting herself locked into the cage downstairs as a punishment.

'I don't want you to talk to her again. Have you got that? She's a lovely one, and you're not going to spoil that. Do you understand what I'm saying? If you do what she does, you won't go far wrong.' Then he added as an afterthought, 'She can be your mother; she looked like you when she was younger.'

He gave her the creeps, the way he always changed his voice to sound like someone different. When he left, he locked Eilise in the cage downstairs. The other woman never answered when Eilise called out to her; she wondered if she couldn't hear her with all the doors closed.

She sometimes caught a little bit of conversation going on between them, sometimes cries of pain and the muffled sounds of sex at all different times of the day and night. Although it was clearly an abusive relationship, she could tell the other woman had no desire to get away.

She wondered if he kept her fed with heroin, too. It would explain why she was so dependent on him.

Chapter 54

Eilise lost track of time. Martin had gone off somewhere, leaving her locked in the cage. She wrapped her hands around the bars and attempted to shake them. *Solid.*

The cupboard door opened and the woman came in carrying a small tray. Eilise watched her as she pushed a drink through the bars. She kept her gaze down.

'So are you married or what?'

She cocked her head to one side, turned to face Eilise and said nothing. She pushed two slices of toast between the bars of the cage.

'He's not here, right? So why won't you talk to me?'

The older woman stood upright; her clothing resembled that of another era. Her dress was dark, floral patterned, knee length. Eilise doubted it had ever seen an iron. The cardigan she wore was baggy and beige. It was dirty. She brushed a lock of dark hair streaked with grey strands away from her face. They made eye contact for the first time. Eilise smiled shyly.

The deep vertical scar on the woman's top lip allowed only a tiny crinkle to form in the corner of her mouth.

'Are you afraid of him?' Eilise said.

She sighed, her shoulders drooping with the exhaled air as if she'd deflated. 'I'm afraid for *you.*' With that, she turned from the cage and shut the door behind her as she left.

With the toast was a small plastic measuring cap, filled to the 15ml mark with what smelled like methadone. Eilise swallowed it; licking the inside of the cap until the sweet taste was no longer present. Wiping her nose on her sleeve, she guessed Martin had been gone for two days. When he came home, he'd give her a proper fix. Her back ached and her skin crawled, the medication would kick in shortly, taking the worst of it away. She made a silent vow. *I'm going to kick this habit when I get out of here.* Strawberry had told her it was like having a monkey on your back; she didn't know what he meant when he said it back then, but she did now. Picking up a piece of toast, she forced herself to eat.

Late in the afternoon, the woman returned with another shot and more food and drink.

'I forgot to ask your name,' Eilise said. 'Will you tell me your name?'

'If he knew you'd been talking, and I talked back—'

'I won't tell him,' Eilise promised.

'He'll ask when he gets back. And if he thinks I'm lying...I don't want him to hurt you.'

'Then let me go.'

'I can't, we're locked in.'

'He keeps you prisoner, too?'

'My name is Cathy.' She raised her jaw defiantly. 'And I don't want to go out. I have everything I need here,' she clipped each word for emphasis.

Eilise watched her mouth as she spoke. Her scarred top lip formed an inverted 'V' where it met with her lower one, the result of poor stitching she imagined, and guessed she'd had an accident when she was younger, must have fallen. A fall like that would have smashed her teeth in. It was probably why she spoke the way she did.

'When's he coming back, Cath?'

'Could be tonight, could be tomorrow, Eliza.' She appeared pleased she'd spoken her name.

'Cath, it's Eilise, not Eliza.'

The older woman nodded and left. Eilise did not take her medicine.

She heard Martin when he came in late that night; he ignored her, going straight upstairs to Cathy. The two of them murmured almost inaudibly for a few minutes. Cathy's voice seemed to be attempting persuasion.

Martin spoke louder than before, 'How did you know that?'

Cathy didn't reply.

Martin then raised his voice, demanding an answer.

'How did you know her name was *Eilise?*' There was a silence and then an accusation. 'You've been talking to her, haven't you?'

Eilise agonised as she heard Cathy's muffled protests and the sounds of a furious struggle, followed by a cry of pain, then deathly quiet.

Eilise listened intently. She couldn't hear a sound.

The door opened, sending in a shaft of light, casting his shadow across the floor.

Martin stood there with blood on his hands and murder in his eyes.

Chapter 55

'I told you not to talk to her. This is your fault!' Martin stomped out and thundered up the stairs. Eilise strained to hear what was happening. He crossed the room above three times in quick succession. Then she heard a sound that made her heart sink. It was the sound of something heavy. A dead weight dragged across the floor.

He'd killed her! Surely, she'd be next.

She looked around her cell, desperately searching for a weapon; there wasn't a single thing that would trouble him if she hit him with it. He was going to kill her and there wasn't a thing she could do about it. Unless she could convince him she was worth keeping.

She'd lost all her dignity years before. If she got through this, she might be able to buy herself the chance to escape later.

She stripped naked, sank onto the bed and waited for him.

An hour later he still hadn't come for her. She was cold and pulled the covers over her. The stress had given her a dull headache. She wanted some scag; she wanted some sleep, and she wanted her nightmare to end. She prayed. Hovering on the brink of consciousness, about to sleep for the first time in weeks unaided by drugs, she thought she'd heard a woman cry. She sat up, listening. Then she heard Martin's voice talking, low and smooth. *She was alive!*

The welcome sound of Cathy's sobbing continued for a full five minutes while he tried to soothe her. Soon all was quiet again.

She lay back down and drew her knees into her chest. She heard the tell-tale stair creak. Eilise kept herself covered. Martin opened the door.

'You almost killed her...what you did.' Words formed in her head, but she dared not speak them.

He pulled the keys from his pocket and unlocked the cage. 'I've got business to attend to. I need you to look after Cathy or she'll die. You owe her.'

'What's wrong with her?'

He shrugged. 'She took a beating, went too far.'

'You should call a doctor.'

'She's a tough one; she'll be all right,' he said, ignoring her advice. 'You can't get out, don't bother trying. Oh, and the place is soundproofed, so don't waste your breath shouting. When I come back, she'd better be alive.'

He's mental; she thought.

He walked out down the corridor. She heard the door slam, the deadbolts turning.

She slipped her T-shirt on and made her way upstairs. The stair creaked. 'I'm coming, Cath,' she said quietly.

Eilise found her propped in bed; her eyes welled up at the sight of her. Her breathing was shallow; although she was breathing through her mouth, a tiny mucous bubble of blood inflated in her left nostril with every exhalation. She looked in a bad way. How a man could do that to a woman was beyond her. Eilise decided to let her sleep. She lay on the bed next to her, listening for her laboured breathing, afraid in case it should stop.

It was almost midnight when Cathy wet the bed.

Oh, great!

Martin was gone for days; she nursed Cathy back to health as best she could. She was still reluctant to talk about him and wouldn't hear a word said against him. He was right about them not getting out. Without tools, there was no way. Eilise wondered what would happen to them if something happened to *him*.

Chapter 56

The caller studied his face in the car's rear-view mirror; he had his father's bony eye sockets, hammered out of shape by many fights, a nose broken so many times it resembled a chimney rock formation. The flinty eyes and bullet head came from his father, too, but he had his mother's mouth, fleshy mashed up lips and teeth that whilst even and white, grew inwards and backwards like a shark's. Few people settled their eyes on him for long. He always got a feeling if someone was looking at him and he'd often swing around and catch them. Most times, once he'd glared at them, they would turn away.

There was something feral and animalistic about him, something familiar, too, like a photo fit, where the top doesn't quite match the bottom. Sometimes, when he was in a mirror gazing mood, he wondered if he'd become what he was because of what he looked like.

Without the benefit of a formal education, he more than made up for it with cunning and deviousness and a sharp intelligence that belied his appearance. Able to imitate voices, he experimented with speaking in different ways; he could sound posh and well educated and as rough and unintelligible as a raging drunk. On top of that, he was also a master of disguise, frequently changing his appearance, especially after significant events in his life. The disguises were something his father had taught him. *Never stay the same...* He used them to cover another genetic trait he shared with his father, for which he hated him.

As Midnight, he'd wear glasses, wigs, beards, moustaches, skin tan lotions. The clothes he wore ranged from lumberjack work shirts through to business suits. Every job he carried out, he engineered with scenes of crime in mind; he knew what they'd be looking for. Unless he wanted to plant something, he left no clues. During his years on the road, he learned to read, and it helped him make sense of the paperwork he would find at people's houses. In an attempt to control his urges, he applied disciplines that diverted his interests elsewhere.

He learned about people and their quirks. Unafraid to experiment with manipulation he observed the different outcomes, and never stopped asking *what if* questions, developing scenarios.

An expert in surveillance, he learned to play chess with other people's lives. His plans came about like evolution.

The pills in the bathroom cabinet, and the smell of the empty glass left on the side of the basin confirmed that gin was her extra poison for the night, a dangerous mix. The blonde wouldn't have woken up if he'd driven a truck through her bedroom.

While she slept, he emptied her safe. When he'd finished counting the money, a little over ninety seven thousand pounds, he'd already worked out how to double it. Unable to believe his luck, after stowing the money away in a Harrods carrier bag, he began leafing through the diary she kept in the safe. *Why keep it in a safe?* Poring over the entries and notes, he found it was a meticulous record of her client's visits. Days, times, what they had done, even what they'd said.

Two in particular drew his attention. One was a police chief inspector who, according to her notes, liked nothing more than having her sing Happy Birthday as part of his foreplay. Alongside his name was the number 1, with a circle drawn around it. The next was someone she described only as the Boss. His name was encircled with the number 2. The other entries too, carried encircled numbers next to them; there were money brokers, city bankers, solicitors. The numbers, he assumed, were based on performance, or the amount of money they paid. He puzzled over it briefly before deciding it wasn't important.

When he'd reached the end, there was a flyleaf with a key to all the numbers listed in sequence. Adjacent to them, were initials and telephone numbers. It took a few seconds for the capital letters to gel in his mind and then he had a moment of enlightenment. *There at the top, next to the phone number, JFK, Mr President. JFK, John F. Kennedy. Could this be DCI Kennedy?* He didn't recognise any of the other initials, but he recognised potential when it presented itself and if it *was* him, by the time he'd finished digging the dirt, if he played his cards right, he would have his revenge. And he'd be untouchable.

Reaching for a new mobile phone, he always kept a new one in the car; he unboxed it and lit a cigarette. After putting the battery in, he switched it on and keyed the telephone number into it.

It answered almost straight away.

He recognised the voice from the television.

'Is that you, Jack?' he said into the handset and disconnected without waiting for a response. *Beware the ides of March, Jack.*

Oh, if his old man could have seen how his apple had grown bigger than the tree.

When Midnight thought about his old man, there wasn't much worth remembering. There were no good times; just the bullshit handed down as if it was the wisdom of the ages.

Old Chinese proverb: He who stands still gets caught. Know when it's time to move on and do it before that!

The fountains of wisdom garnished from a lifetime of lying and cheating were not even correct. His poor mother suffered endlessly, born into a generation where you stood by your man, it never occurred to her that leaving was an option. Her mother's advice would have been. *You just grit your teeth and get on with it.*

She tried to put some decent values into him; her determination to prevent his turning out like his father backfired, and in a way, she helped make him the same because he resented her for it. He was too much of a chip off the old block. He smoked like a trooper, not as much as the old man did, having no money of his own to buy them, he was obliged to smoke his father's dog ends. He would smoke part of the filter too, by his reckoning, it was the best part.

On reaching his teenage years, he had rebelled; no woman was ever going to control him. He exhibited signs of sexual deviancy; he'd spy on neighbours in the hope of catching them undressing, or even catch them having sex, which he occasionally did.

Sometimes, the old man would take him off at night, not coming back until the next morning. When his mother asked where they were going or where they'd been, her husband's thin lips would pull back into a wicked smile, and he'd tap his nose as if she should know better and say. 'Just a bit of night fishing, girl, that's all!'

She knew they were up to no good.

It was easier to say nothing in the end – to turn a blind eye.

So, it was time to move on, he saw it coming clear as day. One more job and that would be him done. No more Mr Nice guy, no more Mr Midnight. Alice Cooper would have been proud of that little addition to his lyrics; he drew his lips back into a wolfish grin.

Having no friends, he kept himself to himself. It was the best way to keep a secret, don't say anything to anyone and stay away from people. His old man taught him that as well and so far it had paid off. He was much more efficient than his old man, though; he had done bird a couple of times, but then, if he hadn't, he wouldn't have been able to pass on what he learned in there, so he supposed it was a good thing.

Yeah, the old man, that shining guiding light. His smile pulled his lips against his teeth so tightly he thought they might split. It faded again as quickly as it appeared.

He wasn't as bad as his old man. He was worse.

When he was almost sixteen, his mother died of lung cancer. She'd never smoked a cigarette in her life.

She kept it from the two of them, and neither of them noticed just how frail she'd become until the end. The old man said she was always going to die young, always had a fuckin' headache, always so sickly.

'Do you know what, Dad? You're so fucking selfish.'

The old man looked at him surprised and considered giving him a beating, but the boy had grown stout; he might turn on him, so he just said, 'If you feel like that, boy, you know what you can do!'

At the funeral, her three estranged sisters paid their last respects. They all knew the reason she had broken contact was because of him; she wouldn't have wanted them to fret. The old man undermined her and cut her off from everyone who was close. One by one, the sisters fell by the wayside and his mother had allowed it to happen, fearful of the consequences of resistance. Before she died, she sent a letter to the eldest, explaining – or at least trying to – in as much as her limited vocabulary would allow, so they knew. Not one of the sisters spoke to the old man, or even looked at him.

'Evil bitches,' the old man muttered out of the corner of his mouth as they stood by the graveside.

There was no wake, but before they left the graveyard, the eldest aunt pulled him to one side. 'Martin, if you want any sort of future that's worth having, you've got to get away from him, we'll help you all we can. You know where we are.'

Afterwards, Martin packed his things into a single holdall and walked to the door. The old man blew smoke after him, and flicked his cigarette end out of the door – right over his head, laughing. 'How do you think you're going to get along without me, eh?' He fished another cigarette from the packet and lighting it, blew a long tantalising plume at the boy, the look on his face, smug. 'You think you're better than me? Well, let me tell you son, the apple don't fall far from the tree.'

At that time, he wasn't sure he knew what he meant. Once outside, he looked down at the smouldering butt and ground it hard into the concrete with his heel.

The old man stood grinning, as if to say, *you'll be back.*

He took one last backward look at him and was gone.

Chapter 57

The caller had resisted the temptation to taunt, but it was time to draw Kennedy into the game. It didn't matter if he got close. If need be, he'd stop him in his tracks. Clearing his throat, he picked up the phone.

He'd seen a film about the Scorpio killer; *he* used to taunt the police, and they never caught him. It was only after he was dead that they thought they knew who he was. The caller's lips pulled into a sneer, revealing his teeth; he flexed his tongue, preparing his voice. His eyes were flat and humourless. *Catch me when I'm dead! I can live with that.*

Tanner took the call; he noted the time as 8:57 a.m.
'Jack Kennedy?'
The question itself was innocent enough, but the tone in which it was spoken, immediately put him on the defensive. There was something familiar about the man's voice. He couldn't quite put his finger on it, but he knew he'd heard it before. 'You mean DCI *John* Kennedy? Who's calling—?'
The caller interrupted him. 'He's Jack to me, all right?' the voice was impatient. 'And I'm calling about the Kathy Bird case.'
Tanner bristled with suppressed anger, but remained calm, his voice smooth. 'Do you have some information for us? I'll have to take your details—'
'No time for that. I know what happened to her,' his voice lowered to a hoarse confidential whisper.
Poised with his pen above his writing pad; the DI noticed a tiny tremor in his fingers as he held it there, becoming more pronounced as he waited for the caller to continue.
'That missing girl, Eliza Staples,' he paused for effect. '*I've* got her.'
'Is she safe?' he asked, scribbling notes and then striking a line through Eliza, correcting it to Eilise.
'You asked for a name. Tell your boss the name is Lee Harvey Oswald.'
His stomach turned over. *This is no crank caller, crazy, maybe, but no crank.* A cold chill ran down his spine. The caller disconnected before he had a chance to ask him anything else. He sat staring bemused at his notebook, he scribbled down the conversation while it was fresh in his mind. When he finished, he rose from his chair and walked out of his office.

It was three minutes past nine in the morning; Theresa had just arrived and was removing her scarf and overcoat by her desk. She caught sight of him looking at her and said, 'Good morning, John, how are you today?'
'I'm very well and you, Theresa?'

'I'm fine, John,' she said it with a slight smile, and he smiled back, somewhat subdued. When the DCI was around, everyone called him Tanner to avoid confusion, but Theresa always called him John, he loved the way she drawled when she said it, making it sound like Shawn, but with a J. He liked her more than he was letting on, and he thought she felt the same. He shook his head to clear the budding fantasy. Kennedy would make his life hell if he knew; then it dawned on him.

The caller. He suddenly knew who he sounded like; he sounded just like Kennedy.

The lights flickered before coming on fully in the DCI's office. He hadn't seen him arrive. With his notebook in his hand, he sauntered over, knowing that, with his latest tidings, he wasn't going to be popular. Yesterday, he had called him a prophet of doom; he had to laugh at that one. *That's a bit rich, coming from you, sir.* He leaned against the wall, attempting to gauge the right moment to go in.

Theresa caught his attention and pulled a mock suspicious face at him, narrowing her eyes and pursing her lips to one side of her face.

He raised his eyebrows at her, and she mouthed a silent question. *What are you doing?*

Waiting for the chief, he mimed back and then grinned at her as he shrugged himself away from the wall. He turned and taking a deep breath, knocked on the door.

Kennedy's voice bellowed, 'Come in!'

The chief glared at him as he stepped into his office, clearly irritated. 'Jesus, Tanner, I've hardly got my jacket off, for crying out loud.'

'I'm sorry, sir, but I can't help it. It's really important.'

'Yes, I'm sure it is, but I need a coffee first.'

He related what the caller had just told him, regardless. The older man froze with his hand on the phone. When he'd finished reading, Kennedy shook his head, blinking in disbelief.

'Jesus,' he said, lifting the receiver.

'Theresa? Morning, love, can you fetch me a coffee – make it black, thank you – oh, and you'd better get one for Tanner, too.'

'Did we get a trace on the call?'

'It's going through now, sir.'

The DCI scratched his head, causing tiny flakes of dandruff to fall. 'You know what's baffling me? This Lee Harvey Oswald business,' he said, brushing off the shoulders of his dark shirt. 'It doesn't take a genius to work out that it's directed at me, but I can't work out why.' He stared at the ceiling as he spoke, at this point merely thinking aloud. He shifted his gaze to his colleague. 'You know what the worst thing is? I don't think it's just some crank.'

'That's exactly what I thought, sir, but there's something else I didn't tell you.'

Turning his attention to Tanner, he said, 'What's that?'

'He sounded just like you, sir.'

'And that's significant is it, Tanner? *You* sound like me on the phone. I haven't got time for idle…' he said, struggling for the right word. 'Piffle.' The look on Tanner's face provoked a new choice of word. 'Bullshit! Happy now? Look, I'm sure hundreds of people sound like me. It's your imagination and nothing more.'

'With respect, sir, you didn't take the call—'

Interrupted by a knock on the door, Kennedy called out, 'Okay.' He put his finger to his lips as the door opened and Theresa came in putting the steaming mugs down on the desk. 'Sugar, John?' she asked.

'We can manage thanks, Theresa,' he said.

She grinned shyly at Tanner before lowering her eyes and leaving the room. Kennedy noticed the smile, and it irritated him.

'You got something going on with her, Tanner?'

Almost choking on his coffee, he quickly put the cup down, eyes bloodshot from where the hot liquid had shot into the back of his nose.

'Let's get that call traced, shall we?' he said and shook his head in dismay.

Tanner picked the cup back up and left with it, walking through the open office area where Theresa and the other girls were working; as he passed; he made eye contact with Theresa, neither of them said a word, but he knew he'd have to start something with her. He allowed himself a faint smile. *Fuck you, Kennedy.*

Later that morning, just before midday, Tanner was back in the DCI's office.

'The call was made on London Bridge; from a phone with a pay as you go SIM card. Needless to say – it wasn't registered, and the signal died immediately after the call. I'm guessing he took the battery out or dropped it into the river.'

Kennedy studied Tanner closely. 'Any CCTV footage?'

'We think we have him,' Tanner said, 'but he was wearing a hoodie if it *was* him, so we couldn't zoom in on his face or anything. There was a problem when we had someone look at the footage.'

'Come on, Tanner, get on with it.'

'There were dozens of people on the bridge making calls at the same time. Miraculously though, only one had a hood over their head and he was stacked like a shit-house. I have a hunch it's him.'

Kennedy sighed. 'Because he was wearing a hoodie?'

'Partly that.'

'Sorry, Tanner,' he said. 'Do you know something? I think you're right. Oh, and Tanner?'

'Yes, sir?'

'We have to catch this guy.'

The statement was obvious, but it meant so much more to Kennedy personally than Tanner could ever guess.

'I know, sir.'

Chapter 58

The Mogadon Melissa took the night before had left her feeling groggy; her mouth was dry and her head pulsed. The 'white' phone rang; she struggled to grab it as much to stop the noise as to answer it.

She picked it up and held it to her ear, gulping the last mouthful of last night's water. A voice crooned a bit of Sinatra down the line. 'Then I go and spoil it all.'

'Oh, Frank, is that you?' she said, speaking before she'd swallowed properly, her voice gurgled – she laughed and almost choked at the same time.

'No, it's Tony. What on earth are you doing?'

'Water. I was drinking when I answered. It nearly went down the wrong way,' she spluttered a bit more, and then giggled. 'What can I do for you?'

'What's today?' he said.

'Friday?' she ventured.

'That's it, you've got it.'

Frank and Tony phoned her every week, each often pretending to be the other one, teasing her for fun, trying to catch her out. Where they'd worked together for so long, they had grown to sound the same, it was difficult to tell their voices apart. Together they formed part of her regular clientele; both were city traders with more money than sense. Tony once told her that footballers would weep if they knew how much money they were making.

In keeping with the Marilyn theme, they pretended to be Frank Sinatra and Tony Curtis. There was a running joke between the three of them; that Tony sang better than Frank and Frank was funnier than Tony was. Sometimes Tony would joke. 'Can I be Frank with you tonight?' *I wish you'd be someone else.* At times, he scared her witless. Tony loved them to undress together, then he'd put her clothes on and tie her up with her own stockings, stark naked. That was the part she found hardest to cope with, she felt so vulnerable; he could do anything and she'd be unable to prevent it. He'd whisper threats into her ear, which he never carried out, but the deviancy of the acts he described to her clearly turned him on. She began to fear he might cross the line and escalate things to a level of kinkiness she couldn't deal with.

She wondered who he was pretending to be, but he paid well and it was all over in an hour. Usually she charged a thousand pounds a session, but he got her down to nine hundred and fifty pounds and then always gave her a fifty pounds tip on top anyway. She guessed it made him feel generous and at the same time; it didn't cost him any more than it would have originally. It was a power thing; Tony just had to have a deal. Working it out, she managed to get by on around five thousand a week and to do that, she needed six or seven punters a week. She had two special clients she never charged for her services. She'd rather not have been in that situation, but in any business you have insurance to pay. This business was no different, except her insurance came in the twin guises of a detective and gang boss.

That afternoon, Max had booked her to open a retro fashion store near Carnaby Street. The appearances he was arranging were getting too much like hard work and she dreaded it. He'd told her she needed to put a reasonable amount of her engagements through the books or she'd have the taxman after her. She suspected the real reason was that he didn't want to lose his cut of the booking fees.

It was the first appearance she'd done since the opening of Lynch's new nightclub earlier in the week. She didn't consider herself outside the law, but Lynch most definitely was and boy, was he making it pay.

She showered and dressed.

That evening, once Tony had come and gone, Melissa was relaxing in the bath listening to Enya playing in the background, she loved mood music. Her flat was spotlessly clean; she kept herself spotlessly clean. Taking a shaver, she neatly trimmed herself, carefully preparing for the arrival of Lynch. He loved her smoothness. She told him she didn't mind if he decided to stay on at the club, after all; it was the first Friday after the opening, but he'd told her, 'That isn't me, all that showing off. I wouldn't miss a tumble with you, babe. I'll be round later.'

He would stay the night; he treated her like a proper girlfriend when he was with her. He knew what she did for a living, but he never talked about it and for her part, she behaved as any normal girlfriend would do. They talked of his plans, the things that bothered him. She listened. He never asked her anything much, how she felt or anything at all. He never asked any normal questions. *It was a strange relationship, but then, with you girl, they all are.*

Melissa dressed all in white; the satin dress, the gloves, the whole ensemble and applying the finishing touches, she dabbed on a little of the perfume he'd brought her and settled down for his arrival.

She kept two mobile phones, one in a white case for everyday use and another in a red case. Only two people had the number for the red-cased telephone. One of those people was Danny Lynch; he'd given her the phone as a gift so he could have exclusive access to her. When it rang, she'd know it was him, and if she didn't answer, she'd better have a legitimate excuse. The other was JFK; he wasn't supposed to have the number, but he'd called himself on it and saved the number while she was in the bathroom one evening.

The first time he called her on it; she thought it was Lynch. 'Mr Lynch,' she said. There was silence for a moment. 'Danny?' she said, thinking he was playing a game with her.

'No, it's not Danny, it's me. Are you seeing Danny Lynch at the same time as me?' He sounded hurt.

'Why no, sugar,' she'd assured him. 'I only see you one at a time.'

Later, when he arrived at her front door with a scowl on his face, she saw it through the viewer. *He was such a child.* Opening the door, she smiled seductively and dragged him off to the bedroom; within a minute or two, he didn't care anymore. After that, he never mentioned Lynch's name again. She wondered why he'd chosen the bachelor life and asked him directly once. He'd said it was to keep the people at work guessing; there were rumours circulating that he was gay, but he did nothing to dispel them.

'If only they knew,' he said.

'Would the truth be less acceptable to them?' she asked.

'What do you think?' he said sarcastically.

'I think that you're such a contradiction, a hypocrite—'

He interrupted. 'I don't pay you to think!'

You don't pay me at all. It irritated her, but she kept her thoughts to herself, him using that phone number meant she had to guard herself whenever she answered it. If Lynch knew someone else had the number, there would be hell to pay. So when he was round, she kept both phones switched off.

The red phone was ringing.

Think of the Devil! He's going to tell me he's staying at the club. She was actually relieved at the thought.

She picked up the receiver. 'Hello?'

'Marilyn?'

Marilyn? The voice didn't belong to Lynch or JFK. She frowned into the receiver. It had to be a wrong number, but still she said, 'Yes.' She thought she knew the voice. She wondered if one of them was pranking her. The next few words unsettled her.

'Or should that be Melissa?'

What the... Only two people knew her real name. Only two people had this number. This wasn't one of them. The caller reminded her of a snake.

'Go and check your safe, and don't hang up or do anything stupid. I'll hang on – I know you have two phones – don't call the police if you want to live.'

Is this really happening? Keeping the phone at her ear, she approached the safe in a daze. The door appeared shut, but the key override was in the lock with her car keys dangling from it.

'You've been in my house?' she said, her thoughts racing. It must have been after she'd returned from the opening. 'You broke into my house in broad daylight! How?'

'Never mind about that; I did – and that's all you need to know.'

You stupid bitch! She cursed herself. She kept the keys with her whenever she left the house, but it never occurred to her that anyone would rob her while she was actually in the house. When she undressed, she left the keys on the bedside table. She never heard a thing. He must have come in while she was in the bath. If he *knew* the people she was screwing...

'You've made a really big mistake, mister. Do you know who—'

He cut her off short. 'I know *exactly* who all your friends are and I don't give a shiny shite. Listen very carefully, Melissa.' The caller accentuated the double 's' in her name with a hiss. 'I want a favour from you, and if you are a good girl, you'll get all your stuff back.'

She listened, too stunned to argue.

'I don't think Mr Lynch is going to be very happy when he hears you've robbed his girlfriend.'

The weariness in the caller's voice implied he didn't actually want to get Lynch involved, not unless he had to. 'Now if you do as I say, he doesn't have to be any the wiser, it's only a small thing I'm going to ask, but you need to consider your position carefully.'

Her stomach churned; she felt sick. The money belonged to Lynch. *Just look after it a bit, while the club gets up and running.* She brazened it out with him. 'What, you stole nearly a hundred grand from me – and now you want to *blackmail* me, as well? You know what? I might just tell him myself.'

'Melissa, you're too smart to do that, besides, according to your notes, ninety thousand belongs to him, apart from that you really aren't thinking straight, are you, *Melissa*?' He read an entry from her diary.

Lynch: *'Your policeman friend protects you doesn't he?'*
You: *'He does.'*
Lynch: *'Good, then the old bill won't come here looking for anything.'*

'Do you remember writing that? *Melissa*, you've overlooked the fact he'll think it was *you* who stole it. It won't be me he's going to come after; he's going to be coming after you.' The caller mocked her with a short, sharp, scared intake of breath. 'Well, that's all right then, but what will our friend say when he finds out you've been keeping a file on him?' A soft sigh, laden with disappointment came down the line. 'What do you think he'll do when he finds out about your friend in the police force? What will he think when he is investigated for the illegal—'

'Okay, okay – I get the picture, but I'm not promising *anything* until I know exactly what it is you are after.'

When he told her, she was incredulous. 'What?'

'Yeah, I know, it seems too easy, doesn't it?'

'I guess you have your reasons, but I want to know what's going on.'

'Trust me, you don't want to know. You want your money back, don't you? You wouldn't *want* Mr Lynch finding out about your diary.'

'No – but how do I know you'll give the money back, I can't trust *you.* You robbed me!'

'Melissa, the way I see it, you have two choices. Either you do or you don't. Now, I want you to post on the wall of your Marilyn Mooner Facebook account as soon as he books in with you again. You will announce, 'Can't wait for more birthday celebrations'. When I see it, I'll call. You will give me the details and time, and I will give you your further instructions. Do we have a deal?'

With little choice but to agree, she told him, 'We have a deal.' She put the phone back in its cradle. A sense of unreality hung over her emotions. She could just as easily have laughed as cried. She felt crazy.

What he wanted was ridiculously easy; she knew everything had a price, but what could he be planning to want *that?*

As she sat thinking, the telephone rang again, interrupting her. She wasn't in the mood, but she composed herself. Taking a deep breath, she picked it up it. The caller, oblivious to her predicament, sent the sounds of heavy breathing down the line. The relief she felt swung her mood to crazy laughter. It was all she could do to prevent herself becoming hysterical; she knew exactly who this was. It was his calling card.

'Jack?' She managed to pull herself together – ever the actress, she turned in a good performance now.

'It's Mr President, to you!' he said, laughing, 'and I'm planning a very private birthday party for tomorrow night. I'd very much like it if I could come over to you.'

A weak smile crossed her lips and her mood lifted. If she'd have told him what was happening, he'd have sorted it, but she was now confident the situation was under her control.

'Cheeky! Well, Mr JFK, let me check my diary. Oh, it looks like I'm free around 11 o'clock tomorrow night.' He had a 'birthday' every week; he reminded her of a man she once saw on the television, who celebrated Christmas three hundred and sixty five days a year. She thanked her lucky stars his sex drive wasn't up to that; it made her smile vaguely. She felt the loose knot in her stomach tighten as her nerves kicked in.

'I'll see you then, Marilyn.'

'Yes, Jack, I'll see you then.'

She put the phone down and walked over to where her laptop sat and posted the message.

A few minutes later, she received a call.

'Tomorrow at 11 p.m.,' she told the caller in a quiet voice. Lynch was due anytime. If he overheard, he'd do more than ask questions.

The phone disconnected. She chided herself. *What are you doing Melissa?*

The doorbell rang. She jumped at the sound. Her nerves jangled. It was Lynch.

Chapter 59

Kennedy's mobile rang. It was unusual for Tanner to ring him on a Saturday unless it was important. He answered it, knowing there was every chance his day off would end in a few minutes. He listened as Tanner requested a meeting with him, away from work.

'What's this about?' he said.

'Not on the phone, sir. We need to meet.'

'Okay. Why don't you come to my house,' he said, checking his watch, 'say, in half an hour's time?'

'I'll see you then, sir.'

Agitated by the proposition Tanner had put to him, he paced up and down his living room.

'Jesus,' he said, chewing on the end of a pencil. 'I can't allow that and you know it!'

Tanner sat forward in the chair to retrieve a glass of water from the coffee table. 'Sir, we have him placed him in the pub where Kathy Bird was drinking that night, then later you saw him in the street with her. Now we have a caller, who not only says he knows what happened to *her,* he's saying he has Eilise Staples as well. What else do you want?'

'John, believe me, I want him nailed as much as you do, but we don't have anything that warrants our going sniffing around in the travelling community. What will we do if it's just some nut that watched both cases on Crimewatch? I can't risk it, especially at the moment; it's a Human Rights hot potato. I need good, reliable evidence.'

'So, you won't allow me to do this.' He finished his water and put the glass back down.

Kennedy studied him carefully for a minute. He didn't take his eyes from his face as he spoke.

'If you do anything without my knowledge, if *anyone* finds out about it there'll be hell to pay. Is that clear?'

There was a mixture of messages in the DCI's expression. The way he offered his hand confirmed it. *He never does that.* They shook hands.

Kennedy wanted him to do it.

Later in the afternoon, Tanner switched on his laptop and started to research the history and culture of bare-knuckle fighting among gypsies. He read for around two hours, totally captivated by a world he hadn't realised still existed. Then he watched a selection of YouTube videos. The fights took place mostly; it seemed, in quiet country lanes, fields and car parks. There was a tradition of settling disputes between families with the fist and not always the fists of those that had the original dispute, but rather more able representatives, usually grown up sons or nephews. It was about honour. The fights were marshalled after a fashion, intervention taking place only if the basic rules were broken, biting being especially frowned upon. The bigger fights had enormous sums of money wagered on the outcome and attracted large crowds. He learned that the venues were never publicised in advance, with arrangements made only in the last moments, because if the police found out they would shut them down. A few of the fighters were clearly legends among the community, but none of them matched the man he was looking for, so he found himself scanning the faces of the people in the crowds. No one bore any resemblance to the E-Fit. No one came close.

He pulled a few strings, someone who owed him a favour who knew someone else. That evening, Tanner got a call back; he was to meet a fighter Sunday lunchtime, at a pub in Tilbury.

Chapter 60

Melissa dressed in his favourite costume, the white sequined gown and examined the fit in the mirror, smoothing it down, adjusting its lines. It would be off in a while, but still, she liked to look authentic. She rehearsed the skippy, happy moves that came just before the end of her singing routine. She practised it to perfection.

The white telephone rang. She jumped at the sound. It was eleven o'clock.

He liked to play these stupid games. She felt apprehensive; she wasn't sure why. Something was happening she couldn't understand and if she wanted her life back, she couldn't do anything but go along with it.

'Hello?' she breathed.

'Are you ready to receive your president? I'm right outside your front door.'

She opened it. 'You could have just rung the bell like anybody else would have.'

He breezed in cheerfully, surveying the passageway with his mobile phone; he pretended to be sweeping for hidden bugging devices. He grinned at her. 'But I'm not just anybody else, am I?' He had already removed his jacket. His face glowed red with the flush of Viagra.

'No, Jack, there's no one else quite like you.' She dimmed the lights. 'Happy birthday, by the way.'

'And there I was, thinking you'd forgotten.' He was now lying on the bed naked, apart from a pair of black socks.

She slinked toward him, beginning his song.

Chapter 61

The caller finalised his plans. He had spent the past week observing the house at random times. The girl was living on her own, which was perfect because although she was only a pawn in his game, she was also exactly his type and lived in exactly the right kind of place, somewhere easy to get into. It had no burglar alarm; it also backed directly onto a park, which proved to be good for covert night time observation, as well as for an alternate escape route – if needed.

The night before, something happened that almost changed his plans. As he approached the rear of her house from the darkness of the park, he saw someone else slipping over her back fence. *The Peeping Tom from outside the blonde's place!*

He observed from behind the fence, standing on tiptoes. The other man spied in on her through the windows, following her as she moved from room to room. After two hours, the lights downstairs turned off one by one until finally the house was in darkness. A moment later, a light from within set the upstairs windows dimly aglow.

When the Peeper finally stole away, he'd worked out a place for him in his plans.

He followed him home.

When he was sure he'd retired for the night, he broke in. He sifted through everything. *These people with mobile phones that never password protect them.* He smirked when he spotted the clumsy efforts to disguise PIN numbers, passwords and usernames.

What's this, a jar of chloroform? What is this guy up to? He contemplated his next move, taking his time.

Looking around, he found an empty bottle of vodka in the glass recycling. Quickly and carefully, he poured half the chloroform into it, then topped up the remainder in the jar with water. He moved out of the room, amazed at how fast such a small amount of vapour had affected him; he shook his head, and once he was clear of the fumes, took a deep breath.

A rare smile touched his lips; he was pleased with how well this unexpected development fitted seamlessly into his plans. When he first saw her come jogging out of the back gate into the park, she was wearing tight Lycra leggings that revealed the shape of her legs, the clearly defined muscles rippled with latent power, and she was only cruising. Black pony-tailed hair swished from side to side, matching the tempo of her pace, checking her watch for the time, she set her dark eyes into a focal point in the distance. Sucking in a deep breath, she upped her pace and her full lips pursed into an O shape with each exhalation.

She was one of the stalker's Facebook friends. Her face instantly recognisable from his photographs, but the poise, the power and grace of her movement, needed witnessing in the flesh for full appreciation.

She was a perfect fit, and now he had a scapegoat.

He felt no guilt; the guy was a pervert anyway. There had to be dozens of photographs of women all over his place. It would be only a question of time before this Peeper raped someone. He was performing a public service. Prevention was better than cure.

Looking back from her gate, it was a distance of three houses to the alleyway. He scooted round to the front quickly, then along the pavement, up to her front door. He rang the doorbell just to be sure no one else was there, using the sleeve of his jumper stretched over his thumb, so as not to leave any prints. There was no answer. He walked casually to the side gate, trying the thumb latch to open it, realising it was secured from the other side; he reached over and undid the bolt. Once through, he observed the property through the rear windows. The inside looked as if she'd just arrived and hadn't finished unpacking, there were half a dozen tea chests filled up to the top with items wrapped in wads of paper. From what he saw, there was no sign of another occupant.

She was definitely alone.

Perfect.

Later that night, he unpacked a box of jam-jars he'd bought from a boot-sale. Cutting a hole in one of the screw-down tin lids, he passed a flexible breather pipe through it and taping it all round with duct tape for an airtight seal, he fitted a mask to the other end and taped that to the pipe as well. He'd reuse the lid, because it would fit any of the jars in the box.

Chapter 62

Reaching over the top of the gate, feeling for the catch, the caller quietly slid the bolt back and slipped undetected into her back garden.

He squatted in the pool of shadow under a tree, and gripping the corner of his jacket raised it like a dark wing to light a cigarette under. His face flared yellow for a second. He blinked and glanced up at the moon. It looked red and otherworldly; he rubbed his eyes. Its appearance didn't change.

He thought it might be an omen, a warning of danger ahead.

It took another half-hour before the lights began switching off, room by room. The last ones were upstairs, the bedroom and bathroom, he guessed. When all the lights were out, he dressed for the job. Putting on his paper boiler suit and over shoes, he taped the joints to the trousers, to stop them coming off and put on his latex gloves. He pulled up the hood, tightening the draw cord, and then fixed his mask in place. Advancing in the shadow cast by the high fence, he crossed the last few feet and paused by the house to look around. He listened up close to the windowpane and satisfied no one was moving around inside, scored the glass with a cutter, using masking tape to prevent any fragments falling noisily onto the ground. He popped the leaded pane with his elbow. A few moments later, he was inside. A large railway style clock on the kitchen wall told him it was just before midnight.

All the lights were out; he navigated his way up to the base of the stairs; the coin-sized beam of his penlight generated a sufficient spill of light to enable him to avoid obstacles like chairs and discarded shoes. He ascended the staircase to the top landing. With all the doors shut, he was reliant on his inner compass to confirm that the door on his far right corresponded with the last light he'd seen turned off. He moved close to it and listened at the hairline gap where the door met the frame. He heard the sound of regular, deep breathing. Two long minutes passed and the first gentle rumblings of snoring began. Once he was sure she was asleep; he took a small bottle of liquid from his pocket. Catching a whiff of its sweet, seductive odour as he unscrewed the lid, he was surprised that such a small exposure could have snatched his breath away. He poured a measure of the solution onto the wadding, folded it and silently opened the door. He made a point of waking her just as the wad covered her nose and mouth.

Her eyes snapped open with sleepy surprise, immediately followed by wide-eyed fear, a futile struggle, momentary disbelief when she finally registered what was happening, and then she succumbed to blissful unconsciousness.

He was already hard and he salivated as he fitted the condom. Seconds later, she was his. The rustling of the paper suit and his own ragged breathing were the only sounds he heard.

When he'd finished, he carefully extricated himself from her. She was still unconscious. Retreating downstairs back to the kitchen, he unscrewed the lid from the makeshift delivery apparatus, leaving the jar on the side in the kitchen.

Once back outside in the garden, he slit the tape from the overshoes, removed the paper suit and gloves and put all of it inside the bin bag. He knotted it tightly.

Crossing the park to the far end in the darkness and checking all round to make sure he was unobserved, he stopped to hide the bag, tucking it right in underneath a timber bridge that crossed over a deep water-filled ditch.

He climbed the park fence, silently dropping down on the other side; he made his way down the alley, back to where he'd left the car, four hundred yards further up the road.

Chapter 63

The telephone rang, insistently edging its way into his consciousness. At first it fitted with the dream he was having, he even interrupted the dream conversation to say. 'I must get that.'

In a sleepy daze, he rolled over onto his side and answered the phone.

'Tanner,' he mumbled.

It was Kennedy. 'Sorry to disturb, but I need you to report to an incident in Blake Street, number 27. Are you listening?'

'Yes, I am,' he said, forcing his eyes to open wide, trying to blink away the cobwebs of sleep.

'Good, only I couldn't hear anything. It's overlooking the park, not far from your place.'

'What's this all about, sir?'

'Number 27 Blake Street,' he repeated. 'A woman was raped tonight in her own home by some freak wearing a gasmask.'

He looked at his watch. 1:29 a.m. *Oh, great!*

He arrived at the scene twenty minutes later.

Outside on the driveway, was an ambulance. Although the curtains were drawn, half a dozen shadowy silhouettes were clearly backlit, moving around purposefully.

The front door opened unexpectedly; Tanner stepped to one side, allowing the exiting paramedics to pass. They carried the victim out on a stretcher, covered with a blanket up to her chin, an oxygen mask over her mouth and nose. She didn't look much older than his daughter. He watched as they loaded her into the back of the ambulance.

'This is going to be a long night,' he muttered wearily.

Chapter 64

Tanner almost overslept. Some internal mechanism dragged him into consciousness and sifting dreamily through his jumbled thoughts; one came crashing to the fore. *It's Sunday.*

The double helping of coffee he drank before he left, did little to help him shrug off the sleepiness that trawled on his senses, it was a state that evaporated the instant he walked into the public bar. At least half the windows had been smashed and then subsequently boarded over. The darkness contrasted sharply with the brightness outside. He guessed the landlord had given up putting glass back in. His eyesight now adjusted to the dim light, he scanned the room. All eyes were on him.

Look out for a dark-haired guy about thirty, wearing a gold belcher chain with a golden boxing gloves charm hanging down. At least two other men fitted the bill, but his man had been looking out for him. Pulling him over to the bar, the boxer said, 'Are you looking for me, boy?' Introducing himself as the writer Ed Quinn, he shook hands with the middleweight. His name was Paul Kelly; he looked far heavier than his fighting weight, but that wasn't uncommon. He knew enough to know that these guys often blew up in weight between fights, and then trained it off a few weeks before the next one.

Kelly's face, bronzed from a life of working outdoors, had stubbly five o'clock shadow on his high flat cheeks, and hair shaven at the back and sides, leaving a crown of longer dark hair slicked back and oily looking. His features were relatively unmarked. *A clever fighter,* he thought.

'So you're writing about the greatest knuckle fighters are you? Will I be in it, boy?'

'If you are a great fighter, you can be sure of it!' Tanner joked.

'Do you want to be finding out?' Kelly looked serious as he indicated the door.

Suddenly, he felt vulnerable; with half a dozen rough looking men now watching them, Tanner rested his hands on the bar.

Kelly put his big hand over one of them and squeezed. 'Don't worry, boy, I'm joshing with you!'

Tanner found it vaguely unsettling that although he was at least ten years older than Kelly, he insisted on calling him 'boy'. They shared an uneasy few pints, with only stilted conversation going on between them, and then Kelly offered to put him in touch with a well-respected elder, a twice crowned, former King of The Gipsies, Archie Brooks.

Introducing himself to Brooks as Edward Quinn, he elaborated on what he was looking for, old photographs, stories and interviews if possible.

Brooks agreed to meet him at his house that evening.

Archie Brooks' house was like a static caravan, all luxury red tasselled velvet cushions, expensive ornaments and mementoes of a life on the road.

'Too old for the travelling,' he explained. 'I been here fifteen year now … don't like it, but the bones creak these days in cold winters, so here I am, stopped off coolin' my heels for a while, before the next big journey up the stairs,' he said, and then rolled his eyes heavenward. 'If he'll take me,' he said with a wry smile.

'Quinn' interviewed him, getting his opinion on who the greatest ever gipsy champion was. They spoke about what these men looked like, their fighting styles, how they fought. Brooks talked him through what seemed like hundreds of rounds.

'Unless you've been a part of it, you don't know what it's like to carry on when every part of you is busted up and bleeding, 'cos you never quit. People like me, you can't quit. It's all about honour. I never made money like they do today and the hands, sweet Mary.' He held them aloft, examining them with pride. The knuckles were deformed; the fingers gnarled like tree roots. 'They used to pickle the hands in vinegar in those days, did it me self. Used to sit there, I did, with each hand sunk in a jar o' the stuff both sides o' me for hours on end. Used to smell like a chip shop, but made the skin like boot leather, see.'

Eventually, he produced a box and took the lid off. He sifted through an old collection of photographs; there were hundreds, all of them well-thumbed. He was careful to keep them in order. They ran through faded sepia to black and white, the newest were coloured ones and they were in all sizes, like the men they portrayed.

'Them old 'uns were my father's – well, would you look at that,' he said, peeling a photo that had stuck to the back of another one. 'I thought I'd lost this one.' His face lit up as he took in all the faces once more. 'This is a group of past champions, taken at a big fight gathering in Plymouth a few years back. Every single one o' them was a champion, in the thirty years before the photo.'

'There are only seventeen of them,' Tanner remarked.

'Aye, a few are dead, a handful has won more than once and this one here…' He tapped his finger on the fighter, who although older than the E-Fit, resembled the man he was looking for. 'He's won it three times.'

Tanner pointed at each of them in turn, asking the names, carefully noting them down. He was only interested in the three-time champion though, Martin 'The Boiler man' Shaw.

He whistled in appreciation. 'Three times, that's quite an achievement.'

'Aye, it is that. The first time he took it; he was just a young man. Then he just disappeared for ten years. Come back, won it again, held it for two years. He quit before some fresh young bull took him down, not like most of 'em, never knowing when to stop. He stood down from the fighting. He's unreliable, anyway, can't hardly find him when you want him. You know; he still fights occasionally, when the urge takes him. He has a terrible temper, that one – he'd suddenly boil up, then he'd let loose.'

Tanner looked closer at the photograph, squinting, then at Brooks. 'Isn't that you, Archie, right next to him in the photo there?'

'Aye, we were stood more or less in the order we held the titles. He took it off me.' He rubbed his chin at the memory. 'I was in me forties, never been beat, not fair and square at any rate.' He pulled his top lip up and back with the crook of his forefinger, revealing the missing teeth down the entire side of his mouth. 'See that – got jumped by ten of 'em, dropped four before someone swung a bat on me. Woke up in hospital, so I did.' He sighed deeply. 'There was no need for it, you know what I mean? It's not how real men deal with things.' He twisted each of the rings on his fingers, so the fronts of all faced forwards. 'Anyways, when he came along, he took everything I threw at him, for the first time in me life I felt the age creeping up on me. He never threw ten shots to land one; he never wasted the power, unless he knew it was landing. He served me with a left that shook me all the way down to me boots, he never says a word, not like some talking' at you all the time, before the fight, during the fight – no, not him. Never says a word, just boils up red with the rage. Now I'm old, I don't mind admitting that's one of the frightingest things about him – you don't know what he's thinking – only sound he makes is Pum! Pum! Pum!' The old man was popping off shots to demonstrate, the look on his face, mean. 'Getting more power that way, punching, punching, punching, everyone a stick o' dynamite – *murderous* – I'd never lie down. Even now, you'd have to put me down and the only way to stop me is to knock me sparko, you know what I mean? I woke up in the middle o' next week! The boys told me he caught me with three punches, the one that shook me, I remember, but the other two...I never saw them coming.'

Tanner took his camera out. 'Would you mind if I take a shot of that for the book?' He pointed to the champion's photograph.

'Put that thing away, will you? Here, take it.' Brooks handed the photograph to Tanner. 'Let me have it back when you've finished.'

Holding the photograph in his hands, he was unsure if it was in his imagination, but he caught the faintest whiff, the smell of horses and saddles, which reminded him of the tack room at the riding school he used to go to as a boy. 'Thanks,' he said. 'Oh, and one other thing. I'd love to talk to the Boiler man, do you think that would be possible?' He looked hopeful. It did not last long.

'You'll be lucky; he don't talk much to his own kind; he's got four words – yes, no and fuck off – keeps himself to himself. Besides, he is a *real* traveller, don't stay long in any place. Only time you ever see him is when he wants to be seen, usually when there's a big fight with money involved.'

'So you don't know where he lives?'

'No, I don't.' His eyes narrowed with suspicion. 'Why would you be asking me that?'

'I'm sorry,' Tanner said quickly. 'I was only thinking about the interview.'

'Let's get one thing straight, Mr Quinn, book or no book, if you want to keep that head of yours on your shoulders, you won't go turning up anywhere without me or my say so, do you know what I mean?'

For a split second, he thought the old man saw right through him. He fixed on his best poker face and replied, 'I wouldn't dream of it. Look, can I get to see an actual fight?'

'For the book? We'll see. Leave your number, Mr Quinn, and I'll call you.'

On arriving home that night, Tanner scanned the photograph and emailed a copy to Kennedy.

Kennedy examined the copy of the photograph closely. Going over the faces with a magnifying glass for a second time, he located the suspect quite quickly. *It's him. I know it!*

A friend of his was working on the national database of mug shots that would soon be available to police forces all over the country, and although it was getting late, he phoned him.

'Malcolm, it's John Kennedy here. Yes…yes, I'm fine and you? Good, listen, I have an old photograph here I'm trying to track. Yes, I know that, but I wondered if I send it, you could…Well, call it an experiment then. It's just that I'm trying to tie up a cold case…You will? Great, give me your email address…Okay, got that. Yeah, we must get together sometime…Yes, I know; it *has* been a while. Let me know how you get on … yeah, thanks. Bye.'

Chapter 65

Monday, 5 March 2007

Tanner entered Kennedy's office just as the DCI flipped his mobile closed.

'Got a new phone, sir?'

'No, it isn't new, it's my personal one,' he said as he drained the last of his tea. Tendrils of steam continued to rise from the empty cup.

How does he manage to drink it when it's that hot? Tanner wondered.

'I'm needed in the cells. Wait here, I'll be two minutes,' he said and grabbed his jacket from the back of the chair. He seemed distracted.

'Shall I come back in a minute?' Tanner said.

'No – wait, just give me a couple of minutes, get Theresa to bring you some tea,' he called back as he left.

Stepping from the DCI's office, Kennedy caught her eye and beckoned her over. As she approached, she looked at him inquisitively.

'What's up, John?' she said.

'Nothing, just wondered if you wouldn't mind making me a tea?'

'Of course not, what about the chief,' she said, barely able to suppress a grin, 'would he like another one?'

Recognising that she had adopted his own derogatory term for the DCI, he grinned widely in return. 'Well, he didn't ask, but you'd better get him one, or he'll only complain,' Tanner said.

'Okay, I'm on it,' she said laughing.

As she walked off, he watched the sway of her behind almost all the way to the tea station; where she turned and caught him looking.

Quickly retreating into Kennedy's office, he sat down. He didn't see the smile that spread over her face as she filled the kettle.

Expecting Kennedy to return at any moment, he looked all round his office, and then his attention settled on the DCI's out-tray, where a folded up copy of the Sun lay. The headline caught his eye. *25-Year-Old Ilford Woman Raped At Home. Police Seek Gas Mask Attacker.* It featured so prominently; he wondered if it was what he had summoned him for.

Who told the papers about the gasmask, Tanner? He imagined him tapping the offending word with his forefinger, and he'd feel defensive, speculating. *With everyone sworn to secrecy, sir – it would have to be the victim.*

The empty seat behind the desk remained as he left it; pushed back, spun halfway round, abandoned in a hurry. Years of use had moulded the back of it into an imprint of Kennedy's posture. *When he goes, the first thing I get rid of is that chair,* he assured himself.

He sighed involuntarily, flipped his pocket book open and began reviewing the notes he'd made the day before.

He rubbed his tired eyes, hoping to rejuvenate them, but only succeeded in blurring his vision. What Tanner needed was a good night's sleep, and he had a feeling he might not be getting one of those for quite some time.

This rape had jumped the queue, and he was only too aware that he still had to trace Martin Shaw. He wondered what had happened in the cells, to warrant the DCI going down there with such apparent urgency.

Finished with his notes, he bookmarked the first page with a pen clipped over it and then shut the pad.

His fingertips drummed on the edge of the desk; he was becoming impatient now. Pulling up his sleeve, he looked at his watch. *Is he ever coming back from those cells?*

The door behind him was open a crack; the bustling sounds of the busy office came through, it seemed there was a spate of telephone calls, most of them had been answered, but a couple of phones rang on insistently – there weren't enough people to answer all the calls. Just to be helpful he considered going out and answering a few calls himself; he'd rather be doing *something* other than wasting time as he waited for the chief's return. He slipped into a kind of non-thinking abstraction.

Theresa appeared, entering backwards with a cup in both hands, she turned and handed him one before putting the other on the desk.

'He still not back?'

'No, but he said he'd only be a couple of minutes.' Tanner shrugged. Now they were alone together in Kennedy's office, awkwardness descended on them, blanking them off from one another. It made for a difficult, stilted conversation, knowing he might walk in at any moment.

She broke first. 'I must get on,' she said.

'Yeah sure, I...thanks for the tea.'

'You're welcome,' she said.

At the door, she hesitated.

'Does the chief seem okay to you?'

'Grumpy as ever,' he said and grinned. 'Why do you ask?'

'Oh, it's probably nothing. He just seems on edge lately. Or is it just me?' she said.

The door jerked open; she snatched her hand from the handle and jumped back.

'Excuse me; I'm not interrupting anything am I?' Kennedy shot her a look as if she'd betrayed him and burned Tanner with a harsh glare.

She saw it and quickly fumbled an explanation. 'I had my hand on the handle, sir, when you pushed it, that's why I jumped away.' It made her sound guilty.

'Theresa?'

She stopped dead in the doorway, her body language defensive. She did not turn.

'You don't have to call me, sir.' He smiled, but it looked forced. He went round the desk, spinning the chair to face forwards before sitting down.

'That was a waste of time. Some nutter claiming to be the Midnight Man, he was as thick as two short planks. I invented a raid and questioned him about it, and he confessed! Right, now where were we?'

Tanner thought about what she had said. The DCI *did* seem on edge, and what he'd just told him sounded implausible, there was something wrong. He knew better than to ask what it was when Kennedy was in this sort of mood. The last thing he needed was to have his balls chewed off. 'I came in to tell you about the interview I had with the victim at the hospital last night,' he said. A small but involuntary cough escaped his lips; he caught it in his cupped right hand and then took a sip of tea. 'Right, sir, what we have so far. I managed to speak to the victim, Natasha Stone, last night. She'd only just moved to that address; she inherited the property from her grandmother. She used to go and stay there most weekends to keep her company, so there was a lot of her stuff already there. Anyway, she moved in straight away, pretty much as soon as her granny died.'

'I don't need her life story. Let's move it on a bit shall we?' He sighed.

'It's all kind of relevant, sir.'

'All right, but let's just speed it up, shall we?'

Before continuing, Tanner cleared his throat and took another sip of tea. 'She'd gone to bed just before midnight, Saturday. She reckoned she'd only been asleep a few minutes when she was woken; she thinks he whispered something to her, but she couldn't recall exactly. She said it might have been her name.' He wasn't actually reading from his notes; he used them more as an aid to his memory; he turned onto the next page. 'When she switched on the light, she saw the intruder was wearing a gas mask. She said she was paralysed with fear. Before she had a chance to recover her senses, he pinned her down and pushed something over her nose and mouth.'

Noting the increasing level of drama, Kennedy looked up from jotting notes of his own as Tanner continued.

'She's a school laboratory technician and she says she recognised the smell straight away – it was chloroform.'

'Chloroform? That isn't used anymore. No one's used that in this country for years. I thought it was banned.' Kennedy scribbled more notes. 'We need to get someone onto to that. Is it still available and do you need a licence?'

'Already done, sir. We had a stroke of luck, because when we started talking about it, she told me one of her colleagues was caught making it at the school and they suspended him immediately. His name is Adam...' The surname eluded him; he started snapping his fingers. 'You know like the park... '

Clearly enjoying his subordinate's rare moment of fallibility, he prompted him unhelpfully. 'Which park – Hyde park, Valentine's park, come on, Tanner, get with it!'

Heat flushed under his collar as he ran his finger down the page. 'There it is... Bletchley, Adam Bletchley.'

Kennedy remained impassive and thoughtful. 'Has anyone managed to speak to this Bletchley?' He analysed the smug look on Tanner's face. 'You moved quickly on this one did you?' he said, a tight smile on his lips.

'Yes, as soon as Natasha gave us a name. His landlady said he left to go out last night and didn't come back. Apparently, he does that quite a lot, staying out until morning. He's a night fisherman, sir.'

He raised an eyebrow at him. 'It's a good excuse to be out all night, I suppose. He fits the bill. Let's have him in for questioning.'

'We're out looking for him, even as we speak, sir.'

The dryness in his throat wasn't just from talking; he was nervous, too. Something about the whole business was disturbing him, and he guessed it disturbed Kennedy, too. He tilted his empty cup; and pulled a face at the thought of drinking the last cold drop.

Kennedy finished his tea and buzzed Theresa to ask for another. *Want another tea?* he mouthed. Tanner nodded.

'Tanner would like another tea, and while you're making him one, could you make one for me?' Although he winked at him as he said it, his humour was just not funny, especially with him hoping to improve his chances with her. It sounded like Kennedy knew and was goading him on purpose.

'Oh, I've got to admit that was very funny coming from you. You don't *really* think she'll believe it was *me* asking for another tea, do you?' His cheeks flushed.

'What are you going on about, Tanner?'

'You, sir,' he said angrily. 'I'm going on about the way you treat women as lesser beings. Like they're just there to serve you.'

'Tanner, I was joking!' Kennedy looked indignant; his expression darkened. 'How dare you presume to judge me – is this because you're jealous? That she does what *I* tell her and not you?'

Back footed, Tanner snorted. 'What? Of course not! I *ask* her.'

The DCI stared at him; the heat of anger suddenly replaced by cold resignation. 'I knew it; you're shagging her, aren't you?'

'Come on, sir, that's out of order!' he said, not quite knowing what else to say.

Kennedy then changed tack so fast; he left Tanner with his mouth agape. 'Did we get anything else from the victim?'

Tanner wet his finger and rifled through his notes quickly. 'We did indeed.' He scanned for the right page and then began again. 'She had a few problems initially with Bletchley, started straight away really. The usual sort of thing, he was a bit creepy and overfriendly, but she dismissed that as him being shy and overcompensating for it. Little by little he wears her down, and she ends up going out with him a couple of times.'

There was a knock at the door behind him.

'Ah, that'll be our tea, get that for me, would you?'

He opened the door; Theresa brought in a tray this time, with biscuits, two mugs of tea, a couple of sugar sachets and a teaspoon. She set the tray down and slipped away without looking at him. He hoped she hadn't heard what Kennedy said.

The more Tanner saw her around, the more he liked her. *Isn't it funny? When you think someone is unavailable, you don't give her a second thought, but since she became available…*Off duty he thought of little else, he'd started thinking about her in quiet moments. Lately, he'd been thinking about her at work, too. She was always so neat and well presented; her full-bodied dark auburn hair not quite touching the shoulders, bouncing as she walked. She had an appealing way about her, kindly, with bright cornflower blue eyes and a vague smile that was never far away from her lips.

Kennedy caught him watching her go out the door and scowled at him, making no secret of his disapproval.

Tanner began to think the chief might be a little jealous.

Kennedy stirred in his sugar first, before taking the spoon in his mouth, drawing it out between pressed lips, sucking it dry. 'Sugar?' he said and offered him the spoon.

Tanner declined, deciding he'd have it without. He tried a sip. It was too hot. Putting the cup down, he continued, 'She said looking back; she shouldn't have done it, but then hindsight is a wonderful thing. He charmed her from the start; she said he seemed too good to be true. Whatever she thought, he said he was thinking too. Whenever she spoke, he would say, "*I was about to say that. Oh, that's just like me – I'm like that!*"'

Kennedy had sat forward and placed his elbows on the desk; for a second Tanner thought he did it because he was interested. Then he put his forehead down on top of the blotter and folded his hands at the back of his head.

He paused and stared at him with disbelief. 'Sir?'

Suddenly Kennedy's mobile vibrated and spun around, causing the surface of the teas to ripple. He snapped it up and opened it.

'I'm going to have to take that. Give me a minute will you, Tanner?'

'Sure,' he said.

The moment Tanner closed the door behind him, he answered it.

Outside Kennedy's office, he debated whether to wait or not as he leaned on the wall next to the door. Something was definitely going on. The chief never usually booted him out while he was on the telephone. The call was on his personal phone again; he hoped his mother was okay.

He stood and watched Theresa over on the other side of the office, on the telephone, writing things down. 'Yes, okay...got that,' she said into the receiver and then looked up from her desk at him and feigned a yawn, flapping her hand in front of her mouth as she did so.

His eyebrows jerked up involuntarily at her; she mirrored him, and he looked away quickly, aware that if anyone noticed the little exchange, the jungle drums would rumble, and the gossip would begin.

He continued with the notes, reading them whilst outside, leaning against Kennedy's wall. He didn't know what was up with him, but there was no way he'd sit through and listen to the entire transcript. He decided to condense the story for the DCI's benefit.

At the hospital the day before, when the nurse showed them down to her room, Natasha Stone was sitting in a chair beside her bed. The bed was unmade. She'd clearly just risen from it. He introduced himself and the WPC with him. He asked if she felt able to answer a few questions. She was located in a side room all to herself. She looked weary and hollow eyed, she fiddled nervously with the belt of her dressing gown, winding it round her fingers tightly, as if to tie her hands, to stifle the story they might tell.

She began hesitantly at first. 'I'm supposed to be grieving for my grandmother and this happens.' She took a deep breath, then the words tumbled out of her in a torrent; Natasha told Tanner the whole sordid story and he listened. He jotted down notes of everything she told him, in case he'd need to refer back to them later.

'I was working with this guy, Adam Bletchley, at the school in the laboratory prep rooms. I wasn't too sure about him; he was just a little bit too nice and it didn't seem natural. He had this plastic smile, if you know what I mean. He hounded me to go out with him and I did a few times, but I wasn't sure it was working or even right for me. He was a bit odd at times. My granny was sick and I think I just let him in under the radar because I needed someone, you know?' He'd asked if she could slow down.

She waited for him to catch up writing before she continued, 'Anyway; I bumped into this girl at the supermarket. Well, not exactly bumped into her, she spotted me and made a beeline, saying, "Hey, you're Natasha, am I right?"' Tanner noticed she put on another voice for the other girl. 'I said, "I'm sorry, do I know you?"' She watched as he scribbled his notes. When he stopped, she began again.

'She said to me, "You're seeing Adam Bletchley, aren't you?" I asked her again, "Do I know you?" She said, "No, you don't, but my friend over there works at your school and she just pointed you out to me." She nods in the direction of her friend. I recognise her and give a little wave. I'm also feeling a bit relieved, because I don't know what this girl wants.' She finished the sentence, making it sound like a question, her voice lilting upwards as she spoke the last word. Her eyes had brimmed with tears.

'Take your time, Natasha,' the WPC said gently.

'Anyway, the first thing she tells me is to give Adam a wide berth.' "I'm warning you as a friend." At this point, I'm thinking, what? Now her friend comes over to join us, she says "Hi," but looks a bit embarrassed. She's one of the chemistry teachers and I always work in the prep room, between her lab and the other one next door. I always prep for her; Adam always preps for the other side. He told me she was a funny woman and that they didn't get on.' She pointed to the jug on the bedside cabinet. 'Excuse me a minute, would you pour me a water? Thank you.'

She gulped a mouthful down. Tanner turned his page over.

'Well, then she starts to tell me about her and Adam. I mean it's crazy. I only went out with him a few times! Anyway, the other girl is now giving me her life story. "I was with Adam for a year. Now that I look at it, it was the worst year of my life. It isn't even over now, but it is getting better." She stuck her hand out for me to shake. "I'm Rainy, by the way."'

'Not even over now. Natasha, what did she mean by that?' the WPC asked her.

'Well, Rainy tells me, "There was nothing so noticeable at first, just the little things. He'd niggle about the clothes I was wearing. You know; that don't suit you; the colours are all wrong, it makes you look big, are you putting on weight? You don't exercise enough, rah, rah, rah!"'

For Tanner, a picture had begun to emerge from her account of things. He wasn't sure how much of it was relevant, but she needed to talk and he let her.

Bletchley had isolated the other girl from her friends; setting up confrontations based on fictitious accounts of something he'd had a disagreement with them about.

He skipped further into the notes he'd made. There were plenty of allegations concerning Bletchley's manipulative ways. There was one occasion, she said, when she challenged him, and it resulted in his saying to her, 'You're not really going to take their word over mine are you? Not after all I've done for you.' Telling her, 'You think she's your best friend, don't you? Well, I never would have spoiled that for you if you hadn't have made me do it, but I'm not sure she really is your best friend, you know.'

When she'd asked him why, he'd explained, 'Oh, it's just that she tried to arrange to meet with me at some hotel while you were at your uncle's funeral that time and I wasn't invited, remember? I never went with her of course, but I thought; poor Rainy thinks that's her best friend and all the time she just wants to screw her boyfriend the minute her back's turned.'

Once Bletchley had alienated all her friends, he began working on isolating her from her family, too. Little by little, he crushed her, making her dependent on him, solely dependent. There was no one else left to turn to.

Tanner did not need a crystal ball to predict the outcome. That was when the abuse really began. Nothing Rainy ever did was good enough. She didn't appreciate him. He began to punish her. He wouldn't allow her out. He made her a prisoner in her own home. He didn't like her talking to other people on the phone. He suspected her of seeing other men. The last thing she had – that he still wanted – was her home. She became convinced it was what he really wanted all along, to take her home from her. He tried to make her change her will in his favour. 'You don't want your relatives, those leeches, inheriting it, do you? Not after the way they've treated you!'

For Rainy, it had been the last straw. Finally, she was able to see him for what he really was. It took a lot of effort for her to escape him, because he was so assertive and confident, he succeeded in undermining her at every turn. No matter how hard she tried to break free, he just kept clawing her back. In the end, with a friend's help, she'd had to take out an injunction on him to keep him away. That was what she meant by 'it's not over yet.'

The other girl had told Natasha enough to convince her to take a backward step. She told Tanner she believed what Rainy told her. Her natural defences were over-ridden by worry over her grandmother's illness. If it hadn't been for that, he'd never have got near her. She told Tanner she particularly remembered how his eyes lit up when she told him her grandmother would leave her everything. She rang and told him she didn't want to see him again. After that, he just kept turning up out of the blue. He seemed to know when she was alone, or where she'd be going with her friends. She began to suspect he was stalking her, even intercepting her emails. 'Sniffing them', as she put it. Last of all she told Tanner. 'The funny thing is as well, isn't it marvellous how you always find these things out afterwards? Apparently, he had a nickname among the men at work. They used to give him a wide berth. They called him "Bletch the Letch".'

Tanner shook his head, incredulous he'd gotten away with it for so long.

He asked her a question. 'Natasha, I want you to think carefully. I know he had a mask on and he very quickly drugged you, but was there anything about him that made you think it was Bletchley; his smell or anything like that?'

'Oh, my God!' Natasha covered her cheeks with both hands. 'Oh, my God. When I smelled the chloroform, I was so sure it was him!' She stared right into Tanner's eyes. 'Now I'm not so sure, because I now remember thinking I could smell cigarettes, and he doesn't smoke.'

'He could have come in from a pub or club though, with the smell on his clothes.' Tanner said.

'No, no. It was much stronger than that. Whoever it was, smoked.'

He closed his notebook; it was all clear in his head now.

A moment later, Kennedy opened his door and seeing Tanner still standing there said, 'There you are. I've been buzzing your office for ages.'

Tanner shrugged. 'You said you'd only be a minute, sir, so I waited here.' He followed Kennedy back inside his office.

'We're going to have to wrap this up quickly. Something else has come up.'

Having just reviewed the whole conversation with the victim, he summed it up in just a few words. 'She went out with Bletchley twice, she found out he was an arrogant, narcissistic, controlling son-of-a-bitch out to get her money. She also suspected he may have been sniffing her mailbox—'

'Where the hell did you pick up a disgusting term like that?'

'Her words, sir, not mine.'

'The sooner we get him in, the better. We'll reconvene on the rest of the report. Get it typed up for me. Let me know what forensics comes up with.' He checked his watch. 'Now, if you'll excuse me, I have to go.'

Tanner stood, shut his notebook and slid it into the baggy left hand side pocket of his jacket.

He left the room, doubt nagging at him.

Chapter 66

While Tanner waited for further developments, he ran a few checks on Martin Shaw.

With no more information, there was little chance of tracking him down through the system. The obvious search string was prize-fighter, followed by his name, but the search revealed nothing.

Without a full name, address or date of birth, he wouldn't even get off the ground with the official channels.

A Google search of newspaper archives came up with a single line reference in the Times. *Crowned Third Time, King of the Gipsies William Martin Shaw refuses post-fight interview*, this was followed by an account of the fight. He noted the reporter's name.

Painstakingly picking articles apart, searching for similarities, dates, anything that would confirm it was the same man. Only ten percent of the articles could be relevant to what he was looking for. Convinced Martin was his middle name; he was then able to verify, under that identity, he hadn't paid any tax, or national insurance, or registered as a professional fighter. He was completely outside the system, an outlaw. *What a waste.* He shook his head. All that work building a reputation, becoming a champion three times, that's no mean achievement and given he did it with a ten year break in between...

Originally he had him pictured as an ignorant brute, now he began to suspect that the opposite might be true. His public image let his fists do the talking, while behind the scenes he was highly intelligent and resourceful. He'd have to be, because if he wasn't, they'd have caught him years ago. *Where did you go, yet stay sharp enough to come back and reclaim your crown after ten years? Prison records! That's it; he'd been in prison.* The new hunch failed to produce anything. *If he'd gone abroad, he'd have to have a passport.* He checked that, too. Nothing. Suddenly he had it; he'd changed his name.

When Tanner had finished checking out his latest lead and drawn yet another blank, it left him with a number of problems. If only he had a clue where to look for him. According to Brooks, no one knew, and if he did find him, he'd have to either bring him in or find a way to get some DNA to run through the national database. *How?*

He felt it in his waters; the guy was in there somewhere, for something, he had to be. His stomach groaned audibly, telling him it was lunchtime. After checking his watch, he reached into his top drawer and pulled out a sandwich. Taking a bite, he stared into the middle of the office wall.

He had to admit, he was stumped.

Chapter 67

Just after lunchtime, Tanner's phone rang. *Kennedy!*

'I thought we were clear about this, no details, everything to be kept under wraps. The last thing we want is for a copycat nutter to latch onto it! Don't you think I've got enough to do without having to worry about whether or not we have a mole in this office?' The thought of another 'Kennedy Inquisition' made his heart sink. *Finally, he'd gotten around to the headline.* By now, of course, he was half-prepared for it.

'I know, sir, but it didn't come from us. I assumed you wanted to talk to me about Bletchley, sir.'

'What about him?'

'He's been arrested; they're bringing him back to the station now.'

'Why did I have to phone *you* to find that out, Tanner?'

He made a face down the phone. 'I thought you might have wanted it kept off the airwaves for now, what with the Gasman headline leak—'

'I just want him in here, Tanner. How long before he gets here?'

'A few minutes yet.'

Kennedy threw the newspaper back in to his out-tray, irritated by the nickname the press had given this character. He knew for sure there'd probably be a string of copycats. That was why they always kept something back, to help weed them out. At least the press hadn't reported about the chloroform and the boiler suit yet.

Tanner knocked on the door and entering Kennedy's office, said, 'Sir, we've just got him booked in downstairs. I imagine you'll want him to sweat a bit before we interview him?' Then he pointed to the headline. 'It's weird, calling him the Gasman; it makes him sound like someone who's coming to take your meter reading.'

The DCI gave him a withering glare. 'I assume Bletchley didn't say anything?'

'He's been cautioned, but he said straight away; he didn't do anything. He hasn't stopped talking, sir. We're just waiting for the search warrant – *then* we'll see what he has to say.'

'Assuming we find something. What have we got from Scenes of Crime so far?'

'Forensically, we have nothing, sir,' he said, swallowing the gum he was chewing.

'Well do we have *anything*?' Kennedy remarked sarcastically.

Tanner looked confused.

'It doesn't matter. Is there a new book out called *How to Commit the Perfect Crime* or something?' he said with a weary sigh.

'They didn't find a single thing, not even a pubic hair. He used a condom and he either flushed it down the toilet, or took it with him. He was dressed in a World War Two gas mask—'

'World War Two!' Kennedy exclaimed. 'The victim recognized that?'

'She identified it from this picture. It might be significant,' Tanner said as he shoved it over the desk.

The DCI was still shaking his head in disbelief. 'Is there anything new from the victim?'

'No, sir, WPC Palmer visited her at home this morning. Miss Stone was unable to describe her assailant in any more detail than yesterday. She did say she thought he was dressed in a white, all-in-one boiler suit. He had the hood up over his head. She described the material, as like one of those reinforced white envelopes they use to deliver important papers. As I said before, he had a gasmask on so she never saw his face. She remembered struggling to breathe, he gassed her with an unknown substance, which we think was probably chloroform, and she certainly thinks it was. The next thing she knows, she can't move, but she's sort of aware of what is happening. He never removed any of his clothing; he kept the full kit on. She was only wearing a nightie.'

'Nice, was it a pink one?' Kennedy's sarcasm caught him unawares as he summarised. 'So we have a gas-masked, boiler-suited fetishist in custody right now, or do we? Make my day; tell me he was arrested with the mask, the suit and a bottle of chloroform.'

Tanner hated it when Kennedy was in one of these moods. 'Unfortunately, sir, he wasn't. We did find an empty Kilner Dual Purpose jar with a cotton pad inside it discarded in her house, though. We're reasonably sure from the faint odour that he used it in the attack. She said it didn't belong to her. I can't think of a reason he should have left it behind, unless he didn't want to run the risk of being stopped with it.' He inhaled deeply. 'Before I go on, I spoke to the hospital and they put me in touch with a retired anaesthetist. When I spoke to him, he told me it's not used for human anaesthesia in the UK any longer. He also said it would have been hit and miss even for someone like him to administer back in his day, so we might be looking for a lab technician with experience of its use in animal experiments or someone else like our suspect, who has some clear knowledge of what it is and how to use it. Either way, it's apparently very volatile and takes a lot of experience to get exactly the right dose.'

Kennedy narrowed his eyes. 'And Belchley, you said he didn't stop talking. I assume someone took notes, what did he say?' Tanner coughed a little ahem in to his fist. He'd have to correct him, but he did not relish it. If he didn't, then later it would come back on him. He sometimes wondered if Kennedy did it on purpose to test his mettle. 'It's Bletchley, sir.'

'Thank you for picking me up on that tiny detail, Tanner.' He glared hotly at him. 'I ask you again. What did he say?'

Tanner returned his gaze.

Kennedy stared at him coolly. For a second, he saw his subordinate's face darken, anger flashing ominously in the younger man's eyes.

Tanner struggled to keep his temper. 'He's admitted he knows Miss Stone, but he has an alibi for the night in question. He was fishing on the lakes in Hadleigh, twenty-five miles away. Two or three other fishermen saw him, he reckons; he's given us two names, Bob and Dave.' The stony expression on Kennedy's face made him want to smile. *It was like working with a teenage child who has had a humour by-pass.* 'We're getting that checked out at the moment. He also readily admits to making chloroform on the school's premises. He's been suspended for it, so it's a bit difficult to deny, but he says he used to make it for an old guy, who used it to gas insect specimens.'

'I don't suppose we have a name there, either,' Kennedy observed dryly.

'You're right. He said he used to make it up occasionally for a guy who collected butterflies and moths since the sixties, but it's frowned on to do it now-the collecting that is, and you can't buy the old substances like those hobbyists used to, not without the relevant safety certificates,' he said as he twirled his pen between his fingers. 'He said he never actually met him.'

'So how did he pass the stuff over to him?'

'I covered that with him already.' He opened his notebook. 'I suggested he was lying. This is what he actually said, "Why would I? Look, he phoned me. He asked me if I could make him up a batch. He told me to put it in the boot of my car and meet him at the Anchor in Benfleet, 9 o'clock that night. £50 cash, no questions, asked. I agreed. I went in and waited half-hour; he never showed, so I left. The following morning, when I unlocked the boot to take the stuff out, it was gone and no money either; can you believe that? He nicked it off me!"'

'It almost sounds believable,' Kennedy remarked dryly.

'That's what I thought. I asked him how he thought this guy had got his number and he said he thought he got it from the school.'

'Had the car been broken into?'

'No, sir, I already asked him that – it hadn't.' Kennedy's phone rang.

'Kennedy,' he said, listened for a moment and then put the phone down.

'The warrant is ready. I don't know about you, Tanner, but I'm itching to get round there.'

Chapter 68

Bletchley lived on the ground floor of a house divided into two flats. His landlady resided upstairs; they obtained a set of keys from Bletchley. Tanner rang her doorbell to let her know what was happening. She was a woman in her early sixties with pink candyfloss hair, wearing eccentric over-sized glasses.

'Mrs Wilkinson? DI John Tanner, we have a warrant to search Adam Bletchley's flat.'

'Okay, what's he done?' She screwed her eyes up at him. 'All that sneaking about in the middle of the night, I knew he was up to no good.'

'We're just making enquiries at this stage, Mrs Wilkinson. We might need a word with you afterwards, if that's all right?'

'Of course, it would be a pleasure,' she said with a wink. 'Call me Vi, it's easier.'

She didn't go back upstairs; instead, she hung around by the front door to Bletchley's flat. Tanner couldn't help noticing she wore pink pom-pom slippers with her jeans.

'Jesus H. Christ,' Kennedy said, gawping. Tanner joined him at the entrance to Bletchley's bedroom.

Inside, one whole wall was a collage of photographs of young women. Hundreds of them arranged in clusters, with each girl as a subject. All had the appearance of classic covertly taken stalker photos. When they were later analysed, they found twenty-six subjects and perhaps unsurprisingly, Natasha Stone was among them. He'd grouped her pictures together in the top left hand corner. There were images of her out jogging, sitting inside McDonalds by the window, out with friends, there was even a photograph taken of her and Bletchley. They also found a list of names and addresses. All they had to do was match the images to the names, to see what that shook out. In the kitchen, they found a large medical type jar. Kennedy put on a pair of latex gloves and opened it. The sweet, cloying smell arrested his intake of air at the nostrils. He knew instinctively it was chloroform. He screwed the lid back down. In a lower base unit at the back of the cupboard, there was a loose panel; behind it was stowed a black plastic bin bag. He reached in and withdrew it carefully. Inside was a roll of duct tape, white boiler suit, a box of latex gloves similar to those he had just put on and a black hood and Stanley knife.

The whole place was crawling with Scenes of Crime officers within the hour.

Chapter 69

They spent the journey back to the police station mostly in silence. They left their crime scene colleagues to pick over every square inch of the flat. The landlady had tried to get some information out of them as they left. Kennedy told her politely, but firmly that if he needed to speak with her, he'd be in touch.

There was something eating Kennedy for sure. A couple of times Tanner had almost asked him directly, but Kennedy was in one of those thoughtful moods of his. He hadn't said more than a few words about Bletchley. Five minutes from the station, he couldn't hold back any longer. 'Is everything all right, sir, you seem like something's on your mind?'

'Tanner, there's always something on my mind.'

'I was reading about sexual deviants once, sir, it's amazing how often they start off like this and escalate, getting bolder…'

'All I know, is that we look likely to have taken a rapist out of circulation. Twenty-seven women on that list, Tanner, imagine if we hadn't caught him now.'

'It doesn't bear thinking about, sir,' he said, turning into the car park at the station. 'Twenty-seven…?'

'That's what I said. What's on your mind?'

He stopped the car. 'Well, as far as I could tell, there were only twenty-six women in the photographs, sir.'

Kennedy slapped him on the thigh. 'Come on; let's see what he has to say.'

In the interview room, Bletchley entered escorted by Tanner and the duty sergeant. Kennedy walked in a minute later.

Kennedy openly studied Bletchley. He was of medium height and build, dark lank hair, a vague unwashed odour about him. Deep-set dark eyes under thick eyebrows, his cheeks were sallow above the beard line; he hadn't shaved for a couple of days. The stubble took on a blue sheen in the harsh lights. His lips were moist, and the lower lip provided a platform for his remaining front tooth to rest on – The other teeth were on a roof-mouth plate, taken from him as a choking hazard. Kennedy imagined him the sort who dribbled in his sleep. If he were convicting on looks alone, this man would be guilty. Bletchley cast a side-glance at Tanner, who was speaking for the benefit of the tape.

He confirmed all present, and informed Bletchley of his right to have legal representation – which he declined. The interview commenced at 6:35 p.m.

'Where were you on the night of Saturday the 3rd of March between midnight and 1:00 am?' Kennedy sat resting his chin on his thumb; his forefinger covered his top lip as he waited for Bletchley's reply.

'I've already told you guys, I was fishing at the old brick-fields in Hadleigh.'

'Can anyone vouch for that?'

'Yes, I met a couple of mates up there.'

Tanner flicked the pages of his notebook back. 'That's right, Bob and Dave. I don't suppose you have any luck remembering their surnames?'

'No. Sorry...' Bletchley shrugged his shoulders sheepishly.

'Do you have a telephone number or address for either of them?'

'No...You see the thing is a lot of the guys that go up there; you know we're mates, and that, but we're just fishing friends.'

Kennedy snorted. 'So you can't verify your story...'

'Err, not unless I can find them. I could get them to come in and make a statement...'

Kennedy produced a photograph of a girl and placed it in front of him on the table. 'Do you know this girl?'

'I've never seen her before in my life.'

'What about this?' It was a telephone number, Kennedy's own personal mobile number.

'No! For God's sake...' Bletchley's hot denial sounded convincing enough, but the tiniest flicker in his eyes betrayed him. Kennedy thought. *He's hiding something.*

'Okay,' Kennedy said as he placed a photograph of Natasha Stone on the table in front of him. 'What about this girl?'

Bletchley licked his lips; his eyes flicked furtively between the two detectives. 'Yes, I know her. She was my girlfriend.'

'Really? Yes – yes of course. What about the other girl, was she your girlfriend, too? Or the other twenty-five women on your wall – are they all girlfriends, too?'

'On my wall?' Bletchley said, looking confused.

'Yes, on your wall.'

'No, wait.' He thought frantically. He'd known they would be searching his place, but he was confident they wouldn't find anything incriminating. The photographs were in a box under a secret panel in the stair cupboard, along with the girls' names and addresses. *On the wall?*

'There are no photographs there, I'm telling you.'

Tanner put a photo showing the collage in position on his wall.

'This is a stitch up!' Bletchley looked directly at Kennedy. 'Look, I misused a few chemicals at school; I made something I shouldn't have made. I've made a mistake; that's all. I had nothing to do with any rape. I'm *not* the gas mask attacker.'

Kennedy fixed him with a look. 'Who said anything about rape or gasmasks?'

'It was in the paper this morning.'

Stunned, Kennedy fired a hostile look at Tanner, as if he held him personally responsible.

'Wait a minute; was it one of those girls that appeared on my wall?'

Kennedy stared at him steadily.

'Oh no, which one?' Bletchley was wringing his hands with anxiety. Tanner thought. *This guy should take up acting.*

'Now, let me see,' Kennedy said. 'I showed you two photographs and you denied knowing one of them. Here she is on your wall.' He pointed at her group of pictures. 'She's about halfway down. The other one is Natasha Stone, your former girlfriend. Look where she is, Bletchley.'

He leaned forwards to see better.

'Can you see her?'

'Of course I can see her.'

'She's at the top isn't she?'

He nodded.

'She was raped in her own home, Saturday night, between midnight and 1:00 a.m. The first on the list.'

'No, no hang on, there's no list, I did not put those photographs up on the wall. I wouldn't be that stupid. If I was…' The next photo Kennedy put down stopped him mid flow.

'Recognise this?'

It was a photograph of a World War II gasmask.

'I think I need a lawyer.'

Tanner stopped the tape, recording the time as 6:55 p.m.

'Too damned right you do!' Kennedy said.

Bletchley looked at him tight lipped.

'Tell me why you have twenty-seven names, but only photographs of twenty-six girls.'

Tanner intervened. 'Sir—'

'Leave him to answer the question, DI Tanner,' he snapped then rounded on Bletchley. 'Well?'

'I know my rights,' he muttered.

'I don't doubt that, son, but you see, the tape is now off and I asked you a fair question. To me it's all about the math. Twenty-six pictures, twenty-seven names. I already know whose picture is missing. I just want you to tell me why.'

'Sir, do you want me to go and get us a coffee?' Tanner leaned towards the suspect. 'With me gone, this'll be the bit where the DCI slaps you up a bit.'

Bletchley had seen enough cop films to believe the possibility. He caved.

'Okay, okay, I'll tell you. I didn't get a photo of her yet.'

Kennedy looked at him with incredulity. 'And that's it?'

'Yes, I only saw her for the first time a few days ago; I haven't had the chance.'

Kennedy considered what he said and wondered where on the list she'd have been if he did have a photograph of her. Did he even need a picture of her to make her the next victim? He felt he might have saved her. When he told her later, she'd be forever grateful. He had to check himself from having a full-blown fantasy about it.

'Go on, Tanner; get him back to the cells. We'll reconvene tomorrow.'

Chapter 70

The following afternoon, with the wind outside buffeting the windows, Kennedy drew the blinds and resumed the interview. Bletchley exercised the right to have legal representation; his appointed solicitor was a Mr Brown.

Brushing a few thin strands of wind-blown hair back into place across the top of his head, Brown began by saying his client had reason to believe someone else had a set of keys to his flat and they'd used them to put his client's private photographs on display, knowing the police planned a raid.

Kennedy shook his head and pinched the bridge of his nose. 'Why does your client think someone would do that?'

Putting his pen down, Brown crossed his arms. 'Look, DCI Kennedy, I'm sure I don't have to tell you that taking photographs isn't a crime.'

'No, Mr Brown you don't. In public places, it isn't, but taken through bedroom windows without permission? Not to mention trespass and the possession of chloroform, which under *any* circumstances without the appropriate licence – whatever the intent – most certainly is.'

'Be that as it may, Mr Kennedy, my client denies he was involved in any assault.'

'It was a rape, Mr Brown,' Kennedy said. 'There's also the question of the paraphernalia found in his flat.'

'He maintains somebody broke in and put it there,' Brown said evenly.

Kennedy turned his head to Bletchley. 'Where's all this coming from?'

'You remember I told you about the guy who wanted the chloroform and didn't turn up? Well I think he broke into my flat *before* that and stole the spare keys from the cupboard in my kitchen. It was only after he stole the chloroform from my boot that I checked and found the keys missing.'

'Why didn't you tell us this yesterday? Why didn't you report it when you suspected a break-in, when you found your keys were missing?'

'Wait a minute; you think because I was watching these women, I must be behind the rape?'

'Bingo!' Kennedy said, sarcastically.

'No, no! Wait a minute. Someone else was watching them as well as me!'

'You never mentioned that yesterday either. Do you have a name?' Kennedy cannot hide his disdain.

'No, I haven't, but I thought he was just like me, you know got his kicks—'

'Who was it, Bletchley?' Kennedy scratched the back of his neck. 'Or hadn't you got round to making each other's acquaintance. Was he watching all of them?'

'No, he wasn't; only Natasha and the other one.'

'What other one, Bletchley?'

'You know which one, the girl that looks like Marilyn Monroe.'

What Bletchley said, overshadowed the sense of relief Kennedy first felt, the knowledge he'd gotten Bletchley in the nick of time. An element of doubt now crept over him.

Kennedy dismissed it as the last desperate efforts of a guilty man trying to shift the blame.

'You'll have to do better than that,' he said.

Chapter 71

With Bletchley returned to the cells, Kennedy said, 'I don't know about you, Tanner, but listening to all that bullshit has made me thirsty.'

On the way home, they called into their regular pub. After a couple of pints, Kennedy forgot about his doubts and became jubilant and puffed up about Bletchley. He even started calling Tanner by his Christian name. 'That's another scumbag off the streets. See, John, that's what good old-fashioned police work is all about. Forget your computers and DNA.'

After his superior had consumed five pints on an empty stomach, Tanner thought on the irony of his earlier words, *his* drunken bullshit had left *him* thirsty, but he couldn't drink, not now that he realised he'd end up having to drop the DCI home.

He continued rambling in the car. 'I mean, John, they always say things like that don't they? "Oh, I admit the photos were mine, but I never stuck them on the wall. I admit the chloroform, but it was for someone else." What about the gasmask and the other deviant paraphylia?' he said, laughing out loud. 'Is that even a word? What does the defendant have to say about that then? "I've never seen them before in my life, your honour." Can you imagine it, John, what the judge will make of *that?*'

'You are absolutely right, as long as he doesn't fall for the "Other Stalker" story.'

Kennedy turned around in his seat to face him. 'What, you mean the *other* stalker, the one he says stole his keys and rearranged the photographs and then planted all that *parafellation?* Anyway, even if it were true, think about it for a minute. Why would anyone do that?'

They were about halfway home; he did not want to spend the rest of the journey treading on eggshells as the DCI became more belligerent, so he changed the subject. 'I don't know about you, sir, but I'm tired, can't wait to get into bed.'

'Bed? Now *that's* a good idea.' He fumbled in his pocket and producing his telephone, called someone.

Tanner assumed it was a woman.

'Hey, it's JFK, are you doing anything? It's just I miss ya,' he laughed. 'No, of course I'm not. I promise I'll be a good boy.'

He clicked off the phone. 'John, my old buddy, do me a favour, will you? Drop me at the end of Petits Lane.'

'Going to the girlfriend's, sir?'

'Mind your fuckin' business, Tanner!' He tapped the end of his nose. 'I don't ask you about fuckin' Theresa, do I?'

Whatever problems had dogged him during the last few days seemed to have disappeared and Tanner was relieved he did not have him in the car for the whole journey; there was something undignified about his behaviour. It had to be the stress coming out. The last he saw of him that night, he was staggering down the road, heading northwards.

Chapter 72

Midnight had no qualms about setting someone up. A few nights before, when he'd seen what he had in his flat, he'd had no doubt whatsoever; he was doing the public a service. 'Sweet mother, this man is a pervert,' he muttered beneath his breath, adding certain items he'd taken in with him, to those belonging to Bletchley.

He located the garage at the end of the garden. The access to it was down a wide alleyway littered with muddy craters. Someone had filled the worst of the potholes with broken brick and chunks of concrete. He made his way down the strips of concrete people had laid outside their own garages, until he reached the one he was looking for. The back gate number confirmed it was the right one. The garage had its metal vehicle door in the alleyway. Beyond the fence, in the garden, a single door led out of the garage, and a concrete pathway ran up to the house. Most of the houses, like this one, were in darkness.

He reached over carefully to unlatch the gate.

Tuning his ears, he listened for any unusual sounds. His eyes had already adjusted to the dim light of the back garden. He shifted the rucksack off his back and squatted by the back door into the garage. He was about to pick the lock, when he tried the handle.

It was unlocked.

Carefully, he opened it. The hinges creaked, but not loud enough to be audible from more than a few feet away. He stole inside, drawing it shut behind him, he clicked on his infrared penlight. There was no car; just a stripped down motorbike, the parts scattered around in a half circle that the mechanic had left to give himself room to work in.

The rest of the concrete floor was clear. There were rows of shelves with labelled boxes containing nails or screws, and adjacent to where he'd just entered at the far end, was a workbench. The bench had a shelf midway between the top and the floor and underneath that, an old army ammunition box. He took a cardboard box out from the rucksack, turned it onto its narrowest side, and carefully slid it out of view, pushing it right back against the wall. Under the shelf, he moved a pile of discarded greasy rags to allow the box to pass behind them, the glass inside rattled, as he adjusted its position, finally satisfied it wasn't visible at a cursory glance.

It contained twelve jars originally; he had reduced the number to seven before he brought the box with him. Of the seven kept elsewhere, one had already been used. Only four more were needed, and then he was done.

He crept back out the way he came in. His victim had a window of opportunity. Check. One move he can still make. After that, there won't be a thing he can do about it. Checkmate.

He paused to look at the back of the house from the other side of the fence. A light switched on in one upstairs room, then in another. It gave the house the appearance of two big square eyes, staring out of a dark face, looking out into the night.

'I'm coming to get ya, Kennedy,' he whispered.

Then he shrank away from the fence and made his way back along the alleyway.

Chapter 73

Early hours, 7 March

As the last lights turned off in the bungalow, the intruder remained in the shadows by the garden summerhouse. He stayed in the same place for a full hour. The frosted window of the bathroom in the house next door came on. The colour of naked flesh caught his eye; it was a dark haired female form, coming close enough to the glass as she cleaned her teeth for him to make out her breasts as they swayed pendulously. A minute later, the light went out.

He moved silently, withdrawing the ladder that he knew was behind the storage shed. *These people that keep unsecured ladders lying around, where would we be without them?* Shaking his head, he rested the ladder against the wall. It was just long enough to project above the roofs edge. He climbed up and formed an opening just above the eaves line, removing only enough tiles to enable him to squeeze through. *Twenty-four inches square should be enough.* He slid them up twisting them out, laying them down, restrained by thin steel anchor straps that he inserted into the tiles either side of the opening. When he'd finished, he would use the same straps re secure the tiles in their original position, to bridge across the void he'd made, then he would put the ladder back as he found it. The tiles would hold, at least until the next strong wind.

He cropped through the exposed timber battens with heavy loppers and sliced a flap through the felt underneath. With his penlight torch in his mouth, he silently squeezed in between the rafters at the far end of the bungalow, away from the bedrooms. Pulling the loose felt down behind him, and then taking the torch from his mouth, he shone it onto the boarded out roof space before him, and then crouched low to avoid banging his head on the timber cross beams, moving forwards slowly; easing his feet down, he shifted his weight with each step, listening intently for tell-tale creaks that might alert the occupants in the rooms below him.

He knew there was little danger of waking either of them, because when he'd scouted the outside of the house the night before, the bins revealed that both of them took something to help them sleep; in the case of one, from the empty whiskey bottles in the recycling, it was alcohol. In the case of the other, it was Tramadol.

The area of the loft closest to the access hatch had shelves built for storage. Stacked in rows of boxes, from the looks of it, were the entire family archives. If he'd had the time, he would quite happily spend all night and day reading up on them and their dealings, absorbing it all for some future campaign. One day, he might come back.

He passed the torch beam across the shelves. All the boxes were labelled with the details of their contents and archived in date order –utility bills, bank statements, appliance guarantees, old vehicle documents and then to one side, two boxes similarly labelled, but marked 'Johns Records' 1963 – 1981 and 1982 – 1992. He peeled the tape off the top of the latter box and lifted out a lever file; he ran his latex covered fingers through the contents. *Not this one.* Pulling another out, he realised the contents were listed on the spine. He had moved a dozen files before he found what he was looking for. The box was full of pay slips, bank statements, old cheque stubs and paying in books, dating back fifteen years or more. He removed a paying in book. A couple of unused slips remained inside; he put them in his pocket. Returning everything to the way he found it, he spotted an old newspaper encapsulated in a clear plastic sheet; the print still looked crisp and fresh. 'Kennedy Assassinated'. After quickly reading the page, he withdrew it from its preserving sleeve and folded it into his inside jacket pocket.

There was another box on the shelf marked 'newspapers and magazines'. It was heavy. Inside, were dozens of True Crime magazine, more newspapers, clippings, scrapbooks. He opened one. The childish scrawl told him who had written it and when. *John Fitzgerald Kennedy, Fall 1976.* 'Somebody's been reading too many American magazines, eh Kennedy?' he whispered to himself as he put the box back.

Shining the torch across the floor, he located the loft access hatch; he levered the sides up with a screwdriver lifting it clear, setting it down quietly, he leaned down and listened. The sounds of two people deeply snoring reached his ears. Each had a distinctive sound. Lowering himself down onto a coffee table, almost slipping on the cloth that covered it, he regained his balance in an instant, then reaching up, replaced the access cover. Stepping down, he crossed the hallway, looking in on both sleepers. Old man Kennedy was flat on his back, mouth open, throat half closed, throttled by the weight of his tongue. Across the passageway in her room, his wife was propped almost upright, snoring through gritted teeth, like waves rolling on the shore. He resisted the temptation to root around in their rooms while they slept.

After a few minutes spent searching the other rooms and hall, he finished with a quick scout through the kitchen cupboards and the bathroom cabinet; there he found an array of medication. He noted that Kennedy senior was on Beta-blockers. *Better not to wake the old git up. I'd not want him to have a heart attack.*

When you tune in to an environment, a sudden silence acts the same way as a warning shout. One of them had stopped snoring. He strained his ears. A creak. *Movement!* Someone was getting out of bed; he cleared out of the bathroom into the spare bedroom with seconds to spare. He heard the soft fall of feet on carpet, then the pad of naked feet on the vinyl in the bathroom, followed by the sound of urination, a hawk and a spit, then the padding of feet again. Five minutes later, the old man's tongue was choking him in his sleep again.

Finally, he found Kennedy junior's room. It was a shrine to someone who had not died, someone who was perhaps expected to arrive back home from college any day now. Baseball posters covered the walls and the shelves stocked with youthful memorabilia, racing cars, figurines from Marvel comics and Star wars. He opened the wardrobe and a stale smell of uncirculated air wafted out, the smell of clothes that needed airing and old shoes; he crinkled his nose as the scent caught in his nostrils. Satisfied he had all he needed; he opened the window and climbed out. He reached back in as an afterthought, to retrieve an object that rested against the wall by the window. Pulling the window behind him, the friction hinges held it closed.

Chapter 74

Late afternoon, Wednesday, 7 March

Theresa Hunter saw the road works traffic build-up just too late to turn off. She cursed herself under her breath. *Why didn't you pay more attention to the advance warning signs when they went up!* The date just hadn't registered. Now she was in the wrong lane, the other was moving faster – she craned her neck round and seeing a gap hopped the car into it, almost slamming into the back of the car in front. The lane she *was* in started moving ahead. If she'd have stayed where she was, she'd be ten cars further down by now and still it kept moving. She remained stationary. *Damn!*

Determined to keep moving, she indicated to change lanes again. No one would let her in. Her temperature began rising. There was a slight opening a few cars back; she could see the lorry driver looking at a map or newspaper. The gap widened further, and she geared herself up to cut into it. She always used to be so critical of other people that lane-hopped, for the first time she understood how saving even a few seconds seemed worth the extra risk.

Terri would soon arrive home from college, and she didn't want that to happen until she was there. If she could have, she'd have picked her up from the college gates, or even a pre-arranged point round the corner, but to do so, would have alerted her to the fact that something was wrong, and the poor kid had had enough to put up with since her father died.

She switched in front of the lorry and congratulated herself on her perfect timing. The lorry driver let her know he didn't agree with a sudden deep, bass blast on his horn and thundered up close behind. She put her slender hand out of the window, and lifted it to say sorry; hoping the realisation that she was a woman would persuade him to back off.

He remained inches from her boot lid, uncomfortably close, intimidating her. The rumbling engine noise and diesel fumes invaded her car, making her wish she'd stayed where she was. Having made his point, he dropped back. With a sigh of relief, she opened the other windows to allow the fumes out.

Ahead, a car had broken down. Beyond that, both lanes were moving steadily. She realised she'd been holding her breath. Emptying her lungs, she inhaled long and deep.

Never one to let problems build up, somehow since the burglary and the subsequent wrong decisions made, she'd done exactly that. For the sake of a quiet life, to shield Terri from any involvement, knowing the anxiety she would feel, she succeeded, but only amplified the effect on herself. She found herself thinking about the past two weeks.

Was it really only two weeks ago? Is that all it was? It seemed as if an eternity had passed since she walked in that evening. It wasn't so much that anything was obvious; there was no sign or clue anything was amiss. The only odd thing she recalled now was that her mother's old tin had been turned around. Joey, the blue and yellow budgerigar whose picture adorned the tin, was facing the wrong way.

She thought about her mother, how she'd always told her from when she was a little girl that while the bird faced outwards, he was looking out for us. Theresa would watch as she reached up to the tall shelf where 'Joey' lived and after she'd taken money from the tin; she was always so meticulous about putting it back *exactly* as it was. That way, she could tell if her no good husband had gotten his hands on it. Sometimes, a terrible row followed, and he'd say, 'I never took no money out, I was only looking to see how much—' and her mother would retort, 'If you *ever* as much as look at that tin again,' She let the words trail, the rolling pin she brandished completed the thought for him.

Her mother would never have left the tin like that. Now that it was her turn to look after it, she'd never have left it like that, either. She was obsessive about things like that. And Terri wouldn't have, either. She too, was obsessively compulsive. It was a big problem for her.

Standing on a chair, she stretched up to get the tin. She lifted the lid; it was all there, no cash missing. How strange, could it have been a mouse? Shuddering at the thought, she put the tin back and faced it the right way. She continued to think about it and it played on her mind. Maybe she *did* borrow a bit of cash without telling her and then put the money back without putting the tin back properly. No, she'd never have done either of those things; she definitely would have put the budgie back facing the right way. It was like having her mum looking out over them. 'No way!' she said it aloud, hoping to break the circle of repetitive thoughts; they retreat for a moment before regrouping in her head.

She thought about asking her, but then realised she'd only freak out. She played out part of the scenario in her head. Terri would be saying. '*Hang on – If I didn't do it and you didn't do it, who did?*' She took a deep breath and fought to control the rising panic she felt. By the third deep inhalation, she'd finally managed to put it to the back of her mind.

The following day, when Terri let herself in, Theresa was just finishing a telephone call. The two of them signalled each other with a series of shrugs, hand gestures and facial expressions as she passed on her way upstairs. Once out of sight, she called down, 'I'm just having a quick bath, Mum.'

Theresa replaced the receiver on the wall-mounted phone.

She caught a glimpse of herself in the mirror on the wall next to it and teased her hair, flicking her fingers through it. She leaned in on tiptoes to examine her teeth. The ornate mirror was another hand-me-down from her mum, the bronze coloured latticework that surrounded it always had notes weaved into it. While pulling the old ones out, she noticed Terri had a doctor's appointment the coming Monday.

'Okay, I'm coming up to see you. How was it last night?'

'Oh, Mum, you wouldn't believe.'

Theresa was three steps up the stairs when the phone rang; she was of two minds whether to answer it. It had already rung five times that morning and every time she answered; silence greeted her. It had to be a wrong number, or one of those auto-dial services.

She turned and went back to the phone, a sense of foreboding unsettled her as she picked it up. Something bad was about to happen.

As she lifted the receiver to her ear, she remembered a trick one of her friends had taught her. *Always let the caller speak first. That way if it's someone you don't want to talk to, you can just say 'wrong number' and bang it back down.*

'Trie? Is that you?' the caller said.

The way he said her name caught her off guard. No one had called her that since her husband died. Trie, as in Tree, he was so drunk the first time they met; he couldn't say her full name. She found herself thinking about him; an affectionate smile graced her lips. She couldn't remember him calling her anything other than that.

It had to be someone who knew her. The voice sounded vaguely familiar, but no one she knew would do that to her. Something was wrong; she sensed it; she couldn't explain. Her chest began to tighten, her mouth suddenly dry.

'I don't know who you are, but please stop calling me Trie.' Her tongue ran over her lips, nervously moistening them. She looked upstairs, half expecting her daughter to come out on the landing, to find out where she was, why she was speaking so quietly. The moment seemed to linger, hanging on what would happen next.

'Oh, I think you *should* know who I am, Trie. I'm the person who paid you a little visit yesterday. Did you not notice I'd been? I left you a clue, Trie; I thought it was only fair.' He puffed theatrically on his cigarette, three little sucking sounds. 'What an interesting lady you are, Trie, and oh, what a lovely daughter you have.' The soft tone of his voice was completely at odds with the menace he generated.

Her mind was racing. *It was him! He had turned the tin!*

'How did you get my number, it's ex-directory?' she whispered, watching the stairs.

'Oh, Trie,' he sounded disappointed. 'I got it from the front of your telephone.'

Okay, but how did you know my pet name? She kept the thought to herself. What happened next put her in a daze.

Terri called down from upstairs, 'Mum, where the hell have you put all my underwear?'

Her blood ran cold.

She wanted to put the phone down immediately and call the police, but something inside stopped her.

'I'm on the phone, Terri!' She surprised herself at how well she suppressed the anger and anxiety in her voice; she stared hard at Terri, willing her to go away.

'Okay, Mum, calm it!' she said and, rolling her eyes, turned away sharply and sloped off.

Theresa regained her composure. 'What do you want from me?'

'Trie, I want you to listen very carefully, your daughter's welfare depends on it.' He veiled his threat behind a softly spoken voice. She suddenly realised how he knew her pet name. He'd read the letters from her late husband.

She listened.

'Three things, Trie, just three small things, that's all I want from you,' his voice was soft and persuasive. 'Now I know you are probably considering calling the police, or thinking you could tell your boss about this conversation, but that wouldn't be wise, Trie, not at all. You know; they've been looking for *me* since before I cannot tell you...a very long time. They won't be able to *find* me, let alone stop me and you telling them about our little situation. Well, it'll only spark a series of problems for you and I know with Terri's *condition*, you won't want that and believe me, you don't want me coming after you.' He reeled it off like friendly advice; she felt an involuntary shiver of revulsion run through her.

'Just get on and tell me what it is you're after,' she said. 'I'm listening.'

When he'd finished telling her, she weighed the options. What he was asking her to do seemed so innocuous. She felt guilty, but when push came to shove, Terri came first. To agree was the easiest thing to do and while she knew it wasn't right, something she'd once heard popped into her head. It was about doing the wrong thing for the right reasons. It puzzled her when she first heard it, but this must be exactly the type of situation they meant when they spoke about it.

'Okay.' She felt a weight lift from her shoulders.

'I'll get the things to you,' he said exhaling.

He's smoking; she thought, as if that explained everything. 'When will you do that?'

He disconnected her.

She didn't see Terri had come halfway downstairs. Terri watched her mother on the phone. The way her mum's face crumpled, as the conversation changed direction was impossible for her to conceal. Terri took the last few steps down and stood in front of her mum. *'What's wrong?'* she mouthed. Her mother shooed her away with her hand, but she stood her ground. When she put the phone down, she smiled a little crazily at Terri. 'I just heard an old friend died. They're going to let me know when the funeral is,' she said smoothly, as she turned on a sad face.

Terri viewed her suspiciously. That wasn't a sad face. That was a worried face and if it was... Why did her mother just lie to her?

'Oh,' she said.

Chapter 75

When Theresa unlocked her car Thursday morning, she noticed a plain manila envelope on the front passenger seat. She unwrapped it and inside was a folded newspaper in a clear plastic sleeve and separately, in a re-sealable polythene bag, a mobile phone.

How on earth did he manage to get into it? The spare key? He must have taken it! She'd checked nothing else was missing after he stole Terri's underwear, but hadn't thought to see if her spare keys were missing.

She remembered what he told her. 'Don't touch any of the items. Tip the newspaper out onto a clear area of his desk, the boot print must be facing up and pointed towards his chair.' He sucked hard on what she assumed was a cigarette and inhaled noisily. 'Are you with me so far, Trie?' Another deeply drawn inhalation. 'The phone, you must put that above his desk in the ceiling void.'

'How am I supposed to do that?' she asked.

The caller issued her with a set of instructions.

Theresa arrived at work a few minutes before 9 a.m.

Contractors had been working in the voids above the suspended ceilings, and the works had been going on for weeks. The builders had set the project up to be completed in such a way as to cause the minimum of inconvenience, but as the project manager had said, when he was defending the things that had gone wrong so far. 'You can't make an omelette without breaking a few eggs!' They were constantly creating dust and setting off smoke sensors, which in turn triggered fire alarms, which in turn led to evacuations. There were broken eggs, but not an omelette in sight.

She pressed the buttons of the mobile through the plastic, as the caller instructed, and waited apprehensively as the phone rang. A male voice answered. Met with silence, the voice demanded. 'Who *is* this? Make it quick, I'm busy!'

Theresa stayed silent; the phone went dead after a few choice expletives. Barely a moment had passed before the man called back. She answered, but said nothing.

'It's you again isn't it?' The voice said, 'You think you can play games with *me?* When I find out who you are, you're a dead man. Do you hear me?' Theresa cut him off.

Out of curiosity, she decided to check the call history. There were ten or twelve numbers recorded there, including the last two calls. Then she spotted something; her telephone number was in the call directory, too. Panicking, she made another wrong decision. She deleted her number.

Next, she climbed onto the desk, pushed up a tile and unfastening the bag containing the phone, tipped it out on top of the adjacent ceiling.

Getting back down, she was surprised how her heart hammered hard in her chest, scared that, at any moment, Kennedy, or someone else might come in. If they did, she'd say she thought she heard something vibrating up there. Lastly, she allowed the folded newspaper to slide out onto the top of the desk. Packing the empty sleeves away and smoothing her clothes down, she wondered what kind of game the caller was playing. *How did you get yourself involved in this?* She reassured herself, if things unfolded badly; she could always come forward and explain. *He put me in an untenable situation. I needed to buy time for my daughter's sake. I didn't understand what he was up to. I had to keep him off my back, while I tried to figure how to bring what was happening to light. They'd understand.*

'After this, there's just one more thing to do, Trie, I want you to get some information for me. I'll call you Monday evening.'

He didn't say what it was that he required.

She was more nervous about this final demand, than she'd been about the ones he'd made before.

She wondered if this last thing would reveal his intentions more clearly. It didn't matter, once she did this; she'd be free from his demands.

You don't realise how much you miss normality until you don't have it anymore.

Theresa couldn't wait to get back to normal. She could see the light at the end of the tunnel.

Chapter 76

When Kennedy arrived at his office, he walked all the way round to the other side of his desk before he noticed the white detritus scattered across the surface. *What on earth?* Curious, he crumbled bits of the debris from the desktop between his thumb and fingers and looked up at the ceiling. There was no light fitting above his desk. That ruled out the electrician doing maintenance. A tile looked as if it hadn't seated correctly. He climbed up onto the desk, and pushed the grid up to adjust it, trying to get it to sit right. When that didn't work, he lifted the tile clear. He wasn't tall enough to see over the grid into the void, even on tiptoes. Finding it difficult to balance, he placed a hand each side of the grid and manoeuvred a book into position with his foot, and using the extra height it gave him, peered in and saw something that looked out of place. He picked it up. It was a mobile phone.

After climbing down, he scratched his head. *How did it get there?*

The last time they refurbished the offices, they'd put in new ceilings. From what he recalled, the void was about two feet high, and there was no way the grid would support a person's weight, so the phone hadn't fallen out of a contractor's pocket.

Someone stood on his desk and put the phone up there, but why? Did they use it as a makeshift torch? That had to be it.

He checked the contacts list on the phone for clues as to who the owner might be. Only two numbers on the phone had names; one read Danny and the other Marilyn. Both were recorded as the most recent calls, but from weeks before. *Why hasn't the battery died?*

His suspicions aroused; he frowned, and checked the date and time on the phone. The time was correct, but the date was set exactly three weeks behind. *If that were right, it would mean the calls had been made less than an hour ago.* A feeling of dread came over him as he selected Marilyn's name to look at the telephone number. *Melissa's! What the hell!?*

It was his window of opportunity, the chance to handle things correctly. He did not know then how much rode on his decision, so he took the path of least resistance, the one he thought was least likely to result in compromising him. He thought frantically. *Who else knows about Marilyn?*

And if that was Marilyn – and it *was* – would it be too much of a coincidence, if 'Danny' turned out to be Danny Lynch?

He already knew the answer as his eyes settled on the newspaper, a distinctive boot print on it just below the headline: *Kennedy Assassinated.*

His blood froze. He thought frantically. Who had access to his office? Who could have left that newspaper and put the phone up there? He felt a small tug of disappointment. If someone else had said it was Tanner, he'd never have believed it – not really, but faced with increasing evidence, it was beginning to look that way. He made no secret of the fact he resented his superior's promotion to DCI over him.

He remembered something his dad always used to say. 'Keep your friends close, but keep your enemies closer.' *Looks like you were right again, Dad.*

Tanner had barely warmed his chair when the telephone buzzed, he clicked the save button on the computer and picked up the phone. 'Tanner,' he said.

'My office, five minutes,' Kennedy said curtly.

'Don't stand on ceremony, sir, not on account of me,' he muttered at the telephone after he'd put it down. He pushed back out of his chair.

Kennedy looked at his colleague strangely, as he entered his office. 'Okay, bring me up to date with everything.'

Tanner reached into his pocket to retrieve his notebook.

'Just for once, leave your notes in your pocket. I'm fed up with the way you hide behind them, when we're speaking.'

'I'm sorry—?' he spluttered, looking as if he'd been slapped.

'Oh, don't pull that stupid face at me, Tanner. Let's get on with it shall we?'

Blinking with surprise and indignation, words formed, he hesitated. *Was there any point trying to reason with the man when he was like this?* He decided, not.

'I have a question for you,' Kennedy said, looking directly into Tanner's eyes, measuring him. 'What do you know about, Danny?'

'Danny? Who's Danny, sir?'

If he's lying, he's a great actor. 'I think he's a friend of Marilyn's.'

'Sir, you've lost me.'

Kennedy looked confused. *If Tanner hadn't put the phone up there, who did?*

A knock came at the door and Theresa opened it, popping her head through the gap. Seeing the two of them in the middle of a conversation, she apologised, 'Sorry. If that's all, sir? I'll get home.'

Kennedy dismissed her with a curt wave of his hand; she made a face and her eyes looked hurt as she withdrew.

'Was that really necessary?'

'No, it wasn't, but she knows what I'm like. I'm just on edge that's all.'

'Speaking of which, in case you've forgotten,' Tanner said, 'she seems to have been on edge herself. We're coming up to the anniversary of her husband's death. I thought you told me you were going to sign her off for a week.'

'Yes, I did have a word with her about that,' Kennedy sounded vague, distracted by something else. 'But she insisted on coming in, said she was better off at work.' The germ of an idea began to bloom in his mind, no longer listening as Tanner spoke again.

'She lost her husband last year, sir; she's certainly been going through it,' he said grim faced. His chin took on a hint of dark blue in the harsh office light.

Kennedy just stared at him.

At the end of the meeting, after Tanner had left, he sat thinking. *What if the two of them, have plotted this together?* He quickly dismissed the likelihood, but something wasn't right and he couldn't fathom what it was.

Chapter 77

John Kennedy senior helped his wife settle down for the night.

Often plagued by the fear she might not wake up in the morning, she was especially anxious because she had a hospital appointment the next day. 'Don't forget what's happening tomorrow,' she reminded him.

As if, I could forget.

He didn't want her to call him for something in the night if he could avoid it, so once he was sure she had everything she might need within reach, he said goodnight. If she disturbed him once he'd consumed his nightly half-bottle of whiskey, and she found out what he did when she was in bed, she'd put a stop to it. The oblivion it brought was his only respite, losing it, did not bear thinking about.

She'd been bedridden over a year, and he was once again reflecting on how cruel and indiscriminate life can be. What she suffered with was late onset Muscular Dystrophy. *Late onset*, for that small mercy they were both grateful, but it was a cruel twist because it happened within a month of his retiring. She would often ask him what he thought she'd done to deserve such a life.

'There are plenty of people out there, far worse off than you or me,' he'd tell her.

'We all have our cross to bear,' he whispered into his whiskey; he did not want her to hear. Raising his glass high, he toasted silently. *To my cross!*

The cross she bore was bigger than the one he carried; lately it seemed to affect her mind. She called out, suddenly scared. 'John! There's someone in the house! I've just seen them go by!'

'You saw someone?'

'A shadow went through the door down the hall...' She looked panicky. Something was always spooking her. Being helpless, sometimes she resorted to attention seeking.

He began a systematic search of the house, thankful it was a bungalow and there was no upstairs to worry about. Going through the motions purely for her benefit, he didn't really think she saw anything at all, but sometimes she succeeded in spooking him, too.

Going down the hall to Johnny's old room, he felt a draught on his face. His door was ajar.

I don't remember leaving that door open and she couldn't have done it. Someone is in there!

John picked up a walking stick from the coat stand in the hall, gripped it tight, took a deep breath and pressed his back against the wall. His heart thumped erratically as it cranked up to a level it hadn't been at for years; he thought his chest might burst, but he was ready for anything. Pushing away from the wall, he jumped through the open door – head turning left and right – half expecting to see someone there.

There was no sign of life. If it weren't for the net curtain, a gossamer sail billowing slowly into the room on the breeze of the open window, there would have been no sign anyone had been in through it at all.

The window was open a crack; he knew it hadn't been before, and *she* couldn't have done it. Someone *had* been in and then left the house that way. The window frame, on close examination, revealed no sign of forced entry. Nothing seemed to be missing, although he thought perhaps Johnny's baseball bat had gone. *That would be crazy. Why would anyone break in to steal a baseball bat?* Then he started thinking his son might have even taken it with him, when he left years ago, he only knew it *used* to be there once. He couldn't quite recall the last time he saw it.

He silently cursed his growing old; he hated what it did to people and their faculties. When Johnny phoned, he'd ask him about it, but would do it in a roundabout way. The last thing he wanted was to be asked, 'What's wrong with you, Dad? I took it with me when I moved out years ago.'

The sound of her voice shook him back from his thoughts. 'John? It's gone quiet, answer me, John. I'm getting scared,' her voice was higher and more fragile than usual; a slight quiver betrayed her fear.

'It's all right, love, nobody's here.'

'But I saw someone.'

'Nobody's here!' he growled.

He thought about calling Johnny, but now wondered if he *might* have opened the window and simply forgotten to close it. She'd managed to spook him; that's all it was.

When John junior called that night, he didn't mention it.

Chapter 78

The night following the Kennedy break-in, he returned to their house. An hour after they'd gone to bed, the intruder crept back inside through the loft, dropping down onto the coffee table. He closed the hatch above and removed a clear plastic sleeve from inside his tunic. It contained a sheet of plain white paper with a boot print on it.

'One I prepared earlier,' he whispered, smirking. The paper slid out of the sleeve as he tipped it onto the white cloth on the table. He put the sleeve back inside his top – it wouldn't be long before the old detective was awake again, checking the whole house, finding the print he'd left for him.

Taking the same route as the previous night, he climbed out of Kennedy junior's window, pushing it home to make it appear closed. The roof temporarily reinstated; he stowed the ladder back behind the shed.

The night was still and quiet; the moon hidden behind clouds. A broom leaned against the wall by the kitchen door. He grabbed it and then held it high above his head, pushing it against the edge of a roof tile, moving it up, so that it grated noisily against the one below it. Inside the roof the noise would reverberate nicely, he was about to do it again, when he heard the tinkling of a bell coming from within. He guessed that must be her summoning the old drunk.

John senior was slipping in and out of wakefulness; he opened his eyes, lay listening on the pillow, unsure if it was an aural hallucination. He was halfway down a darkened country lane in his head, about to check on the activities of two people he saw up to no good in their parked car – *Ting!* The sound of her little bell ringing drew him back; he blinked his eyes. *Must get up!* Allowing one leg to flop to the floor, he rolled out of bed.

She called out to him. 'John, I heard something in the loft!'

He was still gathering his thoughts, not quite knowing where he was or had been. *He'd recognised that car in the lane.*

'John, are you still awake?' The little bell rang again.

'Yes,' he said groggily. He sighed deeply and heaved himself off the bed.

'What is it, love?' he said from the doorway.

'I just heard something.'

Although he'd been drifting off, he felt sure if there had been a noise, he would have heard it.

'Look, love, I know you're scared of one thing and another, but you've got to stop this.'

She looked at him sharply. 'You don't believe me?' She shook her head in disbelief.

'It's not that. It's just, I don't know; there's always...something,' he said, unable to bring himself to spell it out directly. He didn't want to hurt her.

'John, I'm telling you I heard something, didn't you hear it – you were awake, weren't you?'

He stayed in the doorway; he didn't want her to smell the whiskey on his breath. *Now come on, John, you'd have heard it – wouldn't you?* Humouring her, he said, 'I didn't hear a thing, but don't worry, I'll check it out right now!'

He snatched the walking stick from its place on the coat stand. *This is becoming a habit!*

Out in the hall, down by Johnny's room, where the passageway opened up into a circulation area, outside the bathroom and toilet, a sheet of paper with a faint boot print, lay on top of the cloth covering the table, below the access hatch. He hadn't noticed it before; he didn't seem to be noticing much lately.

The week before, she was asking after something he'd put away up there in the loft, he tried first to get up there from the table. He'd moved the cloth. That was one thing he actually could remember, and he'd put it to one side. He didn't want to risk slipping on it, because he worried if he fell... Well, who would look after her? He always used to be able to get up from there, but now that falling was on his mind, he fetched the stepladders.

For a long while, he just stood under the hatch looking at it, his head cocked slightly to one side, listening with his best ear.

She leaned out over the bed and opened the door with the crook of her stick so she could see him.

'What are you doing?' she said.

'It's okay,' he said. 'I'm just listening.'

'Can you hear anything?'

' Shush!' he hissed at her.

'What is it John?' she asked, complaining. 'Nobody talks to me anymore.'

Suddenly, from above there came a sharp scraping noise.

'Call the police!' he shouted.

She fumbled at the phone with thin fingers that shook so badly, they refused to function.

'I can't do it, John!'

He rushed to grab it off her, shouting a warning up at the hatch. 'Don't even think of coming down here, I'm armed!'

From his vantage point across the street, the intruder watched DCI Kennedy arrive, closely followed by the police.

Old man, I'm going to put the bite on your boy so hard. By the time I finish with him, he'll do whatever I tell him.

He slipped away, unnoticed.

Chapter 79

DCI Kennedy stayed the rest of the night with his parents. Reassured by his presence, his father had a few nips of whiskey before bed. When his mother called out several times before she finally drifted off, it was not to his father, but to *him*. She just wanted to know he was alert and still *there*.

Finally, he clambered into bed, turning the light out around three o'clock. He'd already checked it earlier, but he double-checked the window lock again, before adjusting the gap in the curtains with a quick tug to close them. In the lamplight across the street, he thought he saw the figure of a man standing there, legs apart, facing in his direction. Tiredness caused it to register only *after* he drew the curtains. When he whipped them apart again, no one was there.

'You're tired, Kennedy,' he told himself. 'Bone tired.'

His old bedroom didn't feel the same, it did not feel safe and he didn't sleep well. He slipped into a strange level of consciousness and stayed there, not actually sleeping, closer to wakefulness; his eyes flew open at every slight sound.

In the morning, he arranged for scenes of crime officers to conduct a fingertip search from the loft all the way through the bungalow, inside and out. They dusted for prints, took photographs, and checked anything that looked out of place, or unusual.

'Look at this, sir.' One of them called him up into the roof space. He climbed the ladder carefully; lack of sleep had left him feeling edgy, shaky and hung-over. At the top, he stepped onto the floorboards and looked along the dusty racks of shelves; he smiled at his dad's orderliness. In the beam of light against the inside of the roof, the method of entry was clearly visible; the battens were out of line, replaced with metal straps, the felt lining cut through in a rough square.

'So that's how they got in. Not through the unsecured window downstairs, as we thought.'

'That's right, sir, they pushed out a few tiles and just squeezed in.'

'That means they went out through the window downstairs,' he spoke slowly as he considered the evidence. There was something wrong. From what his father had told him, *he* thought someone might have been in the house before and left the window open. *'I didn't want to worry your mum with it, Johnny. I thought it was me going senile.'*

Whoever it was, had been wearing latex type gloves, so apart from a few smudges and the boot print, they found nothing they could use.

Kennedy puzzled over the intrusion at his office with some concern. In both cases, there had been a boot print and in both cases, *he* appeared to be the common factor. Access or apparent access from above; *once is chance, twice is coincidence. It had to be that, just a coincidence. There was a third part to the saying, what was it?*

Being on newspaper, the other footprint was not so distinctive, but from what he could recall, they looked the same. He shook his head at the thought, chastising himself. *You can't say that, Kennedy, all boot prints look similar.*

He couldn't run the risk of implicating himself by mentioning the similarities of both incidents to anyone else, because he hadn't reported the original occurrence. He'd compromised his position. If anyone asked questions, he'd struggle to explain. Deciding he didn't want to be part of the next big police scandal, or newspaper headlines, he made another bad choice; he kept quiet about it.

Kennedy tied off the loose ends one by one; who knew where his parents lived and who had a motive to get at him. The thought shimmered like a phantom taking form. *Tanner?* For the first time, he considered the possibility someone might want him to think it was Tanner and, if that were true, he needed to know why.

Later that morning, a couple of thoughts struck him. The call he'd taken the week before, the single word: *Jack.* He assumed it had been a wrong number. The newspaper left in his office. It couldn't be the same one. Could it?

Climbing back into the loft, he looked through his boxed up magazines. The glassine sleeve that contained it was still there, the newspaper was not.

Chapter 80

Monday, 12 March

Theresa spent the whole evening in a high state of anxiety. Every time the phone rang, she made a mad dash for it. Each time it was someone else calling. She was relieved Terri was out with a boy; at least she didn't have to worry about her. He was a friend of the family, and she knew he'd make sure he bought her home safely.

She sat in her favourite chair. The telephone on the coffee table next to her was plugged into an extension cord. It was now almost bedtime and still she'd not had the call. *Why do people say evening, when they mean night?*

Unable to concentrate on the television any longer, she found herself staring at the phone as if she were somehow able to transfer her force of will down it, to connect to him, to make him call her. It was ridiculous; she decided, so she prepared for bed. Unplugging the phone, she wound up the extension lead and put it away; she didn't need any awkward questions from Terri when she came in. Plugging it back in, it rang immediately. Her heart stopped. She grabbed for it.

The front door opened. It was Terri. She thought she'd burst as she forced herself to say, 'Hi,' as if nothing were wrong. Terri waved with her fingers as she walked by. Theresa half smiled as she echoed her gesture.

'You sound relieved to hear from me. Last but not least,' he said it with an air of finality, but as though he was bored, and the whole thing was a chore to him. 'I want the file on Kathy Bird.'

'I can probably get you a copy.'

'That's all I want. An updated copy of the file, contact details, everything; and once you've done that for me, Trie – you're off the hook.'

A deep sigh subconsciously escaped her. The caller's next words held her remaining breath in check. 'You sound relieved, Trie, but you're not off the hook just yet, not until you deliver. You have until Friday this week.'

He was gone before she could say anything.

She slowly replaced the phone in its cradle. From the very first time he'd telephoned, something about his manner bothered her, now she had an inkling of what was. *He sounded like Kennedy.*

'Hey, Mum, you okay?'

Theresa nodded, smiled and excused any potential suspicions aroused by saying, 'I'm just really tired; that's all.'

The rest of the conversation was carried out in a state of automation; a throwback to how she coped in the days and weeks following her husband's death, one of her friends called it safe mode, functional, but not in possession of all the faculties normally at her disposal.

They watched television together until Terri went to bed at eleven o'clock. Five minutes later, she came back down. 'Aren't you going to bed, Mum?'

'I don't know what's wrong with me. Earlier, I was tired, but now, I don't feel tired at all. It must be my age.'

'You know you're getting old when you start making excuses like that!' Terri said with a smile. 'Goodnight, Mum.'

Stooping to kiss her on the cheek, Terri caught a glimpse of the worry in her mother's eyes. 'Mum, are you sure, you're okay.'

'I'm fine, honestly. You go on up; I'll have a little nightcap, and then I'll go to bed.'

Terri frowned. She knew her mum hadn't been like that since dad died. She shrugged her shoulders. 'Okay, if you say so, Mum.'

Two shots of brandy later and she was ready to sleep.

Theresa's eyes snapped open. She lay with her head on the pillow confused for a moment. Unable to remember getting herself to bed, she glanced at the display on the illuminated clock: 3:01 a.m.

Recalling something from when she was sleeping, she realised the caller had invaded her thoughts. For an instant, she thought she knew what he was up to; it was in her dream. The harder she tried to focus on exactly what it was, the further away it went, she simply could not remember.

She stayed awake for a long time, trying to fathom what the caller was *really* up to.

Chapter 81

Thursday, 15 March

It was Thursday already; the deadline for obtaining the file was looming. Theresa was finding the task harder to fulfil than she'd imagined and for the first time she was worried about what might happen if she didn't deliver. The file wasn't where it was supposed to be. Later in the morning, when she took in Kennedy's coffee, she noticed he had the file she wanted on his desk. Kennedy followed her gaze to the file and slid it into his top drawer without taking his eyes from her.

She smiled awkwardly, and he smiled back.

Later in the afternoon, when Kennedy was out, she opened the drawer; all she needed was a copy for Christ's sake.

The file had gone.

Chapter 82

Almost a week had passed without incident, and DCI Kennedy felt it was safe to return to his own home. John senior began to believe they had just been the victims of some sort of prank, or it could even be a case of mistaken identity. That happened sometimes. In his later years on the force, a killer murdered an innocent man in a revenge attack, simply because he called at the wrong address.

Age had taken its toll on him. If he were honest, the drinking had too; he wasn't as sharp as he used to be. Something was nagging at him, something not quite right about it. Finding a pen and pad, he wrote. *Suspect comes in through roof, goes out window. I find window open. I close it. He comes back in through loft, goes back out window. Both times, he conceals the entry point. Why come back twice? Did he come back more than twice? Was he looking for something he didn't find the first time?*

After concentrating for a few minutes, he gave up, no longer having the wherewithal to figure it out, he thought about Johnny. As so often happens when you think about someone, the telephone rang. *If I had a pound for every time that happened. That'll be Johnny now.*

Half-lifting and part bending down to the receiver; he aligned it with his ear, the arthritis in his arms and shoulders severely limiting his range of movement

'John?' His son's voice took him aback; he'd never addressed him by his Christian name before.

'Johnny?'

'John Kennedy?'

The old man's face creased with consternation. 'This isn't you, Johnny. Is it?'

The caller ignored him, questioning him further. 'John F. Kennedy?'

'No, that's my son. Now, who is this?'

'Don't worry, John. The name is Harvey.'

He considered the chances of someone sounding just like his son making a call of this nature. 'What kind of a game are you playing, Harvey?'

'No game, John, it's Lee Harvey.'

The heat of anger flushed his cheeks, now he was older, it took a lot, but once it was there – he began cranking himself up. *Oswald. Is the caller going to say Oswald?* 'Listen, you've picked the wrong person to play games with. I'm a former chief of police and my son is a DCI and you are calling an ex-directory number, how did you get it?'

It always made him laugh, these people with ex-directory numbers, who left them stuck on the front of their telephones for all to see. Out there on view, for deliverymen, dinner guests, anyone really. Someone, who maybe shouldn't see it. Okay, fair play this one hadn't left the phone on display, but it was still on the front of the old phone they'd discarded in the cupboard.

A full ten seconds passed; he made out the sound of the caller inhaling deeply. *Whoever this is, is smoking a cigarette. He's actually enjoying this.*

'Well, are you going to answer me or not? How did you get my private number?'

The caller exhaled evenly, blowing smoke into the receiver. 'Don't worry, John. It's not *you*, I want. It's your son, *Jack.*'

The phone clicked down.

'Who was that, John?' Rose's voice startled him; he was relieved she hadn't been awake at the beginning of the call. If she had been, she'd have listened in; then there would be a lot of explaining to do.

'Just a wrong number, don't worry. I put him right.'

When she fell asleep again, he quietly returned to the hall. He dialled the number slowly, to keep the noise down. The dial whirred softly each time he released it. It wasn't really an old black Bakelite phone; it was a modern reproduction, a present from Johnny to replace the old one, whose innards were so badly worn it just kept misdialling.

The purr-purr of the dial tone was so loud in the earpiece; he was sure it would wake her at any moment. He tried to muffle the sound by cupping his hand round, holding it tight against his ear.

Come on, Johnny. Pick up the phone!

Finally, he answered.

'Hello, Johnny, is that you?' he half whispered.

'Hi, Dad.' He chuckled. 'You dialled my number, who else is it going to be?' He looked at his watch, 10:30. It was late for him to be calling. 'What's up? Is everything okay?'

'Yes son, everything's fine. I just wanted to make sure *you* were okay.'

'Why do you sound like that, Dad, what's going on?'

'I just had a call from someone pretending to be Lee Oswald, son. Lee *Harvey* Oswald.'

Fear fluttered up from the depths of his stomach, catching in his throat, he fumbled over his words. 'It's all right. I'm okay. It's probably just someone playing silly buggers.'

'But he said he *knew* you.'

'Dad, it's just a nutcase, go to bed now or you'll start worrying Mum.'

'He said your full name. He said he always called you *Jack.*'

The assumed wrong number. Jack. The assassination headline. The pretending to be Lee Harvey Oswald. His heart sank, but he played it down. 'Look, I think it's just a prank caller. We'll keep an eye on it, okay?'

'Do you really think so? I might be getting old and stupid, but it didn't sound that way to me. Anyway, you're a big boy now, if you say it's okay, then it's okay.'

'Yes, really, it's fine. Tell Mum I'll be over tomorrow. Oh, look at the time! I have to be up in a few hours.'

His father chuckled softly down the phone. 'Well *I* haven't!'

'Goodnight, Dad,' he said.

It was past eleven o'clock when Kennedy put the phone down. He walked down the hall turning off the lights, starting with the kitchen as he always did; a routine he carried out automatically, without thinking. He started thinking about how no one else had his mobile number apart from Marilyn. He considered calling her to ask if she'd given his number out. *She's far too discreet to do that.* Then he remembered giving the number as an emergency contact the last time he was with his mum at the hospital. *I'm not often home; I'm a detective.* He'd said it apologetically as if it explained everything. *You can always reach me on this number.* He'd given his name. Was it possible someone with a grudge happened to be within earshot when he did that? He had one foot on the bottom step on his way upstairs. The phone rang and startled him. It reminded him of his old school bell. *No matter how ready you were for it, when it rang; you still jumped.*

Lifting the receiver, he said, 'Okay, Dad, what did you forget to tell me?'

'Is that *you*, JFK?'

Apprehension twisted his stomach into a knot that tightened all the way up into his chest. Kennedy struggled to breathe normally.

'What is it you want?'

'What do I *want*? I want a favour, Jack, I'll be in touch.'

For a moment, he stood still listening to the handset as if he were unsure the caller really had gone. He dialled 1471. A disembodied voice recording played down the line. *You were called today at 11:05 p.m. The caller withheld their number.*

Chapter 83

Sunday Evening, 18 March

The caller's tone was insidious and persuasive. 'Trie, there's something else you need to do to prove your love for your daughter.'

Her natural instinct was to ask who the hell he thought he was to ask her to prove her love for anybody, but Theresa stayed calm.

'What's that?'

'You're going to meet me for sex.'

'That's preposterous, you're sick.'

'Here is my number, write it down.' She did as he asked, and wrote it down on a scrap of paper. Just the number, no name, and then hid it in the index box. She put it under T. Her thinking was Terri wouldn't have to look up her number in the index and with no other name under T that Terri would ever need to call, it seemed as good as place as any.

'You have until tomorrow to decide. Think of it as insurance for your daughter's future. You *are* concerned for her future, aren't you? Oh, and Trie, don't do anything silly, will you?' It wasn't a question. It was an instruction.

If she reported him now, everything would come out, the information she'd planted and the secrets she'd passed. Theresa slumped by the phone considering her options; he had her completely snared. When the police found out, she'd go to prison. When that happened, when little Terri found out, she ran the risk of losing her. She made her decision.

Opening the index, she retrieved the scrap of paper with the number on it, hesitated, then picked up the phone and dialled.

Chapter 84

John Tanner was divorced. He always thought it would be selfish to bring a child into the world and not be there for it. When it became clear to his wife, Maggie, that he wouldn't relent, she left him, apparently returning to Scotland to be closer to her family. It soon emerged she'd started an affair with one of his colleagues. There were some ugly scenes, culminating in a fight, in the station car park.

Originally tipped to take over from Kennedy, his rival's position became untenable, and he managed to pull some strings to get a transfer to headquarters in West Lothian. Once there, it wasn't long before he moved in with Maggie.

At first, Tanner had assumed the chief had helped smooth the transition for him, and he resented him for it. He had the feeling the situation, though not of his making, had harmed his prospects.

They had a son who was now two years old. He wondered what *their* son would have been like, if they'd had one. If only he'd realised Maggie had felt so strongly. Sometimes he questioned his motives. Was it really that he thought it would be selfish to have a child in this job or was it that he couldn't stand the thought of sharing her attentions with someone else, even a child? Either way he'd lost. Better to have loved and lost.

Not like Kennedy, married to the job.

In the evening, he shaved for the first time since he'd been with Maggie, pulling his mouth from the left to right; pursing his lips in the strip lights glare to be sure he hadn't missed any stubble. Then rinsing and drying his face, he applied some aftershave.

What are you doing, Tanner?

He hoped he wasn't setting himself up for a fall.

Chapter 85

Theresa left her house full of trepidation, yet strangely excited at what was about to unfold for her this evening. Getting into her car, she checked her face, started the engine and turning off at the end of her road, she thought about how she'd handle things. She supposed the bright light was what made her look; she saw it coming in her rear view mirror from quite a way back, growing steadily larger and brighter as it came. It hovered bigger and brighter than a full moon, just outside the rear windscreen, close to the boot lid. It filled up her car with light. The roar of the motorcycles powerful engine caught her in the chest and throat, cancelling all other sound from her ears.

She squinted as she tilted the rear view mirror.

Theresa had arranged for Terri to stay with friends for the night, there was no way she'd have left her on her own. The constant pressure Theresa found herself under had worn her down. Caught between the Devil and the deep blue sea of uncharted territory, to survive, she had to make a choice. She chewed on her bottom lip. She worried about what the night would bring.

The oncoming traffic flowed incessantly; the constant stream of lights of varying intensities – bright, brighter, dull, full beam – began to hurt her eyes. The deep drone of the motorcycle, with its big, full moon headlight continued to invade her thoughts, distracting her. *Why do these people always get so close?* She knew if she braked suddenly; he'd have no chance if stopping. She exhaled slowly, trying to keep calm. A long break in the line of traffic ahead meant he'd overtake her in a few seconds. She let another deep breath go. The last car in the line of traffic had passed; she relaxed her foot on the accelerator. The motorcyclist had plenty of time to overtake, but it was something her instructor had drummed into her, when she first learned to drive. *If someone wants to overtake you, let 'em. Easing off the gas as they do it helps.*

The roar of the motorcycle engine overtaking never came. The steady drone and the constant floodlighting of the inside of her car continued. She began to feel a little uncomfortable. He was more than likely going to turn off to her left in a minute. There was a turn coming up in the distance. *Probably didn't think it was worthwhile overtaking.* The gap in the traffic had passed and the cars in the opposite lane were more strung out, less frequent. The left hand turn was approaching; she expected to see a big yellow indicator light come on, then he'd trail off behind her and veer round the corner. Gone. Her headache was rumbling with the rhythm of the low growl of the engine behind her. He did not turn off.

The fear he was following her caught up as insistent as the unwavering headlight beam shining into her car; Theresa felt stripped bare under its light and vulnerable. A roundabout was approaching; she entered it, indicating a right turn. The motorcycle's yellow flasher came on; her hands took on a ghastly hue at the wheel as she drove all the way round past her turning, past her original entry point. The motorcycle did the same. He *was* following her. She forgot about her original destination, part of that journey involved a section of unlit roads. Turning onto a dual carriageway, she frantically thought of where the nearest police station was. The motorcycle stayed tucked in behind her.

It was him. She knew it was him. He was escorting her in such a way he knew she'd be scared witless, willing to do anything. She almost pulled over. *Get it over with, here and now, out there in the cold streets.* It was more fitting to do that, than to do it in a warm, comfortable bed with someone who could... She shuddered. She knew he was dangerous, or she wouldn't have done the things she had so far, she began to indicate to pull in at the next lay by. In the distance, she saw blue flashing lights. She cut the indicator and gunned her engine to catch them up, then realised they weren't actually moving.

She pulled in behind the police car; the officers had two youths out of a black BMW. They looked at her inquisitively as she drew near. The bike slowed. The rider was a big man wearing a full face helmet and glanced in her direction as he roared on past, accelerating so quickly the officers and both youths turned their heads to watch it go. She jotted the registration number down.

One of the officers approached. 'Are you all right, Miss?'

She knew it was *him*. He'd just been letting her know. 'Yes, Officer, I'm fine, although I do have a headache. When I saw all your lights flashing, I thought it seemed like a safe place to stop and grab an aspirin from my bag.'

Twenty minutes later, Theresa arrived at her destination. Her evasion tactics had made her ten minutes late.

Tanner ordered her a drink. She downed it. 'Are you driving?' he said.

'Not if I'm coming back to your place,' she said with a mischievous smile.

'Same again?'

When Theresa had asked Tanner if she could talk to him outside work, he dared to hope, but never dreamed they'd become lovers that night. She'd surprised him with her voracious appetite for him. They were barely inside the house, and had said very little before they devoured each other hungrily. The thick dark auburn hair that framed her face became tangled and bedraggled; her eyes were intense, filled with greedy desire, the enigmatic smile replaced by wicked glee as she whispered in his ear. *Don't tell Kennedy!* He paused at the mention of his name. She giggled, and he laughed, resuming with a new vigour. *Eat your heart out, Kennedy.* She let herself go completely. Two lonely people in need of more than just company, swept away in a tidal wave of passion.

He lay there afterwards, thinking about a possible future and pinched himself. She was all he'd dreamed of and more; he couldn't believe she'd been right under his nose all this time. He never realised just how good she would be for him.

She stroked his chest, lazily running the tips of her fingers across his skin. The sensation soothed him. He kissed her hair and closed his eyes.

'John,' Theresa said, drawling his name in her familiar way, but she sounded different. She sounded scared.

He opened his eyes and stared at the ceiling without saying anything, waiting.
'John, I didn't tell you everything.'

When she'd finished telling him what she'd done, he faced a dilemma. He'd
just begun to picture her in the future with him. Now he had to make a choice.
Would I have done anything different, faced with her choices?

Her next words clinched it for her. 'The thing is, John; I think it's Kennedy
who's been calling me.'

He shook his head and said, 'That's crazy, Theresa, and you know it!'

'Don't you think I know that? You're going to have to bear with me a minute
here. I think Kennedy is the caller. He's compromised me. He thinks he can
demand sex, and I can't do anything about it. But I don't think it started like that. I
think he tried to make me feel sorry for him, that he was being targeted by some
manipulative...*somebody.*'

'Well it's an interesting theory, but what made you come up with such a thing
in the first place? He's never tried anything with you, has he?'

'No, he hasn't, but it's the way he looks at me sometimes, and not only that,
the voice on the phone, it *sounds* like him.'

Tanner froze. A seed of doubt formed in the darkness at the back of his mind.
It would explain the jealousy, the outburst, and what about the call he'd taken.
That caller had sounded like Kennedy too. Where was Kennedy that morning?
Could he have set the whole thing up himself, for reasons that hadn't yet become
clear? He shook his head, more at himself than anything else. To go to such
lengths to get a woman in the sack seemed extreme. He just couldn't see it.

She pulled herself into his arms and squeezed him tight, whispering, 'John,
what are we going to do?'

Chapter 86

When Monday morning came, once Tanner dropped her back to collect her car, she handed him a piece of paper with the telephone number she'd called and the registration number of the motorcycle that tailed her.

One thing was for sure, if they could catch her tormentor, they would be able to keep her off the hook. He put it in his pocket, telling her, 'I'll get those checked out.'

An hour later, when he checked the bike's registration, he couldn't believe his eyes, yet in some crazy way, it made sense to him. He didn't relish the coming confrontation, but he knew he couldn't shrink from it either. The telephone number drew a blank, just as she'd expected.

'Out on our bike the other night, sir, were we?'

'Are you being serious?' Kennedy said, folding his arms.

'Why would I not be?'

'Because my bike is in bits, on my garage floor and has been for months.' Kennedy frowned. 'Why did you ask me that?'

'It looks like someone has cloned your registration, sir.'

'How come?'

'Someone was talking about a road rage incident in my local. They got the registration number, and I thought—'

'I'd have thought you have better things to do with your time, Tanner. What's happening with that fairground boxer you were tracing?'

'Waiting for a call to tell me when he is next fighting, it might take forever. He's an ex-champ who still fights, but rarely these days.'

'Well, get to it, will you. I can't believe you can't trace him until he comes out of the woodwork to fight.'

'There's no official record of him, sir, we only have a twenty-year old photo of him and nobody knows where he lives. So, where exactly do you suggest I start?'

Kennedy seemed deflated as he shrugged. 'Somewhere in the woodwork, I would think.'

Chapter 87

Melissa put down the phone. She confirmed her arrangements with JFK. Moving her laptop in front of her, she signed in to Facebook to post the agreed message. 'I can't wait for more birthday celebrations'. *Almost over now, Mel.*

She'd given up trying to figure out what it was he was up to after the second message. Not that she had time to worry much about it, she was raking in around two and a half, to three thousand in appearance fees and the one night a week with clients was bringing in another six or seven thousand.

If she carried on working extra hard, she'd recuperate most of what was stolen in twelve weeks or so, less her living expenses. If the caller stuck to his word, she'd have the money back a lot sooner. She prayed Lynch wouldn't ask for it in the meantime.

Despite the break-in, she still put her earnings in the safe. *Lightning doesn't strike twice in the same place.* After the break-in, she'd started a new dossier. For her, it was an irresistible urge. Keeping a diary had been a habit from when she was nine years old, when her mum bought her one for her birthday. It was only when she reached later life that she realised the true value of recording days and dates. She recorded every request, right from the caller's first contact with her; she knew what men like him were like. He'd try to spin it out, squeeze another favour from her. If she did it this way, she could say, *you've had your five things you asked for. I know because I wrote it down.*

When the call came this time, a few minutes later, he introduced a new requirement.

She hesitated. It was a bizarre request. She tried to make sense of it. 'I want to know the *reason* you want me to do that.'

'Melissa, we are going to fall out if you keep asking me questions like that, eh?' he said, in a smooth and persuasive voice. 'Do this thing for me and I'll come round with the money and your little black book. Five favours I asked for, and this will be the last. I promise you won't be bothered again by me.'

The tone of his voice reassured her he was telling the truth. 'Okay.'

'Right, when is your next liaison?'

'It's tomorrow night at eight—'

'No, that's too early. Wait a minute.' The caller didn't speak for a moment. 'Okay, we can work with that. At 8:30 p.m. tomorrow, your phone will ring. Do not answer it under any circumstances, is that clear?'

'Yes.' She felt subdued; she didn't have a choice.

'Good and don't listen to the message afterwards. I'll know if you have and if you have, you'll have broken our bargain. You will not get your things back. Do you understand? Now, I want you to call Lynch, tell him you heard this from Kennedy.'

He told her what he wanted her to say. 'Have you got that? Good. After he leaves, the minute he leaves, call this number.' He read it out to her.

She scribbled it down on an old envelope.

'And don't forget my little package. Once I've heard from you, I'll bring your things back as promised.'

He hung up.

Chapter 88

It was Thursday night and a mass of club goers were packed along the length of the building, between the rope barriers, waiting to get in to Lynch's new nightclub. The queue moved slowly, but steadily, a conveyor belt of people would start and stop as the men at the door controlled who came in. Staff turned away only a few, young men mostly, or blatantly under-aged girls. High above the door, a huge array of coloured light bulbs depicted a face that was instantly recognisable, even without the sign that read *Marilyn's*. The crowd below were bathed in the colour of its warm blush. A man emerged seemingly out of nowhere, into the pink hue, apparently intending to jump the queue, a couple of doormen moved to check his progress.

'I'm here on business,' he said, raising both hands above his shoulders, as if protesting innocence.

Neither of them seemed interested. They exchanged looks, respecting the strangers menacing size and appearance by skilfully blocking him and at the same time steering him away with gestures, careful not to touch him.

'Hear me out, fellas.' He stared straight at the head doorman, pitching his voice loud enough to attract his attention. 'I'm hoping to stage a series of White Collar boxing events and I'd love to do them here.'

The head doorman came out and studied the stranger's face. Old, but dangerous looking, he looked like he'd taken part in a few boxing events himself. The stranger caught the look.

'I'm into promotions now.'

'You need to see the boss and he ain't here.'

'Fair enough, anyone else I can see?' he said, knowing Tony, Lynch's right hand man, was in there. He'd seen him arrive five minutes earlier. He inched forward.

'No sorry. Not without an appointment.' The doorman raised his hands to keep him away. A trickle of adrenaline combined with rising apprehension had made him jittery. 'Stand aside for me, will you, I'm trying to run a door here.'

The stranger, now flanked by three bigger men, didn't appear at all concerned. 'Look, I don't want any trouble, but I'm here now – you know what I mean?' His voice softened, 'This'll take about five minutes, that's all, this place would be ideal, but I got another place to see where the staff might be...um, friendlier. I wouldn't have thought your boss wants to be hearing how well the club down the road is doing, because you lost him a great business idea, would you?'

The head doorman spoke to the men either side of the stranger. 'What do you reckon?'

One shrugged. 'I've heard about it, Reg. You know he could be right.'

Reg scratched his chin. 'Okay, take him inside; see if Tony will see him. What's your name?'

'The name's Dyson – as in the Hoover.' His face was deadpan as he added, 'as in clean up.'

'Wait there a minute.' The bouncer pointed him to a navy blue sofa, but he made no effort to sit. The music pounding on the other side of the blue pair of doors seemed to increase tenfold as the doorman opened them to go through.

Left unaccompanied; his attention wandered from the rich, red wallpapered alcove where he sat, to the reception and cloakroom area. The place had a steady stream of people coming in through the doors. He couldn't resist doing the numbers.

You got a tidy little operation here, Lynch.

The doors opened, and Tony came out. He was chewing on gum as if he were in training for a gum chewing competition, the expression on his face fixed as if botoxed. His body jerked sporadically. Either he was suffering from Tourette's, or he'd been mixing too much drink with cocaine. Dyson decided on the latter. Tony couldn't concentrate on the man before him, his eyes continually flicking over at the women coming in.

'Your name Dyson?' He looked contemptuously at the man's ill-fitting suit. 'What we got in mind then, my staff tell me it's to do with staging White Collar boxing nights here, is that right?' Dyson spotted a tiny hint of white powder in Tony's left nostril.

'Tony, that's right. You see there's a market for all kinds of fighting right now, and you know this gives ordinary people a chance to settle their differences in the ring like men. The ring's smaller than a pro ring—'

Tony cut him off short. 'So what do I need you for? I can set this up for myself, and I gotta say to you mate...' Looking at Dyson's weathered and beaten face, he pointed at his spiky, straw-coloured goatee. 'That's the most *fucked up* coloured beard I've ever seen. It doesn't even look real!'

'Tell you what, Sonny.' Dyson's demeanour changed, taking on an air of menace. 'Give it a tug why don't you, see if it comes off.' His lips stretched back baring his teeth. 'If it does, fair play to you, but if it doesn't, I'll smack you up. What do you say to that?' He had his fist up by his jaw, rocking it slowly, his old Foreign Legion tattoo clearly visible left to right across the knuckles of his right hand, spelling out WRAT.

Tony looked at the tattoo – confused for a second, and then his eyes lowered an inch. Inked onto the knuckle of the cocked thumb below, the letter H completed the word for him: *WRATH.*

Tony suddenly felt the chill air of Dyson's menace and as he stepped forward, he gambled the doormen would restrain him, that way not losing face. The bigger doorman planted himself between them; another two appeared out of nowhere.

They showed Dyson the door.

He didn't care; he already had what he wanted.

Lynch answered his phone as he drew into the club car park.

'Mel, you okay? I've just arrived at the club.'

She began hesitantly. 'You know I never talk about Kennedy, 'cause I know you don't like it.' Lynch bunched his fists at the mention of the name. 'But he said something about this operation he's working on.'

'What did he say?'

'I just think you need to watch Tony, that's all.'

'I said, what did *he* say, not what you think. Come on, Mel; let's have the rest of it – *all* of it. '

'The police arrested Billy Wharton a little while back and he talked. Something about a shipment of arms and drugs. I don't know, I couldn't look like I was too interested. Apparently they think Tony is going to hijack the shipment and use the proceeds to start his own operation.'

'Do they now?' he said.

'Danny, what will you do?' After a long pause, she said, 'I don't like it when you go quiet like this, you're not angry with me are you?'

'No, not with you. I'll tell you what I'm going to do; I'm going to give him enough rope. Then we'll see him hang himself.'

Melissa refrained from any comment. She wanted to tell him she'd been instructed under duress to tell him those things, but she dared not. Suddenly, the apprehension she felt about the game she'd been drawn into, moved to a terrifying new level and the consequences scared her more than she'd thought possible.

Relieved she hadn't told him all of it, she was supposed to have said Tony kept coming round to see her behind his back. She shivered at the thought of what he might do if she had told him that.

Lynch sat in the car for a few minutes after the call ended. Why would Kennedy tell her something like that? It had to be a scam to start trouble between him and Tony, but why? He always knew there would come a point in time when the DCI would try to use her against him. In truth, *he'd* considered using her to feed *him* with fake information, just to see if she would. At the beginning, apart from the sex, it was the only reason he kept with her, the possibility of using her like a Mata Hari type figure, but over time he'd grown fond of her. Lately, the possibility of making a respectable woman out of her had crossed his mind with a frequency that disturbed him. Now, he had to find out exactly where her true loyalties lay. Tonight, he was stuck entertaining VIPs from the criminal fraternity tonight. Tomorrow, he'd sort it out with her.

He locked the car and as he walked away, still deep in thought he almost collided with a powerfully built man crammed into an ill-fitting suit. Lynch scowled at him, although he was the one at fault. The man tipped an imaginary cap at him.

For a second, the gangster wondered whose minder he was.

Later, in the club, Tony told his boss about this great idea he'd had. Lynch listened, his eyes narrowing as mumbled his way through a brief outline of his plan.

He clapped Tony on the back. 'You know what, Tony? I can see you going places with ideas like that, mate!' They shook hands vigorously. Lynch called out to a waitress who was hovering attentively nearby.

'Let's have some more shampoo!'

Chapter 89

At precisely 8:30, the telephone rang persistently. Melissa was already with Kennedy and remembered the caller had instructed her not to answer it.

Grunting with irritation, he stretched over to pick it up. She'd anticipated he'd do that, and rolled him back, getting herself on top of him.

'You don't really want me to take a call right now,' she said and reached down between her legs, her hand encircling him. 'Do you?'

'No, I don't think I do now.' He gasped as she manoeuvred herself onto his length. The answer phone seemed to take forever to kick in. She rode him slowly at first, looking deep into his eyes. He stared at her in child-like wonder. Reaching over to the bedside table, she saw a message icon appear on the phone display. Curiosity threatened to get the better of her. The caller had told her she was not to listen to it. Now she was more interested than ever in what it said. Kennedy began thrusting faster, a look of grim determination on his face. She slowed him down.

'Whoa, you forgot to put this on.' She waggled the condom she'd just unwrapped.

'Shit!' he said, as she withdrew herself from him.

'We don't usually?'

'No, but I lost my pills yesterday. I can't take the chance, you know that.'

'Okay,' he whispered. 'Put it on with your mouth.'

Just after ten, Melissa rang the telephone number the caller gave her.

'He's gone. I did as you asked.'

'Excellent, then I'll bring your stuff back to you right away.'

'Hang on a minute, I'm really tired. Can't this wait until the morning?' She wanted her possessions back; she also wanted more time to think. She had toyed with the idea of having a reception committee for him when he came, and she suspected the police would be more than happy to oblige, but she soon dismissed it when she realised she might lose all the money and her dossier on Danny. They'd have a field day and he'd probably kill her. She also thought about having Danny's men meet him, but that was also out of the question. What could she possibly fabricate to tell him without arousing suspicion? Besides, what would happen if one of his men got hold of the files she'd been keeping?

Melissa realised how tightly wrapped the caller had her.

'I'll see you in a couple of minutes.'

If she'd looked through her door viewer, she would have seen him standing there already. Kennedy had left, and he was concerned she hadn't called him straight away.

He couldn't risk her listening to the message he'd left; she might delete it. He rang the bell.

She saw the back of him through the security viewer; he had a carrier bag with him, the same Harrods bag she'd stashed the money away into in the first place.

She let him in.

Face to face and fully in the light, although his ugliness scared her; she found herself strangely turned on by the power he held over her.

They moved down to her lounge. He sat uninvited placing her bag and another one he was carrying between his feet. She noticed he was dressed strangely.

He saw her looking at his taped up wrists and ankles. 'It's okay; I'm on the job, just diverted round here, no time to change.' His lips tightened, baring his teeth. His eyes grew colder.

She'd just begun to read the newspaper when he rang. *Gasman strikes for the third time.*

She was feeling uneasy, bordering on dread; she wanted him out of there as quick as possible.

'That's my money and stuff I presume?' She saw something she was unable to make out in the other bag; it looked floppy the way it laid, reminding her of the deflated armbands she used to carry in a bag to the beach when she was a kid. There was something else in there too, the size of a large tin of beer.

He handed her the money and her files. She looked relieved. 'You see, I keep my promises. Now what do you have for me?'

'I'll get it,' she said, getting up.

In the kitchen, she opened the fridge; it was one of those huge American-style ones with a drinks dispenser and icemaker on one side. She retrieved the package she put there earlier, double wrapped as instructed, the outer layer wrapped in cling film. She closed the fridge door and turned.

He clamped her with a huge gloved hand, sealing her mouth shut, driving her back into the fridge. Her scream was stifled. She realised who he was for the first time.

Her eyes were wide with terror as he explained.

'I told you I'm on a job. I'm here to fix a leak.'

She tried to say, 'What leak?' but only succeeded in mumbling unintelligibly into the muffle of his hand. Seeing him now, newspaper headlines flashed before her. She already knew the answer.

With one hand, he pinned her and poured the liquid into the delivery apparatus with the other. The sweet, cloying, dangerous odour of chloroform snatched her life's breath away.

He held it clamped over her nose and mouth, long after she'd stopped breathing.

Afterwards, he calmly dismantled the Gasman's trademark apparatus and left the jar in the kitchen.

He picked up the money and the diary and then put it back into his own bag.

'I told you I'd give your money back, didn't I?'

Going to her bedroom, he collected her safe keys and robbed her all over again. He pored over the new diary she'd begun, which included him, before taking it. She referred to him simply as the 'Caller', until the last entry; there she referred to him, as 'Condom man'.

He smirked. *The press would have a field day with that name. Dumb blonde.*

He extracted roughly half the semen from the condom with a syringe, transferred it to another; he left a bubble of it in the syringe and inserted it into her vagina, injecting her with it. He stopped to admire her neatly trimmed and shaven pussy. *Now that is neat.* He wondered if she trimmed it to make it look like Monroe's. He began to salivate. Controlling himself, he forced himself to think about what he still had to do.

An echo of his mother's voice sounded in the vast halls of his memories, summoned by the shred of guilt she instilled in him. *Temptation is a trap for the weak. Tell me about weakness, Mother. I'm stronger than you ever were.*

He split the rubber at the end of the original condom, just a tiny nick, big enough to have allowed the seepage into her, small enough to retain the semen. Then he left it, unflushed down the toilet.

Chapter 90

In the darkness at the back of the house, the man pulled on his disposable boiler suit and then his latex gloves. He taped the gloves with masking tape at the wrists, sealing them to the to the paper suit. He repeated the process, taping the over shoes where they joined the trousers at the ankles. Once he'd pulled up the suit's hood and tightened the cord, only his mouth, nose and eyes were visible.

The sound of his breathing changed as he donned the mask, reminiscent of gasping into a cardboard box. He'd spotted her while trawling through Facebook. Nice revealing photographs. She was an aspiring model, happy for anyone to look at her portfolio. Her wall postings revealed she liked to drink, and that made it easy to track her down. Sifting through the photos of places he discovered one of her taken underneath a pub sign, there were other shots throughout the season taken outside in varying locations, but clearly the same place. Concluding she was a regular at the pub, he turned up there on two separate occasions before he finally saw her there. Two hours later, he followed her home. It was that simple. He stalked her over the next few days, getting to know her. She was a drunk. When she wasn't out; she drank to excess in her own home, and she often paraded about the house naked. A couple of times he found himself sorely tempted.

She lived alone, no dog, no cat. The house wasn't alarmed, and it would be a breeze for him to break into. He thought back to how he used to be before he changed his methods. In those days, he'd lay in wait for victims at remote beauty spots around the country. It amazed him how few of the girls ever fought him. It wouldn't have made a difference anyway. He was too powerful. In those days, his unexpected appearance would terrify them, and he'd go to great lengths to ensure he appeared in such a way as to register the shock on their faces, capture the scream in their mouths as it started. The memories stimulated him time and again, and then he would think about her... *The Cornwall Girl*. He'd never left a shred of evidence anywhere until that day. If he hadn't been disturbed, he'd have killed her. No doubt about that. He got away with it and so did she. After that, he changed. It was a warning shot. He learned to get his kicks in other ways. The suits, gloves and overshoes were the same as he wore when he was an asbestos removal contractor. The mask graded suitable for all dusts and fibres especially asbestos. It was also force-ventilated from the inside via a battery pack, so not much chance of him accidentally inhaling any chloroform. He carried his business card with him for the benefit of the police if they stopped and searched him. In his entire life, that had only happened once and that night he'd come close to killing the officer concerned. The urge was on him, but he'd controlled it. The fifth and final Gasman attack was to be the last one. After that, he'd evolve into something else. He rarely grinned, but he congratulated himself on spotting a gap in the market using DNA technology. It was great. He had the sex; someone else would get the blame. With no one else around to hear him, he said aloud, 'You have to agree, you're a genius!'

When he reached her room, she was naked, half out of the bed, he tried to rouse her, but she was so drunk, he probably need not have gassed her.

Gasman strikes twice in one night. He was pleased with himself. When he was finished, he carefully withdrew with his condom intact. He put it into a small plastic bag, to take away with him and sealed it.

He undid the small package he had with him and then transferred the contents of the condom Marilyn had given him into a syringe; which he carefully inserted into her vagina, and then slowly pushing the plunger as he withdrew it, allowed a small amount to dribble down onto the bed beneath her.

Leaving the trademark jar at the scene, he gathered up the rest of the apparatus and took it with him. Later, he stashed it alongside the mask and the seven remaining jars he'd planted in Kennedy's garage some time back.

She was still unconscious when he left.

Chapter 91

It was late. Lynch had been trying to reach Melissa all night. It was unlike her to ignore his calls. At first, he didn't let it bother him. After the fifth successive unanswered call, he decided he'd check up on her. She always took his calls, if not straightaway, she'd get back to him usually within an hour or so. There had to be something wrong.

He arrived a little after eleven o'clock. He'd wanted to talk to her about staying on Saturdays nights as well, he'd tried talking about it earlier, but she became evasive. He imagined what he'd do if he caught her with another man. Then he remembered what she'd told him the night before. Maybe Kennedy was round there, and that was why she wouldn't take his calls. He was firing himself up for trouble.

As he approached the entrance, he looked up. All her lights were on. He pressed redial as he ascended the stairs. Her telephone was ringing. It sounded different, louder, he started taking the steps two at a time without quite knowing why.

The front door was open. A burst of adrenaline surged through him. He bunched his fists and not wanting to alert the neighbours to his presence, pushed the door noiselessly all the way back against the wall.

Satisfied no one was hiding behind it, he called out, 'Melissa – are you there?' Senses in overdrive, he marched down the hallway to the lounge. The TV was on low. A newspaper lay on the couch. An opened bottle of tonic water sat on the coffee table with the lid next to it as if she'd left the room only moments ago. An unfamiliar feeling descended on him. For a moment, he felt afraid. Anxiety evident in his voice, he called out, 'Mel, stop messing about...' He knew, even as he said it that she couldn't be messing around with him. She hadn't known he was coming. He paused in the hallway and looked at her bedroom door; it was ajar, and the light was on. A disembodied question from a TV interviewer filtered down the hall and registered in his consciousness. *'Do you think there was anything you could have done about it at the time?'* The answer failed to register. He cocked his right fist to his shoulder and using his left hand, opened the door fully.

Nobody. No sign of her in the bedroom. No one was hiding behind the bedroom door. He approached the wardrobe where she kept her safe; he wouldn't want someone sneaking out behind him after he left the room. The thought made him check under the bed first.

Nothing. The mirror door rumbled on its runners as he quickly slid it open.

No one. Then he saw the safe door. It was open, the key still in the lock, the safe empty. Apprehension turned to anger in the instant it took for his brain to comprehend. *She's run out on me.* Then he saw her car keys. *Why didn't she take her car?*

He ran out into the hall. Guided by some instinct, he went into the kitchen and there he found her, naked and lifeless, sprawled across the floor.

'Mel!' Lynch was not a man known for expressing any emotion other than anger or hatred, but he cried out for her, raw and without restraint. He sank to his knees next to her; he knew death when he saw it.

Someone had found out about the money. Killed her for the money, and when he found out who it was, they'd better hope the Old Bill got them first.

He needed to think. His hands floated above her body. He wanted to caress her one last time. The urge to touch her was almost too much. Standing up, he looked down at her. 'Jesus, Mel,' he said, wiping his face with his palm. 'I'm going to get whoever did this, I swear – whoever they are.'

On the worktop was an empty plastic shopping bag. He put his hand inside and used it to pick up the red-cased telephone. There were five missed calls, and all of them were his. He checked the call register. There was one number other than his recorded there. *JFK.* Using the camera on his mobile, he photographed the entry on its screen and put it back to where he'd found it. Next, he checked her white phone; there was a message icon on the display. He listened to it. It was Tony trying to smooth his way in with her. 'Listen, I got to be with you again. I'll call round in an hour. See you.'

What Kennedy told her was true, Tony was moving in on him. He disconnected from the message, replaced the phone on the worktop and screwing up the plastic bag, put it in his pocket.

'You know what, my love,' he said, 'I didn't really believe you when you told me, now I'm going to do what I said I'd do. Give him enough rope and then I'll finish him.'

Careful not to touch her, he leaned over and blew a kiss close to her face. She smelled as if she'd had a lozenge. It puzzled him. He'd never known her to eat sweets before, chocolate maybe.

He stood, about to leave. *An empty jar.* It looked out of place. The same sweet, chemical lozenge smell became stronger as he approached it. He leaned over the counter and sniffed. A residual, head-spinning belt from the odour took his breath away. His senses reeled. *What the fuck was she sniffing out here in the kitchen?*

In the morning, the paperboy pushed the paper through the door. It swung open.

Chapter 92

When Lynch heard the message on Melissa's phone, he knew for sure what she told him was true. Tony had gone behind his back, trying to steal his girl. That was just the start, now he was after his business as well. *Jesus!* He punched himself hard in the forehead. He needed time to think. Tony called her at 8:30 p.m. A couple of hours later, she was dead. *Tony! It was Tony. He told her to tell him Kennedy said it.* It made more sense now; all he needed to do was keep himself in check until he understood why. He would do as he said he would. *Give Tony enough rope. All this keeping calm is killing me!* He took a deep breath, picked up the telephone and dialled a number.

'All right, Tony? Anyone seen Billy, he never showed up at the club last night?'

'No, mate, I haven't. You know what he's like when he's got a few quid. Listen, I heard something. I don't know if it's true.'

'Well, spit it out then, I ain't got all day!'

'It's about Melissa.'

'What about Melissa?' he said holding his breath. *How does he know? I ain't told anyone.*

'Oh, fuck, I hope it ain't true.'

'Tell me.'

'I heard she's been murdered by that Gasman.'

Lynch paused. 'Are you sure?' he said, adding with suspicion, 'Where are you hearing this?'

'Err; I heard it from someone who lives down the road to her. Old bill is crawling all over her place.'

The doorbell sounded. He glanced at the CCTV monitor; a man stared into the camera. *Kennedy!* 'I'll get back to you,' he said as he disconnected. He walked out of his lounge, down the long hallway to the front of the house and opened the door.

'What can I do for you, Detective?'

He brushed past without waiting for an invitation to enter. 'Shut the door,' Kennedy said.

Lynch closed it and pointed to one of the armchairs forming a horseshoe shaped reception area around a glass-topped coffee table. 'Have a seat. What's this about?'

The detective remained standing. 'You don't know? You surprise me.'

'I heard about five minutes ago. What are you doing round my place, Kennedy?'

'When was the last time you saw Melissa Lake alive?'

Blowing air in a tuneless whistle, he said, 'She came to the club, two, possibly three days ago.' He levelled his rival with a stare. 'What about you?'

The DCI returned the stare. 'It's not about me, Lynch. It's about you and you telling me anything you know that might help catch her killer.'

'They know about you and her, do they?' The briefest hesitation allowed him to continue. 'Didn't think so, or you'd have come with that sidekick of yours.'

'This isn't helping, Lynch. Wouldn't you like to see us catch the person who did this?'

'The Gasman?' His expression grew dark. 'Do me a favour. Let me catch him before you do, eh? And while I think of it, have you seen Billy Wharton lately?'

'Why would you ask me that?' Kennedy said, trying to look unperturbed.

That look just confirmed it. Lynch thought. 'Nothing, just wondered, that's all.'

Kennedy turned to leave. Lynch called him as he reached the door. 'Kennedy, don't you *feel* anything? She's dead, and it's like you never *knew* her.'

'I was just thinking the same about you.'

He stepped out through the front door, raised his eyes momentarily to the heavens, and then walked away.

Chapter 93

Sunday, 25 March

Kennedy had many unanswered questions. Why would the Gasman kill her and not his other victims? He'd moved on to another one straight after her, and he didn't kill *her*. Was it an accident? Had he starved her of oxygen just too long? Her safe was opened. Did she catch him robbing her, regaining consciousness after he'd gassed and raped her, so he'd gassed her again, overdosing her?

Lynch was wrong about Kennedy. Although he kept outwardly calm, inside he was disconsolate. Because of the nature of his relationship with her, he had to keep it to himself. Apart from losing one of his parents, there wasn't much worse that could happen to him. He sat in the quiet of his office, comparing the loss to the pain he felt, when he first learned of his mother's incurable illness, but this was different. He still had his mother, and anyway, he reasoned, he didn't love Marilyn. She was an infatuation.

When he'd first found out about his mother's illness, Kennedy bought himself a personal mobile phone. Only his parents had the number. He kept it tucked away, set to silent in the inside breast pocket of his jacket, and he carried it everywhere, transferring it from his pocket to the coffee table at home and then to his bedside at night. He tested it to make sure he'd feel it when it rang, hoping he'd not feel that insistent vibration for a long time. He smiled, remembering the day after her diagnosis. His dad had left her to go shopping. She could no longer get about under her own steam for fear of falling over. The phone buzzed urgently in his pocket. He fumbled for it quickly, fearing that this was it – the emergency call.

It was his mother; he could hear her softly crying.

'Mum...Mum? What is it?'

'Oh, Jack, I didn't want to bother you, but I can't get back in bed, I've been trying not to be a bother to anyone, but I'm cold and your father's gone shopping, he never said when he was coming back'

He looked at his watch; it was almost lunchtime, he would, for once, take a break. 'I'll be round in a minute.'

By the time Kennedy arrived and let himself in, she'd somehow managed to get herself back into the bed.

He sat in the armchair looking at her sternly. 'I told you I was on my way, didn't I? You could have fallen and hurt yourself.' She burst into tears and looked at the floor; he realised she hadn't been out of bed at all. He transferred himself onto the bed next to her and put an arm round her shoulders, shocked by how thin she'd become, and as he held her hand he could feel every bone beneath her parchment-like skin. He pulled her into his chest, resting his chin on her head.

'It's all right, Mum,' he said, patting her back as if she were a child.

'I'm sorry, John, I dragged you away from your work and I shouldn't have. I just felt so alone.'

'It's all right, Mum, I'm here now.' It felt so strange to be comforting the one who had given him so much comfort, when he felt scared in the middle of the night, awakened from some bad dream, or when he'd been burning up with a red-hot fever. She was always there and now he was here for her. How life turns around.

The front door opened; a draught blew in briefly.

'I'm back. Sorry it took so long, is everything all right?' His father closed the door behind him and appeared in her bedroom doorway. 'John?' He looked at the two of them. 'What's happened? Is everything all right?' He took in the looks on their faces. The struggle to come to terms with this new phase of her illness etched into them. He moved into the space the other side of her and joined in the circle of three; a trinity of unity.

Nobody said a word for a long time. Finally, she lifted her head and spoke.

'I know about your whiskey, John, and I know you are ashamed. I know because you never were any good at keeping secrets from me, but I don't mind, not as long as I know you can still look after me when I need you in the night.' She smiled the kind of smile that chases clouds away after the rain.

'I'll always look after you,' he said, and then he grinned. 'I love you more than whiskey.' He hugged her extra tight, and they embraced for a long time.

Kennedy didn't think he'd ever forget the image of the two of them that afternoon, each holding the other. He smiled wistfully.

His phone buzzed like an angry bee in his pocket, jolting him from his thoughts, it took him a moment to recognise it was his phone. He fumbled, pulling it out complete with a box of aspirin. He pressed the answer button without looking, as he put the phone to his ear.

Something had happened. 'What is it? What's up?' A sense of mild panic inflected his voice.

'What's the matter, *Jack,* is the job getting to you? No, don't answer. Don't interrupt. A man was arrested early this morning and I will have a real problem if he is charged, Jack. And if he is, *if* he is...then you'll have a big problem, too.'

He hadn't been able to interject; the hypnotic quality of the voice somehow rendered him speechless. Finally, words came. 'Now you listen to me. I know who you are,' he bluffed,

'Stop it, Jack, you're about to make a fool of yourself. You don't know who I am at all, nobody does. I could be the guy outside your office pulling wires or fixing the lift. You wouldn't know, but I know you, Jack, and I mean *really* know you, so you just shut up and listen to me.'

He laughed down the line. 'This is like a scene from a bad movie.'

'Yes, that's *exactly* what it is, a really bad scene. Have you told anyone you were the last person to see Marilyn alive Friday night? No, of course you haven't.

Going to be a bit late now, don't you think?' The click of a cigarette lighter was followed by the sound of the caller inhaling deeply. 'Maybe, maybe not; look, I don't want any trouble, Jack. I have a proposition for you that keeps us all off the hook. I'll call you with the details later.'

Kennedy faced a predicament. If he owned up to his involvement, it would lead to questions. He'd come under suspicion and he couldn't put his parents through that. In their eyes, sleeping with a prostitute would be shame enough, becoming a suspect was not an option he cared to consider.

He would decide what to do once he'd heard the caller's proposition.

Chapter 94

Kennedy jumped, snatching the phone out of his pocket he looked at the display. *Private number. It was him!*

He answered and held the phone to his ear. The caller was already talking, 'Now listen very carefully, Jack. This is what's going to happen. You boys are holding a Billy Wharton in the cells, you'll arrange his release on bail, it shouldn't be too hard when you tell your colleagues what I'm about to tell you. Wharton has a consignment of arms to collect. He'll be getting a call, anytime in the next twenty-four hours. The guns are coming by air via Holland; they will drop them from low level into a remote field somewhere in Essex. I don't have a location yet. Once Wharton's out, you'll have him under surveillance; the rest is up to you. Just think what a feather in your cap it'll be when you and your team close down this nasty little operation.'

'What's in it for you?' he asked.

'For *me*? You surprise me, Jack. Here I am, trying to help you keep a consignment of weapons from falling into the hands of gangsters all over the country and you ask what's in it for *me*? Potentially, you'll be instrumental in saving hundreds of lives from drug and gun related crime. Just be grateful I chose you, my friend.'

The line clicked, cutting the connection.

He didn't bother trying to have the call traced; all the others to him and his parents had been from cheap, disposable mobile phones. They'd managed to match the telephone numbers to prepaid SIM cards and then to the outlets that sold them. CCTV footage enabled them to identify a number of the kids he'd recruited from the streets outside the shops. He'd given them ten pounds to go in and buy the SIM's for him.

None of the descriptions they gave police was the same twice. He was variously dark-haired, clean-shaven, blonde and bearded or shaven headed. The calls were made from different locations, and often many miles apart.

Outmanoeuvred, and trapped in a situation he couldn't afford to have exposed, Kennedy had a sinking feeling. They would not catch this character unless it was red-handed.

With Marilyn gone, he had no one to confide in.

Kennedy wandered down to the cells; he decided he wasn't going to rush into anything until he'd established a few things for himself. He spoke to the custody officer. 'Just the one here tonight, Dawson?'

The officer looked up briefly, before continuing with his paperwork. 'Yes, sir, it's really quiet and even *he* isn't here at the moment. I thought while I have the chance I'd catch up on some admin.'

'So, what's the brief on him, Dawson?'

'He's been arrested on suspicion of handling stolen goods.'

'Where is he now?'

'Drug squad's interviewing him, sir.'

'Drug squad?'

'Yes, sir,' and pre-empting the next question, he volunteered. 'They searched his car, and they not only found a load of jewellery, but they also found a piece of paper hidden in the boot with a phone number on it, sir. No name, just a phone number and he wouldn't say whose number it was – claims he doesn't know.'

'And?'

'They did a reverse check; turns out the phone number was previously used by someone involved in the illegal importation of class A drugs into the country.'

'Really? That's a huge shift from getting picked up for handling stolen goods.'

'And that's not all, sir,' Dawson leaned over the counter, lowering his voice. 'Some of that jewellery has been linked to the Midnight man break-ins.'

'Jesus, Dawson, this could be the break we've been looking for!' Suddenly, he had a hunch. 'I don't suppose you have a record of the telephone number they found on him?'

'No, sir, I don't. All I know is I overheard a DS guy talking about a Danny Lynch.'

What's Danny Lynch got to do with all this?

'Let me know when they bring him back down,' Kennedy said, and turned slowly on his heels to head back to his office, forehead creased with lines of deep contemplation.

Chapter 95

The caller walked into the local branch of Kennedy's bank and made a cash deposit of five thousand pounds. The cashier printed a receipt and handed it to him. Despite the unusually warm weather, she didn't pay any attention to the fact he was wearing black leather gloves.

The next stage of his plan was almost complete and once outside he couldn't resist grinning. His face lit up, but his lips were stretched painfully tight. Concealed behind his moustache, the scar that ran from under his nose down to his upper lip seemed to anchor the lip in place, allowing them to part just enough to reveal his teeth. The backward slope and inwardly slanted arrangement was reminiscent of those of a shark without the sharp tips, but he looked as if he might bite, and if he did, he might not let go. Mostly he kept them concealed. They were not for smiling with. His teeth worked best when they menaced people. His top lip stretched tighter. *All you have to do now is plant the receipt.*

Kennedy paced across the front of the assembled group, addressing them in a loud voice. 'We received a tip off over the weekend. There's to be a shipment of firearms into the country over the next few days,' he said, and even though he held his hands together, a slight tremble remained evident. 'According to our sources, it's a major consignment of semi-automatic weapons, dozens of them; destined for London initially, for onward distribution – Manchester, Bristol, Nottingham – you know the score.' He eyed each one of the officers in turn. 'Following on from the same tip off, we apprehended a man named Billy Wharton. A search of his car revealed him to be in possession of a quantity of stolen jewellery, along with a telephone number used by a major criminal linked to the importation of drugs and arms into the country. Wharton denied knowing anything about the arms, the jewellery or the telephone number. Sound familiar?' he said, attracting a ripple of laughter. 'We're currently in the process of trying to trace or match the jewellery to recent burglaries. Some items have already been linked to the so-called Midnight man robberies. We think the organisation responsible is recycling the proceeds of these crimes into the drugs and arms trade; laundering the cash through pubs and clubs.

'As most of you are aware, we held the suspect in custody for approximately twenty-four hours. We released him without charge yesterday. He's under surveillance and, as we've already been informed of the whereabouts of the rendezvous, arrangements are in hand to stake out the premises. To that end, we've secured the unit next door and we'll have an armed response unit in attendance. We're told Wharton isn't due to make contact with the arms gang until tomorrow, and we're confident the meeting will lead us to the consignment. The intention is to pick them off as discretely as possible, to avoid alerting anyone further up the chain.' Shifting his balance from one foot to the other, he continued. 'Intelligence suggests it's the first of a number of planned drops from planes coming into the remote coastal areas of North Essex and elsewhere. If we can plug this, we have a real chance of disrupting organised crime in the city and giving them a bloody nose. If we can take the ringleaders out, it'll be a feather in our caps, gentlemen. I'm sure I don't have to remind you, we can't afford any mistakes.' He stopped by the desk at the front and picking up a glass of water took a sip from it. His gaze swept across the assembled team. 'We need to be ready the minute the call comes in. I'm sure I don't have to remind you how important it is we get a result here. Any questions?'

Kennedy kept busy trying to keep his mind off things, demanding answers to mundane issues he'd never normally become involved in. Theresa was run ragged fetching paperwork. He chased Tanner on the Archie Brooks connection and then without waiting for an answer, switched back immediately to Lynch. 'We have to bring him in, Tanner,' he'd said, 'I think he's the ring leader of a gang responsible for umpteen major crimes.'

'SOCA is already onto it, sir.'

'I know, but I want to get to him first.'

When Tanner returned to his office, he thought about how jittery and hollow-eyed the chief had looked. He had himself experienced the pain of losing both his parents early on in life. No lingering on, no agonising over each new downward turn. It wasn't good, but it was better than the slow deterioration the DCI was going through with his mother's decline.

Chapter 96

Lynch was agitated. Like a boxer sent to a neutral corner with the scent of victory in his nostrils; he paced one side of the room, barely able to contain himself. Lean, wiry and deceptively strong, many opponents had badly underestimated him on the basis of size alone, finding out to their cost, that looks aren't everything.

When he'd first started out, he had had the face of an angel. Now marred by old wounds, it bore testimony to the long hard-fought battle up through the ranks, and the scars served as a warning to those who didn't know him that he was not a man to be messed with.

In the light of what had happened to Melissa, and after what she'd told him, he'd managed to keep calm against the odds. He needed to weed out the threat against him. One minute Billy Wharton was in custody and then he was out. Once, people could be trusted to keep their mouths shut, but not anymore. When Billy didn't tell him about his arrest, he'd sealed his own fate. He had to get rid of him. Then he'd deal with Tony.

The doorbell rang. Lynch strolled down the hall and opened the door. Terry Bishop stood on the step admiring the spring blooms in the front garden.

'Nice place,' Bishop grinned. 'How're you doing?'

They embraced at the door. 'I'm okay, Tel, good to see you, thanks for coming.' They sauntered into the lounge together, exchanging pleasantries. Released only the day before, he'd taken the rap for his boss in an assault case five years before. If he hadn't, the gangster would have gone down for a lot longer than he did. In return, he secured a promise his family would be looked after, and he'd get a lump sum when he came out.

'Listen, Tel, I got some work for you if you're interested.'

'Could be,' Terry said. 'I ain't doing much else. What is it?'

'It's Tony, mate. He's nicked a hundred grand off me and he's planning to heist me on something else as well.'

Terry whistled. 'A hundred K, how did he manage that?'

'He got in with a girl I was close to, found out she was holding it for me.'

'What about the girl?'

'She's dead.'

'Fuckin' hell, Dan – you *killed* her?' his eyes glazed over.

'No, it wasn't me; someone else did, maybe Tony. I've had to keep the old powder dry, box a bit clever, till I know what he's up to behind my back. It's fucking killing me.' Lynch raised both clenched fists at the ceiling, his eyes blazed with suppressed rage. 'I got a call this morning. He's planning to meet Billy Wharton tomorrow night, to hijack a consignment going to the Hammerson gang.'

'Tommy Hammerson? What's he playing at?'

'He wants to start a war, get me out of the way. I've been watching him all week to find out. Anyway, the caller confirmed it. Which brings me back to you.'

'Dan, I've only just got out.'

'Yeah, I know. The thing is, that hundred grand...a fair bit was earmarked for you, but don't worry, I'll deal with it. Let's get him round for a little reunion get-together.' He paused to think, and closing his eyes, he pinched the bridge of his nose hard, his mouth twisted at the self-inflicted pain, and then he looked straight at his old friend. 'Tell you what, Terry, you phone him. Get him round here. Whatever happens, whether I get the dough back off him or not, at the end of it you'll still get your share, sound fair?'

'I don't know about all this, I've only just got out. How much are we talking, Danny?' he asked.

'Twenty-five grand,' Lynch said.

An hour later, Tony arrived with a bottle of champagne. 'All right, Danny,' he said, as Lynch let him in and led him through to the lounge as he had so many times before. Tony remained oblivious to the menacing undercurrent in the atmosphere.

'Terry! It's good to *see* you. How's life treating you on the outside?'

'Still finding my feet, like I said on the phone I only came out yesterday—'

Lynch interrupted, 'How much money you got on you, mate?'

'Only about six hundred quid, why's that?'

'Where's the rest of it?'

'Eh?' he said, looking puzzled.

He walked right up to him so close he could smell the cocaine on his breath. Lynch had only been on the stuff for a year or so, but he'd become increasingly unpredictable. His words came out all wrong. 'Listen, Danny.'

A one-two-three combination crashed him to the floor. Lynch had him by the hair, pulling hard at the back of his head, forcing him backwards onto his knees; his right fist balled, hovering inches from his face.

'Don't ever *"Listen Danny"* me again, you got that!'

Tony tasted blood in his mouth, his lips felt numb and swollen, teeth, loose and painful.

'Yeah, I got that.' He felt like a dog whose owner had just kicked it.

Lynch pushed him away. 'Last chance; I ain't playing fucking games anymore. Where's the rest of it?'

His former right-hand man protested his innocence.

'How much money have you got in the bank?' A vein on Lynch's temple pulsed.

'What's this about?'

'What's this a-fucking 'bout? You know exactly what it's about; it's about what have you done with my money,' Lynch snarled. 'What have you done with my money?' The vein grew into a throbbing cluster.

'Danny, what's going on?' His voice was desperate.

Lynch erupted into a frenzied attack. Before Terry could do anything, he stabbed Tony in the neck, behind the windpipe. A geyser of blood spurted across the room.

Tony's eyes bulged in disbelief. His hands floundered over the wound in a last desperate attempt to hold onto the blood oozing out between his fingers. His legs kicking and bucking involuntarily as if to escape the wound that was draining his life from him. Lynch stood impassive, covered in blood, watching.

In the bright sunlit room, with its crystal chandeliers and art on the walls, he inexplicably thought of the TV programme 'Through the Keyhole'. *They'd never guess what sort of monster lived here.*

Terry stood in a state of shock. He'd never seen his former boss quite so murderous before. Lynch was still holding the knife when he said, 'Help me clean up this mess, and then I want you to deal with Billy Wharton.'

Chapter 97

With Kennedy increasingly distracted, the strain of getting nowhere fell heavily onto Tanner's shoulders. Once he snapped out of whatever his problem was, he'd be looking for a fall guy, and he knew who that would be. He couldn't remember the last time he'd worked a regular shift, and here he was again, working on a Saturday. Propping his elbow on the desk, he rested his head on the palm of his hand and closed his eyes. An irresistibly sleepy feeling wafted over him, and he floated away. The telephone had rung three or four times before it registered, he answered on instinct, without really knowing where he was.

'Tanner.'

'Mr Quinn?'

It threw him for a second. *Archie Brooks.* 'Oh yes, Quinn speaking. I was expecting a guy called Tanner.'

Brooks seemed hesitant. 'What you was looking for…the fight. It's happening this weekend, and it's a big one, thousands will be there,' he paused. 'Newbury, Sunday morning; find a pub nearby. Wait in the car park. I'll phone you the exact location, half an hour beforehand.'

Tanner suddenly felt nervous. In such a huge crowd someone, he'd arrested before would be bound to recognise him. They'd lynch him before anyone could bail him out. He smiled at the field day his reporter friend would have with that story. *Cop On Unauthorised Surveillance Beaten To Death By Bare-knuckle Crowd!*

She'd love it.

The DCI shook his head in disbelief. 'I don't believe it. With everything else we've got happening, this comes up now.' Kennedy sighed. 'And yes, you are the only one who can do it, Tanner, but I need you back here straight after. The arms shipment is due to be shifted tomorrow. We're just waiting for Wharton to confirm arrangements.'

'He's talking to us?'

'No, we have his phone tapped.'

'Whatever happens tomorrow, sir, I'll be back by evening. I have a feeling they won't try to shift the consignment until nightfall.'

'You're probably right. Make sure you listen out for your phone in all the excitement tomorrow, I might need you beforehand.'

'Okay, will do,' he said as he stopped by the door. 'Sir, have there been any developments with the Gasman?'

'I've just gotten the results back and they confirm the same man raped Melissa Lake *and* Natasha Stone, but there's bad news. The DNA isn't on the National Database. We've hit a brick wall.'

'He's getting careless though, sir, he thinks he's cleverer than us. I think we'll catch him sooner than he thinks.'

'I wish I shared your confidence.'

Kennedy's phone rang. His eyes met with Tanner's and flicked in the direction of the door. The DCI wanted privacy.

He closed the door behind him.

Chapter 98

The following morning, Archie Brooks called to say he'd arrived in Newbury.

'You know what today is, boy? I'll tell you – it's April Fool's day. Fools and their money, ready for parting – What do you *say*, Mr Quinn?'

They met in a pub car park at 11 a.m. Brooks was already outside, waiting. 'Fuckin' signals no good in there and my phone is shite,' Brooks explained, showing him the mobile phone in his hand.

'Thousands will be there today, the betting will be astronomical. There'll be millions placed on the fight.'

Quinn made notes on a hand held recording device.

'You got one of them mobiles with a camera on you? Leave it in the car. I'll send you a few photographs once I've seen your book so far. I might not like it – you know what I mean?' He took a swig of his beer and wiped the froth from his mouth with the back of his hand. 'There's a lot of excitement today, because for the main fight we got "The Boiler man" settling a score with the Flynns. He fell out with the grandfather over a caravan Shaw's father lived in. He says Shaw burnt it down. It's taken him all this time to catch up with him. The grandfather, he's in no fit state to fight, so he's sending his son to do the job for him. The Boiler man's got no kin or he could have passed it on himself. Anyways, the fight is on. The boy is thirty-five, and he's no mug; Shaw is sixty-odd.' He sipped and wiped at his white foam moustache again. 'And there's going to be big money changing hands on that one I'm tellin' you. I'll be having a flutter on it for sure.'

'Will they stop it if the old man gets in trouble?'

Brooks spurted his beer back into his glass. 'Are you trying to have a fuckin' laugh wit me?' He looked with distaste at the foamy head growing on the beer. 'I'm betting on the Boiler man. Jesus the man's got more fight in him than an angry Pit bull, always will have, it will never leave him. They say madness took him over as soon as he was old enough to understand, cursing his father and his mother, too, though he loved her dearly – God rest her soul – because they passed on the hare's curse to him. He got it double.'

'Hare's curse...what is that?'

'What would you call it? A cleft palasy?'

'Palate – I think you mean palate,' Quinn said.

'Palate?' Brooks said it slowly. 'Yes, both of them had it. When he was growing up all the kids bullied him for it, made a fighter out of him, and oh, that temper! Right now, I hear he's madder than hell because he's lost all his cash money on bad bets – he won't lose.' He tilted his beer back, trying without success to drink without dipping his nose in the foam.

While Brooks concentrated on his beer, Tanner was thinking. If Shaw had had an operation on a harelip, he must have had it done with the NHS – and if he did, he had to be traceable.

Brooks took a call and after a short conversation, said, 'Come on, we're going. Leave your car here.'

On the way, Brooks enlightened him with more talk of legends, based on real facts and folklore. Tanner recorded it all with his permission. Occasionally Brooks told him to turn the tape off while he let him in on things he didn't want quoted. 'So, he crossed the street, knocking on his door. When he opened it, he let him have both barrels. We don't tolerate kiddie fiddlers, you see.'

Brooks had a tendency to switch between subjects and now he was back on Shaw. 'I always thought he was smarter than he was lettin' on. Behind his back, people said he was a divvy, but no one would say that to his face.'

'What about women, I bet he had them flocking round.'

'Aye, he did that, but he never seemed interested. Struck me as odd; ugly boy like that turning them down. One or two of the boys thought he might have been a homo; you know what I mean, getting his kicks outside the camp. No one really knew much about him, see, him always away from home and all.'

'Shaw must have made a fortune. Did you say he lost it?'

'Aye, he did that. Although he invested in two, three properties, so I hear. Lucky he did. Had a taste for the gee-gees, you see, only one man wins there.' Taking a cigarette out, he offered him one.

'No, thanks,' he said.

'Well, you won't mind if I do.' Brooks lit it without waiting for a reply. 'Got any money on you, Mr Quinn? If you have, put it all on Shaw. I heard he's got a hundred grand to put on himself.'

'I thought you just said he was broke?'

'Are you trying to catch me out, Mr Quinn? I'm talking about cash money. Might be he sold some property, I don't know. I'm not fuckin' his keeper.'

He decided not to question Brooks' last statement.

After driving miles through the countryside down ever increasingly narrow lanes, they eventually stopped. Caught in the convergence of pick-up trucks, four-wheel drives, BMWs, Mercedes' and horse drawn racing traps, they queued for ten minutes to get off the road. Although he had dressed down for the occasion, he stuck out like a sore thumb. They ranked among the roughest men he'd ever encountered. Peering into the car, they eyed him with open hostility and suspicion as Brooks' passed through a field gate and parked. Tanner felt he'd intruded into an alien world, a world he'd never glimpsed before.

'If we can't get close enough to the fight, I'll get us a copy film of it. Meanwhile, soak up the atmosphere, enjoy it.' Brooks grinned wickedly.

Now he was on his own, no car, no phone, no back-up. The air was charged with excitement and filled with menace, edgy like something bad was about to happen. He couldn't escape the feeling that if something did, it would involve him. Tanner functioned on autopilot, watching himself from a safe distance.

'Stick close to me, boy,' Brooks told him as they moved among the masses of people. Brooks pushed him near to the front. Mounting restlessness added to

Tanner's anxiety, and he couldn't settle, although the mob seemed oblivious to him. Someone was talking about Shaw.

'Just like the old man, just like him. I thought he'd disappeared for good, just like the old man. The mother, though, now she was a lovely woman.'

'Aye, she was that. He fell out with his dad you know.'

'Yeah, I heard. Burned him out of the home when the mother died, didn't he?'

'Yeah, took her maiden name after that.'

'I never knew that,' the other man said. 'What was she? A...' Tanner's ears pricked up. A sudden roar in the crowd drowned the name out, as the fighters appeared. He caught his first glimpse of Shaw. He wore a short and spiky straw-coloured beard and moustache, the gaps between the clumps of coarse hair reminded him of stubble in the fields after harvest. Fearsome looking, Shaw had his head completely shaved, revealing scars that criss-crossed his scalp. From where he stood, Tanner couldn't be sure it was the same man in the E-Fit.

Chapter 99

In the field, the smell of trampled grass, cigarettes and old leather hung in the air, the level of noise already intimidating rose to a crescendo as the fighters appeared. Shaw limbered up slowly; the younger man, Flynn, fired off a series of rapid combinations. The throng roared its approval. Shaw pushed out a lazy left and then doubled it, crossing over with a slow right hand. Brooks was right; money was changing hands left, right and centre. Tanner watched with interest. Shaw still had all the moves, and he clearly kept himself in shape. What struck him most of all was the sense of calm he projected, in contrast to the younger fighter.

Shaw stood ready. He reflected on how he'd created this opportunity for himself. He only had to show his face in front of the Flynns, he knew they'd call him out, knowing he'd have no choice but to fight. Like many a boxer before him, he believed he could go on winning forever.

Fighting was in his blood. *You'll still be picking fights in the graveyard,* his granny used to say to the old man. *Hmmph. The old man.* The fighting kept him out of a lot of trouble. It channelled his propensity for violence and acted as a penance for his wicked ways. Every blow he took a punishment, a point scored for those he'd done wrong to. Apart from settling the score, he hated the Flynns with a vengeance. The younger boys had taken the piss out of him when he was growing up, because of his stutter. He guessed he always knew he'd get a big payday out of it in the future. It was a long time coming, but it was here now.

The stewards struggled to keep the masses back as they surged forward, expecting blood. With the fight moments away, Shaw fired himself up, shuffling and jabbing at the air in a state of adrenaline-fuelled, heightened awareness; a high-octane burst would be on him as soon as the bell went.

His opponent, at only half his age, looked powerful. He was impossibly broad with short arms. They touched fists. 'Short arms' came out swinging. Fists hooking; left first and then right, his short black hair already wet from the pre-fight warm up, shed beads of sweat with each jerky movement.

Faster than the older man had expected, Shaw took a step back and measured him. Flynn's eyes were little black stones that betrayed no emotion. He reminded Shaw of a shark.

So far he'd kept out of range, skipping away, leaning back, arms loose but up in front of him. Shaw didn't like to waste energy. A lazy jab brought Flynn in fast underneath, both fists tearing through the air, knowing at any second he'd connect, and then it would be goodnight Vienna for the Boiler man, who himself slipped a punch, ducked under, half twisting, leaning over from the waist, he whipped a wicked left hook into the ribs just below where Flynn's elbow had been. Wincing, he faltered and drove a shot through the middle into empty air as Shaw circled left, switched to southpaw, jabbing with his right. Flynn deflected, ducked under and caught another vicious left in exactly the same spot. The crowd exhaled as one. *Ooooh!*

Tanner pushed forward. Brooks pulled him back.

Flynn, more cautious this time, couldn't read Shaw, who seemed to be looking off at a point in the distance, unconcerned. He took his chance. Flynn jabbed, doubling it up. Shaw parried the punches with his gloves and then quick as a flash, a left, again downstairs, and a crunching right, down over the top contorted Flynn's face. He was out before he touched the ground.

Tanner had hoped to pick up a towel or something Shaw had used. Maybe even get in close for an autograph, a photo with his arm around him, anything that could yield some DNA material. Shaw took his T-shirt off to wipe his face. *That's it – throw it to the crowd!* He willed him to do it, but he tucked it into his belt, and as he did, Tanner caught a glimpse of the buckle. Suddenly they – the crowd surged forward, sweeping the undercover policeman almost off his feet, almost into touching distance.

In the pandemonium that followed, he and Brooks were separated. He feared for his life. With the stewards overrun, fighting broke out all around them. In the melee, Shaw floored two or three would be attackers. Somebody fired a shotgun. Everything stopped. A loud voice boomed. 'That's enough! Go home, boys.'

The stewards took up positions once more. The crowd began to disperse.

When Brooks found him, he laughed. 'You're as white as a sheet! You okay, Quinn?'

Tanner nodded, but he was thinking about the belt buckle. It looked similar to the sketches drawn by Kennedy and Doherty. It *had* to be him.

A couple of hours later as Brooks drove him back, they discussed the fight they'd seen.

'That was crazy, I've never seen a man of that age move like it,' Tanner said. 'Tell me, Archie, where'd he get the nickname "The Boiler man" from? Was he a ship's stoker or something like that?'

'You know; he could fight *before* he went away, but he came back as a highly trained man. That fight just now, you wouldn't know, but this was over something that happened years ago. 'The Boiler man' came from his mother, her name was Boyle, see. Anyways, when his mother died he fell out with the father and he burnt him out, ran him off the site. Changed his name too, he did, to his mother's maiden name. What was I saying? Oh yeah, after the fire, both the old man and young Boyle went missing. That's how it started.'

'Archie, hang on a minute, I can't keep up. You said he was highly trained and called himself Boyle?'

'Yeah, that's right. Joined the Foreign Legion, he did.' Before Tanner could ask any more questions, Brooks said, 'Did you put any money on him? You should have. I waited till the last minute. After all that shaping up, the boy rattlin' his sabres – I got me some good odds.'

'I got a good story out of it. That's enough for me. So how long was he in the Foreign Legion and what did he do after that?'

'Mr Quinn, is this a story about the great gipsy champions or *The Boiler man?* You see, I don't hear you asking me too many questions about any of those fighters now.'

'I've just seen a fighter in his late sixties beat the favourite, a man half his age and I was impressed. I think a man like that warrants a few words about his background, maybe even warrants a whole book about him, wouldn't you say?'

Brooks pulled into the car park and stopped. He turned to look at Tanner. 'A man like that?' he looked bemused. 'That's as maybe, Mr Quinn, but you'll be getting no more from me. Good day to you.'

Tanner frowned as he stood by his car. *Is Brooks just naturally guarded, or does he know something?*

In order to maintain Quinn's credibility, he'd have to get their story out there. He would pass the tape and his notes on to his friend. She'd do the story for him. After all, she owed him a favour.

Then he called Kennedy to bring him up to date. 'At least we have something to go on now, sir. I'll get straight onto it.'

Kennedy cleared his throat. 'We'll get someone else onto it, you have an assignment tonight. Wharton has confirmed the meet. I'll fill you in with the details when you get to the office.'

Chapter 100

Evening, 1 April

The Sat Nav in Billy Wharton's car took him into the heart of the industrial estate and announced, *You have arrived at your destination.*

The address he sought was actually around the other side of a high security fence. Streetlamps lit the maze of roads with a distinctive soft yellow glow. He drove on taking the next two right turns before completing the circuit with a final turn into the cul de sac he'd seen from the opposite side. The entrance gates were the only ones left open. The long run of linked units appeared deserted. Drawing up to the raised loading apron halfway down, he reversed into position and left the car running. He turned off his lights, not wanting to attract unwelcome attention.

After a few moments, Billy got out of the car to stretch his legs. Deciding he'd hear better without the engine running, he leant back in and turned the ignition off. Distant sounds reached him, workshop motors, shutters rolling up or down, occasional voices, too far off to make out what they were saying. He looked around. Bright yellow lights pooled down onto the area he'd parked in. Penned in by pale grey anti-climb railings, he was alone. He felt claustrophobic. There was only one way out he could see. Back the way he came in.

He took a cigarette from his pocket without removing the pack and lit it. Inhaling deeply, he blew the smoke out, watching as the cloud of yellow smog billowed into the night air, disappearing into the darkness beyond the light. Taking another drag, he blew a further cloud into the night.

The sound of a vehicle's approach alerted him. As it neared, he saw it was a white transit van. The lights swung into view through the gates and it pulled up alongside him.

Billy flicked the cigarette out in a high arc, away from where he stood. He moved round to the driver's door, which was already opening.

Bishop stepped out. Wary, he surveyed the deserted estate around them. He offered a hand. 'Bill.' Wharton took it.

'Terry, I heard you were out. Where's Tony?'

'He's gone on ahead. Are you on your own, Bill?'

'Yeah, he doesn't pay me enough to split it with anyone else; you know what I'm saying?' He grinned. Bishop nodded his assent.

'Bill, we gotta go round the corner mate – someone else is taking us the rest of the way.'

Wharton looked confused. 'I thought it was just me and Tony going, meeting the others.'

'Change of plan, Bill. Come on let's get going.'

Bishop led the way. A few yards down, he turned.

Wharton hadn't moved. He was lighting a cigarette. Holding the pack up, he raised his eyebrows and offered them.

'No, thanks, mate. Are you coming?'

Strange, it's not like the Terry I know to turn a smoke down. He must've given it up in the nick. Putting the cigarettes away, he started after him.

Behind a boarded up window, armed police watched the two men through a slot cut into the sheeting.

Tanner arrived back from the toilet, holding his stomach. 'I had a bad feeling about that kebab I had earlier, and I was right.' He pressed his lips together at each new griping pain.

He peered through the opening. 'Where are they going?'

'Oh, shit! They're heading up towards the corner.'

'Is it just those two, no one else here?'

'No, but that's where our backup is. Shall I tell them to hide?'

The two suspects still had fifty yards to cover before they'd reach the corner.

'Christ! Who told them to plot up there? They'll have to shift – and fast! No wait, they've stopped. What are they doing?'

At the point where the semi-circular arc of brightness gave way to the darkness of the alley; Wharton stopped suddenly. He licked his lips anxiously, eyes filled with trepidation.

'What are you doing, Bill?'

'Where have they parked, mate? Why haven't they parked where we did?' he said, searching Bishop's face for an answer. 'What's going on, mate?'

'Bill, that alleyway leads through to the street the other side. That's where the others are, just up there. See, if anything happened, there's only the one way out round this side. What's the problem?'

'You know I can't go down a dark alley so close to the fence, not with my claustrophobia. I'm going to get the car. I'll meet you round there.'

He turned around and headed back.

'Shit.' Bishop breathed. He hadn't wanted to do it out there in the light, didn't want to have to drag the body out of sight, get covered in blood. He didn't even really want to kill him, but if he didn't, someone else would and he'd be as good as dead himself. He probably would have been dead already if he'd refused. Something had happened with Lynch's state of mind and it wasn't just the coke. *I'll do this job, get the twenty-five grand and then put some distance between him and me. Might even go straight.* The unlikelihood of the last thought had him grinning.

He produced a gun and screwed a silencer onto the end.

'Bill?' He couldn't bring himself to shoot him in the back.

Wharton turned and saw the gun. It all suddenly made sense to him. They'd found out about his arrest somehow. They thought he'd talked. He raised both hands in the air. 'Terry. Don't. I—'

'Sorry, Bill.' Terry sounded genuinely sad as he fired a single shot into his head.

All hell broke loose. Portable arc lights switched on. The team hiding around the corner raced out. Heckler and Koch carbines at shoulders, they advanced on him. Caught in the dazzling light, centre stage, Terry couldn't see. Someone shouted, 'Armed police, drop your weapon!' Shutters rolled up. The sound of approaching heavy boots drummed on the ground.

'What just happened?' Tanner shouted, and threw open the door to join the melee.

'He's just shot Wharton!'

'Oh, shit!'

In the light of recent criticism on the shooting of an innocent man in London and police failure to warn the suspect, Bishop received the benefit of an extra warning.

'Armed police, drop your weapon!'

He couldn't see beyond the dazzling brightness. He lost his sense of direction and perspective. His head spun.

He faced a lifetime in prison if he surrendered.

If I can just get away.

Faced with hard choices, he hesitated a moment longer. Fingers were jittery on triggers. He made a wrong move. Turning quickly in the direction of where he thought he'd left the van, he broke into a sprint. Straight towards the armed officers, the gun was still in his hand.

Two simultaneous shots cut him down. One passed through his head, the other his heart.

At the subsequent inquest, held weeks later, the Specialist Firearms Officers would testify they'd shouted two clear warnings before the suspect raised his gun and ran towards them. Faced with the clear and imminent threat of further loss of life, they'd shot him.

The coroner's court would record a verdict of lawful killing by the police.

Chapter 101

Monday, 2 April

Knowing Kennedy was under increasing pressure from all directions; the caller cranked it up.

'I've got you stitched up tighter than a duck's arse, Jack, and even if you think you can still get out of it, mate, I gotta tell you, you can't. So from now on, whatever I tell you I want done, you do it. Do you understand what I'm saying?'

'You can't blackmail a police officer and think you're going to get away with it,' Kennedy said, but his voice lacked conviction. *He's been ahead of you all the way, Johnny.*

'Get away with it? Jack, what I've done to you is irreversible, incontrovertible.' A cigarette lighter clicked at the other end of the line, followed by the sounds of exaggerated puffing on his cigarette.

A feeling of dread grew within him. The first acid pangs of indigestion assailed his stomach. He instinctively knew whatever it was the caller had in store for him was going to be bad.

The caller outlined the series of predicaments that faced him.

Kennedy recognised more than a grain of truth in the claims. The acid levels increased in line with his rising heartbeat as the caller delivered the events in sequence. Every word was a barb in a line of wire hooking in and tightening.

'They'll investigate you, Jack, you know that,' the caller said.

His thoughts raced. His prospects diminished. Left with nowhere to go, he suddenly remembered Tanner's report; someone had cloned his motorbike registration number, and he realised it was probably the caller who had done that, too.

Ten seconds of silence had passed. 'Are you clear about where we are with all this, Jack?'

Face grim, he said nothing. *I need time to think.* He nodded, forgetting he was on the telephone.

'I said, Jack, *are you clear*?'

Kennedy snapped the phone away from his ear. Stung by the sudden blast of the shout, he looked out through the window in the office partition, worried someone else might have heard it. He switched the phone to the other side of his head and wiggled a finger around inside his damaged ear, hoping to gain some relief for it.

You have to play for time.

'Yes,' he replied.

The line disconnected.

With no idea of the caller's ultimate aim, Kennedy's thought processes had reduced to going round in circles. In frustration, he slammed his fist into the wall, skinning his knuckles. He immediately regretted it as blood welled where skin had been. He didn't hear Theresa knock on the door; he looked up, and she was just … *there*. Opening a drawer quickly, he put his bleeding hand inside, hoping she hadn't seen it.

'Coffee? Are you all right, John, you look like you've seen a ghost.'

He faked a smile. 'Yes – coffee, that'll be fine.'

As she left, Theresa wondered what she'd done to make him so obsessed with her and whether the haunted look in his eyes had something to do with it. *If it did.* Feeling bad enough already, she dismissed the thought. She hadn't asked for any of it.

After she'd confided in Tanner, he said he'd report him. She wondered if he'd already done it. She'd have to check with him, but he wasn't happy with how things had developed after they'd slept together. He said he wanted a couple of days to decide the best way forward. He hadn't said, but she knew from the hurt look in his eyes he felt used.

She was desperate to make it up to him.

Chapter 102

2 April 2007, early evening.

The roadside cafe was bustling with people, when a man walked in. A few heads turned lazily towards him, alerted by the door's opening.

The stranger's eyes swept the interior of the room, scanning faces; nobody met his gaze, or lingered over his appearance for long. Rough and dishevelled looking, he wore a dirty blue boiler suit. His straw-coloured hair didn't look natural, and he had a nose as crooked as a stovepipe revealing the many wars he'd come through, in and out of the ring. Not much over six feet tall and heavily built, he moved with an ease that belied his size and age.

On the far side of the room, no one noticed him at all.

At the counter, he paid for a coffee and picked up a local paper from the rack, tucking it under his arm. He glanced around the room. There wasn't a completely vacant table anywhere, so he selected a table for two which was only half taken.

He pulled a chair back and sat down. A look of exasperation started on the current occupier's face, but before he could object, the stranger's molten eyes settled on him, and he thought better of it. Draining the rest of his cup, he left without a word.

'Something I said?' he asked, raising an eyebrow. He stirred a sugar into the steaming black liquid and unfolded the newspaper.

He'd always taken an interest in the places he passed through. The sleepy towns where nothing much ever happened were the best. The residents were complacent and never expected anything to happen, because nothing ever did.

It was a policy of his never to strike twice in the same place. Not even in a neighbouring county unless you *wanted* to draw attention to yourself. Since the fight, he had no need of work. The breaking and entering here and there was just for fun. It wasn't going to spark a manhunt, and that was the key. Hit a town. Blitz it and then move to the other end of the country and do the same. The police might catch on eventually, but by then, he'd be on to something else. There was *always* something else.

The games no longer held the same appeal, and he understood why many killers felt the need to taunt. It created a challenge, and he was bored.

Whoever had read the newspaper previously, must have dropped it and then put it back together in the wrong order. With the front page apparently missing, he leafed through the pages looking for it. It was there, but reversed, near to the back. He lifted the page out and turned it round.

The headline struck him.

Boy Missing – Police Appeal.

A five-year-old kid on his way to school that morning never arrived. *Five years old!*

What is it with people these days? He sipped the hot coffee. It scalded the oversensitive scar on his top lip. Gritting his teeth in anger, he blamed first the surgeons who hadn't knitted the wound together properly, and then the headline for distracting him.

He blew across the surface of the steaming liquid and continued to read.

He'd noticed over the years on his travels that someone was kidnapping little boys; he'd stumble on the odd headline, hundreds of miles apart. They always started the same. *Boy Missing.*

None of the boys were ever found. He hoped this kid would turn up safe and sound, but he had his doubts. If police suspected a serial killer of children was at large, they were keeping quiet about it. He clenched his fists so hard the knuckles popped.

Criss-crossing the same old roads, he noticed things and he'd look at people more closely. He was more wary of familiar faces than the unfamiliar ones. He developed an expertise in body language, another of the few skills he'd picked up from his father and learned to sense if someone was watching or masking an interest in him. *You feel that, boy? Those people over there are talking about us.*

The same feeling came over him in the café. It was a type of radar, and the two men hunched over on the table in the far corner, blipped onto it. He'd seen them around before. His memory for faces was without equal. Glancing back at the front page, other headlines covering *years* flashed in his mind's eye.

The two were always *there.* Unable to believe he'd never made the connection before, he'd always thought they were just travellers on the lookout for places to rob. He'd known from the look of them they were up to no good, but now he knew exactly what they were.

They were staring back at him; their own radar had kicked in. Something in the way he looked at them gave him away. They exchanged looks, trying to act as if nothing was happening. They talked urgently, occasionally shooting a look in his direction.

What he saw in them, they saw in him. The cold eyes, the sense of detachment and something else, too. The stranger was utterly without fear.

He checked the heat of the coffee, and took another sip, openly watching them.

They were talking about him.

He'd learned to read lips as a boy due to his mother's speech impediment and pieced together what they were saying.

A further quick exchange passed between them so close across the tabletop their faces almost touched. They whispered urgently.

'We can't wait any longer, it's too risky.'

'Are you sure that isn't him?'

'Don't be fucking stupid! *He's* not one of us.'

'Let's just go. That guy over there...he's making me nervous.'

They stood up and left.

He drained the last of his coffee. It made him want to piss, but he daren't go for fear of losing the two men.

Outside they entered a large, dirty white van. He followed at a distance for miles. Eventually, they turned off the main road, driving in the darkness down ever narrowing roads, until they reached a farm track.

Five minutes later, they pulled up outside a rundown house surrounded by old shipping containers.

The stranger had switched his lights off as soon as he'd turned onto the track, navigating by moonlight alone. He pulled up two hundred yards away and observed from his car.

One of the men retrieved a small figure from the back wrapped in a blanket. The other looked around furtively as he slammed the back doors of the van shut. The two men hurried inside with the boy. Dogs barked excitedly. He could tell from the depth and resonance of the barking they were big and there were at least two of them.

Sprinting as fast as he dared in the darkness, he got to within a few yards and then walked the remaining distance on the sides of his feet. He pressed his back against the wall outside the house, next to the door they'd entered.

The low growling informed him the animals had sensed his presence.

Damn dogs! He hadn't fully recovered from the bite he'd received before Christmas. That one had come out of nowhere. Its owner had trained it to go for the nuts. He winced at the painful memory. One day he'd go back for the owner, for what he did to him.

Damned perverts probably think the animals are excited about having a child in the house. No time to lose.

He kicked in the door. *Rottweilers!* The first leapt at him. He buried his knife to the hilt into its head, killing it instantly. He snatched at the knife, pulling up on it hard to retrieve it. The dead dog's head and shoulders rose from the floor. The knife wouldn't come out. It was stuck in deep, right through the bone. *No time!* The second one was on him; hot breath and saliva sprayed his face as he grabbed a front leg. Side stepping away, he pulled and lifted, swinging hard, he smashed it against the wall. He felt its leg break or dislocate; it didn't matter which. He stamped hard on its neck.

Face down on a table, trussed up and crying; the sound muffled by a gag; the boy was trying to turn round to see what was happening.

'Look away, kid!' the stranger commanded.

At first, the men were slow, caught by the shock of how quickly their first line of defence had failed, but now they closed in on the intruder. He stood stock still, ready. They rushed in from both sides as if they'd rehearsed the move, but they could never have anticipated violence on the scale about to be unleashed upon them. The two of them were used to dealing with no more than a child's resistance, and the stranger annihilated them easily with a short series of heavy blows. His gloved fists hooked and hammered away, like a butcher tenderising steaks.

The boy was frozen, stunned into silence, unsure what would become of him.

'Don't turn round, kid.'

He retrieved the baseball bat he'd left outside by the door. When he'd first stolen it, he knew it would come in handy one day. Not quite the use he had in mind for it, but it still fitted in with his overall plans.

One of the men cried out for an end to his misery. The other one was already dead.

Afterwards, he calmly took a mobile phone from one of his victims and dialled 999.

'Stay here, kid. The police are coming to get you out of here, okay?' The boy nodded quickly, obediently not looking at him.

On the way out, he retrieved his knife from the dog's skull. Stuck so tight, he had to use his boot to hold the head in place as he used both hands to twist and wrench the blade free.

He surveyed the carnage. A voice was in his head. *You risked everything to save a kid!*

'It isn't just one kid though, is it? It's for all the other kids those deviants have kidnapped, and for every kid they would have,' he said quietly. He shook his head to clear the voice.

You're going soft.

Chapter 103

West Lothian Police HQ, Scotland.

Detective Michael Brady entered DCI Caulson's office with a report. The DCI didn't turn to look at him. He stood with his hands folded behind his back looking out of the window onto the car park below. Brady was the new, boy, the bright young thing transferred just a few weeks ago from London. Brady sensed the DCI hadn't been particularly impressed with him so far. This could be his chance to shine.

'I have the pathologist's initial findings, sir.'

'Good, leave it on my desk. Shut the door behind you.'

Brady raised his eyebrows, and with a shrug, did as he was told. He could tell from the brusque manner of his dismissal the chief was in a foul mood. He dropped the report into the in-tray. As he reached for the door handle, Caulson spoke again.

'Read it for me, Brady, and not the whole bloody thing. Just pick out the relevant points for me.' The DCI continued looking out of the window.

Brady turned away from the door and approached the desk to retrieve the document. Reaching for it, he realised Caulson could see his every move reflected in the glass against the darkness outside.

'You've read it already, I take it, Brady?'

'Yes, sir, I have.'

'Then don't just read it, *tell* me what it says.'

Brady cleared his throat. 'Well, sir, it confirms the two men were basically beaten to death and violated with a large blunt instrument. We recovered a baseball bat from the scene. In fact, it was protruding.' The chief turned away from the window; he was a pinch-faced man with a stern expression and abrasive manner. Tall and thin, he looked ten years older than his sixty years. He wasn't popular, and Brady was finding out why.

'Sit down, Brady, I know all that already. What else do we have that is relevant to finding this character?'

'Well, there's evidence he actually finished the second man off with the bat, by forcing it so far into him it ruptured everything in its path.'

'You think that's relevant?'

'I do, sir, it tells us that we are dealing with someone who isn't afraid to inflict—'

The DCI did not let him finish. 'So what sort of person are we looking at? The father of a previous victim looking for revenge; a butcher or a psychopathic baseball fan? Tell me about the bat.'

Brady had suddenly become very hot under the spotlight of Caulson's glare. The man wouldn't let him settle, kept catching him off guard. He realised gaining Caulson's respect was going to be nigh on impossible. If he wanted to impress him at all, he'd have to come up with something smart. And quickly.

'The baseball bat has letters carved in just above the handle, spaced out with each one exactly one third of the way round, so the shaft, if rotated, says variously FKJ, KJF or JFK. It's extremely unlikely the initials belong to the assailant. It's also extremely unlikely – given its low value –it's been reported lost or stolen.'

'Anything else?'

'The bat wasn't used to beat the men. Strangely enough, it seems he preferred to do that with his fists. He wore gloves. Apart from tiny pieces of leather scuffed off them and some footprints, we don't have anything else at all.'

'We got nothing from the kid I take it?'

'The man ordered him not to look, but he did see him. He told us there was only one man, and that was about it. He's a wee bit traumatised as you can imagine at only five years old, so I don't—'

'Then don't.' He withered Brady with a harsh glare; he didn't like how the Sassenach tried to ingratiate himself with the use of a Scot's term. 'Any *wee* ideas on how he tracked them down?'

'Not at this stage. He could have been watching them for weeks. We're checking out the computers we found and mobile telephone records. We also found recording equipment, DVDs and so on. Early indications are they were part of a paedophile ring.'

'Sounds like this vigilante did us all a favour.' He lifted a cigarette from the inside pocket of his jacket and put it between his lips. He didn't light it, but he drew through the tobacco deeply. He caught the look Brady had given him. 'Trying to give it up, it's not easy in this job.' He exhaled with a sigh. 'So, in a nutshell, at the moment we don't know if it was revenge, a hate crime, or what the motive was. All we have on him, is he's likely got bruised knuckles.' He drew hard on the cigarette. 'Getting back to those initials.'

'Yes, sir?'

'I want them run through the database, all burglaries where the owners have those combined initials.'

Brady groaned.

'You got a problem with that, Brady?' The chief scowled at him.

'No, sir—'

Caulson cut him off again. 'If we can tie it to a burglary, he might have left some forensic,' he explained, a sudden weariness in his tone.

'How far back are we going with this?'

'Start digging your way backwards, I have a feeling in my water, it won't be too far back.'

'He probably got it from a boot sale.'

Caulson was uncharacteristically patient. 'Maybe...he might have taken it out of a *skip*, but if this turns nothing up, *you'll* follow that line of enquiry afterwards.'

'We could just go public?'

Caulson shook his head. 'At the moment I want it kept quiet, but yes if nothing else turns up...' Caulson was already imagining the spate of copycat nutcases claiming to be the killer.

The chief stood up, signalling the end of their meeting.

'Brady, I want answers. Get your teams working on it right now. We'll reconvene in the morning.'

'Yes, sir,' he said, faking enthusiasm.

Brady returned to his own office. He wondered if Cooper was still around; he could have just walked around the corner to see, but his encounter with Caulson had left him drained. He didn't even bother trying to raise him on the internal phone; he dialled him on his mobile.

Cooper was another ex-Metropolitan man, albeit he'd been in Scotland for ten years.

'You still around? Good. Can you come to my office? Yeah, five minutes?'

Cooper dropped into the chair opposite. 'How was he?' he flicked his eyes in the direction of Caulson's office.

'Is he always that personable?' Brady said.

Cooper laughed, 'He's getting worse. Coming up for retirement, he was already getting a bit flaky – I think he was hoping to get out before anything too drastic presented itself. Go out with a whimper and not a bang. Looks like he's out of luck; the last time something like this happened was twenty years ago, I think he sees it getting out of hand, and you *are* the new boy.'

Brady shrugged. 'He wants these initials checked out.' He pushed a photograph of the handle towards Cooper.

Cooper frowned, 'J.F.K...'

'It's one of three possibilities,' he conceded.

'It's the only one,' said Cooper. 'Look, there's a stop after the J. and the F. There isn't one after the K—'

'Let me see that!' Brady interrupted, grabbing the photos back, irritated he'd missed that detail himself. Cooper was right; there are faint stops after only those letters. 'J.F.K – well that narrows the field. I think we can safely say it's not the former American president's bat.'

Cooper grinned at him. 'That's just narrowed it some more!'

Brady took a swipe at him with the photo. 'Seriously, we need to run a check on lost property – a long shot I know. All victims of burglaries with those initials, find out if they had a bat stolen. If we can find one and tie it in with forensics, that would be great. He doesn't want to go public, so we're stuck with doing it this way.'

'Not a problem,' Cooper said, 'but I'd be surprised if we turn up a single lead.'

'Well, he said to start local and then fan out. Let's get onto it.'

Chapter 104

3 April 2007, late evening.

Paedophile Killings! Police Seek Vigilante Suspect.
The headlines were on billboards and newspapers everywhere. The story spread like wildfire. Aside from regurgitating the original story, the press was unable to do anything to satisfy public demand for the truth. Whoever he was, he'd captured the imagination of people all across the country. From up-market hairdressers to backstreet barbers, bistros, bars and restaurants – everyone was talking. The story quickly topped the list of the most searched news articles on the internet.

If he were to step out of the shadows, he'd become an instant celebrity.

For once, the press was not to blame for the reaction of the public. The stranger couldn't quite believe the things he heard people saying.

'He deserves a medal for what he done.'

'I've heard the police aren't looking for him too hard.'

'I heard they had him, but let him go.'

'It's part of a secret crackdown by the government, costs too much to keep 'em in prison so they're wasting 'em using ex-soldiers.'

'He's ex SAS; he has to be.'

In a pub in North Wales, a stranger sat quiet and unnoticed, nursing a pint of dark ale at a small table, tucked away under the rake of the stairs. There was no room on the other side for another chair. Smoke curled from his cigarette joining the thin grey fug that collected above his head.

He had a way of watching from beneath his eyebrows that wasn't obvious to the casual observer. The object of his attention was a tall, oddly balanced, curly haired man with a high voice who held court among a small crowd at the end of the bar a few feet away. Delivering a punch line he half-twisted and bowed with a burst of laughter, turning to reveal, an empty sleeve pinned to his chest at elbow level. The remaining arm had compensated for the loss and developed to almost the size of his thigh. Those who had known him before his loss would probably have said he'd also developed a bigger personality, and it had helped him to erase the bitterness he felt. Losing an arm was bad enough at any age, but in one so young… It also made him fiercely competitive, always out to prove himself. He was regaling a group of men around him in a loud drunken voice, with a version of how *he* thought the vigilante had pulled off the killings.

'They'd have sent the dogs out first.' He bowled his one arm forward, re-enacting the releasing of the dogs, the thickly braided sinews of his forearm rippled as his hand opened.

'Oh, no, come on, Bryn. You can't know that!'

He shook a huge fist at the interrupter. 'Yes, I can. Shut your mouth while I'm telling it to you, will you. What would be the point of the dogs, if you wouldn't send them out first?'

Someone else agreed with him. 'Oh, he's right about that, what *would* be the point?'

'And then, when he comes right in – after he's done away with the dogs – they know they're in trouble, right?'

While the group of men drunkenly thought it through, Bryn repeated himself. 'They *know* they're in trouble all right!' An unintelligible murmur of agreement rose from the group. All nodded eagerly, waiting for the next dramatization.

'One of them grabs a baseball bat.' The men hung on his every word. 'And he grabs it off him, uses their own baseball bat against them before shoving it up their arses!'

In the brief silence, as they paused on the moment, Owen, who up until now had kept quiet, made a remark. 'I bet they were glad he didn't pick up a frying pan!'

The pub erupted with laughter. Bryn looked exasperated, covering his face with his hand.

When the laughter subsided, eager to take up centre stage once more, Bryn said, 'I don't know about you lot, but if he were to walk in here right now, I'd be the first to shake his hand!'

The murmurs of agreement were almost as enthusiastic as the laughter at Owen's frying pan observation.

Someone noticed the rough looking stranger at the bar behind Bryn. He was holding an almost empty glass. All eyes stared in his direction. The small group fell eerily silent. Bryn, sensing something amiss, turned to follow the direction of their gaze. His eyes settled directly on the man. Dead silence fanned out through the rest of the pub.

The man steadily returned his stare. He was alone, but showed no sign of being intimidated. Lost for words, for once, and in a drunken muddle, Bryn exclaimed, 'It wasn't *you,* was it, boyo?' The bar remained silent as a small crowd drew in around the two men, waiting for the stranger's response.

The stranger took in the crowd and half smiled. His hand slowly extended for Bryn to shake. The whole pub held its breath.

The one-armed man took it. A farm labourer used to using his surviving arm for everything any normal man could do; his arm was at least twice as strong as a normal labourer's, but with a handgrip much stronger and out of all proportion to that. Discounting the likelihood the man was the *actual* vigilante, Bryn turned to the small crowd. His facial expression beaming as if to say, *Are you all watching this?*

Bryn put the grip on the stranger's hand; confident his freak strength would cause the other to buckle up in pain. Rope-like veins stood out among the sinews. The other man was older, but bigger, as wide as a door. His gnarled hands had knuckles that looked full of arthritis. He accepted Bryn's grip, and held firm as he finished the last of his glass with his free hand. Putting the glass down, not taking his eyes off the one-armed man for a second, he squeezed back. A look of surprise flashed in Bryn's eyes. The bones of his hand squashed together, he gritted his teeth to hide the pain; his grin fixed on the verge of becoming a grimace. He maintained eye contact.

A flicker, a narrowing, a dilation of the pupils, something barely perceptible passed between the two men. Recognition. Knowledge. The stronger gave way to the weaker. After all, what value was there in defeating a one-armed man?

The man released him.

Bryn had saved face. He held the stranger's hand aloft alongside his own. 'A draw!' he cried. Releasing the stranger's hand, Bryn shook his own, flexing the stiffened bones, clenching and unclenching his fist. Then he remarked with a humour more befitting Owen, 'If I didn't know better, I'd say you were a one-armed man, too!' Grinning, Bryn, said, 'Tell you what, let me buy you a drink, boyo?'

The man lit a cigarette, tilted his head back and blew a plume of smoke at the ceiling. 'Another time, maybe.'

'Now, Bryn, give him an arm wrestle!' Owen wrapped an arm around Bryn, and pulled him in close, so that they faced the stranger together, square on. 'I'll have my money on my, boyo, here!'

'Sorry, fellas, I got to go. You boys have a drink on me,' he said and put two twenty pound notes on the bar. As the door closed behind him, Owen broke the silence, voicing what they were all thinking, 'You don't think that really *was* him do you?'

Bryn rubbed his aching hand against his chin, thoughtfully. 'You know what, boyo. I think it definitely could have been *someone* like him.'

Two miles down the road the stranger pulled in to offer a hitchhiker a lift. The girl was in her twenties, raven-haired with a heart-shaped, friendly face.

She was relieved to see he was an older man. She'd never have gotten in with a younger man. They couldn't be trusted.

Once inside the car she noticed the boiler suit he was wearing. 'Just finished work?' she said.

'No,' he replied, activating the car's central locking system, 'actually, I'm just about to start.'

Chapter 105

It was already just after 3 p.m. Caulson had deferred their meeting until the afternoon and Brady was dreading it. After spending all day following up what little he had – every avenue had turned into a blind alleyway – he was just finishing his tea. He held the cup against the side of his face for warmth and comfort; an old habit picked up from his father, his thoughts about nothing in particular, when he experienced a eureka moment. Pulling the telephone towards him, he dialled a familiar telephone number. The operator came back to him.

'I'm not getting an answer from that extension, is there anyone else who can help you?'

'Can you try John Tanner?'

She put him through.

'John, it's Michael Brady.'

Through gritted teeth, he said, 'What can I do for you?'

'This is a long shot, but I don't suppose for one minute you'd know if Kennedy owns a baseball bat.'

He knocked on the DCI's door, just as he always did, even when expected. The DCI called, 'Come in.' He opened the door and stepped inside. Kennedy looked up from his desk. He looked tired, the bags under his eyes heavy. 'You wanted to see me?'

Tanner rolled an empty chair back on its castors and sat down. 'Your phone is off the hook.'

'Yes, I know it is,' he said, sounding weary.

'Sir, have you ever owned a baseball bat?'

His eyes narrowed. 'Of course, I have.'

'Stars and Stripes, American style?'

'Yes, I have one like that. Why are you asking?'

'Did you carve your initials—?'

'Tanner, stop pissing about. Get to the point.'

He took a deep breath and explained.

Kennedy couldn't remember seeing the bat when he'd stayed with his parents recently. With a look of consternation, he picked up the telephone and dialled home.

'Dad, can you look in my bedroom for me and see if my baseball bat is still there?' He listened with incredulity. 'You thought I had it? No, I left it there with the gloves and ball. Are they still there? They're not? No, no – don't worry, I must have misplaced them, that's all. Yes, no, don't worry – thanks, I'll call you later. Yes, I will.'

Tanner looked at him expectantly.

'Gone,' he said. There was a thoughtful silence as the two men considered the implications.

Finally, Tanner spoke, 'Where were you on the night of—'

Flushed with anger, Kennedy slammed his hand down hard on the desk. 'This is no time for joking.'

Tanner caught a glimpse of something else in his eyes. Just for a moment, he thought the chief looked afraid.

Chapter 106

When Bletchley's DNA test results came back, they cleared him as a suspect in the Natasha Stone rape case.

They had to let him go; all along his lawyer had argued there was no evidence he actually intended to commit rape – he'd not gone equipped and was entitled to keep the items found within the confines of his own home for his own use if he chose to do so. The decision on whether to prosecute over the illegal possession of chloroform rested with the Director of Public Prosecutions.

Bletchley had waited a few days before returning to his original plan, reasoning the police would never suspect him after his earlier brief incarceration. *I mean, who would be so stupid?* After a few days of painstaking attention to detail, which included setting up alibis for the whole evening, he was at last ready. Dressed all in black, with a yellow fluorescent belt and shoulder strap underneath his outer clothes, he left the house and drove a short distance before parking the car. He stripped off his jacket and jeans and left them inside the car, looking for all intents and purposes like a jogger out for an early evening run.

At the time of his arrest, number twenty-eight on the list did not exist. She'd be home at 8 p.m. and he'd be waiting. Tonight, he wouldn't just watch her through the windows; he would be inside her.

With fifteen minutes to go, he took up his position. From his vantage point, he'd see her get out of the car and walk to the front door. Once her key was in the lock, he'd pounce. Bletchley checked his watch, 7:47. He felt excitement building. *Just a few more minutes.*

A familiar voice suddenly spoke from behind. *Kennedy!*

'You should have left it while you had the chance, you piece of shit.' Bletchley froze, just long enough for a surge of adrenalin to kick through his body. His attempt at breaking into a sprint took too long. He did not move quickly enough to avoid the first blow and, after that, he was a sitting duck.

At just after 8 p.m., number twenty-eight found Bletchley's battered body on her doorstep. Her screams quickly attracted the attention of her neighbours.

Chapter 107

'It looks like we have another vigilante murder, this time on our doorstep.'

Kennedy regarded Tanner with disdain. 'If that was an attempt at humour, it wasn't funny.'

It took a moment for the penny to drop. 'No, sir, of course it wasn't.' He shifted uncomfortably in his seat. 'Preliminary reports show he was beaten to death, just like the victims up North. He had bits of glove leather and a baseball rammed down his throat along with half his teeth while he was still alive by all accounts. The MO seems to indicate it could be the same guy.'

Kennedy mumbled something Tanner couldn't quite catch.

'Sorry, sir, you said something?'

'Don't tell me, Tanner. It was my missing baseball.' *What the fuck is happening to me?*

Clearing his throat, Tanner said, 'Sir, I know it wasn't you, but it would be easier if you *did* have an alibi.'

Kennedy bristled. 'Of course I haven't, and I don't have one for the first incident either!' His bluff face reddened. 'I live on my own and I don't go out much with anybody else. I don't have an alibi for about two hundred nights of the year!' He grabbed his jacket, putting it on as he started walking out of his office. 'Besides, I'd hardly use a bat with my own initials on it and then continue to attract suspicion by giving the murder a baseball theme, would I?'

Kennedy left without hearing the reply. He didn't care anymore.

'No, sir,' Tanner said to the empty room, but he wasn't convinced. The DCI could be using the same type of reverse psychology the cleverer criminals used and he'd been acting strange lately. He wasn't convinced over Theresa either, or the calls she said she'd taken that sounded like him. He'd always suspected the DCI had a secret thing for her. After that motorbike incident, he'd already realised he could have used his own number plates on another bike, but the over-riding question had to be why?

The answer was in his head the following morning. Kennedy had used the alleged caller to manipulate Theresa into doing those things to lay a false trail. So, if he was caught, it would *look* like a set-up. The final piece of the puzzle fitted when he'd asked her for the Stella Bird file in the guise of the caller. Theresa had told him. *'The look on his face when he hid that file, John, the way he looked at me for a reaction, knowing how desperately I needed it. I almost gave the game away, but that was when I knew he had to be the caller.'*

'Did he say anything after that?'

'No, but when he rang – knowing I couldn't get the file because he already had it – he used it to try to blackmail me into sleeping with him.'

Tanner knew he had no choice but to take it higher, yet some little thing niggled at him. *Unless he wore a mask, Theresa would have known it was him and would Kennedy really do all this, just to screw Theresa?*

He decided not to do anything about it until the morning, when he'd had the chance to speak to Kennedy further.

Chapter 108

9:05 p.m. 3 April – Passover.

Miller arrived late for his Passover dinner speech. A traffic snarl coming out of London had held him up, but he arrived with a few moments to spare. En route, he'd kept in constant touch with the school captain, a gangly spotty-faced youth with bright, intelligent eyes who'd met him at the school entrance, and then escorted him into the hallway down the central aisle through the dining tables.

'You'll be sitting there,' the captain informed him, pointing at the vacant place setting as they passed his allocated table. Miller noticed the roll and butter was still intact and wondered if it would last for the duration of his talk. Old friends ribbed him as he made his way through, and he responded by cocking a finger gun and pointing it at them as he walked by.

Nervous, because he hadn't delivered a lecture since his ill-fated series on the supernatural the year before, he'd have loved to have had a few minutes to run through his notes, but there was no time. As he followed him up the five steps onto the stage, the hollow thud of their footsteps echoed into the void beneath. Every year at the annual event triggered a different set of memories.

Aware of the captain introducing him at the lectern, he slipped into autopilot. It was a strange feeling. He felt as if he were looking down on himself from the rafters.

The short applause dissipated. Miller cleared his throat. The microphone picked up the sound, relaying it around the hall. Ripples of laughter reached his ears. The fear he may be about to blush, erythrophobia, bubbled beneath the surface, a fear of manifesting the problem that afflicted his mother all her life. *Don't think about it.* A flush of heat formed a film of perspiration on his forehead. The thought of breaking into a sweat made him more nervous, part of him screamed: *Say something!*

Banishing all conscious thought, he allowed instinct to take over.

Miller leaned on his right elbow and smiled, making it appear the long pause was intentional. His gaze swept the hall and, as he began to speak, a serious expression replaced the smile.

'When I was young and growing up, it seemed the world wasn't such a dangerous place. I'm sure, gentlemen, you read the same news in the papers as I do, hear the same news as I do, and if you are anything like me, you probably wonder what kind of a world we are living in today. What are we coming to?'

A murmur of agreement rolled around the hall. Miller sipped from a glass of water and scanned the crowd.

'If you are the same as me, you probably worry about the state of the world our children are set to inhabit as this twenty first century unfolds.' Both hands gripped the sides of the lectern firmly as he looked around the hall, engaging with his audience.

'If what I'm about to say disturbs you, I apologise in advance. In today's society, we cosset and care for our children on the one hand and then think nothing of allowing them out into the wide-open spaces of the internet from the privacy of their bedrooms, with little control, or supervision. Our children are ill equipped – because they're not ready for it – to deal with the predators that stalk the pages of cyberspace, dressed up like the wolf in Little Red Riding Hood, hiding behind fake photographs and false identities. If we allow the media and other entities to continue to encourage our children to grow up too soon, we'll be taking part in an experiment the likes of which...' He looked down at the ledge behind the lectern, picked up the water jug and topped his glass up, before continuing, 'the likes of which I don't think we've ever seen before.

'I didn't come here tonight to talk about society's ills or what we need to do to make them right. That's a job for someone else better qualified than I am, but I mention these things because I believe they are all related, part and parcel of the same thing. There's a limit to what schools can do in support of parents if they themselves do not observe simple disciplines at home.' He took a sip of water.

'When I left school, I was unsure of what I was going to do. I wanted to do something worthwhile, and I needed to find out for myself what that was. My education at this school, laid the educational foundations, but it wasn't until years after I'd left, that I actually found what it was I was looking for. A chance encounter with a teacher from this school pointed the way for me. I won't bore you with the details, but in a nutshell, as a direct result of that meeting, I chose to become a private investigator and I specialise in tracing missing people.'

He reeled off statistics. 'Every year, around two hundred and fifty thousand people go missing in this country. Happily, most of them turn up again, safe and well, but some people disappear forever. It's a dark, disturbing subject, but fascinating at the same time.'

He turned away from the microphone and coughed once into his cupped hand. 'Excuse me. We all know Fred West and his wife were responsible for the disappearance of – what was it – at least seventeen young people. And because we only find out about the likes of the West's *after* they get caught, we're not in a position to accurately guess how many missing people have fallen victim to opportunistic murderers like them. Serial killers. It's my belief – and I'm not looking to scare anyone – that there are a number of killers out there, so good at what they do they never come onto the radar. They might not *ever* get caught. Obviously, there are links to unexplained, mysterious disappearances of adults and children. In most cases, there are no clues. These people simply – just – vanish. Sometimes, remains are discovered years later.' Miller sipped at his water before continuing. 'New technology, criminal psychology, neuroscience and DNA profiling advancements are evolving all the time, increasing the chances of the eventual arrest and conviction of these killers, but that isn't my job. My job is to find missing people alive, before they disappear forever.' He stepped away from the lectern and bowed to the audience.

A round of applause rippled through the hall accompanied by the hum of male voices raised in conversation, exchanging opinions.

Acknowledging the applause, he raised a hand to doff an imaginary hat and called out, 'Thank you!'

He made his way to the table, stomach churning with after-speech nerves. It seemed ridiculous a veteran of so many talks could still react as if it were his first speech all over again. Before sitting, he ambled round the table shaking hands with old friends, and introducing himself to those he'd not met before.

A waitress approached with a plate of food the kitchen had saved for him. He held his belly in both hands and grimaced at her. 'Thank you all the same, but I think I'll pass. This will do.' Someone had eaten his roll and butter, so he drew a plateful of unleavened bread towards him.

'I'll get you some butter for that,' she said. Her expression echoed the grimace he'd pulled earlier. 'It might make it a bit more appetising for you,' she grinned. 'Oh, and we saved you a portion of fruit salad.'

Miller shook his head, smiled and politely declined. He ate two slices of the dry bread without realising it was there, not just in case a Jewish diner turned up, but as a gesture to mark the first evening of the Passover. Ironically, it had been passed over by the rest of the men at the table in favour of traditional yeast bread rolls. It was all his knotted stomach would allow in any event, perhaps just as well because a steady stream of interested parties approached him at the table, hoping to engage him in conversation; asking questions relating to his talk. He acquired a fistful of business cards, which he stowed in his pocket. The head teacher collared him for almost an hour before he managed to extricate himself from the conversation on the pretext of having to visit the toilet. When he returned, a number of the men at his table had disappeared. They'd either gone home, or drifted onto other tables. He engaged in sporadic conversation with those who remained, and they gradually whittled down in numbers, until only he and one other were left.

'Just waiting for the wife to pick me up,' the other man volunteered.

'Was this the first time you've been back for the reunion?'

'No, I was here once before, years ago. To be honest, I don't enjoy things like this, but an old friend was supposed to show, and he didn't—' he stopped abruptly to answer his mobile.

'Okay, love I'll see you outside.' He stood up. 'I really had best make a move, it's been nice talking to you. Loved your speech by the way.'

Miller stood, and they shook hands. He sat down and gazed around the emptying hall. An hour ago the drone of voices meant they had to raise their own to avoid being drowned out, but now they had to speak quietly or risk being overheard. He smiled at that. No one was having secret conversations here tonight. From what he could make out, they wanted everyone else to know who they were, what they were up to and how well they were doing for themselves. *I might give next year a miss.*

He decided on a top up of red wine. Miraculously, there was still a drop left in one of the bottles, he'd only had half a glass all evening, plus what was left of a small beer, which now looked decidedly flat.

He was aware of a shadow moving into the periphery of his vision. Instinctively, he turned to look.

A stranger stood there smiling at him. 'I tried to get here earlier. You don't remember me, do you?'

Miller scanned his face, trying to imagine what he might have looked like when he was younger. The residual colour of his hair was mid-brown, even reddish, but now mostly grey. His eyes were dark brown, sharp and intelligent looking. He was thinking how much he resembled Brookes as he imagined he might have looked were he alive today, except Brookes had much paler skin and his hair was bright copper coloured, but the bluff face, square jaw and grin were uncannily similar.

'No, I don't, I'm sorry if I should. What's the name?'

'It's John Kennedy. I was a year younger than you.'

Miller scratched his head. A slight crease pinched his forehead between the eyebrows. 'No, I still haven't got you. Did you have a brother in my year or something like that?'

Kennedy offered his hand to shake, and Miller took it. He winced at Miller's grip. 'What have you done to your hand?' Miller asked.

'Oh, it's nothing. I slipped tightening a bolt on my motorbike, scraped it on the garage floor. It's fine, just squeezed it wrong that's all.' Kennedy poured a drop of wine into someone's discarded glass and moved his chair closer to Miller. 'Do you remember that time it rained three days solid? It was so bad they let us into the school hall during lunch break.' Kennedy saw the dawning of recollection in Miller's eyes. 'By the third day of lunch time confinement we were bored out of our minds with listening to Lionel's piano rehearsals. You older guys used to agitate him – get in his light or whatever. I can't recall exactly now, but it didn't matter whether you did or didn't with Lionel. If he dropped a note, and you were anywhere nearby, you got the blame and he'd get incandescent with rage, banging around and scowling. The duty master always sent you to the other side of the hall – well away from him. Do you remember?'

Miller was shaking his head at the returning memory. It lit his face with amusement.

'Then you casually walked up to the base of the steps, we all thought you were going to get on the stage.'

Miller joined in the recollection. 'Let me tell you something. That's exactly what I was planning to do, but then I noticed the access door on the other side of the steps. Unless you walked right up to them, you never would have known it was there. Out of curiosity I tried the handle, and it opened!'

'And because I was the youngest,' Kennedy recalled, 'you had me looking out for the rest of you while you all went in.'

'When we eventually did go in,' Miller twirled the pale remnants of liquid left at the bottom of his glass, examining the patterns it made on the side of it as he reflected on the past. 'It was far larger under there than it looked and so much *warmer* than you'd expect. In the gloom, down a few steps to another level, there was a light and another door. We heard voices coming from behind it and crept further in. I noticed you had followed us. I was suddenly afraid whoever had left the door unlocked – would return to lock it – and we'd be trapped!'

'Yep, you weren't too happy with me!' The two of them slowly shook their heads in disbelief at the follies of youth, both of them quietly remembering.

Kennedy drained his glass. Miller put his down. They were the last of the guests remaining. One or two waitresses were busying themselves clearing the last few tables.

After years of not seeing his long forgotten school friend, he wanted to make the most of it. Shrugging off his earlier tiredness, Miller found a second wind and began speaking more enthusiastically. 'It was so full of old school drama stuff, props and things, theatre swords and shields.'

Kennedy grinned.

'It was an Aladdin's cave to us back then,' Miller said. The years rolled back. He was a child again, yet thinking as an adult about how strange it was you could live in the same town – the same few square miles as some of your old school friends, yet never see them again. Miller had hit his stride. 'And when we crept closer to that door, we could see through the crack, where it had warped in the heat. Down below, I couldn't believe there was this place we never knew about before, but we could see the caretaker and that assistant of his skiving off down there, with their dirty magazines and ashtrays full of cigarettes. You could smell the smoke coming through the gap.'

'You tried to inhale it, as I recall,' Kennedy said.

Miller frowned. 'I don't remember *that*! But I do remember you couldn't hear what they were saying, because the noise of the boiler drowned it out. We'd always imagine they were plotting things, up to no good.'

Then he had a further recollection, one he was not absolutely sure about. 'You went down that ladder once, didn't you?'

'Yeah, I remember that. It was for a dare, and I didn't hear them coming back.'

'That was terrifying, you had about five seconds to hide or they'd have caught you. I still don't know how you so quickly managed to find such a good place to hide under all those smelly boiler suits.' They both laughed. 'So *that* was how you managed to get in with us.'

Kennedy poured from the last of the bottle, sipped it, pulled a sour face and looked squarely at Miller. 'Do you ever think about that accident?'

'Almost every day,' he said lacing his fingers together, looking down at them. 'It's not so bad at night now. I used to wake up in the early hours with it playing through my head, not always the actual incident, but some spin off related to it. It would always end the same though, with me drowning. That's when I'd wake up.'

'Even now?'

'Yes, even now.'

'Do you have a wife and family, John?'

'No, my career came first. I look around at the people I knew, nearly all of them married and then divorced. They have their kids, though, I suppose, but marriage? No, it wasn't for me. I'd have liked to have had a kid, though. I regret that I didn't. What about you?'

'I never married either. I had a girl once, early on.' He chewed on his lower lip. 'But I lost her.'

'Lost her?'

'She was on a ferry; she fell overboard. They never found her.'

'Jesus, Miller, how old we're you then?'

'Nineteen, maybe twenty.'

'Didn't meet anyone else?'

'You know something, after my friends died and I eventually met her; I thought my life was turning round, going to be really good. Then, when that happened to her – the pain of that was a different pain, but I made my mind up. I wasn't going to go through it ever again. So these days, friends, relationships – they don't get so close.' *Ain't no sunshine when she's gone, only darkness every day.* Their favourite song crept into the back of his mind. It always did when he felt wistful and was thinking about her. 'What about you, have you got anyone special?'

'Well, I *had* someone.' He looked around the hall, pausing at the honours board, the crest with the school motto emblazoned beneath in Latin, *Strength through Courage.*

One by one, the tables were denuded of their red cloths. Stripped bare like that they made him think of life and what's left when you lose everything that matters – something once so full, suddenly bare and empty.

Kennedy brightened suddenly. 'Do you ever see any of the others?'

'You missed three of them by minutes.'

'Real shame, I'm glad I bumped into you, though.'

As reticent as ever, Miller just said, 'Yeah.'

They continued to reminisce about old friends, teachers they'd both had. They moved onto their respective careers, realising how similar their chosen professions were. A short period of silence hung between them.

'Oh God, I've just remembered something else!' Kennedy suddenly exclaimed.

Miller's eyes lit up with expectancy.

'That day down in the basement beyond the changing rooms, there was that little office—'

'Are you talking about Kirk and that French mistress?'

'Well, yes, but do you remember that out of the four little unused offices, only the farthest away had a well-polished handle? It didn't make sense; you'd have thought the nearest office would have been the busier, more used. Anyway, we soon found out why. Getting a drink of water from the taps down there, always tasted so much better, like so many other things that are forbidden.'

'We both froze at the first cry we heard. She'd tried to stifle it; you could tell, but it came right out like she was in pain.'

'We looked at each other, scared stiff someone was murdering a woman down there and, after that, it was a soft moaning and we still didn't know, did we?' Both grinned widely as they recalled how they'd sneaked along the corridor close to the wall.

The metal studs on Miller's leather-soled shoes had clicked against the tile floor, so he'd slipped them off. The polished brass knob of the door had been difficult to grip with sweaty hands and operate quietly, but somehow they had managed to get the door open. And there they were, one head above the other, crouched holding the handle, not quite believing what they saw. Kirk had the French mistress on the edge of the desk. Her legs clamped around his back and her ankles crossed above his bare white arse. He was thrusting furiously, and she turned her head from side to side, moaning. Something made her eyelids flutter open. She'd stared straight at them, invitation in her eyes and a knowing smile on her lips. Sensing Kirk might see her staring and turn around; they'd both beaten a hasty retreat.

'After she caught me – *us*, looking…you know every time I saw her after that, I got a hard on, and you know something – she knew it!'

'Now you're stretching things, John.'

'I'm telling you it's true. She asked me if my mother ever told me about never putting your handkerchief in your trouser pocket, then she poked it with her finger and said, "It *is* your handkerchief, non?" The look in her eyes, Miller, she *knew*. It was the first time a woman ever touched me there and to this day I've never forgotten it.'

'I don't remember hearing about that before.'

'Well, you lot were that bit older than me. I don't think I could have put up with the ribbing, so of course I never told you. Oh, what I'd give to be a kid again, eh?' Kennedy seemed troubled. Miller assumed the drink had caught him up in melancholia.

Miller pushed his chair back and stood. 'You coming?' he said. Kennedy lingered.

'No, I think I'll just sit and savour the atmosphere a bit; I haven't been here for so long, it's like going back to church.'

Chapter 109

It was almost midnight. With Miller gone, only Kennedy and three cleaning staff were left in the hall. He reflected back over the evening; he couldn't remember the last time he'd had such an enjoyable time in the company of another man. He wished he'd met him again years ago. *Different roads.* In Miller's company, his predicament had faded for a while. Several times, he'd almost confided in him, but the right moment never quite presented itself. Now sitting alone, his reverie complete, his thoughts returned to his tormentor.

A day earlier, he'd received a telephone call, and before he'd even lifted the receiver to his ear, the caller had started speaking.

'What will you do, *John,* when they find you have been visiting prostitutes?' The voice accentuated his forename to ridiculous effect. 'She kept a diary, you know.'

Kennedy's heart sank, but he responded automatically. 'Now you listen to me!'

The voice talked right over him, mocking him with a lisp. *He's changed his voice yet again.* It sounded tinny. He got straight to the point, and Kennedy listened in stunned silence as the words unfolded.

'What will you do when they find the deleted number of a major criminal on your mobile phone? When the records indicate you called him from right there in your office. That's right. That *is* what I said, from your office and not just the once, either.'

The sound of air sucked through clenched teeth came down the line. 'One whiff, a sniff you are talking to anyone else about these calls, *John* and I will drop you so far in it you'll never see the light of day again. Your father will never be able to forgive you. You know that, don't you, *Johnny*?' Another deeply drawn breath, followed by another well-timed pause.

Kennedy frowned. 'Hey, you, kiss my arse!' There was no response. The caller carried on speaking, regardless.

It's a recording!

'There's also the question of the cash payments into your saving's account, that's right; you never check them do you? You go for those online statements, but you never read them anyway. How are you going to explain the five thousand pounds cash deposit that coincided with Wharton walking free, or the ten thousand put in this morning, *after* he was killed? The cash came from Lynch, by the way. He stashed it in Marilyn's safe, but you know, John, best of all *Johnny* – and you'll like this one… The DNA samples from the Gasman's last two victims … can you guess what they'll find, *Johnny*?' he said, pausing for effect.

Kennedy listened in dismay.

'Of course you can't! The DNA is yours *John*. Do you really think they will listen to your protestations of innocence? What a coincidence it is, that every one of your visits to a murdered prostitute coincided with a Gasman attack?' Another breath. Another silence. The recording continued.

'You have no alibi's now do you, *Johnny?* Do you remember when you said – and you don't even know me, do you, John – *These people are vile*. Do you remember that on television? Well, now you're one of us, *John*. Checkmate.' A millisecond hiss indicated the end of the message. The phone disconnected abruptly. Some of the unanswered questions were resolved. He'd wanted to tell him, '*It wasn't me. I didn't say it. It was Kendricks, and the editors screwed it up*', but he couldn't, of course, because no one was listening at the other end of the line.

The caller disconnected the mobile phone from the laptop. If the police got a fix on the call and triangulated the signal, they'd discover it originated from an area close to the A1 on a pay-as-you-go telephone routed through an auto dialer on a computer. The police wouldn't get that far, but he disposed of the phone anyway. He removed the battery and dropped both parts through the grill of a roadside drain and then sped away.

Although Kennedy had been a detective for long enough to know if a suspect was telling the truth or bluffing, he called his bank anyway. They confirmed two deposits into his account, one of five thousand, and another of ten thousand pounds. His heart sank. The caller had framed him with something from which he couldn't easily extricate himself, if he could at all. It would be only a matter of time before the DNA flagged up a match against the Police Forces DNA database. *How long have you got – possibly a few days? If you are lucky, it might only be a day or two.* It was a problem that over shadowed the rest of the day and weighed heavy on his mind all night. He knew he was screwed. He slept very little.

'Was that really only yesterday?' Kennedy stunned himself with the realisation he'd spoken out loud. Glancing around, he was relieved none of the staff appeared to have heard, they were too busy clearing tablecloths and wiping down the bare tops. They were working their way back down the hall towards him. He had a few minutes before they reached him. The high ceilings, the sedate atmosphere and echoes of a million prayers, did indeed remind him of a church. The walls released memories for him, and he drifted away from his troubles into a higher plane of consciousness.

He knew now with certainty, what he had to do.

Chapter 110

Miller was dreaming. The ghosts of his past slowly paraded before him. They were mostly grey images of the people he missed the most. In the crowd as they passed, he sometimes thought he caught a glimpse of himself. How he was back then. Lost, struggling to find a way back.

In an alternative version of last night's reunion, he saw himself back at the table with Kennedy. This time they spoke of their origins and swapped case notes, laughing at the FBI games his forgotten acquaintance told him he used to play.

'Did anyone ever call you Jack, as in the president?'

The detective reacted slowly and thoughtfully. 'Just a girlfriend I had once and this other *character*. I just started picking up on his trail and then he started playing games with me.' Miller detected sorrow in the other man's eyes. The light faded from them as he continued to speak.

'He called himself Lee Harvey Oswald, pathetic really.' He shook his head sadly. 'I let him get to me. He left a newspaper with the headline "*Kennedy Assassinated*" at the scene of one crime. Not one shred of forensic. Nothing on the paper. No sweat, no nothing. I suppose I had an inkling I was dealing with someone different, not your run-of-the-mill ordinary criminal. I knew he was out to get me. His messages made that perfectly clear from the outset.' He began fiddling with his tie, pulling at the knot, loosening it from his neck.

'Did you ever get him?'

Still fiddling with his tie, he said, 'No, I never did.' And then he asked about Miller's lost friends, the boys who died.

Caught off guard, he bristled at the mention, driven back into his adolescent self where he wrestled with his thoughts. He'd forgotten none of it. It became merely encapsulated in the comfortable blanket time had woven for it. 'Why do you mention that?' he asked.

No longer looking at him, he focused on something beyond where he sat. 'You need to talk about it.'

There was something odd about Kennedy. He couldn't quite put his finger on it. In his head, he fine-tuned his imaginary receiver, but he'd lost him. The dream was no longer in his control. It shifted to a beach ... to a holiday he had long ago.

Then he was back in the hall, where Kennedy waited patiently for his answer. He tilted his head his expression one of query. A half shrug of the other man's shoulders invited an answer. It had been a long moment.

'I'm sorry,' he said, 'I'm just not ready to talk about it.'

Kennedy leant forward, two fingers in the knot of his tie. When he spoke it was with difficulty. 'That happened thirty-five years ago. You should lay those ghosts to rest.'

'I know,' he said simply.

The detective's eyes had become grey. One was narrowed, the other shut. He could have been looking through a telescope. 'I need help, Miller.'

It was late and he was tired. *This is crazy. It's a dream!* He rubbed his eyes. They felt sore. He sparked off an ocular migraine. If he caught it in time and avoided bright lights, he could still prevent the visual aura from manifesting itself.

Kennedy had his back to the light. Miller couldn't look at him.

He felt himself leaving rapidly, floating upwards and backwards. Kennedy's voice briefed him in a blizzard of words he couldn't understand.

Miller woke up and the first thing on his mind was Kennedy's last words. *'So, will you help me?'*

He lay awake for a long time. These shifts in perspective were occurring with greater frequency and now not only when he was asleep. He found if he concentrated hard enough, he could make out in part, what Kennedy had told him. Big trouble, a key and finding a missing girl. No, not a key. She *was* the key. *The key to what?*

He took his pencil and pad from his bedside table and noted it all down. It might make sense later.

Sinking back into sleep just as the birds began to stir, he dreamed about the boys again.

Chapter 111

The following morning Miller woke up, his head filled with strong ideas.

I need help, Miller. Eilise Staples.

He hadn't felt the same way since he'd decided to find Olga Kale, but it didn't worry him. What he was doing was for the good.

Although Nottingham wasn't as far as he thought from London, it was still too far for him to consider driving back the same day. After three and a half hours of boredom, the Sat Nav dumped him a few doors down the road from where he needed to be. He wouldn't have parked right outside anyway.

He grabbed his bag out of the boot and made his way up the path. Eilise's house was in an affluent part of town. Not quite how he'd imagined it, but runaways came from all walks of life. Olga Kale – she'd been a runaway, too. The step up to the front door was freshly scrubbed and still wet, so he stretched up and rang the bell, without standing on it. The door opened almost immediately.

'Mrs Staples?'

'Yes.'

'The name's Miller, I believe you were expecting me?'

'I'm sorry?' Dressed in a floral housecoat, wearing pink marigold gloves and holding a yellow feather duster in her hand, she looked ridiculous, but not self-conscious at all.

'DCI Kennedy arranged for me to come up this morning.'

'Well, he never said anything to me,' she narrowed her eyes. 'Got any ID?'

Miller produced a business card and handed it to her.

'What – the police can't do their own work? They have to call in the private sector to get anywhere?'

'Something like that.' He smiled.

She let him in. 'Come right through.' She steered him into the lounge. 'Would you like some tea, Mr Miller?'

'It's just, Miller and yes, tea would be nice.'

She checked his card. *Miller: Missing Persons Investigator.* 'What an unusual first name. Please call me, Eileen.'

She looked too young to have a daughter of Eilise's age.

'Sit down,' she said.

'Do you mind if I?' He pointed at the collage of photographs that hung on the wall.

'No, no, not at all, feel free.' She left him alone while she fetched the tea.

The mirror above the fireplace opposite reflected the collage. *Two images for the price of one.* A family portrait took pride of place in the collection of photos. He recognised Eilise straight away; she was the older of the two girls. The photo looked recent. The girls stood in front. Mr Staples had a hand on the shoulder of each girl. A six-inch gap was apparent between him and Eileen. Only two family members had happy smiles on their faces, the father and the youngest girl. Miller leaned in for a closer look.

Eileen arrived with the tea. Seeing him looking at the picture, she volunteered, 'That was taken the summer before last.'

'It's a nice photo,' he said.

He sipped his tea, thinking. Eileen Staples and the older girl shared an uncomfortable body language. Their smiles didn't extend beyond the lips, and the eyes of both looked haunted. Mrs Staples' hand was on Eilise's other shoulder. *Family tensions.*

'The photograph was taken just before she ran away the first time,' she explained. 'My husband managed to find her quite quickly, and then for a while we all settled back to normal.'

'Do you know *why* she ran away?' Miller asked.

'Well, you see,' Eileen bit her lower lip thoughtfully, 'Eilise found out she was adopted.'

'So that was why she ran away?'

'It's more complicated than that.'

'I thought it might be.'

'How come?'

'That photograph of you all reveals a lot of secrets.'

She became defensive. 'Oh, *really* is that a fact?' She was an attractive woman, but played it down. In the photograph, she wore no makeup at all.

'Eileen, I'm here to help, but to do that I need your cooperation.'

'Mr Miller, I telephoned DCI Kennedy while I was making tea. He wasn't there, but Inspector Tanner tells me you've quite a reputation in the private sector for finding missing people.'

'That's right, but what he couldn't tell you – because I like to keep this side of things confidential – is that I wouldn't be here if your daughter were dead. You will ask me how I know, and I'll tell you I'm not sure, but the fact is I don't look for dead people.'

She regarded him with suspicion, 'Do you really think you can find her, Miller?'

'I believe so, but first I'll need some help from you, Eileen. You were telling me she ran away the first time because she found out she was adopted, and there was something else?'

'No, she found out she was adopted, and that's all.'

A period of silence ensued. She sat shoulders slumped, her eyes darting nervously about the room. Unable to look at him directly for more than a second, she fidgeted with her fingers, revealing a white ring of untanned skin where her wedding ring had once been.

'Do you want to talk about it?' Miller asked gently.

She'd only been waiting for the right person to come along, waiting for the right moment. The words spilled out of her in a torrent. It was an unburdening. Miller gently placed a hand on her forearm. 'Whoa, slow down. Take your time.'

She paused and took a deep breath. 'I started to notice things going missing. The things you don't notice straight away, things that are out of everyday sight.'

He nodded. It was a familiar story. Taking a pen and pad from his pocket, he made notes.

'She withdrew from us, gradually at first, spending more time alone in her room. She began skipping school. Then she started wanting to go out at odd hours. She always used to go out, but not at such completely random times. People were calling for her who I'd never seen before. In the end, I found out she'd been using drugs. I caught her with the stuff in her bag.' She stopped suddenly as if she might have said too much, unsure if she should go on.

'Does your husband – it's Frank, isn't it? Does he know about any of this?'

She shook her head. He gave her hand a reassuring squeeze. 'Shall I tell you what I see in that photo? It might make it easier for you.'

Her head tipped forward looking at the floor. A single tear ran down her face and dripped from the end of her nose.

'Eileen, the body language in the photo isn't right. It shows sides, and it shows factions, tensions. In short, the family is divided.'

'You can tell all that from a photograph?' She looked bewildered. 'I never knew people could do that just from looking at a photo.'

'Eileen, there's more; you have a reassuring hand placed on Eilise's shoulder and both of you share the same haunted expression. Your husband and youngest daughter look happy. Neither of them knows what secret you and Eilise share.'

Eileen averted her face from Miller's gaze.

'Eilise confided in you, didn't she?'

She made eye contact for the first time since he'd walked into her house.

'As I said, Eilise ran away because she found out she was adopted. She never got very far; it was a cry for help. Frank found her wandering the streets around midnight and brought her home. For a couple of months, everything seemed fine. We explained we'd be happy to help track her mother down if that was what she really wanted, but that she'd probably have to wait until she was eighteen before that could happen. I thought it was the upset of finding out, because you know, that unsettled her. Then I found out about the drugs, and she broke down and told me. Excuse me.' She fled into the kitchen and returned a few moments later dabbing at her eyes with a piece of paper towel.

'She told me Frank was trying it on with her, and getting quite heavy about it, too. In his head because she wasn't blood, I suppose he thought she was fair game. That's no excuse, of course. He told her if she didn't, then he'd do it to our younger daughter. I was planning to help her get her out.' She dabbed her eyes again. 'I'm a mess. Please excuse me.' She rushed out of the room again.

'Who are you?' Frank's sudden appearance startled him.

Miller stood and introduced himself. 'I'm here to help find your daughter. Your wife got a bit upset—'

Frank shook his hand warily. 'I'm Frank,' he said, eyeing the teacups. 'You've been here a while then. Did I miss anything?'

Eileen returned. Frank looked at her suspiciously.

'No,' Miller said. 'I was just running over a few facts to get some background about her runaway tendencies. Now, I understand you adopted her from the earliest age possible. Did she go through school okay, no problems?'

Frank rolled his eyes in exasperation. 'We've been all through this...'

'Not with me though, Frank.'

'Were you expecting him?' he asked Eileen.

'Yes,' she said. 'I got a call to say he was on his way.'

Frank glared at her. 'You never said—'

'Can I see her room?' Miller asked.

Frank turned his attention to him. 'Correct me if I'm wrong, but your job is to find her, am I right? Not to judge or interfere in a family matter.'

'That's correct. Whatever problems or issues arise, they'll be resolved with the close involvement of the authorities. Just to make my position clear – although I'm a private investigator – a senior police officer asked me to assist him and ultimately I'm accountable to him. However, you have my assurance I'll be working on your behalf just as diligently as if you had employed me directly. I *will* find her.'

Frank moved as close to Eileen as he could, wrapping an arm around her stiff shoulders without looking at her. 'That's reassuring to hear, isn't it, love?'

Miller shuffled his feet awkwardly. 'Now, can I see her room?'

At the top of the stairs, off the landing, was a bathroom and toilet. Further down the corridor were four bedrooms. Two each side of the corridor. All the doors were closed. Eileen kept a nice clean house, upstairs it smelled of bleach and polish.

Frank led the way and opened the last door on the left. He stood with one hand wrapped round the door handle and indicated for Miller to go in with a nod of his head.

The brightly painted room was garish. Gothic art posters adorned the walls. For a girl's room, it was a messy one. Eileen explained they'd left it exactly as it was the last time she'd been there. In one corner was a television, a dressing table in the other. There was also a sound system complete with headphones still plugged in.

'Does she have a computer or laptop?' Miller asked.

'She used her phone for everything. Emails and texts. Didn't she, love?' Frank said.

'Actually, she did use the computer next door in the study,' Eileen added.

Frank shot an accusatory look at her. 'You told the police she never used it!'

'Well, she did, but only sometimes.'

'Can I have a look?' Miller backed out of her bedroom and moved into the study next door. If there was going to be anything, it would be on the computer. He'd check with Kennedy to see if they'd taken anything significant away from her room.

'Excuse the mess,' Eileen said. 'The computer's already on. We daren't turn it off. There's something wrong with the switch, so it's on all the time.'

'Who else uses the machine?'

'We all do, but mostly for work or school work.'

Eileen logged in, explaining they had never set up individual user accounts.

'May I?' Miller gestured at the seat in front of the computer and sat before either of them could answer.

He looked at the desktop shortcuts. There were none for Facebook, Myspace or Bebo. Checking the programmes list on the start menu, he saw an unfamiliar red icon. He double clicked it.

It loaded into a social networking site revolving around common interests in music.

Hello, concreteblonde92.

'I'm assuming "concrete blonde" isn't either of you?' Frank scowled at him. 'And from the 92, I guess that's Eilise's birth year?'

The avatar was The Grim Reaper. He looked at the menu buttons and then selected 'Mypage' from the top bar. He saw the last music tracks she'd listened to: All about Eve, Sisters of Mercy, Concrete Blonde and Draconian, among others. According to the site files, she'd last visited thirty-six days before. That meant wherever she was – she'd had access to a computer up until then. Further down the screen was a public messaging service, she had over seventy of them. The most frequent was Strawberry1971. Next to every message was a photo of Paddy Casey, the former Irish busker. Miller had one of his records. *What is a fan of Paddy Casey doing hooked up with a girl whose musical interests seemed to be Goth Rock?*

He looked for her private messages. There weren't any.

'One thing I can tell you is she was last on the site thirty-six days ago. That's after she ran away. I'm guessing she no longer has access to a computer.'

'Will you leave it on there? I'd like to have a look around at it all once you've gone.'

'Of course I will, Eileen.'

After Miller had left, Eileen sat down at the computer and joined Lastfm. She sent a friend request to *concreteblonde92* and left a 'shout' message for her. After that, she took to watching her 'Shoutbox' religiously, waiting for a reply or acceptance of her friend request.

Neither came.

Chapter 112

Miller didn't relish the thought of the long drive back to London straight away, so he stopped for a pint at the oldest pub in England, *Ye Olde Trippe to Jerusalem*. The last time he'd visited the place; he was a young salesman working his way up through the centre of England selling luxury Italian goods. In those days, the women of Nottingham outnumbered the men by three or four to one. The landlady of the guesthouse he'd stayed in near-by had played an active role in pairing him off with her eighteen-year-old daughter and she'd been a willing participant in the arrangement. Afterwards, he left the girl to use the toilet at the other end of the passageway. As he returned to his room, the landlady came out on the landing and dragged him into her bed too. The whole incident was bizarre from start to finish, but he thought of them quite often. Aside from the sex, there had been something endearing about both of them. The memory made him smile. *It all began in Ye Olde Trippe...*

He was half-tempted to check in at the guesthouse again, but he knew the chances were he'd never find it after so many years. Settling down at a table, he switched on his laptop and connected to the internet.

He googled: *'Strawberry1971'*. A fraction of a second later, *'1971' came* up as a hit, listed on several sites. Lastfm, Tripadvisor and eBay all had listings under the same user name. Further down the list were a number of items for sale. *This could be useful.* He logged in to the auction site and did an advanced search.

Got you!

Within minutes, he was looking at the items *1971* had for sale. On over three hundred transactions, his feedback was flawless. Miller was impressed. It reassured him and gave him the feeling he could almost trust him. He scrolled through his seller's history. *There she is...* She'd praised him highly with a five star rating. *Is this how they met? Did they know each other before?* It was possible. She'd purchased a CD by 'The Mission' from him.

His current listings were due to end the following day. One of the items was a hardback copy of the book 'Supernature' by Lyall Watson, which he'd spent years looking out for; and another a bass guitar for a 'Buy It Now' price of fifty pounds. The guitar was available for collection only. The address was in London.

He couldn't believe how easily all this fitted together. Miller completed the transaction for the guitar and then sent an email offering ten pounds cash for the book, if he could collect it at the same time. Later that night, he received a reply.

After a flurry of emails that led right up to midnight, they agreed a time for collection the next day.

It would be late afternoon.

Chapter 113

Miller arrived at one of the bleaker parts of South London soon after lunchtime, pulling up as close to his destination as he could. Getting out, he secured the car. A sign on a lamppost read: *Permit Holders Only*. The car behind his had a clamp on its wheel. He scanned the area for traffic wardens, and seeing none, decided to take a chance.

The flats were arranged in a rectangular horseshoe and had rendered panels on the outside, freshly painted in neutral pastel colours. From a distance, it looked like the sliced end of a Harlequin cake. The attempt to mask the drabness externally did nothing to fix the problems with the people who lived inside. As he strolled, he crossed into the paved area between the enclosing brick walls.

Two youths emerged from somewhere behind and made a beeline for him. They boxed him in with a crude pincer movement. He kept moving.

'What you got for me, man?' The taller one scooted ahead of him and turned walking backwards, nimble, fast and confident. He possessed the look of someone who was beyond caring, like the crack addict who used to hang around near Miller's office with his Staffordshire bull terrier. He disappeared sometime back, and they'd found him stabbed. A single wound to the heart. Rumour had it he owed his dealer eighty pounds. The message carried a clear warning to anyone else who might be thinking about holding out on him. If you do, you die.

The other man was just on the periphery of his vision, slightly behind. More solidly built than his accomplice, he closed in, thinking to take Miller down.

Miller had an advantage. They thought it would be easy. He stopped.

'What have I got for you?' Miller said. 'Nothing you can take.'

They exchanged looks. The taller one flicked his eyes intending to distract Miller into following his gaze.

Darkness gathered, forming shadows. He'd learned long since it signalled something was about to happen. He switched off, allowing pure instinct to take hold. Without warning, a punch slipped by Miller and crashed home. A blur of movement followed, a flurry of blows smacked home.

Miller looked with incredulity at the would-be assailants laid out on the floor. A man stood before him, grinning. Miller came back into focus.

'I don't believe this,' he said.

'Believe,' the other man said simply.

It was Thomas Carney.

Thomas shook his hand. 'I was only thinking about you this morning. How weird is that?'

'I wish I had a pound for every time something like that happened to me.'

Carney stopped to think. He'd obviously had a lot of fights since Miller had last seen him. His nose was as crooked as a stovepipe, and he seemed to have inherited the same flinty-eyed look his trainer had. He sounded a little punchy.

'You know, when you turned up at the gym that night, it worried me because I thought Mickey might decide to take you on, over me. Did you carry on as a fighter?'

'Thomas, I never wanted to be a fighter. Back then, I didn't know much about anything I wanted to do. How about you? For your age, you were really good.'

Thomas laughed. 'You cheeky fucker, you was only about a year older than me. Yeah, I won the ABA middleweight title, had a real career ahead of me, and I threw it away. I can't believe you didn't do anything in the fight game. I could hardly catch you with a shot.'

'That's because I was scared. I didn't want to get hit.'

Carney pressed his lips tightly together and growled, 'I've just remembered all that shit about you not boxing before.'

'It wasn't shit, I was telling the truth. I was just able to read ahead a second or two. My grandfather taught me that. You know – if you do this.' Miller bobbed left. 'It means that.' Miller bobbed right. 'Or this.' He feigned a left hook.

Carney laughed. 'That's too simple. It was more than that; I couldn't fool you with any shots.'

Without warning, Carney unleashed a punch. Miller caught Carney's fist in his hand, two inches from his face.

Carney shook his head. 'Explain to me *exactly* how you knew that was coming.'

'Mu shin. No mind. I can't explain it any other way.'

Thomas stared intently at him. 'In my book that's not an explanation at all.'

'Anyhow, enough about me, Thomas. What was that about you throwing your chances away?'

'I've only just come out of prison for what I did.'

'Oh shit, really?' Although curious, Miller said, 'Listen, Thomas, I have to go see someone, have you got a number? We'll meet and have a proper catch up.'

'Yep, yep, here's my number.' He scrawled it on a piece of paper and handed it over. They shook hands again.

'Be lucky,' Thomas said.

Miller nodded.

At the entrance, someone held the door open for him on their way out and Miller walked in, making his way up the concrete steps to the third floor.

Although he hadn't spoken to the man yet, he already had the strong impression he was Irish.

The south-facing walkway of the council low-rise block was three floors up, and the strength of the wind sweeping along it caught him by surprise. His eyes squinted against the wind-blown dust as he sauntered along checking the door numbers.

It's this one. The material acting as curtains was drab and brown. A scattering of dead flies littered the sill the other side of the glass. They didn't look as if they'd been drawn back for a long time. He looked for a bell or knocker. There was neither, so he hammered on the sun-faded blue door with the side of his fist.

The viewer in the door lit up from behind for a split second and then darkened again.

'Who's there?' The voice had an unmistakable Irish accent.

'Is this Strawberry? The name's Miller. I've come to collect a guitar and a book.'

'Wait a minute!' Something heavy rumbled, scraping over the floor on the other side. A tassel-haired man around forty years old suddenly appeared in the open doorway. Miller was surprised at his age; he'd guessed he would be younger. Apart from his dark complexion, he actually looked like his Paddy Casey avatar.

'Come in.'

Inside, the flat was grim, sparser than it had looked from the outside. Brown blankets secured at the top with multi-coloured map pins formed makeshift curtains. The main room resembled a jumble sale, the windows on the other side of it had no curtains and allowed light to pool over the piles of merchandise. At three floors up, privacy wasn't a problem. No one was going to be peering through those windows without a very long ladder. A heavy timber beam leaned against the wall. Once his visitor was inside, he braced it back into position, raking it off the wall opposite to the underside of the door lock.

Is it only the police he needs to keep out?

'Is there a problem with security around here?' Miller said.

'Well, y'know it, don't you,' he said with a shrug.

The guitar was one of two propped up against the wall, the other, a battered old Spanish guitar, stood alongside it. There were boxes and boxes of stuff stacked off the floor, labelled A – C, D – F and so on. It was an unholy mess.

Pushing his dark tassels away from his face, he leaned over and retrieved a book from a box labelled W – Z, and wiped the top clean with the elbow of his cardigan.

'The guitar's the blue one there, sixty pounds cash to you.'

Miller handed him an envelope.

He opened it to check the cash, unfurling a hand-written note wrapped around the money. It read, *'When did you last see Eilise?'*

'What the fuck!' he spat, his face glowered with unconcealed menace and his fists balled, held at his sides.

'Cool it, fella,' Miller held his hand out palm upwards in front of him, appealing for calm. 'I'm a private investigator and I specialise in finding missing people.'

His face flushed bright red with anger, 'Then find your way out of here, or you'll be the next one going missing!' He pulled a switchblade knife from his pocket, flicking the blade out.

'There's no need for that, really. I just need to know when you last saw her. Her parents are worried about her—'

'Parents? Is that what you call those people?'

'My job is just to find her. The authorities will deal with her family situation.'

'Did you know she ran away, because of what the old man was doing to her? Jesus, Joseph and Mary. The mother *knew* what was happening and did nothing.'

Miller inhaled deeply and then asked, 'Do you know where she is?'

'What, so you can send her back?'

'Look, I know *why* she didn't report him, and I know she won't go to the police herself now—'

'Well would you, if you were in her shoes?'

'Strawberry, it isn't about me. I need your help to find her. Will you do that?'

'Sweet Mary, I never thought I'd see the day. Helping the police,' he said, rolling his eyes heavenward, putting the knife down he crossed himself. 'I wasn't going to stick you with it, only scare you.'

'I know. Look, will you tell me your real name?' Miller yawned. The long drive earlier had taken its toll.

'It's Barry, like in Wales,' he said, pulling a sheepish face. 'Only more interesting.'

'You cut me off before I could tell you. Eilise has gone missing and someone is claiming to be holding her. My job is to find her before she comes to harm.'

Barry looked at him blankly. 'I'd no idea.'

Miller scratched his head. 'When did you last see her?'

'I used to busk up in Nottingham, Paddy Casey songs mostly, hence the look.' His hands were out at the side of his head, framing the hair. 'That's when I met her the first time. She stood watching me play all day long once and afterwards we went back to my digs. We talked, smoked a bit of stuff; she told me what was occurring. She desperately wanted to get away. I felt sorry for her, so I helped her. We came down south, lived on the Farm for a bit, 'bout three months.'

Miller shook his head slowly, bemused. 'Barry, I asked you when you last saw her, not how you met.'

'When I last *saw* her, I was just getting to that. After we left Dale Farm, she didn't want to come here with me, she wanted to find her real mother. I got her dropped off by a friend of mine. That was the last I saw of her.'

'Where did he drop her off?'

'You know, I'm not sure. I think it was Wickford or Benfleet station?'

'Okay, but you're sure he *did* drop her off?'

'No doubt about it. I'd trust him with my life.'

'Did she say what her mother's name was or where she lived?'

'She knew all of that, but she didn't tell me.' He took out a tobacco pouch and began to roll a cigarette. 'Okay, Miller, so who do you think has got her?'

'Someone far more dangerous than you can imagine. I know she's still alive, but she is in grave danger.'

Suddenly, Barry looked serious. The gravity of her situation had only just dawned on him.

Chapter 114

When the DCI didn't show up for work, it seemed to confirm Tanner's worst suspicions, yet still he was reluctant to take matters further until he'd at least had the chance to talk to him. After dialling his home and mobile telephone numbers and getting no answer, he left urgent messages to call him back. By the end of the afternoon, he decided to pay a surprise visit to Kennedy's house.

Unable to get a response at the front door, he ventured round the back. The garage door was unlocked. Inside, Tanner saw the motorbike in bits in the middle of the floor; just as the chief had said it was. Sitting on the workbench was a set of number plates. He picked one up and dislodged a small bolt. It fell and bounced off the end of his shoe. Bending to retrieve it, it wasn't anywhere in sight, he guessed it must have bounced behind a pile of rags. He moved them and discovered a box that contained twelve compartments. There were seven Kilner jars, with five empty spaces. Inside a bag on the floor was a contraption rigged up with tubes complete with a gas mask.

He had the unmistakable feeling someone was staring at him. For one crazy second, he thought someone stood behind him. He turned quickly. There was nobody there. His heart pounded hard in his chest and didn't slow quite some time. He knew he should report what he'd found. Moving the box of jars off the workbench, and without really knowing why, he replaced everything as he'd found it.

Tanner returned to the office. Something had gnawed away at him ever since he left Kennedy's garage. Suddenly, he had a hunch. He checked the CCTV records for the cameras outside the police station. He worked all the way back to the 3rd of January and then he spotted him. The same figure they'd seen on London Bridge, dressed identically, the body posture unmistakable. His face concealed by a hood.

He's been after Kennedy all along.

Chapter 115

5 April

The rapid decline in Ryan's health had nibbled away at his once unshakeable belief. He felt abandoned. Determined to hold on to the last vestiges of hope, he decided to finish a task he'd begun fifteen years ago.

The archiving of his patient files.

The older ones had survived the initial exercise because of their particular interest to him. His thoughts touched on Penny. Pleasant memories bloomed, and then withered quickly as he recalled how their working relationship had turned sour.

After starting a list of files for Stella to prepare for boxing, he decided it would be easier to send them all with the exception of three. One of those files he kept under lock and key. The other two were the files of Bruce Milowski and Jackie Solomons.

Solomons had been the last of his unconventional treatments and a witness to his secret visits to Vera Flynn in those days. Over the years, he'd noticed a correlation between childhood tragedy and the development of resilience in later life. Solomons had undoubtedly fallen into that category. Losing her father at the age of four, she'd been raped and almost murdered, yet she'd gone on to thrive. At one time, he'd considered writing a book on his theories, and although it was prominent on the list of things he had to do, he never got around to it. *It's too late now.*

His thoughts turned to Milowski. He'd been lined up to become the first candidate to receive Vera's remarkable attentions, when his mother suddenly refused any further treatment of her son.

Mrs Milowski...what was her first name again? Ellen, yes that was it. She possessed an innocence that had appealed to Ryan's fatherly nature. He'd wanted more than anything to help her son. The termination of his services had been abrupt. Stung by the recollection for a second time, Ryan moved the file squarely in front of him.

His memories were quite clear.

With Mrs Milowski's permission, he'd hypnotised him, taking him back through the years. He'd asked him to focus on the earliest thing he could remember, something in the past that had perhaps bothered him. Ryan was astounded to learn the boy had fallen into a coal fire at the age of ten months and survived unscathed apart from a few singed hairs. It all came back to him. How, aged four, he had escaped suffocation when a tunnel he'd dug into the sand dunes on a Cornish beach collapsed and buried him. *We found him because his grandfather noticed four of his fingers sticking up above the sand.* At the age of seven, Ryan had seen him as a physician. Only later did he realise the first visit had related to something Bruce never told him at the time. He revealed somebody had chased him in the woods and, from then onwards, he never slept without a light on. The experience had led to his first encounter with the 'shadows' as he called them, but no amount of coercion could get him to reveal more. The boy just locked up, even under hypnosis.

What happened to you, Bruce? Did you make it? Or did you die without me hearing about it?

Ryan drummed his fingers on Solomons' records, lost for a moment, indecisive. Then he put her file and Milowski's on the spare desk, well away from those destined for microfiche.

He pushed his chair back abruptly, straightened his back and then crossed the room. Running his fingers under the lip of the bottom-most shelf, he produced a key. Going from the archive room into his office, he unlocked the top drawer of his personal filing cabinet. The file was right at the back. A plastic tab identified it simply as 'Vera Flynn'.

Ryan removed the brown paper package from its sleeve and placed it on his desk. Inside it, along with her file, was an unopened envelope, containing the last prediction; he recalled how she'd told him not to open it until the time was right.

'But how will I know?' he asked.
'When the time is right, you will know.'
'And then what?'
'You will see.'

He unfolded the packaging and pulled her folder clear, releasing a musty odour. The paperwork had yellowed at the edges; the hand-written notes faded. From beneath them, he retrieved a discoloured buff envelope. The Sellotape securing the flap had dried out and become brittle with age. Holding a corner in each hand, he debated whether to open it.

It wasn't the time.

He drifted back through the years and examined her all over again, with the benefit of a more experienced mind.

Chapter 116

To have believed for thirty-two years that whatever it was she'd predicted would come true was a measure of Ryan's conviction, but it faded as fast as his health declined.

The test of faith she'd set him all those years before, the reason he'd carried on working after Gracie had died… He had to know what it was and whether it had been worth it. More than that, he needed to know she was right. Because if she were, he'd know without a doubt there really *were* more things in heaven than earth, that there truly *could* be a life after death and he'd be reunited with Gracie at last.

It had to be true.

The spectre of self-doubt rose in him. To have waited this long in vain, would mean the end of everything. He was almost ready to accept he might have been wrong, that perhaps The Sister wasn't quite all he thought she was, no more than a clever trickster after all.

Sensing how little time he had left, he made up his mind. As soon as Stella had found a new job, he'd stop fighting just to live another day. He'd just give in and slip quietly and unnoticed out of the back door.

The temptation to open the envelope containing the prediction had never been stronger. He wondered what could happen if he peeked inside. After years of self-control and with time running out, Ryan succumbed and opened it. Pulling out a yellowing sheet of paper, he unfolded it.

Chapter 117

Miller shot forward on the bed gasping for air before he'd even opened his eyes. The folds in his bedcovers restrained him as if he were wearing a lap belt. Gulping another lungful, he realised he actually *had* been holding his breath. His heart hammered so hard against the inside of his ribs, he felt as though a herd of stampeding buffalo were trampling his chest, the heavy beating pounded in his head.

It was just a dream. He flopped down onto his pillows while the effects subsided. There were no curtains or blinds at the windows. The daylight intensified by the whiteness of the walls and ceilings hurt his eyes. He closed them.

During the course of his life, he'd escaped drowning many times, but never before had his sleep been troubled by these apparent flashbacks. Lately his dreams generally had become more frequent and increasingly lucid, their significance progressively disturbing and portentous. Last week he dreamed he was working with a researcher named Michael Simpson, who specialised in the study of brainwashing and its application within cults. Although he'd never seen or heard of him before, his nightly encounters with him had seemed so real. The dreams culminated in a trip to Amsterdam where he'd confided someone was trying to kill him. It was crazy, but he feared for Simpson.

The dreams meant something and, despite endless analysis, he couldn't fathom what. Deep down, he thought they represented a warning.

He switched on his laptop with the intention of googling the meaning of dreams. A news feed caught his eye. He stared in growing disbelief. *Researcher Murdered in Amsterdam.*

Able to guess correctly a good deal of the time, his intuitive powers now seemed to border on the psychic. He knew now with certainty before he read on, what the researcher's name would be.

Stunned, he reached over to the bedside table and checked his watch. Just before nine o' clock. Opening the bedside cabinet drawer, he fumbled through the accumulation of discarded notes and half-empty boxes until he found what he was looking for: a dog-eared old business card. After all these years, he wasn't sure why he still kept it; perhaps he thought he'd need it one day. The area code was an old one, but he knew what it should be, so he added the new digit and keyed the number into his phone.

A few seconds later, it started to ring.

Chapter 118

If he'd been on stage with a magician, he'd have thought it was sleight of hand or some other conjuring trick. The note read: *When a former patient returns, a new church rises from the mountain.*

It wasn't at all what he'd expected. *A former patient returns and a new church. What was all that about?* Ryan always thought it would be something momentous, not something so mundane and cryptic. Guilt weighed heavy on him or was it merely disappointment?

You should have waited.

An uneasy feeling crept over him. He feared the consequences of his actions. *Which former patient? You should have waited, you silly old fool.*

A seemingly random thought popped into his head. A vision appeared of someone he'd not thought about in years.

The telephone rang. Startled, he lifted the receiver. 'Hello, Ryan here.'

'Dr Ryan?'

'Bruce?'

'How did you know it was me?'

His heart leapt at the realisation he'd chosen exactly the right time to open the envelope. Was it a coincidence? *It couldn't be.* For a moment, he worried how he'd tell her and then realised there was no need.

She already knew.

Chapter 119

Miller pulled up in a taxi, paid the driver and stepped out into the unseasonably warm sunshine. From the pavement, the façade of the building didn't appear as imposing as it did when he was last there. The heavy ornate cast-iron gate was secured in the open position with a heel operated counterweighted stay. The stone steps looked familiar, though more dished and worn in the middle than he remembered. High on the wall, the unblinking eye of a CCTV camera lens pointed down, covering the entrance. Arranged vertically, four buzzers shared the same bright alloy speaker panel.

Miller selected the third one up and pressed, the buzzer sounded, and the electronic keep snapped back, allowing him entry. Climbing the stairs, he noticed the creamy-coloured walls were scuffed and scruffy, probably not painted in years.

He made a quick diversion to the men's lavatories before going into reception. He looked at himself in the mirror while washing his hands. Picked out in the harsh glare of fluorescent lighting, the scar on his chin showed white against the peppery stubble. The cut had been so deep his beard no longer grew on it. Miller traced the smooth, inverted scimitar shape with his finger, to where it curved away from just below his lower lip onto his chin.

Donovan Kale had kept Miller's identity a secret from the press, but someone, although unable to get it directly from Kale, had eventually tracked him down. They attacked him on an isolated section of a canal towpath beneath a bridge. The darkness had masked the danger signals, and he hadn't seen the shadows as they'd swirled about him, warning of danger. At the last instant, he caught the dull gleam of a knife as it slashed at his face. *If he hadn't pulled out of the way, now that was a close shave.* He dried his hands and sauntered out across the landing. Opening the door into the reception area, he was surprised to see the layout had not changed. The chairs, coffee tables and magazines lay out exactly as he remembered. He picked up a dog-eared old National Geographic magazine and checked the date: 1970. *Like stepping back in time.*

Ryan emerged from a door behind the reception desk and came around to greet him.

Miller felt the cool, papery texture of his skin as they shook hands. He was shocked at how frail the doctor had become, but gave no sign of it. The psychiatrist looked pleased to see him; his good eye full of mirth.

'Bruce, how are you?' he said, leaning back to get a better look at him. 'How you've grown!'

Miller responded with a laugh. 'I'm fine – you haven't changed a bit!'

Ryan shot him a suspicious look. 'Well, my boy – that can only mean one of two things. Either I look fabulous now or I looked old and decrepit back then.' He indicated a chair.

'Come on, Bruce, sit. We shan't be disturbed.' Both men sat. 'I'm intrigued to know why you've contacted me after all these years.' Ryan rubbed at his good eye. 'You refused to say on the phone, so why are you here?' He gestured, spreading both hands.

'Dr Ryan, people just call me Miller these days. I'll tell you why later.' He coughed into his fist and said, 'I keep dreaming I'm drowning.'

'How often do you have these dreams?'

'Three times in the last week or so.'

'Mm-m.' His hands moved apart and revealed his silver propelling pencil. He rotated the shaft through a variety of angles to catch the best light.

Miller jerked his chin in the direction of the pencil. 'I can't believe you still do that.'

Ryan ignored him. 'It's all a question of timing, you having these dreams, contacting me. There's something else going on. I don't want to run out of time or get too tired to concentrate fully. I tire so easily these days.' A hint of resignation tainted his voice. Since opening the prediction envelope, he felt as if he'd turned an hourglass, and started a countdown on his remaining life. *Why have you set me this puzzle and then left me all alone to solve it?*

Dismissing the fear he may have opened the envelope too soon, he decided to play for time. He retrieved his appointment book from the counter, flicked the pages forwards and then back again.

'Mm-m, now let me see. I might be able to fit you in next week, once I've had the chance to go through your file properly.' In reality, he was hoping to have heard from The Sister by then.

Miller could see the appointment book was empty. 'What about tomorrow?' he said in a voice edged with sarcasm. 'That's if you can fit me in with that busy schedule there?'

Ryan followed his gaze to the diary. 'Aah, perhaps I should explain. This isn't mine – or at least, it isn't up to date. My secretary is looking for a job, you see.'

'You still have the same secretary?'

'No, she left years ago. This one started about three years ago. She's made a few changes, one of which is not keeping my physical diary up to date, she keeps all my appointments on a computer now, so I don't know what's happening if she's not here.'

'Well, how do you know you can fit me in then?'

'The truth is, Bruce, I'm winding down, that's how I know. I'm keeping things going until Stella gets another job. Then I'll call it a day. That's where she is, by the way, at an interview. She's as bright as a button; it won't be long before someone snaps her up.' Ryan didn't tell Bruce about the coincidences involved in looking at his file when he'd telephoned, or the real reason he kept the business open.

'You can't do this afternoon?'

Ryan thought quickly. He felt sure deferring their meeting until the next day was the right thing to do. 'I know we haven't discussed what you came here to talk about. I'd like to cover everything in one go, and to do that I'm going to need to get your file out and read it again, just to refresh myself. Besides, I'm having to man reception while Stella isn't here. I'll ask if she can work tomorrow. If you come in around one o'clock, we'll spend the whole afternoon going through everything.'

Ryan studied him over his silver-rimmed glasses. Miller noticed the pupil of his left eye was milky-blue and unfocused, looking into some distant point. The eye was blind. Most people would have tactfully avoided staring, but Miller was not good at such things. Ryan caught him and stared him out until he averted his gaze.

'Okay, I'll see you tomorrow, Dr Ryan.'

Immersed in writing notes, he didn't look up.

Miller let himself out.

So much to talk about. He'd just have to cover it tomorrow.

Chapter 120

When Stella returned later in the afternoon, Ryan handed her a note reminding her to prepare all the files in the archive room for digitalising, apart from the two he'd separated from the rest.

'How did your interview go?'

'I'm not sure. I think they liked me, but they had another couple of candidates to see and...'

The swirling fog of too many resurrected memories confused him, and he didn't pay much attention to her reply. He needed to sleep.

'I'll leave you to lock up for me,' he said. 'Oh, and there was something else.' Putting a forefinger to his temple, he suddenly remembered. 'That's it! Can you leave the Milowski file on my desk? I'll see you tomorrow.'

'You've forgotten it's Good Friday tomorrow.' She hesitated. 'Are you all right?'

She couldn't believe how much he seemed to have aged suddenly, and she feared he might have left his plans for retirement for too long.

'I'm just really, really tired. I'll be all right after I've had a lie down for a bit. Look, I could really do with your coming in tomorrow. Have a lie-in first, if you like.' His eyes implored her.

She answered without hesitation, 'Of course I will. I'll leave the file for you. I'll see you later in the morning.'

Ryan nodded. He looked utterly drained.

She wasn't convinced he'd actually heard her and knowing she wouldn't see him before she left, she called out, 'Goodnight, Dr Ryan.'

His key was already in the lock, and letting himself through the door at the back of his office; he walked up the stairs to living quarters. He'd divided the house up years before always intending to sell the practice and the accommodation one day and move on, but Grace had died the year before he was supposed to retire. Left without a reason to stop, he'd just worked on. In the hallway at the head of the stairs, he paused before the collage of photographs. The middle one was a portrait of Grace in her prime. He'd arranged all their milestones around it, their wedding day, the first house they'd shared, their first car, anniversaries and holidays. *So many happy moments, but no children. We should have had children.*

'Hello, dear,' he said. He paused in front of her picture and examined her expression. It never ceased to amaze him how the photographer had captured her vivacity at that moment, in that certain light. Viewed from varying angles at different times during the day or under the lamplight glow cast down the hall, he sometimes thought her eyes lit, or her smile shifted, lifting him when he was down, or weary. 'Wonderful thing, the mind, it keeps us alive,' he said as he moved away from the portrait. Glancing back, he thought she looked concerned, so he gave her a reassuring smile, and then tottered along on tired legs down the hall to his bedroom. 'It'll be all right, dear, don't you worry.'

Ryan woke up thinking he'd managed to sleep right through until the next morning. For a few moments, he panicked, and then realised with relief he'd only slept for an hour.

Hauling himself out of bed, he struggled on stiff legs to the kitchen and put a TV dinner into the microwave. He left the food heating while he went into the bathroom and splashed cold water over his face in an effort to freshen up. *This is going to be a long night.*

After his meal, he returned downstairs to his office. Stella had sorted the paperwork from the archive room already. The Milowski file was on his desk.

She'd planted a post-it note on it and written a single word: 'Enjoy!'

A weak smile drew across his lips. He realised how much he'd miss her.

Beneath the note was another, much older one. Although the once royal-blue ink had faded with the passage of time, he recognised the hand that wrote it. The handwriting triggered unpleasant memories of Penny, and reminded him of one of the last tasks she'd ever carried out for him. He dismissed her from his thoughts.

A close examination of the pages revealed they were out of sequence. The temptation to sort them back into order was strong.

How did that happen? I don't have time for this.

After puzzling a moment longer, he decided with some disappointment, that it was just more evidence Penny had failed to maintain her high standards until the end.

He wondered if she'd set it as a sort of time-bomb revenge, knowing he'd look at the files again in the future. Even if she had perceived he'd wronged her, he found it hard to believe she'd have stooped to such pettiness.

He looked for an easy way in, and not finding it straight away, he flashed over each page searching out keywords, attempting to follow the jumbled order of the paperwork before him.

He jotted a few notes from the original text onto a pad. At regular intervals, he paused to reminisce.

In those days, a hypnotherapist by the name of Anderson had worked with him; he recalled the early discussions they'd had. Milowski had maintained his earliest memory was that he'd fallen into a fire when he was less than a year old. A trauma that undoubtedly affected him so deeply he'd volunteered the memory before regression had even begun.

Snippets of conversation returned. Soon he was back in the room with Anderson.

'It's extraordinary he can remember so far back, even taking into account the trauma of falling into a fire. He was ten months old!' Anderson nodded as Ryan continued, 'It isn't acquired false memory syndrome either because I checked that out with his mother immediately afterwards. It actually did happen.' Ryan rubbed at his eyeball. 'Have you made any progress?'

Anderson looked exasperated, 'He's an impossible subject for hypnosis. He just resists no matter what.'

'Call yourself a hypnotherapist?' Ryan said.

'I'd like to see you try!' Anderson retorted.

'Well, actually I did, when he first came in to see me while you were on holiday.' Ryan caught the light on his pencil and continued talking without looking in Anderson's direction. 'Did he say anything significant about the rest of his early life?'

'He spoke freely about everything he could remember leading up to the age of fifteen – it's all in my notes – then he just clammed up for the entire duration of that year. The number of near-death misses he'd had, he seems to remember all of them. He even jokingly said, "I could write a book about the times I nearly died". In every single case, it seemed; he was saved by some timely intervention, and I found that most strange.'

Totally absorbed; he continued to read from his notes.

The boy had survived more than a dozen near fatal incidents, most of them involved rescues from water. His grandfather had turned up to save him virtually every time, but there was one exception.

Milowski had gone with friends to a public pool and was hanging onto the side of the when someone pulled him away for a joke, perhaps thinking it might encourage him to swim, but he'd gone under straight away.

I remember coming up the first time, grabbing a breath, going down. At that stage, it wasn't a problem – I wasn't panicking. I bounced along the bottom and reaching the side; launched myself back up, but I collided with someone's elbow on the way up, swallowed a big lungful of water and panicked. I couldn't get back to the surface. Then someone grabbed me and hauled me out.

The long corridor of his memories led him out into the room with Anderson again. 'What do you think of that?' he'd asked, referring to the many coincidental rescues performed by the grandfather.

Anderson didn't answer.

Ryan rapped his pencil three times on the table.

Startled, the hypnotherapist gabbled, 'I'm sorry, I just...' A puzzled look screwed his face and then he shot an accusatory look at Ryan as he realised what had just happened.

A small, self-satisfied smile creased the corner of Ryan's mouth, and he continued, 'I made a few enquiries and found out a couple of interesting things. Apart from the fact they were remarkably close, it seems the old man had a history of turning up just at the right time, and not only where Bruce was concerned. There's a bit of a list – various friends in the army, his wife. No one quite knows how he was able to just-be-there so many times. It seems he possessed some kind of finely tuned intuition, a sort of radar for picking up distress signals.'

'That's impossible. Didn't you ask him how he did it? You do surprise me,' Anderson said.

Ryan didn't answer at first; he clicked away at the pencil again. Anderson looked at it warily.

'I didn't ask him because he's dead.'

'Oh.' Anderson's lips encircled the word; the O shape remained for a full second as possibilities ran through his mind. 'So, you think his grandfather was somehow alerted by a subconscious link when Bruce was in danger?'

'It's possible. He was thought to be psychic, but he died two weeks before the last incident at the pool. The last rescuer hadn't been among the original party of boys who went to the pool, deciding only at the last minute to go. He told his mother someone had to look out for Bruce. As soon as he arrived at the pool area, he saw Bruce struggling below the water, and he got him out.'

'Who was it?' Anderson asked.

'The rescuer at the swimming pool is most likely the reason the guilt complex is so deeply rooted,' he said, looking directly into Anderson's eyes. 'It was Brookes.'

The accuracy of the recollections Ryan had just experienced amazed him. This was what notes were all about. It was a firm belief of his that not one single thing was ever truly forgotten. All memories lay dormant, just waiting for the right trigger to reactivate them.

He pushed his glasses up, rubbing at his good eye from below the lens allowing them to drop back onto his nose. He toyed with the idea of a cup of tea, but instead poured himself a glass of water from the jug Stella had thoughtfully left him. The water was no longer cold, but it slaked his thirst. Wiping his lips with the back of his hand, he continued sifting through the notes, coming across records of further conversations with Anderson. He drifted back in time, recalling once again.

'You know, Michael, before I decided to become a psychiatrist; I had an overriding interest in the latent powers of the human mind. I spent hours poring over old books and case histories covering impossible feats of strength or endurance.' Anderson appeared more interested in reading his newspaper than listening. Ryan carried on regardless.

'You know the sort of thing I'm talking about. Our bodies are built to last a lifetime at the limits normally placed on them, all of us have a spare capacity we can tap into when survival mode kicks in, and when it does, the mind can override those limits.'

Anderson's lack of attention irritated Ryan, and he did a high, falsetto imitation of Anderson's voice. 'Mm-m. Oh, yes, Doctor Ryan, I know exactly what you mean.'

Anderson sheepishly folded up the paper and sat up attentively.

'I'll give you a couple of examples. A slightly built woman lifts the front of a car to free a child trapped beneath its wheels. A mother slips over the edge of a cliff; her ten-year old son holds onto her with one hand and stops her from falling. They could never do these things normally. It just goes to show when it's really needed, there are people who can tap into something special.'

As he continued, Ryan took to fiddling with his pencil again, click – click – click. The rhythm infiltrated his speech, punctuating the phrases, lending them greater weight than they ordinarily carried.

'Michael, the two incidents I refer to, are borne out by witness statements. After all, in those cases there's at least one other person to corroborate the story. Cases of the individual surviving against all odds are far more commonplace, but not necessarily widely believed, because there are usually no witnesses, and because of that, the chances of survival are reduced. There isn't anyone to help, or call the emergency services, or whatever.' He could see Anderson wondering where he was heading with it all. Ryan held his index finger up. 'At times the mind can also push itself outside of the comfort zone. When the effect of physical pain is too much to endure, the chances of survival diminish unless the mind and body can push through. Michael, some sort of dissociation takes place that allows the body's hardwiring to take over the running of things. Instinct takes over.

'We also have reports suggesting the majority of near-death experiences involving visions occur whilst in this state. Many of these subjects speak of deceased friends and relatives waiting for them at the end of a bright tunnel, their mother and father welcoming them, taking them by the hand to lead them into the light.

'We wouldn't have heard these stories if these witnesses to near death weren't suddenly pulled away, back to earth with a bump. Sometimes the subjects recall viewing themselves from above as they are resuscitated or operated on.'

'Have you got something wrong with that eye?' Anderson said, narrowing his own as if it pained him.

He remembered how at that time, he'd needed to rub that eye with increasing frequency; always intending to have it looked at. He did, but much later, when the damage was irreversible.

In his recollections, he suddenly realised he was seeing with both eyes again.

'You know Michael, in many cases and there were studies – the survivors reported a heightening of the senses that lasted for a long time afterwards,' he paused to push the lead back into the tip of the pencil, brows knitted together; concentrating the way a cat might, when the mouse is in its sights. The set of his jaw, tongue tip poking between his lips, he was intent on instilling orderliness into something as small and insignificant as a pencil lead.

A minute had gone by. He looked up as if awakened from a dream, blinking.

'Where was I? Oh yes, we have studied several cases involving young adolescents or children – cases where serious, life threatening accidents occur with a frequency that exceeds that of chance. In these cases where subjects have survived multiple incidents, they seemed to develop a type of early warning system, something that enables them to continue surviving.' Ryan hesitated briefly, taking a sip of water from his glass. He raised his eyebrows, inviting comment from Anderson, who obliged with the question. 'Are you saying you think he has ESP?' Anderson had the look of a pupil in the presence of a talented and inspiring teacher.

'One of the things that I'm suggesting, is I don't think proper attention is given to the fact a few of these people may be psychic already, and that's how they have the capacity to get themselves out of these situations in the first place. It gives them an edge in the survival stakes.' He reached into his pocket and produced a packet of mints; he took one, and offered the packet to Anderson. 'I think because Milowski was so young when he began experiencing near fatal accidents and surviving them, it triggered the development of a survivor's instinct much earlier than you'd normally expect – and it's grown stronger and stronger with each successive survival.' Ryan considered the implications of what he'd just said. 'He just gets better and better at it.'

'He can't just go on like that, though, can he?'

Ryan's good eye withered him under its gaze.

Anderson squirmed. 'Well, it's obvious isn't it? He'll end up dead.'

'Yes, he may very well have a death wish.' Ryan put his pencil down. 'There's no doubt, subconsciously he sees a bleak future for himself. Scared of any form of human closeness, because he believes people die if they get close to him.'

Anderson continued along the same lines, 'And if he doesn't talk, we can't help him. What do you think will happen to him?'

'He'll die eventually by indirect suicide. Indirect, because he wouldn't knowingly kill himself, but he may very well put himself in a situation that is impossible to survive. In many ways, that's what he's been doing all along.'

'How do you mean?'

'Well, accounting for all the near misses, and given the nature of what I believe was his biggest trauma, there may be some real significance to the fact many of those incidents involved near-drowning.'

'He told me he hates water, why would he continue to go in when he doesn't swim. He should stay away from the stuff.'

'I think he's doing a sort of penance with his life at stake. He will just take greater and greater risks, until one day his luck runs out. Either way, it amounts to the same thing. He has a death wish. He'll die because he wants to.'

'One thing I can't understand is why no one noticed all this years ago. You'd have thought someone would have been saying, 'Look, we have this accident-prone kid, who has nearly killed himself, what, ten or twelve times, possibly more let's have a closer look at him.''

Ryan took a deep breath and sighed. 'We had so many other kids who needed conventional help, and I didn't have time for them all. I tried to shortcut things. He was to have been part of something unconventional. In the end, his mother got wind of the plan, and it was taken out of our hands.'

Anderson looked confused. 'Whose hands, ours? And what unconventional treatment are you talking about?'

'It doesn't matter now.'

A glimmer of understanding darkened Anderson's expression. 'I can't believe you did that without consulting me.'

Looking back now with the benefit of further experience, Ryan realised there was another possibility, one he dismissed as ridiculous almost straight away, but then returned to immediately.

Somewhere in Milowski's notes, he'd written a theory about his grandfather training him. He'd had him guessing cards before he'd turned them over, he would predict what colours the next person coming around the corner would be wearing. He'd taught him to write his dreams down to help remember them, teaching him to make best use of the faculties he believed inherent in everyone. Was it possible the near-death incidents were another form of training, and if that were the case, the question remained, why?

Chapter 121

Ryan screwed his finger knuckles into his closed eyelids in a vain attempt to rejuvenate them. He was no longer sure he could complete reviewing the files in time. It was almost one o' clock. Exhaustion threatened to shut him down. It had been a long, long time since he'd tested himself to such a degree. *Come on, Ryan, you can manage another half an hour.*

Turning over the next page, he plucked up a long fine hair. *Penny had been through the file!* He held it up to the light. It floated like gossamer. It wasn't one of Penny's. 'Mm-m?' he said aloud, and then placed it back between the sheets where he'd found it. An almost invisible bookmark.

It hadn't taken long to get Milowski talking about the accident, he'd managed to hypnotise him before he realised what was happening.

Using the notes as an 'aide-mémoire', he skimmed through until he reached his record of their second meeting. Milowski seemed to realise how he'd duped him the first time, he was guarded and surly. His memory jogged; he found he remembered the scene well.

'Bruce, help me to help you. Tell me about these things that disturb you at night.'

Looking for the notes he'd made when he'd regressed him to four years old, and then seven, Ryan turned the next page and found another out of sequence. He flicked his eyes over it. Once more, he found himself lured into the past.

'So you had this sense of foreboding?'

'If that means I knew beforehand what was going to happen, then yes.'

'Mm-m, you already said it came too late for you to warn them, and obviously you feel bad about that.'

The boy looked at the floor, with his hands clasped together and nodded, the fringe of his hair bobbing in the light coming through the window.

'I want you to think very carefully, back to that exact moment when you first had the sense. Can you remember what it was that made you think something was about to happen?'

Milowski looked up at the psychiatrist. 'I can't explain it, I just knew...' he said, trailing off; face pinched with concentration, pieces of the jigsaw fell into place, suddenly coming together. 'Wait a minute!'

Ryan leaned in closer.

Milowski told him everything.

Foraging further into the notes, he found Anderson again.

'I'm dropping him. He takes up too much time I could be spending helping someone who really needs it. He doesn't need our help; he will outlive both of us.'

'You don't know that. If we can't help him, he'll die and you know it.'

'On the contrary, Michael, I have a friend who knows about these things. The best thing we can do is leave him to find his own feet. If he doesn't, he'll be back here for help anyway.'

Anderson frowned at him.

'Michael, don't worry, I'll explain it like this to his parents: "Sometimes, we create more problems than we solve by mollycoddling our kids. I believe he broke down under unprecedented pressure. Time truly is sometimes the best healer, and I firmly believe that to be the case here."'

Ryan's thoughts shifted into the present. He hadn't said where the name Miller came from. Picking up his pencil, he scribbled a note. He'd ask him tomorrow.

Looking at the clock, he couldn't focus on it properly.

Where was he? Ah, that's it, a note for Stella. I must buy her an Easter egg.

He flipped the light off and stumbled up the stairs past Gracie. Tiredness thickened his tongue as he muttered, 'G'night, m'love.' She stared back coolly.

He managed to undress and then flopped onto his bed.

In spite of his weariness, he didn't sleep for a long time.

Chapter 122

Finding the hair in Miller's file had reminded him of Penny again. At one time, she'd been so indispensable and well trusted; he'd given her a set of keys, not only to the offices, but also to his apartment.

Penny was the first of his patients to have visited Vera. When she was old enough, she sought him out in his new practice, and he'd employed her. Always so pristine and perfect in everything she did, he had nothing but respect and admiration for her. Widowed when she was twenty-five, she poured all her energies into work. Seemingly not interested in meeting another man, she'd worked for Ryan for over ten years.

Not so long after Grace died, Penny changed in her attitude towards him. She became friendlier, more caring, and he appreciated her empathy. Little by little, not so he noticed at first, she began to change. She cut her hair, dying it blonde. Losing weight, she took more care with how she looked; her style of dress became more fashionable and daring. She also started paying Ryan more attention. He was flattered, but he saw no need to tell her he wasn't looking to have a relationship.

One evening, as they were preparing to lock up, she emerged from the ladies' room. She fixed him with a look that left no doubt as to her intentions. The smell of her freshly applied perfume was heady and intoxicating. Completely transformed from the woman he'd known, she sashayed towards him and made a bold play for him. Tempted though he was, he gently turned her down. After that, she turned into someone else, someone he no longer recognised.

He recalled how he'd taken a week off to put some distance between them, to get away from it all and allow things to settle down. When he'd returned, he found she'd slept with someone in his bed – the one he'd shared with Gracie – the love stain left behind on the sheets, plain for him to see. There had been no attempt to clean it up. She'd *wanted* him to know.

He asked her to return his keys. After that, things went from bad to worse. She bullied the other girl in the office remorselessly, took to smoking in the toilets in secret, and worse, she'd hidden a bottle of gin in the cistern. Penny was clearly unwell, but his sense of loyalty – after all she'd given him many years' service – ensured he gave her every opportunity to get better. After what happened, inevitably there was a confrontation, which ended in tears. Ryan agreed to give her another chance on the condition she got help. Ryan remembered noticing through the tear streaked mascara, how pudgy and unhealthy looking she'd become.

Unable to treat her himself, he sent her to another shrink – he hated the term – but the 'shrink' in this particular case, was a friend of his who owed him a long-standing favour.

Ryan telephoned him and, following a brief discussion, he'd agreed to take her on for a couple of free sessions.

Ryan allowed her the time off without deducting her pay. So every Thursday after that, at four o'clock in the afternoon, off she would go to her appointment.

For a while, she seemed to improve, but he had a feeling she was up to something.

'How much do I owe you so far?' he asked his friend about two months later.

His fellow practitioner looked quizzical. 'Owe me? What for?'

'You know, for seeing Penny?'

'Oh,' his friend had replied. 'This is sticky. I can't talk, because she's a *client* of mine.'

'I only asked if I owed you anything.'

Falling silent, he said, 'She's never been.'

When Ryan tackled her about it, she stormed out, and he never saw her again. *Good Penny turned bad.*

Then he drifted back further, almost to the beginning of his career, when he first met Gracie. Lifting the framed photograph of her from the bedside table, he held it tightly to his chest and finally closed his eyes. A deep sigh escaped his lips.

Chapter 123

6 April, Good Friday

Stella had forgotten to set her alarm. Running late, she sped along the pavement balancing her bag in the crook of one arm and her jacket on the other. She couldn't believe how warm it was for early April. Resting her foot on a curl in the front gate's ironwork, she fished in the bag for her keys. Pushing the gate open, she anchored it there, and then made her way up the steps.

She unlocked the door and let herself in. Carefully replacing the keys in her bag she remembered how angry he'd been when she told him she'd lost the original set she was given.

Don't you realise how much it costs to replace a set of keys? If you had to pay for them yourself, you might be more careful!

She couldn't recall an occasion where he'd even raised his voice to her, let alone shouted. Her eyes stung, and she bit her quivering lip as she fought to contain her emotions. Seeing her reaction, he switched his angry expression to one of compassion. Unlocking his cabinet, he'd handed her a spare set, and told her to be more careful. *Don't lose these, and take a letter for me will you...*

She smiled at how guilty he'd felt afterwards and how he'd tried to make up for it by making her a coffee.

Although she was excited at the prospect of a new job, she was also sad. She knew she'd miss Ryan.

Flicking the lights on, she crossed the reception area, and noted the time was 10.55 a.m. She hung her jacket in the corner on the coat tree, and entered the cloakroom to freshen her makeup. A couple of minutes later she stood outside Ryan's office and knocked on the door. There was no answer, so she opened the door. He wasn't there, but he'd left a note on his desk. She picked it up and immediately had the feeling something wasn't quite right.

Dear Stella,

I'm not sure if I'll be awake in the morning when you come. If I'm not, you'll be reading this note :)

Anyway, since you are reading it, I want you to call Miller and ask him to come round to see me straight away.

B. Ryan

She grinned at how he'd caught on to the use of the smiley. He had upgraded his mobile telephone, and she'd introduced him to the fine art of texting. She sent him a short note and ended it with :)

'What on earth is that supposed to be?' He'd said, pointing to the symbol.

'It means you're happy, smiling in a text,' Stella explained.
'Mm-m,' Ryan said as he always did.

Her smile evaporated. She stopped in her tracks. *Dear Stella?* Ryan had never left her a note like that before. His apartment door was ajar; she listened first for any signs of life. Not a sound. She called out to him from the base of the stairs, and when he didn't respond, she ventured up. Gracie's portrait eyes followed her as she walked down the hallway to his bedroom. An uneasy feeling settled on her as she opened the door. 'Dr Ryan?' she said, gingerly poking her head through the gap. 'Are you awake?'

The doctor was lying in his bed, holding a picture face down on his chest. He had one eye fixed open. It looked milkier than ever before. A lop-sided smile had frozen on his face; he looked happy. She wondered if he'd been thinking of Grace. He'd spoken of it often lately, how much he looked forward to seeing her again.

'What if it's just a lie?' she'd asked him.

'Then we're all doomed,' he replied. 'We must not let ourselves believe that, well you can if you want to, but me – I know I'm going to see Gracie again.' She remembered the glint in his eye, the firm set of his jaw when he said it.

She wished she could have shared his absolute faith. For a moment, she saw everything with a new clarity.

'I'll see you again one day,' she whispered and, for the first time, found she believed it. The barrier she'd thrown up against the enormity of it all broke down, and she sank to her knees. She cried, racked by sobs so deep she was hardly able to breathe. She cried for Dr Ryan, and she cried for herself and for all the things she couldn't change.

After a while, she regained her composure and prepared herself to dial 999. The buzzer sounded. *Someone's at the door.*

Numb, she descended the stairs. The electronic drone persisted. She pushed the intercom and answered automatically.

'Who is it?'

'The name's Miller. I have an appointment for one 'o clock.'

'Oh, Miller, Ryan is dead!'

Miller thought he recognised her voice. 'Stella, is that you?'

When the door released, he charged up the stairs two at a time.

Stella was slumped on an armchair in reception when he rushed in. She'd dyed her hair from blonde to black since the last time he'd seen her, but he recognised her instantly. The newly darkened hair matched the black of her smudged mascara.

'Stella, I don't believe this. Where is he?'

She nodded in the direction of the stairs.

He glanced at her as he went through the door and up the stairs. 'Are you all right?'

Her lower lip tugged down at the corners and sadness dulled her eyes. She shrugged and followed him into Ryan's apartment.

Miller stood in the doorway. The psychiatrist's unseeing eye fixed on him, and he felt uncomfortable in its unseeing gaze.

Tears brimmed in her lower eyelids, and she stared at him, knowing with one blink they would fall, afraid if they started, she might never be able to stop them. 'He's dead, isn't he?' she whispered.

Seeing her anguish, he pulled her face into his chest and held her tight. A slight movement caught his eye. 'No, I don't believe he is,' he said. Releasing her, he approached the bed.

Ryan stirred and then tried in vain to sit up. 'Miller, is that you?' he croaked dryly, peering at him with his half-open good eye. His other one seemed to be stuck open. He rubbed it a few times before he could get the lid to close over it.

'Stella, get him some water, please.'

Miller lifted the photograph from the old man's chest and propped him up with an extra pillow. As he tucked it behind, Ryan leaned close and whispered into his ear. 'She read your file, but don't tell her I told you.' The old man gave him a knowing look and tapped the tip of his nose with an unsteady finger.

'Don't worry, I won't.' Miller grinned. 'You gave Stella quite a scare.'

'Why I worked really late and I just overslept, that's all!' He hacked up a cough. 'I'll be fine, just give me a few minutes.'

'You rest, I'll come back later.'

'You can't, what I mean to say is...' Ryan looked distant. 'I'm running out of time, Miller. Now will you both leave the room so I can get dressed?'

'What was he whispering about?' Stella eyed him with curiosity.

'Nothing much, I'll tell you later.'

'What do you mean later? I want you to tell me now!'

Miller raised an eyebrow, unsure if she were joking. She locked her crystal blue eyes onto his and did not waiver. He lowered his eyes. Her mouth was small, but her lips were full, pursed in petulance, rising luxuriant from the creaminess of her face.

'Why are you looking at me like that, have I got something round my mouth?' She wiped her lips. 'Why were you looking at me like that?' she said, inquisitively.

He decided to keep his thoughts to himself. 'I was just thinking how funny it was – me giving you instructions again.'

'If you want to start bossing me around, you'd better give me my old job back,' she said, her face turning a shade of rosy pink.

Miller laughed. 'Come on, get that water sorted out, we haven't got all day.'

She returned with a full glass.

'Stella, wait here while I take this up to him. I need to speak with him in private.'

'Miller, I want to be sure he's all right after that scare he gave me. Shouldn't we call a doctor?'

'He's just tired and old. Once he's had more of a rest, he'll be fine.'

Miller returned upstairs. Stella followed him.

He hadn't made it off the bed. Dressed and propped up on the pillows, he struggled to put his watch on.

'I'm so tired I don't know what's wrong with me, I'm sorry. I just need more sleep, but no time now, I'll catch up tonight.' He rested his wrist against his knee to hold the timepiece in place while he threaded the strap through the buckle. Seeing Stella's eyes on him, he waved her away impatiently, afraid she might offer to help.

'Would you mind leaving us alone, Stella? Miller has to get going, and I've things to tell him in confidence.'

She looked disappointed as she closed the door behind her.

He beckoned Miller to come closer, his voice diminished to little more than a whisper. *Does he think Stella is listening at the door?* Then he realised that wasn't the reason at all; the old man was merely conserving the precious energy even the smallest effort seemed to consume.

'Bruce, I have to know. What really led you to contact me after all these years, you could have phoned anybody. Can you tell me why you chose me?'

'Sure, but something's bothering me from yesterday... How did you know it was me on the phone? When I said my name was Miller, you replied "Bruce" with no hesitation whatsoever.'

Ryan avoided his gaze.

'I never told you I got nicknamed Miller. That came *after* our sessions were over. Have you been watching me?'

Pushing the tips of his index fingers into the corners of his eyes, he rubbed them vigorously. 'Of course I haven't, what a ridiculous thing to suggest.'

'Is it?'

The two men looked at each other, both seeking answers that wouldn't come easily.

Ryan sipped at his water.

'My question, Miller, you haven't answered.'

'Why choose you? I don't know. I kept an old business card of yours for years. It made me feel better knowing I could talk to you again if I needed to. When I first came to see you, I held back on you. I should have told you more, but I was just a kid, and to me you were a just a shrink.'

Ryan winced as if stung by the word. 'Oh, please.'

'Sorry, like I was saying, I was just a kid. I didn't want you to think I was crazy. Do you remember me telling you about the shadows I saw the day of the accident?'

Ryan's eyes widened. He licked his parched lips and said, 'Go on.'

'What I didn't tell you is they'd started to become more than just shadows. I didn't understand it then, and I still don't. They're with me everywhere, like the little floaters you see when you look up at the ceiling staring at nothing in particular. You know they're there. At first you're fascinated, but after a while you don't take any notice.'

Ryan ritualised with his pencil, apparently not listening.

Miller continued, 'Well that's how it used to be. Until recently, if I'd looked at them directly, they'd have disappeared, but when I see them now, I think they're becoming bolder.'

Light gleamed along the shaft of the pencil and the psychiatrist stared at him with such intensity it made his eyes water.

'Are you following me, Doctor?'

'You have my undivided attention. Oh, how I wish you'd told me this before. Please go on, I'm fascinated.' The colour and vigour seemed to have returned to his complexion.

Miller took a deep breath and resumed. 'Well, one evening, and it wasn't dark – I think it was around Easter time – I caught a glimpse from the corner of my eye. It was no big thing as I was telling you before, but this time when I looked at it directly, I realised it wasn't a shadow at all. It was *someone*. Fully formed and in glorious Technicolour, staring right at me.'

Ryan held his pencil lengthways, each end secured between thumbs and index fingers. The light flared against its polished surface. 'Go on.'

'She scared me. I can't explain this very well. She was sad looking, and although I knew she was not from this world – or at least didn't belong in it – I knew she meant me no harm,' A tear rolled down Ryan's cheek. He wiped it away.

'You see, she was an Oriental woman. I was convinced I'd seen her face before, but I couldn't for the life of me remember where. Not then. And there have been others.'

Ryan shook his head, mumbling, 'I knew it. You believed so strongly, you created Tulpa's – thought creatures. If only I'd had this information, I could have studied you. I could have written my book. I wish you'd told me before.'

Miller then said something that completely derailed Ryan's thought train. 'She was the shadow under my bed when I was seven.'

'What? Why didn't you tell me before?'

Chapter 124

Ryan had the look of a man who'd missed the last train home by seconds, arriving on the deserted platform only to see its taillights disappearing into the darkness. Another chance to test his theories missed.

'You should have told me earlier,' he repeated, closely examining his pencil in what little light filtered into the room.

Miller cleared his throat. Ryan snapped out of his distraction with a start.

'That wasn't all of it. As I said, I never told you everything. I held back on you.'

Ryan nodded. 'I know. I guessed as much at the time.'

'I've already told you about the drowning dreams and the shadows.'

'Before we move on, when did you first notice them?'

'The shadows? It wasn't a question of noticing. It was about acknowledgement,' he said, fingering his scar, 'and that came slowly.'

'Go on, Bruce.' He turned over a page of his notepad.

'Bear with me. When I was given the name Miller, I moved ahead and left Bruce behind with all the baggage. Oh, he was still in me, of course he was. The voice of my guilty conscience, the source of my little intuitions; I think it was last year when I finally realised part of me was bigger than I'd care to admit.'

Ryan rubbed so hard at his good eye it turned bloodshot. 'Don't stop on my account,' he said, waving him on. 'I want to hear more.'

'Last year I was on the lecture circuit, speaking about mankind's forgotten abilities and his close relationships with the supernatural. Something happened to interrupt that.' The memory wasn't entirely unhappy. A smile touched his lips. 'I stayed at a haunted house and it started something growing in me.'

Ryan's eye narrowed and he laid his pencil down, saying, 'Tell me.'

'When I arrived there I had a flash of the past, in the old stable block. I'd had fragments of things I couldn't figure out before, nothing like this though. This was a sequence, like a movie scene, but complete with taste, touch and smell.' Miller paused; he looked into a distance beyond Ryan. He closed his eyes and saw the stable boy and the horses form clear in his memory. He shut it out. 'Since then I've noticed other things, and my dreams are becoming a part of that.'

'You dream of drowning, you blocked it out for so many years. The dreams will pass.'

'Or come to pass.'

Ryan recalled his diagnosis of unintentional suicide. 'No, Bruce, you have a purpose here. You have to stop.'

'I'm afraid it's too late for that, Doctor Ryan.' He placed a newspaper page in front of him.

'Last week, I had a series of dreams about a researcher I'd never met culminating in him sharing a secret with me. He told me someone was trying to kill him.'

'Okay-y, but what does this have to do with anything?' Ryan said, holding the paper up.

'Read the headline. It's him, Michael Simpson, from my dreams.'

Leading Authority on Cults in Fatal Collision with Car.

Ryan stared at the page for a full minute after reading the article. A tangle of possibilities hung before him.

Miller interrupted his thoughts. 'Going back to my earlier question, how did you know it was me?'

'Oh that, I knew you were coming, but I learned that literally moments before you called. You see The Sister predicted you would return.'

'The Sister. What are you talking about?'

'You see I first met her in Ireland. I remember it well; it was raining like I'd never known before.' His good eye searched the past, staring into space, lost in far yesterdays. He related the story as if it belonged to someone else; the metronomic click of his pencil a ticking clock, marking time as the story unfolded.

'I'm sorry, Doctor. It's going to take a lot more than that to convince me she knew I'd be coming here this morning.'

'If you'd met her, you wouldn't say that. Besides, we don't have time to work this out now, or at least I don't.' Ryan blinked, his disappointment evident.

'Why are you looking at me like that?'

'You should have told me about the Oriental girl earlier. That was the trouble with you when you were a kid.' He took a breath. 'You never gave me the whole picture. If you had told me earlier, I might have wrestled some sense out of it. I've been trying to write a book, I had a whole chapter planned on phantasms of the living, but it was all anecdotal. I'd never met anyone who had first-hand experience, not that I could truly believe.'

'You think I saw a phantom of someone who is still alive?'

'Yes, I do. Despite the fact you say it was a dream. Questions have been raised about whether a person needs to be sleeping for dreaming to occur.' Ryan shook his head. 'I don't know if I should tell you this, but visions such as you had, are often seen as harbingers of doom. Statistically, there's a one in fifty chance of a death occurring, following a vision of the kind you experienced.'

'Well, those odds are a long shot, and to me it's just a coincidence. Anyway, why do you place such value in what I've told you? As far as you're concerned, it was only a dream after all.'

'True, but the chances of your turning up here at all, are remote after so many years. The fact you turned up right after I opened The Sister's prediction envelope...I'm not even going to try to work the odds out.'

Miller twisted his bracelet around, thinking about his grandfather. Ryan, too, was deep in thought.

Finally, Miller broke the silence. 'Can I just ask you something? Do you believe in ghosts?' Miller guessed, as a psychiatrist, he'd say it was all in the mind.

The doctor answered without hesitation. 'I never did, until I met her. I realised without a God, how would *she* be possible? Now I believe in God and the Devil. I believe in ghosts, and I believe in life after death. After all is said and done, there must be something.' He glanced at his bedside portrait of Grace. 'I have to believe it, or else what has it all been for, these last few years. I believe there's a place for those who believe and a place for those who don't.' He searched Miller's face for a reaction, before continuing. 'Throughout my life, I've noticed the bleaker life is, the more religious the person experiencing it is likely to be, but don't get me started, we haven't got all day!' It occurred to him he might have blown his chances by opening the envelope too soon. She wasn't going to come and knock on the door or drift past on a cloud heralded by trumpets. He'd blown it. Maybe he should try to contact *her*, he wondered if Brenda Flynn was still alive and contactable on her old telephone number.

Ryan's earlier words suddenly registered with Miller. *No, Bruce, you have a purpose here.*

'What purpose?'

'Sorry?' the doctor said.

The telephone rang.

'Pass the phone to me, please.'

Miller obliged.

Wriggling himself upright, he said, 'Dr Ryan here.' He opened his mouth as if to say something, holding its shape as he listened instead, with his eyes on his former patient, he nodded. 'Mm-m, I'll tell him. Can we speak again soon? I'd like that.' He put the receiver down. 'She wants to meet you. You'll go I assume?'

His curiosity aroused; there was only one answer. 'Yes.'

'Rosetta will meet you at 8:30 p.m.'

Miller checked his watch. 'That's plenty of time.'

'No, it isn't. She's assumed you won't fly; apparently, you've developed a phobia. You're to meet her at Waverley railway station.'

'In Edinburgh? That's ridiculous, what if I change my mind?'

Ryan ignored him. 'She sensed you were here, all the way from Scotland. Remarkable.' His face lit with a beatific smile. 'That wasn't her, it was her daughter.' For a moment he thought the doctor was going to say something else, but he was merely moistening his lips.

'I'll get you more water.'

'Thank you,' the doctor whispered. He closed his bad eye with his fingertip.

He headed for the door and yawned, the sight of tired people had that effect on him.

'Bruce?'

He turned back. Ryan had his good eye fixed on him.

'What is it?'

The old man rocked his head from side to side. 'Bruce...Mil...Milwaukee! Is that how you say it? I can't remember.'

'It's close enough, it will do. Are you all right?' he said, showing concern.

'Bruce, Miller – Milwaukee, whatever your name is. Help Stella get a job for me, she's a good girl. And one other thing. Tell her I don't want her to call a doctor under any circumstances. If I am to go, I want it to be on my terms. I don't want to be kept alive. Do you understand? It's important to my beliefs.' His eye beseeching.

Miller turned back from the door and crossing the room, squeezed the old man's shoulder. 'Of course I'll tell her.'

Downstairs, Stella busied herself tidying old files into boxes. At the sight of Miller, she raised her eyebrows and said, 'Well, how is he?'

'He's resting.'

'I think we should call a doctor.'

'He doesn't want that.'

She looked confused. 'What?' she said. 'What do you mean?'

He explained Ryan's wishes; he said it was important to his beliefs.

'He's going to die.' She picked a piece of fluff from her sleeve. 'What did you talk about? I suppose you won't tell me.'

'Stella, I have to go to Edinburgh. I can't explain, I don't know myself yet. Will you be okay?' Although she didn't answer, he knew from her return into his life that she was a part of whatever was going on.

'You have to go now?'

He nodded. 'I'm going back to the hotel to collect my things and then, yes, I'm leaving to catch the train this afternoon.'

She pulled a little girl face, poking her lower lip out as if she might cry at any moment.

'Hey, I'll be back before you know it. I want to talk to you about coming back to work for me.'

She managed a half smile and said, 'It's not the job that's bothering me. What if he dies while you're away?'

'Just give me a call,' he said as he turned on his heel and left, closing the door behind him.

'See you,' she whispered.

He didn't even say goodbye.

Chapter 125

'Ain't the same anymore, this game. Slowly been strangled...see this cab? Got two hundred and fifty thousand miles on the clock.'

The taxi driver hadn't stopped talking from the moment he'd entered his cab. Miller answered perfunctorily, too deep in thought to engage in any meaningful conversation.

Far too many coincidences occurring to be just coincidence. For such a series of events to unfold in such a short space of time, it has to be synchronicity. No time to think about it now.

Arriving back at the hotel at 2:35 p.m. he tipped the driver and then, pushing through the revolving door, crossed the polished marble floor to the reception counter.

The receptionist looked up from her computer screen and watched him approach. She stood to greet him.

'Good afternoon, sir.' She smiled politely.

'Can I have the key for room number 112? I'm sorry; I'll start again.' He smiled apologetically. 'Good afternoon, I'm in a bit of a hurry, would you be able to make my bill up quickly? I have to leave more or less straight away. Oh, and can you get me a taxi for say—' He checked his watch. 'Ten minutes time?'

'Where are you going?'

'Kings Cross station.'

'It'll be quicker by tube.'

'I haven't travelled on the tube for so many years. It's probably changed so much. I think I'll stick with the taxi, but thanks for the suggestion.'

'Yes, of course, sir.' She pushed a button on the telephone and then reached for the key. The sound of the phone came through its loudspeaker, ringing three times before someone answered. She snatched the receiver up as the male voice said, 'Hello.' She maintained a polite smile as she organised the taxi and held out his room key.

As he pressed the button to call the lift, the receptionist called out behind him. 'Ten minutes, Mr Miller, and your taxi will be here!'

He acknowledged her with a smile and a mock salute.

Using the bed as a staging point, he threw his clothes and other belongings onto it. He checked under the bed, scanned the room for anything else and, satisfied everything was there, crammed it all unceremoniously into his bag.

No sooner had he settled the bill, the cab arrived. He slung his bag over his shoulder, opened the door and got in. 'Kings Cross, driver, please.'

'Damn traffic,' he muttered under his breath, checking his watch as the driver dropped him off. He'd missed the three o'clock train. *She was right; I should have taken the tube.* Now he'd have almost an hour to kill before the next train left at 4 p.m. After buying his ticket, he decided to have a look around.

The station had changed beyond recognition since he was last there. Then, it had been old and grimy. Now, it looked clean and new. The journey would take about four and a half hours, which meant he wouldn't arrive much before seven thirty. Suddenly realising it was a bank holiday weekend, he thought about booking a room, at least for a couple of nights. He telephoned directory enquiries and obtained a list of numbers. With no accommodation available at any of the major hotel chains, he worked his way through a list of smaller hotels. He hung on the line with the last of the best-situated hotels; near the town centre. The receptionist was friendly, but chided him for leaving it so late. 'It is a Bank Holiday you know, but let me check; sometimes we get a cancellation.' She came back on the line and confirmed they were fully booked. 'But listen; I used to work at this little place.' She gave him a number to call. 'Ask for Ronnie, tell him you spoke to Glenda. Hang on a minute, someone's speaking to me. Oh, you know, this must be your lucky night; we've just now had a cancellation, would you believe?'

Another coincidence? Shaking his head, he concluded it probably happened all the time and promised himself he'd put all thoughts of chance or fate from his mind. After giving his credit card details to secure the booking, he put his phone away and checked his watch. Still three quarters of an hour to go. Bored with waiting already, he spotted a newspaper discarded on a bench. The headline caught his eye. *Boy 7 Rescued From Paedophile Gang: Two Dead, Police Appeal To Public.* Although the paper was two days old, he picked it up, tucked it under his arm, and went to buy a coffee. Then he sat down to read.

The bodies of two men have been found at an address in West Lothian, following a tip-off. A seven-year-old boy, reported missing early yesterday, was discovered at the scene. He is recovering in hospital. His parents are at his bedside. Police have asked the caller to come forward. Unconfirmed reports suggest it was a vigilante attack.

The coffee tasted sour. He dumped it in the nearest bin and ambled leisurely over to the platform where his train awaited.

Chapter 126

After boarding and finding his seat, Miller placed the paper in his lap. *If only there were more people like that in the world.*

The carriage was unexpectedly quiet for a Bank Holiday; the few people who were on board spread themselves out as the number of seats that wouldn't be taken, became apparent. A young couple put space between themselves and the drunken ramblings of a Scot emanating from the back of the carriage. He was far enough away from Miller not to bother him, but it occurred to him, he'd probably encounter him at some point in the journey. Travelling alone on public transport, he always seemed to attract the drunks and lunatics on board. It was another reason, given the choice he'd have preferred to drive. Although he'd yet to see him, he had a vision of him in his mind's eye. *Not big, no kilt or Tam o' Shanter, pale skin, wiry ginger-blonde hair.* He sighed at the thought.

The train shunted forward. He watched the platform retreating as the train picked up speed.

Miller's corner of the carriage had remained deserted. He was completely at ease in his own company, just him and whatever came up next. Selfish maybe, but he preferred it that way.

He settled into staring out of the window, and wished he could sleep, but he never could in the company of strangers. He closed his eyes and entered a dreamlike state.

Something about the motion of the train jostled memories and started him thinking about painful things, long past. He remembered how he first met Josie, only to lose her to the sea a few years later. The pain still raw, anguish flooded his memory, catching him off guard. Too late, he tried to shut it out. Although he'd been miles away when she went missing, he blamed himself. *You knew you were jinxed, Miller. You shouldn't have got so close to her, shouldn't have allowed it to happen.*

He drifted into thinking about the meaning of unconditional love and how he'd loved unconditionally, experiencing its totality. Losing her the way he did, scarred him far deeper than he could ever have imagined.

Since Josie had disappeared, he kept his mind off women as far as possible, carefully avoiding anything other than superficial involvement. When he felt the need for a woman, it was invariably with someone totally unsuited to him, someone from whom he could stay emotionally detached. He needed sex but avoided love. Pain and love were inextricably woven together, and he didn't want, or need those feelings in his life.

Beyond the window fields flashed by, a movement in the glass caught his eye. Without turning, he saw the reflection of a dark haired woman in her mid-thirties, for the briefest moment, he thought his imagination had conjured it. He'd spent much of his life paying close attention to the periphery of his vision. Sometimes, he saw things that make him aware of other things, like the shadow on the pavement cast by someone coming around the corner before they'd actually arrived in person. His shadows had become fuller, and more defined. Half expecting the woman to be gone when he turned to look at her directly, she remained where she sat. She reminded him of a woman he'd met a few years ago. It wasn't a physical resemblance, more the haughty look she gave him as she turned her face away, with her nose up as if men were beneath her. Now she had his interest, she wasn't looking in his direction at all. She stared out of the window next to her. The train flashed through shade; the light changed. He caught her reflection looking at him. She was a very attractive woman. He turned away.

He was now sure his reflections on the past were linked to the motion of the train, and he wondered absently what would happen if he were travelling backwards. He drifted into thoughts of the woman he'd met years before.

He was in his early thirties; she was at least ten years older than he was, with a good figure and strong, shapely legs. The fit of her clothes hinted at what lay beneath, fascinating him. He used to see her around in the supermarket, always on her own, then after shopping; she'd wait for a taxi to take her home. She was a prime example of *not* his type, but she had a prim and proper air about her that appealed to him, and he *was* in need of a woman. One afternoon, he waited outside for her. When she came out, he introduced himself just as she produced her phone to call a cab.

'Hello, I often see you in here.'

She looked at him suspiciously.

'You're always on your own.' He disarmed her with a warm smile.

The floodgates opened, and soon she was telling him everything. He offered her a lift home, barely getting a word in edgeways. She asked him to stop in the street around the corner to her house.

'The neighbours are awful. If they knew I had a man round my house…'

'Is that an invite?' he asked.

Her face turned pink. 'You know, I'd have invited you in for a coffee, but the gossips around here...'

'That's okay; I'll come back tonight when it's dark. No one will see.'

Pink turned to red. 'Oh, I don't think it's a good idea...'

He leaned over, brushing his lips against her cheek, and whispered close to her ear, 'We could both do with the company.'

Of two minds, she bit her lower lip and grimaced.

'Which house is it?' he said.

She seemed to be holding her breath.

A woman came out from a nearby house carrying a bag of rubbish and saw them sitting there. She moved as far forward as she could before dipping to put the bag down, taking the opportunity to squint right into the car. That simple, single action made her mind up for her.

She gave him her address.

That night, just after dark, he'd turned up with a bottle of wine. She had a lot to say, to tell him about. He listened patiently for half an hour or so; he felt he owed her at least that. She finished her second glass; he reached over with the bottle to refill it. She put her hand out covering the glass. He put the bottle down.

'I'd better not. If I get tipsy, I sometimes do things I regret later.' She stared at the floor, suddenly overtaken by shyness. He took the initiative. Holding both her hands, he pulled her up.

She lifted from the chair without resistance. He looked into her face and eyes. She smiled. He slipped an arm around her waist and pulled her close. They kissed, and a passion exploded right out of her, taking him by surprise; dropping to his knees, he lifted her top to reveal her midriff. He licked and sucked at her belly, French kissing her navel. She went wild.

Both of them were on the floor; her skirt hitched up over her thighs.

He eased his head between her knees and ripped her white panties to one side.

'No! No one's ever done that, it's not allowed!' His tongue alternated up and down each thigh, getting closer to her with each stroke. She arched her back and pulled his head in tighter, clamping her thighs around his ears. She came in a frenzy of denials.

He pulled himself up next to her. She looked at him in wonderment.

'No one has ever done *that* to me before.' She sighed, trying to regain her breath.

He moved his body higher up against her, pulling down on her shoulders so her head was close to his abdomen and began to move her head down, while pushing his hips up.

'What are you *doing?* Oh, no, I'm not doing that. I've never done that to a man before and you can't...'

He pushed himself against her lips; she turned her face left, then right to get away, her lips pressed tight and then suddenly her lips parted and she was on him like a pro.

We never even made it into bed. He smiled at the memory and wondered if she ever met anyone else after that. If he'd awakened a hunger in her. If she were still haughty and aloof around men. Thinking about her had made him a little hard.

The woman from across the aisle now occupied the seat in front of him. She was staring at him, apparently fascinated by the fact he was staring right through her. She made a windscreen wiper gesture with one hand across his line of vision a bemused half smile on her lips. 'Would you like a picture?'

'What?' He squirmed, moving into an upright position. 'Oh, sorry. I do that sometimes, slip into a daydream and, well, I'm sorry.' He flashed a quick embarrassed grin. Her expression remained strangely curious. Miller returned to looking out at the countryside rushing by and thought about the last time he'd almost got into trouble for staring.

Her voice was silky and calm, intruding on him gently. 'Excuse me. A penny for your thoughts?'

Miller turned from the window and regarded her properly.

She had large pale blue eyes, a slight snub nose, her face was both angelic and impish, her poise demure and sophisticated. The expensive boyish bob-cut of her black hair was the only boyish thing about her. The closer he looked, the more her beauty unfolded for him. *Surreal, like the sun on a flower that lifts its bowed head toward the light.* The words he'd written for Josie a lifetime ago sprang to mind.

Uncomfortable that he should be reminded, he turned away. 'You wouldn't want to know.'

She shuffled over on her seat, so she sat directly opposite, leaning forward, she said quietly, 'Come on; help break up this boring journey for me! I don't usually speak to strangers, but you seem okay.' Her hands pressed together, pointing at him as if she were about to pray. 'So – here I am, speaking to a stranger!' She rolled her eyes and, raising her eyebrows, gave a little shrug of the shoulders before allowing her hands to drop into her lap. She waited for his reaction. Miller felt the hook of her velvet claws as she pulled him in. He shrugged at her and looked across the aisle at a young couple wearing headphones. The girl slept; the man with her stared blankly out of the window.

'Do you do this trip often?'

'No, this is my first time.'

'Oh, really?' She arched an eyebrow.

'Yes, it is. Really,' he said, of two minds whether to excuse himself, and just going back to staring out through the window, tripping out on daydreams. The truth was; she'd already turned a key in him and suddenly he became wary of getting to know her any better.

'Given the choice, I'd rather drive,' he said.

'Well, you don't know what you've been missing.' She smiled. 'You can meet some very interesting people on trains.'

'Usually.' He grinned. 'I only ever meet nutcases.'

'Oh? I never have. I suppose I've always been lucky,' she said. 'Tell me what you do for a living?'

'Let's talk about something other than work.'

She arched an eyebrow in his direction. 'We don't know each other well enough to talk about anything other than work.'

A childhood memory sprang to mind. Miller decided to tell it. 'My grandfather used to tell me about a bear he knew from the war.'

'He knew a bear?' She scoffed, an eyebrow arched high.

'Yes, he did – in the Second World War, Voytek his name was.'

'Your grandfather's name?'

'No, the bear!' Miller looked at her closely to be sure she wasn't mocking him.

He'd started the conversation from such an obtuse position; he reeled her in without even trying. She was hooked. It was a story she'd never heard before.

'Anyway,' he rattled off the rest of the bear tale and concluded the story. 'The poor animal died in Edinburgh Zoo.'

'If it's true, that's a very interesting story.'

'Look it up,' he told her. 'You know, my grandfather always said it was a sad irony a bear that fought alongside men for our freedom, was never freer than while the war was on.' He shook his head slowly, his expression the same as his grandfather's had been when he first told him the story years before. 'To have ended up in a cage when it was all over, the poor bear, that's so sad.'

'Well,' she volunteered, 'I guess he wouldn't have been able to survive for long in the wild if they'd let him go, would he?'

'I don't know.' The continuing contemplation on the fate of a bear that died so many years before suddenly seemed irrelevant. He changed the subject. 'So, you travel up often?'

'Once a week, for a long weekend.'

'I'm surprised you don't fly.'

'Sometimes I do, if I'm pushed for time, but if I can, well, I prefer the train. I find it relaxing, and I usually find someone interesting to talk to.' She smiled.

'I hate flying,' he confided in her. 'I hate ferries, and I don't know how you *stand* travelling backwards!'

She looked out of the window at the scenery disappearing forwards into the distance. 'It doesn't bother me. Besides, it's safer if there's a crash.'

'Good point, although I have to say, crashing is not something I would usually associate with a train journey. It's the one thing that surprises me about flying, we don't all face backwards. It would be so much safer than trying to tuck your head down on your knees.'

'Tell me something about yourself.'

'Are you a psychiatrist?' he asked.

'Good heavens, no, I'm a reporter!' She laughed. 'I sometimes think I need one, though.'

They talked about the news. He asked her if she'd read about the vigilante case.

'Funny you should ask that, it's the reason I'm coming up this weekend, to find out more from my police mole.'

Miller was only slightly surprised about how forthcoming she was. People seemed to think they could confide all kinds of things to him. He concluded it must be something about his face.

'Okay?' he said, prolonging the word, inviting her to open up if she chose. She did.

'What the newspapers don't know yet – because the police haven't told them – was that scenes of crime investigators found a baseball bat at the scene. Somebody used it to sodomise both men, and they left it protruding from the backside of one of them. It was obviously used on the other one, as well. Surprisingly enough, it hadn't been used to batter the men, another blunt instrument had been responsible for that – a leather gloved fist.' She reached into her bag, pulled out a pack of gum and offered it to him.

'Thanks,' he said and took one.

She picked up where she left off. 'The only witness was the boy himself, who only caught a quick look at the face of the man before being told to look away. It's thought the man was rough shaven in appearance. He also noticed the man had gloves on. Apart from boot prints and minuscule particles of leather in the mouth of one victim, there was no other forensic evidence. The handle of the bat had a set of initials carved into the end of it.'

'Do you know what they were?' If he wasn't that interested before, she definitely had his interest now.

'Three possible combinations: F.K.J, K.J.F or J.F.K.'

'Like the American president?'

'Yes, somebody else said that, but it's a safe conclusion it didn't belong to him, or the owner of the initials didn't commit the crime.'

She said it so seriously, it made him laugh. She looked slightly offended, but then saw the funny side and laughed with him.

A few moments passed in silence; she regained her previous composure. 'It seems they were part of a paedophile ring and from the information gathered, according to my mole, they're thought to be responsible for over fifty kidnappings and possibly as many murders. They're still analysing computers and things, but it looks like their victims—'

Miller put his hand up to stop her. 'I'm sorry,' he said, his expression pained. 'Look, although I'm interested, as an outsider when it comes to cases like these where kids are involved, that's where I like to stay, outside of it.'

She looked surprised.

'You see; I have a natural inclination to try to solve things, but you know, in the end it's... It becomes an unnecessary distraction for me when I'm working. I mean, the less I know the less chance there is of it distracting me. I don't need anything else clouding my thoughts. Does that sound uncaring?' He paused. 'I can't afford to care.'

'I'm sorry you feel like that,' she said. 'Apparently the kid caught a glimpse of him, the vigilante. He had long hair and was unshaven and older looking than the kid's granddad.' Miller rolled his eyes.

'What's wrong with you?' she said.

'Did you not hear a word I just said?'

'Yes I did, but I've almost finished now, anyway.' She smiled sweetly at him. 'The police are withholding quite a lot of information from the press for now.'

'I don't know why,' Miller said. 'By now he'll be clean shaven, probably with short hair and dyed another colour as well.'

'What makes you say that?' A suspicious look crossed her face. 'Exactly what *is* it you do?'

'I find missing people.'

'What did you say your name was?'

'I didn't!'

'Okay, Mr I – don't – want – *you* to know what my name is!'

He grinned at her. 'I'll tell you my name, it's—'

'No, no, I prefer you without one. *The Man with No Name*, like someone from a mystery novel.'

'Or a Clint Eastwood film?'

She grinned. 'Before my time.' Curiosity got the better of her, and she asked, 'Are you looking for someone right now?'

He hesitated briefly. 'No, I'm meeting someone. I'm between cases, so to speak.'

She didn't press him for details. 'Mmm, I'm interested to know what attracted you to this line of work.'

'Well, the whole story is a long one, so I'll just tell you how it began.'

She laughed. 'This train ride is a long one!'

He explained how he used to stay with his grandfather and how he'd always take a few old copies of True Crime magazine with him, not so much to read, but to study the graphic crime scene photographs.

'They fascinated me. He'd come and sit next to me, asking questions about the scenes, the evidence. It was like playing Cluedo, but with real lives. We'd investigate the unsolved cases, piecing together everything we could get from what we had in front of us, inventing scenarios, postulating. He used to shoot holes in my wild theories. His ones, of course, were airtight. I learned a lot from him.' He reminisced, toyed with the idea of telling her about how his grandfather had psychic abilities. Instead, he just said, 'The old man would have made a great detective.'

'He sounds fascinating. Do you always find the people you look for? I mean; some people disappear, never to be seen again.'

'I don't look for people like that; I only look for people I know I can find.' He looked out of the window as he spoke, at sheep herded by a dog. He couldn't see the shepherd, but he knew he was there.

'I don't see how you can be selective like that, how can you possibly know?'

'It's a waste of time, looking for someone you *know* won't be alive when you find them – and how do I know? *I just do.*'

She looked at him as politely as open disbelief would allow. 'Oh, come on! You don't really think you're going to pass me off with a vague statement like that, do you?'

'Well, I had hoped I might!' He allowed her a small grin.

She thought he looked uncomfortable.

'Look, it's not something that's easy to explain, so it's better not to try at all.'

She looked disappointed, but only for a fleeting moment. She immediately brightened with a new question. 'Tell me about the people you've found then. You must have quite a few stories to tell.'

'Oh, I don't think they'd be anywhere near as exciting as some of the ones you must have. Ladies first, you tell me one of yours, then I'll tell you one of mine.'

'And they say the age of chivalry is dead!' She laughed. 'Okay, where to start? Actually, I'm a freelance reporter. I worked at the News of the World, before going it alone. I didn't want to have to answer to anyone else anymore. While working at the World – I was there for five years – the police were hunting for this character the press dubbed the Midnight Man, because he always struck around midnight. It had become apparent he was active all over the country. At first, they thought more than one individual was carrying out the crimes, maybe working with others using the same MO to throw the police off the trail.

'It didn't take long before they realised it was the work of only one man. Over time, he grew bolder, taking more risks. The crimes had become more and more sexually overt in nature. They realised soon they were going to have a rapist on their hands, maybe even a murderer. Detectives didn't have any forensics, not a thing. So the police joined forces, pooling information and resources to start an elite task force dedicated to tracking him down. I had some close contacts in the force, so I knew a lot more than the public or even the papers.

'Anyway, we received this package one day – it was a video cassette – once the editor became aware of its content, she passed it on to the police, but not until *after* someone made a copy. Anyway, outside of work, I started to collate all the information from previous cases I could get my hands on.

'I was looking for something to break, but it never did. One night, just for fun, I plotted all the known case locations, onto a map, and guess what I came up with? I had more than six or seven hundred flagged points, extending all over the country. One night I was talking to a friend on the phone, just absently doodling with my pencil. I began drawing lines between the dots…all of a sudden; I said to her, *I have to go,* as if it was the most significant discovery since radium or whatever.

'Do you know why? Because what I had subconsciously doodled, was a series of spider webs, covering Manchester, Birmingham, Leeds, Nottingham and London. The spokes, the radials, every one of them running through anchors or links, extending to the far corners of the country, then I noticed something else. The spokes didn't extend to the centres. The city centres were completely empty. For a while I really, really thought I was onto something. He wasn't targeting premises; he was targeting homes; either because they were easier pickings or because he got more of a thrill from what he might find there.' She gestured, rolling a hand, inviting his response.

It was a game, and one he couldn't resist.

'Maybe, but you know what I think?' He paused, a serious look on his face. 'If you have enough dots you can join them together to make almost anything, with a little imagination, even the face of Mickey Mouse.'

She poked the tip of her tongue between her pursed lips and mimed blowing a silent raspberry. Shaking her head slowly, she reached into her bag and produced a piece of paper, which she unfolded and passed to him.

It was a map of Great Britain. On it, she'd marked several overlapping webs; the lowest one had spokes that emanated from around a central location – London. The radials linked to the spokes that extended into the farthest reaches of the map, way beyond the limits of the concentric patterns. What she'd drawn was just as she described to him.

He scratched his head. She was a seasoned reporter; did she really believe this stuff worked outside of films and books?

Yet, *something* struck a chord. 'You know, you just might be *onto* something there.'

'*I know* I am, but I just don't know what.'

'You know what we need?' He looked at her seriously.

'What do we need?'

'We need more information!'

She raised the back of her hand as if to slap him, and he raised a hand and knee in mock defence. They both grinned widely.

'Coming back to this character, you said he might get more of a thrill from what he finds in the homes than presumably he might find in an office? What makes you say that?'

'He only takes what he can carry in his pockets from what I can gather, and there's evidence he spends quite a while in the houses, going through paperwork, private things. He steals sentimental items, and then tries to blackmail the more attractive women into sex in exchange for returning the items, or for keeping quiet about other things he has discovered. I could go on and on with the details. He knows which ones are attractive, presumably from photographs he sees or finds in the house. Anyway, I was telling you about that tape earlier. It's really quite graphic. He lured one victim – I think she had emotional issues – into a meeting. He filmed the whole thing, and he could be heard telling her he was filming it. She even smiled for the camera at one point, unbelievable. He also told her if she notified the police, he'd send the tape to the News of The World. She *did* go to the police and good as his word; he sent the tape.'

'So you've seen it then?'

A slight flush coloured her face. 'Only for professional purposes, but yes, once or twice,' she admitted.

'I assume you couldn't identify him from the film?' He gave her a knowing look.

'Well, of course you don't see his face!' she said hotly. 'I'm sorry, you don't know how much stick I've had to endure as I was the one who saw it originally.'

'It's okay,' he told her, adding with a broad grin, 'did anything stand out?'

She kicked him on the shin.

'Ouch!' he said through gritted teeth. 'That really hurt!'

'That wasn't hard,' she said.

'It doesn't have to be hard to hurt.' He attempted to rub the pain away.

'We digressed; it's a little bit outside my field, but very interesting all the same. I can't believe I hadn't seen it in the press before.'

'If you *are* interested, the press christened him the 'Midnight Man'.'

'I'll look it up,' he said. 'I promise.'

'I hope you meant that, because I'm going to hold you to it.' She laughed. 'And I mean that.'

'I said I'll look it up, and then we'll see.'

The train slowed as it pulled into the station at York. When it stopped, the platform suddenly came alive with the movement of people, passengers disembarking, as others got on. The two of them fell silent as they waited for the resumption of the journey.

He asked himself a question. *Have you ever met someone before that you connect with so completely and utterly, you feel you have known them all your life?* The only time that even came close was when he met Josie, and for the first time since the journey began, he wondered if she might be thinking the same. He turned away from staring out the window, and she had her eyes on him. She smiled warmly as if she'd read his thoughts. He smiled back, but inside he was scared. Afraid he might become involved, not only in the case, but with her, too, and he didn't want to risk losing her.

Chapter 127

After a few minutes, the train resumed its journey. A tall man with a rolled up copy of Der Speigel protruding from the side pocket of his jacket, lurched up to their row of seats, and tried to sit with his rucksack still on his back. Miller exchanged looks with his new companion. She made a drinking gesture with her hand. He nodded agreement. The man decided he couldn't perch on two inches of the seat and stood up to remove the backpack. It swung dangerously close to her as he unhitched it from one shoulder and then the other. He sat across the aisle to her and promptly closed his eyes. She gave him a sharp look, then gestured Miller towards her over the table. She spoke so quietly; Miller had to lean forwards to hear what she was saying.

'Okay, so that was me. What about you?'

'Well, I don't have any unsolved cases as interesting as that. I don't have any unsolved ones, period.'

She pursed her lips and jerked her middle finger up at him.

'A number of years ago I got involved in rescuing a girl from a quasi-religious cult.' He hesitated unsure of how much to tell her.

'Come on,' she urged, 'don't hold out on me.'

An idea formed. 'It's difficult to explain really without going into boring details, but let's just say it all came about because I developed an interest in the brainwashing techniques employed by the Chinese around the time of the Korean War.'

She planted her elbows on the table between them and propped her chin on her thumbs, fingers aligned either side of her nose.

'Whilst researching that I came across an article about cults and their use of the same or similar techniques. They were operating or recruiting in all the major cities. I decided to go to London, on a field trip, and to paraphrase you.' He winked at her. 'You'll never guess what I found.' She opened her mouth to speak, but she wasn't quick enough.

Miller moved on. 'I came across not just one group, but several, all working the tourist attractions. At Piccadilly Circus, there was a group of girls. Every single one of them attractive and they were approaching young men. Openly flirting and waving leaflets at them, they were selling something as well, quasi-religious charms. They parted the men from their money and got them lining up at the edge of the pavement.

'There were two men with them, could have been Asian. One was slim, but athletic looking. The other was bulkier and stood a little back; I think he was probably a minder. He looked dangerous, but anyway the slim guy was about the age I was then. When I looked closer, I realised he was of Mediterranean, possibly even South American appearance. He had a whole harem of girls he'd recruited tucked in behind him like the pied piper. I wanted to get closer to hear what he said to them that worked so well for him,' he said, winking. 'By the time I crossed the road onto the island of Eros; a bus had pulled up, and they ferried them all aboard. He turned as he got on – and I'll never forget this – he had the most unusual eye colouration I've ever seen. Have you ever seen the colour of a lion's eye in the sunshine? What colour would you say that would be?'

'I don't know…a kind of dirty deep golden colour?' She shrugged, her face quizzical.

'Well, that's what his eyes looked like. His skin was bad; pock marked. Not so terrible it ruined his looks, but those eyes and his *magnetism* made him irresistible to young women.'

'Where has he been all my life, he sounds like just what I've been looking for.' She yawned, fanning it with her hand as she slouched in her seat. He shot her a sharp look and then noticed the German had dozed off. She was mimicking his slumped position.

'I'm not bored! My bum has gone to sleep, and it's making me tired, that's all,' she declared, wriggling herself upright.

Miller heard the trolley rattling up the aisle. 'I'm going to have a drink, and it sounds as if you could do with a coffee. Would you like one?'

Her eyes crinkled. 'I'll have tea.'

'Not long after that London trip, I spotted a headline in the paper. *Heiress goes missing in Europe.* The Times ran an in depth article on the family. Her father had made a fortune out of exporting English antiques all over the world, but primarily to the States. When he became rich enough to purchase his own estate, he changed the family name from Lake to Kale; all this had happened before she was born. Her name was Olga, and she'd vanished during a visit to Amsterdam. Apparently, she was fiercely independent and headstrong. It was probably the reason she travelled alone and in denial of her father's wealth. She wanted to believe she was just an ordinary girl, so she dressed like a hippy and hung out with like-minded, disaffected youth.'

The trolley arrived, and Miller paused, not wishing to be overheard.

When it moved off, a drunk shuffled up and fished through his pockets with some difficulty and grabbed a handful of biscuits, which he shoved onto their tray. The biscuits were mostly chipped or broken, and distinctly unappetising. The drunk said in a high, reedy voice, 'A wee biscuit to go wit' your tea?'

They thanked him, and he hovered unsteadily, examining the German with disdain. He raised the back of his hand to his mouth and confided to them. 'Drunk,' he said, jerking a thumb at the sleeping man. He swayed, checking his bearings before finally tottering away, the neck of a bottle of whiskey sticking out of a side pocket in his baggy grey jacket.

She leaned forward and picked a piece of pocket fluff from one of the biscuits. She held it up between her thumb and forefinger. 'Can you believe that?' Her face was a picture of amazement and disgust.

Miller told her the rest of the story.

'Is that it?'

'No, actually that wasn't the end of it. Kale decided to have them shut down. It wasn't easy. It dragged on for a while, but he did it. He obtained evidence they were harvesting vulnerable kids, especially young girls with wealthy parents. Once they'd brainwashed them and bled them dry, they got them working for them; selling all kinds of merchandise, including drugs – selling themselves – they even forced some of them to appear in porn movies. They arrested the leading pastor, but the guy with the lion's eyes and his minder got away.'

'Did they ever get them? You told me you didn't have any unsolved cases.'

'That's true, but he wasn't one of my cases. I'll tell you what I did find out about him, though, and you'd never guess. Not in a month of Sundays.'

'I'm too tired to try guessing, just tell me.'

He beckoned her closer, to whisper in her ear. 'It turned out he was wanted for the assassination of key political figures in Colombia, the Middle East and Africa.'

'You're kidding me!' She checked to make sure she hadn't woken the German.

'I kid you not,' he said, smiling. 'Beat that!'

She shook her head. 'I wish I had my recorder on for all of that. My God, is all that true?'

'He's still out there somewhere. Back then, he was calling himself Carlos. The authorities were obviously very keen to apprehend him, but no one's seen or heard of him since. Apparently, he didn't live on the commune; he and his friend acted as bodyguards for the leader and his recruiters while they were out. At some point, he realised he'd make a good recruiter himself. It was thought he had a vested interest, because so much money was unaccounted for. It had been transferred all over the place, and vast sums had been taken out in cash, that sort of thing.'

The half-empty cups had become cold; the biscuits untouched. 'For a while, I lived under an alias, the police had information my life was in danger.'

'How did you cope with that, it must have been really hard for you?'

'No, not really. I've been living under an alias all my life.'

'What do you mean?' She had a feeling he wasn't going to elaborate. 'Oh, come on. You can't say something like that and then not tell me!'

'Yeah, you're right. I shouldn't have said anything at all.' He couldn't let on he'd worked for Kale since.

She tried to question him further. He divulged and dodged, in equal measure.

In the hope it might encourage him to talk about himself more; she told him more about herself and then dropped a surprise on him.

'You know I told you about that tape?'

'Mm-m.' He stared out of the window.

'Guess what? I didn't tell you everything.'

'You took a copy.'

'Now, how in heavens name could you have known that? Next, you'll be saying you know what was on it!' She stretched her arms out fully and yawned. 'Sorry,' she said.

'That's okay. It's been a long journey.' He looked out of the window, thoughtful. 'But yes, it's a possibility my grandfather could have done. He was the seventh son, not the all-seeing seventh of a seventh, but he had a talent for knowing what was about to happen,' he said, turning back to face her.

She'd fallen asleep. The old devil that cheated him of happiness had intervened once more. He'd been about to ask her about dinner. *Things happen for a reason.* He couldn't afford to get too close; he wouldn't want anything to happen to her.

With her sleeping, the remainder of the journey allowed him introspection. He returned to window gazing, lost in the black holes of forgotten memories. The last three stops passed largely unnoticed.

Five minutes from Waverley, she woke up not knowing at first where she was. She recovered her faculties and asked, 'Why didn't you wake me?'

'To be honest I was enjoying the peace and quiet.'

She narrowed her eyes. 'How's that shin?'

'You looked so peaceful and serene, I guessed you needed it. I should have slept, but I have this thing about not sleeping when there are strangers around.'

'When I go, I sleep anywhere. I don't care.'

'I'm jealous, no really. I can't tell you how many times I arrive in places absolutely worn out because part of me always has to stand guard.'

She laughed. 'What do you think would happen, if you did fall asleep?'

'I don't know, but whatever it is, I'll be awake for it.' The grim look of someone who knew something bad was coming for him passed over his face. He realised he'd probably felt like that for most of his life.

She changed the subject. 'Look I don't know what your plans are now you're here, why don't we meet up a little later?'

'I'd love to, but tomorrow, I have an appointment with destiny.'

'Destiny, who's she?' she said, attempting to make light of it, forcing a smile. 'Yeah, okay. You know, you come across all mysterious and I like that, but I'm going to leave it there because if I found out different, I'd be so disappointed.' She regained her poise. 'But I loved your *stories.*'

'Look, I really enjoyed your company, but what I'm here for… When it... Sorry, I – I'm so tired I'm tongue tied! They weren't just stories. I think you know that anyway.'

She didn't answer, nor even look at him, preferring instead to stare into the distance at the darkened sky.

It's probably better this way. He knew he'd see her again. She'd have loved the bodies in the water story. *Tell her another time. She might even want to do a piece on it.*

As the train pulled in, he suddenly remembered his original plan.

'I don't suppose you heard of the Michael Simpson case?'

'Michael Simpson?' she said, looking quizzical. 'Which case was that?'

He told her, and then added cryptically. 'They think he might have been murdered.'

She arched her eyebrows, raising a silent question.

He touched his nose as if to say he would not, or could not reveal his sources.

She made a note. 'Mmm, that's interesting, I'll look into that one,' she said. 'I haven't been to Amsterdam for a while, and from what you're telling me, it's a hotbed of activity, and it's supposed to be lovely in the springtime.' She suddenly smiled at him; she didn't have to wonder if she'd see him again. She knew. After his earlier rejection, she suddenly felt better.

They exchanged business cards. He walked with her out of the station, and when they got outside, they shook hands.

First, he bowed, and then doffed an imaginary hat.

'I'll be in touch,' she said.

'I'll look forward to that,' he said, and looked at her card: *Carla Black – Freelance Journalist.*

Outside the railway station, he waited for almost half an hour. Rosetta didn't show, so he walked to his hotel and checked in. The receptionist handed him a note. He opened it.

Will call you tomorrow morning, 7:30 – R

He frowned, puzzled. *How could she have known he was coming to this particular hotel? He hadn't booked it until he'd left Ryan's.*

Mounting tiredness and the thought of an early start, led him to consider eating in the hotel restaurant, but he then decided against it. He phoned Ryan to let him know he'd arrived, but he got the answer phone, and hung up without leaving a message; he hated the things. He pulled Carla's business card from his pocket, and dialled the number. When he got to the last digit, his finger hovered over it for a moment. He completed the action.

'Carla?'

'Yes?' she answered sleepily.

'Can we meet tonight?'

There was a long pause. Miller regretted his weakness.

Finally, she said, 'There's a place I know.'

He showered, quickly getting ready. Twenty minutes later, he walked out with a spring in his step. Suddenly he was no longer tired at all.

Chapter 128

Miller found his way into the bar at the bottom of a short flight of steps near the station as Carla had directed him. Once inside, it seemed everybody was talking about the vigilante killer. A conversation between two heavily built workmen wearing tartan lumber-shirts attracted his attention.

'Somebody must've tipped him off what was happening, it's no' like you just *happen* to drop in on a place like that,' he said, wiping beer foam from the straggly tips of his moustache onto the back of his red shirt cuff.

'Aye, you're probably right.' His blue-shirted companion looked thoughtful. 'He could have seen the kidnapping and followed them.'

Red-shirt nodded slowly. 'You know, you might be right, but surely he'd have called the police in?'

'I don't think he wanted the police, but one thing is for sure, he must be one hard-arsed son o' a bitch to go in like that on his own.'

Both men supped their beer.

Red-shirt resumed the discussion. 'Aye, that's for sure. How do you know he was on his own?'

'The boy.' He looked bemused. 'Don't you *read* the papers? Police seek man, no' *men*.' Blue-shirt whispered something in his friend's ear.

Red-shirt sputtered the mouthful of beer he'd just taken back into the glass. Whatever the other man said had clearly shocked him. 'How do you know all this?'

'I have a friend on the force. He told me about it,' he said, smug with one-upmanship.

Miller shut out their talking as he compared what they'd said to what Carla had told him on the train. He wondered if she and Blue-shirt had the same contact. *That would be too much of a coincidence.*

The raised voice of Blue-shirt at the bar drew his focus back to their ongoing exchange.

'Aw c'mon, you wouldn't have wanted to face two Rottweiler dogs and two men, no' on their own turf like that. I mean, what kind o' man would do that?'

'His dad probably would, or an uncle, maybe another relative?' Red-shirt offered.

'No, this was one man, remember. I reckon it was ex-military, someone like that. Besides, the father has an alibi. I know it couldn't be him anyway. He's no' the type.'

'Aye, you're probably right. Another beer?'

Blue-shirt laughed. 'O' go on, twist my arm!'

Red ordered two more beers.

'I mean that business with the bat,' Blue-shirt continued. 'He shoved it right up their arses...*right* up, I'm telling you. I mean, that's got to be some deterrent, that.' He shuddered.

'You know, I thought about that after you whispered it to me. This guy hasn't just come out o' nowhere. I reckon he's done something like this before.'

'Well if he had, the press would have gotten hold o' it and my friend in the force would've told me.'

'I didn't mean exactly that. I meant how easy he did it. You know I'd have taken the law into my own hands if it was one o' mine, but to do that afterwards? For fuck's sake, that's the work of someone who's comfortable around death.'

'I guess you're right, it's got to be someone who's killed before, that's for sure. If I had to stick my neck out, I'd say it was a squaddie, back from Iraq or Afghanistan.'

The men lifted their glasses and drank. Another man approached and asked, 'D'you fancy a nip o' whiskey, boys?'

The two men shrugged at each other and downed their beers in unison. 'Aye, why no'?'

Miller checked his watch. Either he was early, or she was late. It occurred to him she might stand him up. The vigilante talk had intrigued him. After taking a long swig from his pint, he studied the motif on the glass: *Northern Lights.* He drained the rest of the heady brew and put the empty glass down.

The conversation he'd just overheard, called Kirk to mind. Highly trained, cool under fire, it was exactly the sort of thing he'd have been capable of doing. He remembered an incident when he was at school. Three older lads made the mistake of setting about him on their school-leaving day, the last day of term. All three were big and on the school's rugby team. Kirk must have been in his mid-forties. He dropped low, quick as a flash. His hands on the floor between his legs formed a central pivot, about which he spun one leg parallel to the ground, and six inches above it, the extended limb came round like a scythe and chopped the legs from underneath two of the lads. Both hit the ground hard, landing on their backs. Kirk jumped up and caught the third in a painful arm lock, and tightened his grip until the boy arched his back, in a vain attempt to ease the pain.

'Thanks for the game, boys,' he said through gritted teeth.

The boy gasped, 'I surrender!'

'Surrender? We were only playing here, weren't we?' Kirk's eyes were cold, one inch from madness.

Eyes wide, they exchanged worried looks. 'Of course we were, sir!'

Kirk had pulled back from the edge. With eyes still flinty, he released his grip on the boy and pushed him into the other two.

'That's good, but don't ever *play* with me again, sometimes I get carried away,' he said, darkly. 'Now that we're clear, off you go!'

As they left, the tallest boy turned and said, 'How did you *do* that?' There was a hint of admiration in his voice. 'I mean what was that thing you just did, with the legs?'

For a moment, it looked as if Kirk wouldn't reply, but when he did, he said only four words. 'Combat training, Korean style.'

Chapter 129

Miller often wondered what Kirk might be up to now. He hadn't seen him since the early hours of 25th April 1980, when he was nineteen years old. The exact date stuck in his mind because Kirk changed the course of his life that day. The brainwashing, the Korean War, something he told him to do. *Look it up.*

After wondering so many times what had happened to him, he decided to track him down, finally finding him in a nursing home for the elderly. Miller became a regular visitor, and Kirk was always pleased to see him, keen to catch up on the life of his former pupil.

The last time they'd met, Kirk held onto his hand a long time as they shook. The staff had him propped up in bed, his face hollow and gaunt with pain; the steeliness had left his eyes, but the chipped tooth grin was the same.

'Did you live up to your name, Miller?'

The question baffled him, but he kept his confusion to himself. 'I think so, sir.'

Kirk relaxed into his pillow. 'Good, I'm glad. You haven't found yourself a woman, though, have you? You've been avoiding the question ever since you've been coming to see me. You *haven't*, have you?'

Kirk's grip increased perceptibly, the cool and papery texture of his skin more apparent as he did so.

Miller shook his head. 'No.'

'Don't end up like me, son. Alone in bed, waiting for the night to come.' His voice was dry. He licked his lips.

Miller handed him a thin plastic cup of water.

Fixing his gaze on Miller as he sipped, Kirk wiped the wetness from his upper lip. 'There's nothing wrong with you, boy, just moving in the wrong direction, running away when you should be chasing. Get yourself a younger woman.' A light shone in his eyes. 'I had one once, a French mistress at the school, she was younger than me. She'd have looked after me when I got old.' He sighed. 'Didn't work out, though.'

'Why not? What prevented you?'

His eyes dimmed. 'It's a long story and one you wouldn't understand or care for much. Just suffice to say, it was the nights.' He drew a short breath. 'I used to disappear in the night, back into the hell I'd escaped from. It scared her. Don't you let *your* hell hold you back from your destiny.' His eyes, storm no longer on their horizons, were calm and grey. They locked onto Miller's. '*You*...get chasing. Do you understand what I'm saying to you, boy?'

He nodded.

'That's the spirit,' he said, finally relinquishing his grip on Miller's hand.
'Good night, sir.'
'Get chasing, boy,' he said, grimacing, almost folding with pain.

Night came. Kirk was in Korea again. Once more at the fork in the road he'd
come to know so well, and this time instead of turning right, he turned left,
running more or less in the direction of the river. His decision to go south, he
remembered well. It was the road less travelled by, but now of course, the other
direction had become the one less travelled by. Still heading generally south, he
kept above the line of the road higher in the hills, where the tree line more or less
remained intact. He hadn't seen anything other than sporadic Chinese activity for
half a day; he decided to make his way down. He reached a village, a single street
of roughly thatched single storey stone dwellings. It looked deserted, apart from a
few chickens scratching in the dirt and a mangy dog that looked suspiciously at
him, emitting a low growl. Desperate for food, he couldn't chance walking down
the main road; instead, he skirted round the back. Turning a corner, he stopped and
peered down the flank of a storage building. Kirk had yet to see or hear anyone
else. He poked his head round the gap between two buildings. It was clear. He
moved rapidly. He kept low, aware he was exposed. Somebody stepped out quite
suddenly in front of him. A soldier appeared, and he looked as startled as Kirk, but
he seemed friendly, all grinning teeth and a wide flat face.
    Kirk grinned back at him.
    Still grinning, the soldier swung his rifle up and shot him in the chest.
    He fell, clutching at the wound, looking at the heart blood on his hands in
disbelief. Unbelievable pain seared into his chest and right through him, the sky
above bluer than he'd ever known. For some crazy reason, a line from his
favourite Robert Frost poem entered his head and at last, he knew.
    So that's what would have happened if I'd chosen the other way.

Miller returned the following morning, having woken with a start in the
middle of the night. In the brightness of his room, he thought he'd seen Kirk. Tall
and proud, he looked younger than he ever recalled seeing him. He was dressed in
a soldier's uniform. He grinned at Miller and then faded away. Miller lay in bed
unable to sleep for a long time after.

He reported as usual to the office. The matron sat him down; he knew
something had happened to Kirk before she told him. Her mouth was moving in
slow motion it seemed. Her tongue and her teeth working behind her lips
enunciating her vowels, he stared right through her, transfixed.
    'Are you all right, Mr Miller?'
    'Huh? Oh, I'm sorry. I—'
    'You didn't hear a word I said, did you?'
    'Sorry, but yes I did hear you. I do that sometimes, just drift, but I did hear.
Please, carry on.'

'The doctor thinks his heart gave out. He was asleep, he wouldn't have felt a thing.'

Miller wished he'd gotten to know Kirk better. *Why is it we always think like this when it's too late?*

The matron spoke again, 'I think he knew he didn't have long. Last night he handed me this and asked me make sure you got it when you came by.' She held a hardcover book in her hand; she stood, leaned over the desk and passed it to him.

He took it in his hand, surprised at the lightness of it. The dust jacket was missing, but inscribed into the faded blue cover in pale gold leaf, the title and the author's name read:

Mountain Interval.

Robert Frost.

Chapter 130

He'd made his mind up to talk to Carla about the sequence of events that led him to Scotland.

'Daydreaming again were we?' Carla was dressed in a black leather bomber jacket with a synthetic black fur collar that matched her hair in its colour and spikiness perfectly. She looked taller than she had on the train. He stood, and pulled out a chair for her.

She declined his offer to take her jacket. 'It's so cold in here!'

'Are you sure you're a reporter?' The Northern Light's beer he'd consumed too quickly loosened his tongue and lit his eyes with mischief.

A vague smile widened her mouth, the white tips of her even teeth exposed behind lush red cherry lips. 'Why do you ask that?'

'You could be a fashion model.'

She pursed her lips coyly; the lipstick accentuated the fullness of her lips.

He found himself staring at her.

A waiter appeared, and they ordered food and drinks. The meal passed with the sort of conversation that fitted easily in between mouthfuls. The Dutch courage from the beer had dissipated. *If you tell her, will she think you're a nut?*

Carla's nose for a story told her Miller wanted to tell her something. Overriding her natural impatience, she waited. *He'll open up soon.*

The staff had cleared the table of everything but the coffee they were drinking. They were the last people in there.

'I'm curious, Miller, why the change of mind? I mean, I don't usually drop hints to get a guy to take me out, and this is going to sound terribly conceited, but I'm not short on offers.'

Miller looked around at the empty tables and chairs. At last, they could speak without fear of anyone overhearing. 'You only live once, that I know of. I've been going through some changes. I don't know what they're all about, or what they might mean, or even if they are all part of the same thing, but if there's just this *one* shot at things. I mean, if I can't change it, then at least I want to understand it.' He became flustered. 'Can I start at the beginning? I'll try not to bore you.'

'The people who bore me,' Carla reassured him, 'are the ones who presume to think they're interesting. To them, it's unthinkable they might be boring. You don't bore me at all, far from it,' she said. Lifting a handbag onto her lap and fidgeting around inside it, she pulled out a compact mirror and checked both sides of her face before putting it back in the bag. Leaning forwards, her elbows on the table, she supported her chin on her hands and said, 'Go for it.'

He grimaced and scratched the back of his neck, unsure exactly where the beginning was and then inhaled deeply. 'This isn't going to be easy,' he said, exhaled a short puff of air and then began. 'When I was a kid, I was involved in an incident where three of my friends died.'

'That's awful, what happened? How old were you?'

'I was fifteen. We were on a field trip with the school.'

He'd reached the point where the boys had drowned, and he realised he'd tightly twisted the corner of his napkin and wrung it between his hands; he let it go, laying it on the table. Slowly, it unravelled itself.

He stalled and shook his head. 'I don't know if I can just stop there, without telling you about Dr Ryan.'

'So tell me about Dr Ryan!'

He looked at his watch. 'I'm going to have to leave it there; I have to be up early.'

Carla put a hand on his shoulder and squeezed it as she passed him to visit the cloakroom. He called for the bill, and while he waited alone, his thoughts turned to Ryan. In the dim corner of the deserted room, the light from outside threw horizontal bars of light across the table top nearest and up the wall. In the shadows, he imagined Ryan sitting there, one eye narrowed and focused on him.

That book I never wrote, Miller. I never told you this. I had a great interest in the paranormal from an early age; meeting her only fuelled it further. One element that interested me particularly – because it was recurrent – was the part water played in sightings and hauntings. So much testimony down through the years, not provable of course, but to me it made sense. If ghosts, spirits and apparitions are residual traces of energy fired by a tragic or traumatic event – recorded somehow in the fabric of buildings or rocks or places – and if that energy is electrical in some way...I mean, we know people can generate static electricity. We can measure its fields and detect changes in it with polygraphs, EEG and so on. We know people on rare occasions can generate enough power to spontaneously combust, although we don't know how. Water is a conductor of electricity. Could it be then, it aids the playback of whatever impulses have been recorded during extreme circumstances, such as suicides or murders? I think so, and I think it goes a long way to explain why you see your apparitions most clearly in the rain. And here's another fascinating thought for you I seem to have overlooked until now. Your friends perished on 15th July, St Swithun's day.

Miller shrugged at the shadowy corner. 'Is that supposed to mean something to me?'

It marks the anniversary of the mine disaster that took place nearby in 1857. It rained so hard it flooded the workings, killing dozens of people. Your friends drowned on St Swithun's day.

'You've lost me, what's the significance?'

Local superstition has had it for years, on that day, the ghosts from the mine return to walk among the living. Belief is a powerful thing, Miller. If you believe in something strongly enough, anything is possible.

'Ryan, that's just fairy tale stuff.'

Is it? Consider the Tibetans – they've mastered a technique based entirely on the belief they can create a thought creature. A Tulpa they call it. Other people can see these things, as well. There was a documented case, where an English woman was able to create one following the prescribed methods, but she lacked the inner spirituality to control it, she had to get help to get rid of it. Do you believe in ghosts, Miller?

He laughed. 'It's a bit late for me to be in denial!'

'Who were you talking to?' Carla cast her eyes about the room.

'Was I talking?' Miller drew his hand across his face and said, 'Phew! Thank heavens I only had one of those beers. I've got to go.'

Chapter 131

Outside, Miller checked his watch. 'I'll walk you to your hotel. You're only five minutes from mine. I haven't stopped talking about myself all evening. We really should have talked more about you, Carla.'

'Don't worry about it.' She smiled. 'I want to hear more about you.'

'I don't think we have time.'

'Come on, at least until we get to my hotel.'

'It was July 15th, a Tuesday,' a voice rose within him, circumventing all barriers to it, catching him unawares. His story, rarely told, tripped off his tongue. *What are you doing, Bruce? I'm never drinking Northern Lights again!*

The recollections were vivid; he brought them to life for her. 'The tragedy was bad enough, but when they started pulling these old skeletons out of the water from years before...'

As they arrived outside her hotel ten minutes later, he was still talking. 'I don't know what's happening to me. It's like everything converging at once, outside my control. I can't make any real sense of it.' He stared up into the yellow haze that held back the darkness around the streetlight. 'It's like everything has been coming to this. Whatever it is. That's why I called Doctor Ryan.'

'What did he think was happening to you?'

'Look, I've said too much already.'

'Miller, I want to know what's happening to you.'

'Strange dreams, that's all.'

'You're not going to tell me?' She seemed disappointed.

He took a sharp intake of breath. His lips pressed tight together.

'Come on, Miller, answer the question.'

'It's complicated.' He exhaled.

'I don't care, *tell* me.'

He focused on her. 'I keep having nightmares where I wake up on the point of drowning and that's not all. Lately, I've found if I concentrate hard enough, I can almost tell what people are thinking. Not with everybody, and not all the time.' He told her everything he'd told Ryan, with the exception of the Simpson dream. 'Do you think I'm going crazy?' He was staring at her the way he did on the train – not seeing her – but seeing *through* her. His eyes came back into focus. He looked exhausted.

She'd been tempted to interrupt him, but she held off, not wanting to stifle the words flowing out of him. It had been like watching a self-imposed exorcism.

'Holy shit,' she said, and whistled low.

Miller trembled.

Suddenly she wanted nothing more than to hold him.

They'd been outside her hotel for a quarter of an hour; she shivered in the dropping temperature. 'Are you going to come in?' she said, and reaching for his hand pulled him up the steps.

'Carla, listen. I have an appointment tomorrow with someone who apparently holds the key to my destiny and it's so late.' He left her by the entrance doors. He was ten feet away before she even thought of protesting.

He blew her a kiss. 'There's nothing I want more than to come in with you, but it's going to have to wait, at least until I get back.'

She called out after him, 'I won't be here when you get back!'

Carla slipped into her room and dropped her handbag onto the seat of the armchair. Removing her shoes and jacket, she then wriggled out of her jeans. Semi-naked, she admired herself in the mirror, and then leaned down into her bag to pull out her voice recorder. It was no bigger than a pack of ten cigarettes. She pushed the rewind button, held it close to her ear and clicked play.

When she decided to pass the time of day with Miller on the train, she'd not expected to find a potential story in him. As the journey and the conversation progressed, she discovered there were at least two, and as she reflected on the content of the tape, she realised Miller *himself* was a story. His reticence annoyed her; she was going to have to get closer. She hadn't had a challenge in a long time, but first she had to get to grips with the Vigilante case.

Putting the recorder down, she picked up her phone, selected a name from the menu and pressed the connect button. She knew it was late, but Michael Brady never slept before one o'clock in the morning.

'Hello, Michael, it's Carla.'

'Carla? Oh, Carla *Blue!* It's been such a long time... Is it really you?'

'Yes, it's really me.' *Carla Blue.* When the tape turned up at The News of The World, he'd been an officer in the Met and had heard through the grapevine she'd watched it. He called her at work to talk about it. Afterwards, they had a brief fling. It didn't last, he outlived his usefulness, but she remained on good terms with him. She never fell out with people like him. *In her job, you never knew when you might need them again.*

'You still there?'

'Yes, I am. I was just thinking, when are you lot ever going to let me live that down?'

He chuckled down the other end of the line. 'Well, how are you?'

'I'm very well and you?' She didn't allow him to answer, getting straight to the point. 'Michael, I'm putting a piece together on the Vigilante murders and I'm struggling to get information. Is that something you can help with?' She held her breath.

'Oh, Carla, you're putting me on the spot here.'

'Michael, I'm sorry, but I don't have anyone else I can ask. If you help me, I'll owe you one,' she lowered her voice suggestively.

'Look, Carla, they're keeping this one under wraps from the press, if anything gets out...it could get sticky.'

'Michael, all I want is to be there with a finger on the button, so when the story does break…'

He sighed. 'I wish there was a way I could help you. Where are you?'

'I'm in Edinburgh.'

'Do you want me to come over?' He sounded hopeful.

'Have you anything for me, information wise?'

Brady spun it out. 'I might have.'

'Oh, come on, Michael, don't hold back on me.' She paused and then said, 'How are things with you and Maggie, by the way?' Met with silence, she bit her lip.

'I've got one thing, but you must promise you never heard it from me. You remember I used to work with John Kennedy at the Met?'

'Vaguely,' she lied.

'Well, it turns out the baseball bat recovered from the scene of the killings used to belong to him.'

After putting the phone down, she pulled out the 'Midnight Man' cobweb map and studied it again. It helped her think outside the box, and it always seemed to work best when she was a little bit unfocused, but it wasn't working tonight.

She thought about Miller. *What are you really doing in Scotland?* She knew he wanted her, but whatever it was he was here for, was more important. Her curiosity was aroused. *I have an appointment with destiny.*

What she'd said to him about being disappointed if he turned out to be a bull-shitter was true. She'd spent half her life avoiding womanisers. She could smell them a mile off, but Miller. He was a mystery.

She poured a second glass of wine and returned to studying Midnight's movements.

When she'd first started, it was obvious the patterns centred around cities because of the road systems, but the more she thought about it, the more she realised, when you have over seven hundred points to join up, there's a good chance the *appearance* of a pattern would form. What Miller had said somewhere along the line on the train, came back to her.

The only reason this character has avoided city centres is because they are mostly business premises protected by alarms and CCTV cameras. There are cameras that cover the streets. London has one of the highest levels of street surveillance in the world, and he likes to move around, blending in. He knows he'll be caught somewhere on a camera. He won't risk breaking into those houses, or flats within city centres like London, because they're usually owned by the very wealthy, who protect themselves and their property with sophisticated security systems, even guards.

There had been a number of Midnight attacks in the suburbs surrounding London. She still had a contact in the Met, and he'd told her there was evidence to suggest he sometimes targeted individuals connected to victims of previous burglaries. Her reporter's nose caught a whiff of something. She was unsure what it was. *He put strangers together just for the fun of it.*

Carla started folding the map to put it away, thinking how impossible it was to predict where he'd strike next. She wondered what his motives were, recalling what Miller said on the train. *You have so many dots you could join them all together and make the face of Mickey Mouse.*

She glanced at her phone. *A text from her man in the Met. How strange.* She'd literally just thought about him, remembering a call she owed him from months back.

Off the record, they quite often helped each other, and now he'd provided her with the location of the latest confirmed activities of the Midnight man. *He's in Scotland!*

Quickly unfolding the map again, she located the town. She took her coloured pencil and marked it. A shiver of excitement ran through her. It was less than ten miles from the vigilante attack and it had occurred earlier on the same day. There were so many dots on the map, though not many in Scotland. *Surely, that's too close for coincidence?*

Something he'd discovered during the burglary might have led him to the paedophiles. He could have set an accomplice onto them, or he might have done it himself. It could be him.

Coincidence. Miller had said it was partly the reason he was in Scotland. Now she'd had a run of them herself. She googled the word and read several articles on the subject, but none summed it up better than the one line quote she'd read first of all. *Coincidence, if traced far enough back, becomes inevitable.*

She couldn't remember a man turning her down before. The urge to ring Miller became overwhelming. Bemused, even angry, she conceded he was different. He'd aroused her curiosity on many levels.

She imagined what would happen if she picked up the phone and called him. *I'm laying here all warm and soft, fresh from the bath. I've rubbed moisturising lotion all over my body. I've shaved myself for you, imagine. I'm guessing you'll love how smooth it is. I'm wearing just a thong. I was wondering if you'd help me with something.* Would Miller agonise at the other end of the line? She allowed the fantasy to evaporate. He was just too much for her to fathom right now and she didn't want to face rejection. *Carla, I'd love to, but right now, I need to sleep.*

She bit into her lower lip, and her imagination sparked another fantasy. 'Oh, boy, Miller,' she breathed to herself. 'I haven't even got *started* with you yet.'

Miller turned his phone off. *If anyone needs me, it can wait till morning.*

Waves of exhaustion swept over him, each stronger than the last. He slipped deep into slumber and then awoke unsure of how long he'd slept. He inspected his watch. The luminous dial showed it was almost two in the morning. Just when he most needed sleep, he found himself embarking on one of his restless phases, waking in the night, limbs surging with electrical activity that drove him from bed to pace around the room. He believed it to be a side effect of extended celibacy, an effect that was sometimes beneficial in gaining insights, or problem solving. Tonight it was counter-productive. *You need a woman.*

Usually it took two months before the symptoms became intolerable. This particular sojourn had crept up on him; he should have known from some of the wilder dreams. He lay on the bed and thought about Carla. *You know the quickest way for you to get to sleep, Miller.*

He rolled off the bed and started deep knee squatting until his thigh muscles burned and then got back in. He plugged in his headphones and listened to an achingly beautiful song that personified the loneliness he felt from his self-imposed abstinence from meaningful relationships, a kind of penance.

When you have no one, none can hurt you.

A burgeoning realisation crept up on him. Kirk was right; he'd cheated himself out of happiness for long enough. *Too tired to think anymore.*

He drifted into the soft embrace of sleep.

Chapter 132

The following morning, Carla phoned Tanner.

'Hello, John? It's Carla,' she said, sounding sheepish.

Tanner flipped his pad back to its first page. He'd titled it *New Year, new pad.* Four months later, dog-eared and filled with notes, he was on the verge of starting a new one. He found the entry he was looking for two pages in. *4th January – Carla?* The question mark was large and florid.

'Carla?' he said, the sarcasm in his voice, undisguised. 'I only called you three months ago.'

'I'm so sorry, you know how it is. I was working on this story, getting nowhere fast.'

'You should have said. I might have been able to help.'

'I don't think so, John. It's way out of your area, Newcastle, as a matter of fact.'

'Newcastle? That's way out of your area, too, surely?'

'You know me, I'll go anywhere there's a potential story.'

Tanner racked his brains, and tried to figure out what he'd heard from up there lately. *January?* 'You've got me, Carla. What was it you were working on?

'Oh, it doesn't matter now. I'm onto something else, and I suddenly remembered I owed you a call. Did you get anywhere with that gipsy you were trying to trace?'

'God, Carla, where to start. The short answer is no. We're still looking for him.'

'Remind me. What was the background to it?'

When he'd finished, she whistled a single, low note. 'Now that's interesting – if you are still stuck in a bit, I'd love to look at it off the record, you know.'

'We'll see. What are you on at the moment then?'

'Have you heard about the Vigilante case recently that happened up North?'

'You're up north again, Carla?' His heart sank a dread realisation upon him. 'What's the attraction up there?' *Brady.* He recalled their uneasy conversation of a few days before. 'I guess you've been talking to Brady.'

'Well, of course I have!' She knew all about his rivalry with Brady, how much he despised him for winning promotion over him, how he'd blamed Kennedy for making it easy for him to join his ex-wife in Scotland.

'John, listen to me. I only ever maintain professional relationships with my contacts these days. He was a mistake, you know that, but I have to ask you something about Kennedy.'

'Kennedy?' Tanner sounded surprised. 'How have we got onto him?'

'John, has he said anything about the Vigilante case, anything at all?'

Puzzled by the question, he hesitated.

She heard him draw breath at the other end of the line.

'I'm pretty sure he said something like, "We've got enough problems of our own, so they can bloody-well keep him", why do you ask?'

'I heard the men who kidnapped the boy had been mutilated with a baseball bat.'

'I heard that, too. Let the punishment fit the crime, so to speak. Hang on a minute.' Theresa entered his office with tea for him. He winked his thanks and she smiled. His old feelings for Carla disappeared as he watched her leave. He lifted the cup to his lips and blew across the hot liquid before he sipped.

'Are you there?' Carla demanded. 'The bat had the initials JFK on it.'

Tanner almost choked on his tea.

The first time she'd met Tanner, the police wanted to interview her because she was the one who'd taken delivery of the package and she'd seen the suspect. She remembered it well.

'Carla Black?' He didn't wait for confirmation. 'I'm Detective Inspector Michael Brady, and this is DI John Tanner. We need to ask you a few questions, if you don't mind. We have him on CCTV, but it isn't the best image. We're having it enhanced as we speak. Did he say anything to you?'

'He said, "That's one for the internet". I didn't know what he was talking about; he just handed it to me and left.'

'You got a close-up look at him, though. How old would you say he was? Were there any distinguishing features you could tell us about, any moles, scars? Anything?'

'No, not really, other than he was heavily built and hard-eyed. He looked like he'd been in a few scrapes, and he was older up close than he looked when I first saw him approaching. I realised it was because he'd either dyed his hair or had a black wig on.'

'What makes you say that?'

'From the lines on his face, he should have had at least *some* grey hair.'

'And that's it?'

'Yes, I'm afraid it is.' Her eyes narrowed as a memory drew into focus. 'Wait a minute. This is going to sound daft, but I've just remembered. He sounded just like Clint Eastwood,' she paused. 'He also had the same hands as the guy on the DVD.'

The detectives exchanged looks. 'Did he?' Brady said.

Why do you say these things, Carla? Her simple statement had given away she'd watched the film. Quickly trying to distance herself from the remark, saying with a thin smile, 'Well, that's what I heard, anyway.' As she showed the two detectives out, each slipped her a card without the other one's knowledge.

She accepted both.

Chapter 133

Saturday Morning, 7 April 2007.

Miller's eyes snapped open. His mobile was buzzing and spinning around on the dressing table. It took him a moment to remember where he was.

He rolled onto his back, pulled his arm out from under the pillow and squinted at his watch. *7:30 a.m.*

He scooted down to the foot of the bed, leaned over to the dressing table and answered it.

'Miller, it's Rosetta. Be ready in half an hour.'

'Okay,' he said, and inwardly groaned. *Half an hour!*

He flopped back onto the bed and collected his thoughts. After looking at his watch a second time, he sprang up off the bed and started getting ready. Whenever he was away, he left his watch on all night, always. He had an irrational fear something might happen and he'd have to dash out and leave it behind. Yet when he was at home, he left it off. *What's the difference? You're crazy, Miller.*

He hadn't slept well at all; the shadows had plagued him all night from the dark recesses of the hotel room in ways they'd not done since he was a child. Then, they had scared the life out of him. He'd see them scurry just out of his line of sight, and no matter how quickly he turned to look, they would be gone. It was years before he could sleep with the light off. Yet still their occasional whispers would wake him, and he'd sit bolt upright in bed listening hard to the fading sounds that seemed to come from within his own ears. Once he'd realised they were harmless, beneficial even, he began to see them in a different light.

It was another reason for not having a relationship. What sort of woman would understand such things without judging him crazy? It was a question not many other men had to face. It was easier to avoid the issue.

Lately, the shadows had been more active, conspiring with his dreams, and warning him of something. He hadn't yet figured out what it was.

It took ten minutes to shower and pack. In reception, he discovered breakfast was included, so he checked out first, and wandered through to the restaurant with barely enough time for a fresh juice, coffee and croissant. Once finished, he picked up his holdall and made his way out and down the steps to the pavement.

A Range Rover with blacked out windows drew up, the passenger window rolled down. The driver was a young woman. She leaned towards him.

'Miller, get in, I don't think you were followed. I'm Rosetta, by the way.'

Followed? Who would have followed him? Her appearance wasn't as he'd expected. He'd imagined she'd be matronly looking. It would be easy to forgive someone for thinking the daughter of a former nun might look frumpy, wearing loose old-fashioned clothes that concealed an ample frame. She was quite the opposite, slim, flat chested and fashionably dressed; her hair gathered and tied up in a Japanese style topknot. He peered at her through the window. She reminded him of someone he couldn't quite place.

'Well, what are you waiting for? Get in the back.'

He opened the door, stowed the holdall on the back seat and stepped in next to it.

'Sorry about that, it's early for me. I haven't woken up properly.'

Her laugh was a melody. 'Where I come from, the day starts at first light.'

She looked at the rear view and side mirrors, and indicated to pull out. Her hair was a pale strawberry colour. It fascinated him. The insides of her lips showed pink as she pursed them, deep in concentration as she slipped out into the traffic. The car accelerated smoothly into a suitable gap.

'Have we got far to go?'

'It'll take less than half an hour, probably twenty minutes, that's all. We're just outside Edinburgh. Once we clear the city, I'm going to have to ask you to put this on.'

She passed him a black hood over her shoulder.

'It's a precaution,' she explained. 'Mother has people looking for her all over the place, some of them just want a reading.'

'And the others?'

'It's complicated, but let's just say, it's to do with the church. We lived in Brighton for years, at least until I was five years old.' She laughed. 'I prefer the clean Scottish air and acid rain here.'

'I guessed from your accent you must have been here for a long time. What about the neighbours where you live?'

'Nobody knows. She rarely sees anyone else these days. You're the first in years.'

'So, what does she want to see me for that's so urgent?'

'In a little while you can ask her yourself.'

They travelled more or less in a straight line heading south. Looking out through the window at the city streets, he'd always imagined Edinburgh was on a scale comparable to London, but already the area was becoming less populated as they neared the outskirts.

'Miller, lie down and put the hood on for me now, will you?'

He did as she asked.

Ten minutes later, the car bumped down an unmade road. He woke with a jolt into the enveloping darkness of the hood. He put his hands up to his face and felt the cloth as if to check he actually was awake.

'You can take that off in a minute, we're nearly there,' she told him.

'I must have fallen asleep.'

She chuckled. 'You do a fair impression of a big motorbike, snoring away, you were.'

The car came to a halt. Rosetta killed the engine.

'I'm really sorry about this, but I can't let you take the hood off yet, not until we're inside.' She opened the door, took his arm, helped him out and led him to the front door.

'Step in two paces,' she warned.

He raised his foot gingerly.

'Okay, we're there; you can put your foot down.'

He lowered the foot. The air inside the hood was stale and warm; he could still smell the coffee on his breath. The door creaked open, it sounded heavy on its hinges. A gloved hand touched his and pulled him forward; his sense of direction became confused. He hadn't noticed before she was wearing gloves.

'You can take it off now.' Rosetta's voice no longer came from in front of him.

Miller removed it, and blinked at the light; a woman's outline was silhouetted against the brightness pouring in from the window behind. It took a moment for his eyes to adjust. The woman in front looked just like Rosetta, perhaps a year or two older.

'You didn't say you had a sister,' he said over his shoulder.

'I'm Rosetta's mother. Sorry about the hood, I told her there was no need, but she gets these things in her head.' The light of the window permeated the loose strands of her hair and they floated, charged with static, fine and fairy-like in a golden aura.

He didn't need to be told he was in the presence of The Sister, she held out a silken-gloved hand, and he took it. She led him down the crooked hall into an oak-beamed drawing room, where hand-carved linen-fold oak panelling extended halfway up the walls. The small windowpanes broke up the light and threw corners and recesses into shadow and cast shapes across the swirling autumnal patterned carpet.

She motioned for him to sit down at a small round table. There were two chairs; she took the one opposite.

Some of Ryan's reverence for her had rubbed off on him and he felt in awe of her.

She had avoided eye contact until they were seated, but now settled them on him. Calm, green and all seeing, she held his attention easily. Her face oval, with skin smooth and pale as alabaster, she exuded warmth. Miller couldn't detect a single age line in her complexion; her hair was devoid of grey. If Rosetta were twenty-five years old, The Sister would have to be at least in her early forties, based on the assumption that, as a good catholic girl, she was of consenting age when she became pregnant.

'Finished?' A curious smile played on her lips.

There could be no secrets in the presence of The Sister. What Ryan had said was true.

'Don't be afraid. There's no need. I've been waiting for you a long time.' She shifted her gaze to watch the approach of Rosetta, who brought them tea. She placed his cup on a saucer in front of him. Tiny swirls of steamy mist converged from the edge of the cup into the centre, where rising up it formed an ethereal spire of vapour. The scent found its way into his nostrils. *Lemon tea.*

'I haven't had a cup of that type of tea since my grandfather died,' he said wistfully.

'You miss him, don't you?' Her voice was warm, a lilting Irish brogue, soft as the summer drizzle he'd felt when they put his grandfather in the ground, buried with the two ounces of Polish soil he'd carried with him everywhere, so he never felt far from home.

He nodded slowly.

'Every one of us has a purpose in this life; it's like a rope. It pulls us through and binds us all together as we head along its length. We are the fibres that twist, turn and eventually break away. Some of us meet along the way, our strands entwine, and we share the journey, sometimes for a long time. Some will twist away around the bend and never meet with the other again. I see all these things, and it hurts me to sit on my hands, to have to watch it go by as it will. I can't interfere, not directly.

'I know how it *feels* when a wildlife cameraman is compelled to watch while nature takes its course, knowing he so easily could have rescued the calf which is about to be devoured. It's why I had to wait for you to come to me. I first spied you out in a vision I had many years ago, our strands touched for the first time. Did you feel it? Your grandfather did, but he was weakened, and not long for this world.

'I tried to link with you many times, but wanting to forget what you saw, you switched yourself off. You were in denial. In truth, you couldn't know, you were too young. It's only right you should come now, when you're ready. We are all born, and we all die eventually. Those things are facts. We cannot change the end, but we can change the journey, not go to our fate in a straight line, go round the houses a little bit, and enjoy the view.'

She took a breath; he hadn't noticed her breathing before.

'We don't always see our purpose from the ground, wrapped up as we are in the struggle to just keep going. When we are in the rope, in the coils, it's as if we are going round and round, going nowhere. When we start our ascent, we might see it if we look back and have the where-with-all to figure it out. Everyone has a part to play; they may not see it right now. They may *never* see it. Many don't make sense of it until their last days. Some will see it just as the light fades from their eyes. There are others, like you, blessed with second chances, a third or even more, given a chance to grow. There have been, and there will be times, when you can make no sense of any of it, but you were made to be strong, as were we all. You must find your strength.

'The course of your life changed years ago, and it's taken all this time to find your way back. You have a lot of catching up to do. It is why coincidence grows around you every day, why synchronicity dogs your footsteps. Part of you always knew. Your grandfather knew. Why do you think he taught you the things he did? You are slowly remembering. It is why you chose your profession. It is why you dream the way you do. You are coming out of the coils, ascending the rope toward your destiny.'

Miller took a sip of his tea. It tasted exactly as his grandfather used to make it.

'Can I ask a couple of questions?' He didn't wait for an answer. 'You're not just avoiding people who want their palms read without an appointment.' Miller scrutinised her face. 'You're hiding here, aren't you?'

Her eyes wavered almost imperceptibly as she glanced over his shoulder to Rosetta, who nodded her approval.

'To answer one of your questions, we are not hiding, but we don't want to be found. The Catholic Church has been trying to persuade me for *years* to return to the fold. I don't need the hassle. And now there are people looking for us, or more particularly, for something they believe we have.' She paused, her curious smile deepened. 'To answer your other question, Vera is a part of me that is long past, to use that name you'd have to have known me back then. When the Church employed me, I was Sister Verity, and when I left them to work for the poor, I became known as The Sister. Just call me Sister, that'll be fine by me.'

Lifting his tea to his lips, Miller met her gaze. He hadn't asked the second question, he'd only thought it.

For a minute, they sat in silence.

Chapter 134

Stella stood at the side of Ryan's bed as he drifted in and out of consciousness, watching over him. His breathing shallow and low in his abdomen, she had to stare intently to check it was still moving. He looked peaceful. Occasionally, the skin of his eyelids revealed movement beneath, as if his eyes watched something on the big screen of his mind. She wondered what he dreamed about.

Miller had passed on Ryan's wish that he should be left to die. She knew she wouldn't be able to stay and comply with his wishes. She had to go. 'Good night, Dr Ryan,' she whispered, and quietly shut the door behind her.

His memories unfurled one after another. In his dream, he couldn't control them, couldn't prevent them rolling out, and all seemed to focus on failure. Could he have done things better? He felt miserable and dejected, just as the whiskey priest made famous by Graham Greene did in his final moments facing the firing squad, knowing with crystal clarity that he could have achieved so much more.

What was it all for?

His good eyelid opened with reluctance. He was alone; he thought he caught a whiff of Gracie's perfume.

What was it all for?

His strength ebbing; he scrawled two messages on his pad and then signed them. With nothing else to hand, he placed them in a faded old envelope.

His mood changed. The line between consciousness and dreams blurred. Giddy and light on his feet, he moved, but he wasn't walking; freed from the constraints of friction he travelled fast towards an unknown destination, he was afraid. *You know at the end you don't see your whole life flashing by, but if you're lucky, you get to make some sense of it.* Bruce Milowski's words from years before flashed into his brain. Although they were advanced for such a young boy, he never gave them a second thought. Here, he paused, and sense came. They weren't the boy's words, they were his grandfather's. *Satori...so this is what it feels like.* Self-doubt washed away; he bathed in a shimmering and ethereal light. *This is it, Ryan, your faith tested, your soul naked.* A hand slipped through the crook of his arm and hardly daring to hope, he turned. *It's Gracie!*

She'd come to meet him. Leading him on, she held on tight to his forearm and leaned her head against his shoulder. 'I've been waiting for you, Mr Ryan,' she said.

Miller continued to drink his tea in small sips, his telephone buzzed from the depths of his pocket.

He retrieved it and glanced at the display. *It's Stella.*

'I should take this,' he said.

'That's okay,' she affirmed. 'Ryan's dead, by the way.'

It took a moment for what she'd said to register.

'Hello, Stella.'

'Oh, Miller, it's Ryan. He just died.'

He calmed her the best he could from the end of the telephone, and gave her instructions about what to do, who to call. 'No, listen…don't worry. If you need to talk, I'm right here…only a phone call away. I'll be back soon. No, I'm not sure, could be tonight, more likely tomorrow, in the afternoon. I will. I'll—'

Stella interrupted, blurting out, 'I need to see you.'

Her words carried an urgency that took him aback. '*See* me? What for?'

'There's something I need to ask you and something I want to tell you.'

'Look, Stella, I can't talk now.'

'No, not now, tomorrow, when you get back. Come round.'

'Okay.' He couldn't imagine why she wanted to see him. 'I'll call you—'

The phone cut off. *No signal.* He shrugged his shoulders. 'I lost the signal.' Ryan's words came back to haunt him. S*ee if you still have your cynicism, after you've met her.* The idea *she* might have had something to do with the signal loss entered his head.

'You're here, and you are needed there,' she said, an enigmatic smile touching her lips. 'She needs your help in more ways than you know.'

'Ryan said the same thing.'

'That isn't what I'm referring to.'

'Well, that sounds very mysterious. What do you mean?'

'I see three women in your life; one is no good for you, the other two…either would do for you. Miller, you are going to have to choose, and choices can be painful sometimes.'

'Sister, what if I choose not to?'

'I'm only telling you what *might* be, what you do about it, is up to you.'

A polished black stone slightly larger than a toy marble appeared in her hand. It bent the reflection of the window behind across its spherical surface.

'I want you to hold this for a moment. What it is, I don't rightly know, but it is something unique, a gift from God.'

Miller viewed it with suspicion.

'Don't worry,' Sister explained. 'We can go all round the houses, with me plucking things about you from the air, or we can shortcut things.'

'With that?' he asked.

'It's something I found years ago, when I was a wee young girl. It helps me focus on people…what they carry inside; it helps me understand what makes them tick. I want you to put your hand out, focus for a minute.'

Both stared at the stone.

It was empty when she first found it, readable only after others had touched it. It never occurred to her it wasn't *empty*. There had just been nothing new to transfer into *her*. If she'd have been of a remotely scientific disposition, she'd have had an inkling of how it worked sooner. She knew she was an aberration. In human terms, she was off the scale, the amplification of her senses out of all proportion to evolutionary needs. She recognised Miller was mildly psychic, but if he were a dog, she was a bloodhound. Her extra perception covered all the senses, and gave rise to the existence of something else in her. A sixth sense.

She removed her glove and held the stone in her naked fingers, above his out-turned hand. Her eyes danced. 'Are you ready?' she said and dropped the stone into his palm. She closed her eyes.

The weight of it surprised him. His hand dropped a fraction as he compensated for the weight. He was still wondering how such a tiny thing could be so heavy, when he felt something stir. Energy held inside passed through beyond its form and detonated. Miller couldn't have explained the effect in any other way; it started a chain reaction of his sense. A hurricane wind blew right through the depths of him. Tiny particles of shape or form gathered from nothingness to somethingness. The Sister was aware the instant the transference began because what passed into him, transmitted through the airwaves, back to her. Her eyes flew open.

Miller reeled and looked startled as a blur of past events churned through his mind. He had the look of someone who'd seen inside Pandora's Box. Fragments linked; pieces fit. His expression was one of horror.

'Stop!' she commanded, clapping her hands together. 'You were not supposed to *see*. I underestimated you. I should never have allowed you to touch the stone!' She snatched the stone back from him.

'Then why did you?'

'Because I cannot touch you directly, it would be too overwhelming, even painful. The stone does the same thing without the pain.'

They sat bemused, and stared at each other.

Finally, Miller spoke, 'Jesus, Mary and Joseph, what is that thing?'

'When I first found it I thought it was a meteorite, now I'm not sure. Whatever it is, I believe it to be a gift from God.' She rolled the stone between her thumb and forefinger while he observed. Jet black and naturally shiny, it was a perfect sphere. *What are the odds of it naturally forming that way?*

She removed the second glove, and holding the stone clasped in one hand, wrapped the other around it and absorbing what it had taken from him. Consternation crossed her face. 'I know you saw the priest.'

Unsure of exactly what he'd seen, he nodded. 'I saw something.' He closed his eyes. He was in a graveyard.

'Miller, please put those thoughts from your mind. You were not supposed to see.' She moved, her form radiant in the light of the window. He squinted as he searched her face.

'What the hell was that all about?'

'Oh, Miller, how best to tell you?'

A trickle of blood dewed on his nose tip, he wiped it away on the back of his hand. Confused, he grabbed a tissue from his pocket. *I never get nosebleeds.*

Sister thought rapidly. This was the first time she hadn't known exactly what to do since she became an adult. Some other things...well, she couldn't control everything. In many ways it reminded her of what happened with Mick when they'd touched, when she'd had the image of him falling in front of a train on a railway crossing. She'd seen his death coming, but she didn't know when, where, how, or even that it would actually happen. She could do no more than tell him to be careful.

After that experience, she'd always worn gloves around people. If her mind was Wi-Fi, her skin was hard wire and the stone a medium in between, its transmission by touch similar in principle to plugging a USB stick into a computer. It was a quirk of fate that only certain people could read it. Already she picked up on Miller's latest thoughts. He was thinking the stone was not a meteorite, or a gift from God. *No, he was examining the possibility it could be alien technology. God is an Alien?*

It never ceased to amaze her how people denied the existence of God, yet readily embraced the possibility of alien life. There was no time to tell him everything. She reached out without warning and touched him.

If the stone had sparked an explosion, her touch was like planets colliding, an atom bomb. All resistance fell before it, scorching his senses; his thoughts flattened like trees as her experiences translated into impressions and came in a blizzard of wind, raining down on him from the Armageddon inside of her. He felt like a man who had tasted the sweet, heady nectar of life for the very first time. It enveloped him, and he wanted more.

Their histories exchanged in a matter of seconds, but this time she lost all control over what passed. Connections forged between them, which could not be undone.

Echoes of her past mingled with his. The black hole in his memory swallowed them up and regurgitated them as his own, there was no way of knowing if they actually belonged to him. It meant it would be a long time before he could pick them apart again.

Random voices and images ran through his consciousness.

A garish, modern, neon lit church appeared. A voice followed, 'You must find another place to live or he'll find you!'

Me or her?

'There are many devils that walk this earth, and he is one of them. He has many faces.'

Pain, sorrow and guilt chained him with unhappiness and held him down; a vision formed of a choirboy sitting on a pew outside a confessional. He'd deliberately timed his confession, moving back in the queue three times, so remained the last to go in. *How do I know this?* A scene from the past played out in his head.

'Bless me, Father, for I have sinned, it's been too long since my last full confession. Since then I've decided you'll not be manipulating me into any more of your vile practices, Father. I didn't know before, I was only ten years old, but I know it's wrong now.'

The priest was calm. 'You want to turn your back on all the special privileges your position brings? You no longer want to be in the choir?'

The boy blurted, 'I'll not be doing those things anymore. It's against God and nature, and it stops now!'

The priest hissed through the grille, 'It stops when I say it stops—'

'No, Father, it stops now or I go to the police!'

'Then go to the police, do you think they will take the word of an illegitimate orphan against the word of a priest?'

The boy didn't make it out of the church grounds. The priest murdered him.

Miller saw it all. Head between his knees, he covered his face and then sat up abruptly at the gravelly sound of his grandfather's voice. 'Sometimes you find stray thoughts and tune in. Sometimes they are like ghosts in the air. Strong like they were from one hour ago, or yesterday. Only the strong ones mean anything; otherwise they wouldn't be out there.'

He was in freefall. Thoughts manifested; scenes unfolded. Not all belonged to him. A man dressed in khaki, a tall girl. *Bruce, I told you not to go off! Where are you? Bruce!* His mother's voice. *What is she doing here?* Wandering absently, he telescoped skywards, a birds-eye view looking down. A little boy tripped over, jumping stones. Faces, hidden for years by time and trauma, came back to him. More and more was stacking up; he couldn't process the information fast enough.

'Move on now, and tell no one,' Sister said. The enigma that was her smile became clearer.

Moving on... Miller had been planning to do that for years, the perfect excuse to indulge his dark side at last, he felt as powerful as her. A crazily related thought popped into his head. *How would you like to come back to my place for drinks? You would? How lovely. Just pop that sack on your head for me. Oh, boy!*

His head spun with impossible velocity and just as he thought he'd pass out, it stopped abruptly.

All track of time had been lost. They stared at each other. Miller had a curious smile on his lips. He was first to break the silence.

'So that's what happened to you. .When Ryan tried to contact you again, you had left for Rome. The church recognised you were gifted and they trained you, effectively to use the gift for the good of people.' He had a better grip on how the information had transferred itself into him.

'That's right.' Her eyes shone. 'They wouldn't have wanted me to work for the other side now, would they?'

'It might have been easier,' Miller joked.

She smiled at him; eyes wide with warmth, green and bright as the newest leaves that caught the light of the sun in the treetops. 'Aye, it might, but I chose the right way. I had to ask myself, would I give my soul to have everything in the here and now knowing I'd be damned forever? It was, as they say, no contest.'

The church had had enough of damaging publicity and was looking for ways to fight back. Vera had arrived at just the right time. Besieged by claims of child abuse and at a time when congregations were diminishing year on year; they needed someone capable of sniffing out the corrupt priests and the bishops that protected them. She became a soldier of the church. Known as The Sister; she answered directly to Rome. She became disillusioned with the way they dealt with the priests she handed them on a plate. They had sent them off to work in other parishes, where after a period of grace, the abuse would begin all over again. She'd lost confidence in the Church's ability to punish their own. Preferring, it seemed, to rely on the day of judgement to administer their justice. The final straw was Father O' Donohue. She'd exposed him, and all they did was send him to another parish. She tried to leave; they refused her resignation. In despair, she ran away. She never forgot Father O' Donohue. *He, who would become a child killer.* Forbidden to intervene, she had to watch like a wildlife cameraman. Some things had to happen, before other things could.

'Sister,' Miller said, 'The killer priest, Father O' Donohue. I get the feeling you want to see him brought to justice?'

'I did not *tell* you about him. Do what you will, I cannot help you.'

A garish looking neon cross over a modern church. *He'll find you.* Miller frowned as the last vestiges of swirling thought drained from his mind.

'I saw something that didn't make sense to me just now. It tells me you're in danger. Is there something I can do to help you, Sister?'

She shook her head. 'Not now, but when the time comes, Miller, you will know.'

Miller tried to force himself to see more. He succeeded only in wearing himself out.

Rosetta drove him back to the hotel. Drained, he dozed for the whole journey. *Sister has an external power source I don't have.* He'd recharge his batteries overnight, and leave for home in the morning.

As he drifted into sleep, he thought about Carla. *You should call her, Miller.* In his head, another voice argued. *What would be the point in this somnambulant state?*

He sank into oblivion.

The Sister was in his head, in his dreams. She taught him something he'd never have thought possible. When he returned home, he found he'd developed a psychometric ability with photographs, and if he held one, echoes of the sounds captured at the moment the picture was taken, were replayed. A snapshot was exactly that, a snap of sound that lasted a split second. He found it too fantastic to believe until he discovered he could also see beyond the periphery of the photographs.

It took a while for him to realise he was tuning in to the mind of whoever had taken the photograph, but who would believe him? It was another thing to keep quiet about. *Who could you tell that to without them thinking you're a crank?*

Strangely enough, three names cropped up, and they were all women.

Chapter 135

Stella found him the next morning, in bed where she'd left him.

He lay motionless, illuminated under the saintly halo of light the bedside lampshade deflected around his head and shoulders, a beatific smile frozen on his lips. Ryan looked as if he'd been happy in his last moments.

She felt for a pulse, but already knew this time he was gone for sure.

After Miller had left, he'd told her how happy he felt that his long days had finally drawn to a close. He'd confided he was afraid of something she'd put to him several times, in past discussions. *What if you are right, Stella? What if this life after death, this meeting your loved ones again – what if it's all a big lie?* She'd squeezed his hand. 'You have to believe in it now, Doctor Ryan,' she told him. 'Or what hope is there for the rest of us?'

From the look on his face, he could have been winking at her; his good eye closed and that frozen smile... Stella guessed he'd found the truth.

'I wish I could have had your faith,' she whispered.

She mused about the rewards of unwavering belief. How good would that have been after living a life believing there'd be a call, a letter, or a knock at the front door one day. She imagined that beautiful moment, when uncertainty was swept away, her sister alive at the door. Her parents had given up and she had, too, save for a spark that wouldn't die. In denial, she was alone, without faith, and it was killing her. She'd never confided in Ryan. Once he'd said something to her, following one of their philosophical discussions. *Many people deny the existence of God all their lives, and then acknowledge his existence by praying to him in their last moments. It's never too late. Remember the crucifixion scene? Where the thief tells Jesus he believes in him and Christ says, 'Today you shall be with me in Paradise.'*

Despite what Ryan had said, he had wavered. Real inspiration was what she needed to restore her faith, not just a passage from the Bible. The worm of denial was dug deep in her. Eating away bit by bit, it was destroying her chances of happiness.

She collected herself and reaching to turn the light out, saw a crumpled old envelope sticking out from under the lamp's base. It was addressed to her. She opened it. Inside she found his precious pencil and a note. With shaking hands, she took the note out and read it.

The realisation that even as he'd faced his last moments, he'd still taken the time to think about her and Miller, made her cry. The writing, spidery and child-like, was still recognisably his.

'My Dear Stella,

Something for you, in recognition of your loyal service and in lieu of notice! Please ensure Miller gets to have my pencil.

I'll see you again one day :-)
B Ryan'

Also in the envelope was a cheque made out to her for ten thousand pounds.
She called Miller.

The whole day rolled by as if she were an onlooker until suddenly, without
remembering the journey; she found herself back home. Looking out of her
window, reflecting on Ryan, she hoped he hadn't died during the night, but rather
in the morning. Good Friday morning.

Unsure what to do with herself, she removed the office keys from her key
ring. She didn't know what to do with them.

Everyone close to her had now died. Miller hadn't answered her last call, and
she was desperate to speak to someone.

Vodka was a last resort. It was a place to go when the pain became too much.
She lifted the scabbed edges of her old wounds, and then cauterised them with
alcohol, before packing her new pain back down into them, sealing them off again.

She conducted yet another post-mortem on her feelings.

Her mother was obsessed to the point of irrationality. Her dad, in supporting
her obsessions, caught them as well, like a contagious disease. The bombardment
was relentless. *You never support me; you don't believe it enough to make it
happen.*

What it was that kept her immune, she couldn't be sure. It was probably the
fact she'd never met her sister. She'd only known her from photographs, or from
what her mother tried to indoctrinate into her, or punish her with. *You should be
grateful... Your sister would have loved that if she were here... She'd never have
let us down like that!*

Stella's personality was rebellious by nature, so she railed against the guilt
and angst, knowing it held the key to her mental stability. All the while she was
growing up, her dependence kept her mother sane. When she reached her mid-
teens, her mum began to change. Stella noticed her flaky irritability, never far
away, would come upon her more easily; the slightest thing setting her off. She'd
feel guilty afterwards, but she chipped a little of Stella's tolerance away each time.
By the time she was eighteen, she was ready to strike out on her own

She studied psychology and gained an understanding of it all. She found
herself led down the path of looking at cults; the idea of becoming part of one big
happy family was appealing. To give and receive unconditional love, to feel
valued and worthy, to be with others who were as disaffected as she was.
Compared to her own life, it would be heaven, but then she realised she'd be living
life on somebody else's terms, the same as she was now.

She'd be living a lie, and she needed to get away from that.

When she was in her third year at university, her parents, having been so
strong all the way through, collapsed in on themselves. The train that carried their
hopes derailed suddenly and so unexpectedly.

Looking back, it was only ever a house of cards. One collapsed, and the other
followed.

She never did get to qualify.

She joined the care professions herself, looking after old people, qualifying as a nurse.

Then one day, feeling unfulfilled and insecure, she answered an ad in the local paper completely on impulse.

She managed to secure herself a job, working for Miller's missing person's agency. She had this crazy idea she might help herself by helping others find their lost loved ones, and she harboured a hope she might finally find out what had happened to her sister.

In drink, she had tried to pluck up the courage to ask for help, but in going about things the wrong way, she felt compelled to leave. Next, she landed a job working for the elderly Dr Ryan and at last began to feel the pieces of her life coming back together. She learned a lot from Ryan without actually being a patient of his. He helped her; he had a knack for understanding people, a natural affinity with them. He understood the way her losses had affected her, there was no need for her to say.

She could never have brought herself to seek psychiatric help. He understood that, too.

When he told her he was finally in the last furlongs of his working life, he illustrated his points of view with her, passing on some philosophies and stories. He told her about Gracie, how he knew one day they'd be reunited.

'A day that's getting closer,' he added with a smile.

She sensed in the same way she had with her parents, that she wasn't quite getting the full story from him. In her last days with him, he'd encouraged her to go out and find another job. He hadn't wanted her to miss out.

When Miller walked into the reception at Ryan's office, she knew she'd come full circle.

Chapter 136

Miller phoned Stella from the train on the way back from Edinburgh. Her answer-phone activated a drunken message. *Hi, ish Shtella here, if I don't answer the phone ish 'cosh I've on the vodka. I migh' be gone shome time.* At the end of the recording, a series of muffled fumbling noises came down the line and then the message disconnected.

On his arrival home, he tried calling her again, but she still didn't pick up. Bone tired, he was relieved. He'd call her later.

Miller unpacked his holdall and set the few clothing items to one side ready for the washing machine. Upstairs, he flopped on top of his bed. He closed his eyes, hovering in the transition between waking and sleeping for the briefest moment until he heard a familiar gravelly voice. He descended further.

Far, far down he found his grandfather with his back towards him, tending the soil in his back garden. Without turning, he scooped a handful up into a sieve and shook it into an old tobacco tin until it was full and put the lid on. He offered the tin over his shoulder, still without turning. 'So, you never feel far from home. Take it.' The weight of it surprised him. It was just like the one his grandfather carried everywhere until he died. 'Granddad?' he said, but the old man faded before his eyes and he slept for the first time he could remember untroubled by his dreams.

He didn't wake up until after 9 a.m. The first thing he did was telephone Stella. Her drunken voice answered; he hesitated; thumb poised ready to disconnect. *I'll have to go round there.*

The phone transmitted rattling sounds and then she spoke. 'Hello?'

'Stella, are you okay?'

'Oh, Miller, I got myself into a mess last night.' She coughed dryly. 'Sorry, I have something for you that Ryan left. Can you come round later this afternoon, once I've had a chance to get my act together?'

When Stella opened the door, he had a bunch of flowers behind his back. 'I thought these might help to cheer you up,' he said as he whipped them out, presenting them to her.

She took them and managed a weak smile. 'Thank you, very thoughtful of you.'

He noted how pink and puffy her eyes were. 'Are you sure you're okay, do you want me to come back?'

'That is *exactly* what I don't want. Come in.' She motioned him in with a slight jerk of her head and turned down her hallway. He entered and closed the door behind him.

Upstairs, there was a commotion going on, raised voices, rumbling noises, things moving and scraping across the floor. Miller looked up at the ceiling. She caught his eye.

'That,' she said, pointing her finger at the flat above, 'is them upstairs getting ready to go on holiday.' She sighed. 'I'll be glad of the peace and quiet. Lovely, I can't wait.' She smiled at the thought.

'Are they always that noisy?'

'Like you wouldn't believe.' She drew out a stool for him at the breakfast bar in the kitchen. 'Drink?'

'Have you got water?'

She turned the tap on. 'Yes, we have water.'

'Bottled water?' He shrugged.

She opened the fridge and pulled a chilled bottle out. 'Would you like a glass and ice?'

'Is it bottled ice?' He grinned and took the bottle. 'This'll do fine.'

She poured herself a fruit juice. He waited for her to sit, before doing so himself.

'I can see you've done a lot of crying, Stella, are you okay?' His voice was quiet and comforting.

She glanced at him and then quickly turned away, fanning her face with both hands. 'I'm a bit all over the place with my emotions.' She sipped at her drink. 'I don't like losing people. Ryan was like my grandfather.' She covered her eyes with one hand and tried to compose herself. 'I'm sorry,' she said, wiping tears from her face.

Miller laid his hand over hers. 'I know he meant a lot to you. Take your time, tell me everything.'

She withdrew her hand and started at the point where her sister, Kathy, had been missing for a year. As she spoke, her hands fluttered up in front of her and helped articulate her words.

'At first, it drew them much closer together. I don't know all of it, but they were well on the road to splitting up when it happened. Their grief reunited them. That's where I came in. When I was born, I was a distraction for them, you know. It gave them a reason not to fill up their entire lives with the searching. Having me gave them an anchor, helped them balance their lives. I grew up in the shadow of someone who disappeared before I was a gleam in my father's eye and even though my sister was no longer there, I played second fiddle to her.' She picked up a tissue and dabbed her eyes.

'As I grew up, I began to understand it better. The candle – that candle mum kept burning in her old room day and night. We never took holidays because she had to be the one who kept it alive, transferring it from the last candle to the next, like she was the Keeper of the Eternal Flame.' Stella's hand found the tissue again. She twisted it between her fingers as Miller looked on. He let her speak without interruption.

'When I reached the same age as *she* was, I became a nurse at the same hospital. I wanted to see what it was like to walk in her shoes, go out to the same pubs and clubs, and listen to the same music she did. Looking back now, I think I wanted to be the daughter they missed so much, but I couldn't replace her.

'When I got to twenty-one-years old, they... No, *she* decided to kick it all in.' She dabbed at her eyes again. 'At first, I kept that candle burning. I rummaged through boxes and boxes of old newspapers, cuttings, posters and notes. You know there were letters from people who claimed to have *seen* her. There were letters from people who had *dreamed* about her. Letters from clairvoyants that *knew* what had happened...where she was...that she was still alive. Some of them even tried to exchange further information for money, and it was clear mum and dad had paid more than a few of them in their desperation to get results.' She stared at the backs of her hands and examined her bitten nails with disdain.

'As well as becoming a nurse, I studied psychology, criminology and anything else that might help me to understand it all, to come to terms with it.' She turned to face him and said, 'Miller, I've lost someone I never even met, but I felt her loss every single day through them. And when I was old enough to understand, it became my duty to share it with them.

'Now they're gone, too. I lost them. What was it, three years ago? I lose track. I've been in denial. You know, after the funeral, I allowed that candle to go out. I told myself it didn't matter. It was only symbolic, pointless. It made no difference in reality. It was a focus for mum's prayers and hopes. I'm still looking for answers. It seems to have become a duty for me I can't shake off, and it fucks me up. None of my relationships work out because of it. I've given up trying.' Her hands settled back into her lap. 'I'm so sorry, putting all this on you. Ryan's gone. There's no one left who understands, not that I can talk to.'

'Stella, you're talking to me and I'm listening. You really mustn't worry.'

Her face contorted as she stifled a yawn, and staggered into the lounge, plonking herself on the sofa. 'I'm so tired. I need to sleep, but...'

'But what, what is it?'

'Miller, will you stay until I wake up?'

He nodded. 'Of course I will.' He felt almost as drained as she did.

She allowed herself to tip over to one side, lying down, curling her knees up into her body, her hands and fingers woven together, thumbs to her lips. She closed her eyes and was asleep within seconds.

Poor kid.

He watched over her from where he was sitting. His eyelids felt droopy. He closed them. Listening to her slow, steady breathing lulled him. He slept, too.

With no idea what the time was, he opened first one eye and then the other, guessing from the total lack of sound outside that it must be just before dawn. He looked at his watch; it was 9:30 p.m. *You were asleep for three hours.* Disorientated, he decided not to wake her, and slowly eased himself away from the cushions. She detected his movement and sat up blinking, her face crumpled at the light. 'Where are you going?' she said, stretching her arms wide, yawning.

'I didn't mean to wake you, I should get going. I've got a busy day tomorrow.'

'You must think I'm awful, falling asleep like that. I never even offered you a proper drink. Do you want a drink?'

Miller checked his watch again, pleased she seemed brighter. 'Okay, just a quick one.'

'Sometimes the quick ones are the best.' She laughed. 'I take it you wouldn't mind Bacardi. I think I drank all the vodka last night.'

She continued speaking to him from the kitchen down the hall; he struggled to hear, so he went to join her there. 'I'm sorry, you were saying?'

'I was saying, Ryan left something for you. I'll get it in a minute.'

'What is it?'

She touched her nose. 'I thought I was the impatient one.' She passed his drink over to him. 'I assumed you wouldn't mind it mixed with coke.'

'No, not at all – cheers.' They touched glasses.

Miller sipped. It took his breath away. 'Jesus, Stella, that's strong!'

'Oh sorry, must have mixed it up with mine.' She handed him the other one.

He tasted it cautiously. *Even stronger than the first!* Returning it with a wry smile, he said, 'After all you've been through, dealing with Ryan dying, I guess you need it more than I do.'

She turned her glass around and looked through it at him; her eye magnified and her face elongated. 'Things look different when you've had a drink. More palatable, I think. Ryan helped me see something; he *showed* me something. Do you believe in life after death, Miller?'

He considered the question. 'Yes, I do. There was a time when I didn't, but now… Yes, I do.'

'Have you ever lost anyone close, in tragic circumstances, Miller?'

Miller stared hard at her. He already knew she'd read his file. Was she testing him to see how truthful he was on the subject? He decided to tell her about Josie.

'Stella, I had a girlfriend once. She vanished while at sea on a ferry. They never recovered her body. I'm not sure if it's relevant now, I'm too close to the heart of things to see properly, but I thought I saw her once, seven years after she disappeared.

'I was on the tube coming back from Piccadilly Circus. I had a notion I might write a book about the tide of human misery that lurks just out of sight below the mainstream life of the capital. The sex, the drugs, the runaways. I decided there and then I'd always make time for the genuinely needy, to help them track down missing loved ones, for free.

'Anyway, at around half past seven the train pulled into Russell Square. I was on my way to Finsbury Park, meeting a friend there, and I saw her quite clearly. The shadows were playing up that morning, but I wasn't on an assignment or anything dangerous, so I thought nothing of it. He paused. *She's read your file, so she knows about the shadows.*

'She was further up the carriage, sitting alone in a gloomy corner. The light above her kept flickering. I got this strong feeling. I can't explain it, but when I focused properly – it was her. She smiled. Not the way I remember her smiling. Her lips stayed together, but immediately we made eye contact; she turned and rushed straight out of the carriage, just as the doors closed. I thrust my hand between them, activated the auto release and then ran out after her. I wanted an explanation. I called out after her. I wasn't sure she heard me. She wasn't actually running, but I had to – or I wouldn't have kept up. She rushed up the stairs and then outside, always just in sight. I called out after her a couple more times, but she'd disappeared.

'I was devastated as you can imagine. Convinced she was alive, I stopped off at a café to collect my thoughts. All these questions ran through my head, but mostly – why? Someone came in and started talking to the lady behind the counter. "Have you heard about the fire? There's been a disaster at Kings Cross station."'

Stella's lips parted; she looked stunned.

'That's when I knew. All those near misses, more lives than a cat – I had some sort of early warning system working for me. I could still slip on a banana peel and yet I had this *radar* that would warn me if I were in grave danger. What it is, I can only guess, but after I saw Josie that time...' He stretched out his fingers and stared into the palm of his hand.

'Did you ever see her again?'

'No, I never did.'

'You didn't tell Ryan about any of this, did you?'

Miller stared at her with surprise. 'How would you know that?'

She grinned mischievously. 'It wasn't in your notes.'

A grin touched his lips. 'He'd have loved that story, but it happened in the intervening years. I wish I'd remembered it the other day. Besides, I never told him everything.'

'Why not?'

'I didn't want him to think I was a basket case.'

Confusion creased her brow. 'But he *was* a psychiatrist! Do you think if you had known more about your "radar" when your friends died, you'd have been able to save them?'

'Possibly. It still hurts to think I might have been able to...but then, things happen for a reason don't they? How did this come up, we were supposed to be talking about you. Talking about this doesn't make me feel better. It never will. That's why I keep it inside, out of sight.'

'Out of mind,' Stella finished for him.

'Stella, I have to go.' He wasn't sure if the drink he'd had would put him over the limit, but he knew if he stayed, there could be a repeat of Christmas three years ago.

'Okay,' she said.

Miller sat bolt upright in bed, the pull of the sheets restrained him at the waist. Heart racing, eyes bulging; it was only a dream, but the worst yet. He traced the sequence back in his mind. It was a dream that had no beginning.

His sudden move had woken Stella. 'Miller, you scared me. What the hell is going on?' Her eyes narrowed. 'Do you trust me?'

'Of course I do.'

'You do? That's good. Would you remove your silver for me?'

'What?' he asked suspiciously. Where she was concerned, there was always an angle.

'Take your silver *off* for me!' Her face darkened; her voice deepened. 'Take it off!' she commanded. She locked eyes with him and, smiling demonically, began to writhe seductively on the bed. 'Will you take it off?' she said, cajoling.

He slid one arm underneath her and pulled her on top of him. He was aroused. She kept him at bay. 'Answer me!' she whispered harshly.

What kind of game is this? 'Of course I would.'

'Then do it, show me. Prove it to me.'

He removed all of it, with the exception of his crucifix and torc bracelet.

'The bracelet and the cross!' She spat the last word.

Surprised at her role-playing abilities, he said, 'No, never. When they were given to me, I was made to promise I would never remove them. I never have. He rolled himself on top of her. 'If you continue to ask me to remove them, I will have to say, *"Who is this that asks me to break a promise,"'* he said the last few words in a deep, guttural, demonic growl. He scared her.

She put a finger over his lips. 'Shush silly, you always get carried away.' She laughed, her eyes crinkled to match her smile. 'Wow, you've never taken it off since you put it on?'

'That's right,' he said.

'Can I see it?'

He held his arm out to her. She turned his wrist. The torc glowed in the moonlight, polished and smoothed by years of wear. 'It's beautiful,' she said finally, and then manoeuvred herself under his arm. With her back turned, spooning into him, she drew it down against her breast and held it there. He felt the warmth of her breath as she dreamily said something he couldn't quite make out so he leaned in to hear her better.

You're not in bed, a voice whispered. He rose into consciousness. His head was on the cushion of the sofa. He turned. Stella was staring at him with curiosity. *A dream within a dream. What the hell?*

'Stella? I thought I'd gone home.'

Her lips pursed. 'Mm-m, you don't remember? What's wrong with you, Miller, are you for real?'

Miller looked up. In the grey light of early morning, shadows played across the ceiling as the headlights of a car passed by.

He couldn't remember.

He nursed a glass of water. 'This is why I tend not to drink,' he said apologetically.

'It's okay,' she said. 'I'm used to it.'

'Well, I'm sorry, I said I'd listen and I fell asleep. You were saying you didn't believe in the existence of an afterlife.'

'It doesn't matter now. I'm tired and a little bit wasted. I've come this far.' She turned away, tears rolling down her cheeks.

What's wrong with me? I don't know what's wrong with me. I can't get through. I shouldn't have had that drink.

'So, suppose I told you about a girl I once knew.'

'Miller, come on, what is that going to prove? Some second-hand story isn't going to convert me. I need proof, actual proof.'

'Just listen, then you can make up your own mind.'

'Fire away,' she said, sounding as if she'd already made up her mind that it was bullshit.

'After you'd left, I tried to get someone else to replace you, but it wasn't easy. I'd almost given up, and then one Friday afternoon I took a call from someone asking if the job was still open. I said it was and, within the hour, I had this girl in. She couldn't get a babysitter, so she brought her son with her. She was a little flaky. I wasn't sure she'd be right for the job, but I...when I saw her boy, I knew I had to give her a chance. He was a little blonde, angel-faced boy. He had a penny whistle and he thrust it into my face. I tried to take it, but he snatched it back out of reach, hiding it behind his back, which made his mother laugh. "You can look, but you can't touch," she told me.

'What's his name?' I asked.

"It's Bobby," she said. "He's autistic." With that, the little boy takes his penny whistle to his lips and begins to play.' Miller smiled at the recollection. 'I'd prepared myself to cover my ears, but you know what? He played that thing like a little maestro. The sound, the tune – I'd heard it before somewhere – a couple more notes and I had it. He was playing *Mother Nature's Son,* an old Beatles number. So I joined in quietly. Now, I can't sing, but when it comes to singing along to that song...well, that's what I did. Mumbling along with what words I could remember *Born a poor young country boy, Mother Nature's son, all day long I'm sitting singing songs for everyone*. Singing along to the penny whistle. The delight shining in that little boy's eyes was quite something. In those moments, there was a connection between him and me. I looked at his mum. She was weeping and smiling, all at the same time. I knew I wanted to be a part of his life, if I could. It touched me so deeply.'

'I want to meet Bobby,' Stella said wistfully. 'He just sounds so sweet!'

Miller continued.

'She started with me the following Monday. I ran through the job with her, and then handed her an "idiot sheet" covering everything. I noticed she'd gotten a tattoo on the inside of her wrist. It was inked in with a washed out green, hand-written script. I couldn't read it properly, and she caught me looking.' He drifted back to that day.

'You're looking at my tattoo,' she said, and held her arm out.

'It's a nice tattoo, but what does it say?'

'*Aparta de mi lado esos seres malvados* – In English: Keep me safe from evil things – or something like that.' She appeared distant, her eyes out of focus. 'I had a Spanish boyfriend who used to carry one of those little devotional prayer cards they sell in the cathedrals and churches over there.' She paused to sip her drink before continuing. 'Anyway, I had this awful dream one night. I can't tell you what it was about, but I woke up scared and upset. When I told him about it, he gave me the card. The prayer was to Santa Barbara. He told me it would keep me safe from bad things. And I felt better, you know, like straight away. I'm not religious, or superstitious, but you know something? He died the next day. After that, I had the tattoo done and ever since then I've carried the card around with me as well.'

She undid her purse, took the card out and handed it to Miller to look at. The picture showed the saint bathed in golden light, her face serene, around her crowned head a golden glow. She held a cup and a sword. The prayer was lengthy, and Miller could see why she used only part of it for the tattoo, but, *Oh Dios* would hardly have taken any more room on her wrist.

'Why did you omit "Oh Dios" from the tattoo?'

She took the card back. 'Because I didn't just want to limit the plea to God. It leaves me free to appeal to *anyone* out there to keep me safe!'

Miller turned away from his recollections, back to Stella. 'It was a talisman of words, a verbal amulet etched in green, the colour of life. If she believes hard enough that it will keep her safe, then it will. Belief is a powerful ally.'

'Okay, Miller, it all sounds very intriguing, except I'm not convinced.'

'Have you ever experienced coincidence?'

'Well, of course I have.'

'Have you ever wondered why certain events are apparently linked by a series of coincidences?'

'I can't say I have ever had first-hand experience of anything like that.'

'Well, I have.'

'What – real first-hand experience or just another story you heard from someone else? What you just told me wasn't your experience. It belonged to someone else!'

'So if I tell you something direct from my experience, would you believe it then?'

'I'd believe *you* believed it.'

'There's none so blind—' he retorted.

'You think I don't want to see? Do you think I should just *accept* what you say as gospel without question?' Her mood changed; he'd touched a nerve.

'Stella, you read my file and accepted *that* as gospel.'

'Hey—,' she said angrily. 'Why do you keep bringing that up?'

He scratched his head. He'd not mentioned it before, but he hadn't intended to make her angry.

'What more do you want from me?' she said hotly. 'Another apology?'

'Okay, Stella, where's *your* file, so I can have a good look at you?'

'Now you're trying to make me feel guilty about it? Well, I don't have one.'

Miller reached out unexpectedly and grabbed her hand too quickly for her to resist. He held it tight. Heat flowed between them. It came from him.

'Why are you looking at me like that?' she asked.

'I've just read your file.'

Her mouth was half-open. 'You're kidding me, aren't you?' She wasn't sure she should believe him; her eyes were round with incredulity. 'Are you saying you can read people? I don't believe you!'

Suddenly she felt immensely tired. It washed over her as if she'd worked too hard, for too long without a break. 'I wish you'd told me you were going to do that.'

'Well then, now you know how it feels.'

'I still can't believe you did that!'

'I didn't, I just told you I did.'

Stella frowned. 'Stop playing games with me, Miller. I *have* to know the truth. Can you honestly read people, can you tell the future?'

He hesitated and then said, 'Sometimes, it's a bit of a story. I didn't used to be able to do anything much at all. Lately, it seems I can.' Pausing, he searched for the right words. 'I always had good intuition – I could tell if someone was lying to me and all that.' He thought about the shadows that had dogged him most of his life. He'd gone from fear to apprehension, at some point knowing they looked out for him, whispering in the night, influencing his dreams. *How can I tell her I have to sleep with the light on to get a decent night's sleep?*

'I suppose the truth is, if I can do it at all, it only works when it matters,' he said, and then after a moments reflection, added, 'Lately, there have been lots of times when it really seems to matter.'

'So did it matter so much just now that you felt you needed to grab my hand?'

'I just had this overwhelming need to convince you, but I don't know why.'

Stella didn't look convinced.

'I can't say any more than that, really. If the truth were told, mostly it's intuition. Reading reactions, tiny changes of expression, it isn't anything special.'

'You say it's nothing special!' She shook her head in amazement. 'It is exactly what Ryan referred to in his notes. He thought you had a greater ability to survive because you may have been psychic, or that each subsequent survival made you psychic. I didn't believe it when I read it, but now I think he might have been onto something,' she said, her mood turning dark. 'So all the time, when I knew you before, you might have been able to help me and you never said anything?'

'I didn't understand it as much as I do now, and anyway, if you needed my help to find your sister – why didn't you just ask?'

Stella was astounded. 'So you can?'

Miller deflected her with a serious look. 'Do you know what I'm going to say to Ryan, when I see him in the great hereafter?'

'Of course I don't!'

'I'm going to tell him to make sure he keeps my file locked away from you!'

Her face softened. Almost smiling, she raised the middle finger of her right hand and screwed it around in the air.

Chapter 137

'I don't want to go to his funeral, I hate anything like that.'

'So do I, but if you don't go, you'll regret it.'

'Do you think he'll mind if I don't?' Stella said, avoiding his gaze.

'I'm sure he wouldn't mind a bit.' Miller lifted her chin. 'But to not go when you could have...'

She turned to face him. 'Is what?'

'Running away. And I think he'd mind that.'

Afterwards, at the wake in Ryan's favourite gastro-pub, they stood together, shoulder to shoulder with dignitaries from the world of psychiatry, ex-colleagues, associates – most of his friends were also doctors. A few former patients were there. Ryan's solicitor, who was also his friend, announced it was Ryan's dearest wish they should all come together for food, drink and merriment and to that end he'd left one thousand pounds. There was a good, lively atmosphere, generally, however, a diminutive and dapper grey-suited elderly man with silver hair and a light Scottish brogue approached them, his face suitably solemn. 'Are you from the medical world?' Miller didn't quite catch what the man said and asked him to repeat it. He got his wires crossed and thought the man was asking if he was with a newspaper called 'Medical World'.

The man walked away, still solemn, but bemused.

Stella came out from hiding behind Miller's back; eyes filled with mirth. 'I don't know how you managed to keep a straight face, I was wetting myself!'

He grinned at her, happy she was happy and then confided, 'I had my hand in my pocket, pinching myself.'

The man had circulated and latched onto another hapless victim, a woman who looked just as confused as Miller had; she searched the room for an escape route. Catching Miller's eye, she made her excuses, pointing in his direction, and then made a beeline for him, grinning from ear to ear as she came over.

They had a quick exchange about the man. 'The trouble was that he was so softly spoken, and with his accent, I couldn't understand a word he was on about.' The three of them all joined in laughing.

'It's strange, but I'm getting the feeling I know you. Have we met before?' he said.

She introduced herself, 'Jackie Solomons. I was a patient of his.'

He shook her hand, 'Miller. I was, too.'

Stella shrugged her shoulders, feeling somewhat left out and extended her hand. 'My name's Stella. I just *worked* for him.'

The entrance door opened and a veiled woman stepped in. Framed in the shaft of light, she closed the door behind. Dressed in funereal black, her presence was striking. Wisps of rosé tinged hair protruded from beneath the hooded cape she wore. A few people stared at her, before returning to their conversations.

'Who's that?' Stella said, transfixed by her appearance.

Jackie answered, 'That's The Sister. Oh, my God, I haven't seen her for years. I once caught Ryan visiting her.' She told them the whole story. 'And she had this jet-black stone, plopped it into the palm of my hand and, well—'

Miller coughed discreetly, his eyes flashing theatrical caution at Jackie as The Sister approached from behind.

'Talking about me, are you? Only nice things I hope,' she said, her smile barely perceptible.

'You didn't say you were coming to the funeral,' Miller said.

'I tend not to announce my movements in advance, what with the church pursuing me and all.'

Miller was sure she winked at him from beneath the veil. Surprised she should mention such a thing aloud, he found himself double-checking he hadn't just heard it in his head, but she was closed to him.

'It's a long way to come for a funeral.'

'Aye, it is. I have unfinished business to look after. You know some things have to happen, for other things to happen.' She touched her nose, her eyes bright, alive and knowing, clearly visible, despite her dark veil.

Apart from The Sister, none of them seemed to notice the petite, blonde woman in her late fifties who stood by the bar next to them, listening to every word they said.

Penny, intrigued by all she'd just heard, put together a picture in her head of The Sister and Ryan. *That medium, turning up dressed in black like his widow.* She seethed and for a second looked directly at the woman in black. Calm, the green eyes captured her miniature image and held her there. Unable to maintain eye contact, an idea bloomed. She suddenly knew exactly what to do.

On arriving home, Penny decided she'd report her to the church. She hadn't any idea why they were looking for her, but it was about time they clamped down on seedy seaside fortune-tellers. Knowing the local priest wouldn't be interested, she switched on her computer and googled to whom she should report the woman's whereabouts.

Two thirds of the way down the screen, an interesting thread came up. *The Church of the Resurrectionists of Monte Cristo, known among its members as 'The Church'. A shadowy organisation, links to corrupt political leaders, one of its bodyguards wanted for the recent assassination of an African Bishop.*

She thought awhile before digging deeper. *Monte Cristo, Mountain of Christ, second comings.* Although she realised this was not the church that was looking for The Sister – if she told them about the stone and the fortune teller's alleged abilities, the Resurrectionists might just want to find her, too.

Chapter 138

Penny contacted the Resurrectionists and, after an exchange of emails – the last one had requested her telephone number – she awaited the arrival of a man who had assured her he was a very distinguished member of The Church.

Unbeknown to Ryan, when he'd written asking for the return of her keys, she'd had them copied and kept the duplicate set. The original alarm was key-operated and had been for years. If she knew Ryan at all, he wouldn't have wanted to spend money upgrading the system. Always keen to make a good impression on any man, Penny had dolled herself up for the visit. When the doorbell rang, she had no misgivings about letting the man in. She found herself quite excited at the prospect of time alone with him, he seemed friendly enough, but there was a distinct air of danger about him. Penny toyed with the idea of holding out on the information and using it as a bargaining chip. *Who knows what might happen?*

The Churchman didn't take long in getting to the bottom of the story; she told him about the file she'd seen.

Twenty minutes later, the swarthy looking man returned to his hire car and placed a set of keys on the passenger seat. Within an hour, he was in possession of the file.

Penny had started a sequence of events she could not have foreseen when she contacted the Resurrectionists. The files they'd stolen illuminated a trail for them to follow. One by one, they would pick off their targets.

In Ireland, a black Fiat drove between the pillars of a rundown dry-stone wall into the front driveway area and bumped into a large pothole. The tall man in the passenger seat hit his head on the inside lining of the roof with a dull thunk, he shot a look of displeasure at the driver.

Brenda Flynn looked out of her window as the car parked. *It's late for visitors.*

Brenda had had two or three of these visits over the years since Vera disappeared, emissaries of Rome looking for her. *You'd a thought they'd a given up by now.* When the two men arrived at her door, she was already waiting the other side. Opening it at the first knock, the unexpected visitors drove her backwards inside.

The shorter, swarthy-looking beady-eyed man held onto her while the tall, thin man looked around, moving down the hallway.

'I don't have anything worth taking,' Brenda informed them coolly. 'But you're welcome to look, why don't you!'

'Your niece, where is she?' the swarthy man demanded.

'Who are you, and what do you want?'

'Just tell us where she is and we'll be gone.'

'Vera? I haven't seen her in years.' Brenda glared at them defiantly. 'And even if I had, I'd not be telling you!'

'Which one is her room?'

'What do you want to know that for?' Brenda asked, genuinely bemused.

'It's this one,' the taller man said, dipping his head slightly as he stepped through the door.

Brenda struggled to break free, but the swarthy looking man held her easily.

'Get off me!' she yelled. 'What are you doing in there – get out of my house!'

'Stop struggling, old woman, we don't want to hurt you.'

The tall man emerged from Vera's old room and nodded at his accomplice. 'I know where she is,' he said.

On the way out the taller one stopped by the front door and held his left hand out, hovering where once the water butt had been.

Once they'd gone, a mystified Brenda Flynn walked into Vera's old room. She never changed it at all, dusting round occasionally. Nothing seemed out of place. Except for the bed, it looked as if someone had laid on it.

Why would that be?

She notified the police.

Chapter 139

Tuesday, 10 April

Wind blew through the air with a vengeance, twisting sheets of rain into phantom forms and sweeping the car park, filled it with puddles in seconds. The sunny spirits of the past few days were dampened, replaced by pervasive gloom. Trapped by the weather in the car, Miller and Kennedy waited for the rain to ease.

'By the way, there was a break-in at Dr Ryan's last night. I thought you might like to know,' Kennedy said, looking grim.

'Well, that's good of you, but what does it have to do with me?'

'They broke into his filing cabinet and took several files. According to the index, one of them was yours.'

'Mmm, you say they broke into his filing cabinet. Did they not break into his office?'

'No, they had keys, they left them behind. We ran a couple of checks; Stella Bird still has her keys. We found the name Penny McAllister on the key holder records from a long time back. I think we can be reasonably sure they were hers.'

'Reasonably sure – how can you be?' Miller said, perturbed. Kennedy was one of those people he just couldn't read at all.

'Because when we called to talk to her, we found her dead, strangled with one of her own stockings.'

Miller whistled. 'Jesus, is there any chance you can tell me who the other files were?'

'Patient confidentiality, it wouldn't be right to tell you.' Kennedy tapped his nose. 'Anyway, why are you so interested?'

'I'm not sure really, just yes or no, was one of the missing files that of Vera Flynn, or The Sister or someone like that?'

'Yes,' Kennedy said, 'it was. Why do you ask?'

'Just curious. I don't suppose you'll tell me which others are missing?'

Kennedy cleared his throat. 'No other files were missing.'

Miller sat in silent contemplation.

The detective continued, 'We have intelligence from a good source that a pseudo-religious group is planning to kidnap her.'

'Really? And why would they want to do that?'

'I don't know, but something's going on. Her aunt reported a strange incident yesterday. Two men forced their way into her home; they didn't take anything, but according to her, one of them said, after he'd been in Vera Flynn's bedroom: *I know where she is,* and when you take that piece of information, along with the email correspondence found on McAllister's computer, I think we can safely say

Vera Flynn is in danger.' Kennedy brightened. 'Hey, look the rain's stopping. Give it another couple of minutes, we can go inside.'

Miller looked at Kennedy and shook his head in mock dismay. 'You're unreal.'

'Before I forget, I didn't tell you about Jackie Solomons did I? She was in the cabinet at Dr Ryan's too—'

'Wait a minute; I met her at Ryan's funeral—'

'And?' the detective said.

'Nothing. Just seems a strange coincidence, that's all.'

'Where was I? Oh, yes. Do you know something, Miller? The man that tried to kill her – she said he reeked of tobacco smoke. It stuck in my mind for ages afterwards. It was such a general thing, not much of a clue, but she kept saying it to me back then as if she didn't want to forget.'

Miller half-turned towards him in the driver's seat, his stomach growling with hunger, he couldn't wait for the rain to stop so they could continue the discussion over breakfast. It was such a cold case; there wasn't any need to worry if someone eavesdropped on them.

'And after the reek of tobacco, it was how big his hands were.' His frown deepened as he struggled to recall the details; he was doing well without any notes. 'No, not his actual hands, but the knuckles. They were big and scarred, like the knuckles of a boxer or bare fist fighter. She never got a look at his face; he ordered her to look down. Her friends weren't close enough for a good look, so all we had was three things.'

'Three things?'

'That's right. He's a fighter; he smokes, and he left his semen at the scene of the crime, in a manner of speaking,' Kennedy said, with an apologetic grin. He looked for a reaction, but Miller remained impassive. He cut a smear with the edge of his palm and peered through the condensation on the windscreen, looking skyward to see if the rain showed any signs of stopping. Miller settled back into his seat, before finally making a statement.

'No matches, even after all these years.' His head shook from side to side, in silent disapproval. 'To my way of thinking, there are a number of things to consider—'

Kennedy interrupted him. 'There was actually something else she said; it was a really hot day, but he wore a boiler suit. At the time, we guessed he might be a mechanic or something like that.'

Miller paused, thought about what Kennedy had just said, and continued, holding up the forefinger of his right hand. 'Whether or not it was the first and only time he intended to kill that day, he dressed for it – to avoid cross-contamination between them. He inseminated her so we can conclude he intended to dispose of the body quickly. If her friends hadn't intervened, you wouldn't have found her. I believe he's done this before. This man has never come up on the radar, never had a sample taken.' He fixed Kennedy with an intense stare. 'Do you know how many young women go missing without a trace every year? This character could have killed many times before.'

Kennedy sighed. 'We considered all those things and more. It's also possible he died before committing another crime, before we got to him.'

Staring up into the dark clouds, Miller didn't hesitate in his response, 'He's not dead.'

'*You* can't say that, Miller,' Kennedy retorted. 'Not without a shred of evidence.' He stared through the misted glass. 'I, on the other hand, can. You know, a few weeks ag, I was in a lift with a character, a big, rough looking man. I'd never seen him before. There was only him and me. He was looking down, but I noticed him watching me, caught the devilish glint of them from under his eyebrows. And I noticed the smell of stale tobacco, so strong and overpowering I didn't need to look at his hands. I *knew* what I'd see. Yes, that's right – the hands of a bare-knuckle fighter. My gut told me I was in the presence of the man who had committed that crime. I just knew it. If you could arrest someone on a gut feeling, I'd have arrested him there and then. We made the briefest eye contact. I knew then he was going to attack me, but the lift stopped and more people got on. He hesitated, and then got off.

'Afterwards, I tried to disregard my instincts, but you know what? I remembered a case in Gibraltar in the late eighties; the SAS had shadowed some IRA suspects. One of the SAS men exchanged a look with one of the suspects a split second before the shooting began. At the inquest afterwards, the soldier testified there was recognition on both sides of what was about to happen. *He seemed to know.*

'It was the same in that lift. The minute I laid eyes on his knuckles, and he saw me looking, *he knew.* Whether he left the lift early because of that, I couldn't say, but I know it was him and although I curse I missed my chance, I also know he wouldn't have come quietly. It would have been like a ten-year-old trying to arrest a full-grown man. I also got the impression,' he paused for reflection, 'that he knew me, not from any kind of instinct, though. I think he knew my face; I got that feeling as well.'

Miller looked sideways at him. 'So *you* get a *feeling,* and that's okay?'

'You know, you've just reminded me. It didn't seem so important at the time; I mean we are talking about a lot of years ago now.' His eyes looked slightly out of focus; he rubbed them with his knuckles until they were pink and bloodshot. 'I was just a rookie detective back when Jackie Solomons was attacked. I checked the records to see if there had been any reports of any other incidents around that time, in the few months before. I can remember being in the pub just talking generally, making enquiries.'

Miller looked at his watch.

'Am I boring you?'

'No, no,' Miller said, tapping to show the time on the watch. 'But if we don't make a run for it now, we're going to miss breakfast.'

Inside the cafe, they located a table in a relatively quiet corner. The place was busy, a sign of good food. Miller placed their orders at the counter. A young girl in a bibbed red and white striped apron brought over the order. Kennedy heaped a spoonful of sugar into his steaming mug.

'Would you like my toast?' Kennedy asked. 'It's too heavily buttered for my liking.'

'No, what I have is plenty enough, thanks.'

'I hope you don't mind if I slip out of my detective's overcoat and talk to you as a friend,' Kennedy said. 'It just *might* be easier to forget I ever was a detective and listen to the story I'm about to tell you.'

Well, this is a new one, thought Miller. Inside, the cafe was steamier than it had been in the car. The windows had previously served as a shop front. With too much cold glass, they ran with condensation.

'You know, I'm going to try to tell it as a bystander from back then, if you'll indulge me.' Kennedy's eyes appeared grey, devoid of any depth.

Miller checked his watch; he had time. 'Well, why not...'

Kennedy nodded and began his story. 'So, as I was saying. I was in this pub; not much bigger than someone's front room. I was off duty, but I got talking to one of the locals there. Vince, his name was, and the youngest in there apart from me. Anyway, he'd seen me around, and he knew I was a detective. I told him I was investigating the rape of a young girl. 'I heard about that', he said. I asked him eventually if he'd heard about anyone acting suspiciously anywhere around. He looked at me thoughtfully. 'Are you talking about the area around Devils Pond? If you are, it wouldn't have been anyone from round here.'' Kennedy blew at his tea.

'When I asked him why, the whole room went quiet. It seemed they were looking at each other, deciding whether or not he should tell me.' He stirred more sugar into his mug.

Miller sat forward attentively. 'Come on, John, get to the point.'

'Well, he told me no one goes there anymore because the place has a jinx.'

'*Jinxed* – is that all you got, you gave me the impression there was more.'

'Patience, Miller, there's more. You know; Vince was a caver, been all round the whole of Devon, Cornwall, Somerset, potholing, exploring old mines and caves. He told me he'd never have gone anywhere near the place. From a caver's point of view, it was just too dangerous. Unstable, water that rises out of nowhere, underground collapses. Not to mention gas pockets. You know, Miller; I was there, waist deep in my imagination, as Vince continued.

'I'll tell you what, John, it was John wasn't it? Well anyway, a little team of us gathered there once. I've been in some creepy caves, and mines so dark, the imagination can take hold and spook you out, the unexpected sound of dripping in an enclosed space, shadows that seem to come and go, and your headlamp only makes it worse. The eerie atmosphere outside this place was enough to put us off, but then the gas detector was picking up methane, hydrogen sulphide gases, all kinds. We decided not to go any further. Afterwards, we heard at least two explorers who'd been there before had died, succumbed to the gas. Round here, it has a reputation for people disappearing, so yes, the only people who would go there would be outsiders; I'd say that quite definitely.

'Then Vince pointed to a little alcove in the corner, Cyril's Corner, he told me. Cyril must have been around ninety years old. Vince said, "What's your name again?" I repeated it, and he took me over to meet him. "Cyril, this is John. He wants to know about the Devils Pond." The old man looked at me; one of his eyes was withered and cloudy, and the other bore right into me. "That pond is cursed; the whole place down there is – always has been. My grandfather died there in the mine; they reckon he was swept away underground. They never found his body, most of them drowned, or crushed. Twenty-three souls were taken in one go. All that rain and water finding its way into subterranean channels, did something to the ground. The following morning, Devils Pond, appeared. Kids kept drowning in that pool, I don't think they found them all. Too deep, too dark...only one person goes there now from round these parts." I asked him who it was, and he said, "Whoever it is that marks the old Whitethorn tree with clooties." He noticed my puzzled look, and explained, "They are offerings to the spirit that lives there, wiped with the pain of the sufferer, with the hope the spirit will take it away." He turned the handle of his empty mug towards me. "Used to think it was one for every soul that perished there." He leaned in and beckoned me closer. "When I was a kid I went down there for a dare one night in July, they say the people who died in the mine all those years ago, walk again on that night." Did you go? The old man nodded solemnly. What happened? I asked. The old man paused to sip from his mug, and with some theatrics, showed me it was empty. He sat there with his arms crossed, and made it clear he'd say no more until he got another drink.

'I got him another beer, and he sipped at it, obviously deep in thought. Well, what happened? I asked him again. He looked so serious I thought it would be something horrendous. He slapped his leg. "Not a damn thing!" He guffawed, and then coughed so badly, I thought he might choke on the spot. When his cough settled, I asked Cyril who put the clooties there. Cyril told me no one knows. "There were twenty-three of them that night, the clooties, that is." Then completely unexpected, he asked if I'd heard about the three boys that died there.'

Miller listened intently. *This cannot be a coincidence.*

'I told him, I might have heard something. It was a lie, but I didn't want him to hold out on me.'

Miller couldn't take his eyes off Kennedy. Is he playing a game with me? Does he know?

Kennedy continued, 'He told me while they were dredging for the bodies, they found so many skeletons in there, all shapes and sizes. Most of them were miners, men and boys. They also found a few female skeletons, five of them, weighed down with rocks and boiler suits tied around them – and two men dressed up the same.'

Miller's thoughts reeled. 'If he hadn't been disturbed, Jackie would've ended up in there, too, wrapped in the boiler suit he was wearing that day.'

'Most likely,' Kennedy said. 'Incidentally, did I tell you how many clooties were tied up when I last visited the place? It was forty-nine.'

Miller looked incredulous.

'The twenty-three original rags Cyril saw and a further twenty-six; if you take the original mine bodies, the seven murder victims and the three boys off, that leaves thirty-nine. So what is it those clooties represent?'

Confused by rapid developments, Miller needed time to digest the question.

'And I haven't finished yet, there's one more thing,' Kennedy said.

'What's that?'

'After the boys died, and the place had been thoroughly searched, Cyril told me the locals clubbed together to have the pool filled in and fenced off more securely by the local farmer.' He leaned in closer. 'You know, when I visited there that morning, sixteen years after they'd said it was filled in, it was back again. The pool was *there* again. I'd gone with Cyril and Vince in his Land Rover. We drove as close as we could. The last bit took an absolute age. Neither of them would go that last few yards with me, so I crossed the field on my own, stepped between the top and middle wire of the fence. It struck me straight away, what Cyril had said about the locals. They knew its boundaries and kept away. You'd know it if you ever went there. It's a spooky place, and the people around are superstitious. You have to remember, we're in a land where they still believe in Pixies, a land full of Iron and Bronze Age burial chambers. Cyril told me he reckoned those miners cut through something, some invisible barrier that let something out; it was released with such a terrible cry that those who heard it said it was the sound of tortured human souls – like nothing on earth, a thousand voices pent up in misery.'

Miller turned away, unsettled. He looked out of the window, deep in thought. 'John, I have to ask you this – you knew I was the fourth boy from that day...so what are you trying to say?' Through the pain, the only clear thing he could remember was the futility of throwing his beloved seashell to Brookes.

When he turned back, Kennedy had gone.

Chapter 140

Wednesday, 11 April

The doorbell rang; it was early morning, and the bright daylight stung Miller's eyes as he opened the door. The postman had a package that required signing for. Miller scrawled his signature hastily and thanked him.

'Have a nice day,' he said and sauntered back to his van.

The large brown envelope felt bulky; he examined the outside trying to guess what the contents could be. The red franking mark bore the school's coat of arms. The postmark revealed it had been posted the previous day, 10th April 2007. *A thank-you letter for the speech the other night, I'll bet, and they've thrown in a copy of the school magazine, as well.*

He closed the door and tore open the envelope. Inside, was a letter and another smaller envelope marked for his attention: 'STRICTLY PRIVATE AND PERSONAL'. First, he read the letter from the head teacher...*and finally, I would like to thank you for a most engaging talk on an interesting subject. And I do hope you will be able to join us at the reunion dinner next year. You will find within the larger envelope; another discovered by a cleaner behind the lectern on the stage in the hall the morning after your engagement.*

Miller scratched his head. *But that was over a week ago.* He double-checked the postmark and then opened the smaller envelope. Inside was a note from Kennedy and a further sealed note addressed to John Tanner.

Bruce,

Seeing you again tonight made me realise how much I miss close friendships with old friends; you know – people you can trust, people you can confide in. I wanted to tell you something face to face, but we were having such a good time reminiscing I didn't want to spoil it. It's something I regret, because it now falls on me to try to convey it all in writing, but before you read on – you must promise on your life that you won't divulge the contents of this letter to anyone else for the moment.

I've compromised myself. I made a few bad choices, did some immoral things, but nothing criminal. I'm stitched up so tight, I can't breathe. I can do nothing apart from disappear for a while. Let things take their course.

This person obtained my semen from Melissa Lake, a woman I was seeing. She was a prostitute, but I never really saw her that way. I never paid her and I think she was as fond of me as I was of her. Anyway, back to my blackmailer. He used my DNA to implicate me in a number of rapes carried out by the Gasman. He planted, fabricated and tampered with God knows how much other evidence. My father is a retired Chief Constable. It would kill him if this got out. I'm in no position to do anything about it, not without running the risk of exposure. He tipped me off about a shipment of guns and drugs; I was hoping to retire early as I'd mentioned to you. It would have been a real feather in my cap if I'd pulled it off, but it was a set-up. He used me. The result was two people dead. A gangland informer and his executioner. Nice and neat, but there were no drugs or arms. He phoned me the day after to thank me! Then he asked how I was going to explain the large sum of money deposited in my bank account that morning.

Oh, and it gets worse. I took part in a Crimewatch reconstruction late last year; there was a mix up with the edit. I now believe the kidnapper of Kathy Bird was watching the programme. Someone said something off camera – I didn't say it, but he blamed me. My blackmailer is the kidnapper, and I'm sure he's involved with the Gasman, and maybe even Midnight, too. He also claims to have kidnapped the missing girl, Eilise Staples. I think she's the key to all this and, if I'm right, when she is found, the rest will unravel.

When you and I met again last night, I realised you just might be the one person who can get me out of this mess. It's a lot to ask someone so quickly after our re-acquaintance, but I can't involve the police.

I've assumed you will agree.

You need to watch out for this character; he's very clever. He pressured me into giving him the address of Kathy Bird's sister; I was trying to buy myself some time. I have a feeling he might be planning to emulate what he did to her sister. Find him, find the Gasman and clear my name. We have to stop him.

I can't believe I'm writing this, sitting in our old school hall and in my best handwriting, too! You will need to speak to my colleague, John Tanner. There's a separate note enclosed to give him. Tell him you met me at the old school reunion, and I asked for your help. He will want to know where I am.

Do not try to find me at this stage.

Keep this letter in a safe place; you might need it to explain your actions later on. I will try to get in touch with you soon.

John.

PS. After all this, you won't forget me again as quickly as last time!

He finally moved away from the front door to the kitchen, pulled out a chair and sat at the small round table thinking. There was one thing he couldn't understand, something that bothered him. *If Kennedy had written that letter over a week ago, why didn't he ask if he'd received it when he'd seen him at the cafe?*

Puzzled, he rested his chin on his hand. *And why didn't you warn me about Stella when I saw you yesterday?*

He observed the milling shadows as darkness gathered about him, yet sensed no danger to himself. *You need to warn her!*

In the bedroom, he unplugged his mobile phone from the charger; it vibrated suddenly in his hand and he almost dropped it. The display said *Stella*.

'Hello, Stella, you're early, what's up? Couldn't you sleep?'

After short pause, a man's voice spoke through the handset. 'Oh, she's sleeping well. I gave her something to help her. Now you listen to me!' he shouted.

Miller jerked the phone away from his ear. 'I'm listening,' he said, calmly. There was no need to ask who was calling, he already knew.

'Aren't you going to ask me who I am?' the caller asked.

'Tell me or don't, it doesn't make any difference. I'm only interested in why you called me from Stella's phone, and that she's safe. What is it you want me to listen to that you had to shout like that?'

'Miller, *Mr* Miller, I got your number off her phone. Did you know you were the last person she rang? I've been researching you, Mr Miller. I know you like to find missing people. Well, let me tell you something, Mr Miller; she is most definitely missing and now here's the rub. If you try to find her, if I get the slightest whiff of you or the police coming near, I'll kill her.'

Something about his growling style of speech set Miller to thinking. *He sounds like Clint Eastwood!* It didn't occur to him that the vocal similarity was deliberate.

'What are you planning to do with her?'

'Oh, don't worry, Mr Miller. I only want to make her happy,' the caller exhaled audibly. 'As the saying goes, what do we do now?' Then he was gone.

Miller shuddered. I can't just leave her, but where the hell do I start?

His mind began to race.

The caller thought back to the day before; the ease with which he took her was scary, even by his standards. He grabbed her in through the side door of his van. Clamping her mouth, he chloroformed her from behind, just enough to put her out. He checked the street for witnesses, nobody there. 'That was easy,' he said to himself, and slid the door shut.

He trussed and gagged her in the back and, when he was done, rolled her onto her side and then stroked the inside of her thigh. 'No time for that!' he chided himself in a strict voice. Removing his hand, he climbed through into the driver's seat.

Outside a remote country pub, Miller sat waiting. It was the sort of place where people having affairs met up for a drink before going off into the seclusion of the nearby lanes. The chances of bumping into anyone you might know were unlikely. Miller, too, had chosen the pub for its seclusion. Nestled at the end of a country lane, the long straight stretch of road leading up to it meant you couldn't be followed by a car or motorbike without noticing.

The sound of a vehicle approaching drifted in on the wind before the car itself became visible. It was Tanner.

They introduced themselves and once inside, brought drinks, and found a dim corner, well away from the half a dozen or so drinkers collected around the bar.

'Thanks for agreeing to meet me so quickly.'

'That's okay, you said it was urgent.' He held his glass up and tipped it in Miller's direction. 'Cheers.'

Miller echoed the gesture.

Tanner swallowed a mouthful and exhaled loudly enough for a couple of people to turn and look at him.

'You know, I never even knew this place existed.' He looked around the pub and took in the five-hundred-year-old detailing. Just the sort of pub he'd love to acquire on retirement. He nodded to himself approvingly. 'Right, so what's all this about then?' Tanner switched his attention to Miller abruptly.

Miller twiddled a beer mat in his hand and then leaned forward, dropping his voice so he was only just audible. 'Kennedy told me someone was framing him and this character had him stitched up so tight he'd have to disappear for a while.'

'I don't see how disappearing is going to help him clear his name.'

'Can I trust you, Tanner?'

'What do you mean by that?' Tanner looked offended. 'More to the point, you're Kennedy's friend, so how do I know I can trust you?'

Miller looked Tanner square in the face. 'Fair comment, but listen, although we went to the same school, we weren't friends. I met him for the first time in years at a Passover dinner. I was giving a talk there; he turned up on my table, and we started talking.'

'What date was that?'

April the third, a Tuesday night, why?'

He looked at Miller, gauging his sincerity. 'No one has seen him since; he never showed for work in the morning, isn't taking my telephone calls.' Tanner hesitated. 'Miller, I paid a visit to his house when he didn't answer my calls.'

Miller stared.

Tanner had something on his mind. 'I don't know whether I should tell you this, but I'm going to anyway.' When Tanner had finished, he looked for Miller's reaction.

'You know you said no one has seen Kennedy since he didn't show for work?' he said, examining the detective's face.

'You've seen him, haven't you, Miller?' he said, steadily returning his gaze. 'Okay, let's hear it.'

'Yes, you're right, I have seen him.'

'Where did you see him?'

'At a roadside cafe, just before you get on the A130. I was waiting in my car for the rain to stop, and he just got into my car.'

'You arranged to meet him there?'

'No, he just turned up, as I said.'

Tanner scrutinised Miller with a look that bordered on disbelief.

'Did he tell you anything?'

'He's been following up some interesting leads since going AWOL.'

Tanner eyed Miller suspiciously. 'But why is he talking to you?'

'Oh, come on, Tanner, surely you can see. He doesn't want to risk getting arrested!'

'That's not what I meant. I meant, why choose you?'

'I don't know, perhaps it's because I have a friendly face, but you know what? I believe him.'

Tanner nodded; his lips pressed tightly together. 'It's out of my hands, Miller. Now, if you know where he is?'

'That's the thing; I have seen him, but I don't know where he is or when he'll appear next. He didn't say,' he paused for a moment. 'Oh, and that's the other thing. He asked me to give you this.' He produced an envelope from his pocket.

Tanner opened it and read the note inside. 'He wants you to take over the search for Eilise Staples in his absence. Under the circumstances, I don't think I can follow his instructions.'

'John, that's fine, but I have to tell you I've already started looking for her. He asked me to do that *before* I got the letter. All of what you've told me...if he *was* set-up, then this character has done a good job of it. Kennedy needs help to clear his name, but in the meantime, he's still thinking about the job. I'm a specialist in my field; he trusts me. There's a lot of intuition involved in the work we all do, mine works differently to yours. Not better or worse, just different, and it's telling me there's a connection here. It could be the key.'

Tanner softened. 'I'll give you such information on the case as is available in the public domain. I know a journalist who can brief you. Do you have a card?' Miller fished a business card from his inside jacket pocket and handed it over. Tanner retrieved his own number from his mobile and wrote it down. No name, just a number. Miller looked at it and raised an eyebrow. It looked familiar to him.

'Who does the number belong to? You didn't put a name.'

'I know,' said Tanner. 'I'll call her tonight and tell her to expect your call. Her name is Carla, by the way.'

'All this is great, John, but there's something else. I had to know I could trust you. The guy who was blackmailing Kennedy has now kidnapped Stella Bird.'

'The sister of Kathy Bird? Stone me. I don't believe this!'

'Kennedy warned me he'd been forced to give his blackmailer her details. And now the kidnapper has contacted me. Clearly, I'd have reported it, but he's threatened to kill her if anyone goes after him.'

Chapter 141

Unable to feel anything at all that might give him a clue to her whereabouts, Miller was at a complete loss. The faculties he'd previously possessed, including those he'd most recently become aware of, had deserted him. He emptied his mind of all conscious thought, a technique his grandfather had called, pusty umysł: *In Polish, Bruce, means no mind or mu shin in Japanese. Now you know in three languages. No mind.* When he had first succeeded in achieving this state, he was able to tune in and receive snatches of lower frequencies in much the same way a short-wave radio receiver might. *How can it let me down when I need it most?* Of all the possibilities that nagged at him, there was one he refused to believe. *If she was dead, I'd know it, wouldn't I?*

Exhausted from his efforts, he tried again without success and then it suddenly dawned on him; The Sister had something to do with his connectivity problem. *You must learn to respect the space and barriers other people put up.* Had she taken something away from him to teach him that?

He dialled a number into his telephone. A sleepy sounding female voice answered.

'Carla, can I count on your discretion?'

'Why, what's happened?'

Miller related everything he could think of to her. She listened patiently to the whole story without interrupting.

'Needless to say, if he gets wind I'm looking for him or he finds out the police are involved; he'll kill her.'

'Who else knows about this letter from Kennedy?'

'No one, apart from one of his colleagues, John Tanner.'

'I know him,' she said. 'You say Kennedy told you he thought the man blackmailing him was the kidnapper of at least two women, and could have links to the Gasman, and the Midnight man? You know something, Bruce; I've been looking for a story to break on this guy ever since that tape turned up when I was at the News of the World.'

'Carla, that's great, but we haven't got a thing to go on and I really need to find him.'

'I have a name.' The simple statement dropped it on him like a bomb.

'You have a name? Why didn't you say so before? Who is it?'

'Until you finished I couldn't be sure – it's William Shaw, also known as Martin Boyle. We had a hell of a time tracing him.'

'Wait a minute – who's *we?*'

'A contact I have in the job.'

'In the police?'

'Yes.' She knew he'd ask anyway, so she told him. 'It's Tanner.'

Since Tanner had given him Carla's number, he was only mildly surprised. 'Carla, have we got an address?'

'No, we found out who he is, but he's always on the move, even his own people never know where he is. He's a bare-knuckle fighter, at least he was. Something of a legend, by all accounts. It's rumoured he owns several properties, but we haven't been able to trace any so far. Not under that name.'

'I'm sure you have already, but I have to ask; have you checked under his mother's maiden name?'

'No, but what makes you ask?'

'It's just a hunch, that's all.'

'I'll see what I can find out.'

'Carla...you and Tanner?' He let the question hang.

'Oh, Bruce.' She laughed. 'I didn't know you cared.' Although she didn't deny it, she did not confirm it either.

No nearer to finding Stella, an odd mix of emotion washed over him. Desperation and despondency combined with relief and elation, as he finished the call.

Chapter 142

Stella woke up on a filthy mattress on the floor. At first she didn't move. She checked her body over, mentally feeling for anything untoward. *I'd know if he'd raped me, wouldn't I?* She couldn't be sure. Her head pounded in a strange way. She felt disconnected and numb.

Looking around, she realised she was effectively in a cage; the front wall of her enclosure consisted of floor to ceiling round steel bars; the heavy drape curtain the other side, kept them hidden. She tried to call out, but her dry throat managed only a hoarse whisper.

She noticed a bucket next to the toilet on the back wall. *There's water in it!* The film of scum on top revealed it wasn't fresh.

She tried to produce enough saliva to lubricate her throat without success. She took a deep breath and put a hand into the bucket, wetting it and cautiously sniffing it before scooping a handful to her mouth and sipping. It tasted like goldfish water; she resisted the urge to spew it back out and swallowed.

She realised she couldn't seem to focus for more than a few seconds at a time. *How did I get here?* Pinching the bridge of her nose used to help her concentrate when she was at school; she squeezed hard. *That's it!* A large white van had pulled up next to her as she came out of her garden gate onto the street; she thought it was a delivery for someone else. She heard the rumble of the side door sliding back. Somebody had grabbed her, hauled her inside. Something put over her mouth…couldn't breathe...and now she was here.

She tried to shake the fuzziness from her head – so damn tired! She sank back to the floor, dragged down into sleep again.

A metallic clunk followed by the dry scraping of a heavy bolt roused her. He pulled the curtain open only enough to allow him in, he was holding something; she backed away into a corner as he grabbed her by the back of her neck. He pushed her face down into the filthy mattress; she gagged dryly as he penetrated her forearm with a sharp needle.

She bucked against him. He pinned her with his weight. The vacuum from the syringe drew out a swirl of her blood into the mixture, filling its chamber before he plunged it back into her.

'What's that you've just put in me?' she demanded, outraged.

'That? Don't you worry about that!' He cupped his groin. 'When I recover from this dog bite, you'll get a better injection than that, if you know what I mean. You'll be begging me for it soon enough.' His eyes were cold; his fleshy lips pulled tight against his teeth, baring them. 'It hurts too much, but it's nothing a Viagra couldn't sort out.'

She shrank into the corner of the cage, terrified.

He taunted her in a camp voice, 'Frankie says, *relax.* Enjoy the ride.'

Frankie? Who the hell is Frankie? A wave of nausea washed over her. She only just made it to the toilet before the contents of her stomach expelled themselves.

With no windows, her sleep patterns disrupted, Stella lost track of how long she'd been there; it could have been days, or even a week. He'd bring small portions of food and water three times a day as far as she could tell and stay to watch while she ate. After, he'd inject her before leaving. She realised it was pointless to resist. The combined food, drink, injection routine had a strange effect on her. She began to look forward to it and the warm escape to oblivion that followed.

At first, she told herself Miller would find her quickly. He'd miss her, realise she'd gone and start on her trail, after all that was what he did – find missing people. *Where are you, Miller?*

Had he even *realised* she was missing? Her mind strayed into other areas of possibility, opening up new thoughts, but never for long. The drug he'd given her made it impossible to think about *anything* for any length of time. She concluded it must be heroin. *Is he trying to make me an addict?*

It was the last thought she had before drifting out of consciousness. She dreamt she was a little girl again, eight years old and on holiday with her parents; she ran over the shale on the beach, eager to reach them, so happy to see them again. She slipped on the gravel and grazed her knee. Her father scooped her up, and she wrapped her arms around him, weeping softly into his neck. 'Daddy, it hurts so much!'

'I know sweetheart, I know, but when something hurts you,' the thickening in his throat caught his voice, 'think about happy days and shake it off. It works for me.'

She opened her eyes, wiped them, and rolled closer to the bars. Her dad had marched through hell to get to the other side. He just kept going. Her thoughts touched on the mystery of their suicide pact. She still couldn't bring herself to believe he'd just given up. He'd have never done that. No matter how bad things were, he'd have steered them out, carrying her mother with him on his back and holding Stella's hand. *Why did you have to persuade him to do it, Mum?* She steeled herself. *I have to get out of here!*

She crawled to the bars that imprisoned her. From what she was able to see under the curtains, she was in a box within a box behind a caged wall, beyond that was a locked door.

While waiting for him to come with food, drink and her next fix, she positioned herself so she could see beyond the curtains from different angles when he drew back the curtain. A gleaming polished pole ran between floor and ceiling in one corner. Too substantial for a pole dancer's; it was more like a fire fighter's pole. It had thick rubber crash mats at the foot of it. So far, she'd not seen what was at the top of it, there was obviously a doorway onto it from upstairs.

Why would you have one of those in your house?

She soon became aware she wasn't the only woman held captive. There were others, but they never spoke until he was out. When the mouse-squeak of a step on the stairs was followed by the sound of the front door closing shortly after, the voice of the 'Urger' would start.

Stella couldn't make out exactly what she was saying; she seemed to be trying to get the other woman to talk to her, but she wouldn't. This continued until eventually the Urger was warned to be quiet. There wasn't any conversational flow. One would urge, the other would warn.

The voices came from above her.

He clearly kept them separated from each other. She imagined from the muffled level of sound that there were at least two doors between her and them. She decided to take a chance and called out into the void beyond the curtain. 'Hello. Can anybody hear me?'

She waited for an answer; the silence hung for what seemed an eternity. She called out again, louder this time. 'Can *anybody* hear me?'

The Urger's voice whispered cautiously. Although barely audible, her words were unmistakable. 'Who's there?'

'Shush!' the Warner's voice insisted.

The front door slammed, cutting the tentative exchange short.

He was back!

Chapter 143

Without a word, Martin stripped off and went straight into the shower. A few minutes later, he emerged with a towel around his waist and a devilish glint in his eye. 'Here, Cath, look at this.'

She stared at the protrusion; her expression remained impassive, but the apprehension she felt filled with her with dread. She said nothing.

'Jesus, this is the first time since,' he said, removing the towel. 'Look at that!'

She'd known it was only a matter of time. He brushed past her and returned to the bathroom where he removed a key from the pocket of his discarded jeans. Her eyes followed him. He stopped at Eilise's door and unlocked it.

She knew she had to do something. 'Martin, it's been such a long time.' She took him in her hand, stroking.

He shoved her to one side. 'Get out of my way; I've kept her waiting for long enough!'

She leapt onto his back wrapping her arms and legs around him. He stumbled one, two, three steps, and then regained his balance. He twisted around and launched backwards, crashing her against the wall. The collision knocked the wind out of her, but she hung on. He reached back over his head and grabbed her hair. Her nails dug deep into his hand as she tried to release his grip. With his free hand, he opened the door and pitched forwards at the waist, almost taking her scalp off as he threw her over his shoulder into the void. As she fell, she grasped in vain at the pole.

He thought he heard a sound behind him, hesitating; he listened intently at Eilise's door and then relocked it. He stooped to where his jeans lay, replaced the key in the pocket, and then drew the belt out from the waistband. In three strides, he crossed the room, wrapped himself around the polished steel pole and slid down after Cathy.

The sudden unlatching sound of a door opening reached Stella's ears. Low grunts of exertion, followed by the cry of a woman in pain, the rustling of clothes and the scrape of feet dragging across the floor above.

'No, Martin!' The intensity of the voice startled Stella. She held her breath, afraid of what might happen next.

Something thudded onto the crash mats. Stella gasped at the sight.

A woman laid there, crumpled, her back towards Stella. She whimpered pitifully.

Stella pressed flatter on the floor and lifted the edge of the curtain. A grating sound, metal on metal rasped down the pole. A pair of booted feet dropped into view and landed square on the crash mat.

Stella withdrew, terrified he'd see her.

'You know what you're going to get now, don't you?'

She whimpered louder.

'Martin, please,' she implored. 'I was jealous. I'm sorry. Oh, Martin, my leg. It really hurts.' Her vowels sounded as if her tongue were a large pebble. *Maybe he'd hit her there.*

He grabbed the back of her top and ripped it from her.

'No – *please* don't!' she said, her voice cracked, and no longer restrained. She cried openly.

Stella peered under the curtain and bit her lip. Long angry scars criss-crossed the woman's back. A belt buckle dangled into view. Suspended, it turned slowly until it revealed the grotesque effigy emblazoned on the other side of it. A screaming skull wreathed by laurels. It created an air of menace almost as unbearable as the pain about to be inflicted. He paused, and seeming to consider which end to strike with.

She stood slowly, terrified he might hear. With one hand over her mouth, she stifled the sound of her ragged breathing. The silence, impossibly stretched, broke. The belt cut through the air. Swoosh – crack. The woman cried out.

Stella backed away; eyes squeezed shut. She knew she should do something. At least *say* something, but the fear she'd be next sapped her courage.

Swoosh – crack! Swoosh – crack! With every vicious strike against her bare flesh, the woman cried out and wailed in dread expectation of the next.

Stella had retreated, slid to her haunches against the wall. Knees drawn up, hands over ears, she prayed for the nightmare to end. A vision of her father came to mind. *What would he have done in her situation?*

Her eyes opened. She rose, approached the curtain and spoke loud, her voice filled with authority. 'For God's sake – leave her alone!'

For the second time in as many minutes, menacing silence reigned. Her bladder puckered with fear, threatening her resolve.

The curtain swished back, and Martin's dead black eyes bored into hers, his face flushed and contorted with hatred. Defiant, she stared back. A droplet of urine moistened her pants. About to fall apart, she wrestled with the voices in her head and finding one strong enough, spat at him through the bars. 'Well, what are you going to do – *kill* me?'

He moved with deliberate slowness to the cabinet that housed the key to her cell. Inserting it into the lock, he turned it.

'Yes – but first I'm going to give you something to remember me by.'

He swung open the gate.

Stella had backed herself into a corner, if she could feint left and quickly go right, duck under his reach, she might just have a chance to escape. She prayed the lower door wasn't locked.

He was almost on her. *Time to make that choice, Stella. Look at his eyes, look the way you want him to think you'll go and then go in the opposite direction.*

With both avenues cut off by his direct approach, her only remaining chance was to dive beneath the spread of his arms. She took a deep breath.

Barely perceptible, a high squeak came from beyond the door. He heard it and stopped, listened with head tilted. *Someone is on the stairs!* He dashed for the cupboard door; the flayed woman grabbed at his ankle and he stumbled. She wrapped both hands around his shin and held on fast. He lashed out at her with his free leg.

'Let go, Cath!' he yelled.

Still she held on. He dispatched her with a grunt, rabbit punching her behind the ear. She exhaled and rolled over unconscious.

Without exiting the cupboard, he listened intently. No one was on the stairs, and the front door remained shut. Satisfied nothing was amiss, he returned to Stella. A snarl tightened the skin across his face, and the broken bones of his nose showed white beneath the skin, black eyes blazing with the only emotion that ever touched them. Rage.

'Now you're going to pay,' he said, grabbing onto her arm so tightly she thought it would break. His grip stopped the circulation to her fingers, and they felt cold and numb. She fought back, tried to snatch away. He rewarded her with the same punch he'd dealt Cath. Stella tried not to let the lights go out, fought against losing consciousness and lost.

Stella opened her eyes. On her knees unable to move, he'd tied her arms by the wrists behind her back, secured them to her heels and left her half slumped against the sofa. She realised with horror he'd undressed her, and she tried to focus on how she felt *down there*. She couldn't feel anything. *He hasn't raped me.* Her elation lasted for the only briefest moment; it was a temporary reprieve. It was coming.

He re-entered the room holding a syringe; he tapped the air bubbles to the top, shooting them out. He knelt beside her. She thought about her father once more. *That happy holiday.* She smiled vaguely.

'What did I tell you? You've been looking forward to this now, haven't you?'

He pushed the needle into her. The drug rushed through her veins with a power that shut her down systematically. She knew instinctively he'd given her too much, but she no longer cared. She was resigned to her fate. No one was coming for her. She closed her eyes and prayed for sweet release, hoping she'd feel no pain. She smiled.

The half-smile was still on her lips when he tied the stocking gag tightly around her face.

Chapter 144

Miller suddenly realised what day it was – Friday the thirteenth. Although not normally superstitious, he felt wary. The sky darkened as he pulled into the car park beside the café, a single splat of water struck the windshield so hard it jarred him from his thoughts. The aqueous explosion was a mere precursor to what would come next. The wind rose up out of nowhere, whipping up a machine gun burst of similar sized drops that pounded the car and ricocheted off in all directions.

He couldn't recall another time he'd experienced rain like it apart from the time Kirk had given him a lift many years before. *Kennedy! The last time I saw him it rained like this.*

Whichever way he turned in his investigations into Stella's kidnapping he couldn't tune in, and he couldn't focus. The awareness that trickled in through dreams, the shadowy perceptions – had all left him. All signals were jammed.

His car door suddenly opened, and a soaking wet Kennedy got in.

Miller clutched at his chest. 'You nearly gave me a heart attack! We're going to have to stop meeting like this, John.'

'Yes, I've been trying to reach you for a few days – couldn't get through,' he chuckled. 'Listen, I know where Stella is.'

Miller turned his full attention to the DCI. 'Where?'

'We don't have much time. Come on, drive. I'll show you where.'

Miller crunched out of the car park.

'Turn left,' Kennedy said.

'Where am I heading?'

'Grays.'

Once on the main road Miller put his foot down. For the first time since she'd vanished, he felt connected to her. She was alive, but in great danger.

With Stella securely bound and gagged upstairs, Boyle decided to check on Cathy. She was still unconscious. Turning to go back up, he reached the bottom step and froze. *The bolts on the inside face of the door are drawn back!* Puzzled, he knew he'd secured them when he returned earlier. He climbed the stairs, pausing on the loose step, shifting his weight. *That squeak from just now – it cannot be.* He sped up the remaining treads and checked Eilise's door. *Locked!*

'Eliza, are you in there? Answer me.' Met with silence, he unlocked the door feverishly. He howled in disbelief when he saw that she'd gone. He thundered across the floor looking everywhere for her. Cathy mercifully remained unconscious, Stella, hovering on the brink of another world, imagined she heard him cursing and growling. The thread she'd floated away on tautened. She stopped, held in limbo. *Something is happening.* She didn't want to die. Hand over imaginary hand she began clawing her way back.

Martin was in Eilise's room. She'd been unable to escape with her bags; he'd rifled through her meagre possessions before, but he had no reason to look beyond what was in front of him. This time he tipped everything out onto the floor and began sifting through everything, examining her clothes, turning out pockets on a hunch. He was amazed at how little she possessed; even for a runaway. She'd obviously packed only what she needed. He held up a pair of patchwork jeans that were clearly too small for her. *What did she need these for?* His hands crumpled over every inch of them, and then turning them inside out; he found a secret pocket had been stitched in, using an old silken scarf. He felt something under his fingers, and defined the edges before tearing the lining away to reveal the contents. A note, folded in half, written on the smallest piece of paper possible, revealed a name and address. He scratched his head and pondered. *Why hide it? If you lost your jeans and wanted them back, you'd put the address in an obvious place.* The answer dawned on him quite suddenly. *I know where you're going, and I'm coming to get you back.*

But first, he'd fuck Cathy's sister. With Eilise gone, the prospect now excited him more than anything; his upper lip pained as he grinned. *They had no idea how close they'd come to being reunited.*

He couldn't wait to see the look on Stella's face when he told her.

Chapter 145

'There! Over there. That's the block of flats.' Kennedy pointed to a parking space. 'Pull in here.'

Miller brought the car to an abrupt halt. The two men leapt from the car and ran up to the entrance; the DCI unlocked the communal door with a fire brigade key. Once inside they charged through the lobby, hesitated by the lift and decided to take the stairs.

'You go on ahead, Miller,' he said, already breathless. 'It's on the seventh floor. Number seventy-one. Quickly!'

All that working out on the treadmill is paying off today, he thought as he left Kennedy behind. After what seemed an eternity, he reached the seventh floor and burst out of the lobby into the corridor looking left and right for the flat numbers. Someone had removed them from the walls. He started in the wrong direction. Kennedy emerged behind him. 'It's that way,' he said with a jerk of his thumb.

Although the numerals were missing, Miller located the door easily.

'Do I knock?' He looked at Kennedy.

'No time. Break it down!' Miller shouldered the door; it gave much easier than he expected, and he stumbled half-falling into the passageway.

'She's upstairs!' Kennedy shouted.

He took the stairs two at a time and sprang through the first open door.

Boyle towered naked and fully erect over Stella, with his unbuckled belt in his hand. A thin trickle of blood ran down the inside of her forearm, an empty syringe lay discarded beside her. Bound hand and foot, and stripped of her clothes, she leaned sideward against the sofa, her face filled with fright and desperation. Her eyes fluttering as she tried to stay conscious, lit briefly as she recognised him, and then shut. Her head slumped forward.

Boyle turned, calmly wrapping the belt around the fist of his right hand, confident the smaller man was no threat to him. 'I told you didn't I?' he snarled, licking his lips, 'if you came looking, I'd kill her. I've given her enough horse to stop a fuckin' rhino. Now, it's your turn.' Cold-eyed and ugly, he fixed Miller with a stare and advanced towards him.

Miller felt terror tugging at his knees. Boyle had to be in his late sixties, but he looked no older than a fifty-year-old. An abhorrence; a freak of nature, muscular and lean, faced with a man like that, most people would have turned and run, but with Stella's fate in his hands, he had no choice. Deprived of any semblance of his previous abilities, he didn't know what to do. Four words came to him, *pusty umysł...no mind.* A blue flash of lightning illuminated the room. Thunder rolled. It started to rain.

He'd hesitated a moment too long. Boyle's huge belt-wrapped fist hurtled towards his face, faster than a cannonball.

With only a millisecond to go until impact, the shadows returned, seeming to slow down time. The shadow-shape of a man formed on the wall opposite and dropped, spinning on the axis of his hands. *Copy me, boy!* Miller aped the movements of the shadow with lightning speed. He spun, palms down on the floor scribing a wide arc in a blur of movement anti-clockwise, his right leg like a scythe, took the other man's legs out from under him. He crashed down hard onto his back. Winded, he raised his head off the floor.

Miller gave him no chance to recover. He shot up driving the heel of his foot with full force into Boyle's face; his head smacked hard against the floor. He glanced at the shadow on the wall. It echoed his posture.

With his opponent out on the floor sprawled on the floor unconscious, Miller knew he had to work fast. *No time to untie or dress her. He had to get her to the hospital right away.* The nearest was five minutes away. He couldn't risk the wait for an ambulance, so he scooped her into a fireman's lift and ran, surrounded by shadows and darkness down seven floors of stairs, surprised at how weightless she felt.

Once he'd got her into the car; he drove at high speed. If she were to survive, every second would count. There was a bus in front. He caught it up and veering round to get past it, immediately pulled back. *Two of them!* He couldn't risk overtaking both buses at the same time. Frustrated, he banged his hand down hard on the steering wheel and gauged the chances of forcing the oncoming traffic to let him pass. He indicated to overtake. The bus directly in front pulled in at a stop. Jubilant, he shouted, 'Yes!'

The chance to get by the remaining bus had suddenly become a realistic prospect, and he edged out to overtake.

An elderly woman lurched unexpectedly off the pavement into the road. Hitting the brakes, he narrowly avoided her. The bus in front had stopped. If she'd only hurry out of his way – he could get in front of it before it pulled out again. She took what seemed like forever to finish crossing in front of him, staring balefully into the car, muttering something about inconsiderate drivers.

Come on! The bus indicated to pull out and started rolling forwards. Miller gunned the car like a kamikaze pilot, out around the front of the bus and into the path of the oncoming traffic, before swerving back into his own lane. He felt the adrenaline surging through his system. His neck felt hot under his collar.

Two minutes later, he arrived at A & E.

An hour later, Miller was at her bedside. It had taken two Naloxone injections to wipe out the effects of the heroin, she'd renarcotised after the first. Although she appeared stable, the doctors wanted her kept under observation.

The corners of her mouth lifted when she saw him, relieved to be in the hands of someone she trusted, but she didn't feel much like smiling. She felt spaced out and peculiar and on top of that, more than anything, though she'd never ask for it, she needed sympathy. She yawned, long and loud.

'Oh, Miller, I can't stop *yawning,*' she said. 'I thought you'd abandoned me. What took you so long?'

'Stella, you need to rest.'

'What about the other girls – what happened to them? Are they okay?'

'The police found one of them. The other one escaped. They haven't found her yet.'

'And what about him…they have arrested him, right? I was so scared when he tied me up like that – I thought – you know; I thought I would die.' She blinked rapidly, holding back tears.

'Come on now, you rest.'

Although she was still fuzzy and out of it, she needed to talk. 'Those were the things I've dreaded the most in my life since Kathy went missing. Kidnap, rape, murder, tied up. I never expected to suffer all those things at once.' She looked dejected and sad, but Miller beamed.

'Why are you grinning at me like that? It's not funny.' Her shoulders slumped, deflated.

'Well, unless something else happened you didn't tell me about, you got away with at least two of the things you just mentioned.'

'*And* injected with a drugs overdose,' she added it to the list without emotion. He stopped her.

'Okay, okay, you have every right to feel sorry for yourself. Did I tell you about the time I got murdered once?'

She poked her tongue at him. 'He *was* going to rape me, if he hadn't been bitten in the crotch by a guard dog, if he'd been functioning – it doesn't bear thinking about. Miller, he was a complete schizo. By the way, you kept that one quiet, didn't you?'

Miller looked confused. 'What?'

'Just before I passed out, that move…you didn't tell me you could do *that* stuff! When I saw you do that, I knew we were going to be okay. I mean – what the hell was that?'

He laughed. 'Oh that,' he said, modestly, 'was combat, Korean style!'

'Miller?'

'Yes?'

'Thank you.' With tears brimming, her lips quivered, and she bit the top one, holding herself in check. 'This has all been such a nightmare.'

He wasn't sure now was the time to tell her. She saw the look on his face. 'You didn't answer me just now. They did get him, didn't they?'

'Stella, there's a police guard outside the door. They told me when they got there, Boyle was gone.' Miller's words took a moment to sink in.

'Oh no, that means...'

'Stella, he'd have to be crazy to come after us again, the police would catch him straight away.'

'But that means it isn't over.' Stella's eyes looked haunted. 'Doesn't it?'

The door knocked, opening simultaneously. Tanner strolled in with a female officer, and despite making a beeline for Miller, he addressed Stella without looking at her. 'I'm sorry it couldn't wait. We're keen to pick this scumbag up as soon as possible. This is DI Wright,' he said, pointing to her. 'So if you're up to it, we have a few questions we'd like you to answer.'

Pulling Miller to one side, he said, 'How did you get there before we did?'

'Well, I have to confess, I had a little help from a friend on the inside.'

'What, working with Boyle?'

'No, working with you – only you didn't know it.'

'Don't smart-arse me, Miller. I'm not in the mood. Who was it?'

'It was Kennedy. He showed me how to get there—'

'You were *with* Kennedy. Where is he now?'

'He disappeared after he showed me where Boyle was holding Stella. I guess he didn't want to get involved, not until he's sorted his mess out.' He stopped himself short; he had a flash of the first time he ran into Kennedy at the cafe.

It was raining like Armageddon that day as well; he recalled how Kennedy disappeared. The look on the girl's face in the café when he'd asked where Kennedy had gone. *'Who?'* she'd said.

He examined Kennedy in his mind's eye. Seeing him again after the reunion dinner – in the cafe the first time – he couldn't *read* him or anything else when he was near. It all began to fall into place. The DCI had shadowed Miller ever since he disappeared. It was something to do with the rain, but what, he didn't know.

'Miller, I haven't got all day – who was it?' Tanner sounded irritated.

'I'm not sure I can tell you *that* at the moment, but I think I know where Kennedy is.'

'This had better be good,' Tanner said.

'I think you'd better come with me, John,' Miller said, softly.

The clues had been there all along; even the letter had spelled it out. *Do not try to find me at this stage.*

The following day, the local newspaper carried the headline: *Missing DCI. Police identify body.*

Inside the paper, the article was brief. *Police confirmed the identity of a body found hanging beneath the stage in a disused basement area of a local school as being the missing DCI John Kennedy; police have ruled out foul play. The family has requested their privacy be respected at this difficult time.*

Chapter 146

As soon as she heard him flaying poor Cathy, Eilise rose from her hiding place behind the sofa. In the melee a few moments before, she'd crept unseen out of her room, before he'd locked it again.

She sneaked down the stairs; every step taken painfully slow – she didn't know exactly which one creaked. She held on to the banister and took the steps two at a time. She'd worked out it would decrease her chances of landing on the creaky step by fifty percent, plus it sped her descent.

Too late, she froze at the first tiny creak. She stabilised her weight across the step, the handrail above, lent some support, but she didn't have the strength to prevent herself from applying more downward pressure on her foot. She shifted slowly onto the one below, realising it wasn't the weight going onto it that triggered the sound; it was the weight coming off. The stair chose a lull in the proceedings to issue its distressed rodent-like screech.

He'd have heard that! No time to make it back upstairs – no time to get out of the front door. With the keys she'd lifted from his jeans, she would need at least a minute to unlock the door quietly. With nowhere else to hide, she tucked herself behind the swing of the cupboard door and prayed he wouldn't find her.

The door swung back. She pressed herself flat against the wall. If the door touched her, he'd feel it. The wheeze from his exertions passed across the edge of the door in the direction of the stairs. *Three breaths.* She imagined his face the other side, turning then to check the front door.

Keen to get on with the business of beating Cathy, he didn't step out into the passageway. Her lungs on the verge of bursting, a cough tickled at her throat. In a desperate effort to suppress it, she desperately sucked a glob of saliva from her dry mouth and swallowed hard.

Finally, he withdrew, shutting the door behind him. She exhaled long and slow and then with her ear to the door, listened. As the sounds of further punishment inflicted on Cathy seeped from the room, she made her escape.

Out on the street, she familiarised herself with where she was. She couldn't see a telephone booth anywhere, but there was a McDonalds only a few hundred yards away. She ran all the way, stopping outside to compose herself, and then walked in to steal a mobile phone from a young mum too busy feeding her child to notice.

She dialled 999 and asked the operator for the police.

'Listen, my name is Eilise Staples. I've just escaped from a kidnapper.'

The operator tried to slow her down.

'There's no time! Two women are about to be murdered. You've got to hurry!' She gave the address, adding, 'It's on the seventh floor, number seventy-one.'

She calmly returned to the table where the young mother continued to sit and bent down to the floor. She held out the phone she'd retrieved.

'I just found this on the floor, is it yours?'

At the railway station, Eilise debated whether to bunk the fare, but decided she couldn't afford to fall into the hands of the authorities. Not yet. She cadged enough money to buy a ticket and within half an hour was on a train heading for Romford. The journey would be a short one.

Once on the train, Eilise recalled how she'd obtained her mother's address.

She'd stared at the piece of paper for ages, not quite believing she held the key to her future in her hands. She memorised it, then terrified she might forget, decided to hide it, but where?

The last thing she wanted was for her foster parents to find it. She moved it around, trying several places, starting with between the pages of a book, but, after putting it back on the shelf, she stared at it for a while, not happy. What if her sister came in and took that book, choosing it from all the others on the shelf? Her eyes settled on the dressing table. Squatting, she pulled out a drawer and held it up, looking underneath. She could tape it to the underside. It would have to be at the bottom, otherwise the clothes from a lower one could snag it. She put the note in her pocket and went to look for some tape in the kitchen.

Staring out of the train window, Eilise dug her fingernails into the fabric of her jeans, pinching the flesh of her thigh beneath, hoping the hurt would stifle her stream of thought, but she was too far gone to be able to stop.

Her foster father had come up behind her, uncomfortably close. Pulling away, she noticed he had this funny expression in his eyes; she'd seen it more and more lately. She didn't know what it was, but she didn't like it. She continued opening drawers, systematically rummaging through before moving on to the next one.

'What are you looking for?' His voice was low, guttural.

'I'm just...I'm hoping to find some sellotape.' Then, realising he'd probably ask what for, she added quickly, 'The binding on my homework book is coming apart.'

'Well, you should have said. I've got something that will do the job nicely, I think.' He reached up into the top cupboard over the coffee machine and grabbed a thick roll of metallic coloured tape. 'Let's go and have a look, shall we?'

She recalled it as if it were yesterday. She tried to fob him off, the colour was wrong for a schoolbook. Her friends would laugh, but he was having none of it. He was now in her room.

'Now let's have a look at that book, shall we?'

She opened her bag and pulled it out.

He looked closely from the roll of tape to her. 'You're lying to me,' he said. 'You weren't that desperate to find tape to fix a book that's still in your bag.' His eyes gleamed. He seemed to know something.

She blushed. The tape rasped as he pulled a strip from the roll and tore it off.

'You know this stuff has all kinds of uses.' His eyes had become defocused as he moved towards her. He stuck the tape over her mouth. Her turn had come. Her

foster mother was out. She realised in her excitement over finding the address, she hadn't yet seen her sister come home.

When it was over, he pulled the tape from her lips roughly. 'Only way to do it and that's quickly.'

The tape took a small piece of skin from her lip and made it bleed. Too numb to feel pain, she glanced about her; not quite believing what had just happened was real. Touching her mouth, she looked at the thin smear of blood on her fingers. He adjusted his clothing and leaning down to see in the mirror, smoothed his hair.

'It'll be better next time, if you're a good girl, we won't use the tape.' He offered her a tissue he'd taken from his pocket. Eilise turned away sharply.

'Don't get any ideas about telling anyone,' he said with an air of menace. 'If you say anything, I'll kill you and tell them you must have run away.' At the door, he paused. 'If your mother asks about the lip, you accidentally bit it. Got that?'

As soon as he left the room, she broke down. Silent tears blurred her vision, and she trembled, fighting back the urge to scream. She looked for the patched jeans that were once her favourites. They didn't fit anymore, so she stitched a patch made from a silky scarf to form a pocket on the inside and taking the note, placed it inside. She stitched it closed, sealing it in. Before turning the jeans out the right way, Eilise wiped herself on them and then hung them in the farthest dark corner of her wardrobe. There they would stay until she needed them. She was just fourteen.

When her foster mother had come home, she knew something had happened; the guilt showed through in his over-attentiveness and Eilise's detachment. His threat still inhabited her ears. *If you say anything, I'll kill you and tell them you must have run away.*

Soon afterwards, she did exactly that; she ran away for the first time. In her head, they were all dry runs, seeing how far she could get before they caught up with her. It would be another year before she actually got away; carrying everything she needed in two black bin bags including the patchwork jeans, concealing the note she'd use, to get him for what he did.

As for the note, hidden away as it was, it reminded her of her objective. She didn't know what would happen when she arrived there. The possibility of rejection was a risk, but if she never tried, she'd never know. The one thing she was certain of was that she didn't want to wake up one day when she was older; when it was maybe too late, thinking; *why didn't I go to my mum's while I was young, and had a chance for us both to make something of it.*

Eilise arrived exhausted and bedraggled, soaked right through. Never in a million years had she imagined her real mother lived in a place like this. She checked the number fixed on the gate, unfastened the catch and walked up the pathway. The double frontage with imposing old leadlight windows was set back among creeping ivy, neatly clipped, but still threatening to take over the last exposed areas of deep red brickwork.

At the door, under an open porch area out of the rain, she raised her hand to grasp the knocker, it reminded her of an antique pistol handle; she drew it back and let it go. The weight of it delivered a resounding bang on the black striking plate. She held her breath without realising while she waited for an answer.

A shape appeared in the bulls-eye window. The face distorted unexpectedly as it leaned forward to peer out, so one eye appeared as if it were looking through a magnifying glass.

'Who is it?' said a female voice.

This is going to be a toughie, she thought.

Chapter 147

The moment she'd rehearsed so often was upon her, the many variations practiced played through her head: *Hello, Mum, I'm your daughter...Hi, Mum, I was your little girl ...I'm the little girl you gave away, all grown up now...*

The door opened. All her words were chased away.

'Can I help you?' The woman's eyes narrowed with suspicion. 'I think you must have knocked at the wrong house.'

'If you are not Jackie Solomons then you're right – I've knocked at the wrong house, I'm pretty sure you're Jackie, though,' she took a deep breath. 'You gave me up for adoption. I don't suppose you remember me do you?'

Jackie always knew this time would come. Lost for words, she looked Eilise up and down, taking in the scruffy clothes, the unwashed hair, and her hollow, haunted eyes. The girl on her doorstep didn't stop looking back over her shoulder.

'You'd better come in,' she said. 'What shall I call you?'

'Eilise,' she murmured, almost ashamed. Then she told her everything. A long silence ensued.

For whose benefit did I give you up all those years ago – was it for you? Or did I do it for me? Jackie scoured her conscience. Because she couldn't face living with the offspring of her rapist, she'd consigned her into the hands of a child abuser. *An innocent young girl; she didn't deserve that. Would things have turned out better if I'd done something different?* It was something new to haunt her.

Should I be feeling something for her? Numb, that's what I feel. She studied Eilise and saw something of herself in those lost eyes. *She has my eyes!*

Eilise stared at her, and waited for the one thing that might change everything. A tiny crescent lifted the corner of her mouth into a smile that didn't reach her eyes.

She knew Jackie never wanted her. In her heart, she knew nothing would change that, even after all she'd just told her. She'd had to come though, if only to see who'd carried her for nine months until she was ready to enter the world. At least they had that between them. It seemed there was nothing else to say. *You shouldn't have expected anything else, not really.* She stood, ready to leave.

'What are you doing?' Jackie asked.

'Sorry, I shouldn't have come.'

'Wait, Eilise.' She wasn't yet comfortable saying her name. It didn't roll the way it should from her tongue. 'There's something I should tell you.' The instant she'd said it she regretted it. She'd not even told Tina; she looked for a way out. She had no idea how Tina would react when she finally heard the truth.

'Come on; follow me upstairs, I'll run you a bath,' Jackie said.

On the way up, one of the steps creaked, and Eilise flinched, gasping aloud. Jackie turned. 'Don't worry,' she said, 'you won't fall through. I'll sort you out some clothes for when you come out.'

With Eilise in the bath, she crept downstairs, stepping over the noisy one. She'd been meaning to get it fixed for ages; until Eilise reacted like that, she'd forgotten all about it.

She picked up the phone and rang the police; the girl was underage after all.

The bluesy sound of female vocals started up in the bathroom. Jackie looked up at the ceiling and smiled.

Emergency, which service do you require... she put the phone down.

She needed time to work things out; she couldn't just put her back into a system that had failed her.

A taxi pulled up. *Thank God, Tina's home.*

She opened the front door to let her in and caught the whiff of stale cigarettes. Five discarded cigarette butts on the ground. One of them still smouldered. *Someone has been having a cigarette right by the porch! Who the hell has been smoking outside my front door like that?* She shuddered involuntarily. 'Tina quick, get inside.'

'What's wrong, Mum?'

'I'm not sure.'

She glanced around, nerves jangling before closing the door in a hurry and double locking it.

The strains of Eilise singing in the bath reached Tina's ears.

'Is that a new record, Mum?' she asked.

Sometimes, Jackie put music on upstairs while running the bath, or whilst getting ready. Focused on Eilise singing away upstairs, Jackie realised she actually had a very good voice.

'No, Tina, it isn't a record. It's a visitor. Someone I should have told you about years ago.'

'What are you talking about?' She started for the stairs.

'Tina, love, let's wait for her to come down.'

She took a step back and let her hand slide off the banister. 'Okay, but who is it?'

Jackie sat down, her hands clasped between her knees; not looking at Tina as she told her, 'It's your half-sister.'

Tina, displaying a maturity beyond her years, moved next to her and placed a hand on her shoulder.

'It's okay, Mum. Tell me all about it.'

The creaking stair behind announced Eilise had come down.

At first, Jackie was uneasy. She told them both what happened to her. There wasn't a point in the next half an hour where none of them cried. Eilise was a tough nut to crack, but she joined in when Jackie told them how she'd lost Harry.

And then Eilise described what had happened to her.

'You should get the police, Mum,' Tina said.

'The police would have got the other two girls out of there,' Jackie said. 'If I call them now—'

'If you do that, I'm going right now.'

Jackie could see she meant it. 'Don't worry, Eilise, we'll work something out in the morning, I promise.'

Later, while Eilise changed for bed, Tina asked, 'What will happen to her, Mum?'

'For now, she'll stay with us. In the morning – well, we'll just have to see.' Jackie cocked her head at her younger daughter, suddenly thoughtful. 'Tina, you don't mind if Eilise shares your room? It's just I wouldn't want her sneaking off in the night … she's a runaway you see and—'

'That's okay, Mum; I'll keep an eye on her.'

Jackie couldn't quite believe how well it had gone. The pills she'd popped an hour ago were dragging her into sleep. She pressed the fob to set the alarm. The activation light flashed. She cleaned her teeth, listening over the sound of the electric toothbrush for the beep to confirm the alarm had set. *Now what's wrong with this?* The power in the toothbrush ran out. She padded heavy-eyed, to the spare room to place it on charge.

In her room at last, she turned out the light and closed her eyes.

They've seen you; they know who you are. The game had turned against him, yet he was unafraid. Strange, but this new turn of events excited him in a way he'd not experienced in years.

Whether Eliza had come here or not, he decided he was going to have her mother. He calculated his chances; after what happened earlier, no one would expect him to turn up here and with Kennedy in hiding, not answering his phone, it was the perfect opportunity to fit him up one more time before exposing him.

There was no time to plan fully; his observations covered only a matter of hours. He noted the alarm was an old type, easily nobbled by a burglar of his ability. There was no sign of a man or dog, in occupation. He'd seen the mother when the young girl pulled up in a taxi. With all the curtains drawn, he couldn't see anything going on inside. Snippets of muffled conversation found their way into his ears, but he couldn't make out the words. Then he heard the singing. Rich and soulful, it had to be the mother. *Sing for me baby.* He'd overcome them all, one by one with the gas. They wouldn't know a thing until later, and by then he'd be long gone. He'd make up his mind about taking the girl back to another safe house later. *Shouldn't have ignored me, Kennedy.*

He went to fetch his equipment.

In the back garden, he finished his final cigarette and changed into his suit. Moving quickly with barely a sound, he masked up and struck a small windowpane with his elbow. The way he was hyped-up, he'd hear a pin drop, or feel the air pressure change if a door opened.

He felt supreme, superhuman.

Jackie often awoke with a start, sitting upright, not quite sure where she was. Despite the passing of time, the dreams still occurred with unpredictable frequency. Anything could spark them off. Sometimes, she knew it was because she'd seen a news report or a headline, or watched a film, but whatever it was, it was always the same. She'd wake up choking and gasping for air after he'd throttled her in yet another nightmare.

Tonight was different. Something woke her before she'd reached the end. The last vestiges of a sound replayed in her consciousness. *What was that? It sounded as if someone had popped a paper bag.* The noise came from downstairs.

She reassured herself. The house alarm would have sounded. It's nothing. Silent trepidation stretched on like the space between lightning and thunder – waiting for the rumble that confirmed it was far away.

Once inside, the intruder eased his way up the stairs; a tread groaned as he put weight onto it. He froze, listening for any sign that the movement had been detected. Easing his foot from the step, he continued his ascent.

Jackie lifted her head she thought she'd heard the stair tread complain. It was the step. She knew it. Knew *exactly* which one it was. The girls were in bed, so how? *When the toothbrush had run out of charge, and I'd...* A feeling of dread came over her. *The alarm! I never heard it beep when I set it.*

'Oh no,' she whispered, on the edge of panic. 'There's someone down there!'

Frantically, she started fumbling to open the bottom drawer, searching inside for her panic alarm, and the knife she kept in there. She knocked the table lamp over and caught it, but not before the base rocked loudly against the tabletop.

The intruder, almost at the top, hesitated. *Someone's moving around!*

Accelerating up the remaining stairs two at a time, he turned as he reached the landing; with eyes acclimatised to the darkness, he spotted a door handle turning. He moved up right outside and pressed himself flat against the wall.

Jackie opened the bedroom door.

He swung into view, startling her.

The Gasman!

She fell backwards over her own feet in her haste to get away, stunned by how quickly he'd gotten to her room. She struggled up into a sitting position, trying to catch her breath. She gasped in terror when she saw him in the light of her bedroom.

Then he was on her.

'Oh, n—ummph!' A huge hand clamped over her mouth.

'Is she here?' The voice was low, distorted by the mask. Her situation and the menace he managed to inject into just three words left her wide-eyed with fear. She shook her head at the question, desperate to protect Tina and Eilise.

He pushed himself closer. The cold perspex touched her face. 'I'll kill you if you're lying!'

She could smell his smoker's breath through the mask. A wave of revulsion washed over her, quickly overtaken by terror. She was about to be raped and murdered. The ordeal she'd endured years ago came back in an instant, crippling her limbs; she couldn't move. Jackie – the girl who vowed never to be a victim again, the girl who'd decked a soldier once – had gone to pieces, her muscles turned to jelly.

Her vulnerability excited him; he was too far gone to turn back now. He forgot about gassing her, there was only one thing on his mind.

His breathing ragged and amplified by the mask, he squatted next to her and parting her knees easily, ran a latex gloved hand up the inside of her thigh, hooking a finger into the crotch of her panties; she gagged dryly – a double retch.

Of all his victims, only one other had reacted that way. His mind accelerated back in time. He pushed her hair back with his free hand, scrutinising her closely. *It was her! Older, plumper, but her. The one that got away. The Cornwall Girl!* His penis stiffened as blood surged into it, throbbing in anticipation.

Jackie caught a movement in the corner of her eye. *Was it one of the girls?* She fixed her stare on the masked face holding his attention. He stared back with an all-consuming intensity and ripped off her knickers.

'Do-not-touch-me!' she shouted, no longer worried about waking the girls, the words empowered her limbs; she struggled wildly as his weight pressed down on her.

He ignored her efforts to fight back, overpowering her with ease. Only one thing was on his mind, as a cat fixed on its prey; nothing could distract him.

The Gasman pinned her to the floor. He wrestled himself into a position where he could easily control her with an arm barred across her neck. Her flailing hands didn't bother him. He didn't even care about the noise now. His free hand unbuckled his belt and started down his fly.

Jackie's eyes bulged as she strained against choking; her voice sounded strangulated, but the words were clear. 'For God's sake get it over with!'

Behind the mask, the man sneered.

An explosion went off inside his head.

'Leave – my – mum – alone!'

The girl's voice… What the…! She'd hit him with something. Instinct kicked in; he rolled over and caught himself on one knee, not quite going down. A ten count started in his head. *Ten-nine. Got to get up!* He closed his eyes. An unbearable brightness scorched them and intensified in the same way a light bulb flares before it dies. *S-she's b-broken your head!* A stuttering voice told him. In no position to defend himself, he had to get out.

Eilise brought the rounders bat down hard again, catching him on the shoulder as he stumbled to his feet. Through a bloody mist, he saw Eilise with a younger girl behind her. Jackie was on her feet screaming, 'Get out. GET OUT!' Her tiny fists bunched; her face contorted with anger; she activated the screamer.

For a few seconds, he stared balefully, gathering his senses. Eilise raised the bat above her head to warn him off. He faltered as he turned unsteadily, loping off. Eilise followed a few feet behind, to make sure he really did leave the house.

Chapter 148

S-she's b-broken your head! His father's voice ridiculed him from where he hid in the dark recesses of his mind. *Won't be long now, son, and you'll be stood before your maker. Remember who that was? Yeah, that's right, me. And I'll judge you. I ain't forgotten what you did to me...*

Boyle lurched the last few yards to where he'd left the car. He had trouble unlocking it. Once inside, he settled into the back of his seat. *You're concussed, don't go to sleep. She's stoved your head in.* His fingertips gently traced the source of the pain; an area of his skull felt dished. *Maybe it was always like that.* He couldn't be sure. The sticky dampness of his fingers confirmed what he'd already guessed; he was bleeding. *Got to get out, got to keep moving...* Starting the engine, he drove carefully to his lock-up situated in a quiet and respectable part of town.

The drive took a matter of minutes. He clambered from the car and opened the garage door. Once inside he stripped his outer garments leaving him wearing jeans and a sweatshirt. He threw the gasmask and the suit into a corner and then wheeled his motorbike out. Somewhat revived by the crisp night air, he scanned the windows of nearby houses, absently wondering if the pounding in his head could take the pummeling of a lengthy motorcycle ride. *Just got to do it.* He put the car away, shut the doors and donned his crash helmet, flinching as the inner lining scraped over his wound. He turned the key and pressed the starter button. The engine purred into life and then he roared out into the night.

The motorcycle's steady drone did nothing to ease the throbbing pain in his skull. He summoned thoughts to take his mind off it. Amidst the myriad of memories to choose from, one kept returning. He couldn't shake it out. After his mother's funeral, he'd left home, but returned a few days after to see his father...

I was thinking about the other day—

Why do you always speak wit' anyone else's voice but your own? Fucks me off something chronic the way you do that. You ashamed of your voice, sonny, is that what it is?

I'm g-going f-fish-fishing. D-down C-Cornwall f-for a f-few days. C-Camping out. I-I t-thought y-you m-might l-like to c-come—

What, wit' you? I don't think so!

On the long drive down, his father didn't stop babbling on at him. A couple of times he pulled over to check the boot, make sure he hadn't come back like Lazarus.

He humped him all the way down the hill from the barn at the top, down to the pond. In the early morning mist, visibility was down to twenty yards. The dew clung to his clothes and sparkled like diamonds. He wrapped him up and weighed him down. Smoked a last cigarette in his company and then heaved him into the black water. The font of all his dark obsessions gone, he wondered if he'd ever be free.

    A couple of hours later, in the countryside not far from where he was born, he followed a footpath for a short distance, until he came to a fence with a stile. Crossing over the top, he veered immediately to his right, into a row of bushes at the top of a deep ditch, exactly five paces from the style. Lighting a smoke, he inhaled deeply, and then used the lighter to locate the protruding head of a tent guy pin pushed deep into the ground. He withdrew it and with it dug out a buried biscuit tin. The metal had started rusting, but the plastic sandwich box within was intact. The waterproof container held the only tickets he needed to start a new life, a new passport and driving licence, a razor for shaving his head and a blonde moustache. Peeling the lid off, the orange glow of his cigarette tip revealed other contents. His fingers found five slim bundles of fifty-pound notes and lingered over a well-wrapped gramme of heroin. He thought about his head and grinned as far as his lips would allow. Another drag revealed something else in there, too. *Forty cigarettes, he'd thought of everything.*

Chapter 149

Eilise struck the intruder with such force it opened up a gash in the back of his head, which bled profusely. When they checked the blood against the national database, the DNA wasn't a match for that previously left by the Gasman. Tanner immediately thought there was a copycat on the loose. He thought about Kennedy. It was a significant piece of evidence, but not conclusive. He still might have a copycat on his hands. When Kennedy dropped off the face of the earth, and with everything else stacked against him, it seemed his guilt was assured. Yet something niggled at Tanner; he'd never really believed it was Kennedy enough to take it further. He didn't report the case to his superiors.

Half an hour later, a contact of his in the Forensic Science service called him.

'We've got a match for that sample. It's a match for DNA recovered from a rape, which took place in Cornwall in 1991. It's quite incredible really as we've only just reviewed that particular evidence using the new technology—'

'Have you got a name?'

'No, it's unidentified.'

'I've got to go. Ping me an email with the details you do have.'

Tanner was in a contemplative mood; he pondered on how Kennedy's fate had been hastened and sealed by wrong assumptions and bad decisions. If he hadn't allowed the blind desire for Theresa and the resentment of Kennedy to get in the way, he might have handled things differently. Although he knew self-recrimination would make no difference, he couldn't shake its heavy mantle from his shoulders.

The computer chimed its electronic delivery tone, announcing the arrival of a new message. He opened it. The contents proved Kennedy was no rapist, but raised disturbing questions. *First things first.*

He picked up the phone and dialled.

'Mrs Solomons, there's been an important development regarding the blood sample we analysed from your house. I think it's best if we talk about this face to face.'

'Is it that serious? Look, I'm not leaving Tina,' she said firmly. 'Can you come here?'

'I don't want to worry you unnecessarily, but it's best I see you. Are you there for an hour or so?'

Tanner arrived within the hour, and she let him in. Tina stood protectively by her side. 'Mrs Solomons.' He glanced at Tina. 'We need to speak in private.'

'Call me Jackie.' She turned Tina to face the stairs. 'Wait upstairs for me; this will only take a minute.'

'What's going on, John?'

'I think you'd better sit down,' he said, steering her towards the couch. 'You won't believe this, but the DNA we took from your house. It's a match with the sample taken from you, from when you were raped sixteen years ago.'

A stunned silence reigned for a complete minute while Jackie struggled to comprehend.

'But that must mean…' Tears welled, and she wiped them away on her sleeve. 'John, I need to get my daughter back from social services. Will you help me?'

'As soon as I get back, I'll have someone call you. Are you sure you'll be okay, just you and your daughter … she seems a bit young.'

'We'll be fine; I just need a moment alone.'

He let himself out and strolled to the car. *So, Kennedy was no rapist.*

After the suicide verdict, Kennedy's funeral took place on a wild, wet and windy day. Over a hundred people packed into the tiny church for the service. Tanner welcomed the invitation by Rose and John Kennedy to deliver a eulogy on behalf of his friends and colleagues.

'Not many people knew John Kennedy like I did.'

Tanner spoke of him warmly. His eyes settled on Kennedy's parents, Rose in a wheelchair, and John senior as always, by her side. He thought they'd diminished in physical stature, seemed to have shrunk since the last time he saw them. Their wet eyes shone with pride, as Tanner listed their son's many achievements.

'…and he was a great friend, and I wish he could have confided his troubles in someone, but that was the sort of man he was, fiercely private. He wouldn't have wanted to burden anybody else with his problems.' He looked up, eyes focused on an infinity beyond the roof of the church. 'John, heaven will be a safer place now you're there, and knowing you it won't be long before you start going after the top job.' Faces lit with smiles through the tears. 'Rest in peace my friend.'

Theresa dabbed at her eyes with a tissue.

Miller didn't venture far inside, preferring to observe the proceedings from behind everyone else.

The discovery of Melissa Lake's diaries in a hollowed out section of Boyle's bathroom door had exonerated Kennedy of all suspicion over the Gasman attacks. The detailed chronicles she'd kept as *her* life insurance, proved to be the salvation of Kennedy's reputation.

After the burial, Tanner caught up with Miller in the car park and confided in him.

'I can't tell you how bad Theresa and I felt suspecting Kennedy was behind a lot of the things that were going on.'

'Such a shame for his parents,' Theresa lamented.

'It wasn't all bad,' Miller told them. 'It led to the arrest and conviction of Danny Lynch and the key members if his gang.' He folded down his fingers as he continued. 'What happened to Kennedy led directly to the rescue of Stella Bird, and the release of her long lost sister. It brought about the reunion of the missing girl, Eilise Staples, and her real mother. And one other thing...' Miller paused. *Some things have to happen, before other things can happen. Was she behind all this?* He wondered just how far she'd have had to stretch her self-imposed 'cameraman' limits to engineer all those things.

Tanner interrupted his thoughts. 'I'm still waiting for the report on how you found Boyle's flat...' he winked, 'and let's not forget, we solved a lot of old cases out of it too. Even if Boyle *is* still out there.'

Miller nodded. 'Yes, that's true. Something I have to say to you though Tanner. I know you think Kennedy was the Vigilante killer.'

'Who told you that?'

'I just know,' he said, shrugging his shoulders. 'It wasn't him, it was Boyle again. He knew Kennedy would likely struggle with an alibi, so it was another way of keeping the poor guy under pressure... The thing is – and I know it's a bit controversial, but it's just us talking here – in those cases, Boyle actually did some good.'

Tanner shook his head. 'I can't say I disagree with the sentiment, but I can still see Kennedy doing it. Anyway, the official line is that those killings remain unsolved.'

Miller ran his fingertip over the scar on his chin, thoughtfully, and raised his eyebrows at Tanner.

'What are you looking at me like that for?'

'You didn't ask me what the other thing was.'

'Come on, Miller, don't beat around the bush.'

'A little bird tells me you two are getting married.'

'How did you know that? We haven't told anyone yet'

Miller touched his nose and winked.

He smiled as he walked off. *Sometimes, Sister, surely the wildlife cameraman should be allowed some fun.*

He didn't attend the wake afterwards, preferring instead to go for a long walk in the rain. Along the treeline, out of his line of sight, someone walked with him.

In court months later, Eilise gave evidence against her foster parents. Eileen received a reprimand in the strongest possible terms for her failure to act. Frank Staples was gaoled for seven years. The day of the sentencing would be the last time she ever saw them.

Jackie started a process she could have never foreseen a few months earlier; she applied to adopt the daughter she'd given up for adoption sixteen years before. *We'll hire a private tutor to finish off your education. On Saturdays, you'll come and work in one of my agencies.*

Eilise already felt she belonged more with her than she did with the Staples' family. Closing her eyes, she shut the memories out. She had a new life now, with her real mother, and a half-sister to get to know.

Eilise made a solemn vow. She'd never touch drugs again.

Chapter 150

They arrived in the weak yellow sunshine of early morning from opposite directions and within minutes met as arranged, at a fashionable pavement café near Kew Gardens.

Carla caught sight of him first. 'Hey, Miller!' she called.

He turned at the sound of her voice. Her hair was longer than he remembered, but still short and spiky enough to bounce with every movement of her head.

'Miller, how are you?' She held out an elegant hand and raised both eyebrows, greeting him. A smile started in her eyes and spread quickly over her face, the friendliness and warmth genuine.

He'd forgotten how long her fingers were; he took her fingertips and folded them over his, so the back of her hand faced upward. Returning her smile, he bent and kissed it. 'I'm very well and you?'

'Careful, Miller, I might start to think you're a gentleman and you know what that means?'

Miller cocked his head to one side. 'No, but I'm sure you're going to tell me.'

'You'll have to start treating me like a Lady,' she said.

'I don't think I'd have too much trouble with that.' Her fingers slowly slid away from his.

'It's good to see you again. It seems like forever ago.'

'I know what you mean. I've been run ragged. Are you hungry?'

'I'm Hank Marvin.'

He queried her with a raised eyebrow.

'Starvin',' Carla said, laughing. 'Surely you've heard that expression before?'

'Nope, never heard that one before.' He pulled a chair out for her and moved around the table to sit opposite. 'Are you sure you're okay with sitting outside?'

'When I can see the sun it always makes me feel warm, even if I'm not.' She zipped her bomber jacket right up into the collar. 'I'm fine, really I am.'

'Remember that story you told me about, on the train, about the lake with all the bodies in?'

'Yes, I do. It's not something I'll ever forget.' He laid his menu back on the table. 'What about it?'

He turned to signal a waiter, who approached. They ordered breakfast.

Half-barrels planted with shrubs surrounded by brightly coloured flowers, helped screen them from the bustling pavement. Birds hopped between unoccupied tables beneath a green and white awning. What she was about to tell him was to be her next big article; she held back until the waiter was out of earshot.

'I've been digging and delving since we last met. There were a couple of things you got me into, and since I stalled on the vigilante story—'

'You stalled on it?' He couldn't hide his surprise.

Carla explained, 'I needed more than what I had. I can't just do half a piece. Anyway getting back to Devils Pond, in amongst the bodies they recovered was an Australian student. The police had identified him as the caver who went missing a couple of weeks before his girlfriend vanished.' Breakfast arrived, interrupting her. She stopped to butter some toast and then resumed speaking. 'Well, guess what?' Pleased with herself, a lop-sided grin etched a line into her cheek.

'They found her in the lake with him.' Miller echoed her smile.

'How do you do that?' She shook her head, bemused. 'Anyway, that's right. She was in there, too. She was the key to identifying not only him, but a missing German woman as well.'

Miller began writing in a notebook he'd taken from his pocket.

'She was wearing an amulet, a five poisons charm. It was on a chain around her waist; her name inscribed around the edge in Chinese – the killer must have missed it – no other jewellery was recovered from any of the other bodies. As you can imagine, there wasn't much left of the boyfriend by the time they pulled him out. They had to use dental records.' Carla watched as Miller finished the last of his food and lifted the teapot ready to pour.

'You know, I think I'd prefer coffee.'

He tried to get the waiter's attention. She laid a hand on his forearm; it felt cool against his skin. 'It's okay; since it's already here, I'll stick with the tea.'

Miller glanced at her hand; she drew it away softly. Her touch sent a pleasant tingle up his arm. For a split second, their eyes met.

'You're really quite shy, aren't you?' she said. Miller's tiny smile seemed to confirm it. 'Where were we? Oh yes, there was her and the boyfriend and another girl, all dating from around the same time. The other boiler-suited bodies had been in there significantly longer. Weighted down with rocks, the legs and arms of the suits were wrapped around them, and tied up in knots. Except for Lei Liang – that was her name – she had only the legs of the suit tied around her, which seems odd.'

'The whole thing is odd!' Miller laughed.

She wrinkled her nose at him. 'Odd for him is what I meant. Maybe he was disturbed, or some other reason. Who knows with these people? Anyway, the boyfriend was fully clothed under the suit, as you might expect, but so were the women. We know when he didn't come back, a team was called in to search a nearby mine. They assumed he'd died in a roof collapse, buried under tons of rock.' She stirred a sugar into her tea.

Deep lines of concentration creased Miller's forehead while he ran possibility against probability. He didn't want to reveal he knew more than he was letting on. 'So, how did he come to be in the water wrapped up in a boiler suit?' he said.

She laughed. 'You're the investigator, you tell me!'

He took a sip of tea; he looked serious.

Carla realised she'd led him into reliving part of his childhood ordeal. Her smile evaporated. She kicked herself for being so insensitive.

'It's all right Carla.' He seemed to know what she was thinking. 'I knew the second I laid eyes on that place, with the boys that day. I knew it wasn't right. I didn't know enough about things then to warn them in time.' Miller looked at a spot in the mid-distance and drained his cup. Topping it up, he held the pot out to her.

'No thanks,' she said.

Stirring the cup helped him think. 'From what you have told me, we know he was a caver who was into exploring old mines.'

She nodded. 'That's pretty much what I found out.'

'People like that don't go off doing things like that alone, it's too dangerous. Normally there would be at least two of them. Did you find out who the other girl was?'

'She was identified as Christina Fischer, a German national. Reported missing a few days after the Australian disappeared. He met her and Lei Liang at university; they were all very close…'

Full of admiration for the way Carla had put it all together, he couldn't add anything to what she'd already found out.

'I spoke to the caver's brother in Australia. He'd heard about this spooky place; a mine shut down after a disaster a hundred and fifty years ago. Now, from what I can gather from speaking to her mother in Germany, Christina just told her that she'd planned to go on a little trip somewhere, but it was all very secretive. She said she'd tell her all about it when she came home. Of course, she never did. My theory is they were lovers – did I tell you she was Lei's best friend?' she asked, raising a querulous eyebrow. 'Anyway, at some point, after they pitched camp, the killer attacked them. He left the tent in place, taking all the caving equipment, everything, deep into the heart of the old workings, where he caused a collapse. The bodies were then disposed of in the lake.' She settled her gaze on him. 'If it hadn't been for the unfortunate demise of your friends, we might never have known…'

Miller nodded.

'And I couldn't believe nobody had missed these people at the time they disappeared,' she said, looking incredulous.

'I suppose because they were all foreign students, people just assumed they'd gone home for the summer?' Miller suggested.

'Maybe, but quite how Lei came to be there, is a bit of a mystery.'

He gave her a sideways look. 'You put all this together through speaking to the brother?'

'That's right; I built up a background, found out what friends he spoke of, girlfriends and so on. Then I found out all three were connected and had all gone missing within the same ten-day period. It makes you wonder how the police missed it at the time, doesn't it?'

A blizzard of thoughts blew into his mind, as if a door had opened during a snowstorm, before slamming shut. Part of what had made no sense when he'd seen inside The Sister's head came together now. The pieces were in the air; he watched them as they settled into place.

Irritated that he appeared to have lost interest, Carla, trying to catch his eye, noticed them flickering, and leaned in to get a better look. It seemed to her he'd slipped into a trance-like state. She waved her hand in front of his face. His eyes remained focused on something only he could see.

'Miller, what the hell are you doing? Are you having a fit or something?' At first, Carla thought he was just play-acting. He was scaring her now. 'Miller!'

He snapped out of it, allowing his mind to refocus. His gaze returned to her. 'His name was Thomas; he met up with Christina Fischer; they were going to explore the mine together. They were secret lovers. The killer caught them on the rocks by the river, down from the pit entrance. He smashed the Australian's head in from behind, with a rock. Christina trapped beneath the body. A sitting duck... I don't think I have to tell you the rest.'

'His head *was* smashed in from behind. How did you know that? Have you been doing your homework without telling me?'

Miller didn't answer.

She stared at him suspiciously. 'Well, how else could you have known, unless you read my mind?' Carla's mouth gaped as her thoughts illuminated with possibilities. 'You're scaring me a little bit here, *tell* me.'

'I got the information from an eyewitness,' he said.

'Miller, you have got to be kidding me. An eye witness from forty years ago?' She sat back with her arms folded across her chest and raised an inquisitive eyebrow. 'Who is it?'

'It's actually two people, and one of them is me, although I only saw part of it at the time.'

'Miller,' she shook her head in disbelief. 'What is this bullshit?'

'Carla, if you knew how hard this was to convey.' He pinched the bridge of his nose. 'Bear with me; I'm going to give it a try. It's a little bit like coming out of suspended animation, or at least, what I *think* that would be like. Little by little, I seem to be remembering things. At the moment, I can't explain it any better than that.'

'Miller, you said you were one of two people and you didn't see it all. I'm assuming that means that the other person did. Do you realise that with this, on top of everything else? The judge would throw away the key.'

'Carla, there's one or two problems here. The police have to catch him first, and the other person — witnessed it from two hundred miles away.'

She slapped her hand down hard, making the cutlery bounce on the table top. 'I'm not in the mood for this, Miller!' A few heads turned in their direction. When she saw how weary he suddenly looked, she couldn't help but feel sorry for him. 'I freaked out there.' She placed her hand on his arm. 'I apologise. Who's the witness?'

'When you've finished, we'll get into that.' The focus of his eyes shifted. He looked confused.

'Are you sure you're all right? You look exhausted.'

He squeezed her hand and smiled reassurance. 'Did you find out any anymore?'

She seemed to have caught some of his weariness, but she smiled and cleared her throat. 'I was trying to get a bit more background,' she took a sip of tea. 'I called the brother in Australia again. He told me at first he simply refused to believe it was Thomas. He wouldn't have believed it unless dental records proved otherwise. When I asked him how he could be so sure it wasn't his brother, he told me. 'Simple, although by then he was just a pile of bones, he always wore this leather belt, see. I brought it for his eighteenth birthday, before he left for Europe, and they never found it. Even if the leather had perished, when they went over the site with a fine tooth comb, with metal detectors, or whatever they use, they'd have at least found the buckle.' He sent me a photograph he'd taken before the trip. Thomas posing in a new bush hat and Tee shirt, with the belt worn around a new pair of Levis. You'll never guess what?'

'Carla, I'm too tired for guessing games,' he said with a thin smile.

'Oh, Miller, I'm sorry. I had the photo enhanced. It looks like he was wearing the same belt Midnight had on in the video he sent to the News of The World. If it *is* the same man and it *is* the same belt.'

Coming alive with enthusiasm, he said, 'You know something, Carla? I think you're on the verge of a big story here, well done.'

She looked pleased and fluffed herself up with pride. 'Speaking of stories, you've been keeping something back from me. The witness and that business just now, I want to know what's going on. And you never did tell me what you were doing in Scotland.'

He rubbed his chin with his thumb and forefinger. 'Okay, I could have told you more,' he said, looking tired again. 'The thing is I don't confide in people really, not like I should. I just got into the habit of not doing it.' He took a deep breath. 'When I was seven years old, I saw him – the killer, and he had the Chinese girl slung over his shoulder. He chased me.' He raised a hand and waved to the waiter. 'I don't know about you, but I need a coffee.'

She shook her head, anxious to hear the rest.

'It took the accident with the boys to unlock the door to the earlier memories, if it hadn't been for that, I'd never have visited Dr Ryan, and if I hadn't visited him...' Miller struggled to find the right words.

'Yes,' she said, patiently.

'When I said I didn't understand the rest of it...' Miller searched for the right words. 'It was like automatic writing, or something like that.' A look of consternation crossed her face. 'Well, how else do I put it?' Miller said. 'I'm just opening up and letting whatever it is come through. All I know for sure – is something started happening before I contacted Ryan, and since I went to Scotland a few weeks ago, it's turned into something else.'

'You're talking about the day after you left me?'

'That's right.'

'What happened?'

'Can I trust you, Carla?'

'Of course you can,' she said with sincerity.

His coffee arrived. He left it black, stirring in a single sugar, while she rummaged in her bag for something. She pulled out a Kleenex and a compact mirror.

'Something in my eye,' she explained, dabbing at it.

He waited until he had her full attention.

'Carla, I just asked if I could trust you, and you told me, yes.' Miller scrutinised her face.

Although she flinched, it was almost imperceptible. She met his gaze, chin out, defiant, but she shifted, no longer comfortable in her chair. *He knows.*

'Why are you taping this conversation without telling me, Carla?'

'Because I don't want to forget anything you say, and because I want to play it back over and over, looking for clues.' She bit her bottom lip and looked at the ground.

'All you had to do was ask. I wouldn't have refused,' he said, disappointment evident in his voice.

'I don't suppose you trust me now, do you?' She half-smiled. 'I'm a reporter, sometimes I forget there are more important things...' she trailed off, hoping for another chance.

After a moment's contemplation, he said, 'Come on, let's get out of here.'

He paid the bill.

'Does this mean you're not going to tell me what you were about to confide?'

Miller put his finger to his lips and held it upright.

Steering her to the right as they left the cafe, they walked in silence for several hundred yards, before she asked where they were going.

'We're going back to my hotel,' he said, accelerating into a brisk stroll. She confirmed her willingness by clattering along behind, on heels not designed for the pace. She stopped and slipped them off.

When she finally caught him up, she asked, 'You will tell me what you were going to say, won't you?'

They swept up the steps to the main entrance. Miller held the door open for her. 'Of course I will, afterwards.' He pushed the lift button. The doors opened straight away, and he stepped inside.

Her head turned away. Pushing her full lips into a petulant pout, she followed him in.

Once in the room, Miller poured them a drink from the mini bar.

Carla sidled up to him and then moulded herself into his body. He felt the beat of her heart through his shirt. With one hand, he scrunched the hair at the back of her neck. She placed a finger between their lips. 'Wait, I don't want to be distracted from this with your secret on my mind. Tell me *now*.'

Miller didn't need to be clairvoyant to know what would happen in the next few minutes.

'Okay, when I left you in Edinburgh I went to meet a former nun, but she wasn't like any nun I'd ever met before. She's known as The Sister and has the power to heal, read the past and help to put wrong things right. She can also tell the future.'

'I can do that,' Carla said with a wicked grin.

'Whereas I saw Boyle carrying Lei, she witnessed the actual crime from her home in Ireland. She touched me and sparked a sort of transference of knowledge and experience from me to her.'

Her eyes narrowed. 'Are you bull-shitting me?'

'No, she wasn't expecting what happened next. I got a flash of something from her. She tried to stop it, but it was too late. I'm still making sense of it now. Are you following me?' She nodded. 'Anyway, the point is; she wants me to help her in some way. She has this power, but she's forbidden to interfere directly with fate.'

'So what does that mean?'

'I'm not sure, but I think it was no accident I connected with her. I've seen another murder through that connection, and I've seen the man who did it. A priest murdered a choirboy and got away with it, because she couldn't break her vow of silence. It's not my normal line of work, but I'm going to see justice done.'

'That's very commendable.' Carla hardly dared to believe him. If what he said were true, he was well on the way to providing her with more great stories than any other source.

'Do you mind if I have a shower?' she said, already closing the bathroom door.

'No, you go ahead.' He turned, and saw in the mirrored wall opposite that she'd left the door open a few inches. The powerful jets of water thundered against the toughened glass cubicle. Carla called out to him above the roar. 'Are you coming?'

Miller stripped out of his clothes and went to her. The cubicle door popped open. She let him in. The sight of her shapely body stirred him; each beat of the heart increased his desire. She held him. They kissed, tentative at first, and then consumed by a hunger, devoured each other. Her breasts were pert, and slightly upturned, with nipples like rosebuds. The water dribbling off them made them stiffen, and stand out more erect; he nibbled each in turn, tracing a line down through her belly. He tongued her navel; her hands grasped the back of his head, guiding him down to her lower abdomen, she was shaven and smooth, with a fine, black tattooed line of tiny words running down to her clitoris. He struggled to make out what they said in the trickling rivulets of water.

M

e

l

é

c

h

e

r

Carla arched, thrusting herself forward, expectant. She sensed his hesitation and looked down. 'What are you *doing*, Miller, it doesn't say *read me* in French, it says me lécher – *lick me.*'

Carla gasped as he obliged, whispering, 'I *knew* you were going to do that.'

Afterwards, he asked if she was worried she might come to some sort of harm because of what he told her about people dying around him.

'Oh, I see, it was a health warning was it. I don't take much notice of things like that. How can you live a rich and fulfilling life, if you worry about every little thing?'

'Look, my three best friends, my girlfriend.'

'It was just bad luck; that's all. How many millions of people smoke and don't get cancer?'

'Hardly the same thing.'

She arched her brow at him and traced the outline of his tattoo with a well-manicured fingernail. 'With all the excitement over *my* tattoo, I forgot to ask you about yours. Tell me, what does it mean?'

'It means, 'Keep me away from wicked things' or something like that.'

Carla licked his chest and nibbled at him; throwing the covers off she went further down. 'Well it hasn't worked has it?' she said, as she took him in her mouth.

Chapter 151

Hot water from the shower pummelled his upturned face with needle-like jets, as he moved around in a clockwise circle offering his head, neck and shoulders the benefits of the same high-pressure treatment. Without opening his eyes, he fumbled for the shampoo he'd balanced on the soap dish. Locating it, he squeezed a blob of the viscous liquid into his palm and washed his hair. He thought about Stella, the last time they'd spoken she told him she'd be in touch when she was ready. *I'll give it until the end of the day and then if I don't hear anything; I'm calling her.*

He was drying himself off, when the telephone rang; quickly wiping his hands, he answered it.

'Carla?' He dried around his neck and nestled the phone between his jaw and shoulder.

'You know you told me about that case, the researcher on cults, Michael Simpson?' The question was slanted with suspicion.

'Yes, is everything all right?' he said, sipping from a bottle of mineral water.

'Well, no actually. There I was asking all kinds of questions about his murder and you got me arrested—'

'What!' he spluttered, almost choking.

'That's right; the post-mortem revealed he was murdered.'

'I told you someone was trying to kill him and then he was found dead—'

''Yes you did, but you didn't tell me no one else knew that, did you? I got arrested, thank you very much, Mr Miller!'

'Whoa. When I gave you that tip off, I didn't expect that you'd go in like a bull in a china shop.'

'I haven't finished yet!' she said through clenched teeth. 'The police wanted to know why I was asking questions related to a murder enquiry that had not been officially announced. As far as the press was concerned, it was an accident. And they wanted to know where I got my information from.'

'You didn't tell them!' The few seconds she took to answer was intended to keep him in suspense.

'You'll be relieved to know I didn't, I blagged my way out of it, saying it was a hunch, but the thing is... How did *you* know? You told me on the train three weeks ago, before you'd had your meeting with The Sister, so I'm a little bit confused about what the truth is here.'

Miller cleared his throat, unsure of the best way to tell her. 'Carla, look, it's complicated.'

'How did I know it would be? We'll come back to the question in a minute. Anyway, I've done some digging; it seems he was investigating a religious cult in Spain.'

Miller felt a cold chill creeping over him; an electrifying wave swept over his flesh, across the follicles of his skin. The hair on his forearms stood on end. He had a sense of foreboding. *What's going on with you lately, Miller, have you turned into a magnet for strange coincidences?*

'Apparently, he wrote a book about cults in the early eighties and he'd returned to researching to see how they'd moved with modern times. His studies show…' Carla carried on talking in the background…*The larger ones have done very well, might even be regarded as respectable.* Her voice faded as Miller's perceptions shifted, triggered by something she said. He had a glimpse, a view he recognised. It was a trail that led him back through his memories… he was in the car with Kirk again that rainy night when he was nineteen…*Look it up …* he transported himself into the morning after, back into the library, the book in his hands in his mind's eye…he folded it shut. He focused on the author's name on the front. *Michael Simpson!*

Carla hadn't noticed his mind was on something else. He tuned into her voice once more as he returned to his normal self.

'This particular one seems to have been resurrected and rebranded from an older version. In other words, only the name has changed. The questionable practices are the same. I've heard rumours they launder and recycle money in the same way as drug cartels. In fact, according to my sources, there's evidence to support the supposition that this cult is under the control of a major criminal. Simpson was in Amsterdam unravelling connections to the drugs and arms trade, when he met with his *accident*. I think I'm going to need help on this one.'

Miller bit his lip, unsure about her continuing with the investigation he'd set her off on. He knew she wouldn't just drop it, he'd have to do something, but he couldn't afford to compromise his position with the work he was doing for Kale. He needed more answers. 'Did you find out anything else, Carla?'

'Okay, the top guy was taking these heiresses. Once they'd been bled dry, he was running them as high class whores. Got them addicted to religion. Got them hooked on drugs. By then, they'd do anything he wanted.'

Miller asked himself. *What is my life but a series of coincidences? It can't be the same one, can it?* In his heart, he already knew. All these things had come full circle, and they weren't finished yet.

'You didn't say what they call themselves now.'

'To give them their full name: The Resurrectionists of Monte Cristo. Have you heard of them?'

He remained silent.

'Sometimes they're referred to as simply 'The Church''.

'The Church,' Miller repeated, struck by a moment of epiphany. The garish neon Church image and the disembodied voice he heard when The Sister touched him came alive inside his head. *You must find another place to live, or he'll find you! That's who is looking for The Sister, not the Catholic Church at all.*

Several times since Kennedy's funeral, he'd deliberated the question: *How far could she go without direct intervention?* A series of mini revelations played through his head. All the unlikely coincidences pointed to the hand of The Sister working indirectly behind the scenes. Boyle, Kirk, Ryan, Olga Kale the cult and everything else, her fingerprints were all over them.

A steely look crossed his face. 'You know something, Carla? I'd like to shut them down once and for all.'

'But how would you manage to do that?' she said.

'I know a man who will help me.'

'Tell me it's not Tanner!'

'No, it isn't. It's Donovan Kale.'

Chapter 152

When Miller arrived at Stella's house, it was already mid-afternoon. The sky was leaden, pregnant with storm, and the atmosphere had stalled between high and low pressure, keeping the rain at bay. Looking up at the heavens, he muttered, 'Why don't you just rain and get it over with.' *She didn't sound herself at all when we spoke a few hours ago. It can't be easy, being reunited with someone you've never met before.* From the gate, he saw the curtains were still drawn.

She'd been through hell over the last few weeks, but insisted she be left to deal with it alone.

At the door, he paused and questioned his motives, unsure whether he should turn and walk away. His brief re-acquaintance with her had led her into danger, the old pattern. On the step, half-turned away, he hesitated, sensing what she was going through was beyond her own capacity for self-healing. Carla was different; she was streetwise. Stella, for all her hard exterior, was soft and vulnerable inside. He identified with her on that level, acknowledging his own persona was just an act to cover for the child in him that never grew up.

He thought back on all that had happened over the last three weeks. When they'd first found Kathy, she didn't want to go with them; she'd fought her rescuers with the ferocity of a wild animal.

At first, Stella refused to believe she was her sister. The futility of her parent's suicide heightened the anguish she felt. It was the eyes that first drew her back to Kathy's photograph. Twenty-three years had passed, and no matter what else in her appearance had changed, she still had those eyes. Denial was no longer an option; the last doubts disappeared. It *was* Kathy.

At the hospital after Kathy's initial appraisal, the psychiatrist explained she'd developed Stockholm syndrome – where the captive bonds with the captor in order to ensure their survival. He'd held her for so long she actually believed she loved him; the clear evidence of abuse and beatings hadn't diminished that belief. She'd become institutionalised, and to complicate matters further, she had signs of brain damage; more tests were needed.

Miller had gone with Stella; she didn't have anyone else. He'd asked what the forecast was for the future.

The psychiatrist, Dr Marshall, looked at them both over the top of his glasses and explained conventional methods would take a long time to get anywhere. 'I suspect she had a blow the head, or some kind asphyxiation that deprived the brain of oxygen. Physical abuse, drug abuse, they're all on the radar. To cut to the chase, you'll be better trying the alternative route.'

He referred Stella to a friend of his in Norwich, a specialist in NLP and hypnotherapy; he wrote the details on a card and passed it to her. She thanked him and taking it, noted the name, Victor, followed by a telephone number.

It was a few days before the hospital allowed Kathy to go out with them. They collected her early in the morning. Stella sat next to her in the back seat; all attempts at conversation failed. Miller observed her in the rear view mirror; she looked distressed.

In Norwich, the therapist, Victor, was a kindly looking man with a shaven head and gentle voice. A female chaperone sat unobtrusively in a far corner for the session. They left Kathy, knowing she was in good hands for the next two hours, while they went to have breakfast in a department store nearby. Stella remained subdued and uncommunicative throughout. Although he tried to break through the self-imposed barrier she'd erected, he was unable to find a way. His efforts left him exhausted.

When they returned, the therapist left Kathy in his office with the chaperone, while he delivered his appraisal. 'I can help her; that's the good news. The bad news is, well, it's going to be a long hard road.'

Stella began, 'But, Mr Marshall—'

Victor interrupted, his voice becoming firm and authoritative.' She doesn't know who she was before; there's absolutely no recollection, even under hypnosis. So we're dealing with amnesia as well as captive bonding. Tests have shown she is brain damaged, but perhaps worse than that...for you at any rate, she really believes she is Cathy Boyle,' he said grimly. 'And that's just for starters.'

Miller kept quiet. Stella did the talking. 'Surely she remembers something about who she was – *is*, I mean Cathy and Kath, they're too close for coincidence?'

'That's true. Maybe the kidnapper named her after the ID she had with her?'

Stella was firm. 'No, that never happened. You see they found her bag; she didn't have it with her.'

Victor studied her face, concerned. 'It's a dilemma – do we rehabilitate her as Cathy Shaw or Cathy Boyle, or do we try to re-establish her original identity, Kathy Bird, one she hasn't existed in for twenty odd years?'

After a quick exchange of looks, Miller spoke at last. 'Whichever one gives her the best chance of a future.'

The therapist stroked the top of his shaven head with the palm of his hand, and looked at Stella, eyes filled with compassion. 'She did remember one thing under hypnosis, I didn't want to tell you just yet, you've had enough to cope with, but it might just help you to decide.'

'What is it?' she said, agitated. 'I want to know.'

'That scar on her top lip. At first, I thought it was an old one, you know, from a harelip. Well, I asked her about it when I had her regressed, and suggestible. She – she remembers him doing it with a pair of scissors.'

With each new revelation, little by little, Stella had come undone. She broke down.

By the time they left the therapist's office, she was in a state of shock. They returned Kathy to the hospital.

Miller had driven Stella home. She barely said a word.

He'd been unable to volunteer his point of view, while Kathy was in the car, so he said, 'To me it's obvious. She has no future as Cathy Boyle. That part of her life is over now, it wasn't real. She needs to be Kathy Bird again, even if it means dealing with the loss of your parents and everything else that's happened in between'

Stella didn't answer him, and he didn't push her.

Arriving back at her house, he entered with her to check the house was clear. The telephone rang. It was the hospital. Not long after they'd left, Kathy had gone into a catatonic state.

Miller asked if there was anybody she could call, who could stay with her. Stella regarded him with a strange, hurt look. 'No, no, I'll be fine. I just need to be alone for a few days.'

She didn't ask you to come now. It's a mistake. You should have respected her wishes and left her alone. He decided to come back another time.

The door opened. He hadn't knocked. Surprised at the sight of him half-turned away from her doorstep, she shot Miller a hurt look. Apart from the pain in her eyes, her face was expressionless. Still in her dressing gown, the face pale with dark rings below her eyes, the unbrushed hair combined to tell a story. A whiff of alcohol caught on his inward breath; he tasted her despair. 'Oh, Stella,' was all he managed to say.

Without answering, she turned from the door; he followed her in, closing it behind him.

In the gloom of the lounge, she flopped onto the sofa and stared unseeing at the television. A strange carnival of lights projected onto her face from soundless pictures.

Stood in the doorway, he sought a connection with her. None came. Purposefully he strode across the room and swished the curtains back. Light flooded in. Despite its greyness, she cowered, her eyes squinted against it.

'Do-o-on't' she said, in a cracked, parched voice that lacked conviction.

'Stella, look at me.'

She turned to face him, her gaze on his cheekbones, avoiding eye contact.

'Talk to me, Stella – I can help.'

A moment passed; she took a deep breath and exhaled it as a sigh. 'I look a right junkie mess, don't I?' She turned her arms out, exposing the forearms, allowing a brief glimpse before lowering them again.

Track marks! The visible scars of her brief captivity had all but disappeared, but deeper wounds were left for her to deal with.

'Considering what you've been through, I think that's the least of your worries.' Miller took a seat next to her on the sofa, and clasping his hands firmly together, held them between his knees.

'Shall I get us some tea?'

'I don't want anything.'

'Have you eaten?'

She didn't turn, but sought him briefly, looking out from the corner of her eye. 'Do I look like I'm in the mood to eat anything?'

'No, but that's why I asked. You should have something; it'll help,' he said.

'Help me with what? I was better off not knowing what happened!' Her face flushed with anger. 'And I feel so *guilty* about how I feel!' She wrung her hands together. 'God, I hate myself for how I feel!'

'Stella, none of this was your fault, but you've got to move on for your own sake and Kathy's, too. You were looking for work before Ryan died, a lot has happened between times I know, but how about starting back with me. I've got a job that's going to keep me busy for a while, and I could do with someone I can trust to look after things. What do you say?'

'I'm not sure.' Her fingers twisted into knots.

'Please, Stella,' he said, not wanting to press her too hard. 'I'll be at the office in the morning. I could do with your help.'

Chapter 153

Early the next day, Miller let himself into his office. Although he'd seldom worked from there over the past year, the cleaner still came in once a week to keep the dust and cobwebs at bay. Paperwork in unsorted piles covered every available spare desk space. *Jesus, this place, is a mess. Coffee, that's what I'll start with.*

In the kitchen, waiting for the kettle to boil, he wondered if Stella would show. Images of other secretaries came and went; he smiled at the memories.

The worktop rumbled as the water boiled; the button clicked off. About to pour the contents into his cup, the sound of the entry buzzer jarred him into almost scalding himself.

On the way to the door, he glanced at the CCTV monitor. His heart lifted. Stella had arrived.

In the weeks that followed, she re-established herself quickly, reminding Miller of why he'd once considered her his finest secretary. She glanced up and caught him looking at her.

'What?' she said, with a bemused smile.

'You look happy, and I'm glad. Want tea?'

The telephone in his pocket vibrated urgently. 'Excuse me,' he withdrew it and answered as he advanced down the corridor to his office.

'Carla, any news?' He'd taken to ribbing her with newspaper-style clichés. 'Anything to report?'

'As a matter of fact, I have. While you've been playing nursemaid, I've found out something very interesting.'

What she'd just said managed to irritate and intrigue in equal measure. 'Come on, Carla, that's unfair—'

'It's the truth. You should be here in Amsterdam with me, but it's okay,' she sighed. 'I do understand, but this is *your* job. Kale is paying you, not me,' she said her voice dropping, 'what if I went to him directly?'

Miller laughed, 'If I don't get paid, neither will you. So, what have you found?'

'Carlos, that's not his real name.'

He detected something other than pride in her tone. 'That doesn't surprise me much,' he said, with an air of nonchalance. 'What is it?'

'Come over here and I'll tell you.' *Click.*

'Carla, are you still there?' *She's put the phone down on you.*

Sunlight slanted across the window, finding its way into his office, the slab of light it cast onto the wall adjacent widened perceptibly as he watched it, warming the room as it grew. *She's right. You should be there. He'd get Stella to book him a flight for this afternoon.*

'Who's Carla? I don't think I've met her...' Stella's eyes gave little away, but her voice was too measured, unnatural. 'And I haven't seen any paperwork concerning her...'

'I'll explain. She's working with me in an unofficial capacity. She's a reporter, but no ordinary one...'

When he'd finished explaining, Stella said, 'I'm not sure about this new direction you're taking, it sounds dangerous.'

'I'll be back before you know it, and anyway,' he held his mobile phone up and shook it. 'If you need me just call.'

The hotel was a former canal house, arranged over three storeys. Inside, the décor was a sumptuous blend of modern and traditional furnishings, light streamed in through arch-top windows. *This must be costing a packet.* She'd booked him a room opposite hers. They met in the bar.

'I'm impressed, Carla. You're doing well to afford to stay in a place like this.'

Her eyes sparkled in the light. 'It's all on expenses, Miller. Remember?'

'Jesus Christ, what on earth makes you think—?'

'Shush, silly,' she looked around furtively. 'He's staying here. On the top floor.'

Speaking in hushed tones, she brought him up to date. '...As far as I can establish his real name is Jubal Khan. His bodyguard Hasan got himself into trouble in Afghanistan; Khan did a deal with the Taliban. In exchange for killing a high ranking official, they would help get Hasan out.'

'Jubal Khan... Sounds familiar to me, now where have I heard that name before?' Two men of Middle Eastern appearance entered the bar. Miller flashed a warning with his eyes.

'Not them,' she whispered, grabbing her drink. 'Let's carry on this discussion in my room.' She slid off her stool, winked and gestured with a tilt of her head. 'Come on.'

Miller drained the rest of his glass and followed her.

Once in her room, the conversation continued; she seemed to have acquired a thirst for alcohol and raided the mini-bar with a regularity that astonished him.

'As the story goes, he got himself into Kandahar prison just so that he could get Hasan out. His contacts blew a hole in the outer wall near the guardhouse, stormed in, machine-gunned the few guards that had survived the blast and set half the prisoners free, mainly to hide the fact that they'd orchestrated the whole thing just to get those two out.'

'Who told you all this?'

'Now, that would be telling, but it's enough to say one of the other escapee's works in a nearby bar. Apparently, he followed them for quite a while after the escape, before Khan set Hasan onto him. He lived to tell the tale, obviously, but he told me he'd spotted "The Mute" as he called him coming into this hotel a couple of weeks ago with Khan.'

His mind wandered back to the first time he'd seen Carlos with his bodyguard in Piccadilly. Three questions formed. *Could it really be him? Could it be the same minder? Would they recognise him after all these years?* 'If what you say is true, I'm beginning to think we might be in over our heads—'

'Think about the money, Miller.' Although Carla's eyes gleamed, they'd taken on a glassy appearance.

Miller encircled the thumb of his left hand with his fingertips and contemplated them. 'Money isn't everything,' he said, thoughtfully. 'It alleviates some worries for sure, but the acquisition of wealth…'

'So it's selfish to want money for security, if it brings happiness?'

'That's not what I'm saying. I'm talking about the true happiness that comes from contentment. It shouldn't be complicated by selfish needs. I'm talking about people who give without expecting something in return, because if you do that – if you expect nothing, and you get nothing – how can you be disappointed?' The alcohol clouded his thoughts. 'We shouldn't be selling ourselves to the highest bidder. If everything is for sale, then where do we stop? If supply and demand is all that matters, then what price do we place on our souls?' Miller's telephone rang. He ignored it.

She swallowed the last of her drink. 'I don't care about any of that,' she said. 'Miller, can I ask you something?'

'Sure, fire away.'

'Do you want to fuck me?'

The sound of tinkling cutlery, faint, but unmistakable, reached his ears. Dull pain pushed into his eyeballs from behind; he opened them seeking release and turned his head on the pillow. Carla remained asleep next to him. 'Never drinking like that again,' he mumbled and sat up.

She stirred, and lazily ran a fingertip down his spine. 'What are you doing?'

'I'm going home. Are you coming?'

'Why?'

'I told you last night. It's not worth the money and Stella needs my help.'

'What about me?'

'Come home.'

She bit her lip and sat forwards, holding the quilt under her chin. 'I'm in too deep. I'm sticking with the story. You go on though, run home and wet-nurse your little girl.'

'Carla, it's not that at all. It's too dangerous.'

'It's okay, I'm a big girl. I know what I'm doing. Leave me.'

For most of the journey home, he thought about her, and wondered if he'd done the right thing. To her it was all a game. She might want him, but she didn't need him. Sooner or later hurt would come knocking. *What would be the point in that?*

On Friday the 13th July, he returned from the Netherlands and reported to Donovan Kale.

The billionaire pushed his seat away from the desk, clasping his hands together, and resting them on his crotch. 'I thought you told me you wouldn't stop, until you had the job done.'

'It's true; I did say that, and I've helped you to shut down almost every major cult operating in Europe. That leaves only one of any size and a rapidly growing pseudo religious organisation. I'm going to have to terminate my involvement.'

'Miller, we've known each other a long time so let me ask you … why the change? You like the money don't you?'

'Donovan, this isn't about money. This is about a couple of things that have crept onto the radar, and I can't just walk away without resolving them.'

'What are they?'

Miller explained, and when he'd finished, Kale sat forward abruptly.

'This other business, it needs to be out of the way. What was the name of this pseudo religion as you put it?'

'They call themselves the Resurrectionists of Monte Cristo —'

'Leave them – they're crackpots!'

'You wanted to find out more about Carlos?'

'Forget him, he's just a mercenary. Besides, he's too dangerous. I want you focused on bringing this last organisation to heel. I want the leader. If we don't take him out, the whole thing will just start up again. This other business – what is it, and how long do you need?'

Didn't I just quit? Miller thought, but decided not to press the point for now. 'I need to get Kathy out of the hospital and up to Scotland.'

'Kathy? Scotland?'

Miller pressed his lips together. Although Kale was one of the few people he could trust, he decided it best not to mention Carla. 'Donovan, it's a long story, so I'll condense it for you…'

A few minutes later, Kale stopped him. 'I've heard enough, take the time you need and then get back to me, yes? A few days won't hurt.'

With her bag clutched under her arm, Stella swept around the corner, and up the driveway. Suddenly she stopped and turned to look at the gates. A smile crossed her face, and a bounce came into her step as she timed the last three paces to land on the step outside the door. She pressed the buzzer.

'So, how was Amsterdam?' She smiled, and her cheeks dimpled.

Guilt, a feeling he wasn't comfortable with, rose suddenly and flickered in his eyes. 'I couldn't wait to get back,' he said, 'I've got some plans for you.'

'Really?' she searched his face to see if it were true.

'You know what I said when we found Kathy?' Miller said.

'Yes…?'

'Well, Stella, I haven't finished yet, but don't get your hopes up.'

'Don't!' She leaned forward and pushed him away. 'I know what you're trying to do.'

'Stella, I think I know someone who can help her.'

'What do you mean?'

Miller silently studied her face; one eye beamed brighter than the other.

'What? Oh, come on.' She jigged up and down on the spot, and then her eyes lit up. A nervous giggle sounded in her throat. 'The deprogrammer you used on the Olga Kale case? We could use him if he hasn't retired?'

'No, I have someone else in mind.' He took a deep breath and held it.

'The Sister!' she exclaimed.

'How did you guess? I'm not sure how I can persuade her, though.'

'It wasn't a guess, I just knew somehow! And you *will* persuade her,' she said. 'I just know it!'

A bemused smile fixed on Miller's face. *You didn't think this one through, did you? You don't even know where she lives!* Stella was so buoyant, that when he confided in her about Amsterdam and the reasons for keeping the trip secret, she was barely listening.

He and Stella collected Kathy on Sunday morning from the hospital to take her out as they had previously, as part of her rehabilitation.

Marshall pulled him to one side. 'Listen, Miller, it's been almost three months now, we've been working hard, but progress has been minimal. Her physical condition has improved no end, when she gets on the treadmill there's no stopping her. It must be a reaction to being cooped up all that time.' Handing him Kathy's medication, he continued. 'I know you're following Victor's advice, and I wish you the best of luck with that. She's still trapped in that sick relationship, pining for him, like a lovelorn teenager. We need to work on it. Until we get through that, I don't think we'll get any further and don't forget – it's only a weekend pass.'

Miller shook the psychiatrist's hand. 'Thanks, Marshall, we'll see if Stella can't start working on rebuilding Kathy's memories straight away.'

Once on the train, it was inevitable Miller cast his mind back to how he first met Carla Black. He was on his way to see The Sister then, and he recalled the secrecy with which the former nun surrounded herself. He began to doubt she'd see him, or any of them unannounced, even if they could find her. When they got closer, he might be able to communicate with her. With luck, if she hadn't locked herself down, she'd sense he was close by. His developing perception meant she was always guarding against him finding out too much about her. The blanket she'd thrown over his senses didn't cover them completely, occasionally it would shift, and he could peek out from under it.

Kathy was quiet, and spent most of her time staring out through the window. Every so often, when the light was right, her reflection would show in the glass. More than once, when he glanced at her mirrored there, he noticed she was looking at him.

This is the longest and most boring four hours you've ever spent, surely, Miller. After all this, you'd better be sure The Sister will see you.

Stella had tried to engage with Kathy earlier, but without success. Now, only half an hour from Edinburgh she decided to resume her efforts, talking about her early life, her mum and dad, how much they'd missed her and how pleased they would have been to see her back again.

Finally, she spoke, her impediment clearly evident. 'Why does everyone keep saying that to me?'

'Because it's true, look – here you are in a photograph just before you were taken.'

'I wasn't taken.'

'Yes you were.' She offered her the photo. 'Go on, look at it.'

Her eyes narrowed as she examined the picture. She stroked the uniform with the tip of her finger, wistfully. 'I always wanted to be a nurse, but that is not *me,* and I don't know who *you* are.'

Stella was visibly upset. Miller tried another angle. 'You and Martin, how did you meet?'

Her eyes misted at the mention of his name. 'We met after a dance. He told me I reminded him of his mother.' She stared out at the landscape flashing by the window.

Pointing to his own upper lip, he said sympathetically, 'Is that why he did that to you, Kathy, because you reminded him of his mother.'

She looked frightened.

'He *wanted* you to speak like that – didn't he? You don't have to do that anymore, you're safe and with us, now,' he said softly.

For a full thirty seconds, she didn't utter a sound. Agitated by some inner turmoil, she suddenly looked anxious.

Freed from the encumbrance of habit, her own voice unfamiliar, she spoke, 'Why did you say *would* have been pleased to see me back again?'

'Oh, Kathy.' Stella told her the whole story. When she'd finished, she reached for her sister's hand. Then Kathy screamed. Stella immediately embraced her, pulling her head in tight to her breast.

A bull-necked, shaven-headed man, ears adorned by thick gold-hoop earrings approached. Two women appeared, behind him craning their necks around his shoulders to get a better view. A further group of onlookers gathered, pushing forwards.

'What's going on here?' He glowered at Miller and without taking his eyes off him, turned his head slightly towards Kathy. 'Did he hurt you, lovey?'

Stella whispered soothing words, tears rolling down her cheeks.

Miller stayed seated and spoke softly, 'Twenty-three years ago; this poor woman was kidnapped, and as you can see, she's still traumatised. We don't need any kind of scene.' The murmuring fell into a hush. He shifted his gaze from the man and glanced over the faces of the small pack beyond his shoulders. 'I know how it looks, but we are taking her to get specialist help just outside Edinburgh. You can all go back to your seats now.'

'Oh God,' one of the women cried, 'it's that poor lass who was on the news a few weeks ago. They thought she was dead.' Faces filled with sympathy and heads bobbed around, trying to get a better look at her. The man relaxed his stance. 'I'm sorry; I'm no' one to stand by, y'know?' He shrugged.

'That's okay,' Miller said. The man lingered for a moment, perhaps wondering if there were anything he could do, he turned and ushered everyone behind him back their seats. 'Good luck wi' that,' he said over his shoulder.

The train reached Waverley just after lunchtime. Kathy still wore a troubled expression. Stella watched her carefully, and kept her between herself and Miller as they traipsed out of the station on legs still stiff from the journey. Once outside, as they were about to get in a taxi, Miller's mobile rang and he gestured for them to wait, while he turned his back to the wind so he could hear better. It was Tanner.

'I called at the hospital to interview Kathy, and she's not there. And you know why? Because she's with you. What the hell do you think you're playing at, running off with my witness? You had better get back with her, right now!'

'John, we cleared it with the hospital. I'm sorry you were inconvenienced, you should have called Marshall. Besides, she isn't up to a police interrogation at the moment. She's here with us because we're helping her. You can wait.'

'Miller, I don't think you understood me—'

'We're back tomorrow; you either wait or come up here.' He snapped his phone shut.

'Can you believe that?' He turned and found Stella on the kerb, on her hands and knees.

'Jesus, Stella. Are you okay?' He helped her to her feet.

'She jumped me! I can't believe it. My own sister jumped me!'

'Did you see where she went?'

'No, it all happened so fast.'

'Don't worry, we'll find her. She can't get far without any money.'

'She's taken my handbag,' she said, her face grim.

Together, they looked in all directions. No sight of her. They spotted an elderly man at the rank and rushed over to him. 'Did you see a woman, dark hair ... no, half grey. Scar on her lip, dressed in a black, hooded tracksuit?'

'Did she have the hood up or down?' the old man said. 'I didn't see any face, but someone dressed in black with a hood up, just jumped in that taxi over there.' He pointed down the street.

'Stella, quick, she's in that cab!'

They dove into the next one, brushing aside a young couple who were about to get in. Once inside, the doors locked. Outside, the man banged on the windows, protesting.

The driver sat up abruptly, holding up a two-pound coin he'd retrieved from his footwell. 'Thought I'd lost that!' he said gleefully. 'What's all the commotion?'

'Follow that cab,' Miller said. 'I'll explain as we go.'

'Where to?' the driver asked with a shrug.

Miller exchanged exasperated glances with Stella. 'Just follow it and there's a nice drink in it for you if you catch up with them.'

The driver gunned the engine. They began to gain ground. Kathy watched them anxiously through the rear window. The next set of traffic lights turned red. Forced to stop, they watched the car disappear from view.

'Come on!' Stella bounced impatiently on her seat.

Seconds later, the lights changed.

They'd lost her.

'What now?' The driver asked.

'Keep going,' Miller said. 'How far does this road go south?' Not waiting for an answer, he turned to Stella and said, 'How much money do you have in your purse?'

'You don't think she's trying to get back to London?'

'No, I just think she's trying to get away. How much have you got?'

'About fifty or sixty quid.'

'Driver, can you find out who's got her, the woman in the black tracksuit, in their cab?'

'Okay, I'll have a word.'

'Tell who ever it is to stall her somewhere, until we get there. There's fifty quid in it for them.'

Stella was impressed with his idea. A smile appeared on her face for the first time in what seemed like hours. It was short lived. She realised he'd promised her fifty pounds as the reward money.

After a few minutes of radio chatter, the driver said, 'Okay, we got her, but you need to tell me what this is all about before we go any further with this.'

'I'll explain,' Miller said.

The other driver had taken her to a nearby golf club and pulled into the car park. He popped the bonnet on pretext of checking the water. 'The radiator, it's just started losing water the last couple of days, getting worse.'

While he played for time, she saw the other cab approaching from behind. Quickly realising she was about to be trapped; she took off onto the golf course, and made for the cover of trees.

Miller took all the paper money from his back pocket, seventy pounds altogether and put it into the driver's hand. 'Sort that out between you,' he said and ran off in hot pursuit.

'Wait for me!' Stella cried out after him, slowing at the edge of the car park, as she realised she couldn't maintain his pace.

Running downhill in as straight a line as possible, he saw Kathy ahead. He was confident he'd catch her. The ground away from the fairways undulated, and he narrowly escaped falling several times as he pitched forwards through the rough grass. He slowed down.

Where on earth, does she think she's going?

She disappeared into a grove of trees as he reached a flat and even fire road. He put the hammer down, driving his arms faster than ever; his hands came up straight, like blades slashing through the air, legs pumping harder still, desperate to narrow the gap. He ran as if his life depended on it. Clearing the trees, thirty, forty seconds behind her, he couldn't see her.

A group of elderly golfers gathered around the shore of a lake, agitated and pointing. Someone pushed a small boat out. He yelled out to them, without breaking stride. 'Have you seen a woman?'

'She's in there, gone under. She just waded in!'

He took the scene in a split second of clarity; the black water trail parted through the green chickweed to the middle, where she'd waded and then gone down. Five more paces to the bank. If he leapt hard enough, he judged he'd make it most of the way. A voice inside his head reminded him. *You can't swim!*

Three, two, one – Miller took off.

It was a mighty leap, his trajectory Olympian. The flight – three beats of his pounding heart – exhilarated him. He plunged into the water, taking a last desperate gasp of air with him as he sank below the surface.

He didn't attempt to swim, instead feeling the churn of the water around him, he opened his eyes. The water stung them closed. He couldn't see.

Wading along below the water, the weight of his wet clothes kept him down. *You don't have long, Bruce.* The gasp reflex was almost upon him.

Something brushed against his leg; he reached down, his fingers running through a tangle of hair. *It's her!* As he struggled to stay calm, he inwardly thanked the Lord for all the times he'd practiced holding his breath; it was something he'd always done as a child, a habit he'd continued into adulthood. Gripping her under the arms, he launched himself upwards, dragging her; sensing the right moment, and as it came, he bent, and with the strength that desperation had brought to him, swung her upwards. The momentum forced him down. She left his arms; he felt her body surge through the water.

Although he couldn't swim, he was strangely calm. The will to survive had taken over everything. Every pounding heartbeat reminded him he was alive. His last breath, desperately snatched breaking for the surface the third time, was stale, exhausted by his exertions, but still he held it in.

A pulse inside his temple throbbed; his ears split with pain as the pressure built; the muffled beat of his heart grew louder as he continued to sink, and the murky light above slipped further away. All thought must disappear – *mu shin no shin, mu shin* – empty mind, *pusty umysl*. His life depended on his ability to forestall the gulp reflex, to buy time against the odds in the hope of rescue.

All thought disappeared. Autopilot kicked in and at last; he was in survivor mode. Feet touched the bottom first. Knees folded; every ounce of power directed into powerful thighs. Driving up from his haunches, he surged through the water, a human missile shooting for the surface. The initial burst of acceleration died quickly. The mass of water held him down. He battled the last few inches. Getting his face out into the air, he sucked a quick shot into his lungs. It wasn't enough.

Sinking back to the bottom for the fourth time, thoughts intruded. *You should have learned to swim.*

He had to save his strength for one final burst. *Mu shin, no shin. Pusty umysl.* All thought must disappear.

Touching the bottom again; his legs folded until his fingers touched the mud; he drove up hard for the surface, again.

Miller's mind was empty, but his heart knew if he didn't make it this time, he was finished. His face pushed up under the surface of the water, an inch short; he flailed his arms to get higher. His efforts in vain; the chance missed, going under again. His heart sank; he was at the limit of his conscious ability to withstand the body's pre-programmed gulp reaction. He would take in water. Lungs burned, on fire, ready to explode. Desperately refocusing – *Mu shin* – It was too late. The fight was lost.

A thought popped into his head. *In those last moments, you don't see your whole life flashing by, but if you're lucky, you get to make some sense of it all.*

Reflex took over. Gagging on the first influx of water, he didn't have the strength to do anything but die.

Chapter 154

His world rose within a bubble, mercurial, ballooning upward, dark waters kept at bay, as breath and air deserted him.

The water no longer stung his eyes. A last trail of silver bubbles escaped his lips and nostrils. He watched them go.

With no hope of rescue, he resigned himself to Fate. He'd always known when the end came it would come by water…the end of living on borrowed time.

At last, he felt redeemed. *Did you save her? Maybe not, but at least I would have died trying.*

The water churned about him. A funnel formed, dragged him along in its vortex. All the things he'd ever done flashed before him fast, faster, running backwards. *You are receding…*

It all made sense.

A strange sensation crept over him. Detachment, but in a way he'd never experienced before. His cold and heavy clothing fell away as the rope of life unwound, releasing him strand by strand, thread by thread. For a moment, he floated above himself, free and untethered, but not wanting to let go. From the corner of his eye, a bright copper bloom appeared in the murk of the water beneath him. He sensed rather than felt something press into the palm of his hand, and he willed his fingers with all his might, overriding disconnected synapses, to hold onto it. Spirit hadn't left him yet. Words formed in his head. *I've got you mate…*

Darkness stole him away into nothingness.

A void, black and unyielding held him fast. *How long have I been here?* In the distance, he thought he heard Stella's voice. *Is she here too?* Heart filled with dread; he searched for her in vain.

His father was laughing. Out in the field they picnicked. Bruce laid on his front; face turned into the grass, studying the fine ribbed detailing of its blades close-up, imagining himself as an explorer in the jungle, hacking his way through, beating off monstrous ants and spiders. A feeling descended upon him. Thoughts, not his, intruded. It was the first time he could remember having the sensation of being watched. He rolled over and stared up at blue skies that stretched out forever. High above, a tiny cross-shaped fleck rode the air. He blinked against the brightness, and holding his eyes closed, suddenly felt lighter, more buoyant than the breeze. In his mind's eye, he could see himself and his family far below on the ground. *I am the bird!* Soaring higher, he scoured the land with eyes sharper than a telescope, taking in rocks and trees; everything came into focus in a way he'd never experienced before. Finally, he zoomed in on a girl in a purple dress marching purposefully down the hill into the valley below; she stopped to remove her rucksack—

The sound of his mother's voice drew him back.

Don't go any further, Bruce!

Miller opened his eyes; the glare forced him to shut them again. Blinking, he tried to sit up.

'Don't.' Stella leaned over and restrained him with light fingertips against his chest. 'You almost died, you need to rest.'

His voice lodged in the dryness of his throat and failed. He swallowed hard and winced at the soreness in his chest. Confused, he pinched at the skin of his thigh beneath the bedclothes. Not entirely satisfied he wasn't in the throes of some elaborate dream he'd concocted to fool himself into thinking he was still alive; he pinched again, this time harder.

Noticing the movement under the covers, she said, 'What are you doing under there?'

'Just checking to see if I'm still alive.' The last jumbled remnants of his memory jostled to make sense. 'But how...how long have I been here?'

'Since yesterday,' she said.

'What happened to Kathy?'

'You saved her.'

Almost overcome with relief, voice barely above a whisper, he said, 'I did? Thank God.'

'Yes, you did. I thought you told me you couldn't swim.'

He frowned and said, 'I can't.'

'Well, you did a good job of pretending you could when you swam—'

'Whoa, I did not swim,' he insisted, concentration knitting his brow as he collected his thoughts. 'I bounced along the bottom, and then pushed her up out of the water, that's what happened. I didn't swim!'

'But you *did*, you were struggling on your back with one arm round her, holding her head clear. Don't you remember? You got her as near to the shore as you could, then you both went under. You must have panicked. I don't know how you did it. You propelled her up out of the water – a guy in a boat grabbed her, but then you went under again. You were gone for ages. When help arrived, they found you half out of the water in the reeds on the other side, unconscious. If you didn't swim, how did you get there?'

'I don't remember exactly.' A shape, a form, just before he'd let go in the murky waters... A flashbulb went off in his memory – *The bright copper coloured hair. No, it couldn't have been. That would be crazy.*

'I think you're mistaken about what happened,' he said.

'Still in denial, eh?'

Miller changed the subject. 'Where's Kathy? Is she here, in the hospital?'

'No, she isn't, as I was coming down the hill; a four wheel drive with blacked out windows came past on a fire road; they'd almost caught you up before you went in.' Stella poured herself a plastic cup full of water. 'As soon as Kathy was out, they resuscitated her and took her with them.'

'Who did?'

'The Sister and a younger woman, I'm guessing her daughter.'

'Where was I?'

'You were still in the water. By that time, the emergency services were coming down the fire road. I think they just wanted to get out before anyone challenged what they were doing.'

'You saw her?'

'Yes, I recognised her from Ryan's funeral.' Stella looked at Miller and paused, as if considering the credibility of her next statement. 'I didn't try to stop them taking her. I know this probably sounds odd, but I just felt everything would be all right.'

'It will be. She's like the last survivor of a forgotten tribe...' Miller's voice trailed off as his thoughts caught up. 'I often wonder why it is God made such people. Was it by design, or accident?'

'You're getting too deep for me now. Come on, you need to rest,' she said. Picking up her bag, she stood, ready to leave.

'Wait, she – they – Tanner and Marshall, what's happening about that? They must have said something about Kathy?' he asked.

'I telephoned Marshall and asked if we could extend the paperwork to cover a few more days and after I'd told him she was responding very well to being with us, he agreed.'

His thoughts touched on Tanner. If Marshall had agreed to a few more days, he might not like it, but he couldn't object.

Miller sighed. 'I'm so tired; I could sleep for a week, but at least we know she's in good hands.'

'I'll leave you to get some rest. I'll be back later.' She took no more than six paces and stopped, delving into her handbag. 'Oh, by the way, they gave me this.' Stella held out a clear, sealed plastic wallet.

'What is it?' he said, raising himself onto an elbow.

'They told me you were holding it so tightly in your hand, they had to prise it from you.' She patted his arm. 'I'll leave you to it.'

Mystified, he took the bag and held it up in front of him. Something inside was wrapped in tissue paper. His forehead creased in puzzlement, as he pulled the seal apart and reached in to retrieve the object. Placing it on the bedclothes in front of him, he slowly stripped the thick layers away. An edge exposed; he hardly dared to conceive its meaning, his heart hammered, expectant. *What?* Feverish, his fingers tore at the rest of the paper, setting the object free. Joy and confusion mixed with surprise when he realised what it meant. His face lit with wonderment, and he beamed as he held it, felt its curve against the inside of his palm.

It was his seashell.

The meaning of many things he'd never understood before became clear. He'd cheated death so many times. Now, what Kirk had said to him once summed it up perfectly. *I escaped, but I never got away.*

'Kirk, old friend,' he whispered. 'Maybe that's so. Maybe I'm not *meant* to get away. Maybe this is my life; only ever a heartbeat away from dying. Maybe I haven't escaped, but I have bought myself some more time.

An hour later, he discharged himself from the hospital.

The jangling sound of a telephone infiltrated Miller's dream, louder and louder, until finally he sat up, exasperated at the thought a dream phone call could wake him. His mobile buzzed almost immediately, spinning in a clockwise arc on the bedside table. The caller display told him it was Tanner; he disconnected the call. It immediately rang again.

'Yes!' Miller barked, and was met with silence. He checked the display. It wasn't Tanner. He softened his voice. 'Sister...is that you?'

'No, it's Rosetta. I'm coming to collect you. Bring Kathy's sister. It's time to set things right.'

'How is Kathy?'

'She's better. I'll see you soon.'

Miller dressed quickly and left his room. Crossing the hotel passageway,he knocked on the door opposite. He looked at his watch. *Come on, Stella.*

A two-inch gap opened; the frown on her face disappeared when she saw who it was. She'd turbaned her hair in a towel, and she checked it was securely wrapped, before stepping back to allow him into the room.

'Are you coming in? I have to warn you, the place is a mess—'

'Stella, Rosetta is on her way to pick us up to see Kathy. We need to be ready.'

'I'll race you,' she said and shut the door.

With just enough time to freshen up, pack and ping a quick email to Carla, he checked his watch. *No way would she beat him.* He turned on the shower.

Using his phone, he drafted an email and pressed the send button.

Hi, just touching base. I haven't heard from you for a while. I won't call you in case you're spying on someone, ha ha. Ring me this evening.

Miller.

He debated on whether to add an 'x', and decided not. As he pressed the send button, there was a knock. Throwing the last of his belongings into a small carrier bag, he opened the door.

Stella had beaten him in getting ready. She looked immaculate in the clothes she'd been wearing the day before; hair tucked up into a silken scarf; make-up faultlessly applied.

'How did you—?'

'When I have to get going, I don't mess about. Unlike some.' She grinned.

An hour later, they were on the road. The trip didn't seem to take anywhere near as long as Miller's blindfolded journey.

'You decided you can trust us enough not to tell anyone where you live then?'

Rosetta glanced sideways at him. 'It was never a question of trust. What you don't know, you can't tell anyone else. After this, we are moving on, so it really doesn't matter.'

Miller looked at Stella, turned down one corner of his mouth and shrugged his shoulders. She mirrored his gestures and raised an eyebrow.

Rosetta smiled, crinkling her eyes, and met Stella's gaze in the rear-view mirror. 'Your sister is so much better,' she said.

'It would be a miracle if that were true.'

Rosetta's eyes came back from the road to the mirror again, still smiling. 'Oh, ye of little faith.'

Open heath gave way to woods and then forest; where the sun streamed flickering beams through passing trees; light and dark strobed in and out in equal measure. Miller, drawn by the rhythm into abstract thought, glanced at Stella. She appeared to be sleeping. He closed his eyes.

Rosetta slowed, and without indicating, turned from the road into a narrow lane. Deeper into the woods the density of the trees increased, closing up their leafy overhead canopies until the sky could be seen no more. Gloominess prevailed. The uneven road bounced and jarred him from his daydream. Miller opened his eyes. Stella stretched her arms wide, fists clenched and shivered. Guessing they were close, she remained silent, contemplating. A narrow gap in the earthen bank presented itself, and Rosetta turned into it. Ahead, the track led out into the sunshine.

'How does the postman find you?' he laughed.

'Nobody finds us. We have no need of mail delivery. What we send, we deliver ourselves, one way or another.' Her eyes blinked at the sudden increase in brightness. 'And what we need, we collect.'

Tyres crunched over gravel as she slowed, wildflowers and weeds, overgrown and undisturbed by traffic, brushed against both sides of the car with a gentle rasp.

Around a long slow bend, nestled among a copse of trees, a house came into view. With walls of stone and leaded windows, under a heavy slate roof, it was an oasis of civilisation amongst the wilds, its gardens neat and clipped. A flash of light reflected from a lower window, dazzling him. Vision blurred; he leaned back into the seat to avoid the glare, and watched his own arrival in his mind's eye. He sat forward with a start. On the cusp, understanding lingered at the edge of his consciousness, as elusive as the shadows that had dogged him all his life. *Pusty umysl.* He cleared it all from his mind.

The car drew to a halt. Miller appeared to be in a trance. Stella glanced at him and waved a hand before his eyes. He was gone, yet still he followed Rosetta, in through the front door, past the lobby into the hall. At the first door on the left hand side, she turned to Stella and said, 'Sit in there, please.'

'Is he all right, Rosetta?'

'He'll be fine,' she said and smiling reassurance, led Miller down the narrow passageway towards the last door on the right as she'd done before. At the end of the corridor, brilliant light shone through the window and fuzzed his vision. Kaleidoscope colours preceded Sister's appearance in the doorway. As he advanced towards her, his viewpoint switched, and he watched himself coming forwards. Rosetta withdrew from his side, trailing behind. Shadows formed and gathered to the left and right of him. Three dimensional and no longer dark, they emerged from the washed-out watercolour hues of hair and clothes and creamy flesh, becoming lit and exposed in the brightening light, as he neared the window. *Am I seeing through her eyes?*

With only two paces remaining between them, his view switched back. The shadows at his shoulders resumed their darkness on the periphery of his vision, but he felt no danger. Her gloved hand extended; she smiled at him. *I know what to do!* Snatching her hand, he gripped her wrist. Eyes flashed. Receding. Caught between here and there, he understood at last. *I wasn't controlling the bird that day. She was.*

'Where's Kathy?' Stella asked when Rosetta returned.

'She's upstairs, sleeping in the room right above us.' She lifted her face to the bowed ceiling.

'How can you be sure? We've only just walked in,' Stella said. 'And you've been gone at least three quarters of an hour.'

'Oh, Stella, you'll be seeing her soon enough. I think it's best my mother enlightens you.'

Stella fell silent. Intrigued, but reluctant to push for an answer, she changed the subject. 'I'd go crazy if I had to live all the way out here, away from it all. Doesn't it drive you mad?'

Rosetta considered the question. 'No, not at all, there's always something to do.' She indicated a tray in the far corner of the room. 'See that?'

'What about it?'

'One of the first things I learned from my mother. You don't need props, but some people like it, if you have them.'

'What do you mean?'

'Have you ever been to a medium?'

'No. I don't believe in them.' She recalled how her parents had been cheated by fake offers to track Kathy down. 'Your mother, The Sister, she isn't a medium is she? She's more than that.'

'Yes, she is.' Her eyes twinkled. 'She won't be long now. Do you want to play with the sands while we're waiting?'

The Sister twisted herself away from his grasp. 'Do not touch me,' she said, and then fixed him with fierce intensity, her eyes piercing him, connecting...

A young girl lay on a bed in the grip of a fever. Hair, unwashed and bedraggled, the palest ginger he'd ever seen spread about the pillow around her head. He watched her, watching herself from a point, he guessed, that must be just below the level of the ceiling, her mother by her bedside, damping her forehead with a flannel, stroking and soothing. All colour left her skin. She disappeared from view as he was pulled backwards, high above the house, soaring into the stratosphere, spinning and wheeling. From dizzying height, he looked down. I know this place. A man and a woman pitching a tent. Through her eyes, he witnessed their murder, the strange ritual the killer followed in disposing of the bodies. Whisked back in moments, he found himself looking up at her mother as she smiled and caressed her face. *You're back.*

The passing of time was marked in seconds rather than weeks as doctors and priests came and went.

The girl in the purple dress he now knew was Lei Liang... The killer lying in wait – he wanted to scream out, to warn her, as if his voice could carry back through the years. *Wait!*

A small boy skipped along from stone to stone by a stream. *That's me!* He watched it all from his bird's eye view. His mother scared, looking all around, crying out his name, panicking, running in circles tethered to the spot by his little sister. His grandfather rising, turning and tapping his father. *Come on!* The race against time... Lei Liang's strangled face... his slip. Boyle as he looked for him... The body hurled into the water, and more things than he could possibly have seen for himself that day. Moments. Stolen moments. Stolen lives. The killer had done more than steal the lives he took; he'd stolen a part of the lives of those who had seen him, too. Tumbling through time, echoes of long forgotten words trailed him. *You're back...*

The truth dawned on him. 'So all those times, all those near-death incidents and near misses, the interventions, you engineered them, didn't you?'

She shook her head. 'No, not me. I'm not allowed to intervene, remember?'

'Then who?'

Whispers, like those he heard in the night sometimes, rose from behind. A chorus of droning voices murmured, coming through, male and female, old and young.

'Look around you,' she said, gesturing expansively at the congregation she'd assembled for him. 'These are the shadows that intervened for you in life, as well as in death.' Grandfather, Lei Liang, Brookes, Josie, Kirk and Kennedy, all were there.

Turning, he faced them and shook his head. 'They're not real.'

'You will see.'

Each matched the last memory he had of them exactly. *Somehow, she's able to read my thoughts and project images back to me.*

Gossamer strands of hair floated, charged with static electricity, surrounding her head in a rosy, beatific golden glow. Her eyes shimmered and fixed upon him. A maelstrom of complex feelings tore through his emotions, overwhelming him. Struggling to pick them apart, he saw Josie on a ship's deck alone at the rail. A man approached from behind and savagely attacked her. Spared the entire ordeal, for him it was over in seconds. The man heaved her overboard, into the sea.

Miller wept.

'You were among her last thoughts,' Sister said.

'Don't.' He shielded his face behind a raised hand as he composed himself. 'Can they see me? Can I talk to them? I feel them stronger than ever before.'

'You closed yourself to them. Only in your dreams do you hear. Only through your mind can you speak to them.'

'I have so many things I want to say.'

'They know. There's no time now, soon I have to leave.'

'Sister, I need more answers. Just give me a few more minutes, please.'

She smiled, and her eyes sparkled. 'I bring water to within sight of the horse. Then he must find his own way to drink. Moments, you have moments.'

He scanned their faces. Aside from one, all others averted their eyes. *Brookes. Perhaps he holds the key to the most recent mystery.* He hadn't changed since he'd last seen him alive. The shy smile, his hair the same bright copper hue, the creamy face and biscuit coloured freckles, all the same. He felt in his pocket; his fingers found his seashell. Pulling it out, he held it in front of him. 'Chris, how did you give this back?'

The Sister answered for him. 'The answer is beyond our comprehension.'

'Does that mean I'll never understand? Answer me this. Did you send them to look out for me?'

'Heavens, no, they did that for themselves. As for understanding, I have shown you the water.'

Aware that time was running out, he *felt* it from her. The water glimmered on the horizon as elusive as an oasis, and yet...

'Are they happy?' Miller said, indicating the small group.

'They're not unhappy.'

'If you laid them to rest, would it mean I'd never see them again?'

The Sister smiled serenely. 'In your heart, they will always be near you.'

His former shadows bloomed into full Technicolour for the first time, faithful in every detail to the pictures that hung in the gallery of his mind. He scoured their impassive faces for a clue. *What do you want me to do?* No answer came. He searched for guidance in the depths of his soul. At last, he said, 'Always in my heart? Then let them be at peace.'

They faded from his view.

'Sister, I can't feel them anymore, have they really gone?' he said, looking troubled.

'Nothing is ever really gone, unless you believe it to be so.'

A strange sensation tugged at his senses like the moon pulling on tides, and he was struck with a sudden realisation: Dr Ryan was Rosetta's father. It came through so strong; he knew she had wanted him to know. They exchanged glances.

'I lost my powers for a long time after that happened. I didn't think they'd come back, but they did.' She fondled the stone wistfully and smiled. 'You absorbed something of me; you had a part to play. No more, I'm setting you free, go,' she said waving him away. 'Now it's time I saw Stella.'

Rosetta had risen from her seat before Miller arrived, already taking Stella by the hand as he walked into the room. He looked exhausted, but managed a half-hearted grin before he sat down in the warm seat vacated by Stella.

She took a deep breath as Rosetta led her down to the end of the long passageway.

The door was open. She entered the room.

'Come, Stella, sit with me.' Sister moved from the gloom nearer to the window, where a small round table with two chairs was conveniently located. 'It's my reading table,' she explained. 'Close enough to the light to see, not too close so as to burn me. I have this condition, see. It stops me living life to the full.' She stretched across the table and took Stella's hand. Closing her gloved fingers around it, she squeezed reassurance. 'What's your excuse?'

'I'm sorry?' Stella said, looking straight into The Sister's face. Seeing neither lines nor any blemish on her skin, she shifted her gaze to her eyes. What she saw frightened her. Eyes that were previously green now shone with opalescence, shimmering, changing colour. Stella tried to look away, but a peculiar magnetism locked her in. Her hair stood on end, as The Sister's rose in harmony, haloing her head.

If the Sister had had reason to delve into Stella's past at Ryan's funeral, she would have seen the truth as it now presented itself. The truth of what really happened to her parents. *Stella doesn't know.* Allowing her perceptions to form fully, she reached into the past.

Her eyelids fluttered; static stormed across the surface of her skin. Energy sparked needles through her gloved hand into Stella's, and the shock jolted her into letting go.

Sister stood witness in her parent's bedroom on a night blacker than she'd ever seen.

Her father was having a nightmare, muttering in his sleep; a sheen of perspiration covered his face. Suddenly he called out, crystal clear. 'Don't you touch my child!'

Her mother stirred and laid a hand on his chest, gently reassuring him. 'What is it?' she said.

'Something's happened to Kathy!'

His eyes were wet and tinged with sadness. Wiping tears, he blinked hard. 'We're never going to see her again, are we?'

'Don't say that, love, don't say that.' A strange light was in her eyes. 'One day we will see her again. Together. Do you believe in God?'

He nodded; teeth clenched; eyes closed.

'Then, whatever happens, one day, we-will-see-her-again.'

The following day, her mother had brought home a large dose of horse tranquillisers from the vets where they worked and waited until her husband had fallen asleep, before injecting him first and then herself. Sister, viewing ahead, held onto the vision. She remembered once asking Father O'Malley when she was a child. *'A white lie isn't a sin, is it Father?'*

His eyes narrowed suspiciously. 'A sin is a sin. What is the sin we're talking about here?'

'Keeping quiet about something to spare someone's feelings.'

'Are you talking about shielding someone's feelings here, now? It's most likely a venial sin.' His eyes softened. 'I don't think anyone would get overexcited if you told a lie like that.'

Sister decided she should spare Stella's feelings.

'Your mother wrote you a letter the night before the suicide; you never read it did you?'

Stella shook her head.

Giving her no choice, Sister recited from the image in her mind.

My dearest Stella,
I'm so very sorry, but by the time you read this, dad and I will have gone. There's nothing I can say that will change anything now. Your father had a

nightmare, and I knew after that, we couldn't carry on. It would have been unfair
to burden you with our loss anymore. Sometimes you have to be cruel to be kind.
I hope you can forgive us.
Mum. xxx

Stella's eyes brimmed with tears. 'How did hearing that help me?'

'You can't hide behind the not knowing now, can you? I used to ask people if they wanted the truth, but you know something. Sometimes you're better off without it. The truth has the power to hurt as well as heal. Open another tin of worms, what for?'

The former nun removed her gloves and revealed a polished black stone. 'One more thing to do, Stella. I'm going to put this in your hand. Hold it out for me.'

Rosetta raked the sands, levelling them across the tray with the edge of her hand. 'You sure you don't want to do this with me, Miller?'

'Positive.'

'You might see something, I already can. Three women in your life, Miller, and only one is any good for you.'

'Is that right?' He grinned. 'Is one of them a stranger, tall and dark?'

'See for yourself.' Her eyes flashed green and brilliant. 'Make sure you choose wisely.'

He laughed. 'I can't see anything. Your mother switches me on and off like a video link.'

'She does? How does she do that then— wait, what's that?' Rosetta defocused and stared across the surface. 'You see that cross? They're coming.'

The weight of the stone surprised her. Stella had the sensation of something drawn out from her, as if she were donating blood; the feeling lasted for the briefest moment and then was gone.

Sister retrieved the stone and held on to it, smiling an enigmatic smile. 'You always said you needed more than anecdotal evidence and that you needed an experience of your own and nothing short of a miracle would change your mind.'

Stella stared at her transfixed.

'You also said if there were a God, if there was such a being, then he was the God of grief and sadness, disappointment and loneliness. You just ploughed your furrow through life, dealing with whatever it threw up, looking forward to the next hundred yards,'

Stella couldn't take her eyes off her.

'Yours was not life, it was a mere existence. A condition bestowed on you by something that happened before you were born.'

'How do you know all that? I wrote that in my diary when I was seventeen-years-old, and then I ripped the page out and threw it away. How could you know?'

'The only thing that matters is that your sister is back to where she was before she was taken. She has the memories you shared with your mum and dad, inside her now. She understands they've gone, and she understands she was away, but she has no concept of time. In her head, she missed nothing at all. Kathy's time starts now. Can you understand that? You must help her. After all, she is your sister.'

Stella gazed at the autumnal pattern in the carpet.

Rosetta burst through the door. 'They're coming!'

The Sister smiled. 'I know.'

Chapter 155

Reacting to the gravity in Rosetta's voice, Stella got to her feet, frowning apprehension. 'Who's coming?' she said. 'Will someone tell me what's going on?'

Sister remained calm, seated. 'Miller, go. Take the sisters with you.'

Worried lines appeared on Stella's face. 'What's happening?' she asked nervously, looking at each of the others in the room, she waited for an answer.

'The Church, not the Catholic Church – another one – they're coming for her,' Miller said, taking her arm and steering her out of the door. 'Go and get Kathy. She's upstairs, right?' He looked at Rosetta. She nodded.

Stella lingered, uncertain. 'What do you mean they're coming for her?'

'I'll explain later. You need to get Kathy,' he repeated and then turning, he said, 'Come on, Sister, let's get you out of here.'

She smiled serenely. 'Miller, Rosetta will drop you all to Waverley, you can get the train back to London. Rosetta, is your emergency bag packed?'

'It's been packed for days—'

'Good, now get these people out of here.'

Miller squatted in front of her by the table. 'Are you not coming?'

'If I do and they catch up with us, there will be blood. Just go. You don't owe me anything.'

Without taking his eyes from her, he said to Rosetta over his shoulder, 'Bring the car round.'

She looked to her mother for confirmation. 'Do it, Rosetta,' she said.

'What are you doing, Miller?' Rosetta said.

'If she's not going, I'm staying with her.'

'Miller, you cannot. I have to do this on my own. It's one of the things fate has always had in store for me. Get your bag, Rosetta.'

'You can't make me leave, besides I have a plan,' he said.

She raised an eyebrow. A light shone in her emerald eyes and the hint of a smile graced her lips. 'I guessed you might.'

Rosetta left the room for a few moments and reappeared carrying a small suitcase. Kathy stood behind her, bleary-eyed, next to Stella.

'I hope you know what you're doing, Miller,' Stella said.

He stepped forward and embracing her, whispered in her ear, 'I'll see you soon.'

She squeezed him hard before they parted, he hesitated and then awkwardly shifted direction, leaning back in to kiss her cheek, and she turned her face at the same time. Her lips brushed against his. 'Soon,' she murmured.

Kathy looked embarrassed as he took her hand and kissed the back of it lightly. Winking, he said, 'Take care of each other. I'll see you both soon.'

Sister hugged her daughter in a lingering, warm embrace, and whispered in her ear. They held onto each other's hands, reluctant to let go. Unseen, she palmed something into Rosetta's hand before finally parting with her.

'Where is the tall man?' Carlos said, as he slid into the passenger seat.

Hasan took the notepad from the dashboard, scribbled on it, and pushed it toward his companion. *He is already in Scotland.*

'Always, he is one step ahead of us. He wants the stone for himself. Drive, Hasan. I will speak, and you will listen…'

The Sister had known for years the cult's popularity would grow. Always moving behind the scenes, she'd severed many reptiles from the head of the new Medusa, but no matter how many she removed, others sprang up to take their place. The leader remained elusive, hidden behind many facades, his identity unknown to but a handful of trusted allies, and her. In a world where people were leaving the traditional church in droves, he'd built a new congregation founded on blind faith and mind control. With the power and wealth he'd accumulated, almost beyond compare, it seemed nothing could stand in his way.

Miller knew the key to stopping them was Carlos, but Kale had warned him off. With the Resurrectionists less than a few hours away, he telephoned Kale.

'Donovan, it's Miller. I need your help with something. Remember I told you about that business I had in Scotland? Well…'

When he'd finished explaining everything, Kale was silent for only a moment.

'This is what I suggest: The Vatican,' he said, 'it's the only place she'll truly be safe, and from what I can gather, they'll welcome her back with open arms, the Resurrectionists wouldn't dare to follow her there.'

'That's great, Donovan, but we need to move quickly.'

'Scotland, you say? Whereabouts?'

'Not far from Edinburgh.' Miller replied.

'I can have my plane there within two hours. There's a private airfield about twenty miles out. Can you get her there?'

Miller covered the receiver. 'Is there another car here?'

She nodded.

'I don't know how this is going to work, Donovan, but yes, give me the postcode, and we'll get there.'

'I'll have it sent to you by text. Two hours. See you there.' Kale hung up.

'Come on, Sister; let's get you packed and ready.' He followed her along the passageway to the lobby, where a suitcase sat waiting for her.

'You weren't ever planning to wait for them, were you?' he said, studying her face. Tiny creases at the corners of her eyes gave her away. *I should have known!* 'How did they find you?'

'Oh, I knew they would, eventually. My ability to resist those who pry was somehow doubled by the stone, but the closer someone gets, the harder it is to stay concealed.' Her fingers sought from habit to roll a missing object. 'And he is close.'

'Who?'

'The tall man. The seer. I feel him.' She donned her cape and gloves, pulling the hood up and lowering the veil over her face. 'Miller, we must go now. He'll kill you if he finds you here. He wants only me and the stone.'

'Now where's this car?' he said.

The tall man stopped the elderly red Citroen, opened the driver's door and then half-getting out, he stood, holding it ajar. With one foot on the road and the other still in the vehicle, he turned and looked south. *The stone. It's no longer here.* He'd gone ahead to try to obtain it for himself. With it, his would be the ultimate power. There would be no need for The Sister. With it, he'd be able to read the future in addition to reading the past. *Miller is with her.* He got back into the car, considering his next move.

Bumping up the lane in an old, battleship-grey army jeep, they rounded the first bend. The sun cast a red glow across the lane onto the wild flowers. *A car is coming! No, it isn't moving.* It was stationary and empty.

'I don't think I can get round it,' Miller said. 'I'll see if I can move it.'

'Be careful,' she said, laying a gloved hand on his forearm. 'He is near.'

With no one else in sight, Miller got out and looked into the abandoned vehicle. The door was unlocked. *No keys.* He remembered a gap they'd passed in the bushes further up, on their way in earlier, a passing point.

'Sister, you're going to have to drive the jeep, push this French banger backwards. I'll steer it.'

The hedgerow quivered and then suddenly parted as a man clambered through the foliage. 'Move away from the car, Miller.' He held a pistol.

'You!' Miller exclaimed, recognising him as one of the men who'd tried to kill him a year ago. *The tall man.*

He brushed along between the vegetation and the side of the car, keeping the gun levelled on him.

'Move away down the passenger side and get in,' he commanded.

The gap between them was six feet. *You'll never do it.*

'Don't even think about it,' the other man sneered. 'You, Sister, out! I know you no longer have the stone. Where is it? Tell me!' he said, aiming the pistol. 'Or I'll kill him.'

He knows where it is. Her thoughts came from Miller's head.

The seer looked from one to the other. *What sort of trick is this?*

Her eyes flickered behind her veil. Miller saw himself through her eyes.

The gun swept round to aim at her. 'Last warning. Where is the stone?'

A shadow formed. *Taekkyon!* His mind emptied in the blink of an eye. He took two steps, ducking under the pistol arm as it swung to follow him. His hand coming around from below, he gripped the seer's wrist, knee against calf, folding the leg backwards, at the same time forcing the gun hand away from him. Miller stepped up onto the lowered thigh using it as a springboard and drove his knee straight up into his adversary's face. The gun went off. Birds scattered from nearby trees. The Sister fell to the ground.

Oh, no – she's been shot! Fearful, he rushed to her stricken form. Dropping to his knees beside her, he cried her name. She didn't move. One leg had folded and tucked half beneath the upper calf of the other; he unfastened the silken cape, looking for a wound, and finding none, pressed his ear against her chest, listening for a heartbeat.

'What are you doing, man?' She pushed his head away. 'I fainted, that's all! I can't bear violence.'

With no time for ceremony, he yanked her to her feet and then crouched by the unconscious man, searching his pockets for the car keys. Finding them, he threw the gun over the hedge. 'Quick, get in the car.'

The car screamed in reverse gear as he swung it into the passing point. Backwards, forwards, back again, turning enough to face forwards, he then drove as quickly as the car's suspension would allow them to go. Shadows gathered about him.

'I thought you'd laid them to rest,' he said, grinning.

'So did I,' she said, a hint of a smile on her lips.

Miller dropped her off an hour later, at the airfield. One of Kale's bodyguards met them in the car park, and they followed him to where a private jet awaited her. After helping her aboard with her luggage, Miller embraced her.

'Will I ever see you again, Sister?' he asked.

She rested her forefinger on his chest, right above his tattoo. 'Si Dios quiere,' she said, and even though her hand was gloved, and he was wearing a jumper and shirt, her touch burned into him.

'I'll see you again, Sister,' he whispered and walked back down the steps onto the concrete taxiway.

She watched his back as he descended, smiled enigmatically and turning, entered the plane.

A female flight attendant introduced herself and showed her inside.

Kale emerged from the cockpit and took over, asking, 'Isn't your daughter coming with you?'

'Rosetta is making her own way.'

Sister smiled as Kale's face darkened. 'But they're after her, too!'

'I know,' she sighed. 'But you know how it is with the young.'

'When did she leave?'

She knew there was a time for truth and a time for lies; there was only one option. 'An hour ago.'

'Excuse me.' Kale turned on his heel. 'I'll be back in a moment.'

Taking a seat, she looked out of the aircraft's window. Head down, Miller crossed the strip, on his way back to the car park. She blew a kiss after him.

The distant figure of Miller stopped abruptly and turned. The jet shone in the late evening sunshine, its whole length illuminated, radiating a beam, so bright everything else paled against it. *It looks like Ryan's pencil!* Shielding his eyes, he squinted, looking for her at the window. Something in his perception changed, and he saw his tiny figure standing out alone, by the runway. The link forged all those years ago, no longer denied, still in existence.

He googled the telephone number of the nearest taxi firms while he waited. Only when the plane was airborne did he call a cab. His finger poised above the keypad to make his next call, he hesitated. *If she'd wanted the police involved, she would have told you.*

Selecting Tanner from his contacts menu, he telephoned him.

'John, it's Miller. Look I'm sorry about the last few days.' He held his mobile away from his ear while Tanner turned the air blue with a tirade.

'Stella's on the train with Kathy, heading for King's Cross, I don't know which train they caught, but they should be back in two or three hours, I would have thought. Any luck with finding Boyle, by the way?'

'Don't you read the papers? We're in the middle of the biggest manhunt this country has seen for years,' Tanner said. 'Where are you?'

'It's a bit of a story, John, but if Boyle is still at large, it might be an idea to get the girls picked up from the station when they arrive, make sure they're safe. I'll call Stella and find out how far away they are and let you know.'

'Between you and me, I think he's long gone, but let me know what time and I'll get someone to meet them.'

'Thanks, John, I'll call you back.'

Taking a deep breath, he phoned Stella.

'Hi, Stella, it's me. Is everything okay?'

'Jesus, Miller, what was that all about. I couldn't get anything out of Rosetta, what is it about you? I'm beginning to believe you when you say you're dangerous to know!'

'I haven't got time to explain it now. The main thing is you and Kathy are okay. How much longer before you arrive in London? Tanner is going to send someone to meet you, but listen, do me a favour. Don't say anything about what happened with The Sister.'

'How can I say anything? I can hardly remember a thing.' She laughed nervously.

The taxi arrived.

Deciding to catch the train home in the morning, he checked into the nearest hotel to the railway station as he could.

Moments later, his phone rang. *Carla.*

'Miller, where are you?'

'I'm in a little room at a hotel in Edinburgh—'

'I called you straight away. Guess what? No, don't bother. I've just discovered Michael Simpson posted some documents into an email account he'd set up under an alias. I'll explain everything later, but I now know who killed him, and why.'

'I thought we were clear—'

She interrupted, 'Yes, but you'll never believe what I found out.'

'Oh, Carla, *please* just tell me.'

'It's Kale – he's the leader of the Resurrectionists.'

For a moment, he didn't answer. Despite everything else that came before, he'd not seen *that* coming.

Pinching the bridge of his nose, he said, 'Carla, give me a minute, I'll call you back.' He disconnected her.

His mind raced. When Vera had touched him, and he'd seen those things: the neon sign, the garish cross over the church glowing high on the mountain.

It all became clear.

The Sister had her reasons for throwing a blanket over his senses, and he realised she'd known her destiny all along and used him to do what she couldn't do directly herself.

He'd unwittingly helped her to get inside; now she would at last finish the task fate had set her long ago.

Miller wondered if he'd ever see her again, and then he smiled.

Calling Carla back, he laid his cards on the table. 'Listen, you're going to have to drop the investigation—'

'Miller, are you kidding me? No way!'

'Will you just hear me out? You have a great story, and we both know that, but to leak it now benefits no one, puts lives in danger and spoils whatever chances there might be of a better one, and besides, what's happened about Carlos?'

'Trail's gone cold. I haven't enough for a story really. I have some more on his background, but I don't do half a job.'

'That's exactly what I'm saying.'

'Okay, okay, I'll drop it for now. I was thinking about writing a book about Boyle.'

'Boyle? There's a story there, but you can't finish that one either.'

'Oh, I think I can,' she said.

Rosetta stepped off the train into the cool night air and made her way towards the seafront.

The buildings in the side street leading towards it were derelict, boarded up; most of them had been that way for years. Only the dregs of society, drug addicts, winos and the down-on-their luck used them now. It was almost midnight.

It was safer on the streets during the day, while most of them slept off the effects of the night before. After dark, it was a place best avoided.

Two rough sleepers sat facing each other, with their backs against the red brick wall of a porch. At the bottom of the stone steps leading up to it, was a black iron gate with three-foot railings each side of it. It was a visible deterrent to invasion, which although not unassailable, made them feel safer.

One was Irish, the other Czechoslovakian. They took turns guarding their snug in the daytime. They hadn't left it unattended, since a couple of Romanian gypsies had laid claim to it some time ago. It hadn't been easy to get it back. One would go off to forage for money, drink and food, while the other stayed behind. The arrangement worked well.

When they spoke, it was quietly, to avoid drawing attention to themselves. They finished the last of the drink; it was the trigger – knowing there was no more – to descend into oblivion. It beckoned the Czech first, as always, and the conversation dwindled to almost nothing.

It was the same every night.

'She's not coming, is she?' the Irishman said, out of the blue.

The Czech's head tipped back as he drained the last drops from the purple tin in his hand; he rolled his eyes in his companion's direction without moving his head.

He spoke from the corner of his mouth, as he swallowed. 'Who's not—' His chest heaved, interrupted by a choking spasm. His lips pressed tightly together to prevent the loss of any precious liquid, his eyes bulged as he struggled to regain control of the reflex. Finally swallowing, he coughed a piece of phlegm and spat it over the wall. '— not coming?'

The Irishman shook his head in dismay. 'Did your mother not tell you never to speak wit' your mouth full?'

The advice was lost on the Czech as he wiped his mouth on the back of his hand, eyes red and streaming. 'I don' remember my mother!' he said, with a hoarse voice.

'Shame on you, Czech.'

'An' shame to you!'

The sound of footsteps in the narrow street silenced them. The only light was the moon. Knocked out on a nightly basis, the council had given up replacing the streetlights years ago. Boarded up buildings lined both sides of the street, but the security measure didn't prevent the former hotel opposite being used as a drug den. A large corner of corrugated iron sheet covering a ground floor window pushed out. A pair of feet appeared, followed by legs and the rest of the body, which eased down to the pavement beneath. The owner of the footsteps they'd heard held the sheet open, before climbing in himself. There was always someone coming or going.

They never bothered the two men; they didn't have anything they needed.

'She hasn't been since last year,' the Irishman said.

The Czech slipped further down against the wall, so that his back was almost on the floor, while his head remained upright, leaning against it. From the side, he was almost L shaped. His neck would ache in the morning, but he was too far gone to move. He closed his eyes, mumbling, 'Crazy Irish, lemme sleep.'

'Things were different when she was around. I didn't need this *shit* when she was around.' He looked at the half-empty bottle with disdain. Turning it to catch the moonlight, it revealed the tiniest smear of liquid still inside.

He licked his lips and almost sensually pushed his tongue into the bottle's smooth neck, tipping it up, waiting patiently for last of the moisture to dribble over his taste buds. It warmed his mouth, and he slumped back against the wall, eyes slowly drifting out of focus.

The gate creaked. Heart pounding, he sat up rubbing his eyes as he looked warily down the steps.

The figure of a woman, dressed in a light grey cape, came towards him, her pale face and rosé coloured hair coming alive in the silvery light.

She looked younger than the last time he'd seen her.

'Czech, wake up; she's here. Our Lady is resurrectified.'

She smiled enigmatically. 'Hello, Paddy.'

Hollow crumpling sounds came from the thin metal sheets as they pushed back from the window behind her, she looked over as a gangly youth slid out, looking around furtively before going on his way.

The smile was still on her lips, but her face couldn't mask the sadness she felt at the plight of those around her.

Paddy was on his feet, wiping his hands against his clothes, smoothing his hair. 'What is it, what's wrong?'

She turned to face him. 'It's okay, Paddy. I was just thinking, that's all.'

Every year at Easter, no matter what, her mother had returned to Brighton. She'd have loved to have helped them all, but she recalled her words. *You can't grow seeds in a barren land; they won't take.* A question formed in her head. *But what if you bring fertile soil with you?*

She rolled the stone between her thumb and forefinger. Manipulating it into her palm, she closed her grip on it. The impressions it contained had long since passed into her, but the energy it possessed amazed her, firing her body and soul.

She thought about her mother again, but she was shut down to her. Rosetta couldn't connect.

'When the time comes,' her mother had said, 'and the Resurrectionists come for you; seek out Miller. He'll know what to do.'

She puzzled over the advice. *Why not you, Mum?* It was the one area they hadn't covered in the plan. A thought seeded in her mind, designed to seek out the light when the time came, germinated. *If she uses the wavelengths, the tall man, he will know.*

Chapter 156

Monday 27 August

The improvement in Kathy had occurred almost overnight. The hospital released her on the proviso she stayed with her sister, and Miller had insisted Stella took six weeks off work to help with her rehabilitation. He'd kept in regular touch with her throughout, and during her absence; she'd volunteered – if time permitted – to create a new website for him. On Saturday afternoon, she'd telephoned to say she would be in on Monday. Desperate for the change in direction an enhanced presence on the internet could bring, he hadn't argued. Quite apart from that, he needed her back.

The gates were already open. She was already in. As he strolled up the driveway, he noticed she was playing music. *She must be in a good mood.* He was looking forward to seeing her. Unable to suppress a grin, he pressed the buzzer. The alloy speaker panel crackled, and the bolt mechanism disengaged. Pulling the door open, he entered.

Stella's face lit with a smile. 'Hi, stranger,' she said, switching the radio off. She got to her feet and came around to the front of the desk, encircling him with her arms.

He squeezed her tight and said, 'Good to see you back at last. How's Kathy?'

Pulling away, she looked almost disappointed.

'And you – how are you?' He shrugged, embarrassed. 'I'm sorry; I've had so much on my mind I've forgotten my etiquette.'

'We're both okay,' she said, 'Kathy goes to a day centre now. I'm a bit worried because she's talking about becoming a nun, which is hardly surprising after everything she's been through. Doctor Marshall said her recovery was nothing short of a miracle, but he was inclined to believe she'd faked at least some of her earlier symptoms. Do you think he's right?' she said, cocking her head to one side inquisitively.

'It isn't important. She's so much better, and that's all that counts.'

'True, but what he said is a cop-out. Why not just admit that whatever The Sister did, it worked?' She dipped her head and looked up at him from below her fringe. 'Now that I've got you face to face, you've got a lot of explaining to do.'

'Can I have a coffee first?'

'Of course, I'll join you.' She plucked her cup from the top of her desk and said, 'I'll put the kettle on.'

Miller followed her to the kitchen. 'How's the website going?' he said.

'It's all done, just needs you to look it over and give it your stamp of approval.' She held up a teaspoon. 'Still taking sugar? You chop and change so much I never know.' She bit her bottom lip and looked at him, tears welling. 'I'm sorry. I still haven't quite got over everything.'

'Hey, if you need some more time?'

'No, really, I've had more than enough, I – it's time I got back into normality.' She took a tissue from under her sleeve and dabbed at her eyes before throwing it into the waste bin.

The kettle rumbled steam spewing from its spout. The button popped out, and the vibration slowly subsided. She poured the water and stirred. 'I'm having mine black, you?'

'Same.' He picked his coffee up from the worktop and wandered out into the main office area, with no one else present to worry about, he said, 'What did you want me to explain?'

'All of it. I want to know why The Sister had to flee like that, and what this church you spoke about wants her for. Did she get away?'

She sat behind her desk. He perched on the corner.

'She did what she set out to do. I helped her. Beyond that, I don't know anything else.' He stared into a distance she couldn't see. Kale had betrayed the trust he'd put in him. Isolated from the abilities that had grown within him all his life, the other acquisitions, sharpness of mind and intuition hadn't left him. Conclusions, once based on probabilities, chances and possibilities: he'd have to learn to put faith in those deductions again. Although cut off and cast adrift from all previous perceptions, he was acutely aware he was missing something. More and more, he'd thought about what Rosetta had told him. *I see three women. Only one is good for you.* With Stella sitting adjacent to him, the thought drifted into his mind.

She waved her hand in front of his face.

He shook his head and then clapping his hands together, said, 'Right, let's see what you've done with this website.'

'I didn't realise you could do all that,' he said after she'd run through the pages. 'The last site we had running was just static, do you remember?'

'Do I,' she groaned. 'Okay, so you're happy with the layout, what about contact details, you said you were going to think about those—' Interrupted by the sound of his mobile ringing, she paused as he answered the call.

'Good morning,' he said, deliberately withholding her name. 'Is everything okay?'

'Miller, I need your help.'

'Can we talk about it later?'

Stella, detecting a level of tension in his voice, stared at him, and listened for clues that would give the caller's identity away.

'It's to do with Boyle,' Carla said.

'He's long gone,' he said, calmly, but without conviction. He didn't want to spook Stella.

'Is he? Are you sure about that? I know you got Tanner to meet the two sisters when they came back from Scotland.'

'That was weeks ago, he's either skipped the country, or he's dead. Eilise hit him so hard she swears she left a dent in his head.'

'Still, you can't be sure, can you?'

Stella got to her feet and moved closer to him. Looking at her, he half smiled and grimaced at the same time. He moved from the corner of the desk, and ambled towards his office, mouthing to her; *I won't be a minute.*

'I can't, you're right, I can't.' He mourned the passing of the powers Sister kept cloaked from him. He sat on the corner of his desk.

'It's a nice little job, Miller. A jaunt down country, an overnight stay with me?'

'What does any of that have to do with Boyle? I'm right in the middle of setting up a new website in the office.' He sighed. 'I'm trying to get away from all that. I want to take a new direction, a less dangerous one.'

Carla's voice cooled and became distant. 'A few months ago, you'd have jumped at the chance to stay overnight somewhere with me. It's that new secretary of yours, isn't it? You can't bear to leave her, can you?'

He considered what she said. There was some truth in it. He definitely felt more of an affinity with Stella since he'd taken her to Scotland.

Carla goaded him. 'Not denying it then?'

He laughed. 'So silence is agreement is it?'

'Never mind,' she said, her tone matter-of-fact. 'I've got a prediction for you. Can you guess what it is?'

A small measure of irritation crept into his voice. 'Sadly, no. Just tell me, will you?'

'You're so boring lately, Miller. There was a time you'd have had a guess, and it would have been right.'

'Carla, stop messing around and just tell me.'

A low whistle came down the line. 'Okay. You will come with me to Devils Pond.'

'You're wrong about that,' he said.

'For my book, I have to solve the mystery of those clooties that appear every year. I have a theory and only one chance to prove or disprove it for another year. August the 27th, ghost day.'

'You've got the date wrong, it's the 15th July.'

'No, that's St Swithun's day. The anniversary of the mine disaster, the day the locals believe the pond releases those ghosts to walk again. I'm talking about the Chinese; they celebrate ghost day more or less a month later.'

'All very interesting Carla, but I've laid my ghosts to rest. I won't be coming with you. Find someone else.'

Stella appeared in his doorway, watching him, cool eyes gauging his reactions. He shrugged his shoulders at her and mouthed, *I'm not going.*

'Miller, I've dug up a lot of stuff for the book we didn't know about Boyle before,' Carla allowed a stream of air to escape her lips. 'The night Josie disappeared...' she trailed into silence.

He stood upright, curiosity lining his face. 'What about it?'

'Boyle was on the same ferry.' Her voice softened. 'If we can find out who puts those silken rags up every year, we will have another piece of the jigsaw. We might get closer to finding out—'

'When are we going?'

'Today.'

He listened as she told him the plan.

Stella shook her head in dismay. 'Tell me you haven't agreed to do something with that woman. She's bad news.'

'Look, Stella, it's just one night—'

'I don't care, I'm coming with you. When is it?'

'Tonight, I have to go. She's doing a book about Boyle. Do you remember me telling you about Josie, my first love, how she vanished at sea, and they never recovered her body?'

'I do, but aren't we all supposed to be moving on?'

'If what she just said is true, it will help me to do that. She told me Boyle was on the boat when Josie disappeared that night.' A faraway look was in his eyes.

'And you're going after him?'

He stared into the depths of her crystal blue eyes and registered the concern there. 'Stella, if I knew where he was, I'd go in a heartbeat,' he said, through clenched teeth. 'For what he did to her and what he did to Kennedy. I'd kill him.'

Stella's hand sought his, to reassure, provide comfort. Her touch electrified him. A solar wind blew through his senses, and he saw something he hadn't realised before. When The Sister had given Stella the stone, part of him was contained within it. She'd known it would pass into Stella. Now he had it back. Not as strong as it had been, just like an echo. Closing his eyes for a moment, he rested his other hand on top of hers. Something else came through. She felt it too.

He pulled away.

'I don't want you to go,' she said.

An awkward silence followed.

'Miller, what happened just now? I know you felt it. The same thing happened when I held the stone at the Sister's house; something was taken from me.' Her voice seemed disoriented. 'And now I feel strange, as if I've known you for years.'

'I'd love to be able to explain it, but I wouldn't know where to begin.'

The Sister. All this was meant to be, according to her vision. She'd stripped him of his extra-sensory abilities so he wouldn't see through her plans for infiltrating the Resurrectionists and through Stella, she'd given a part of that back and in doing so had created a bond between them.

I see three women. Only one is good for you.

'I've got to go,' he said.

She stepped into the doorway and barred his exit.

Getting closer to her, he said, 'Okay, I'll squeeze past.' She did not attempt to move. A look passed between them as he crossed the invisible line into her personal space. Clear, crystal blue eyes, larger than he'd ever seen them before locked with his. Her arms found their way around his neck. Hesitant at first, they kissed with a passion that threatened to engulf them with its flames. She felt for him, and gasped as he nibbled her neck.

'Stella,' he whispered. 'What are we doing?'

'I want to be sure you'll come back to me.'

Miller knew that to get safely close to the pond in the dark; he'd need a four-wheeled drive vehicle. He hired a Land Rover and picked Carla up just before four in the afternoon. A fresh and lovely fragrance preceded her as she got into the car with an overnight bag.

'Ready?' he said.

'I'm always ready,' she breathed.

His right eyebrow rose, out of her line of sight. 'You were going to tell me how you found out about Josie.'

'It was quite a simple exercise to trawl the records. To be honest, the connection came out of the blue. I knew Boyle had joined the Foreign Legion, and I knew he had French connections, among others dating back to those times. To cut a long one short, I went to France to see if I could track any of them down and I did. Tanner came with me.'

A pang of jealousy soured the taste in his mouth. 'How did you get him involved?'

'Oh, he owed me a favour. We'd done some research on the best travelling fighters in an effort to track Boyle down earlier, and we interviewed a number of past Kings of the Gipsies. The whole story is in my book, but we ended up talking to this guy in Marseilles and it turned out he'd seen Boyle for the last time, quite by chance in Boulogne, waiting for the ferry on the night Josie vanished. We checked the passenger records. Boule – the name he adopted in the Legion – was among them, and so was she. Coincidence? I think not.'

In his mind, he replayed the snapshot the Sister had shared with him. His jaw tightened, grinding his teeth together. *It was him. I know it was him.*

'Are you okay?' she asked, breaking the silence.

'I have to be,' he said, changing the subject. 'You didn't tell me how you'd drawn the conclusion the Clootie Fairy only appears on ghost day, and that being so, how do they avoid detection on each anniversary?'

'Ghost day is never the same day in consecutive years. I pieced everything else together, but something still bothered me about this part of the story. The locals had tried periodically, to catch whoever it was tying the silks up, wrongly assuming whoever it was, was marking the anniversary of the mine disaster. I went there the other day, what a creepy place it is… I counted all the clooties, some of them were old, bleached white, green with mould, rotting; just the knotted part around the branches had survived. Someone had tied up a pair of red socks, so clearly a few of these offerings are just random, but then I counted the silk ones separately, and there were thirty-one of those.'

He struggled to recall the numbers of rags Kennedy had quoted him. 'Carla, when Kennedy was last there, he accounted for twenty-three mine deaths, the seven murder victims and my three friends. At that time, the number he'd seen tied up was forty-nine. I'm sure of it.'

'Maybe, but how many silk ones? Anyway, the penny dropped. There was one of those for every year since the bodies were discovered.'

'I see where you're coming from, and Lei Liang was Chinese.'

'Exactly, and the extra clooties only started manifesting themselves after her remains were identified.'

Driving on auto-pilot, Miller slipped into deeper thought. Ryan had told him about the local legends surrounding Devils Pond, the locals believing it released its spirits on July 15th every year. *Thirty-one. Silks. Every year.* He was on the verge of figuring it out when Carla spoke again.

'Did you know one of the skeletons pulled out matched Boyle's DNA profile? We reckon it was his father. He disappeared not long after his wife – Boyle's mother – died. It looks like he killed him, too. His own father.'

'What else have you found out about him?'

She laughed and stroked the back of his neck. 'You'll just have to wait for the book to find out.'

They arrived at almost eleven o'clock. He drove slowly down a farm track that led to within a quarter of a mile of the pond and switched off the engine and lights.

'Shouldn't we get nearer?' she said.

'If anyone comes, they'll need a torch to see in this dark, so we'll spot them easily enough. No, we'll wait here.'

At just before midnight, Carla caught a glimpse of a low light in the darkness, moving slowly through the trees. Miller had dropped off, snoring gently.

'Come on, Miller,' Carla said, shaking him violently. 'Quick! There's someone over there!'

He woke, not quite knowing where he was.

Carla was already out of the car. If it really were the Clootie Fairy, she wanted to be the first see who it was. The leaden cloud cover broke, allowing moonlight to illuminate the surrounding land to some degree. Miller got out and ran after her.

Keeping under cover, they followed the shadow as it carried its dim light close to the waters. The dark clad figure put the lamp down and tied a fresh clootie in place, and turning picked up the lantern and moved closer to the water.

From behind, the figure was so small; Carla thought it was a child, but it couldn't be. The clooties had appeared every year for over thirty years.

Carla's torch gave her away. The figure froze on seeing the pool of light, and made no attempt at escape, instead, a thin voice rasped, 'Who are you?' *It was a woman!* She continued talking without waiting for an answer. 'Every year on night of Ghost Day, I mark anniversary of death of my child in this place. When I hear of custom to tie rag wiped with hurt, and I see much old rag rot in the wind. I tear sleeve and leave there first time. After, I bring always finest silk. You know pain, it never go away.'

She turned to face Carla and Miller. In the torchlight, she looked younger than her years. Miller did the maths; she had to be in her late seventies, but could easily pass for a woman in her sixties.

Carla spoke to her softly. 'Are you Lei Liang's mother?'

'Yes, I am.' The old woman said, proudly raising her chin. 'You didn't tell me, who are you?'

'My name is Carla Black and I'm hoping to solve the mystery of what happened to your daughter and the other people who died here.' She indicated Miller. 'This man is an investigator and I'm a reporter. We are not far off catching the man who did this.'

'You know Lei is not here. I do not know where is she, but not here. I am glad. My gift to her was Five Poison amulet. Here in body, but spirit free, saved by charm from water demon.'

Lei Liang's mother moved to the edge of the bank. Taking a telescopic pole with a hook, she extended it, hanging a small paper boat on the end. She lit a taper in the boat before pushing it out, placing it in the water, unhooking it with great care. The three of them stood silent, watching the ritual.

The flame in the tiny vessel flared and shooting upward disappeared into the gloom, leaving only ripples. The moonlight laid a path across the dark waters.

From the corner of his eye, Miller sensed movement. A shadow stepped from behind into his line of sight. Lei Liang shimmered in the moonlight in all her beautiful glory.

Her mother gasped at the sight and clasped her hands in joy. She spoke rapidly in a mixture of Chinese and English.

'Lei, is it really you?' She fell to her knees before the vision.

The projection lasted for several minutes as mother and daughter communed. The manifestation was so strong, Carla saw it, too.

Afterwards, Miller looked drained.

'You didn't tell me you could do that,' Carla said.

'I didn't,' he replied. 'Something used me.'

Miller's doorbell rang as he made himself a coffee. He checked his watch. *9:05 a.m.* Wiping his hands on a towel, he walked to the front door. The silhouette in the bulls-eye window revealed it was the postman. 'Morning,' he said as he opened it.

'Morning, I have this for you; it wouldn't fit through the box, and I didn't want to leave it on the step in the rain…'

'Thanks,' he said, taking the parcel. 'You don't need a signature?'

'No, whoever sent it, posted first class. I checked the label. Luckily, it only took two days,' he said. 'I've known second class post to arrive before first lately. Post office is going to pot! You have a good day.'

'Thanks. You, too.'

The style of writing on the address label was broad and florid. He thought he recognised it. He picked up his coffee and took the parcel into his conservatory. Setting the cup down, he carefully unwrapped the package. Carla's face stared up at him from the back cover. He was familiar with the photograph; he remembered telling her when she'd first showed it to him and told him of her intention to use it for her book. *If you put that photograph on the cover of the book – it would sell millions.*

He quickly scanned the words on the back and then turned the book over to read the front cover. The picture struck fear into his heart. It was of a man wearing a gas mask, dressed in a navy-blue boiler suit. The title read:

The Boilerman Killings -
The Life and Times of William Martin Boyle

By Carla Black

He smiled. *She has guts.* Picking up his coffee, he began to read.

He called her at around lunchtime. She couldn't keep the excitement from her voice. 'Well, what did you think?'

'It's very good,' he said, hesitance dampening his enthusiasm.

'You don't have to say that if you don't mean it.'

'I *do* mean it, it's very good, and I loved that photograph of you on the back.'

'Thank you,' she said. 'You sound as if you're going to say, but...'

'I'm just not sure about the ending.'

'How so?'

'*He remains at large,*' Miller paused. 'I prefer to think of him dead.'

The sound of her sucking air between her teeth came down the line. 'Miller, you must *know* he's still alive.'

'Maybe. You know if he sees this, he'll come after you.'

'I'm banking on it.' She giggled. 'Can you imagine what a story *that* would make?'

'Always the story, Carla. Don't you ever think about anything else?'

She laughed. 'I think you know that I do. How about dinner tonight? We have a lot of catching up to do. Boyle's in Morocco. I think I know where to find him. We'll talk about it later, yes?'

Morocco. A voice inside told him not to go.

'Carla, not tonight. I'm busy. I'll call you tomorrow.' He turned the phone off. His thoughts drifted. *I see three women. Only one is good for you...*

Three women... Who were they? He liked Carla a lot, but he knew they'd only find trouble together. He'd not had feelings for anyone since Josie the way he felt for Stella, but would she turn out to be wrong for him, too? He didn't want to hurt, or be hurt. What if the as yet unknown woman came along and blew him away?

He shook his head, and then grinned. In his heart, he knew the answer.

The Road Not Taken

Two roads diverged in a yellow wood,
And sorry I could not travel both
And be one traveller, long I stood
And looked down one as far as I could
To where it bent in the undergrowth;

Then took the other, as just as fair,
And having perhaps the better claim,
Because it was grassy, and wanted wear;
Though as for that the passing there
Had worn them really about the same,

And both that morning equally lay
In leaves no step had trodden black.
Oh, I kept the first for another day!
Yet knowing how way leads on to way,
I doubted if I should ever come back.

I shall be telling this with a sigh
Somewhere ages, and ages hence:
Two roads diverged in a wood, and I—
I took the one less travelled by,
And that has made all the difference.

Robert Frost (1874–1963) – Mountain Interval

A note from the author

I hope you enjoyed my debut novel, and if you did, would you please consider leaving a short review on Amazon? Reviews help independent authors like me gain recognition and ultimately, provide us with encouragement to keep writing.

Thank you for your support. It is much appreciated.

Max.

The Life and Times of William Boule, a spin-off book featuring several characters from this one, and is available in ebook and paperback format on amazon.

If you'd like to be notified of future book releases, please email:
notify@skinnybirdproductions.com

7340231R00290

Printed in Germany
by Amazon Distribution
GmbH, Leipzig